ORMOND;
or
THE SECRET WITNESS

with Related Texts

Constance / blind
father, she supports
him, company (pharare
fails - apprentice (Craig)
embezzles, they go poor,
yellow fiver epidemic,
Philidelphia, bumps into
Craig, follows him to house,
owned by Ormond

Charles Brockden Brown

ORMOND;
or
THE SECRET WITNESS

with Related Texts

Edited, with an Introduction and Notes, by
Philip Barnard and Stephen Shapiro

Hackett Publishing Company, Inc.
Indianapolis/Cambridge

14 13 12 11 10 09   1 2 3 4 5 6

For further information, please address
  Hackett Publishing Company, Inc.
  P.O. Box 44937
  Indianapolis, IN 46244-0937

  www.hackettpublishing.com

Cover design by Abigail Coyle
Text design by Carrie Wagner
Composition by Professional Book Compositors
Printed at Sheridan Books, Inc.

Library of Congress Cataloging-in-Publication Data

Brown, Charles Brockden, 1771-1810.
  Ormond, or, The secret witness : with related texts / Charles Brockden Brown ;
edited with an introduction and notes by Philip Barnard and Stephen Shapiro.
    p. cm.
  Includes bibliographical references.
  ISBN 978-1-60384-126-9 (cloth) -- ISBN 978-1-60384-125-2 (pbk.)
  1. Young women--Fiction. 2. Philadelphia (Pa.)—History—19th century—Fiction.   I. Barnard, Philip, 1951– II. Shapiro, Stephen, 1964– III. Title. IV. Title: Ormond. V. Title: Secret witness.
  PS1134.O76 2009
  813'.2--dc22

                                                    2009025796

The paper used in this publication meets the minimum requirements of
American National Standard for Information Sciences—
Permanence of Paper for Printed Library Materials,
ANSI Z39.48-1984

CONTENTS

ACKNOWLEDGMENTS

We thank the Department of English, University of Kansas, and the Department of English and Comparative Literary Studies, University of Warwick, for support throughout the preparation of this volume. Special thanks go to Professor Carol Rutter, Susan Brock, and everyone at the CAPITAL (Creativity and Performance in Teaching and Learning) Centre at Warwick for arrangements during a Warwick/ RSC Fellowship in Creativity and Performance, and to the Head of Department Professor Thomas Docherty for sustained encouragement. The College of Arts and Sciences at Kansas provided generous support for archival research.

For access to their digitized text of the first edition of *Ormond* we acknowledge and thank the University of Virginia Libraries and their Early American Fiction Collection project. The analysis of textual data provided by S.W. Reid in the 1977 Kent State Bicentennial Edition of the novel has been a basic source of information for our work.

For permission to reprint material from the Diary of Elihu Hubbard Smith, we thank the American Philosophical Society. The staffs of the University of Kansas Libraries and The Spencer Research Library rare book collection have been generous sources of textual materials. For additional help with texts and images, we thank Janie Morris and Eleanor Mills at the Perkins Library, Duke University; Ana Guimaraes at the Rare Book and Manuscript Division of the Kroch Library, Cornell University; and the staff of the Historical Society of Pennsylvania.

We are thoroughly indebted to the community of scholars who work on Brown and early modern culture, and to colleagues in the Charles Brockden Brown Society, whose insights and advice have helped form our ideas about and approach to this and other writings by Brown. The collective effort of the Brown Society has been especially enlivened by the forthcoming scholarship of current and recent graduate student colleagues Sarah Blythe, Lana Finley, Anthony Galluzzo, Tiziana Pagan, Joe Shapiro, Abigail Smith, and Tamika Nadine Walker. For new information on the sources for Brown's piece, "Terrific Novels," we thank Michael Cody; for help with particular information on Brown's correspondence in the 1790s, we thank John Holmes; and for information on Giustiniana Wynne, Countess Rosenberg, we are indebted to Nancy Isenberg.

For guidance and support with the editorial process at Hackett, once again we acknowledge the good works of Rick Todhunter, without whom this volume and the three that preceded it would never have happened. Carrie Wagner, Abigail Coyle, and Christina Kowalewski have made essential contributions to the design and quality of this text and, likewise, to the entire series of Brown novels at Hackett. It has been a pleasure and career highlight working with them.

Personal thanks and Woldwinite relations of reason and desire link us to Anne Schwan, Cheryl Lester, and Julia Barnard.

Ormond,

oder

der geheime Zeuge.

Aus dem Englischen des Godwin

frei übersetzt

von

Friedrich von Oertel.

Leipzig,
bei Johann Gottlob Beygang,
1802.

Title page from the 1802 German translation of *Ormond*, the first U.S. novel to be translated and republished in Europe. Note that the novel is falsely attributed to William Godwin (possibly to help sales); this "error" thus recognizes the Woldwinite context for Brown's novel. The copy reads: "Ormond, or the Secret Witness. Freely translated from the English of Godwin by Friedrich von Oertel. Leipzig: Johann Gottlob Beygang, 1802." Image courtesy of the Rare Book, Manuscript, and Special Collections Library, Duke University.

INTRODUCTION

Women, wake up; the tocsin of reason sounds throughout the universe; recognize your rights. The powerful empire of nature is no longer surrounded by prejudice, fanaticism, superstition, and lies. The torch of truth has dispersed all the clouds of folly and usurpation. Enslaved man has multiplied his force and needs yours to break his chains. Having become free, he has become unjust toward his companion. Oh women! Women, when will you cease to be blind? What advantages have you gathered in the Revolution?

Olympe de Gouges, *Declaration of the Rights of Woman and the Female Citizen* (September 1791)

Charles Brockden Brown's *Ormond; or The Secret Witness* is perhaps the most self-consciously radical fiction written in the United States before *Moby-Dick* or the later phase of modernism. Brown's novel deserves this kind of reading not only because it affirms radical perspectives on women's lives and the revolutionary age, or because its interest in radical positioning extends to the level of literary form as it builds a repudiation of the period's novelistic strategies of conservative containment into its narrative frame. In addition to all of its remarkable thematic and formal features, *Ormond* deserves to be read in this manner because it also explores the active, dynamic constitution of radical thinking and society.

Most progressive Enlightenment-era fictions seek to illustrate a relatively static set of ethical positions or themes, in which the corruption and immorality of the old regime can be denounced, replaced, and, in a narrative sense, resolved. Brown's novel, by contrast, emphasizes the process through which individuals change and develop new forms of political and social consciousness. In *Ormond*, characters develop new ways of thinking and relating to the social order through an often-uneven assimilation of radical ideas, and through a series of realizations that help them resituate themselves within alternative networks. The novel's primarily female characters experience processes of self-transformation and incorporation within new social forms that occur in the crucible of ongoing history, as their efforts at self-education are shaped by and respond to the violently partisan and rapidly changing conditions during the 1790s.

All of Brown's novels employ formal and thematic complexity toward their artistic, intellectual, and wider political ends, but *Ormond* makes more demands on the reader in this respect than Brown's other fictions. From its earliest reception to the present, the novel has fascinated and puzzled readers who have responded on the one hand to its revolutionary thematics, and on the other to its insistently challenging narrative form and theatricality, which even for readers familiar with Brown constitute one of the most intriguing aspects of the novel.

First published in January 1799, after being composed in about four to six week's time beginning in late November 1798,[1] *Ormond* tells the story of Constantia Dudley, from her family's catastrophic financial collapse in New York and subsequent suffering during the epic Philadelphia yellow fever epidemic of 1793, to her encounters with cosmopolitan revolutionaries who connect her with the currents of circum-Atlantic social and political upheaval in the 1790s. While the tale's surface action follows Constantia as she surmounts a series of crises and obstacles, its backstories, subplots, and narrative frame develop a sustained meditation on late-Enlightenment debates concerning political liberty, women's rights, conventions of sex and gender, and their relation to the reshaping of an Atlantic world in the throes of transformation.

This Introduction is intended to orient the reader to the world of *Ormond* by providing tools for understanding Brown and his novel. A sketch of Brown's life and the novel's late-1790s context, and a discussion of Brown's understanding of novels as instruments of political education, will provide general background. Information on central motifs and emphases—from theatrical masquerade and the 1793 yellow fever epidemic to contrasting models of womanhood, female transvestism in the revolutionary era, responses to the French émigré community in the period's U.S. urban culture, and the fate of radicalism in a time of reaction—will lead to a discussion of the ways that the novel develops its primary social, psychological, and political concerns.

Brown's Life and the Context of the 1790s

Brown was born into a Philadelphia Quaker merchant family on January 17, 1771. Philadelphia, the capital of the newly formed United States during the 1790s and then the largest, wealthiest, most culturally and politically diverse city in North America, was his home for most of his life. Beginning in the mid-1790s and particularly during the intense 1797–1800 period when he was writing his novels, however, Brown also lived in New York and moved in a cosmopolitan circle of young upper-class intellectuals who circulated and debated the latest medical-scientific, political, and cultural information, and produced writings on a wide variety of subjects.

---

[1] There is little information in Brown's correspondence, the diaries of his friends, or other sources, concerning details of the novel's composition. Timing suggests that composition did not begin before late November and, in a letter to his brother James on December 20, 1798, Brown writes:

"What excuse to make for my long silence I know not, unless the simple truth be sufficient for the purpose. Some time since I bargained with the publisher of Wieland for a new performance, part of which only was written, and the publication commencing immediately, I was obliged to apply with the utmost diligence to the pen, in order to keep pace with the press. Absorbed in this employment, I was scarcely conscious of the lapse of time, and when the day's task was finished, felt myself thoroughly weary and unfit for a continuance of the same employment in any new shape.

I call my book Ormond, or the Secret Witness. I hope to finish the writing and the publication together before new-year's day, when I shall have a breathing spell."

Growing up a Philadelphia Quaker (members of The Religious Society of Friends are commonly known as "Quakers" or "Friends"), Brown was shaped by that community's history of dissenting relations to mainstream Protestant and Anglo-American culture, and by Philadelphia's importance as both a political center and a major port connected with Atlantic and global mercantile networks. Brown had a classical education at the elite Friend's Latin School in Philadelphia and seems to have taught briefly at the Friends Grammar School in the early 1790s, but did not, like male friends in his New York circle, attend a university, since many Quakers and other dissenters in the U.S. and England did not patronize the educational institutions that served dominant Protestant groups. Although Brown's adult years led him from his Philadelphia origins to the intellectual world of the radical Enlightenment, his Quaker background nonetheless marks his development in fundamental ways. Quaker traditions and doctrines concerning egalitarianism and equal authority for women in the Quaker community contributed to Brown's lifelong commitment to female education and equality.[2] Similarly, Quaker leadership in antislavery organization is part of the background for the implicit and explicit reflections on slavery and African American experience in *Ormond*, the novel *Arthur Mervyn*, and other writings. Interestingly, after having grown up as Quakers in the increasingly diversified Philadelphia of the late eighteenth century, Brown and all his siblings but one married non-Quakers (Brown's youngest brother, Elijah Jr., remained unmarried), an increasingly common trend for Quakers at this time. Consequently, Brown was formally dissociated from the Quaker meeting in Philadelphia when he married Elizabeth Linn, daughter of a Presbyterian minister, in 1804.

Growing up the fourth of five brothers and seven surviving siblings total in a merchant family,[3] Brown's life was shaped by the mercantile culture of Philadelphia during the revolutionary era. The merchant careers of Brown's father and four brothers made him intimately familiar with the circum-Atlantic import-export commerce that was the main business of Philadelphia's port.[4] Brown's father Elijah came to Philadelphia as a young man from Chester County, Pennsylvania, and had a checkered business career mainly as a conveyancer, a broker and manager for real estate, mortgage, and other transactions. In 1777–1778, during the American Revolution, he was arrested and interned in Virginia as one of a group of Quakers deemed "dangerous to the State" for refusing on religious grounds to sign oaths of allegiance. In 1784, he was humiliatingly imprisoned for debt. Through all this, the father struggled to

---

[2] See Fleischmann, *A Right View of the Subject: Feminism in the Works of Charles Brockden Brown and John Neal*.

[3] Kafer, *Charles Brockden Brown's Revolution*, provides the numbers we use here, i.e. five brothers and two sisters who survived to adulthood, plus three siblings who died at birth or in early infancy (45, 210n36, 221n25).

[4] See the accounts of Brown family business interests in Warfel, *Charles Brockden Brown*, 16–18, 23, 204; Clark, *Charles Brockden Brown*, 108–9, 194–95; and Kafer, *Charles Brockden Brown's Revolution*, 26–37, 45–46, 162, 214n15. Brown's brothers Joseph and Elijah, Jr. voyaged throughout the Atlantic and Mediterranean worlds as merchant importers.

continue in business, partly sustained by the real-estate holdings and financial interests of Brown's maternal aunt, Elizabeth Armitt.

Although his family intended for him to become a lawyer, Brown abandoned his
Philadelphia law apprenticeship in 1793, complaining that the language of law existed to deny rather than enact justice, and moved toward the circle of young, New
York-based intellectuals who helped launch his literary career and, with Brown as one
of their group, enacted progressive Enlightenment ideals of conversation, intellectual
inquiry, and companionship.[5] The New York group included a number of young
male professionals who called themselves The Friendly Club, along with female rela-
tives and friends who were equally invested in progressive intellectual exchange and
enlightened models for same-sex and other-sex companionship. This progressive
model of companionship based on "reason and desire" expressed through a "republic
of letters" is a crucial context for Brown's astonishing burst of novel writing between
1798 and 1801. The key figure in this group was Elihu Hubbard Smith (1771–1798),
a Yale-educated physician and writer who met Brown in Philadelphia in 1790, and
helped catalyze his literary ambitions. Aspects of Smith's life, from his abolitionism
and Deism[6] to his efforts to treat yellow-fever victims and other progressive political
and social positions, figure as models for characters and events in Brown's novels
Edgar Huntly (1799) and *Arthur Mervyn* (1799–1800).[7]

As one of this circle, Brown developed his knowledge of like-minded British radical-
democratic writers of the period—above all William Godwin and Mary Wollstonecraft (whose books were already in Brown's household as a youth, before he met
Smith)—as well as medical and physiological knowledges drawn from the Scottish
Enlightenment (notably Erasmus Darwin), the French Naturalists, and other streams
of continental Enlightenment thought. The circle was committed to abolitionist activism and many of the male members of the group were officers in abolition societies and free schools for African Americans. The circle's interest in similar groups of
progressive British thinkers was strong enough that they established contact through
correspondence with scientist Erasmus Darwin (via Smith), novelist Thomas Holcroft, and Godwin himself (via Dunlap and Godwin's ward Thomas Cooper, an

---

[5] For discussions of this circle, see Waterman, *Republic of Intellect* and Teute, "A 'Republic of Intellect'" and "The Loves of the Plants." The diaries of William Dunlap and Elihu Hubbard Smith provide detailed records of Brown's activities and relations within this circle.

[6] "Deism" is a progressive eighteenth-century response to Christianity. It affirms the existence of a
"supreme being," but rejects revelation, supernatural doctrines, and any notion of divine intervention in human affairs. Reason and science, rather than scripture and dogma, are the basis for religious belief. Late-eighteenth-century writers often adopt a deistic stance as part of their general
secular and rationalist critique of earlier institutions. Deism is associated with "natural religion" and
the well-known metaphor of the deity as a "clock-maker" who creates the universe but makes no
further intervention in it. Many leaders of the American revolutionary generation were Deists, notably Benjamin Franklin and Thomas Jefferson. See Walters, *Rational Infidels: The American Deists*.

[7] For more on E. H. Smith, see the excerpts and discussion in Related Texts, and Waterman, *Republic of Intellect*.

actor who emigrated to the U.S. and moved in Brown's circles). Thus Brown's interest in European developments led him to participate in a network of like-minded endeavors, but his progressive, modernizing ideals meant that he felt little or no need to emulate Europe or the past as superior cultures.

If Brown's intellectual circle in New York constitutes one part of the context for his period of novel writing, the other crucial element in this context is the explosive political atmosphere of the revolutionary 1790s as it culminated in the reactionary backlash of 1797–1800. Throughout the decade, events and discussions in New York and Philadelphia were closely intertwined with the ongoing processes of the French Revolution (1789–1798), the Haitian Revolution (1791–1804), and events leading to the Irish uprisings of 1796–1798. Refugees and participants from these revolutionary events filled the streets of 1790s Philadelphia and New York with émigrés of every stripe and color, from Royalist French aristocrats and planters from the Caribbean fleeing ongoing revolutions, to enslaved "French negroes" or "wild Irish" revolutionary activists and intellectuals.[8]

By the end of the decade a severe reaction against the period's progressive ideals spread through the Atlantic world and was especially powerful in England, Germany, and the recently formed United States. During the administration of the second U.S. President, John Adams (1796–1800), the ruling Federalist Party presided over a partisan and repressive response to real and imagined threats of revolutionary subversion and potential conflict with France.[9] Enacting the now-infamous Alien and Sedition Acts (1798), for example, Federalists made it illegal to criticize the Adams administration and legitimated the arrest and deportation of those deemed enemies of the state (i.e., primarily recent French and Irish émigrés). Paranoid countersubversive fantasies about conspiracies led by mysterious groups like the Illuminati (a secret society ostensibly plotting to overthrow church and state institutions), as well as panic by ruling elites about newly articulated ideals of universal democracy, including female equality and slave emancipation, contributed to this crisis. Traces of the Illuminati scare are evident in *Ormond*, as well as in *Wieland* and its "prequel" *Memoirs of Carwin the Biloquist*.[10] Although these excesses led to the Federalist's defeat and the election of their Democratic-Republican opponent Jefferson in the 1800 election, this conservative convulsion nevertheless helped put an

---

[8] For more on the period's émigré culture, see "Portrait of an Emigrant" and selections by Moreau de Saint-Méry, Watson, and C. F. Volney in Related Texts.

[9] In the political party terminology of the 1790s, Federalists are the more Anglophile, moneyed elite, and conservative party (the party of the Washington and Adams administrations), and Democratic-Republicans are the more socially and regionally heterogeneous Francophile party (which comes to power after 1800 in the Jefferson and Madison administrations). See the discussions of this backlash and its implications in Cotlar, "The Federalists' Transatlantic Cultural Offensive of 1798"; Elkins and McKitrick, *The Age of Federalism*; Fischer, *The Revolution of American Conservatism*; Miller, *Crisis in Freedom: The Alien and Sedition Acts;* and Tise, *The American Counterrevolution.*

[10] For more on the scare and the period's counterrevolutionary activism, see "Illuminati Debates" in Related Texts.

end to the revolutionary era and laid the foundations for the more staid cultural order of the early nineteenth century.

Brown's efforts to establish himself as a professional writer in this period of action and reaction were impressive indeed. After several years of experimentation with poetry and literary narratives that remained unfinished, Brown's novelistic phase began with the 1798 feminist dialogue *Alcuin; A Dialogue* (included in Related Texts here), a text that is closely related to *Ormond's* focus on women's lives and ideologies of sex and gender, and continued unabated through the composition of eight novels by late 1801. Throughout this period, in addition to work on his novels, Brown was editing the New York *Monthly Magazine* (April 1799–December 1800) and publishing numerous essays, tales, and reviews. As noted earlier, the four "gothic" novels for which Brown is best known—*Wieland, Ormond, Arthur Mervyn*, and *Edgar Huntly*—were all published between September 1798 and September 1799 (*Mervyn, Second Part* appeared in September, 1800), and there was a period in 1798 when all four were under way at once.

Although Cold-War-era commentators often presented Brown as a writer who renounces his literary and progressive political ideals when he stops publishing novels in 1801, a more plausible explanation for Brown's subsequent shift toward other forms of writing is that his novels did not make money, the particular conditions that fueled the intense novelistic burst from 1798 to 1801 changed (who could sustain such a rhythm of production?), and he became interested in new literary outlets. Like his older counterpart Godwin in England, Brown moves away from the novel because he feels it no longer offers an effective mode of argumentation in the increasingly conservative cultural and political environment that emerges after 1800. Had Brown lived longer, he may conceivably have returned to novel writing, as Godwin did in the later 1810s.

Brown's later literary career builds continuously on the novels and earlier writings. Between 1801 and his death from tuberculosis in 1810, Brown edited two important periodicals: *The Literary Magazine* (1803–1807), a literary and cultural miscellany that renewed his experience with the earlier *Monthly Magazine* and which he filled with his own essays and fiction; and *The American Register* (1807–1809), a historical and political periodical that featured Brown's "Annals of Europe and America," a comprehensive narrative of Napoleonic-era geopolitics. In addition, he undertook a novel-length historical fiction known as the *Historical Sketches* (1803–1806) that was published only posthumously; a now-lost play; and several lengthy, quasi-novelistic pamphlets on expansion into the Louisiana territory and Jefferson's embargo policies (1803, 1809).

These writings continue Brown's career-long concern with the link between historical and fictional ("romance") writing, and extend the earlier program of "reason and desire" that makes writing an instrument of progressive, educational principles in the public sphere. Rather than dramatizing the ways individuals are shaped by social pressures and crisis contexts, as he did in his novels, the later Brown explores forms of historical narrative and the larger historical world that made up the allusive backdrop of the earlier fiction. The critical perspective on global webs of imperial warfare, colonialism, and revolutionary change that figures in *Ormond*'s backstories, for example, becomes explicit and is explored in detail in the later historical writings and essays.

The Woldwinite Writers and Brown's Novelistic Method

The world of *Ormond* and Brown's other novels, with their gothic emotional intensities, disorienting psychological and social violence, and embedded backstories and subplots, may be difficult to sort out on first encounter. Understanding some basics about Brown's primary intellectual and political sources, and his well-defined novelistic method, however, can help the reader understand features of his novels that might otherwise seem difficult to grasp.

Unlike many authors of eighteenth-century fiction, Brown had a well-developed methodology and set of themes for writing novels. His method draws on and further develops the ideas of the British radical-democratic writers of the period. Brown's enthusiastic reception of these Woldwinite[11] ("Anglo-Jacobin") writers—above all Mary Wollstonecraft, William Godwin, Thomas Holcroft, Robert Bage, and Thomas Paine—undergirds his entire literary project after the mid-1790s. The British "Dissenter" culture of highly educated middle-class professionals and the clubs and academies from which these writers emerge is the wider context of Brown's own Philadelphia Quaker community. Brown was exposed to the Woldwinite writers through his father's copies of their works even before he moved into the New York circle and explored their writings in greater detail.[12]

The Woldwinite agenda rests on three basic arguments that draw together the main strands of knowledge and critique in the late, radical Enlightenment. Drawing on well-established eighteenth-century arguments and themes such as associative sentiment (the idea that emotions are communicated from one individual to another and may be used to encourage constructive, progressive behavior), these arguments sum up this group's rejection of the pre-revolutionary order and their conviction that social progress may be achieved by altering dominant ways of thinking through peaceful

---

[11] We use the term Woldwinite to highlight, through an abbreviation of Wollstonecraft and Godwin, this group's special place among the British radical democrats of the 1790s. The term "Godwinians" erases the crucial role of Wollstonecraft and other women in this group, a role that was particularly important for Brown and many other writers. Similarly, these British writers are also discussed as "Jacobins" or "Anglo-Jacobins," a name used by opponents to demonize them by association with the Jacobin faction in the French revolution, but the group explicitly rejected the "Jacobin" position in favor of its own distinct set of cultural-political positions. For the distinction of "Jacobin" and "Girondin" in the culture wars of the period, see "Narratives of French Girondin Heroism" in Related Texts. For studies of literary Woldwinism, see: Pamela Clemit, *The Godwinian Novel*; Gary Kelly, *The English Jacobin Novel 1780–1805* and *English Fiction of the Romantic Period, 1789–1830*; Marilyn Butler, *Jane Austen and the War of Ideas*; and J. M. S. Tompkins, *The Popular Novel in England, 1770–1800*.

[12] For the Woldwinite writings in Brown's household, see Warfel, 17–18, 27; Clark, 16; Kafer, 46, 66–72.

cultural means such as literature. First, the social order of the old regime (monarchy and feudalism) is to be rejected because it is artificial and illegitimate, violating the natural equality of humanity by imposing coercive hierarchies of caste and faith. Second, given that the old regime maintained its domination through an obscurantist mythology of territorialized race, priestly tricks, and a politics of secret plots, conspiracies, and lies, a new social order will require the development of more rational, constructive, and transparent institutions and practices. Third, the illustration of progressive behavior, in print and other media, will multiply to generate larger social transformation because society works through chains of associative sentiment and emulation. These cultural relays generate progressive change as the illustration of virtuous behaviors and results spreads through imitation, with each individual learning and transmitting new and improved ways of acting by observing others. Proceeding from these assumptions, the Woldwinites' critique leads to their antistatism, their distrust of institutions, and their use of cultural forms such as literature to advance their program. Because they believe in the natural propulsion of cooperative behavior and the guidance of critical reason, these writers see social change as resulting from the amplification of transformed local, interpersonal, or intersubjective relations.[13] Thus, as we say today, the personal is political.

In their assumption that global historical change begins from the bottom up with the premeditated transformation of relations among a small circle, the Woldwinites are an early instance of the belief in a cultural avant-garde that aims to develop means of worldly social revolution through arts and manners rather than political parties or state institutions. In contemporary terms, the Woldwinites introduce a relatively straightforward, albeit limited idea of environmental or social construction, the notion that individuals are shaped or conditioned by their social environments and circumstances. Their ideas about social construction are limited in that they position themselves as innocent participants and do not always recognize the dilemmas implicit in their own social program (particularly its assumptions about sentiment, benevolence, and associative imitation, for example), and insofar as they direct their critique mainly at the hierarchical inequalities of the old regime while neglecting new modes of inequality that are part of the emergent structures of liberal capitalism. Brown adopts their environmentalist argument but also, as a second-wave Woldwinite, recognizes that these ideas about social construction and action are incomplete. His fiction attempts to think through their limitations and implications in ways that we will explore in greater detail when we turn to the plot of *Ormond* in what follows.

Building on these basic Woldwinite ideas, Brown's fictional method is articulated in several key essays on narrative technique and the social role of the novel that appear at the height of his novelistic phase, notably "Walstein's School of History" (August–September, 1799) and "The Difference between History and Romance" (April, 1800).[14] To summarize this method, we can say that Brown's novels combine

---

[13] For more on Wollstonecraft and Godwin, see the discussions and selections in Related Texts.

[14] These essays are included in Related Texts.

elements of history and fiction, placing his characters in situations of social and historical distress as a means of engaging a wider audience into considerations of progressive behavior. His novels explore how contemporary subjects—whether relatively elite actors such as *Ormond*'s narrator Sophia Courtland or relatively lower status or disempowered individuals like protagonist Constantia Dudley—respond to damaging social conditions caused by defects in dominant ideas and practices. Through their interconnected patterns of socially conditioned behavior, dramatic suspense, and gothic intensities, Brown's fictions urge readers to reflect on how to overcome corruption in order to construct a more "virtuous," more equal and fulfilling society.

This approach begins with Brown's understanding of the relation between historical and fictional ("romance") writing. History and fiction, he argues, are not different because one deals with factual and the other with fictional materials. Rather, they are intrinsically connected as two sides of one coin: history describes and documents the results of actions, while fiction investigates the relations between actions, speculating on the possible motives and circumstances that cause and explain them. Fictions are thus narrative experiments that tease out possible preconditions and consequences of historical events or behaviors, and that reason through social problems presented as hypothetical situations; they are a form of conjectural or counterfactual history. Whereas history describes events, romance analyzes and projects the probable causes, conditions, and preconditions of events.

The "Walstein" essay builds on this distinction and develops a three-fold plan for novel writing, providing a fuller account of the rationale and essential themes that inform Brown's fiction. In the essay, the historian Walstein combines history and romance in such as way as to promote "moral and political" engagement while rejecting universal truths, stressing the situatedness of engaged political response in noble and classical figures such as the Roman statesman Cicero. Walstein's pupil Engel then modernizes and develops the theory by adding that a romance, to be effective in today's world, must be addressed to a wide popular audience and draw its characters not from the elite, but from the same middling and lower status groups that will read and be moved by the work. History and romance alike must address issues and situations familiar to their modern audience, notably the common inequalities arising from relations of sex and property.

Thus, a modern literature will insert ordinary individuals such as Constantia Dudley, rather than elite actors like Cicero, into crisis situations in which they must negotiate contemporary conflicts involving social status and property, and erotic desire or gender relations. Finally, Brown's essay emphasizes that a thrilling style and form are crucial, since a romance capable of moving its audience to considerations of progressive action must "be so arranged as to inspire, at once, curiosity and belief, to fasten the attention, and thrill the heart." In this manner, Brown's method uses the twists and turns of his intentionally challenging plots, as well as dramatic crisis conditions including endemic prejudice, rape, catastrophic bankruptcy, and yellow fever epidemics, as ways to illustrate and think through interrelated social problems and encourage an engaged response to them.

Secret Witnessing and Transnational Forms

In *Ormond*, Brown explores questions that arise when we consider the transformation of identity less as a punctual event stemming from a single crisis or epiphany, than as a continual, multistaged process, a cascading wave that combines the consequences of multiple effects. We might say that Brown's novel, as it draws on and extends its Woldwinite models, provides an early illustration of the belief that a cultural revolution of the mind must precede a political one of society. Brown's tale of radical insight includes more elements than this innovation alone, however. Unlike some of the period's more insistent commentators, this novel does not call for an automatic rejection of the past. Throughout *Ormond*, younger female characters repeatedly gain empowering educations in spite of hostile environments and the action of psychologically damaged and damaging parental figures. Read allegorically, these examples of educational experiences that overcome dysfunctional relationships with elders seem to convey Brown's dual understanding about the conditions for growing radicalism. On the one hand, an emerging push for human liberty, conventionally depicted in the figure of an imperiled young woman, cannot simply emerge from nothing, like a modern Venus from the half shell or the fully empowered Athena from the brow of Zeus. Any spontaneous, unplanned attempt at a thoroughly new-made society will rest on a precarious, fragile foundation. In this light, progressives must learn to select judiciously from the past and endure its unpalatable aspects in order to forge intellectual instruments that may be put to good use even if the context from which they emerged must be rejected or surpassed.

On the other hand, Brown suggests, the clothing of the past may also serve as protective cover if innovative energies are in danger of becoming overshadowed by counterrevolutionary forces, by a more powerful resurgence of dominant interests threatened by change. *Ormond*, therefore, goes beyond the affirmation of radical principles to narrate the need for tactical sophistication in response to a relatively inhospitable social ecology. In other words, it dramatizes the need for discovering a mode of operation that can allow radical spirit the time it needs to nourish itself and survive political currents such as the reactionary wave that swept over Brown and his generation in the late 1790s, when the progressive ferment of the decade's early years was pushed backward by the renewed violence of dominant monarchical and imperial-commercial interests throughout the Atlantic world.

From *Ormond*'s first pages and opening references to Stephen Dudley's artistic education, one of the ways that Brown articulates his position on radical tactics is to emphasize the contrast between two different politicized aesthetic modes or styles, often positioning the novel's characters in terms of affinities for one or the other. Classicism, often referred to as Augustan style, emphasizes order and regularity by governing expression with formal "laws" that emphasize balance, harmony, geometrical regularity, and veneration for precedents and preexisting order. Classicism's "other" goes by many names, including romantic or gothic in this era, and prioritizes expression over its regulation, emphasizing irregularity, sensuality tied to bodily and emotional intensities, and forms that are new, surprising, or unprecedented, as opposed to conventional and well-established.[15] Contrasts between idealized form and materialized feeling recur frequently throughout the novel, presented as combinations of aesthetic predispositions with social and political outlooks. While relatively static neoclassical ideals are marshaled in support of existing order, forces of dynamic expression look to utopian reformulations. At several points in *Ormond* Brown alludes to the Roman poet Ovid's well-known tales of mythological transformation, the *Metamorphoses*. Ovid's poem establishes a narrative template for signaling the difference between outward, bodily form and the inward rush of desire and new identity. This divorce of form and content can be taken as an underlying theme that Brown wants his readers to "secretly" witness through the novel's frame narrative as it is presented by the character Sophia Courtland.

An awareness of *Ormond*'s formal complexity, its ruse of meaning actively constructed against, through, or in spite of formal appearances, helps explain why the novel has received the least and most contradictory commentary of Brown's quartet of best known and almost simultaneously published novels. For most of the twentieth century, scholars looked to Brown as the "founder" or "father," albeit a frustratingly unconventional one, of a uniquely American literary tradition. As long as nationalist exceptionalism and normative aesthetics were the grids through which the novel was to be evaluated, then *Ormond* surely appeared as an incomprehensibly misguided experiment or outright failure.[16] At least two basic types of information are necessary to overcome the limitations of this approach.

First, *Ormond* is the product of a tremendously cosmopolitan horizon. It draws on the progressive English political theory of the Woldwinites (itself often delivered in novelistic garb); combines its political reflections with features adapted from popular gothic and sensational novels from Germany (the *Schauerroman* or "shudder" novel); and refers additionally, specifically, and in detail, to French utopian, libertine, and pornographic fictions, as well as particular Italianate traditions in music and the visual arts. Because Brown is so thoroughly embedded in international or transnational networks, his readers are best served by coming to his texts with a working sense of his rich influences and context, which this edition attempts to convey with this Introduction and a selection of Related Texts.

Second, as a writer who can be challenging on several levels, Brown intentionally introduces additional complications in the case of *Ormond*. Even readers familiar with Brown's core beliefs and general literary techniques soon discover that these

---

[15] For the dynamic historical distinction between Classicism and its others, and its relation to discussions of form and genre in wider intellectual history, see the seminal essay by E. H. Gombrich, "Norm and Form: The Stylistic Categories of Art History and their Origins in Renaissance Ideals"; Lukács, "Schiller's Theory of Modern Literature"; Debord, *The Society of the Spectacle*; and Lacoue-Labarthe and Nancy, *The Literary Absolute*.

[16] For earlier commentary concerning the novel's disjunctions and paradoxes, and readings that often attribute them to haste or other defects in composition, see for example Krause, "*Ormond*: How Rapidly and How Well 'Composed, Arranged, and Delivered'"; Nye, "Historical Essay"; Rodgers, "Brown's *Ormond*: The Fruits of Improvisation"; and Watts, *The Romance of Real Life*.

guidelines are not always sufficient to unravel this novel's maze of backstories and false identities, or to resolve the questions posed by its remarkable manipulations of narrative perspective. Hence it becomes necessary to explore Brown's strategies in narrative and argumentation, and to ask how these are related to the novel's insistent narrative frame. Partly due to his own upbringing within the Quaker (Society of Friends) community, Brown habitually abjures a belligerent rhetorical style. When he wants to indicate disagreement with other authors or critics, he often does so by formulating gentle or discrete asides that suggest that there are other ways of considering the question, or by presenting alternatives through double negatives and other rhetorical turns, including Latinate word choice and sentence construction, that detach disagreement from emotional intensity. Indeed, in keeping with this discursive pacifism, Brown's writings likewise embrace a thematic pacifism by consistently criticizing militarism and deflating the prestige traditionally connected with male rituals of "honor" in warfare and violence.

Considered against this background, with an awareness of Brown's career-long aversion to direct political and discursive antagonism, how is the reader to approach the novel's many—and manifest—paradoxes? How is it, for example, that *Ormond*'s characters enthusiastically endorse and enact revolutionary violence, deliver intemperate reactionary denunciations at odds with the novel's underlying radicalism, and enact nonnormative pairings, all without having their ideas or actions negated by any of the period's conventional fictional techniques for signaling and containing "dangerous" or undesirable positions? Most novels condemn or punish undesirable characters and the positions they represent with a variety of conventional gestures, from symbolic expulsion in death to explicit negation by narrators or other characters.

Similarly, how is it that *Ormond* seems to violate or obfuscate certain principles and conventions that figure as reliable signposts in Brown's other fictions? Given that Brown repeatedly takes up the programmatic Woldwinite slogan of sincerity in other fictions, and personally emphasized the need for such truth-telling even when it led to discomfort among friends, it is striking that *Ormond* presents a world in which virtually no one is sincere. Regardless of gender, social status, or political outlook, all of the novel's significant characters engage in various types and degrees of imposture. They indulge in assumed identities; the distribution of gossip, rumor, and hearsay; acts of secret surveillance bordering on and including voyeurism; the manipulation of knowledge and withholding of information; bodily masquerade; and the circulation of forged or counterfeit documents and currency. In the world of *Ormond*, a character's insistence on her or his honesty and interpersonal transparency usually signals the very opposite. Yet rather than simply condemning, satirizing, moralizing on, or raging against the universality of hypocrisy and deceit in a hopelessly fallen world, Brown's novel seems to encourage the reader to accept this dynamic, and possibly to learn to negotiate its pitfalls, or realize its hidden promise. Brown's carefully formulated position is neither moralizing negation nor cynical acceptance, but, perhaps, a reflection on the conditions of disabused action in a world where progress requires strategy and forethought, and in which new energies meet with tremendous and at times overwhelming resistance.

The development of the novel's initially disorienting complexities suggests a concerted pattern at the heart of Brown's purpose and, understood in its literary and historical context, implies that Brown imagines his readership to be a bifurcated one. He assumes, that is, that his desired, ideal audience will perceive and respond to some aspects of the novel more attentively than other, more casual readers. Using *Ormond*'s own language, we can say that Brown's manner of writing in this novel seems to seek an audience of secret witnesses. Because of the unconventional narrative strategies and twists that Brown uses to inscribe implicit meaning in a space between the novel's surface plot and an encoded or half-hidden one, however, it is difficult to discuss the novel in detail without having a full awareness of its events and structure. For readers who prefer not to know what happens before they have experienced the text for themselves, we therefore recommend that you finish reading the entire novel before continuing with this Introduction.

The Theater and its Double

One indication of Brown's double-tongued approach comes early on, as the novel's first pages introduce us to Stephen Dudley, father of the novel's protagonist Constantia. Dudley is the son of a New York merchant who has studied painting in Italy and England. When his own father dies, Dudley puts aside artistic ambition and turns his mind to commerce, even as he pines for an eventual return to his earlier interests. His hard-won fortune, however, is entirely lost, embezzled by a young con artist who fabricates an English identity and wins Dudley's trust. Dudley goes on to suffer blindness in the miserable aftermath of this financial collapse, but his sight and former mansion in Perth Amboy, New Jersey, are both later returned to him.

For Brown's expected readers, the middle-class men and women of Philadelphia and New York, this description evoked the biography of one of Brown's closest associates, William Dunlap. Dunlap was the son of a New Jersey merchant who moved to New York during the War for Independence. Blind in one eye due to a childhood accident, Dunlap went on to study painting in London under Benjamin West. Returning to the United States, Dunlap was unsuccessful as a painter and joined his father's business. On the father's death, Dunlap inherited a Perth Amboy home and invested his inheritance in a quarter-share of the new Park Theater in New York, where he worked as manager, directed plays, and endured the slings and arrows of English actors.[17]

Yet despite the similarity of their names and certain biographical details, it is certain that Dunlap was never an abusive alcoholic or victim of massive embezzlement, like Dudley at his lowest point; Dunlap would not declare bankruptcy until 1805, six years after *Ormond*'s publication. It might be expected that adding such traits to a character modeled on Dunlap and publishing them in a widely circulated novel

---

[17] On Dunlap, see Coad, *William Dunlap*.

would cause some degree of scandal for Dunlap or possibly a rift with Brown. Yet Dunlap remained one of Brown's closest friends and advocates throughout his life.[18] In literature, a novel in which real people are presented as characters with fictionalized names is called a *roman à clef,* literally a novel with a key: if readers know the characters' real names, they possess the interpretive "key" to the novel's hidden meaning. Given Brown's ready use of a character that combines recognizable biographical information with extravagantly negative fictional details—details that were obviously perceived as untrue by anyone familiar with the real person—we might by analogy call *Ormond* a novel of play or *roman de jeu,* a novel in which outlandish characterizations of associates are not only unobjectionable, but even enjoyable because they are taken not literally but as a surface to be "read through," a bit like elaborate insults at a contemporary "roast" event.

In such a situation, the audience takes pleasure in their ability to recognize and focus on the difference between surface and depth, the gap between offensive characterizations and an obscured signature whose intention and effect is quite different. Considered as a formal innovation of sorts, this mechanism of openhanded forgery may be one of Brown's particular contributions to literary technique, especially as he deploys it in *Ormond,* where it signals an extended critique of the power relations hidden within an aesthetic of sentimentality, or the notion that a person or social situation can be seen and understood instantaneously and intuitively, without consideration or questioning of the context or originating structural conditions of social inequality that led to the scene or the individual's present state.

Ekphrasis is the technical, rhetorical name for using one medium of art to describe the effects of another, for example the use of a painting to represent a scene from a play, or the use of a poem to represent a painting. To an exceptional degree, *Ormond* invites its readers to imagine and experience the dynamic reception of other artistic media. The effects of painting, music, and song are repeatedly invoked and enacted in its pages. But the medium to which Brown refers most centrally in *Ormond* is drama.[19] "Theatre" is a key word repeatedly invoked by the novel's characters to

---

[18] See Kafer's remarks on the allusions to Dunlap and other aspects of *Ormond* that would be legible to Brown's close circle, in *Charles Brockden Brown's Revolution,* 156–65.

[19] As a close associate of Dunlap and others, Brown was keenly aware of and engaged in theater. Dunlap was an active translator of German drama for his own productions, and Brown's close friend Smith also tried his hand, without great success, at staging an opera. Although he never brought a drama of his own to the stage, Brown tried his hand at play writing at least twice. In 1797, with Dunlap and Smith, he planned to collaborate on a never-completed adaptation of Woldwinite writer Robert Bage's novel *Hermsprong* (1796). Some years later, as we know from the account given by British actor John Bernard, Brown wrote and then burnt the manuscript of a play apparently concerning an Egyptian magician, his Persian apprentice, and a "Greek girl, who attempted to combat the magician's influence." See Bernard, *Retrospections of America, 1797–1811,* 250–55.

Brown seems to have reviewed only one staged play, his future brother-in-law John Blair Linn's now-lost *Bourville Castle; or, the Gallic Orphan* (*New York Minerva,* Jan. 18, 1797). But he developed critical and theoretical reflections on drama in numerous articles that considered the relative efficacy of different translations and both the negative and positive effects of theater (according to

describe the impact of contemporary events swirling around them, for example when Constantia arrives at her friend Sarah's home during the yellow fever epidemic in Chapter 6 and discovers a "theatre of suffering"; or when "the progress of action and opinion" are described in Chapter 19 in the "theatre of France and Poland." Beyond simply invoking a concept, however, the novel adapts the logic and machinery of theater, emphasizing its antisentimental split between actors' personalities and the characters they embody; its visual separation of space between the stage and the still visible offstage margins; the distinction between stage and audience; and different possible perspectives on the action from widely separated orchestra or balcony seats, divisions that the audience may simultaneously ignore and observe.[20]

Drama is the preeminent model for *Ormond*'s novelistic theatrics because, by overlapping different scenes onto a single space (the stage), it allows the cumulative registration of social exchanges developing through time. While it might be said that picaresque novels, with their tireless succession of scenes and episodes, achieve aspects of this effect, the medium of theater possesses an arguably unique ability to exploit artifice while simultaneously highlighting the illusory effects of this artifice, bringing out the play within the play. It is this theatrical potential that seems to become an attractive model for Brown as he organizes his novel. The witnessed masquerade stands as an early instance of what Bertolt Brecht, in the early twentieth century, described as the prerequisite for the modern theater, its ability to create an "alienation effect" for the viewer who is encouraged to both recognize the theatrical apparatus, its generated artifice, and to use this recognition as a cognitive space, a new cultural opportunity and encouragement, for critical reflection on a social conflict.[21]

Brown looks to theater not simply because it is well suited for emphasizing the difference between depiction and facticity, form and insight, or representation and reality, but because it suits his purpose in presenting specific political questions. That is, Brown may literally and rightly regard politics in the 1790s as histrionic and dependent on techniques of illusion in propaganda and the struggle over interpretations. But in a more incisive sense, he seems to adopt a theatrical model for political inquiry in this novel because sensational drama may provide a mechanism for exploring an experience and phenomenon for which analytical concepts or terminology had not yet been devised: the condition of progressive thought in retreat after an initial period of success.

Enlightenment-era political theory had well-developed ideas concerning the primary forces that retarded political progress—the heavy hand of the aristocratic, undemocratized State and the mystifying authority of institutionalized religion—but

---

its content and purpose) on middle-class audiences. See, for example, "On the Effects of Theatric Exhibitions," in the Philadelphia *Weekly Magazine* 1.12 (April 21, 1798), 357–60; and "On the Flavian Ampitheatre at Rome," in the *Literary Magazine* 3.18 (March 1805), 167–69, which relates the architectural structure of a spectacular space to its social effects.

[20] For a related argument concerning the novel's theatricality, see Richards, "Tales of the Philadelphia Theatre: *Ormond*, National Performance, and Supranational Identity."

[21] For alienation effect, see the essays in Brecht, *Brecht on Theatre: The Development of an Aesthetic*.

far fewer means for thinking through the lived experience of progressives in the early 1790s whose aspirations were turned back by the renewed bourgeois conservatism that emerged and became a major cultural force after 1797. Additionally, and crucially, most of the period's progressives had no theoretical language or analysis for explaining the rise of a form of middle-class reaction against the energies they themselves unleashed in the act of overthrowing the old social order. Certainly, one of *Ormond's* principle themes is the exploration of the cultural codes of this reaction, particularly of ostensibly power-free sentiment, that an increasingly dominant middle class would use to retard the force of social change and widening human emancipation.

It is vastly oversimplifying matters to say that the novel in Brown's hands is simply the continuation or articulation of a set of progressive ideals initially put forward by Anglo-European thinkers. Rather, *Ormond*, perhaps even more acutely than Brown's other fictions, attempts to put these ideals under stress in order to see how well they can survive the period's newly emerging hostility to Enlightenment ideals by nonaristocratic or Church officials, and hostile or antagonistic conditions, and to imagine how they might be transmitted in an increasingly inhospitable environment. *Ormond* is less a didactic novel than a tutelary or educational one, in that it highlights literary techniques that analyze and enact the ways in which radical perspectives can be circulated throughout certain parts of society and transmitted across generations in the face of resurgent conservatism.

The Middle Class in Crisis

After the opening of the novel's frame by narrator Sophia Courtland, the story she tells about her friend Constantia Dudley begins with a conventional plot line immediately recognizable to the period's readers. A businessman's reliance on sentimental appearances, his trust in an associate based on honest looks and reputation, is catastrophically misplaced. The comfortable security of mercantile routine is consequently undermined by deceit and the victim's safety net consists in the insulation provided by the private resources of the family (as opposed to the public negotiation of law), in this case a dutiful and extraordinarily resourceful daughter. Thus Stephen Dudley goes bankrupt after he trusts and relies on his apprentice Thomas Craig, and the series of events set in motion by this crisis brings the novel's protagonist Constantia to the fore. But even in the novel's presentation of this initial collapse stemming from Craig's duplicity, masquerade, and forgeries, it seems to depart significantly from predictable genre conventions in order to develop a counterexplanation of the mercantile family's crisis.

It soon becomes evident that Dudley's sudden downfall is a consequence of much more than gullibility and misplaced trust. On a literal reading, it follows from Craig's dishonesty and additionally from Dudley's more subtle inclination to resort to strategies of masquerade and secret surveillance himself, instead of confronting Craig with straightforward questions. Thus a conventional didactic lesson might be the importance of sincerity, an implication that the crisis could have been averted had Dudley himself refused to engage in duplicity. But this reading silences the force of class antagonisms, especially the resentment of a man born into the laboring class against the assumed privilege of the mercantile elite's comfort, seen in Dudley's openly declared "prejudice" against labor. Brown, does not, however, allow the libertine Craig to declare his hostility overtly, perhaps because he perceives the risks of open complaints against the social group from which his own readers are drawn. Instead, he broaches the theme obliquely in two ways: first by arranging for the Dudleys themselves to experience the heartless distrust to which those with Craig's class origins are subjected, and, second, by staging a refusal to uphold the behavioral codes and social arrangements that the middle class uses to distinguish and protect itself.

After Constantia and her father are thrown from their previously unexamined professional-class levels of comfort and privilege, they experience a brutal and brutalizing world that mixes them with heartless landlords, impoverished laborers, other low-prestige status groups, continual exposure to the degrading force of prejudice, and close brushes with death. The family falls into abject poverty and indigence despite the presence of wealthy former business associates nearby, and Constantia and her father are forced to pawn their last remaining comforts simply to survive the winter cold. The Dudleys must struggle to gain a modicum of security because, seen as poor, they are assumed to be disreputable and untrustworthy. While the social death that the Dudleys experience might initially be felt as a consequence of Stephen Dudley's own prideful shame, the onset of the yellow fever epidemic reveals that his "theatre of suffering" is more determined by class and ethno-racial conflict than by natural disaster, especially as the damage strikes unequally throughout American society.

The fever scenes in *Ormond*'s Chapters 3–7 are not as elaborately developed as the better known ones in *Arthur Mervyn* (published two or three months after *Ormond* in April or May, 1799). But in both cases this dramatic setting juxtaposes the biological corruption of the fever with the rampant commercial and social-economic corruption of a society that makes it easy for the wealthy to escape the fever in summer homes outside the urban center (like the landlord M'Crea in Chapter 8), but that abandons the poor to either little more than the modest support that they can offer one other or, conversely, a survival of the fittest as class and status gradations emerge even amongst themselves.[22]

Late-summer yellow fever epidemics were a periodic feature of life in North American cities at this time, and the 1793 Philadelphia episode fictionalized here became the best known and most frequently evoked of any in American accounts. This was

---

[22] For the relation between fever and market crisis in Brown and his context, see Anthony, "Banking on Emotion: Financial Panic and the Logic of Male Submission in the Jacksonian Gothic"; Christophersen, *The Apparition in the Glass: Charles Brockden Brown's American Gothic*; Ellis, "Charles Brockden Brown's *Ormond*, Property Exchange, and the Literary Marketplace in the Early American Republic"; Gould, "Race, Commerce, and the Literature of Yellow Fever in Early National Philadelphia"; Ditz, "Shipwrecked; or, Masculinity Imperiled: Mercantile Representations of Failure and Gendered Self in Eighteenth-Century Philadelphia."

partly because of its sheer magnitude and devastation (about 5,000 died and 17,000 fled a city whose population was roughly 55,000) but also, just as importantly, because it became a flash point for struggles concerning race, class, and immigration. Because the disease's etiology and transmission by mosquitoes was not yet understood, for example, many debates racialized the fever, supposing that its nature and virulence varied according to race and that Africans were less susceptible than Europeans. A variant xenophobic fantasy speculated that the French might be less susceptible than Anglos or other Protestant Europeans, and that international commerce with the French Caribbean was responsible for the fever's arrival.[23]

All of these attitudes and debates are dramatized in *Ormond*. The city's free blacks were on the front lines of emergency care, often used as nurses and undertakers on the mistaken assumption that they were immune to contagion. Shortly after the epidemic ended, these black Philadelphians faced ungrateful accusations that they used their positions to steal from stricken whites or extort money for their services. Brown implicitly counters these racially motivated claims in Chapter 5 by highlighting Constantia's interaction with an African woodcarter who is a reliable and entirely trustworthy partner in coping with the death of Constantia's friend Mary Whiston.[24]

Similar prejudices emerge in Chapter 7, in which the old soldier Baxter secretly witnesses a midnight burial in the garden of a neighboring house. Baxter is an elderly, impoverished ex-soldier (retired after service in British imperial wars) who has taken work as a night watchman and guard to survive the financial downturn and layoffs that occur as the fever depopulates the city. As he gazes through keyholes, windows, and over fences in order to spy on a mysterious female struggling to bury an older male, his train of thought is structured by a variety of irrational dislikes. He is "deeply and rancourously prejudiced" against the French (he has even adopted the xenophobic idea that they are immune to yellow fever) and it is this casual Francophobia that makes him disinclined to help his neighbor ("a frog-eating Frenchman") despite evident suffering and need. Although Baxter's ignorance and prejudice initially seem quite distinct from the thinking of the middle-class characters who animate the later chapters, his embodiment of social and ideological fault lines, as well

---

[23] Statistics concerning the 1793 epidemic vary significantly in different sources; we use numbers from Estes and Smith, *A Melancholy Scene of Devastation: The Public Response to the 1793 Yellow Fever Epidemic*. For general accounts of the epidemic, see Powell, *Bring Out Your Dead: The Great Plague of Yellow Fever in Philadelphia in 1793*; and the Web-based resources in Arnebeck, *Destroying Angel: Benjamin Rush, Yellow Fever and the Birth of Modern Medicine* (http://www.geocities.com/bobarnebeck/fever1793.html). For historical discussions of the fever's social and political implications, see the essays in Estes and Smith, *A Melancholy Scene of Devastation*; Kornfield, "Crisis in the Capital: The Cultural Significance of Philadelphia's Great Yellow Fever Epidemic"; and Taylor, *"We Live in the Midst of Death": Yellow Fever, Moral Economy, and Public Health in Philadelphia, 1793–1805*.

[24] For more on the ways that the fever affected the city's free black community and generated debates about the social inclusion of Africans in U.S. civil society, see Nash, *First City: Philadelphia and the Forging of Historical Memory*; and Estes and Smith, *A Melancholy Scene of Devastation*.

as his example of prejudicial interpreting, will be repeated in ever more significant forms by wealthier and more established characters. The perceived pattern thus indicates a dominant reality of conflict that is obscured by a public rhetoric of sympathetic care. Brown, however, mainly investigates this split indirectly by teasing out the pressures embedded within the middle class's own preferred narrative mode of fiction at that time, a sentimental tale of a young woman in distress.

Constantia and Generic Models of Womanhood

Although Stephen Dudley introduces the problem of the bourgeoisie or commercial middle class in crisis, it falls to his daughter, the conventional focus of sentimental fiction, to bear the burden of reconstructing their lost status as he retreats into self-protective isolation. During the family's experience of laboring class misery, Constantia's role, as her name suggests, is to be constant, faithful, and dutiful. Even in the absence of paternal authority and credibility, it is Constantia who must labor to restore the knowability and reliability of social and commercial value on which bourgeois society rests, by adhering to the traditional role of women as objects of exchange trafficked between men. As Brown and the Woldwinites argue, this is the traditional function of marriage, and this is what makes marriage effectively a form of genteel slavery for women.[25]

As a commodity for male desire, Constantia and implicitly all women are constantly on display and available for male observation. To use this novel's keywords, they are constantly being witnessed or observed in a quasitheatrical manner. In this optics and the economic relations it literalizes, women are judged mainly for their erotic and status appeal to men and the perceived value of their sexual sympathy is monetarized like other commodities. At its extreme, this principle corresponds to Constantia's disgust at being assumed to be a prostitute or a target for rape when she circulates in the public arena of the city's streets, but it also governs relatively "civil" exchanges such as the courtship of Scottish merchant Balfour (Chapter 9), the banter between Craig and Ormond about Constantia that facilitates Craig's handling of Ormond's money (Chapter 11), and the behavior of male servants and the otherwise virtuous Magistrate Melbourne, who observes Constantia in ways that hint that he is taking stock of her sexual availability (Chapters 10–11). Women, in this world, are available for visual inspection and an unwelcome, penetrating intrusion into their

---

[25] For commentary on the novel's feminism and exploration of the conditions of women's lives, see Fleischmann, "Charles Brockden Brown: Feminism in Fiction"; Hinds, *Private Property: Charles Brockden Brown's Gendered Economics of Virtue*; Krause, "Brockden Brown's Feminism in Fact and Fiction"; Layson, "Rape and Revolution: Feminism, Antijacobinism, and the Politics of Injured Innocence in Brockden Brown's *Ormond*"; Stern, "The State of 'Women' in *Ormond*; or, Patricide in the New Nation"; Waterman, *Republic of Intellect*; Wicke, "Sophia, Martinette, et Constantia: Des femmes exemplaires?"; and Zhang, "The Liberation of Women in America and the Three Female Characters in *Ormond*."

private spaces. Because Constantia is not conventionally beautiful, with her relatively large frame and "less … delicate" complexion (as described by the narrator Sophia as she compares Constantia to the striking features of Ursula Monrose in Chapter 8), the novel's emphasis on this repeated surveillance implicitly argues that *all* women are subject to this dynamic, not simply those deemed physically attractive.

Yet something unexpected happens when the Dudleys meet with an opportunity to escape their poverty and regain some aspect of their former status, when Constantia is saved by the respectable merchant Balfour from the possibility of a street rape by working-class toughs. Balfour is attracted to Constantia's reliability and utility as helpmate to his commercial life, and proposes marriage. Constantia's rejection of Balfour, against her father's wishes, like her first rejection of an unworthy suitor before the novel's action began, underlines her larger rejection of the cultural script that is expected to govern her life. Had she accepted Balfour's proposal, the novel would have a conventional outcome and expected forms of structural balance. The damage initiated by Craig's imposture would be restored by the mediocre Balfour, whose very conventionality makes him profoundly uninteresting and at the same time representative of an entire middling lifeworld.[26] But Constantia rejects these formal expectations out of hand. In marked contrast to conventional novelistic and sentimental heroines, Constantia will neither marry nor die. *Ormond* thus moves beyond conventional expectations and generic models for female identity, and, along with Craig's return, Constantia's decision to refuse a suitor marks the conclusion of *Ormond*'s first narrative segment.

With this blow against conventional expectations, Brown both introduces and extends the critique of female disempowerment that was developed in Woldwinite writings, most notably Mary Wollstonecraft's 1792 *Vindication of the Rights of Woman*. Wollstonecraft argued that women have been denied equality by a set of infantilizing social customs and institutions, and provided an early analysis of the way that the rhetoric of romantic love turns women into silent objects over which men contend. Her analysis highlights a series of themes that illustrate and document female subordination. The behaviors associated with female beauty constrain women's activity and force them into concerns with fashionable dress that in turn generate juvenile thinking. Traditional practices of female education exclude the male-associated topics of politics, science, and history, limiting women to the less analytical, more affective or emotionalized fields of languages and the arts (painting, music, dance). Additionally, the ideology of heterosexual marriage legitimates a form of contractual servitude likened to that of African slavery (and here the period's Orientalist fascination with the seraglio and harem conflated slavery and sexual submission). In *Alcuin*, his first extended prose publication, Brown conveyed these arguments in

---

[26] "Lifeworld" describes the way that the combined force of social and cultural institutions and their associated practices create a shared world of common sense and perceived reality. Roughly speaking, our "lifeworld" is the sum of the assumptions, meanings, and norms that we absorb from our social environment.

dialogic form and suggested their implication within the realm of rights and juridical empowerment.[27]

In *Ormond*, Brown expands Wollstonecraft's arguments in two significant ways. Though his moment lacks the terms and concepts later developed to address these questions, he uses Constantia's trials to develop a wider definition of gender horizons than Woldwinite writings. It is not simply Constantia's clothing and appearance that is disempowering, for example when poverty forces her to adopt a different style of dress in the early chapters, but the wider fact that she is trapped by a "social address" of femininity. Regardless of how she presents herself, she is restrained by normative expectations concerning womanhood, and these conditions define her location in the social field. But secondly, even if this constraining girdle of convention were removed, the absence of these restraints would not in itself be enough to make her free. After all, Constantia has received a "male" education and demands the freedom to think outside the doctrines of organized religious dogma. Here Brown rejects the notions of "equality feminism," or the idea that access to formal legal rights alone is an adequate condition for freedom. Like liberal political economy, this approach to women's lives presents the problem of disempowerment as the laissez-faire need for the removal of blockages or interferences, such as prejudice or legal inequities, and considers that this removal will level the playing field to make all presumably autonomous individuals equal to compete in the marketplace. This is the "possessive individualism" that is economic and political liberalism's answer to disempowerment.

In *Ormond*, however, the female protagonist realizes that gaining equal access to rights, or even to rights and knowledge together, is not enough. For Constantia, a "stranger to pusillanimity" or fear, the problem is having the courage and will to enact this knowledge, especially in the public sphere and in relation to men. The difficulty that she faces, because she is a woman, is the need to overcome internalized fear and the long-standing sense of female inferiority that has been instilled in her as the natural ideal of submissive womanhood. To use Wollstonecraftian language, she needs to summon "masculine" courage. This is to say that Brown realizes that a mental revolution must occur for genuine liberation to take place, and that this cultural transformation must precede legal or political affirmation because the former creates the necessary conditions for the latter.

Although Brown's particular focus in *Ormond* is on women, the need for a new cultural consciousness preceding the legal conditions of equality is a precept that Brown emphasizes repeatedly in his writings on all forms of social domination, including ethnic or racial subordination. This is the reason why he often brings these two categories together in particular characters or incidents (such as Constantia's encounter with the woodcarter), or in his analytical arguments. Brown consistently refused the idea that the accident of birth determines one's fate, that biology determines destiny as it delivers a permanent social death or disability. For Brown, if slaves behave lazily

---

[27] For more on Wollstonecraft and Brown's development of Woldwinite arguments concerning women, see *Alcuin* and the selections from Wollstonecraft and Godwin in Related Texts.

and seem to lack the will to excel, this diffidence is not the consequence of racial nature, but the imposed condition of slavery, which strips away basic levels of dignity and imposes a multigenerational system of subordination.

Constantia's problem, then, is that even though she is restored to her accustomed middle-class privilege, and even though she distinguishes herself by a "male" education and exceptional courage and fortitude, none of this is enough to take her beyond the conventional horizons of a sentimental heroine. The dilemma she faces is that it is not enough to be free from those who would trick and exploit her. She must also free herself from mental slavery and a hesitation to act.

This process of discovering and forging new ways of womanhood, as one instance of personhood in general, is a fundamental theme of *Ormond*. In many ways the novel's initial chapters may be read as an implicit pastiche and critique of early American sentimental fiction and the ways in which sentimental texts participate in the objectification of women by presenting them primarily as bearers of emotional distress whose crises illustrate but do little to suggest ways of resisting or altering existing states of domination. *Ormond*'s departure from these models is openly advertised in its insistence on qualitative changes in the development and mentalities of its primary female characters, and the qualitative differences between them.

As Constantia encounters the novel's title character Ormond and the women Helena Cleves, Martinette de Beauvais, and narrator Sophia Courtland in the novel's second and third segments, the narrative shifts to a startlingly different tableau of alternative models and potentials for female experience. If the narrative of self-development is categorized as the *Bildungsroman*, the genre that narrates an individual's self-formation, cultivation, and education (the three basic senses of the term *Bildung*), then *Ormond* should be regarded as one of the first revisions of this model. The interior narrative of women's thinking, doubts, and aspirations was already highly developed in the tradition of sentimental or "seduction" novels that developed the models of intensive self-reflection established in Samuel Richardson's *Clarissa* (1748) and its influential successor, Jean-Jacques Rousseau's *Julie; or the New Heloise* (1761). *Ormond* refers to these models, but reduces their emphasis on psychological interiority and authenticity, both to question the class assumptions inherent in sentimentalist models, and to connect the question of development into new stages or forms to matters of collective social and political transformation.

Brown's move toward an alternative generic model to explore women's lives takes on additional significance if we consider that it focuses on a character whose "social address" or location is different than that of the genre's customary male protagonists, for such a focus on a nonnormative protagonist implicitly shifts and questions the form's conventional presuppositions. For example, literary historian Franco Moretti argues that that the *Bildungsroman*'s focus on normative European male heroes makes them individually distinctive yet, ultimately, in the form's typical narrative resolutions, representatives or proxies for communal norms of dominant society. The genre's primary function is thus to engineer the end of the narrative so that it provides, as many have observed, an imaginary resolution to real contradictions. Typical or conventional novelistic endings, in other words, resolve crisis into normality. They answer the formulaic question, how much development is necessary for a tale to be concluded in ways that will not threaten preexisting bourgeois structures and aspirational values for advancement *and* security?[28]

But while these observations are undoubtedly valid for narratives concerning conventional male and European protagonists, they nevertheless leave two other trajectories unexplored. First, Moretti's model does not ask what might happen if, rather than delivering parables of individualism, such narratives of self-development redirected their audiences toward the collective and utopian. Second, and consequently, this alternative community might not have an "end." Its energy might be directed toward further change, and thus become a narrative about ongoing, enlarging, or permanent revolution. These are the questions that *Ormond* begins to raise after Constantia's refusal to marry, and after Brown's refusal to make her a sentimental heroine who embodies comic harmony in marriage or tragic catharsis in death.

The Community of Sorrow and its Vicissitudes

Constantia's first experience of new social potentials draws her toward an emotionally saturated idea or imagination of female community. As her friendships with deferential laboring-class women such as her maid Lucy, Mary Whiston, and Sarah Baxter suggest, these relations often transcend class barriers both upward and downward, so that she is spontaneously comfortable in addressing, quickly befriending, and identifying with women she has not previously encountered. As she learns about the fate of other women, she rushes to consider them similar to herself so that, for example, when imaging the suffering imposed during the yellow fever in Chapter 6, Constantia's imagination constructs the misery around her specifically as a crisis of women in pain, afflicted by the loss of husbands and children. In a certain sense, in fact, Constantia seems to relish the paradoxical freedom opened up by plague conditions, as she becomes more comfortable walking through the city's streets once they have been depopulated and the men who ordinarily dominate these spaces have disappeared. The female community that she initially imagines is based on the sympathetic bond of tears or emotions.

This community of sorrow is most fully developed in her relationship with Helena Cleves, aka Mrs. Eden. In accordance with the logic of sympathetic identification, Helena closely mirrors Constantia's circumstances. Both women come from mercantile-family backgrounds in New York, and both lose this world due to financial turbulence. They both find themselves living under pseudonyms in Philadelphia, where their inability to achieve social inclusion is illustrated in the way they are physically cloistered in small apartments controlled by unfeeling males, and psychologically contained by their own internalized fears of social encounters that would expose them to disapproval and shame. Helena particularly illustrates the condition of women who are imprisoned and damaged by socially conditioned norms of femininity. She

---

[28] For the *Bildungsroman* and its cultural politics, see Moretti, *The Way of the World*.

is literally and figuratively imprisoned because her dedication to maintaining the prestige of luxurious dress and living conditions has led her to objectify herself as a "kept" woman, a mistress. Helena's devotion to this emotional ideal appears in her facility with a feminized and aesthetic style associated with modern Italianate forms, in opposition to the figuratively stoic rigor of Constantia's "Roman," classical, and male-associated knowledge.

If Constantia was initially reluctant to contradict or resist male authority, she finds it easier to do so when she is acting on behalf of a sisterly figure in distress. In this situation, Constantia and the novel's readers may begin to consider that psychological and social growth results not from selfishness, the cultivation of individual interests, but from social action, the politics of collective and mutually beneficial organization. If Constantia's encounter with Helena thus provides a test case for this initial turn toward a woman's community of feeling, Helena's suicide quickly literalizes the weakness and fragility of this position and its potential. In an allegorical sense, Helena's inability or refusal to face life's rigors suggests the intrinsically narrow limits and self-imposed limitations of female identity understood as shared trauma. If it teaches Constantia the weakness of this position, it also presents her with an opportunity to overcome her own self-imposed limitations.

In the Helena episode Brown seems to reject strategies or politics based on essentializing sympathy circulated among the victimized. This phase of Constantia's development may additionally be seen as Brown's indication that there are greater structural impediments to (female) empowerment, and an implicit argument about the need to free oneself from past models. For Brown was all too aware of the degree to which even the period's leading feminist writers, female and male alike, found it difficult to extricate themselves from the psychologizing grip of "romance." Mary Wollstonecraft and Maria Hays, for example, two authors read and admired by Brown and his associates, were widely discussed as progressive females prone to heartbreak caused by the libertine deceit of men with whom they had fallen in love.

Wollstonecraft's ill-fated romance with Gilbert Imlay, which resulted in an out-of-wedlock child and suicide attempt, was a well-known recent case in point. Wollstonecraft's husband, William Godwin, described these experiences in a posthumous biography which had the unexpected effect of blasting her reputation for decades. In his biographical *Memoirs of the Author of a Vindication of the Rights of Woman* (1797), Godwin also describes how a Helena-like figure, Frances ("Fanny") Blood, represented for Wollstonecraft the ideal of female sympathetic community. Yet despite Wollstonecraft's plans to live with and financially support Blood, the latter chose the conventional path of matrimony and motherhood. Wollstonecraft's affection for Fanny was such that she named her first child (a daughter who later committed suicide) after her.[29] Hays was similarly incapacitated by a romance with an unfeeling man, in much the same way that Helena sacrifices herself to Ormond.

---

[29] For more on Wollstonecraft's relationship with Frances Blood and its significance for *Ormond,* see the Godwin selection in Related Texts.

Constantia seems to acknowledge the fragility of sympathy when, after Helena's death, she again behaves in a manner that few readers would expect: she continues her relationship with Ormond, even after it becomes clear that his actions and declaration of erotic interest in her were the catalyst for Helena's suicide. In terms of novelistic or generic conventions, Constantia's refusal to simply condemn Ormond is extremely unusual or even scandalous behavior, as the London *Anti-Jacobin Review* indicated when it rejected *Ormond* categorically, citing its refusal to condemn suicide and related "disgusting and pernicious nonsense" as evidence of its unsuitability for readers.[30] From the perspective of most assumed readers of sentimental or romantic novels in this period, it is remarkable that Constantia behaves as she does, and doubly remarkable that Ormond is neither overwhelmed by guilt nor symbolically punished for his part in Helena's demise.

To a certain degree, the refusal to blame Ormond follows Brown's career-long interest in writing against the principles of revenge and retribution, which he, like the Woldwinites, saw as a set of destructive values that belong to the corrupt machinery of feudal society. Because the rejection of revenge as a self-destructive passion recurs on numerous levels in Brown's novels *Wieland*, *Edgar Huntly*, and *Arthur Mervyn*, it is hardly surprising to find it here. Yet within the context of Constantia's development, her continued affinity for and meetings with Ormond underlines her rejection of woman-centered sentimentality as an affect that is insufficient in the struggle against the old regime and as one that might, in fact, be complicit with its maintenance and reproduction.

Ormond: International Man of Mystery

Constantia's first turn away from sentimental relations comes in her encounter with Ormond's dogmatic refusal of sympathy and its certainties. At all levels, Ormond is brusque, insensitive, and infuriatingly contradictory. A fierce opponent of behavioral hierarchy and the display of politeness that obscures social inequalities, he is nevertheless arrogant, self-aggrandizing, and a firm believer in the superiority of men over women. He professes social transparency, but uses arcane skills as a ventriloquist and master of disguise to secretly examine others and use them with or without their knowledge to influence society, for example when he watches and evaluates Constantia to determine whether she merits receiving (disguised and indirect) financial support. He is antipatriarchal but demands obedience and patronizes those around him. Although Ormond's background and larger ambitions remain mysterious in their detail, not least because the narrator Sophia openly acknowledges that her politicized belligerence toward Ormond colors her descriptions of him, he seems to belong to an international secret society that seeks to distribute enlightenment values through opaque means that are as oppressive as the forces they seek to dismantle. For example, Ormond's group may act as an Inquisition-like secret tribunal that envisions imperialist occupation of non-European lands.

---

[30] *The Anti-Jacobin Review* 6.26 (August 1800), 451.

However, what Ormond stands for seems less significant than the effect of his manner of conveying it to Constantia. His relationship with her proceeds through a series of action and reaction spirals, in which his initial offensiveness inevitably acts to pull her closer. This pedagogy is unorthodox and transforms Constantia's attitudes through abrupt, often insulting psychic shocks, rather than nurturing encouragement. With this antisentimental schooling through adversity, Ormond raises the question for Constantia of whether one can learn from and in a hostile environment. Can one draw knowledge from established authorities, take what is useful from the past, and then use it to extricate oneself from their rule? As mentioned, this third, interstitial position, caught between the extremes of total subordination to authority and totally spontaneous revolt also suggests the need for a tactics of subterfuge or a guerilla-like existence within a larger social fabric.

Furthermore, Ormond's indeterminacy, the continual difficulty of determining with certainty what he actually believes, who he is, or where he has been, provides a model of what it might mean to exist in a time of rapid transition, in a moment in which it becomes difficult, if not actually a liability, to believe in a firm or permanent sense of the (individual) self. Can one live with the challenge of being comfortable with indeterminacy, without dependence on ideas of authenticity in settled forms of (gendered, regional, ethnic, denominational) identity, while still negotiating a critical engagement with the world? Does having an embodied identity help one live and learn from the play of history, even if this history is traumatic, degrading, and disreputable? Or more simply put: Can there be a progressive cultural politics that radically frees itself from the need for an identifying social location, from the particularities of body, race, and nationality?

The possibility of this divide comes with the challenge that Ormond's shapeshifting, in his masquerades as an African American chimney sweep or possibly as the charlatan Martynne, presents to the physiognomic assumption and sentimental idea that the body's surface is the register on which interior personality can be found and reliably interpreted. While the novel's characters frequently gaze on each other as a means of ascertaining the relative risks of interaction, Ormond refuses to be read so simply. Ormond's inscrutability comes on the heels of Craig's, but unlike Craig, whose imposture was perceived in wholly negative terms, Ormond's is simultaneously abrasive and seductive for Constantia. For despite his complicity in Helena's suicide and the fracturing of female community, Constantia is magnetized by Ormond as he presents an initially disconcerting, but also compelling possibility of breaking away from the social conventions and identities which may imprison us even as they provide the security of the known.

Female Antisentimentality: Martinette and the Politics of Enlightenment

Although Ormond's name gives the novel its title, Martinette de Beauvais may be its most remarkable figure and is certainly the character who provides Constantia the greatest tutelage in alternative modes of being (female) in the modern world. Because she appears in disguise as the mysterious Ursula Monrose (the figure secretly witnessed by the old soldier Baxter in Chapter 7, and subsequently glimpsed and described in Chapter 9) before being revealed as Martinette, this French-speaking émigré functions as a sort of hidden vortex around which Constantia swirls until she has developed to the point where meeting Martinette will have maximum impact.

When Sarah Baxter first tells Constantia the story of an apparently impoverished immigrant woman who disappears after old Baxter witnessed her burying an elderly man presumed to be her father, the American woman's first response typifies the codes of sentimental emotion. She yearns to meet this woman who, in her habitual imagination of female community, doubles and amplifies the conditions of her own suffering. Similarly, when Constantia encounters the foreigner in a shop in Chapter 8, she feels a powerfully magnetic, yet still inarticulate attraction to the stranger. When Constantia finally does encounter and speak with Martinette outside her initial disguise, however, this long-standing code of sympathetic attraction is abandoned for an elective affinity, an intentional and purposive bond, that is riddled with ambiguity and tension because it is based on the rational evaluation of possibilities and challenges that individuals encounter in the modern world's political and social turbulence. Above all, Martinette represents the enactment of a dynamic response to the liberating opportunities presented by revolutionary social change.

Like Ormond, Martinette is emphatically cosmopolitan; she speaks many languages, and has traveled and lived throughout the Mediterranean, European, and Atlantic worlds. She is comfortable existing within and accommodating herself to the kinds of complex conditions that characterize a historical period in rapid and violent fluctuation, and this facility is signaled by the multiple names and social conditions her character bears in successive stages of her life. Intellectually and politically, she is a fierce advocate of the progressive and radical Enlightenment. Like Ormond, she is almost twice Constantia's age and assumes a commanding role whenever she meets the younger woman. Martinette's abrupt appearances and disappearances mean that she dictates the tempo of their relationship, and her wide knowledge and personal, bodily engagement in contemporary international politics as lived experience means that Constantia looks to her for concrete education about the disruptions of the modern world, in contrast to her previous, more abstract study of classical history and culture. Yet in comparison with the contradictory mixture of opportunities and obstacles Constantia encounters in Ormond, Martinette provides a more influential and accessible model. Martinette's concrete embodiment of liberatory possibilities provides the information and example that will be necessary to cross the barrier of gender constraints that has blocked Constantia's horizons to this point.

Unlike Constantia, Martinette seems to be beautiful in the conventional terms determined by male evaluations of female appearance. As Sophia's detailed verbal "portrait" in Chapter 8 suggests, Martinette is small, delicate, graceful, and smoothly complexioned. But unlike Helena, the novel's other conventionally beautiful and delicate woman, Martinette refuses to allow the accident of her appearance or exterior biological apparatus—her female sex—to predetermine or define her social potential and actions. Martinette's rejection of the imprisonment of gender is most clearly explained when Constantia quizzically wonders how this exotic foreigner could have experienced so much in contrast to her own relatively localized and banal past. Martinette replies with unapologetic vigor: "You grew and flourished, like a frail Mimosa, in the spot where destiny had planted you. Thank my stars, I am somewhat better than a vegetable. Necessity, it is true, and not choice, set me in motion, but I am not sorry for the consequences." This reply affirms the value of cosmopolitan circulation over nativist isolation, as Martinette refuses to be fixed or defined by the accident of being born into a particular region, language, class, or body.

In contrast to Constantia, Martinette is unwilling to be constant or true to dominant ideals of femininity. In what is a prescient, point-by-point refutation of the values cultural historians would later define as the nineteenth-century "Cult of True Womanhood,"[31] Martinette rejects domesticity, religious piety, sexual purity, and submissiveness to male dictates and expectations. Significantly, and almost shockingly for the period's fictions, Martinette is a woman who is comfortable with the enactment of female sexuality and who is never punished or humiliated for it.[32] Free from debilitating shame, she unhesitatingly recounts a past rich in erotic experiences with multiple partners outside the policing oversight of theocratic authorities. She has little or no interest in maternity and certainly does not consider her widowhood as her final identity or an event worthy of morbid preoccupation.

Martinette's backstory, recounted in Chapters 19–21, primarily emphasizes her ability to elude the prescriptive force of conventional scripts for women's lives and, crucially, to elude them precisely because she abandons sentimentality. When she buries the man assumed to be her father, the old soldier Baxter is as shocked by her lack of tears as he is by the moonlit burial itself. Martinette's freedom from rule by feminizing emotion means that she can be schooled by adversity rather than constructing herself as its victim. She has antagonistic relations with her elderly female governess Madame Roselli and, even more so, with the priestly tutor Father Bartoli (Chapter 20). Yet despite the priest's attempt to seduce (or rape) and dominate her, Martinette manages to invert the scenario and empower herself instead, by focusing on useful aspects of the situation, notably the tutor's ability to transmit to her the male-associated disciplines of science and history.

Martinette's tactical refusal of sentimentality and embrace of an assertive perspective on her life's challenges is articulated most clearly in the passage in Chapter 21 in which she unapologetically recounts her earlier plan to assassinate a Royalist general hostile to the French Revolution. Constantia is initially shocked by her friend's enthusiastic endorsement of violence toward revolutionary goals, but Martinette makes it clear that she believes social emancipation can only occur in the moment of crisis.

---

[31] For this formation, see Welter, "The Cult of True Womanhood, 1820–1850."

[32] See Lewis, "Attaining Masculinity: Charles Brockden Brown and Woman Warriors of the 1790s."

For Martinette, these are the times that try women's souls. As Constantia marvels at the idea of acting in "a scene of so much danger," Martinette replies:

> Danger my girl? It is my element. I am an adorer of liberty, and liberty without peril can never exist … . Have women, I beseech thee, no capacity to reason and infer? Are they less open than men to the influence of habit? My hand never faultered when liberty demanded the victim.

By rejecting ideals of pacific, evolutionary reform and celebrating the arena of emergency because it provides the best opportunities for previously disempowered groups to throw off their shackles, Martinette exemplifies trust in revolutionary dynamics.

Martinette's commitment to a politics and pedagogy of decisive ruptures is typified by her serial acts of transvestism in the service of the American and French Revolutions. Martinette's cross-dressing, a feature of the novel that was drawn from a popular period subgenre of military female-transvestism narratives, is much more than a simple proclivity to masquerade.[33] It offers a new mode for combining antiaristocratic and antipatriarchal politics, since transvestism is an attack on the standing order of the body as the most fundamental "social address" of status. Furthermore, Martinette relates the story as the mechanism of her own liberation from normative internalized fear. While fighting in military drag for American independence, she discovers that "the timidity that commonly attends women gradually vanished," and relates that she gradually became "embued by a soul that was a stranger to the sexual distinction." Emancipation from internalized fear is, of course, what Constantia herself has been consistently struggling to achieve.

Numerous commentators have noted Constantia's initial recoil from Martinette's ferocity, and often insist that this momentary aversion should be understood as Constantia's (and Brown's) final word on the question of revolution.[34] But this interpretation seems to ignore both Constantia's ensuing desire to learn more from Martinette, and Martinette's larger claim that change occurs through antisentimental shocks, whether these be Ormond's scandalous statements or Martinette's willingness to thrust herself into scenarios of risk and danger. Martinette's list of the reasons why some women cross-dressed to participate in revolutionary wars shows Brown's

---

[33] For more on the revolutionary-era genre of female transvestism tales, see the selections concerning Louise Françoise de Houssay and Deborah Sampson in Related Texts, and the commentary in Dekker and Van de Pol, *The Tradition of Female Transvestism in Early Modern Europe*; Dugaw, "Female Sailors Bold: Transvestite Heroines and the Markers of Gender and Class"; Friedli, "'Passing Women': A Study of Gender Boundaries in the Eighteenth Century"; Garber, *Vested Interests: Cross-Dressing and Cultural Anxiety*; Gustafson, "The Genders of Nationalism: Patriotic Violence, Patriot Sentiment in the Performances of Deborah Sampson Gannett"; Wheelwright, *Amazons and Military Maids: Women who Dressed as Men in Pursuit of Life, Liberty and Happiness*; and Young, *Masquerade: The Life and Times of Deborah Sampson, Continental Soldier*.

[34] See for example Marchand, "Introduction"; Levine, *Conspiracy and Romance: Studies in Brockden Brown, Cooper, Hawthorne, and Melville*; Comment, "Charles Brockden Brown's *Ormond* and Lesbian Possibility in the Early Republic."

awareness of the period's rumors and accounts of female transvestism, but Martinette's final rationale—the "contagion of example"—indicates her awareness that the communication of possibilities may catalyze their imitation and further enactment.

Readers may assume that Martinette's account of her past is inauthentic or carefully manipulated in part or in whole, given her self-admitted experience in imposture and masqueraded identities. As Constantia realizes in Chapter 19, "an impenetrable veil was drawn over her [Martinette's] own condition." But to discount the importance of her example for Constantia on this grounds would be to mistake the greater lesson that this experienced and knowledgeable foreigner—"a woman thus fearless and sagacious"—extends to the young American. For Martinette provides a master class in how to refuse body-based government of all kinds, whether the rules in question are those of aristocratic lineage, male authority, or racial prejudice.

Martinette's rejection of the old regime of feudalism and priestly fraud is most obvious with her active engagement in the French and American revolutions. Her antipatriarchal gestures are inherent in her easy appropriation of male authority, which goes beyond her practice of transvestism to include her staging of moments that reverse the normative sexual economy in which women are trafficked between men. For example, when the still-disguised and as yet unknown Martinette stands next to Constantia before a shopkeeper handling the trade of a lute, she pretends not to speak English, forcing the male merchant to shuttle between the two women. In early modern iconography, the lute is a familiar attribute of female sexuality. In singing to this instrument's accompaniment, the female voice circulates among male listeners in much the same way that Helena Cleve's musicality marks her as female and available. But in this scene, as Martinette implicitly arranges it, a male voice becomes an object circulated between women, and male desire (since the lute is Stephen Dudley's tool of pleasure) is subordinated to a discretely signaled affinity between two females. Similarly, no matter what conditions led to the death of Roselli, the man that Martinette buried in Chapter 7, the unceremonious and tear-free burial enacts the "death" of the patriarch, especially insofar as it frees Martinette from a woman's linkage to the home so that she can move at will, in striking contrast to Constantia's domestic cloistration during these same chapters as a "good daughter" enacting filial piety toward her moody, emotionally abusive father.

Additionally, Brown hints at one more possible register of freedom with this character by suggesting potential connections to the condition of slavery and the situation of racially mixed women. The suggestion of possible racial mixture in Martinette appears with Chapter 8's description of her skin color ("the shade was remarkably deep," comments the narrator Sophia) and delicate frame, both qualities that may gesture toward period stereotypes in which mixed-race women were held to be more feminine, dainty, and elegant than either blacks or whites of "pure" or less mixed ancestry. Although Martinette relates an elaborate backstory concerning her Eastern Mediterranean origins, there is no independent confirmation of this tale and claims of southern European identity were in fact one of the alibis used for racial passing (a later example is the fugitive slave George in Stowe's 1851 *Uncle Tom's Cabin*, who passes with a "Spanish complexion"). Considering that Martinette's last port of call before arriving in Philadelphia was the Caribbean slave colony Haiti, and that her companion Roselli oversees colonial possessions in another slave colony, Cayenne, French Guiana, it may well be that she has a more than passing connection to the world of slavery, a possibility additionally suggested by her name's resemblance to Martinique, an important French sugar colony.

In the racial hierarchies of Haiti, mixed-race subjects had a different social status than individuals with full African parentage. Many of these "free people of color" became wealthy plantation and even slave owners in their own right. Mixed race or "mulatta" women from his planter class then frequently exchanged wealth for status by marrying poorer white Creoles, much as English aristocrats married the daughters of American robber barons in the later nineteenth century. Consequently, if the relation between Roselli and Martinette was that of a former master and slave, or of a European Creole and a free woman of color, then Martinette's tearless burial may connect with a number of other scenarios, from the murder of an extortionate master to a fortuitous opportunity for freedom brought about by the chaos of the fever epidemic. Martinette's burial of the father may thereby hint at a kind of racial uprising or a violent refusal of the kind of "kept" status that Helena experienced in a more self-destructive fashion.

In a French Position: Culture and Political Contagion

As it presents Martinette's activities in Philadelphia and develops the implications of her impact on Constantia, *Ormond* also registers and provides commentary on the more diffuse cultural wave of transformation that occurred when large numbers of Francophone refugees from the ongoing revolutions in Paris and Haiti arrived in the city. Throughout the 1790s, and above all during the 1793–1794 period of extreme political and social crisis that corresponds to the dates of the novel's action, French exiles arrived in U.S. port cities and had an immediate impact on American culture far out of proportion to their relatively small size as an emigrant group. Like Martinette, who plans to leave Philadelphia to rejoin the revolutionary struggle after learning of Robespierre's death in Chapter 21, many of these refugees considered themselves temporary exiles, waiting out the revolutionary storm that was underway in metropolitan France or colonial Haiti.[35]

Unlike the mainly agricultural and laboring-class background of earlier and larger northern-European emigrant groups such as the Germans and Scots-Irish, these Francophone exiles of the 1790s belonged largely to the middle class and planter

---

[35] For commentary on the period's Francophone wave, see Branson and Patrick, "Etrangers Dans Un Pays Etrange: Saint-Domingan Refugees of Color in Philadelphia"; Meadows, "Engineering Exile: Social Networks and the French Atlantic Community, 1789–1809"; Nash, "Reverberations of Haiti in North America: Black Saint Dominguans in Philadelphia"; Potofsky, "The 'Non-Aligned Status' of French Emigrés and Refugees in Philadelphia, 1793–1798"; and Wiener, *The French Exiles, 1789–1815*.

elites, and consequently tended to be more literate, financially comfortable, and less familiar with manual labor than earlier immigrant communities. With little experience in crafts, the refugees scrambled to survive by helping establish a market for consumer pleasures—often involving the commercialization of physical appearance and behavior—as hairdressers, dressmakers, cooks, dance instructors, book sellers, and music and theater performers. As they brought a new code of manners and personal dress styles to the plainer, predominately Protestant cultures of American cities, the French strangers were arguably important catalysts or accelerators in this period's shift from self-sufficient, agrarian, household economies toward more modern patterns in which individuals fashion their identity not by adherence to family or village origins, but through consumer choices in clothes, books, and other cultural commodities. Not only did these French emigrants make new kinds of consumer objects and behaviors available to Americans, they also embodied and modeled for locals a radically new mentality involving comfort with lifeways based on a consumer economy, an orientation that is dramatically different than Puritan ideals of asceticism or Quaker moderation.

While these refugees often arrived with little money, they did come with considerable cultural capital, as highly literate individuals often accustomed to managing others as merchants, lawyers, or property owners. Perhaps not since the New England Puritans had North America experienced the arrival of so bourgeois and educated a group as these Francophone émigrés. They introduced fashionable consumer and dress styles including relatively relaxed codes concerning the display of sexual desire and behavior, such as the open presence of mixed-race mistresses in the street. As they introduced a new repertoire of cultural outlooks to the early U.S., they positioned themselves as "educators" who could guide the American public in their experience of these new styles. In this manner, the period's French-speaking émigrés also began to create something that had not previously occurred in the U.S., a bridge between classes based on a new set of cultural and political outlooks.[36]

While there was already a long-standing dynamic of prestigious French contributions to early U.S. culture, previous exchanges tended to focus on relations between elites, for example the Marquis de Lafayette's friendship with Washington, or Franklin and Jefferson's exchanges with French scientists and intellectuals during their diplomatic assignments in Paris. The French refugees of the 1790s, by contrast, encountered a wide spectrum of Americans, and their new conditions of unexpected social decline meant that high-status Francophone exiles found it necessary to live and work among middling and laboring-class Americans. Brown accurately captures this mixture when he presents Martinette, during her period of disguise as Ursula Monrose, living among the Philadelphia working class, and later has her explain her travels to Constantia by citing the geographical writings of C. F. Volney, another of the refugees who took up residence in Philadelphia during this period and became

---

[36] In Related Texts, see Brown's "Portrait of an Emigrant" and the selections by Moreau de Saint-Méry, Watson, and C. F. Volney.

well known to Brown's circle.[37] It was the French immigrants' potential for introducing a new set of "irregular" cultural ideals, as well as their ability to circulate these practices through the lower strata of the city outside the control of the standing political and social order, that made them so threatening to conservative forces and the sitting Federalist government during these years.

Conservative anxieties concerning the period's multifaceted wave of French cultural influences are critically dramatized throughout *Ormond* in more and less obvious ways, from the plebian Francophobia of the old soldier Baxter to narrator Sophia Courtland's more sophisticated but no less pronounced antipathy to all things French. What Brown is inscribing in the novel with this motif, in general terms, is the way that the period's vitriolic revolution debates corresponded to partisan divisions in the U.S. political climate at the time the novel was written. The Federalist Party in power in the U.S. during the 1790s supported England rather than France and feared the effects of European revolutions, but the greater and more lasting threat that the period's conservatives associated with French immigrants to the United States perhaps lay in this immigrant community's tendency to hasten a new "democratic" consensus and fusion between the political elites of the opposition Democratic-Republican Party (Virginia and New York property holders such as Madison, Jefferson, and George Clinton, Vice President to Jefferson and Madison) and a large stratum of artisans, mechanics, and itinerant laborers then seeking organizational opportunities. When the Federalist administration of then-President John Adams enacted the Alien and Sedition Acts in 1798, the year that Brown's novelistic phase began, their target was not simply to repress explicit political radicalism (allegorically, such as Ormond's), but also to contain what they perceived as the threat of alternative cultural outlooks that might link together otherwise isolated non-Federalist groups (allegorically, such as Martinette's alliance with Constantia). In this light, it is not Ormond alone who elicits a reactionary response in the narrative's framing of events, but Martinette as well. The relatively greater anxiety provoked by Martinette's influence may be inferred, perhaps, by the fact that it is only after she establishes her connection with Constantia, and not after Ormond's entrance, that the novel's narrative flow is unexpectedly interrupted.

Reactionary Regulation: Sophia and Counterrevolutionary Sentiment

All of Brown's novels present sudden and initially disorienting breaks in their plotting and narrative development. These breaks tend to divide the narratives into seemingly irreconcilable parts (often halves, or binaries), to suggest contending or contradictory energies, to heighten the reader's awareness of the limitations of the narrator's point of view, and to shock the reader generally, reshaping the sense of the

---

[37] For more on Volney and his relation to 1790s Philadelphia, see Related Texts.

novel's action that readers have presumably built up or assumed before the break occurs. As a result of such breaks, *Wieland* shifts from a tale about a lower-class wanderer and mysterious voices at a wealthy estate, to a terrifying account of insanity and patriarchal family murder. *Edgar Huntly* begins as a story about an enlightened Quaker's rural benevolence, but ends with uncontrollable sleepwalking, barbaric cycles of settler-Indian revenge violence, and profound insecurity. *Arthur Mervyn* opens with a panorama of overwhelming institutional corruption literalized in the 1793 yellow fever epidemic, but ends with an unexpectedly hopeful tale of romance between figures from different classes and ethnicities. In all of these novels, the abrupt juxtaposition of superficially different elements has a logical purpose for Brown as he uses one dimension of the narrative to reveal tensions that underpin and inform another. Thus, we might say, the narrative segments are not ruptures or breaks so much as efforts to turn the narrative upside down so that readers will see a social underbelly or infrastructure that is otherwise missed or too easily ignored. *Ormond* not only follows this pattern of emplotment through the introduction of new perspectives and story lines, but its overall narrative frame is arguably Brown's most insistent and complicated use of this technique.

The effects of this frame are evident throughout the novel, although the manner in which its influence is gradually intensified and revealed means that readers are not obligated to notice it until Sophia Courtland, the narrator of the entire performance, steps out from the behind the authorial curtain in Chapter 23 and exchanges her relatively understated shaping of the narrative's meanings up to that point for an overt, explicit intervention in its drama of contending revolutionary and reactionary energies. Sophia, as "S.C.," establishes and acknowledges her control over the narrative on the novel's first page, when she addresses it to a "German" reader identified as I. E. Rosenberg, admits that her portraits of Constantia and Ormond will be neither objective nor complete, and intimates that the narrative's fictional purpose is to account for Constantia's "defects" and "errors" in such a way as to make her a suitable partner for an elite marriage. Even in the novel's early chapters, Sophia intervenes to address the reader and editorialize, usually in ways that implicitly claim she is more intimate with the protagonist Constantia, and a more authoritative source of knowledge about her, than any of the other characters with whom Constantia interacts, above all Ormond and Martinette. In Chapter 2, for example, Sophia establishes her emotional authority as a member of Constantia's community of suffering and claims special proximity to the protagonist with her assertion that "my eyes almost wept themselves dry over this part of her tale."

A striking example of this style of intervention occurs in Chapter 8, a sort of tour de force of narrative insinuation in which Sophia rhetorically balances Constantia's loss of a visual portrait of Sophia herself (claiming that this loss constitutes a deep psychological and sympathetic wound for Constantia) against her own production of a verbal portrait of Martinette, her future rival in Constantia's affections, who at this point is still in disguise as Ursula Monrose. Even before she uses her narratorial powers to reveal to the reader that Monrose is in fact Martinette, Sophia is already attempting to limit and qualify Constantia's interest in Martinette by insinuating that

Constantia's real dilemma (presented as a crisis of interior psychological authenticity of the kind that occurs in sentimental novels) concerns herself, Sophia, rather than the fascinating woman Constantia is encountering and becoming attracted to. A picture is worth a thousand words, as the saying goes, and thus Chapter 8's performance of what we might call "narrative narcissism" need not be noticed by the reader, even though it prefigures the more blatant instances of prejudicial interpretation that will emerge in the novel's later narrative segments. The old soldier Baxter and the predatory Ormond, more attentive readers may realize, are not the novel's only deeply prejudiced and antagonistic secret witnesses.

By the point that Constantia forms her friendship with Martinette, the novel has implicitly charted her increasing awareness of the possibility of emancipating herself from the gender constraints of conventional femininity and womanhood. In this regard, Martinette's presence and example is more influential than that of Ormond. The emergence of this crucial influence, therefore, may explain why Sophia waits until after Martinette's full-blown arrival, rather than her own melodramatic and alarmist introduction of Ormond, to unmask herself as Sophia Westwyn Courtland and step onto the stage of the tale's events.

Sophia is perhaps best understood as a sort of mirror opposite to Martinette. Both characters share similar transnational and tumultuous life conditions, but they embody diametrically opposed ideological interpretations of the contemporary moment. Martinette is cosmopolitan, a freethinker, willing to engage with social change, socially and politically radical. Sophia is nativist, territorial and provincial, dedicated to religious dogma, hostile to change, socially conservative, and politically reactionary. Like Martinette, Sophia is taken abroad by a damaging maternal figure she does not like, but whereas Martinette used travel as a means of learning, Sophia spends her time complaining and avoiding her new surroundings. While Martinette transforms herself through social intercourse in different cultures, including marrying men of different nationalities, Sophia is a petulant American abroad who spends her time grousing that Europe is not like home and is never happier than when she finds compatriots to reminisce with.

On returning to the U.S., Sophia writes in Chapter 24, she found that "the difference between Europe and America, lay chiefly in this; that, in the former, all things tended to extremes, whereas, in the latter, all things tended to the same level. Genius and virtue, and happiness, on these shores, were distinguished by a sort of mediocrity. Conditions were less unequal, and men were strangers to the heights of enjoyment and the depths of misery, to which the inhabitants of Europe are accustomed." With this insistence on social conformity, Sophia's superficially patriotic affirmation celebrates America as the land of internalized discipline. Deeply provincial, she employs the language of patriotism as a means of reinforcing existing forms of social relations while repressing social differences and the possibilities of Enlightenment liberation that Ormond and Martinette illuminate for Constantia. Further, she channels a contemporary conservative argument about the difference between America and Europe that was then associated with the ruling Francophobic Federalist Party. Ventriloquizing future U.S. President John Quincy Adams, who wrote from

Berlin in 1800 to assert that the difference between the American and French Revolutions was simply "the difference between *right* and *wrong*," Sophia asserts a qualitative distinction between the two revolutions in order to draw Constantia's imagination back to the limited horizons and perspectives that defined it before she met Ormond and Martinette.[38]

Up until Sophia steps onto the stage in Chapter 23, her narrative perspective and political views have been more implicit than explicit. Once she reveals her identity and recounts her backstory by way of establishing herself as a childhood friend and protector of Constantia, however, her narrative provides an increasingly tendentious and argumentative denunciation of the past and present activities of both Ormond and Martinette, presenting them as the destructive careers of pathologically imbalanced minds and the consequences of progressive and radical political principles.

Sophia's narrative authority and interventionist role in the novel's conclusions pose basic questions of interpretation. Some readers have agreed with critics like William Hedges, who argues that Sophia's "actual presence [is] the sure sign that the novel will tolerate no deviance from accepted views," or with Robert S. Levine's suggestion that Brown introduces Sophia to affirm that "the preservation of liberty may require a 'reactionary' power."[39] There is no question that Sophia represents a counterrevolutionary outlook, but it is much less certain that Brown intends readers to hear Sophia's rants as his own, rather than as illustrations of the ways that conservative and reactionary claims are commonly presented as neutral, commonsensical, or unquestionable affirmations of "natural" order.

What seems clear, by the time Sophia begins to intervene actively in the novel's action, is that she uses her role as narrator to present herself as an objective and omniscient commentator when she is anything but. Simultaneously claiming that she has constructed her narrative solely from Constantia's letters and that she has secret sources of information that she cannot clarify, Sophia never mentions that almost all of its events, from Dudley's bankruptcy to her own return shortly after the father's death to assume his monitory role, occur during Constantia's Philadelphia exile when there was no communication between the two women. At best the narrative is a retrospective reconstruction of events that occurs after Ormond and Martinette are no longer present to counterbalance Sophia's admittedly prejudicial representations. She asserts special knowledge about Ormond in her prefatory note to Rosenberg and in Chapter 12, but withholds any information that might confirm her claims, rationalizing this narrative strategy with the assertion that it is not "prudent to unfold *all* the means by which I gained a knowledge of his actions; but these means, though

---

[38] John Quincy Adams, "Preface" (p. 4) to his translation of Friedrich von Gentz's counterrevolutionary tract comparing the "origins and principles" of the American and French Revolutions (1800). For Brown's explicitly argued rejection of this position and its associations in the U.S., see his review of this pamphlet in Related Texts.

[39] William Hedges, "Charles Brockden Brown and the Culture of Contradictions," 118; Levine, *Conspiracy and Romance*, 49.

singularly fortunate and accurate, could not be unerring and compleat." Even as she delivers her sensationalized denunciations, in other words, Sophia confesses to the reader that she cannot or will not provide evidence beyond her own words to justify her portrait of the novel's title character. In contemporary parlance, we might say that Sophia practices "stonewalling": she delays, misdirects, and ultimately refuses to answer implied questions about the validity of extraordinary claims.

Critic William Scheick, for example, notes how Sophia's "revelations frequently clarify little for the reader; rather they generate other questions.... Often, she brings the reader to the verge of understanding, only to distract his attention by the urgency of a new present moment, leaving his comprehension of events incomplete."[40] This narrative practice of misdirection and willful obfuscation is intentional, for it allows Sophia a relatively subtle means of amplifying a sense of need in the reader that legitimates her own claims to be a superintending figure whose authority is natural and unquestionably authentic. Thus it is crucial to recognize Sophia's dedication to controlling the flow of information throughout the tale, especially because so much of our perception of Ormond, for example Chapters 21, 26, and 27's anecdotes concerning his barbarity during the Russo-Turkish wars, comes only from Sophia, who has never met Ormond in person, but who targets him for vilification because of his political ideals.

The accelerating tempo of events in the novel's final segment, from Dudley's death in Chapter 22 to Ormond's in Chapter 29, in which the narrative's rhythms pulse ever more rapidly and produce more inscrutability than even the events of the yellow fever epidemic, occurs only after Sophia's emergence into the novel's action. Neither of the violent deaths that punctuate this final act are witnessed, and the interpretation of both is literally and figuratively managed by the narrator. Sophia seems to use this shift in dramatic pacing and velocity to distance Constantia from Martinette and to portray Ormond as an immediate danger, even though Ormond and Constantia have already established placid relations despite strong intellectual differences. For it is only after Sophia's physical arrival in Philadelphia that Ormond will be presented as a violent, maniacal rapist intent on possessing Constantia dead or alive. At the same time, however, in an unexpected and additional narrative turn, this staging of Ormond's libertine sexual violence as both the consequence and literalization of his radical politics allows Sophia to present her own attraction to Constantia as an alternative sexuality.

Female-Female Sexuality: The Desire that Shall Remain Nameless

As early as the 1940s, scholars were already commenting, albeit briefly, on the thematization of female same-sex desire in *Ormond*. For the next several decades, this

---

[40] Scheick, "The Problem of Origination in Brown's *Ormond*," 133.

feature of the novel was often skirted and frequently dismissed with the assumption that the novel's outlook is unquestionably heterosexual.[41] Beginning with Lillian Faderman in the early 1980s and the ensuing rise of literary, cultural, and historical studies on same-sex sexual expression and communities, however, *Ormond's* treatment of female relations and erotic contexts has become foregrounded as readers have increasingly noted the erotic charge that binds the novel's women, and debated the ways in which the novel seems to reflect on (proto)-lesbian desire.[42]

For example, Constantia's search for an alternative script for female personhood presents implicit reflections on marriage as a form of slavery and on the mind-numbing commodification of women as objects to be trafficked between men. These aspects of the novel already harbor an implicitly critical perspective on compulsory heterosexuality, since they imply that normative codes and categories of womanhood are not "natural" states but rather an imposed regime of subordination. The example of Constantia's briefly glimpsed mother, who in Chapter 2 "died a victim to discontent," exemplifies the ways that normative wifedom can expose women to physical and psychological forms of domestic violence and everyday practices of depersonalization. Constantia's insistence on displaying sympathy directed mainly to women, and her experiences of annoyance and endangerment as a result of male supervision and intrusion into her private sphere, are also parts of this pattern of reflection. These everyday forms of cultural background noise, the "normal" conditions of existence in Constantia's world, are continually amplified by Sophia's heart-rending shrieks of deep romantic friendship for the subject of her narrative. Sophia never ceases to advertise her emotionalized bonds with Constantia, insists that the two should spend their lives together, and immediately after getting married abandons her husband in Europe to travel perilously across the Atlantic and search for her long-lost friend, even when there is no certainty that Constantia is even alive.

Sophia's emotionally saturated claims made her relationship with Constantia the realm of most critical focus until the 1990s, when scholars who had become more

---

[41] Warfel, in *Charles Brockden Brown* (1949), writes that in Sophia and Constantia "Brown recognized ... an abnormal relationship" (132). Of Constantia, he suggests, "Emotions of normal love are alien to her nature, and there seems to be a homosexual tendency in her conduct. She rejects all suitors, and in the end no husband awaits her" (130). The 1952 Clark biography replied by arguing that there is no evidence "that Constantia was the victim of homosexuality" (173).

[42] The argument here draws from Shapiro, "In a French Position: Radical Pornography and Homoerotic Society in Charles Brockden Brown's *Ormond or the Secret Witness*." In *Surpassing the Love of Men: Romantic Friendship and Love Between Women From the Renaissance to the Present* (1981), Faderman opened a new phase in discussions of the novel when she argued that "In *Ormond* the female-female love [i.e., the bond between Sophia and Constantia], despite the title of the work, is the central and most powerful relationship in the book, and it provides the happy ending" (155,n433). For recent scholarship and commentary, see Comment, "Charles Brockden Brown's *Ormond* and Lesbian Possibility in the Early Republic"; Layson, "Rape and Revolution"; Lewis, "Attaining Masculinity"; Smyth, "'Imperfect Disclosures': Cross-Dressing and Containment in Charles Brockden Brown's *Ormond*"; and Roulston, "Having it Both Ways? The Eighteenth-Century Menage-à-Trois."

attuned to the cultural politics of transvestism as a medium for communicating same-sex sexual desire began to examine the links between Martinette and Constantia. It is Sophia herself who first reveals the affinity between the two in Chapter 8's previously mentioned artful contrast between her own claims on Constantia and the magnetism of a still-disguised Martinette, during the exchange of a lute and its erotic connotations. Sophia's description of the two women exchanging the lute bypasses the level of explicit, linguistically coded assertions to concentrate on "interpreting the language of features and looks." In this context, the reader may well find Sophia's insistence on the resemblance of the two women initially confusing, given the superficial difference she notes between their ages, physiques, and public comportment. But her suggestion of an unstated yet nevertheless visible attraction conveyed in forms that go unnoticed to bystanders will be repeated and made plainer in subsequent chapters. When Martinette explains why large numbers of women are serving covertly in the Revolutionary army, for example, she says that, among other reasons, some of these disguised fighters are simply following other women into a setting which may, despite its potential dangers, offer greater possibilities for female-female intimacy. Similarly, when Martinette explains the ease with which she was able to take refuge in Philadelphia's émigré community at a time of emergency, her evocation of a secret city with little-known subcultures hints at the presence of wider erotic possibilities as well.

The presence of same-sex practices and subcultures was well known to Brown and, historically, it is well documented in the Philadelphia of the 1790s. Indeed, Brown was the first U.S. writer to inscribe male same-sex relations in fiction. The protagonist of his serially published *Memoirs of Stephen Calvert* (1799–1800) is a man who suddenly and inexplicably loses interest in his fiancée and falls in love with an exotic, cloistered immigrant. When he proposes, the woman tells him that she is already married and explains that, soon after her marriage, she discovered her husband having sex with another man.[43] Brown's later magazine article on the Persian poet Hafiz

---

[43] *Memoirs of Stephen Calvert* (*Monthly Magazine* 2.4, April 1800, 265–66) sets out the crucial passage concerning the husband's behavior in these terms:

"At length, various circumstances set the depravity of my husband in a new light. For a long time I was blind to the obvious inferences which a person, much acquainted with the world, could not fail to have drawn from appearances. My husband's negligence of me I naturally ascribed to his attachment to some other woman. I could not readily believe what yet appeared to be true, that his associates were wholly of his own sex; and I gave him credit for a rectitude of conduct, in one respect, which was little in unison with other parts of his deportment.

This illusion came, at length, to an end. Belgrave's contempt and hatred of me exceeded even his own regard for his own reputation, and to his own safety, from the animadversions of the law. So open, so shameless was his conduct, that, at length, my own eyes were allowed to witness—.

I cannot utter it—I was frozen with horror. I doubted whether hideous phantoms, produced by my own imagination, had not deceived me; till my memory, putting past incidents together, convinced me that they were real."

Brown echoes the pre-twentieth-century code phrase *peccatum illud horribile, inter Christianos non nominandum* (that horrible sin not to be named among Christians). Nineteenth-century editions of Brown that included *Stephen Calvert* excised this passage.

openly acknowledges the male poet's desires for young men.[44] Besides the complexity of its own action, *Ormond* refers to other contemporary codings of female-female sexuality, for example in its footnoted allusion in Chapter 14 to a fictional account of the life of Orientalist adventurer Edward Wortley Montagu. That narrative begins with an allegorical scene in which Montagu's mother, the Bluestocking intellectual Lady Mary Wortley Montagu, enters a Turkish harem and witnesses explicitly sexual, all-female "oriental" dancing, before being forcibly impregnated by the Sultan, as if to compensate for her indulgence in non-normative erotics. In this period, the historical Lady Montagu was famously the object of slanderous attacks by Augustan poet Alexander Pope and others that associated her with same-sex sexual practices.[45] French émigré bookseller Moreau de Saint-Méry, in passages included in Related Texts here, also noted and reflected on female-female sexuality in 1790s Philadelphia.[46]

Because critics and historians are still learning how to read the period's discourse of same-sex affections and how to understand its description of a spectrum of possibilities extending from homosocial friendship to explicit homosexuality, readers must still decide for themselves whether they see *Ormond* as a text of sexual longing and alternative or oppositional reflections on female-female sexual companionship. If we choose to read the novel in ways that include historically-attuned awareness of female-female eroticism and its representations, then the important question, perhaps, is less whether Constantia is more attracted to Sophia or to Martinette, than whether these two relationships may encode different styles of same-sex attraction that together chart out conditions and possibilities for future relationships. If the purpose of Sophia's narrative is indeed to prepare a marriage to the never-explained figure I. E. Rosenberg, then her longing for proximity to Constantia will implicitly be restrained, privatizing, and protected by the coverture[47] of marriage. Martinette's style of behavior, on the other hand, unapologetically transgresses conventional codes for female behavior and is frankly radical in its political outlook. Contemporary readers

---

[44] See "On Persian poetry and Hafiz" in Brown's *Literary Magazine* 3.21 (June 1805), 419–23.

[45] For more on Montagu and the fictional account of his life, see Notes to Chapter 14 and the discussion in Related Texts of female transvestism in the revolutionary era.

[46] For a fuller discussion of the cultural politics of sex-gender in 1790s Philadelphia, see Lyons, *Sex Among the Rabble: An Intimate History of Gender & Power in the Age of Revolution, Philadelphia, 1730–1830*.

[47] Laws of coverture are the body of early modern English common law regulating women's legal status and personhood in this period. Under Anglo-American common law, women had no legal personhood or formal, statutory independence. A woman's legal identity (and consequently her right to own property, sign contracts, and so on) was absorbed into or "covered" by that of her father, husband, or other male guardian. In the Anglo-Norman legal terminology of this system an unmarried woman was a *feme sole* (a woman alone), a married woman a *feme covert* (a covered woman). Although it abolished titles and primogeniture, the American Revolution did not change these laws concerning women's subordination. For discussions of coverture and its relation to the period's U.S. reading culture, see Kerber, *Women of the Republic: Intellect and Ideology in Revolutionary America*; and Davidson, *Revolution and the Word*.

might find the latter more appealing and, depending on how we read the final scenes, it may well be that Brown shared this perspective.

Conventional Endings and Uncommon Sense

Brown's encoding of nondominant forms of gender and sexuality helps us consider the implications of the novel's violent and puzzling final act. Throughout *Ormond* Brown has staged tensions between two aesthetic and political worldviews. One seeks to reaffirm traditional social order and gender roles, and lends itself to expression through the codes of classicism, with their concern for maintaining balance, simplicity, and symmetry. The other, which embraces political transformation and the forging of new behavioral roles, is linked to an expressionistic and mobilizing aesthetics that favors irregularity and embodied performance. As the tale is drawn toward its conclusions, these two tendencies may usefully guide different ways of reading its final pages.

On its surface, the plot seems clear. A vertiginously imbalanced Ormond uses the surrogate fraudster Thomas Craig as an intermediary to accomplish the murder of Stephen Dudley, then seeks physical control over Constantia through rape. Acting in self-defense, Constantia kills Ormond in her paternal mansion before Sophia can arrive to protect her. The classic sentimental confrontation between a virtuous woman and a predatory rake is not actually witnessed, but generically resolved by Sophia's uncanny ability to submerge all status differences and social tensions into the "ultimate restoration to tranquillity" that is invoked on the novel's final page. Sophia's aggressive management of Constantia's affairs will implicitly prevent any further encounters with radicals, advocates of social change, or other forces of imbalance, for she transports her friend to London, the geopolitical fulcrum of Anglo-American counterrevolutionary order, where her new life is such that she "has experienced little variation."

Sophia ensures that Martinette and her Francophone influence remain distant by reporting, once again on the novel's final page, that her own husband, the suggestively named Courtland, has communicated startling new revelations after meeting with Martinette in revolutionary Paris and simultaneously denying Martinette new information about Constantia, because he "thought proper to with-hold from her the knowledge he possessed." Sophia's brief assertion, seemingly an afterthought, that Martinette was secretly the sister of Ormond, effectively ends the text by fusing and demonizing both of the novel's radical figures, erasing any significant distinctions between them. As the curtain falls, then, Sophia has returned Constantia to where she began the story, cloistered within domestic tedium. The tale's protagonist seems destined for marriage with the mysterious I. E. Rosenberg, an event that may transpire as soon as her virtue is legitimated (her "errors" and "defects" erased) by Sophia's embedded narrative, which is *Ormond* itself. With generic assumptions of conventional melodrama and compulsory heterosexuality assured, all's well that ends well and the novel seems to provide the reader with a "proper" ending, the finale and imaginary resolution that the drama "ought" to have, and might more easily have had, if Constantia had never strayed from conventional expectations and scripts.

Yet the puzzling rough edges that Sophia's narrative does not succeed in smoothing away seem to leave the reader with many suggestive possibilities and a persistent sense that the narrative's highly conventional conclusion does not, in the end, satisfactorily account for the novel's wider suggestions and willful irregularities. Coming as they do at the end of a tale that repeatedly illustrates how its characters indulge in charades of transparency while enacting stratagems of hidden surveillance and imposture, *Ormond*'s final pages hint that they too engage in dramatic misdirection, and suggest that a more careful reading may qualify the conclusions that Sophia has presented to her reader.

For example, in the novel's world of dizzying inversions, where the rich, white Ormond passes as a poor, black chimney sweep, or the physically delicate female Martinette successfully masquerades as a male soldier, readers have ample reason to wonder about the authenticity of the novel's strangely veiled and melodramatic death scene, as well as the identity of the mysterious I. E. Rosenberg, whose name, as Wil Verhoeven notes, is a German inversion of the French meaning of Martinette's earlier pseudonym. That is, both Rosenberg (in German) and Monrose (in French) mean the same thing: red—or pink, rose-colored—mountain.[48] If Sophia writes to Rosenberg in order to hand Constantia over to this figure, then could she be wittingly or unwittingly writing to someone, such as Martinette, who is arranging for Constantia's final movement toward a French position?

To consider only the theatricality of Ormond's death, it is notable that Sophia does not witness the scene and never presents it dramatically to the reader, but only glimpses the aftermath through a keyhole, a bit like the old soldier Baxter spying on Martinette in Chapter 7, and draws a rapid conclusion as to its import. The scene that she discovers, with two male figures draped over one another, seems knowingly posed or staged, a hyperbolic possibility suggested by Ormond's own quotation of Hamlet dragging the body of Polonius, as he brings out Craig's corpse. Ormond's strange death mask also intimates a hidden joke as a "smile of disdain still sat upon his features. The wound, by which he fell, was secret, and was scarcely betrayed by the effusion of a drop of blood." What could an imperceptibly wounded Ormond be laughing about?

In short, since every other compilation of letters in the novel is composed of frauds and forgeries (Craig's letters, accounting, and bank notes; Martinette's unseen autobiography; and Martynne's reference letters), the novel's overall logic suggests that Sophia's narrative must likewise fall under suspicion of duplicity. Whether we distinguish terminologically between the "novel" and the "narrative," between the text's surface and depth, or between literal and figural levels of reference or figuration, it seems clear that Brown has designed *Ormond* in such a manner as to bring out a

---

[48] See Verhoeven, "Displacing the Discontinuous; or, The Labyrinths of Reason: Fictional Design and Eighteenth-Century Thought in Charles Brockden Brown's *Ormond*."

readerly awareness of the difference between Sophia's scripted narrative and the wider potentials it attempts to contain. Allegorically, it may well be that Constantia's murder of Ormond completes her initiation into the worldview that Martinette had previously championed. Given the novel's logic of theatricality, it is plausible to speculate that, like Martinette, Constantia has learned through adversity, under the tutelage of a predatory male, and figuratively buries his corpse in the paternal garden, right under the nose and spying eye of a prejudicially inclined agent of public order.

Brown's novels often suggest struggles to clarify meaning in the midst of such duality as his characters search through disorienting architectural or other spaces in which important texts and other secrets are hidden.[49] Novelistic devices of inscrutable or hidden manuscripts were already commonplace elsewhere in the period's gothic fiction and were used to great purpose, for example, by William Godwin in his *Caleb Williams*, which Brown's contemporaries commonly understood as a model for *Ormond*.[50] The period's conventional use of this motif, however, referred to secrets about the past, so that novelistic discovery tended to reveal feudal crimes and subterranean horrors of the old regime. Brown's writing seems to take a different approach, one mainly suggested by the period's libertine and pornographic fictions, in which the known-but-unacknowledged secrets refer to alternative societies *in the present moment*.[51] In *Ormond*, such allusive references to alternative social arrangements includes Martinette's comment about a Francophone Philadelphia that remains hidden in plain sight to Anglo eyes, or Ormond's revelation that Constantia's father's closet opens into rooms beyond her apartment's apparent limits. Brown's combination of texts, spaces, and utopian possibilities that are obscure to mainstream eyes but visible to those who can perceive them suggests that he has articulated *Ormond*'s entire narrative in this fashion.

Ormond, then, may be read as two narratives, one familiar and conventionally digestible, and another more subtly radical in its subterranean codes. Given the interpenetration of aesthetics and politics that characterizes it so thoroughly, Brown's use and abuse of generic forms in this novel is best understood from our perspective at the outset of the twenty-first century as a political allegory in which Brown indicates that, by the end of the 1790s, the forces of reaction, the Sophia-like embodiments of common sense and conventional wisdom (*sophia*, in Greek), have become strong enough to exert control over the mechanisms of public expression, the narrative form

---

[49] See McNutt, *Urban Revelations: Images of Ruin in the American City, 1790–1860*.

[50] See Verhoeven, "Opening the Text: The Locked-Trunk Motif in Late Eighteenth-Century British and American Gothic Fiction." Contemporaries understood the connection with Godwin to such a degree that the 1802 German translation of *Ormond* could be intentionally or unintentionally attributed to Godwin himself, and Brown's earliest biographer Paul Allen could remark, "Constantia appears to be little more than Godwin's hero in a female dress." See Allen, *The Life of Charles Brockden Brown*, 389–91.

[51] See the image from Restif de la Bretonne's *The Perverted Peasant* (1776) in Related Texts, and the commentary in Shapiro, "In a French Position: Radical Pornography and Homoerotic Society in Charles Brockden Brown's *Ormond or the Secret Witness*."

itself. In a situation of weakness, he seems to suggest, radicals are well advised to wait for the arrival of a more progressive phase, and in the meantime to inscribe their meanings in encoded forms that may be transmitted to distant or future actors.

This strategy of nonsubmissive submergence, or artful insubordination, would be true for the surviving Woldwinites, like Godwin, who quietly waited until the next generation, when figures such as his daughter Mary and Percy Shelley would relay a radical spirit and attempt to resurrect an older progressivism that had been left for dead by the period's counterrevolutionaries. Shelley's friend Thomas Love Peacock reported that Shelley avidly read Brown's novels and considered that Constantia Dudley was his finest achievement.[52] Mary Shelley, the daughter of Wollstonecraft and Godwin, and Shelley's wife and partner before his death, likewise read Brown's novels and famously spun a tale, in her novel *Frankenstein* (1818), about the arrival of the undead in the form of a creature created from graveyard limbs, in a manner that suggests the challenges of representing a resurrected progressivism. Brown, of course, would not live to see the next phase, due to his untimely death from tuberculosis in 1810. *Ormond*, however, can be read as a document of his developing political and narrative tactics, a tale about the strategic need to wait until better days. Accordingly, as readers of *Ormond*, we are the secret witnesses of progressivism long delayed, but not destroyed.

---

[52] Peacock, "Memoir of Percy Bysshe Shelley," 409.

A NOTE ON THE TEXT

Ormond; or The Secret Witness was first published in mid-January 1799. New York French émigré bookseller Hocquet Caritat was the publisher, and George Forman the printer. Caritat, who had published Brown's novel *Wieland; or the Transformation* just four months earlier, applied for a copyright on January 16 and the book was being advertised by January 21.

The novel appeared in London in 1800, printed by William Lane for his Minerva Press. Shortly after the first U.S. publication, Caritat advertised a 1799 translation by John Davis into French as *Ormond, ou le témoin secret* that would make it and *Wieland* (translated and published in France in 1808) the earliest U.S. novels to appear in French. No copies of the Caritat-Davis French translation exist, however, and scholars are uncertain as to whether it appeared. In 1802, *Ormond* became the first U.S. novel translated into German, when it was published in Leipzig by Johann Gottlob Beygang as *Ormond; oder der geheime Zeuge*, "freely translated from the English of Godwin" by Friedrich von Oertel.

The Kent State "Bicentennial" edition of *Ormond*, published in 1982, is the modern scholarly text of the novel and provides a "Textual Essay" and "List of Emendations" that document copy-text and provide a rationale for selecting between variants. This Hackett edition uses the first, Forman printing as its copy-text, silently correcting that edition's obvious typographical errors. We regularize the first edition's irregular dashes and ellipses but otherwise make no modernization of alternative spellings or usage. For a full discussion of the novel's textual history, see the textual essay, notes, and appendices by S. W. Reid in the Kent State edition.

Brown's *Alcuin; A Dialogue* is also edited in a modern scholarly form as part of the Kent State "Bicentennial" edition, with a complete apparatus of variants, as well as historical and textual essays that are the most complete source of information on that text's complex publication history. The copy-text for Parts I and II in this Hackett edition is the first, 1798 edition of *Alcuin*, published by Brown's associate Elihu Hubbard Smith and printed by T. & J. Swords, who also printed numerous other works by Smith, Brown, and their circle, including *Wieland*. Copy-text for Part III of the dialogue is the first printing of that section, which appeared in Paul Allen and William Dunlap's 1815 posthumous biographical miscellany, *The Life of Charles Brockden Brown*.

For other texts by Brown, this edition uses as copy-texts the first printings from Brown's New York *Monthly Magazine* and its successor, *The American Review*, as well as his Philadelphia *Literary Magazine*. More information on the publication history of these texts is available in the Related Text headnotes concerning them.

Similarly, the other Related Texts in this volume are drawn from first or, where indicated, other contemporary printings, and are not modernized. Our translation of excerpts from Moreau de Saint-Méry's *Voyage* benefits from the precedents of the 1947 English version by Kenneth and Anna Roberts, published as *Moreau de St. Méry's American Journey, 1793–98,* but is based on Moreau's French text as it appears in the 1913 Sims edition, *Voyage aux Etats-Unis d'Amérique, 1793–1798.*

ORMOND;

OR THE

SECRET WITNESS.

———

BY THE AUTHOR OF WIELAND; OR THE
TRANSFORMATION.

———

NEW-YORK:
Printed by G. FORMAN, for H. CARITAT.
—1799.—

TO

I. E. ROSENBERG.[1]

YOU are anxious to obtain some knowledge of the history of Constantia Dudley. I am well acquainted with your motives, and allow that they justify your curiosity.[2] I am willing, to the utmost of my power, to comply with your request, and will now dedicate what leisure I have to the composition of her story.

My narrative will have little of that merit which flows from unity of design. You are desirous of hearing an authentic, and not a fictitious tale. It will, therefore, be my duty to relate events in no artificial or elaborate order, and without that harmonious congruity and luminous amplification, which might justly be displayed in a tale flowing merely from invention. It will be little more than a biographical sketch, in which the facts are distributed and amplified, not as a poetical taste would prescribe,

---

[1] "To I. E. Rosenberg": the novel begins by establishing an important framing device. This prefatory note from the narrator, "S.C.," addresses the narrative to an I. E. Rosenberg, whose identity is unexplained. The footnote indicates that Rosenberg is "German," a word that in this period designates a large number of German-speaking sovereign territories, from Free Imperial Cities and small duchies to kingdoms, throughout Central and Northern Europe.

While there is no explicit allusion to particular individuals or texts, readers in circles like Brown's in the 1790s might recall the name Rosenberg in several ways. At this time, Rosenberg was known as an elite family name in the Austrian Habsburg Empire; the family's holdings were concentered in the Austrian province of Carinthia. In this connection, Brown may intend the name to echo that of Giustiniana Wynne, Countess Rosenberg (1736–1791), then a widely reviewed Anglo-Venetian author of enlightened essays that defend female education and resistance to female subordination. Wynne-Rosenberg was also connected by reputation to numerous transnational intrigues. For possible allusions to Wynne-Rosenberg in Chapter 20, see note 20.20.

"Rosenberg" would also have resonated with Brown as a family name used in a new English version of Friedrich Schiller's 1784 play *Kabale und Liebe* (Intrigue and Love), then being read by Brown's circle and staged in New York by Brown's close friend, theater manager William Dunlap. Schiller's play was both commercially successful and banned in Germany, and typifies the *Sturm und Drang* (Storm and Stress) themes of emotionally saturated, often irrational defiance against the standing (aristocratic) political and social order. Its plot concerns a romance of secret misalliance between an aristocrat's son and a bourgeois woman, against the noble father's wishes, ending tragically with a *Romeo and Juliet*-like accidental double suicide. The play was initially translated into English in 1796, but Matthew Lewis published a new version in 1797, titling it *The Minister* to distinguish it from the rival version. Lewis' version changed the name of the plot's noble family to Rosenberg, possibly alluding to the prominent Austrian family mentioned above. Schiller's play is best known today in its adaptation as an opera, Verdi's *Luisa Miller* (1849).

[2] "Your motives … justify your curiosity": the implication, recalled in the final paragraphs at the end of the novel, is that Rosenberg is a suitor who has "motives" and justifiable "curiosity" concerning Constantia's history and reputation as a possible prelude to a marriage proposal.

but as the materials afforded me, sometimes abundant and sometimes scanty, would permit.

Constance,[3] like all the beings made known to us, not by fancy, but experience, has numerous defects. You will readily perceive, that her tale is told by her friend, but I hope you will not discover many or glaring proofs of a disposition to extenuate her errors or falsify her character.

Ormond will, perhaps, appear to you a contradictory or unintelligible being. I pretend not to the infallibility of inspiration. He is not a creature of fancy. It was not prudent to unfold *all* the means by which I gained a knowledge of his actions; but these means, though singularly fortunate and accurate, could not be unerring and compleat.[4] I have shewn him to you as he appeared, on different occasions and at successive periods, to me. This is all that you will demand from a faithful biographer.

If you were not deeply interested in the fate of my friend, yet my undertaking will not be useless, inasmuch as it will introduce you to scenes to which you have been hitherto a stranger. The modes of life, the influence of public events upon the character and happiness of individuals in America, are new to you. The distinctions of birth, the artificial degrees of esteem or contempt which connect themselves with different professions and ranks in your native country,* are but little known among us. Society and manners[5] constitute your favorite study, and I am willing to believe, that my relation will supply you with knowledge, on these heads, not to be otherwise obtained. If these details be, in that respect, unsatisfactory, all that I can add, is, my counsel to go and examine for yourself.

S.C.

*Germany.

---

[3] "Constance": in the opening sentence above, the narrator initially referred to the novel's protagonist using the full form of her name: "Constantia." Her use of a more familiar form now, and intermittently throughout the rest of the novel, may subtly insinuate that her relationship with and knowledge about Constantia is more authoritative or intimate than that of other characters in the novel, above all Ormond. For more on this contrast, compare Ormond's turn to this form of Constantia's name in Chapter 16 (note 16.4).

[4] "Not prudent to unfold *all* the means … compleat": the narrator acknowledges that her portrait of Ormond will be incomplete and prejudicial, and states that her sources of information about him must remain secret. This claim introduces the ensuing themes of secret witnessing, voyeuristic knowledge, and interpersonal insincerity and imposture.

[5] "Influence of public events upon … individuals in America … Society and manners": the narrator's claim for the wider social and historical value of her narrative places the novel in the genre of enlightened social observation and anthropology. This emphasis highlights the idea, common to Brown and his Woldwinite models, that social and historical circumstances shape individuals: the narrative will tell Constantia's story, but will also develop a portrait of "society and manners" in a postrevolutionary republic, i.e., a social order that has rejected old regime hierarchies and institutions, and deference to the authority of nobles and priests.

ORMOND;
OR THE SECRET WITNESS

Chapter I

STEPHEN DUDLEY was a native of New-York. He was educated to the profession of a painter. His father's trade was that of an apothecary. But this son, manifesting an attachment to the pencil, he was resolved that it should be gratified. For this end Stephen was sent at an early age to Europe, and not only enjoyed the instructions of Fuzeli and Bartolozzi,[1] but spent a considerable period in Italy, in studying the Augustan and Medicean monuments.[2] It was intended that he should practise his art in his native city, but the young man, though reconciled to this scheme by deference to paternal authority, and by a sense of its propriety, was willing, as long as possible to postpone it. The liberality of his father relieved him from all pecuniary cares. His whole time was devoted to the improvement of his skill in his favorite art, and the

---

[1] "Fuzeli and Bartolozzi": (Johann) Henry Fuseli (1741–1825), a Swiss painter and writer, and Francesco Bartolozzi (1725–1815), an Italian engraver and artist. Both were leading figures in elite and progressive London art and literary circles in the 1780s–1790s; both associated and worked with notable female intellectuals and artists (among others, Fuseli with Mary Wollstonecraft, and Bartolozzi with Swiss-Austrian painter Angelica Kauffmann, who will be mentioned in Chapter 13). Both artists produced work that associated them with the gothic wave in Anglophone literature and art in the late 1790s.

[2] "Augustan and Medicean monuments": shorthand for Italianate Classical and Renaissance sources in art and architecture. The "Augustan" age is that of the first Roman emperor Caesar Augustus (63 B.C.E.–14 C.E.) and his massive building projects. Augustus is supposed to have said on his deathbed, "I found Rome of bricks; I leave it to you of marble." Medicean monuments are those created by Medici family patronage in fifteenth and sixteenth century Florence and Tuscany, at the height of the Italian Renaissance. The Medicis were patrons, for example, of Michelangelo and Leonardo da Vinci (see note 27.4). The "neoclassical" culture of the early eighteenth century in England (e.g., the poetry of Alexander Pope or prose of Samuel Johnson) is commonly referred to as "Augustan" because it emulates these Classical sources and models and favors harmony, symmetry, and "order," poised balance achieved through regulating formal devices of mirroring repetition; a (Protestant-minded) emphasis on simple lines and curves, rather than the irregularity of (Catholic) baroque; and the creation of emotional poise in the viewer or reader. By contrast, the Italianate Renaissance involved a more sensual aesthetics, involving voluptuous contrasts of light and dark and the bravura display of idiosyncratic ("wild") feeling and experiences. With these references, Dudley's artistic training becomes the first of the novel's many references to 1790s tensions between social realms conceived according to neoclassical orderliness, or according to seemingly sociopathic and revolutionary gothic or other modernizing styles. These two perspectives are roughly divided between those that create clinical abstraction rather than emotional intensities in the reader. For more remarks on classical, Italianate art, see notes 19.2 and 27.4–5.

enriching of his mind with every valuable accomplishment. He was endowed with a comprehensive genius and indefatigable industry. His progress was proportionably rapid, and he passed his time without much regard to futurity, being too well satisfied with the present to anticipate a change. A change however was unavoidable, and he was obliged at length to pay a reluctant obedience to his father's repeated summons. The death of his wife had rendered his society still more necessary to the old gentleman.

He married before his return. The woman whom he had selected was an unportioned orphan, and was recommended merely by her moral qualities.[3] These, however, were eminent, and secured to her, till the end of her life, the affection of her husband. Though painting was capable of fully gratifying his taste as matter of amusement, he quickly found that, in his new situation it would not answer the ends of a profession. His father supported himself by the profits of his shop, but with all his industry he could do no more than procure a subsistence for himself and his son.

Till his father's death young Dudley attached himself to painting. His gains were slender but he loved the art, and his father's profession rendered his own exertions in a great degree superfluous. The death of the elder Dudley introduced an important change in his situation. It thenceforth became necessary to strike into some new path, to deny himself the indulgence of his inclinations, and regulate his future exertions by a view to nothing but gain. There was little room for choice. His habits had disqualified him for mechanical employments. He could not stoop to the imaginary indignity which attended them, nor spare the time necessary to obtain the requisite degree of skill. His father died in possession of some stock, and a sufficient portion of credit to supply its annual decays. He lived at what they call a *good stand*, and enjoyed a certain quantity of permanent custom. The knowledge that was required was as easily obtained as the elements of any other profession, and was not wholly unallied to the pursuits in which he had sometimes engaged. Hence he could not hesitate long in forming his resolution, but assumed the management of his father's concerns with a cheerful and determined spirit.

The knowledge of his business was acquired in no long time. He was stimulated to the acquisition by a sense of duty, he was inured to habits of industry, and there were few things capable to resist a strenuous exertion of his faculties. Knowledge of whatever kind afforded a compensation to labour, but the task being finished, that which remained, which, in ordinary apprehensions would have been esteemed an easy and smooth path, was to him insupportably disgustful. The drudgery of a shop, where all

---

[3] "Unportioned orphan … moral qualities": Constantia's mother will remain nameless. Dudley's marriage to a European woman is mentioned only briefly, in three places, and first noted here as a misalliance between a wealthy young American and a European girl without an inheritance. The mother's sudden death in the family's initial crisis will be mentioned, again very briefly, in Chapter 2, and in Chapter 24 the narrator will note that she was a French woman who escaped from a convent in Amiens to marry Dudley (see note 24.2). Although little emphasis is made of it on the surface of the narrative, it may be significant that, in terms of her parentage, Constantia is half-French, for Anglophile-Francophile tensions and Francophobia will play an important role in what follows.

the faculties were at a stand, and one day was an unvaried repetition of the foregoing, was too incongenial to his disposition not to be a source of discontent. This was an evil which it was the tendency of time to increase rather than diminish. The longer he endured it the less tolerable it became. He could not forbear comparing his present situation with his former, and deriving from the contrast perpetual food for melancholy.

The indulgence of his father had contributed to instill into him prejudices, in consequence of which a certain species of disgrace was annexed to every employment of which the only purpose was gain. His present situation not only precluded all those pursuits which exalt and harmonize the feelings, but was detested by him as something humiliating and ignominious.[4] His wife was of a pliant temper, and her condition less influenced by this change than that of her husband. She was qualified to be his comforter, but instead of dispelling his gloom by judicious arguments, or a seasonable example of vivacity, she caught the infection that preyed upon his mind and augmented his anxieties by partaking in them.

By enlarging in some degree, the foundation on which his father had built, he had provided the means of a future secession, and might console himself with the prospect of enjoying his darling ease at some period of his life. This period was necessarily too remote for his wishes, and had not certain occurrences taken place, by which he was flattered with the immediate possession of ease, it is far from being certain that he would not have fallen a victim to his growing disquietudes.

He was one morning engaged behind his counter as usual, when a youth came into his shop, and, in terms that bespoke the union of fearlessness and frankness, enquired whether he could be engaged as an apprentice. A proposal of this kind could not be suddenly rejected or adopted. He stood in need of assistance, the youth was manly and blooming, and exhibited a modest and ingenuous aspect. It was possible that he was, in every respect, qualified for the post for which he applied, but it was previously necessary to ascertain these qualifications. For this end he requested the youth to call at his house in the evening, when he should be at leisure to converse with him and furnished him with suitable directions.

The youth came according to appointment. On being questioned as to his birthplace and origin, he stated that he was a native of Wakefield, in Yorkshire;[5] that his family were honest, and his education not mean; that he was the eldest of many children, and having attained an age at which he conceived it his duty to provide for himself, he had, with the concurrence of his friends, come to America, in search of the means of independant subsistence; that he had just arrived in a ship which he named, and, his scanty stock of money being likely to be speedily consumed, this had been the first effort he had made to procure employment.

---

[4] "Humiliating and ignominious": Dudley affirms the period's privileged-class notion that commerce is inherently degrading or less honorable than living from inherited wealth, interest, or rents. The events that follow suggest that these "prejudices" will contribute to his downfall.

[5] "Wakefield, in Yorkshire": a small town in north-central England.

His tale was circumstantial and consistent, and his veracity appeared liable to no doubt. He was master of his book and his pen, and had acquired more than the rudiments of Latin. Mr. Dudley did not require much time to deliberate. In a few days the youth was established as a member of his family, and as a coadjutor in his shop, nothing but food, clothing, and lodging being stipulated as the reward of his services.

The young man improved daily in the good opinion of his master. His apprehension was quick, his sobriety invariable, and his application incessant. Tho' by no means presumptuous or arrogant, he was not wanting in a suitable degree of self-confidence. All his propensities appeared to concentre in his occupation and the promotion of his master's interest, from which he was drawn aside by no allurements of sensual or intellectual pleasure. In a short time he was able to relieve his master of most of the toils of his profession, and Mr. Dudley a thousand times congratulated himself on possessing a servant equally qualified by his talents and his probity.[6] He gradually remitted his attention to his own concerns, and placed more absolute reliance on the fidelity of his dependant.

Young Craig, that was the name of the youth, maintained a punctual correspondence with his family, and confided to his patron, not only copies of all the letters which he himself wrote, but those which, from time to time, he received. He had several correspondents, but the chief of those were his mother and his eldest sister. The sentiments contained in their letters breathed the most appropriate simplicity and tenderness, and flowed with the nicest propriety, from the different relationships of mother and sister. The style and even the penmanship were distinct and characteristical.

One of the first of these epistles, was written by the mother to Mr. Dudley, on being informed by her son of his present engagement. It was dictated by that concern for the welfare of her child befitting the maternal character. Gratitude, for the ready acceptance of the youth's services, and for the benignity of his deportment towards him, a just representation of which had been received by her from the boy himself, was expressed with no inconsiderable elegance; as well as her earnest wishes that Mr. Dudley should extend to him not only the indulgence, but the moral superintendance of a parent.

To this Mr. Dudley conceived it incumbent upon him to return a consenting answer, and letters were in this manner occasionally interchanged between them.

Things remained in this situation for three years, during which period every day enhanced the reputation of Craig, for stability and integrity. A sort of provisional engagement had been made between the parents, unattended however by any legal or formal act, that things should remain on their present footing for three years. When this period terminated, it seemed as if a new engagement had become necessary. Craig expressed the utmost willingness to renew the former contract, but his master began to think that the services of his pupil merited a higher recompence. He ascribed the prosperity that had hitherto attended him, to the disinterested exertions of

---

[6] "Probity": honesty, integrity, trustworthiness.

his apprentice. His social and literary gratifications had been increased by the increase of his leisure. These were capable of being still more enlarged. He had not yet acquired what he deemed a sufficiency,[7] and could not therefore wholly relieve himself from the turmoils and humiliation of a professional life. He concluded that he should at once consult his own interest and perform no more than an act of justice to a faithful servant, by making Craig his partner, and allowing him a share of the profits, on condition of his discharging all the duties of the trade.

When this scheme was proposed to Craig, he professed unbounded gratitude, considered all that he had done as amply rewarded by the pleasure of performance, and as being nothing more than was prescribed by his duty. He promised that this change in his situation should have no other effect, than to furnish new incitements to diligence and fidelity, in the promotion of an interest, which would then become in a still higher degree than formerly, a common one. Mr. Dudley communicated his intention to Craig's mother, who, in addition to many grateful acknowledgements, stated that a kinsman of her son, had enabled him, in case of entering into partnership, to add a small sum to the common stock, and that for this sum, Craig was authorized to draw upon a London banker.

The proposed arrangement was speedily effected. Craig was charged with the management of all affairs, and Mr. Dudley retired to the enjoyment of still greater leisure. Two years elapsed and nothing occurred to interrupt the harmony that subsisted between the partners. Mr. Dudley's condition might be esteemed prosperous. His wealth was constantly accumulating. He had nearly attained all that he wished, and his wishes still aimed at nothing less than splendid opulence. He had annually increased the permanent sources of his revenue. His daughter was the only survivor of many children, who perished in their infancy, before habit and maturity bad rendered the parental tie difficult to break. This daughter had already exhibited proofs of a mind susceptible of high improvement, and the loveliness of her person promised to keep pace with her mental acquisitions. He charged himself with the care of her education, and found no weariness or satiety in this task that might not be amply relieved by the recreations of science and literature. He flattered himself that his career,[8] which had hitherto been exempt from any considerable impediment, would terminate in tranquility. Few men might, with more propriety, have discarded all apprehensions respecting futurity.

Craig had several sisters and one brother younger than himself. Mr. Dudley desirous of promoting the happiness of this family, proposed to send for this brother, and have him educated to his own profession, insinuating to his partner that at the time when the boy should have gained sufficient stability and knowledge, he himself might be disposed to relinquish the profession altogether, on terms particularly advantageous to the two brothers who might thenceforth conduct their business

---

[7] "Sufficiency": wealth adequate to meet one's financial obligations, allowing one to live without the necessity of earning wages.

[8] "Career": in this usage, the course of his entire life.

jointly. Craig had been eloquent in praise of this lad, and his testimony had, from time to time, been confirmed by that of his mother and sister. He had often expressed his wishes for the prosperity of the lad, and when his mother had expressed her doubts as to the best method of disposing of him, modestly requested Mr. Dudley's advice on this head. The proposal therefore, might be supposed to be particularly acceptable, and yet Craig expressed reluctance to concur with it. This reluctance was accompanied with certain tokens which sufficiently shewed whence it arose. Craig appeared unwilling to increase those obligations under which he already laboured. His sense of gratitude was too acute to allow him to heighten it by the reception of new benefits.

It might be imagined that this objection would be easily removed; but the obstinacy of Craig's opposition was invincible. Mr. Dudley could not relinquish a scheme to which no stronger objection could be made. And, since his partner could not be prevailed upon to make this proposal to the friends of the lad, he was determined to do it himself. He maintained an intercourse by letters with several of those friends which he formed in his youth. One of them usually resided in London. From him he received about this time, a letter, in which, among other information, the writer mentioned his intention of setting out on a tour through Yorkshire and the Scottish highlands. Mr. Dudley thought this a suitable opportunity for executing his design in favor of young Craig. He entertained no doubts about the worth and condition of this family, but was still desirous of obtaining some information on this head from one who would pass through this town where they resided, who would examine with his own eyes, and on whose discernment and integrity he could place an implicit reliance. He concealed this intention from his partner, and entrusted his letter to a friend who was just embarking for Europe. In due season he received an answer, confirming, in all respects, Craig's representations, but informing him that the lad had been lately disposed of in a way not equally advantageous with that which Mr. Dudley had proposed, but such as would not admit of change.

If doubts could possibly be entertained respecting the character and views of Craig, this evidence would have dispelled them: But plans however skilfully contrived, if founded on imposture, cannot fail of being sometimes detected. Craig had occasion to be absent from the city for some weeks. Meanwhile a letter had been left at his lodgings by one who merely enquired if that were the dwelling of Mr. Dudley, and being answered by the servant in the affirmative, left the letter without further parley. It was superscribed with a name unknown to any of the family, and in a hand which its badness rendered almost illegible. The servant placed it in a situation to be seen by his master.

Mr. Dudley allowed it to remain unopened for a considerable time. At length, deeming it excusable to discover, by any means, the person to whom it was addressed, he ventured to unseal it. It was dated at Portsmouth in New Hampshire. The signature was Mary Mansfield. It was addressed to her son, and was a curious specimen of illiterateness. Mary herself was unable to write, as she reminds her son, and had therefore procured the assistance of Mrs. Dewitt, for whose family she washed. The amanuensis[9] was but little superior in the arts of penmanship to her principal. The contents of the epistle were made out with some difficulty. This was the substance of it.

Mary reproaches her son for deserting her, and letting five years pass away without allowing her to hear from him. She informed him of her distresses as they flowed from sickness and poverty, and were aggravated by the loss of her son who was so handsome and promising a lad. She related her marriage with Zekel Hackney, who first brought her tidings of her boy. He was master, it seems, of a fishing smack,[10] and voyaged sometimes to New-York. In one of his visits to this city, he met a mighty spry young man, in whom he thought he recognized his wife's son. He had traced him to the house of Mr. Dudley, and on enquiry, discovered that the lad resided here. On his return he communicated the tidings to his spouse, who had now written to reproach him for his neglect of his poor old mother, and to intreat his assistance to relieve her from the necessity of drudging for her livelihood.

This letter was capable of an obvious construction. It was, no doubt, founded in mistake, though, it was to be acknowledged, that the mistake was singular. Such was the conclusion immediately formed by Mr. Dudley. He quietly replaced the letter on the mantlepiece, where it had before stood, and dismissed the affair from his thoughts.

Next day Craig returned from his journey. Mr. Dudley was employed in examining some papers in a desk that stood behind the door, in the apartment in which the letter was placed. There was no other person in the room when Craig entered it. He did not perceive Mr. Dudley, who was screened from observation, by his silence and by an open door. As soon as he entered, Mr. Dudley looked at him, and made no haste to speak. The letter whose superscription was turned towards him, immediately attracted Craig's attention. He seized it with some degree of eagerness, and observing the broken seal, thrust it hastily into his pocket, muttering, at the same time, in a tone, betokening a mixture of consternation and anger, "Damn it."—He immediately left the room, still uninformed of the presence of Mr. Dudley, who began to muse, with some earnestness, on what he had seen. Soon after he left this room and went into another, in which the family usually sat. In about twenty minutes, Craig made his appearance with his usual freedom and plausibility. Complimentary and customary topics were discussed. Mrs. Dudley and her daughter were likewise present. The uneasiness which the incident just mentioned had occasioned in the mind of Mr. Dudley, was at first dispelled by the disembarrassed behaviour of his partner, but new matter of suspicion was speedily afforded him. He observed that his partner spoke of his present entrance as of the first since his arrival, and that when the lady mentioned that he had been the subject of a curious mistake, a letter being directed

---

[9] "Amanuensis": a secretarial assistant who copies or writes from dictation.

[10] "Smack": a single-masted boat for coastal commerce and fishing, with an onboard well for keeping fish alive until delivery to harbor markets.

to him by a strange name, and left there during his absence, he pretended total ignorance of the circumstance. The young lady was immediately directed by her mother to bring the letter which lay, she said, on the mantle-tree in the next room.

During this scene Mr. Dudley was silent. He anticipated the disappointment of the messenger, believing the letter to have been removed. What then was his surprise when the messenger returned bearing the letter in her hand! Craig examined and read it and commented, with great mirth, on the contents, acting, all the while, as if he had never seen it before. These appearances were not qualified to quiet suspicion. The more Dudley brooded over them, the more dissatisfied he became. He, however, concealed his thoughts as well from Craig himself as his family, impatiently waiting for some new occurrence to arise by which he might square his future proceedings.

During Craig's absence, Mrs. Dudley had thought this a proper occasion for cleaning his apartment. The furniture, and among the rest, a large chest strongly fastened, was removed into an adjoining room which was otherwise unoccupied, and which was usually kept locked. When the cleansing was finished, the furniture was replaced, except this trunk, which its bulk, the indolence of the servant, and her opinion of its uselessness, occasioned her to leave in the closet.

About a week after this, on a Saturday evening, Craig invited to sup with him a friend who was to embark, on the ensuing Monday, for Jamaica. During supper, at which the family were present, the discourse turned on the voyage on which the guest was about to enter. In the course of talk, the stranger expressed how much he stood in need of a strong and commodious chest, in which he might safely deposit his cloaths and papers. Not being apprized of the early departure of the vessel, he had deferred till it was too late, applying to an artizan.

Craig desired him to set himself at rest on that head, for that he had, in his possession, just such a trunk as he described. It was of no use to him, being long filled with nothing better than refuse and lumber, and that, if he would, he might send for it the next morning. He turned to Mrs. Dudley and observed, that the trunk to which he alluded was in her possession, and he would thank her to direct its removal into his own apartment, that he might empty it of its present contents, and prepare it for the service of his friend. To this she readily assented.

There was nothing mysterious in this affair, but the mind of Mr. Dudley was pained with doubts. He was now as prone to suspect, as he was formerly disposed to confidence. This evening he put the key of the closet in his own pocket. When enquired for the next day, it was, of course, missing. It could not be found on the most diligent search. The occasion was not of such moment as to justify breaking the door. Mr. Dudley imagined that he saw, in Craig, more uneasiness at this disappointment, than he was willing to express. There was no remedy. The chest remained where it was, and, next morning, the ship departed on her voyage.

Craig accompanied his friend on board, was prevailed upon to go to sea with him, designing to return with the pilot-boat, but when the pilot was preparing to leave the vessel, such was this man's complaisance to the wishes of his friend, that he concluded to perform the remainder of the voyage in his company. The consequences are easily seen. Craig had gone with a resolution of never returning. The unhappy

Dudley was left to deplore the total ruin of his fortune which had fallen a prey to the arts of a subtle imposter.

The chest was opened, and the part which Craig had been playing for some years, with so much success, was perfectly explained. It appeared that the sum which Craig had contributed to the common stock, when first admitted into partnership, had been previously purloined from the daily receipts of his shop, of which an exact register was kept. Craig had been so indiscrete as to preserve this accusing record, and it was discovered in this depository: He was the son of Mary Mansfield and a native of Portsmouth. The history of the Wakefield family, specious[11] and complicated as it was, was entirely fictitious. The letters had been forged, and the correspondence supported by his own dexterity. Here was found the letter which Mr. Dudley had written to his friend requesting him to make certain enquiries at Wakefield, and which he imagined that he had delivered with his own hands to a trusty bearer. Here was the original draught of the answer he received. The manner in which this stratagem had been accomplished came gradually to light. The letter which was written to the Yorkshire traveller had been purloined, and another, with a similar superscription, in which the hand of Dudley was exactly imitated, and containing only brief and general remarks, had been placed in its stead. Craig must have suspected its contents, and by this suspicion have been incited to the theft. The answer which the Englishman had really written, and which sufficiently corresponded with the forged letter, had been intercepted by Craig, and furnished him a model from which he might construct an answer adapted to his own purposes.

This imposture had not been sustained for a trivial purpose. He had embezzled a large share of the stock, and had employed the credit of the house to procure extensive remittances to be made to an agent at a distance, by whom the property was effectually secured. Craig had gone to participate these spoils, while the whole estate of Mr. Dudley was insufficient to pay the demands that were consequently made upon him.

It was his lot to fall into the grasp of men, who squared their actions by no other standard than law, and who esteemed every claim to be incontestably just, that could plead that sanction. They did not indeed throw him into prison. When they had despoiled him of every remnant of his property, they deemed themselves entitled to his gratitude for leaving his person unmolested.

---

[11] "Specious": outwardly plausible or attractive, but of little real value.

Chapter II

THUS in a moment was this man thrown from the summit of affluence to the lowest indigence. He had been habituated to independance and ease. This reverse, therefore, was the harder to bear. His present situation was much worse than at his father's death. Then he was sanguine with youth and glowing with health. He possessed a fund on which he could commence his operations. Materials were at hand, and nothing was wanted but skill to use them. Now he had advanced in life. His frame was not exempt from infirmity. He had so long reposed on the bosom of opulence and enjoyed the respect attendant on wealth, that he felt himself totally incapacitated for a new station. His misfortune had not been foreseen. It was imbittered by the consciousness of his own imprudence, and by recollecting that the serpent which had stung him, was nurtured in his own bosom.

It was not merely frugal fare and an humble dwelling to which he was condemned. The evils to be dreaded were beggary and contempt. Luxury and leisure were not merely denied him. He must bend all his efforts to procure cloathing and food, to preserve his family from nakedness and famine. His spirit would not brook dependance. To live upon charity, or to take advantage of the compassion of his friends, was a destiny far worse than any other. To this therefore he would not consent. However irksome and painful it might prove, he determined to procure his bread by the labour of his hands.

But to what scene or kind of employment should he betake himself? He could not endure to exhibit this reverse[1] of fortune on the same theatre which had witnessed his prosperity. One of his first measures was to remove from New-York to Philadelphia. How should he employ himself in his new abode? Painting, the art in which he was expert, would not afford him the means of subsistence. Tho' no despicable musician, he did not esteem himself qualified to be a teacher of this art. This profession, besides, was treated by his new neighbours, with general, though unmerited contempt. There were few things on which he prided himself more than on the facilities and elegances of his penmanship. He was besides well acquainted with arithmetic and accompting. He concluded therefore, to offer his services as a writer in a public office. This employment demanded little bodily exertion. He had spent much of his time at the book and the desk: his new occupation, therefore, was further recommended by its resemblance to his ancient modes of life.

The first situation of this kind, for which he applied, he obtained. The duties were constant, but not otherwise toilsome or arduous. The emoluments were slender, but by contracting, within limits as narrow as possible, his expenses, they could be made subservient to the mere purposes of subsistence. He hired a small house in the suburbs

---

[1] "Could not endure to exhibit this reverse … New-York to Philadelphia": to lessen the perceived shame of bankruptcy and humiliation of lower-class status and wage-work, Dudley hides himself and his family by moving to another city where they are unknown and, the reader learns later, by changing his name (see note 11.4).

of the city. It consisted of a room above and below, and a kitchen. His wife, daughter and one girl, composed its inhabitants.

As long as his mind was occupied in projecting and executing these arrangements, it was diverted from uneasy contemplations. When his life became uniform, and day followed day in monotonous succession, and the novelty of his employment had disappeared, his cheerfulness began likewise to fade, and was succeeded by unconquerable melancholy. His present condition was in every respect the contrast of his former. His servitude was intolerable. He was associated with sordid hirelings, gross and uneducated, who treated his age with rude familiarity, and insulted his ears with ribaldry and scurril[2] jests. He was subject to command, and had his portion of daily drudgery allotted to him, to be performed for a pittance no more than would buy the bread which he daily consumed. The task assigned him was technical and formal. He was perpetually encumbered with the rubbish of law, and waded with laborious steps through its endless tautologies, its impertinent circuities, its lying assertions, and hateful artifices. Nothing occurred to relieve or diversify the scene. It was one tedious round of scrawling and jargon; a tissue made up of the shreds and remnants of barbarous antiquity, polluted with the rust of ages, and patched by the stupidity of modern workmen, into new deformity.[3]

When the day's task was finished, jaded spirits, and a body enfeebled by reluctant application, were but little adapted to domestic enjoyments. These indeed were incompatible with a temper like his, to whom the privation of the comforts that attended his former condition, was equivalent to the loss of life. These privations were still more painful to his wife, and her death added one more calamity to those under which he already groaned. He had always loved her with the tenderest affection, and he justly regarded this evil as surpassing all his former woes.

But his destiny seemed never weary of persecuting him. It was not enough that he should fall a victim to the most atrocious arts, that he should wear out his days in solitude and drudgery, that he should feel not only the personal restraints and hardships attendant upon indigence, but the keener pangs that result from negligence and contumely. He was imperfectly recovered from the shock occasioned by the death of his wife, when his sight was invaded by a cataract. Its progress was rapid, and terminated in total blindness.

He was now disabled from pursuing his usual occupation. He was shut out from the light of heaven, and debarred of every human comfort. Condemned to eternal dark, and worse than the helplessness of infancy, he was dependant for the meanest offices on the kindness of others, and he who had formerly abounded in the gifts of fortune, thought only of ending his days in a gaol or an alms-house.

---

[2] "Scurril": scurrilous, coarse, indecent.

[3] "Rubbish of law … hateful artifices … new deformity": a scathing description of law as a technology of ruling-class power, used to confuse and control rather than to produce a more just and equitable society. Although his family intended for him to become an attorney, Brown abandoned his Philadelphia law apprenticeship in 1793, similarly complaining that the language of law existed to deny rather than enact justice. For a second remark on this head, see note 10.1.

His situation however was alleviated by one circumstance. He had a daughter whom I have formerly mentioned, as the only survivor of many children. She was sixteen years of age when the storm of adversity fell upon her father's house. It may be thought that one educated as she had been, in the gratification of all her wishes, and at an age of timidity and inexperience, would have been less fitted than her father for encountering misfortune, and yet when the task of comforter fell upon her, her strength was not found wanting. Her fortitude was immediately put to the test. This reverse did not only affect her obliquely and through the medium of her family, but directly and in one way usually very distressful to female feelings.

Her fortune and character had attracted many admirers. One of them had some reason to flatter himself with success. Miss Dudley's notions had little in common with those around her. She had learned to square her conduct, in a considerable degree, not by the hasty impulses of inclination, but by the dictates of truth. She yielded nothing to caprice or passion. Not that she was perfectly exempt from intervals of weakness, or from the necessity of painful struggles, but these intervals were transient, and these struggles always successful. She was no stranger to the pleadings of love from the lips of others, and in her own bosom, but its tumults were brief, and speedily gave place to quiet thoughts and steadfast purposes.

She had listened to the solicitations of one, not unworthy in himself, and amply recommended by the circumstances of family and fortune.[4] He was young and therefore impetuous. Of the good that he sought, he was not willing to delay the acquisition for a moment. She had been taught a very different lesson. Marriage included vows of irrevocable affection and obedience. It was a contract to endure for life. To form this connection in extreme youth, before time had unfolded and modelled the characters of the parties, was, in her opinion, a proof of pernicious and opprobrious temerity.[5] Not to perceive the propriety of delay in this case, or to be regardless of the motives that would enjoin upon us a deliberate procedure, furnished an unanswerable objection to any man's pretensions. She was sensible, however, that this, like other mistakes, was curable. If her arguments failed to remove it, time, it was likely, would effect this purpose. If she rejected a matrimonial proposal for the present, it was for reasons that might not preclude her future acceptance of it.

Her scruples, in the present case, did not relate to the temper or person, or understanding of her lover, but to his age, to the imperfectness of their acquaintance, and to the want of that permanence of character, which can flow only from the progress of time and knowledge. These objections, which so rarely exist, were conclusive with her. There was no danger of her relinquishing them in compliance

---

[4] "The solicitations of one ... of family and fortune": that is, Constantia has already turned down one marriage proposal from a wealthy but immature suitor. As the previous paragraph suggests, this information is presented as evidence of Constantia's intelligence and courage. This is the first of three male suitors Constantia will reject in the course of the novel (see note 9.8).

[5] "Opprobrious temerity": shameful recklessness. Temerity is unreasonable disregard for danger or negative consequences; "rashness, foolhardiness, recklessness" (*OED*).

with the remonstrances[6] of parents and the solicitations of her lover, though the one and the other were urged with all the force of authority and insinuation. The prescriptions of duty were too clear to allow her to hesitate and waver, but the consciousness of rectitude could not secure her from temporary vexations.

Her parents were blemished with some of the frailties of that character. They held themselves entitled to prescribe in this article, but they forbore to exert their power. They condescended to persuade, but it was manifest, that they regarded their own conduct as a relaxation of right, and had not the lover's importunities suddenly ceased, it is not possible to tell how far the happiness of Miss Dudley might have been endangered. The misfortunes of her father were no sooner publicly known, than the youth forbore his visits, and embarked on a voyage which he had long projected, but which had been hitherto delayed by a superior regard to the interests of his passion.

It must be allowed that the lady had not foreseen this event. She had exercised her judgment upon his character, and had not been deceived. Before this desertion, had it been clearly stated to her apprehension, she would have readily admitted it to be probable. She knew the fascination of wealth, and the delusiveness of self-confidence. She was superior to the folly of supposing him exempt from sinister influences, and deaf to the whispers of ambition, and yet the manner in which she was affected by this event, convinced her that her heart had a larger share than her reason in dictating her expectations.

Yet it must not be supposed that she suffered any very acute distress on this account. She was grieved less for her own sake than his. She had no design of entering into marriage, in less than seven years from this period.[7] Not a single hope, relative to her own condition, had been frustrated. She had only been mistaken in her favourable conceptions of another. He had exhibited less constancy and virtue than her heart had taught her to expect.

With those opinions, she could devote herself, with a single heart, to the alleviation of her parents' sorrows. This change in her condition she treated lightly, and retained her cheerfulness unimpaired. This happened because, in a rational estimate, and so far as it affected herself, the misfortune was slight, and because her dejection would only tend to augment the disconsolateness of her parents, while, on the other hand, her serenity was calculated to infuse the same confidence into them. She indulged herself in no fits of exclamation or moodiness. She listened in silence to their

---

[6] "Remonstrances": strenuous objections or complaints.

[7] "In less than seven years from this period": if Constantia is 16 at the time of her father's bankruptcy (established six paragraphs earlier), her plan is to wait until age 23 before considering marriage. Rejecting conventional wisdom on female passion and a woman's desire for comfort, Constantia instead invokes the "masculine" virtues of rational composure. By refusing to subordinate herself as an object that can be transferred according to the wishes of her parents, male suitors, or narrow economic self-interest, she suffers heartache but escapes the possible life-long damage of marriage to a selfish, emotional impostor. For more, see the discussions of marriage in Chapter 9 (note 9.6) and in Brown's *Alcuin* in Related Texts.

invectives and laments, and seized every opportunity that offered to inspire them with courage, to set before them the good as well as ill, to which they were reserved, to suggest expedients for improving their condition, and to soften the asperities of his new mode of life, to her father, by every species of blandishment and tenderness.

She refused no personal exertion to the common benefit. She incited her father to diligence, as well by her example, as by her exhortations; suggested plans, and superintended or assisted in the execution of them. The infirmities of sex and age vanished before the motives to courage and activity flowing from her new situation. When settled in his new abode, and profession, she began to deliberate what conduct was incumbent on herself, how she might participate with her father, the burthen of the common maintainance, and blunt the edge of this calamity by the resources of a powerful and cultivated mind.

 In the first place, she disposed of every superfluous garb and trinket. She reduced her wardrobe to the plainest and cheapest establishment. By this means alone, she supplied her father's necessities with a considerable sum. Her music and even her books were not spared, not from the slight esteem in which these were held by her, but because she was thenceforth to become an economist of time as well as of money, because musical instruments are not necessary to the practice of this art in its highest perfection, and because, books, when she should procure leisure to read, or money to purchase them, might be obtained in a cheaper and more commodious form, than those costly and splendid volumes, with which her father's munificence had formerly supplied her.

To make her expences as limited as possible was her next care. For this end she assumed the province of cook, the washing of house and cloaths, and the cleansing of furniture. Their house was small, the family consisted of no more than four persons, and all formality and expensiveness were studiously discarded, but her strength was unequal to unavoidable tasks. A vigorous constitution could not supply the place of laborious habits, and this part of her plan must have been changed for one less frugal. The aid of a servant must have been hired, if it had not been furnished by gratitude.

Some years before this misfortune, her mother had taken under her protection a girl, the daughter of a poor woman, who subsisted by labour, and who dying, left this child without friend or protector. This girl possessed no very improveable capacity, and therefore, could not benefit by the benevolent exertions of her young mistress as much as the latter desired, but her temper was artless and affectionate, and she attached herself to Constance with the most entire devotion. In this change of fortune she would not consent to be separated, and Miss Dudley, influenced by her affection to her Lucy, and reflecting that on the whole it was most to her advantage to share with her, at once, her kindness and her poverty, retained her as her companion. With this girl she shared the domestic duties, scrupling not to divide with her the meanest and most rugged, as well as the lightest offices.

This was not all. She, in the next place, considered whether her ability extended no farther than to save. Could she not by the employment of her hands increase the income as well as diminish the expense? Why should she be precluded from all lucrative occupation? She soon came to a resolution. She was mistress of her needle, and this skill she conceived herself bound to employ for her own subsistence.

Cloathing is one of the necessaries of human existence. The art of the taylor is scarcely of less use than that of the tiller of the ground. There are few the gains of which are better merited, and less injurious to the principles of human society. She resolved therefore to become a workwoman, and to employ in this way, the leisure she possessed from household avocations. To this scheme she was obliged to reconcile not only herself but her parents. The conquest of their prejudices was no easy task,[8] but her patience and skill finally succeeded, and she procured needle work in sufficient quantity to enable her to enhance in no trivial degree, the common fund.

It is one thing barely to comply with the urgencies of the case, and to do that which, in necessitous circumstances is best. But to conform with grace and cheerfulness, to yield no place to fruitless recriminations and repinings, to contract the evils into as small a compass as possible, and extract from our condition all possible good, is a task of a different kind.

Mr. Dudley's situation required from him frugality and diligence. He was regular and unintermitted in his application to his pen. He was frugal. His slender income was administered agreeably to the maxims of his daughter: but he was unhappy. He experienced in its full extent the bitterness of disappointment.

He gave himself up for the most part to a listless melancholy. Sometimes his impatience would produce effects less excusable; and conjure up an accusing and irascible spirit. His wife and even his daughter he would make the objects of peevish and absurd reproaches. These were moments when her heart drooped indeed, and her tears could not be restrained from flowing. These fits were transitory and rare, and when they had passed, the father seldom failed to mingle tokens of contrition and repentance with the tears of his daughter. Her arguments and soothings were seldom disappointed of success. Her mother's disposition was soft and pliant, but she could not accommodate herself to the necessity of her husband's affairs. She was obliged to endure the want of some indulgences, but she reserved to herself the liberty of complaining, and to subdue this spirit in her was found utterly impracticable. She died a victim to discontent.

This event deepened the gloom that shrouded the soul of her father, and rendered the task of consolation still more difficult. She did not despair. Her sweetness and patience was invincible by any thing that had already happened, but her fortitude did not exceed the standard of human nature. Evils now began to menace her, to which it is likely she would have yielded, had not their approach been intercepted by an evil of a different kind.

---

[8] "The conquest of their prejudices was no easy task": as the family experiences laboring-class poverty, Constantia's willingness to work to help her family and others must first overcome her family's elite "prejudices" against wage-earning and labor. For Dudley's earlier condemnation of work, see note 1.4.

The pressure of grief is sometimes such as to prompt us to seek a refuge in voluntary death.[9] We must lay aside the burthen which we cannot sustain. If thought degenerate into a vehicle of pain, what remains but to destroy that vehicle? For this end, death is the obvious, but not the only, or morally speaking, the worst means. There is one method of obtaining the bliss of forgetfulness, in comparison with which suicide is innocent.

The strongest mind is swayed by circumstances. There is no firmness of integrity, perhaps, able to repel every species of temptation, which is produced by the present constitution of human affairs, and yet temptation is successful, chiefly by virtue of its gradual and invisible approaches. We rush into danger, because we are not aware of its existence, and have not therefore provided the means of safety, and the dæmon that seizes us is hourly reinforced by habit. Our opposition grows fainter in proportion as our adversary acquires new strength, and the man becomes enslaved by the most sordid vices, whose fall would, at a former period, have been deemed impossible, or who would have been imagined liable to any species of depravity, more than to this.

Mr. Dudley's education had entailed upon him many errors, yet who would have supposed it possible for him to be enslaved by a depraved appetite; to be enamoured of low debauchery, and to grasp at the happiness that intoxication had to bestow? This was a mournful period in Constantia's history. My feelings will not suffer me to dwell upon it. I cannot describe the manner in which she was affected by the first symptoms of this depravity, the struggles which she made to counteract this dreadful infatuation, and the grief which she experienced from the repeated miscarriage of her efforts. I will not detail her various expedients for this end, the appeals which she made to his understanding, to his sense of honor and dread of infamy, to the gratitude to which she was entitled, and to the injunctions of parental duty. I will not detail his fits of remorse, his fruitless penitence, and continual relapses, nor depict the heart-breaking scenes of uproar and violence, and foul disgrace that accompanied his paroxysms of drunkenness.

The only intellectual amusement which this lady allowed herself was writing. She enjoyed one distant friend, with whom she maintained an uninterrupted correspondence, and to whom she confided a circumstantial and copious relation of all these particulars. That friend is the writer of these memoirs. It is not impossible but that these letters may be communicated to the world, at some future period. The picture which they exhibit is hourly exemplified and realized, though, in the many-coloured scenes of human life, none surpasses it in disastrousness and horror. My eyes almost wept themselves dry over this part of her tale.[10]

---

[9] "Voluntary death": the first of the novel's many references to suicide. Following Godwin's *Enquiry Concerning Political Justice* (1793), Brown rejects religious dogma that condemns suicide, and considers it justified in certain circumstances.

[10] "That friend is the writer of these memoirs ... My eyes almost wept themselves dry over this part of her tale": in this and the previous paragraph, the narrator Sophia Courtland again emphasizes her control over the narrative and makes the first of many overt editorial interventions.

In this state of things Mr. Dudley's blindness might justly be accounted, even in its immediate effects, a fortunate event. It dissolved the spell, by which he was bound, and which, it is probable, would never have been otherwise broken. It restored him to himself and shewed him, with a distinctness which made him shudder, the gulf to which he was hastening. But nothing can compensate to the sufferer the evils of blindness. It was the business of Constantia's life to alleviate those sufferings, to cherish and console her father, and to rescue him, by the labour of her hands from dependance on public charity. For this end, her industry and solicitude were never at rest. She was able, by that industry, to provide him and herself with necessaries. Their portion was scanty, and, if it sometimes exceeded the standard of their wants, not less frequently fell short of it. For all her toils and disquietudes she esteemed herself fully compensated by the smiles of her father. He indeed could seldom be prompted to smile, or to suppress the dictates of that despair which flowed from his sense of this new calamity, and the aggravations of hardship which his recent insobrieties had occasioned to his daughter.

She purchased what books her scanty stock would allow, and borrowed others. These she read to him when her engagements would permit. At other times she was accustomed to solace herself with her own music. The lute which her father had purchased in Italy, and which had been disposed of among the rest of his effects, at public sale, had been gratuitously restored to him by the purchaser, on condition of his retaining it in his possession. His blindness and inoccupation now broke the long silence to which this instrument had been condemned, and afforded an accompaniment to the young lady's voice.

Her chief employment was conversation. She resorted to this as the best means of breaking the monotony of the scene; but this purpose was not only accomplished, but other benefits of the highest value accrued from it. The habits of a painter eminently tended to vivify and make exact her father's conceptions and delineations of visible objects. The sphere of his youthful observation comprised more ingredients of the picturesque, than any other sphere. The most precious materials of the moral history of mankind, are derived from the revolutions of Italy. Italian features and landscape, constitute the chosen field of the artist. No one had more carefully explored this field than Mr. Dudley. His time, when abroad, had been divided between residence at Rome, and excursions to Calabria and Tuscany.[11] Few impressions were

---

[11] "Calabria and Tuscany": regions to the south and the north of Rome along the west coast of the Italian peninsula. Calabria is the southwestern toe of the peninsula, the area south of Naples and closest to Sicily, noted for rugged mountain landscapes and underdeveloped agrarian economy. Tuscany is the region around Florence north of Rome, notable as an artistic, cultural, and commercial center from the Renaissance to the present. Dudley's cultural formation is symbolically oriented around Rome and Italy, the epicenter of Latinate and culturally "classical" forms from the Roman Empire to the modern revolutionary age. With Rome as his focal point, Dudley's journeys in either direction contrast more Enlightened, modernizing northern Italian regions with a relatively impoverished south (then the Kingdom of the Two Sicilies), usually depicted as culturally backward, superstitious, and crime-ridden: stereotypes that continue even today.

effaced from his capacious register, and these were now rendered by his eloquence, nearly as conspicuous to his companion as to himself.

She was imbued with an ardent thirst of knowledge, and by the acuteness of her remarks, and the judiciousness of her enquiries, reflected back upon his understanding as much improvement as she received. These efforts to render his calamity tolerable, and enure him to the profiting by his own resources, were aided by time, and, when reconciled by habit to unrespited gloom, he was, sometimes, visited by gleams of cheerfulness, and drew advantageous comparisons between his present and former situation. A stillness not unakin to happiness, frequently diffused itself over their winter evenings. Constance enjoyed, in their full extent, the felicities of health and self-approbation. The genius and eloquence of her father, nourished by perpetual exercise, and undiverted from its purpose by the intrusion of visible objects, frequently afforded her a delight in comparison with which all other pleasures were mean.

Chapter III

THIS period of tranquillity was short. Poverty hovered at their threshold, and in a state precarious as their's, could not be long excluded. The lady was more accustomed to anticipate good than evil, but she was not unconscious that the winter, which was hastening, would bring with it numerous inconveniences. Wants during that season are multiplied, while the means of supplying them either fail or are diminished. Fuel is alone, a cause of expense equal to all other articles of subsistence. Her dwelling was old, crazy,[1] and full of avenues to air. It was evident that neither fire nor cloathing would, in an habitation like that, attemper the chilling blasts. Her scanty gains were equal to their needs, during summer, but would probably fall short during the prevalence of cold.

These reflections could not fail sometimes to intrude. She indulged them as long as they served merely to suggest expedients and provisions for the future, but laboured to call away her attention when they merely produced anxiety. This she more easily effected, as some months of summer were still to come, and her knowledge of the vicissitudes to which human life is subject, taught her to rely upon the occurrence of some fortunate, though unforeseen event.

Accident suggested an expedient of this kind. Passing through an alley, in the upper part of the town, her eye was caught by a label on the door of a small house, signifying that it was to be let. It was smaller than that she at present occupied, but it had an aspect of much greater comfort and neatness. Its situation, near the centre of the city, in a quiet, cleanly, and well paved alley, was far preferable to that of her present habitation, in the suburbs, scarcely accessible in winter for pools and gullies, and in a neighbourhood abounding with indigence and profligacy. She likewise considered that the rent of this might be less, and that the proprietor of this might have more forbearance and benignity than she had hitherto met with.

Unconversant as she was with the world, imbued with the timidity of her sex and her youth, many enterprizes were arduous to her, which would, to age and experience, have been easy. Her reluctances, however, when required by necessity, were overcome, and all the measures which her situation prescribed, executed with address and dispatch. One, marking her deportment, would have perceived nothing but dignity and courage. He would have regarded these as the fruits of habitual independence and exertion, whereas they were merely the results of clear perceptions and inflexible resolves.

The proprietor of this mansion was immediately sought out, and a bargain, favorable as she could reasonably desire, concluded. Possession was to be taken in a week. For this end carters and draymen were to be engaged, household implements to be prepared for removal, and negligence and knavery prevented by scrupulous attention. The duties of superintendence and execution devolved upon her. Her father's blindness rendered him powerless. His personal case required no small portion of

---

[1] "Crazy": "full of cracks or flaws ... liable to break apart or fall to pieces" (*OED*).

care. Household and professional functions were not to be omitted. She stood alone in the world. There was none whose services or counsel she could claim. Tortured by multiplicity of cares, shrinking from exposure to rude eyes, and from contention with refractory and insolent spirits, and overpowered with fatigue and disgust, she was yet compelled to retain a cheerful tone in her father's presence, and to struggle with his regrets and his peevishness.

O my friend! Methinks I now see thee,[2] encountering the sneers and obstinacy of the meanest of mankind, subjecting that frame of thine, so exquisitely delicate, and therefore so feeble, to the vilest drudgery. I see thee, leading thy unhappy father to his new dwelling, and stifling the sign produced by his fruitless repinings and unseasonable scruples—Why was I not partaker of thy cares and labours? Why was I severed from thee by the ocean, and kept in ignorance of thy state? I was not without motives to anxiety, for I was friendless as thou, but how unlike to thine was my condition! I reposed upon down and tissue, never moved but with obsequious attendance and pompous equipage,[3] painting and music were consolations ever at hand, and my cabinet was stored with poetry and science. These, indeed, were insufficient to exclude care, and with regard to the past, I have no wish but that I had shared with my friend her toilsome and humiliating lot. However an erroneous world might judge, thy life was full of dignity, and thy moments of happiness not few, since happiness is only attendant on the performance of our duty.

A toilsome and sultry week was terminated by a sabbath of repose. Her new dwelling possessed indisputable advantages over her old. Not the least of these benefits consisted in the vicinity of people, peaceable and honest, though poor. She was no longer shocked by the clamours of debauchery, and exposed, by her situation, to the danger of being mistaken by the profligate of either sex, for one of their own class.[4] It was reasonable to consider this change of abode, as fortunate, and yet, circumstances quickly occurred which suggested a very different conclusion.

She had no intercourse, which necessity did not prescribe, with the rest of the world. She screened herself as much as possible from intercourse with prying and loquacious neighbours. Her father's inclinations in this respect coincided with her own, though their love of seclusion was prompted by different motives. Visitants were hated by the father, because his dignity was hurt by communication with the vulgar. The daughter set too much value upon time willingly to waste it upon trifles

---

[2] "O my friend! … thee": here and periodically throughout the rest of the novel, the narrator adopts the familiar pronouns "thee" and "thou" and forms of poetic diction already archaic in the 1790s, seemingly as a means of insinuating that she is on more intimate or familiar terms with Constantia than any of the novel's other characters. Usage of thee and thou was still common among Quakers at the time, but in this context it registers heightened emotionality. Other characters will also occasionally switch to thee and thou usage at moments of heightened emotionality and crisis throughout the narrative.

[3] "Equipage": in this usage, "a carriage and horses, with the attendant servants" (*OED*). This paragraph is another example of the narrator's emotionalized editorial framing of Constantia's story.

[4] "For one of their own class": Constantia moves to avoid being seen as a prostitute.

and triflers. She had no pride to subdue, and therefore never escaped from well meant importunity[5] at the expense of politeness and good humour. In her moments of leisure, she betook herself to the poet and the moralist for relief.

She could not at all times, suppress the consciousness of the evils which surrounded and threatened her. She could not but rightly estimate the absorbing and brutifying nature of that toil to which she was condemned. Literature had hitherto been regarded as her solace. She knew that meditation and converse as well as books and the pen, are instruments of knowledge, but her musing thoughts were too often fixed upon her own condition. Her father's soaring moods and luminous intervals grew less frequent. Conversation was too rarely abstracted from personal considerations, and strayed less often than before into the wilds of fancy or the mazes of analysis.

These circumstances led her to reflect whether subsistence might not be obtained by occupations purely intellectual. Instruction was needed by the young of both sexes. Females frequently performed the office of teachers. Was there no branch of her present knowledge which she might claim wages for imparting to others? Was there no art within her reach to acquire, convertible into means of gain? Women are generally limited to what is sensual and ornamental: Music and painting, and the Italian and French languages, are bounds which they seldom pass. In these pursuits it is not possible, nor is it expected, that they should arrive at the skill of adepts. The education of Constance had been regulated by the peculiar views of her father, who sought to make her, not alluring and voluptuous, but eloquent and wise. He therefore limited her studies to Latin and English. Instead of familiarizing her with the amorous effusions of Petrarcha and Racine, he made her thoroughly conversant with Tacitus and Milton.[6] Instead of making her a practical musician or pencilist, he conducted her to the school of Newton and Hartley,[7] unveiled to her the mathematical

---

[5] "Well meant importunity": bothersome but well-intended interruptions.

[6] "Petrarcha and Racine ... Tacitus and Milton": the contrast is between (stereotypically) "soft" and "feminine" arts, associated with Italian and French belles-lettres—the sonnets of Italian poet Petrarch (Francesco Petrarca, 1304–1374) and the dramas of French tragedian Jean Racine (1639–1699)—and (stereotypically) "robust" and "masculine" forms of history and poetry associated with Roman historian Tacitus (Publius Cornelius Tacitus, c. 56–117) and English epic poet John Milton (1608–1674). The opposition between presumably "softer" Italian and French forms and "harder" Roman and English ones is a self-evidently Anglophile, imperialist perspective during the revolutionary period, when the British Empire was challenging France (in both pre- and postrevolutionary forms) for domination in all fields political, economic, military, and cultural.

[7] "Newton and Hartley": Isaac Newton (1642–1727), the English mathematician and physicist who first outlined the theory of gravity, and David Hartley (1705–1757), English philosopher and psychologist whose work was important in the development of "associationist" psychology, or the theory that consciousness and ideas derive from empirical sensations, not preexisting or innate ideas. Again, the point is that Dudley has given Constantia an unusually "masculine" and intellectually rigorous education. Rather than merely decorative arts ("musician or pencilist") that copy or imitate preexisting nature, she has learned to inquire about the "principles and progress of human society," to analyze historical processes of social and cultural change. And again, the points of comparison offered by the narrator Sophia are suggestively Anglophile.

properties of light and sound, taught her as a metaphysician and anatomist, the structure and power of the senses, and discussed with her the principles and progress of human society.

These accomplishments tended to render her superior to the rest of women, but in no degree qualified her for the post of a female instructor. She saw and lamented her deficiencies, and gradually formed the resolution of supplying them. Her knowledge of the Latin tongue and of grammatical principles, rendered easy the acquisition of Italian and French, these being merely Scions from the Roman stock.

Having had occasion, previous to her change of dwelling, to purchase paper at a bookseller's, the man had offered her at a very low price, a second-hand copy of Veneroni's grammar[8] The offer had been declined, her views at that time being otherwise directed. Now, however, this incident was remembered, and a resolution instantly formed to purchase the book. As soon as the light declined, and her daily task at the needle had drawn to a close, she set out to execute this purpose. Arriving at the house of the bookseller, she perceived that the doors and windows were closed. Night having not yet arrived, the conjecture easily occurred, that some one had died in the house. She had always dealt with this man for books and paper, and had always been treated with civility. Her heart readily admitted some sympathy with his distress, and to remove her doubts, she turned to a person who stood at the entrance of the next house, and who held a cloth steeped in vinegar to his nostrils. In reply to her question, the stranger said in a tone of the deepest consternation—Mr. Watson[9] do you mean? He is dead: He died last night of the *yellow fever*.[10]

The name of this disease was not absolutely new to her ears. She had been apprized of its rapid and destructive progress in one quarter of the city, but, hitherto, it had existed, with regard to her, chiefly in the form of rumour. She had not realized the nature or probable extent of the evil. She lived at no great distance from the seat of the malady, but her neighbourhood had been hitherto exempt. So wholly unused was

---

[8] "Veneroni's grammar": a widely used Italian language instruction guide by Jean Vigneron (pen name Giovanni Veneroni) first published in French in 1678, translated into English by 1729 as *The Complete Italian Master; containing the best and easiest rules for attaining that language. By Signor Veneroni*, etc. Editions appeared throughout the eighteenth century and into the 1790s, when the book was commonly available in Philadelphia bookshops.

[9] "Watson": Brown uses the name Watson again for another character whose death initiates significant events in both parts of the novel *Arthur Mervyn* (1799–1800). In both cases the reported death of a character with this name marks important new stages of the narrative.

[10] "*Yellow fever*": the onset of the Philadelphia yellow fever epidemic of August–October 1793 places this scene in August of that year. The 1793 Philadelphia epidemic is the best known and most devastating of many episodes in the Atlantic harbor cities of North America in the late eighteenth century. Brown studied accounts of yellow fever epidemics with others in his New York circle, lived through the New York epidemic of August–September 1798 just prior to writing *Ormond*, and published a series of fictions using yellow fever epidemics as a setting, culminating in *Ormond* and his next novel *Arthur Mervyn*. For more on Brown's use of this crisis setting to explore issues concerning the social order, see the Introduction.

she to contemplate pestilence except at a distance, that its actual existence in the bosom of this city was incredible.

Contagious diseases, she well knew, periodically visited and laid waste the Greek and Egyptian cities.[11] It constituted no small part of that mass of evil, political and physical, by which that portion of the world has been so long afflicted. That a pest equally malignant had assailed the metropolis of her own country, a town famous for the salubrity of its airs and the perfection of its police, had something in it so wild and uncouth that she could not reconcile herself to the possibility of such an event.

The death of Watson, however, filled her mind with awful reflections. The purpose of her walk was forgotten amidst more momentous considerations. She bent her steps pensively homeward. She had now leisure to remark the symptoms of terror with which all ranks appeared to have been seized. The streets were as much frequented as ever, but there were few passengers whose countenances did not betray alarm, and who did not employ the imaginary antidote to infection, vinegar.

Having reached home, she quickly discovered in her father, an unusual solemnity and thoughtfulness. He had no power to conceal his emotions from his daughter, when her efforts to discover them were earnestly exerted. She learned that, during her absence he had been visited by his next neighbour, a thrifty, sober and well meaning, but ignorant and meddling person, by name Whiston. This person, being equally inquisitive into other men's affairs, and communicative of his own, was always an unwelcome visitant. On this occasion, he had come to disburthen on Mr. Dudley his fears of disease and death. His tale of the origin and progress of the epidemic, of the number and suddenness of recent deaths was delivered with endless prolixity. With this account he mingled prognostics of the future, counselled Mr. Dudley to fly from the scene of danger, and stated his own schemes and resolutions. After having thoroughly affrighted and wearied his companion he took his leave. Constance endeavoured to remove the impression which had been thus needlessly made. She urged her doubts as to the truth of Whiston's representations, and endeavoured, in various ways, to extenuate the danger.

Nay, my child, said her father, thou needest not reason on the subject. I am not afraid. At least, on my own account I fear nothing. What is life to me that I should dread to lose it? If on any account I should tremble it is on thine, my angelic girl. Thou dost not deserve thus early to perish: And yet if my love for thee were rational, perhaps, I ought to wish it. An evil destiny will pursue thee to the close of thy life, be it never so long.

I know that ignorance and folly breed the phantoms by which themselves are perplexed and terrified, and that Whiston is a fool, but here the truth is too plain to be disguised. This malady is pestilential. Havock and despair will accompany its

---

[11] "Contagious diseases … Greek and Egyptian cities": Brown's closest friend, physician Elihu Hubbard Smith, wrote a lengthy reconstruction and analysis of the "Plague of Athens" in 430 B.C.E. in the group's journal *The Medical Repository of Original Essays and Intelligence* 1.1 (August 1, 1797). Smith later died, in Brown's presence, while tending to fever victims during the New York epidemic of September 1798, shortly before Brown began work on this novel.

progress and its progress will be rapid. The tragedies of Marseilles and Messina will be reacted on this stage.[12]

For a time, we in this quarter will be exempt, but it will surely reach us at last, and then, whither shall we fly? For the rich, the whole world is a safe asylum, but for us, indigent and wretched, what fate is reserved but to stay and perish?[13] If the disease spare us, we must perish by neglect and famine. Alarm will be far and wide diffused. Fear will hinder those who supply the market, from entering the city. The price of food will become exorbitant. Our present source of subsistence, ignominious and scanty as it is, will be cut off. Traffic and labour of every kind will be at an end. We shall die, but not until we have witnessed and endured horrors that surpass thy powers of conception.

I know full well the enormity of this evil. I have been at Messina, and talked with many who witnessed the state of that city in 1743. I will not freeze thy blood with the recital. Anticipation has a tendency to lessen or prevent some evils, but pestilence is not of that number. Strange untowardness of destiny! That thou and I should be cast upon a scene like this!

Mr. Dudley joined with uncommon powers of discernment, a species of perverseness not easily accounted for. He acted as if the inevitable evils of her lot was not sufficient for the trial of his daughter's patience. Instead of comforter and counsellor, he fostered impatience in himself, and endeavoured, with the utmost diligence, to undermine her fortitude and disconcert her schemes. The task was assigned to her, not only of subduing her own fears, but of maintaining the contest with his disastrous eloquence. In most cases she had not failed of success. Hitherto their causes of anxiety, her own observation had, in some degree, enabled her to estimate at their just value. The rueful pictures which his imagination was wont to pourtray, affected her for a moment; but deliberate scrutiny commonly enabled her to detect and demonstrate their falacy. Now, however, the theme was new. Panick and foreboding found their way to her heart in defiance of her struggles. She had no experience by which to counteract this impulse. All that remained was to beguile her own and her father's cares by counterfeiting cheerfulness and introducing new topics.

This panic,[14] stifled for a time, renewed its sway when she retired to her chamber. Never did futurity wear, to her fancy, so dark an hue. Never did her condition appear

---

[12] "Tragedies of Marseilles and Messina": two earlier epidemics or plagues, assumed to be akin to yellow fever, that devastated Marseilles, the Mediterranean port in the south of France, in 1720–1721, and Messina, in Sicily, in 1743. Previous epidemics from classical antiquity to the modern era were familiar to Brown and his associates through the medical literature on yellow fever that they read and discussed in their New York circle.

[13] "For the rich, the whole world is a safe asylum, but for us … perish": the city's elites avoided the ravages of the fever by retiring to country estates and arranging to be away during the epidemics, whereas the laboring poor, the coopers, woodcarters, laundresses, and others who will appear in these chapters were left to their own devices. This is another aspect of the Dudleys' new experiences during their plunge into laboring class conditions.

[14] "This panic": panic and fear, emphasized throughout this chapter's final paragraphs, were regarded by Brown and his circle as destructive side effects of the epidemic, and as physiological forces

to her in a light so dreary and forlorn. To fly from the danger was impossible. How should accommodation at a distance, be procured? The means of subsistence were indissolubly connected with her present residence, but the progress of this disease would cut off these means, and leave her to be beset not only with pestilence but famine. What provision could she make against an evil like this?

---

that made potential fever victims weaker and more susceptible to infection (the mechanism of which was not then understood). Whiston's fearmongering, mentioned earlier, or Baxter's in Chapter 7, provide examples of the dangers of succumbing to fear, and Constantia's strength of character is illustrated in the manner in which she resists it, one of several instances of her development and lack of female timidity.

Just as the biological corruption of the fever parallels the social corruption of the city, Brown's novel implicitly juxtaposes the negative effects of fear and panic in the fever context with the effects of political fear and panic in the charged atmosphere of the Illuminati scare and other episodes to which this novel will allude. For more on the novel's response to the social and political panics of the late 1790s, see the Introduction and Related Texts.

Chapter IV

THE terms on which she had been admitted into this house, included the advance of one quarter's rent and the monthly payment of subsequent dues. The requisite sum had been with difficulty collected, the landlord had twice called to remind her of her stipulation, and this day had been fixed for the discharge of this debt. He had omitted, contrary to her expectations and her wishes, to come. It was probable, however, that they should meet on the ensuing day. If he should fail in this respect, it appeared to be her duty to carry the money to his house, and this it had been her resolution to perform.

Now, however, new views were suggested to her thoughts. By the payment of this debt she should leave herself nearly destitute. The flight and terror of the citizens would deprive her of employment. Want of food was an immediate and inevitable evil which the payment of this sum would produce. Was it just to incur this evil? To retain the means of luxurious gratification would be wrong, but to bereave herself and her father of bare subsistence was surely no dictate of duty.

It is true the penalty of nonpayment was always in the landlord's hands. He was empowered by the law to sell their moveables and expel them from his house. It was now no time for a penalty like this to be incurred. But from this treatment it was reasonable to hope that his lenity would save them. Was it not right to wait till the alternative of expulsion or payment was imposed? Meanwhile, however, she was subjected to the torments of suspense and to the guilt of a broken promise. These consequences were to be eluded only in one way: By visiting her landlord and stating her true condition, it was possible that his compassion would remit claims which were, in themselves, unreasonable and uncommon. The tender of the money accompanied by representations sufficiently earnest and pathetic, might possibly be declined.

These reflections were, next morning, submitted to her father. Her decision in this case was of less importance in his eyes, than in those of his daughter. Should the money be retained, it was, in his opinion, a pittance too small to afford them effectual support. Supposing provisions to be had at any price, which was, itself improbable, that price would be exorbitant. The general confusion would probably last for months, and thirty dollars would be devoured in a few weeks even in a time of safety. To give or to keep was indifferent for another reason. It was absurd for those to consult about means of subsistence for the next month, when it was fixed that they should die to-morrow—The true proceeding was obvious. The landlord's character was well known to him by means of the plaints and invectives of their neighbours, most of whom were tenants of the same man. If the money were offered his avarice would receive it, in spite of all the pleas that she should urge. If it were detained without lieve, an officer of justice would quickly be dispatched to claim it.

This statement was sufficient to take away from Constance the hope that she had fostered. What then, said she, after a pause, is my father's advice? Shall I go forthwith and deliver the money?

No, said he, stay till he sends for it. Have you forgotten that Mathews resides in the very midst of this disease. There is no need to thrust yourself within its fangs. They will reach us time enough. It is likely his messenger will be an agent of the law. No matter. The debt will be merely increased by a few charges. In a state like ours, the miserable remnant is not worth caring for.

This reasoning, did not impart conviction to the lady. The danger, flowing from a tainted atmosphere was not small, but to incur that danger was wiser than to exasperate their landlord, to augment the debt and to encounter the disgrace, accruing from a constable's visits. The conversation was dropped and, presently after, she set out on a visit to Mathews.

She fully estimated the importance to her happiness of the sum which she was going to pay. The general panic had already, in some degree, produced the effect she chiefly dreaded; the failure of employment for her needle. Her father had, with his usual diligence at self-torment, supplied her with sufficient proofs of the covetous and obdurate temper of her creditor. Insupportable, however, as the evil of payment was, it was better to incur it spontaneously, than by means of legal process. The desperateness of this proceeding therefore, did not prevent her from adopting it, but it filled her heart with the bitterest sensations. Absorbed as she past along, by these, she was nearly insensible to the vacancy which now prevailed in a quarter which formerly resounded with the din of voices and carriages.

As she approached the house to which she was going, her reluctance to proceed increased. Frequently she paused to recollect the motives that had prescribed this task, and to reinforce her purposes. At length she arrived at the house. Now, for the first time, her attention was excited by the silence and desolation that surrounded her. This evidence of fear and of danger struck upon her heart. All appeared to have fled from the presence of this unseen and terrible foe. The temerity of adventuring thus into the jaws of the pest, now appeared to her in glaring colours.

Appearances suggested a reflection which had not previously occurred and which tended to console her. Was it not probable that Mathews had likewise flown? His habits were calculated to endear to him his life: He would scarcely be among the last to shun perils like these: The omission of his promised visit on the preceding day, might be owing to his absence from the city, and thus, without subjection to any painful alternative, she might be suffered to retain the money.

To give certainty to this hope, she cast her eye towards the house opposite to which she now stood. Her heart drooped on perceiving proofs that the dwelling was still inhabited. The door was open and the windows in the second and third story were raised. Near the entrance, in the street, stood a cart. The horse attached to it, in his form and furniture and attitude, was an emblem of torpor and decay. His gaunt sides, motionless limbs, his gummy and dead eyes, and his head hanging to the ground, were in unison with the craziness of the vehicle to which he belonged, and the paltry and bedusted harness which covered him. No attendant nor any human face was visible. The stillness, though at an hour customarily busy, was uninterrupted except by the sound of wheels moving at an almost indistinguishable distance.

She paused for a moment to contemplate this unwonted spectacle. Her trepidations were mingled with emotions not unakin to sublimity, but the consciousness of danger speedily prevailed, and she hastened to acquit herself of her engagement. She approached the door for this purpose, but before she could draw the bell her motions were arrested by sounds from within. The staircase was opposite the door. Two persons were now discovered descending the stair. They lifted between them an heavy mass, which was presently discerned to be a coffin. Shocked by this discovery and trembling she withdrew from the entrance.

At this moment a door on the opposite side of the street opened and a female came out. Constance approached her involuntarily and her appearance not being unattractive, adventured, more by gestures than by words, to enquire whose obsequies were thus unceremoniously conducted. The woman informed her that the dead was Mathews, who, two days before, was walking about, indifferent to, and braving danger. She cut short the narrative which her companion seemed willing to prolong, and to embellish with all its circumstances, and hastened home with her utmost expedition.

The mind of Constance was a stranger to pusillanimity.[1] Death, as the common lot of all, was regarded by her without perturbation. The value of life, though not annihilated, was certainly diminished by adversity. With whatever solemnity contemplated, it excited on her own account, no aversion or inquietude. For her father's sake only, death was an evil to be ardently deprecated. The nature of the prevalent disease, the limits and modes of its influence, the risque that is incurred by approaching the sick or the dead, or by breathing the surrounding element, were subjects foreign to her education. She judged like the mass of mankind from the most obvious appearances, and was subject like them to impulses which disdained the controul of her reason. With all her complacency for death and speculative resignation to the fate that governs the world, disquiet and alarm pervaded her bosom on this occasion.

The deplorable state to which her father would be reduced by her death, was seen and lamented, but her tremulous sensations flowed not from this source. They were, in some sort, inexplicable and mechanical. In spite of recollection and reflection, they bewildered and harassed her, and subsided only of their own accord.

The death of Mathews was productive of one desirable consequence. Till the present tumult were passed, and his representatives had leisure to inspect his affairs, his debtors would probably remain unmolested. He, likewise, who should succeed to the inheritance, might possess very different qualities, and he as much distinguished for equity as Mathews had been for extortion. These reflections lightened her footsteps as she hied homeward. The knowledge she had gained, she hoped would counterpoise, in her father's apprehension, the perils, which accompanied the acquisition of it.

She had scarcely passed her own threshhold, when she was followed by Whiston. This man pursued the occupation of a Cooper. He performed journey-work[2] in a

---

[1] "Pusillanimity": cowardice.

[2] "Cooper … journey-work": a cooper "makes and repairs wooden vessels formed of staves and hoops, as casks, buckets, tubs" (*OED*). "Journey-work" is artisanal work done for daily wages or for hire. In the period's hierarchy of skilled crafts work, a journeyman is above the apprentice, who is like an indentured servant in that he receives food, board, and clothing but not wages, but below the "master" who works for himself or has enough funds to take on apprentices. A journeyman was so

shop, which, unfortunately for him, was situated near the water, and at a small distance from the scene of original infection. This day his employer had dismissed his workman, and Whiston was at liberty to retire from the city; a scheme, which had been the theme of deliberation and discussion during the preceding fortnight.

Hitherto his apprehensions seemed to have molested others more than himself. The rumours and conjectures industriously collected during the day, were, in the evening, copiously detailed to his neighbours, and his own mind appeared to be disburthened of its cares, in proportion as he filled others with terror and inquietude. The predictions of physicians, the measures of precaution prescribed by the government, the progress of the malady, and the history of the victims who were hourly destroyed by it, were communicated with tormenting prolixity and terrifying minuteness.

On these accounts as well as on others, no one's visits were more unwelcome than his. As his deportment was sober and honest, and his intentions harmless, he was always treated, by Constantia, with politeness, though his entrance always produced a momentary depression of her spirits. On this evening she was less fitted than ever to repel those anxieties which his conversation was qualified to produce. His entrance, therefore, was observed with sincere regret.

Contrary, however, to her expectation, Whiston brought with him new manners and a new expression of countenance. He was silent, abstracted, his eye was full of inquietude, and wandered with perpetual restlessness. On these tokens being remarked, he expressed, in faultering accents his belief, that he had contracted this disease, and that now it was too late for him to leave the city.

Mr. Dudley's education was somewhat medical. He was so far interested in his guest as to enquire into his sensations. They were such as were commonly the preludes to fever. Mr. Dudley, while he endeavoured by cheerful tones, to banish his dejection, exhorted him to go home, and to take some hot and wholesome draught, in consequence of which, he might rise tomorrow with his usual health. This advice was gratefully received, and Whiston put a period to his visit much sooner than was customary.

Mr. Dudley entertained no doubts that Whiston was seized with the reigning disease, and extinguished the faint hope which his daughter had cherished, that their district would escape. Whiston's habitation was nearly opposite their own, but as

---

called because craftsmen above the apprentice level would often travel for a period to gain more experience and look for locations where a new master was needed, since craft conventions implied that masters would not directly compete against or undercut each other. At this time, advancement to master status was becoming increasingly difficult, forcing grown men to remain at the "journeyman" level for years. Additionally, artisan structures were eroding as small-shop crafts were increasingly conglomerated and proletarianized. Thus Whiston is increasingly dependant on insecure, temporary employment. His basic financial insecurity is created by changing labor conditions that occur as the poorly recognized forces of encroaching capitalism are doubled by the biological insecurity of the yellow fever that he faces by working so near the waterfront where the epidemic begins. For more, see Salinger, "Artists, Journeymen, and the Transformation of Labor in Late Eighteenth-Century Philadelphia."

they made no use of their front room, they had seldom an opportunity of observing the transactions of their neighbours. This distance and seclusion were congenial with her feelings, and she derived pleasure from her father's confession, that they contributed to personal security.

Constance was accustomed to rise with the dawn, and traverse, for an hour, the State-house Mall.[3] As she took her walk the next morning, she pondered with astonishment on the present situation of the city. The air was bright and pure, and apparently salubrious. Security and silence seemed to hover over the scene. She was only reminded of the true state of things by the occasional appearance of carriages loaded with household utensils tending towards the country, and by the odour of vinegar[4] by which every passenger was accompanied. The public walk was cool and fragrant as formerly, skirted by verdure as bright, and shaded by foliage as luxuriant, but it was no longer frequented by lively steps and cheerful countenances. Its solitude was uninterrupted by any but herself.

This day passed without furnishing any occasion to leave the house. She was less sedulously employed than usual, as the cloaths, on which she was engaged, belonged to a family who had precipitately left the city. She had leisure therefore to ruminate. She could not but feel some concern in the fate of Whiston. He was a young man who subsisted on the fruits of his labour, and divided his gains with an only sister who lived with him, and who performed every household office.

This girl was humble and innocent, and of a temper affectionate and mild. Casual intercourse only had taken place between her and Constance. They were too dissimilar for any pleasure to arise from communication, but the latter was sufficiently disposed to extend to her harmless neighbour, the sympathy and succour which she needed. Whiston had come from a distant part of the country, and his sister was the only person in the city with whom he was connected by ties of kindred. In case of his sickness, therefore, their condition would be helpless and deplorable.

Evening arrived, and Whiston failed to pay his customary visit. She mentioned this omission to her father, and expressed her apprehension as to the cause of it. He did not discountenance the inference which she drew from this circumstance, and assented to the justice of the picture which she drew of the calamitous state to which Whiston and his sister would be reduced by the indisposition of either. She then

---

[3] "State-house Mall": gardens behind the State House, present-day Independence Hall, on Chestnut Street between Fifth and Sixth Streets. The building was first completed in 1732 as the State House of the Province of Pennsylvania and still commonly known by that name in the 1790s, when it was renamed "Independence Hall" after the U.S. Declaration of Independence and Constitution were drafted and signed there. On her daily walks, Constantia notes that the city is being depopulated by the fever.

[4] "Vinegar": vinegar was popularly thought to defend against yellow fever. Many believed that its acrid smell would clarify the atmospheric medium of the disease by discharging the air's "taint" (mentioned a few pages earlier). This idea of disinfection through odor discharges remained popular well into the next century, when it led, for example, to the firing of cannons to circulate the smell of gunpowder or to the burning of tar as public health measures against the fever.

ventured to suggest the propriety of visiting the house, and of thus ascertaining the truth.

To this proposal Mr. Dudley urged the most vehement objections. What purpose could be served by entering their dwelling? What benefit would flow but the gratification of a dangerous curiosity? Constance was disabled from furnishing pecuniary aid. She could not act the part of physician or nurse. Her father stood in need of a thousand personal services, and the drudgery of cleansing and cooking, already exceeded the bounds of her strength. The hazard of contracting the disease by conversing with the sick, was imminent. What services was she able to render equivalent to the consequences of her own sickness and death?

These representations had temporary influence. They recalled her for a moment, from her purpose, but this purpose was speedily re-embraced. She reflected that the evil to herself, formidable as it was, was barely problematical. That converse with the sick would impart this disease, was by no means certain. Whiston might at least be visited. Perhaps she should find him well. If sick, his disease might be unepidemical, or curable by seasonable assistance. He might stand in need of a physician, and she was more able than his sister, to summon this aid.

Her father listened calmly to her reasonings. After a pause, he gave his consent. In doing this he was influenced not by the conviction that his daughter's safety would be exposed to no hazard, but from a belief that though she might shun infection for the present, it would inevitably seize her during some period of the progress of this pest.

Chapter V

IT WAS now dusk and she hastened to perform this duty. Whiston's dwelling was wooden and of small dimensions. She lifted the latch softly and entered. The lower room was unoccupied. She advanced to the foot of a narrow staircase, and knocked and listened, but no answer was returned to the summons. Hence there was reason to infer that no one was within, but this, from other considerations, was extremely improbable. The truth could be ascertained only by ascending the stair. Some feminine scruples were to be subdued before this proceeding could be adopted.

After some hesitation, she determined to ascend. The staircase was terminated by a door at which she again knocked, for admission, but in vain. She listened and presently heard the motion as of some one in bed. This was succeeded by tokens of vehement exertions to vomit. These signs convincing her that the house was not without a tenant, she could not hesitate to enter the room.

Lying in a tattered bed, she now discovered Mary Whiston. Her face was flushed and swelled, her eyes closed and some power appeared to have laid a leaden hand upon her faculties. The floor was moistened and stained by the effusion from her stomach. Constance touched her hand, and endeavoured to rouse her. It was with difficulty that her attention was excited. Her languid eyes were scarcely opened before they again closed and she sunk into forgetfulness.

Repeated efforts, however, at length recalled her to herself, and extorted from her some account of her condition. On the day before, at noon, her stomach became diseased, her head dizzy, and her limbs unable to support her. Her brother was absent, and her drowsiness, interrupted only by paroxysms of vomiting, continued till his return late in the evening. He had then shewn himself, for a few minutes, at her bedside, had made some enquiries and precipitately retired, since when he had not reappeared.

It was natural to imagine that Whiston had gone to procure medical assistance. That he had not returned, during a day and a half was matter of surprize. His own indisposition was recollected and his absence could only be accounted for by supposing that sickness had disabled him from regaining his own house. What was his real destiny, it was impossible to conjecture. It was not till some months after this period that satisfactory intelligence was gained upon this head.

It appeared that Whiston had allowed his terrors to overpower the sense of what was due to his sister and to humanity. On discovering the condition of the unhappy girl, he left the house, and, instead of seeking a physician, he turned his steps towards the country. After travelling some hours, being exhausted by want of food, by fatigue, and by mental as well as bodily anguish, he laid himself down under the shelter of an hayrick, in a vacant field. Here he was discovered in the morning by the inhabitants of a neighbouring farm house. These people had too much regard for their own safety to accommodate him under their roof, or even to approach within fifty paces of his person.

A passenger whose attention and compassion had been excited by this incident, was endowed with more courage. He lifted the stranger in his arms, and carried him from this unwholesome spot to a barn. This was the only service which the passenger was able to perform. Whiston, deserted by every human creature, burning with fever, tormented into madness by thirst, spent three miserable days in agony. When dead, no one would cover his body with earth, but he was suffered to decay by piecemeal.[1]

The dwelling, being at no great distance from the barn, could not be wholly screened from the malignant vapour which a corpse, thus neglected, could not fail to produce. The inhabitants were preparing on this account, to change their abode, but, on the eve of their departure, the master of the family became sick. He was, in a short time, followed to the grave by his mother, his wife and four children.

They probably imbibed their disease from the tainted atmosphere around them. The life of Whiston and their own lives, might have been saved by affording the wanderer an asylum and suitable treatment, or at least, their own deaths might have been avoided by interring his remains.

Meanwhile Constantia was occupied with reflecting on the scene before her. Not only a physician but a nurse was wanting. The last province it was more easy for her to supply than the former. She was acquainted with the abode but of one physician. He lived at no small distance from this spot. To him she immediately hastened, but he was absent, and his numerous engagements left it wholly uncertain when he would return and whether he would consent to increase the number of his patients. Direction was obtained to the residence of another, who was happily disengaged, and who promised to attend immediately. Satisfied with this assurance, she neglected to request directions, by which she might regulate herself on his failing to come.

During her return her thoughts were painfully employed in considering the mode proper for her to pursue, in her present perplexing situation. She was for the most part unacquainted with the character of those who composed her neighbourhood. That any would be willing to undertake the tendance of this girl was by no means probable. As wives and mothers, it would perhaps be unjust to require or permit it. As to herself there were labours and duties of her own sufficient to engross her faculties, yet, by whatever foreign cares or tasks she was oppressed, she felt that, to desert this being, was impossible.

In the absence of her friend, Mary's state exhibited no change. Constance, on regaining the house, lighted the remnant of a candle, and resumed her place by the bed side of the sick girl. She impatiently waited for the arrival of the physician, but hour succeeded hour and he came not. All hope of his coming being extinguished, she bethought herself that her father might be able to inform her of the best manner of proceeding. It was likewise her duty to relieve him from the suspence in which her absence would unavoidably plunge him.

---

[1] "Decay by piecemeal": contemporary accounts of the epidemic provide sensational (and stereotypical) anecdotes of similar incidents, in which fever victims fleeing the city were shunned, abandoned to die, or attacked as a result of panic and fear of infection. Brown could draw such scenes from well-known sources such as Mathew Carey's *A Short Account of the Malignant Fever, Lately Prevalent in Philadelphia* (1793).

On entering her own apartment she found a stranger in company with Mr. Dudley. The latter perceiving that she had returned, speedily acquainted her with the views of their guest. His name was M'Crea; he was the nephew of their landlord and was now become, by reversion, the proprietor of the house which they occupied. Mathews had been buried the preceding day, and M'Crea, being well acquainted with the engagements which subsisted between the deceased and Mr. Dudley, had come, thus unseasonably, to demand the rent. He was not unconscious of the inhumanity and sordidness of this proceeding, and therefore, endeavoured to disguise it by the usual pretences. All his funds were exhausted. He came not only in his own name, but in that of Mrs. Mathews his aunt, who was destitute of money to procure daily and indispensible provision, and who was striving to collect a sufficient sum to enable her and the remains of her family, to fly from a spot where their lives were in perpetual danger.

These excuses were abundantly fallacious, but Mr. Dudley was too proud to solicit the forbearance of a man like this. He recollected that the engagement on his part was voluntary and explicit, and he disdained to urge his present exigences as reasons for retracting it. He expressed the utmost readiness to comply with the demand, and merely desired him to wait till Miss Dudley returned. From the inquietudes with which the unusual duration of her absence had filled him, he was now relieved by her entrance.

With an indignant and desponding heart, she complied with her father's directions, and the money being reluctantly delivered, M'Crea took an hasty leave. She was too deeply interested in the fate of Mary Whiston, to allow her thoughts to be diverted for the present into a new channel. She described the desolate condition of the girl to her father, and besought him to think of something suitable to her relief.

Mr. Dudley's humanity would not suffer him to disapprove of his daughter's proceeding. He imagined that the symptoms of the patient portended a fatal issue. There were certain complicated remedies which might possibly be beneficial, but these were too costly, and the application would demand more strength than his daughter could bestow. He was unwilling, however, to leave any thing within his power, untried. Pharmacy had been his trade,[2] and he had reserved, for domestic use, some of the most powerful evacuants.[3] Constantia was supplied with some of these,

---

[2] "Pharmacy had been his trade": the type of shop that Mr. Dudley inherited from his father was never specified in Chapter 1, but this passage indicates that it was a pharmacist's shop, or apothecary. The grinding of raw materials into powders and admixture of alcohols into liquids required in this profession are not dissimilar from the oil paint preparation techniques Dudley learned in his earlier training as an artist.

[3] "Evacuants": purgatives or emetics, vomit-inducing substances. Along with bleeding (which required the expense of a surgeon or attendant), purgatives were mainstays of treatments advocated by mainly British-trained physicians such as Benjamin Rush. The idea was to induce a cathartic shock to the body that would catalyze its defenses. The approach was highly controversial and contrary to the approach associated with French-trained physicians or others with prior experience in the Caribbean, who were more familiar with the disease and favored a rest cure in the belief that the

and he consented that she should spend the night with her patient, and watch their operation.

The unhappy Mary received whatever was offered, but her stomach refused to retain it. The night was passed by Constantia without closing her eyes. As soon as the day dawned, she prepared once more to summon the physician, who had failed to comply with his promise. She had scarcely left the house, however, before she met him. He pleaded his numerous engagements in excuse for his last night's negligence, and desired her to make haste to conduct him to the patient.

Having scrutinized her symptoms, he expressed his hopelessness of her recovery. Being informed of the mode in which she had been treated, he declared his approbation of it, but intimated, that these being unsuccessful, all that remained was to furnish her with any liquid she might chuse to demand, and wait patiently for the event. During this interview, the physician surveyed the person and dress of Constance with an inquisitive eye.[4] His countenance betrayed marks of curiosity and compassion, and had he made any approaches to confidence and friendliness, Constance would not have repelled them. His air was benevolent and candid, and she estimated highly the usefulness of a counsellor and friend in her present circumstances. Some motive, however, hindered him from tendering his service, and, in a few moments, he withdrew.

Mary's condition hourly grew worse. A corroded and gangrenous stomach was quickly testified by the dark hue and poisonous malignity of the matter which was frequently ejected from it. Her stupor gave place to some degree of peevishness and restlessness. She drank the water that was held to her lips with unspeakable avidity, and derived from this source a momentary alleviation of her pangs. Fortunately for her attendant, her agonies were not of long duration. Constantia was absent from her bedside as rarely, and for periods as short as possible. On the succeeding night, the sufferings of the patient terminated in death.

This event took place at two o'clock in the morning. An hour whose customary stillness was, if possible, increased tenfold by the desolation of the city. The poverty of Mary and of her nurse, had deprived the former of the benefits resulting from the change of bed and cloaths. Every thing about her was in a condition noisome and detestable. Her yellowish and haggard visage, conspicuous by a feeble light, an atmosphere freighted with malignant vapours, and reminding Constance at every instant, of the perils which encompassed her, the consciousness of solitude and sensations of deadly sickness in her own frame, were sufficient to intimidate a soul of firmer texture than her's.

---

body needed to conserve its energies to fight the disease rather than direct them outward. This debate over treatments was often blurred by physicians on the ground who used both approaches. For example, while Brown's closest medical associate, Dr. Elihu Hubbard Smith, studied under and frequently consulted with Rush, he also seems to have followed a version of the French-associated approach. For more on the controversy, see Estes and Smith, *A Melancholy Scene of Devastation*.

[4] "Surveyed … inquisitive eye": the doctor's male gaze provides an example of the way Constantia's body is voyeuristically evaluated by men. Although the doctor is "benevolent," the language used here nevertheless intimates an undertone of sexual coercion.

She was sinking fast into helplessness, when a new train of reflections shewed her the necessity of perseverance. All that remained was to consign the corpse to the grave. She knew that vehicles for this end were provided at the public expense, that notice being given of the occasion there was for their attendance, a receptacle and carriage for the dead would be instantly provided. Application, at this hour, she imagined would be unseasonable. It must be deferred till the morning which was yet at some distance.

Meanwhile to remain at her present post, was equally useless and dangerous. She endeavoured to stifle the conviction, that some mortal sickness had seized upon her own frame. Her anxieties of head and stomach, she was willing to impute to extraordinary fatigue and watchfulness; and hoped that they would be dissipated by an hour's unmolested repose. She formed the resolution of seeking her own chamber.

At this moment, however, the universal silence underwent a slight interruption. The sound was familiar to her ears. It was a signal frequently repeated at the midnight hour during this season of calamity. It was the slow movement of an hearse, apparently passing along the street, in which the alley, where Mr. Dudley resided, terminated. At first, this sound had no other effect than to aggravate the dreariness of all around her. Presently it occurred to her that this vehicle might be disengaged. She conceived herself bound to see the last offices performed for the deceased Mary. The sooner so irksome a duty was discharged the better. Every hour might augment her incapacity for exertion. Should she be unable when the morning arrived, to go as far as the city-hall,[5] and give the necessary information, the most shocking consequences would ensue. Whiston's house and her own were opposite each other, and not connected with any on the same side. A narrow space divided them, and her own chamber was within the sphere of the contagion which would flow, in consequence of such neglect, from that of her neighbour.

Influenced by these considerations she passed into the street, and gained the corner of the alley, just as the carriage, whose movements she had heard, arrived at the same spot. It was accompanied by two men, negroes, who listened to her tale with respect. Having already a burthen of this kind, they could not immediately comply with this request. They promised that, having disposed of their present charge, they would return forthwith and be ready to execute her orders.

Happily one of these persons was known to her. At other seasons his occupation was that of *woodcarter*, and as such he had performed some services for Mr. Dudley. His temper was gentle and obliging. The character of Constance had been viewed by him with reverence, and his kindness had relieved her from many painful offices. His old occupation being laid aside for a time, he had betaken himself, like many others of his colour and rank, to the conveyance and burial of the dead.[6]

---

[5] "City-hall": the newly built (1790) City Hall at Fifth and Chestnut Streets, in the same complex of administrative buildings with the State House mentioned in the previous chapter (see note 4.3). After 1791, this building was also the first home of the U.S. Supreme Court.

[6] "His old occupation being laid aside for a time … others of his colour and rank … burial of the dead": by having a black volunteer help Constantia in an especially generous manner, doubling

At Constantia's request, he accompanied her to Whiston's house, and promised to bring with him such assistance, as would render her further exertions and attendance unnecessary. Glad to be absolved from any new task, she now retired to her own chamber. In spite of her distempered frame, she presently sunk into sweet sleep. She awoke not till the day had made considerable progress, and found herself invigorated and refreshed. On re-entering Whiston's house, she discovered that her humble friend had faithfully performed his promise, the dead body having disappeared. She deemed it unsafe, as well as unnecessary, to examine the cloaths and other property remaining, but leaving every thing in the condition in which it had been found, she fastened the windows and doors, and thenceforth kept as distant from the house as possible.

Constantia's own selfless heroism, Brown takes an implicit position in debates concerning the work of free blacks as nurses and undertakers during the 1793 epidemic. Partly because of mistaken notions that Africans (and, in some version, the French) were immune to yellow fever, the city's free black community (the largest and most significant in North America at this time) was pressed into emergency service on the front lines of medical care during the 1793 epidemic. When the third edition of Mathew Carey's influential account of the epidemic (*A Short Account of the Malignant Fever*, mentioned in note 5.1) accused some of these black workers of stealing from victims or extorting excessive payments for their services, free black community leaders Absalom Jones and Richard Allen defended the community and refuted Carey's charges with their pamphlet, *A Narrative of the Proceedings of the Black People during the Late Awful Calamity in Philadelphia in the Year 1793* (1794). In this and the next paragraph, the volunteer's generosity, as Constantia's "humble friend," implicitly supports the Jones-Allen version of events and rejects racialist attacks on the black volunteers.

Chapter VI

CONSTANTIA had now leisure to ruminate upon her own condition. Every day added to the devastation and confusion of the city. The most populous streets were deserted and silent. The greater number of inhabitants had fled, and those who remained were occupied with no cares but those which related to their own safety. The labours of the artizan and the speculations of the merchant were suspended. All shops, but those of the apothecaries were shut. No carriage but the herse was seen, and this was employed, night and day, in the removal of the dead. The customary sources of subsistence were cut off. Those, whose fortunes enabled them to leave the city, but who had deferred till now their retreat, were denied an asylum by the terror which pervaded the adjacent country, and by the cruel prohibitions which the neighbouring towns and cities thought it necessary to adopt. Those who lived by the fruits of their daily labour were subjected, in this total inactivity, to the alternative of starving, or of subsisting upon public charity.

The meditations of Constance, suggested no alternative but this. The exactions of M'Crea had reduced her whole fortune to five dollars. This would rapidly decay, and her utmost ingenuity could discover no means of procuring a new supply. All the habits of their life had combined to fill both her father and herself with aversion to the acceptance of charity. Yet this avenue, opprobrious and disgustful as it was, afforded the only means of escaping from the worst extremes of famine.

In this state of mind it was obvious to consider in what way the sum remaining might be most usefully expended. Every species of provision was not equally nutritious or equally cheap. Her mind, active in the pursuit of knowledge and fertile of resources, had lately been engaged, in discussing with her father, the best means of retaining health, in a time of pestilence. On occasions, when the malignity of contagious diseases has been most signal, some individuals have escaped. For their safety, they were doubtless indebted to some peculiarities in their constitution or habits. Their diet, their dress, their kind and degree of exercise, must some-what have contributed to their exemption from the common destiny. These, perhaps, could be ascertained, and when known it was surely proper to conform to them.

In discussing these ideas, Mr. Dudley introduced the mention of a Benedictine of Messina,[1] who, during the prevalence of the plague in that city, was incessantly engaged in administering assistance to those who needed. Notwithstanding his perpetual hazards, he retained perfect health, and was living thirty years after this event. During this period, he fostered a tranquil, fearless, and benevolent spirit, and restricted his diet to water and pollenta. Spices, and meats, and liquors, and all complexities of cookery were utterly discarded.

---

[1] "A Benedictine of Messina": a member of the Benedictine monastic order, in the Sicilian city Messina, already noted in Chapter 3 as a previous outbreak of pestilence witnessed by Dudley while he lived in Italy (see note 3.12). This is likely an invented detail, not a reference to any historically attested figure, serving to connect observations about polenta in the following passage with Dudley's knowledge of an earlier epidemic in the Mediterranean world.

These facts now occurred to Constantia's reflections with new vividness, and led to interesting consequences. Pollenta[2] and hasty-pudding or samp, are preparations of the same substance; a substance which she needed not the experience of others to convince her was no less grateful than nutritive. Indian meal was procurable at ninety cents per bushel. By recollecting former experiments, she knew that this quantity, with no accompaniment but salt, would supply wholesome and plentiful food for four months to one person.* The inference was palpable. Three persons were now to

*See this useful fact explained and demonstrated in Count Rumford's Essays.[3]

---

[2] "Pollenta": meal or flour ground from corn and boiled into a simple, inexpensive porridge. Polenta was originally used in Venetian cooking and in this period was recommended as wholesome, inexpensive food for the poor, slaves, and other indigents. "Hasty-pudding" and "samp" are other terms for this dish or slight variations. An article with instructions for cooking polenta, "Account of the Cultivation and Uses of Indian Corn in Italy [By a respectable Physician, of that Country, now in this City]" was published in the Philadelphia *Weekly Magazine*, July 21, 1798, just after Brown finished publishing the reviews of Rumford's essays discussed in note 6.3.

[3] "Count Rumford's Essays": *"Essays, Political, Economical, and Philosophical"* (4 vols., 1796–1798), by the Massachusetts-born Benjamin Thompson (1753–1814). An eclectic scientist, civil administrator, and author, known for inventions such as a convection stove and new theories for the management of the poor, Rumford was a loyalist spy in Washington's officer cadre, who left North America for England during the Revolution before he could be captured. In England, he became an important scientist in what would later be known as thermodynamics. His work mainly involved improving the efficiency of heat (caloric) transfers and its military applications for munitions. After his British mentors become enmeshed in scandals, he left to work as an administrative manager and innovator for the Munich-based Elector of Bavaria, who ennobled him as "Count Rumford." In Munich, he successfully reorganized the Bavarian military, designed the "English Garden" that remains a central feature of Munich's landscape, and operated a model workhouse for the poor. Most workhouses of this period insisted that their inhabitants display "morality" and operated at a deficit. Thomson abandoned this moral imperative and instead provided adequate clothes, heat, and food for the workhouse inhabitants, while making these comforts affordable by implementing his experience in efficiency systematics. He published his findings, which were widely reviewed in British journals.

In May–June 1798, six months before the appearance of *Ormond*, Brown published a multipart review of Rumford's *Essays* in the Philadelphia *Weekly Magazine*. He again published a series of review articles on Rumford in the New York *Monthly Magazine* beginning in July 1799. One of these reviews discusses Rumford's recommendation of polenta as an inexpensive food for the poor: "Among all kinds of vegetable food, Count Rumford assigns the preference to Indian corn. The extensive use of it in Italy, under the name of Pollenta, and in North-America, evinces its nutritiousness and wholesomeness. In the countries cultivated by negro slaves, it is generally preferred by them to rice, which they account the more fugitive and less substantial food. In addition to this, it is known to be producible in larger quantities than other grain; hence the propriety of encouraging the cultivation and extending the use of it" (*Monthly Magazine*, July 1799, 302). Brown continued to publish articles on Rumford through his later career, for example "Anecdotes of Benjamin Count Rumford" (*Literary Magazine*, Dec. 1803); and "Economy of Light" (*Literary Magazine*, Sept. 1804). Brown does not seem to have recognized, however, that Thompson was politically reactionary, or that his social welfare schemes were introduced only to forestall popular support in Bavaria for the republican ideals enacted in the French Revolution.

be supplied with food, and this supply could be furnished, during four months, at the trivial expence of three dollars. This expedient was at once so uncommon and so desirable, as to be regarded with temporary disbelief. She was inclined to suspect some latent error in her calculation. That a sum thus applied, should suffice for the subsistence of a year, which, in ordinary cases, is expended in a few days, was scarcely credible. The more closely, however, the subject was examined, the more incontestably did this inference flow. The mode of preparation was simple and easy, and productive of the fewest toils and inconveniences. The attention of her Lucy was sufficient to this end, and the drudgery of marketing was wholly precluded.

She easily obtained the concurrence of her father and the scheme was found as practicable and beneficial as her fondest expectations had predicted. Infallible security was thus provided against hunger. This was the only care that was urgent and immediate. While they had food and were exempt from disease, they could live, and were not without their portion of comfort. Her hands were unemployed, but her mind was kept in continual activity. To seclude herself as much as possible from others, was the best means of avoiding infection. Spectacles of misery which she was unable to relieve, would merely tend to harrass her with useless disquietudes and make her frame more accessible to disease. Her father's instructions were sufficient to give her a competent acquaintance with the Italian and French languages.[4] His dreary hours were beguiled by this employment, and her mind was furnished with a species of knowledge, which she hoped, in future, to make subservient to a more respectable and plentiful subsistence than she had hitherto enjoyed.

Meanwhile the season advanced, and the havoc which this fatal malady produced, increased with portentous rapidity. In alleys and narrow streets, in which the houses were smaller, the inhabitants more numerous and indigent, and the air pent up within unwholesome limits, it raged with greatest violence.[5] Few of Constantia's neighbours possessed the means of removing from the danger. The inhabitants of this alley consisted of three hundred persons. Of these eight or ten experienced no interruption of their health. Of the rest two hundred were destroyed in the course of three weeks. Among so many victims, it may be supposed that this disease assumed every terrific and agonizing shape.

It was impossible for Constantia to shut out every token of a calamity thus enormous and thus near. Night was the season usually selected for the removal of the

---

[4] "French and Italian languages": since she was not able to buy the Italian primer mentioned in Chapter 3, Constantia relies on her father to educate her in these languages. Given her later inability to comprehend French speakers in Chapter 8, her father's instruction may not have been successful, or the French may be a Caribbean dialect.

[5] "Season advanced ... greatest violence": the 1793 epidemic reached its height in late September–early October, peaking at more than 100 fatalities per day between October 9 and 12. As Brown indicates, the crowded, cramped alleys near the Delaware River wharves were the sites of greatest mortality. This was partly due to inadequate drainage and sewage, which allowed plague-carrying mosquitoes to breed, and partly to crowded conditions, since poor who lived in these alleys could not afford to flee the city.

dead. The sound of wheels thus employed was incessant. This, and the images with which it was sure to be accompanied, bereaved her of repose. The shrieks and laments of survivors, who could not be prevented from attending the remains of an husband or child to the place of interment, frequently struck her senses.[6] Sometimes urged by a furious delirium, the sick would break from their attendants, rush into the streets, and expire on the pavement, amidst frantic outcries and gestures. By these she was often roused from imperfect sleep, and called to reflect upon the fate which impended over her father and herself.

To preserve health in an atmosphere thus infected, and to ward off terror and dismay in a scene of horrors thus hourly accumulating, was impossible. Constance found it vain to contend against the inroads of sadness. Amidst so dreadful a mortality, it was irrational to cherish the hope that she or her father would escape. Her sensations, in no long time, seemed to justify her apprehensions. Her appetite forsook her, her strength failed, the thirst and lassitude of fever invaded her, and the grave seemed to open for her reception.

Lucy was assailed by the same symptoms at the same time. Household offices were unavoidably neglected. Mr. Dudley retained his health, but he was able only to prepare his scanty food, and supply the cravings of his child, with water from the well. His imagination marked him out for the next victim. He could not be blind to the consequences of his own indisposition, at a period so critical. Disabled from contributing to each other's assistance, destitute of medicine and food, and even of water to quench their tormenting thirst, unvisited, unknown, and perishing in frightful solitude!—These images had a tendency to prostrate the mind, and generate or ripen the seeds of this fatal malady, which, no doubt, at this period of its progress, every one had imbibed.

Contrary to all his fears, he awoke each morning free from pain, though not without an increase of debility. Abstinence from food, and the liberal use of cold water seemed to have a medicinal operation on the sick. Their pulse gradually resumed its healthful tenor, their strength and their appetite slowly returned, and in ten days they were able to congratulate each other on their restoration.

I will not recount that series of disastrous thoughts which occupied the mind of Constance during this period. Her lingering and sleepless hours were regarded by her as preludes to death. Though at so immature an age, she had gained large experience of the evils which are allotted to man. Death, which, in her prosperous state, was peculiarly abhorrent to her feelings, was now disrobed of terror. As an entrance into scenes of lightsome and imperishable being, it was the goal of all her wishes. As a passage to oblivion it was still desirable, since forgetfulness was better than the life which she had hitherto led, and which, should her existence be prolonged, it was likely that she could continue to lead.

---

[6] "Shrieks ... husband or child ... senses": Constantia sympathetically "feels" the city in pain, but her perception is a feminized one. She imagines the survivors as women, wives or mothers, and not as men.

These gloomy meditations were derived from the langours of her frame. When these disappeared, her cheerfulness and fortitude revived. She regarded with astonishment and delight, the continuance of her father's health and her own restoration. That trial seemed to have been safely undergone, to which the life of every one was subject. The air which till now had been arid and sultry, was changed into cool and moist.[7] The pestilence had reached its utmost height, and now symptoms of remission and decline began to appear. Its declension was more rapid than its progress, and every day added vigour to hope.

When her strength was somewhat retrieved, Constantia called to mind a good woman who lived in her former neighbourhood, and from whom she had received many proofs of artless affection. This woman's name was Sarah Baxter. She lived within a small distance of Constantia's former dwelling. The trade of her husband was that of porter, and she pursued, in addition to the care of a numerous family, the business of a Laundress.[8] The superior knowledge and address of Constance, had enabled her to be serviceable to this woman in certain painful and perplexing circumstances.

This service was repaid with the utmost gratitude. Sarah regarded her benefactress with a species of devotion. She could not endure to behold one, whom every accent and gesture proved to have once enjoyed affluence and dignity, performing any servile office. In spite of her own multiplied engagements, she compelled Constance to accept her assistance on many occasions, and could scarcely be prevailed upon to receive any compensation for her labour. Washing cloaths was her trade, and from this task she insisted on relieving her lovely patronness.

Constantia's change of dwelling produced much regret in the kind Sarah. She did not allow it to make any change in their previous arrangements, but punctually visited the Dudleys once a week, and carried home with her whatever stood in need of ablution. When the prevalence of disease disabled Constance from paying her the usual wages, she would, by no means, consent to be absolved from this task. Her earnestness on this head was not to be eluded, and Constance, in consenting that her work should, for the present, be performed gratuitously, solaced herself with the prospect of being able, by some future change of fortune, amply to reward her.

Sarah's abode was distant from danger, and her fears were turbulent. She was, nevertheless, punctual in her visits to the Dudleys, and anxious for their safety. In case of their sickness, she had declared her resolution to be their attendant and nurse.

---

[7] "Cool and moist … symptoms of remission and decline began to appear": with the onset of cooler weather (killing the mosquitoes that carried the fever), the epidemic fell off sharply after the year's first frost on October 28. By November 10 the epidemic had ended.

[8] "Porter … Laundress": the Baxters' social status is below that of mechanics or artisans like Whiston. As someone whose job is to move objects (presumably shipping cargo), Baxter is an unskilled day laborer, and his wife, similarly, depends on labor that requires manual exertion rather than the skill of a seamstress, for example. Since both depend on the city's economy they cannot easily leave, despite the epidemic, while there remains any possible work to be had. When the harbor traffic stops, leaving nothing for Baxter to carry, he must find work as a night watchman.

Suddenly, however, her visits ceased. The day on which her usual visit was paid, was the same with that on which Constantia sickened, but her coming was expected in vain. Her absence was, on some accounts, regarded with pleasure, as it probably secured her from the danger connected with the office of a nurse, but it added to Constantia's cares, inasmuch as her own sickness, or that of some of her family, was the only cause of her detention.

To remove her doubts, the first use which Constantia made of her recovered strength, was to visit her laundress: Sarah's house was a theatre of suffering.[9] Her husband was the first of his family assailed by the reigning disease. Two daughters, nearly grown to womanhood, well disposed and modest girls, the pride and support of their mother, and who lived at service, returned home, sick, at the same time, and died in a few days. Her husband had struggled for eleven days with his disease, and was seized, just before Constantia's arrival, with the pangs of death.

Baxter was endowed with great robustness and activity. This disease did not vanquish him but with tedious and painful struggles. His muscular force now exhausted itself in ghastly contortions, and the house resounded with his ravings. Sarah's courage had yielded to so rapid a succession of evils. Constantia found her shut up in a chamber, distant from that of her dying husband, in a paroxysm of grief, and surrounded by her younger children.

Constantia's entrance was like that of an angelic comforter. Sarah was unqualified for any office but that of complaint. With great difficulty she was made to communicate the knowledge of her situation. Her visitant then passed into Baxter's apartment. She forced herself to endure this tremendous scene long enough to discover that it was hastening to a close. She left the house, and hastening to the proper office, engaged the immediate attendance of an hearse. Before the lapse of an hour, Baxter's lifeless remains were thrust into a coffin and conveyed away.

Constance now exerted herself to comfort and encourage the survivors. Her remonstrances incited Sarah to perform with alacrity the measures which prudence dictates on these occasions. The house was purified by the admission of air and the sprinkling of vinegar. Constantia applied her own hand to these tasks, and set her humble friend an example of forethought and activity. Sarah would not consent to part with her till a late hour in the evening.

These exertions had like to have been fatally injurious to Constance. Her health was not sufficiently confirmed to sustain offices so arduous. In the course of the night her fatigue terminated in fever. In the present more salubrious state of the atmosphere, it assumed no malignant symptoms, and shortly disappeared. During her indisposition, she was attended by Sarah, in whose honest bosom no sentiment was more lively than gratitude. Constantia having promised to renew her visit the next day, had been impatiently expected, and Sarah had come to her dwelling in the evening, full of foreboding and anxiety, to ascertain the cause of her delay. Having gained the bedside of her patronness, no consideration could induce her to retire from it.

---

[9] "Theatre of suffering": the misery of Baxter's home is described as if it were a melodramatic scene in a play, a suggestive metaphor that is extended through the chapter and novel.

Constantia's curiosity was naturally excited as to the causes of Baxter's disease. The simple-hearted Sarah was prolix and minute in the history of her own affairs. No theme was more congenial to her temper than that which was now proposed. In spite of redundance and obscurity in the style of the narrative, Constantia found in it powerful excitements of her sympathy.[10] The tale, on its own account, as well as from the connection of some of its incidents with a subsequent part of these memoirs, is worthy to be here inserted. However foreign the destiny of Monrose[11] may at present appear to the story of the Dudleys, there will hereafter be discovered an intimate connection between them.

---

[10] "Sympathy": sympathy and its cognate sensibility are interrelated keywords that are frequently debated in this period and that play important roles in the writings of Brown and his Woldwinite models. They identify an immediate emotional-physical relation or response to other individuals, often celebrated as replacing older, prerevolutionary or aristocratic modes of deference with new, more modern and implicitly egalitarian models for interpersonal behavior and cooperation. Here the emotions aroused by a moving story like Baxter's can be mobilized to generate emotional connections and possibly encourage the reader, like Constantia, to benevolent action.

[11] "The destiny of Monrose": the first use of the name Monrose. The following episode concerning Sarah Baxter's husband and his encounter with mysterious neighbors named Monrose was first developed in an earlier form in Parts 4–5 of Brown's 13-part essay series "The Man at Home," in the Philadelphia *Weekly Magazine* (February–April 1798). This new version of the episode retains the name Baxter for the old soldier, but gives a new name, Monrose, to the father and daughter next door (in the 1798 version their name was De Moivre). Brown's choice of the name may echo the protagonist Monrose in the 1798 comedy *Knave or Not?* by Woldwinite Thomas Holcroft, a writer that Brown and his circle corresponded with and followed closely. The Monrose character in that play was generally understood as a mouthpiece for Holcroft's radical-democratic criticism of the British ruling class. In act 3 scene 5, for example, Monrose inveighs against the wealthy as "legal robbers ... that plunder the defenceless, strip the widow, and defraud the orphan: yet assume to themselves the port of justice, and condemn wretches in rags by wholesale, ay to the gallows, for petty three farthing thefts; while their own enormities are dressed out in authority, and law is made the guardian of great crimes and the merciless punisher of the unprotected." In his preface to published versions of the play, Holcroft claimed that the play's commercial failure was the result of the political persecution of progressive writers in the mid and late 1790s.

The description also recalls Brown's sketch, *Portrait of an Emigrant*, presented here in Related Texts.

Chapter VII

ADJACENT to the house occupied by Baxter was an antique brick tenement. It was one of the first erections made by the followers of William Penn. It had the honor to be used as the temporary residence of that venerable person.[1] Its moss-grown penthouse, crumbling walls, and ruinous *porch*, made it an interesting and picturesque object. Notwithstanding its age, it was still tenable.

This house was occupied, during the preceding months, by a Frenchman. His dress and demeanour were respectable. His mode of life was frugal almost to penuriousness, and his only companion was a daughter. The lady seemed not much less than thirty years of age, but was of a small and delicate frame.[2] It was she that performed every household office. She brought water from the pump and provisions from the market. Their house had no visitants, and was almost always closed. Duly, as the morning returned, a venerable figure was seen issuing from his door, dressed in the same style of tarnished splendour and old-fashioned preciseness. At the dinner hour he as regularly returned. For the rest of the day he was invisible.

The habitations in this quarter are few and scattered. The pestilence soon shewed itself here, and the flight of most of the inhabitants, augmented its desolateness and

---

[1] "Antique tenement … Penn … residence of that venerable person": Brown locates the incident to be recounted in this chapter in a house that, by tradition, was the first local residence of Pennsylvania's founder William Penn (1644–1718), during Penn's initial visit to found the colony in 1682–1684. The house is a historical link with the founding of Philadelphia and the colony of Pennsylvania in 1682, and thus allegorically an emblem of the city's history. Penn had reserved space in the layout of the city for a property he intended to bequeath to his daughter Laetitia, and consequently the small court in which this house was built, extending south from Market Street between Front and Second Streets, was called Laetitia Court (present-day South Letitia Street).

The choice may supply an ironic or critical context for an incident that will exemplify groundless xenophobic fears and fantasies about foreigners on the part of Baxter, a former British imperial soldier and emigrant himself. Similarly, in his 1799 novel *Edgar Huntly*, Brown associated that novel's settler-Indian violence with the legendary Penn's Elm that was reputed to memorialize the colony's mythically harmonious relations with the Native American Delaware who were displaced by the colonial founding in 1682. In both cases, icons of the founding are belied by insistent and ongoing conflicts between Anglo settlers and perceived ethno-racial and national others. This setting may additionally involve inside references, since the Philadelphia publisher who would handle Brown's novels *Arthur Mervyn* and *Edgar Huntly* later in 1799 was H. Maxwell, whose offices were at 3 Laetitia Court.

[2] "Lady … of a small and delicate frame": the first mention of the character later identified as Martinette de Beauvais. The fact that the mysterious Miss Monrose of this chapter will turn out be an important figure known by another name in the novel's second half is the "intimate connection" between this story and the Dudleys that was noted at the end of the previous chapter. Baxter's perceptions of this woman will turn out to be wildly inaccurate, seemingly constructed according to the numerous prejudices and fears described in the paragraphs that follow. Here, described in her first appearance as "small and delicate," she seems to be caring for a father figure in much the same way Constantia cares for her father Stephen Dudley. At around thirty, however, she is much older than Constantia.

dreariness. For some time, Monrose, that was his name, made his usual appearance in the morning. At length the neighbours remarked that he no longer came forth as usual. Baxter had a notion that Frenchmen were exempt from this disease.[3] He was, besides, deeply and rancorously prejudiced against that nation.[4] There will be no difficulty in accounting for this, when it is known that he had been an English grenadier at Dettingen and Minden.[5] It must likewise be added, that he was considerably timid, and had sickness in his own family. Hence it was that the disappearance of Monrose excited in him no inquisitiveness as to the cause. He did not even mention this circumstance to others.

The lady was occasionally seen as usual in the street. There were always remarkable peculiarities in her behaviour. In the midst of grave and disconsolate looks, she never laid aside an air of solemn dignity. She seemed to shrink from the observation of

---

[3] "A notion that Frenchmen were exempt from this disease": Baxter believes irrational rumors that Africans and the French are immune to yellow fever. The idea likely arose because some Africans and French Creoles, arriving in Philadelphia in 1793 to flee ongoing slave revolution in Haiti, had developed resistance to the disease by being infected with it either in Africa or while living in the Caribbean. Patients who survive a minor yellow fever infection (as Brown himself did after contracting a mild case in the New York epidemic of 1798) develop a lifelong immunity against further infection.

[4] "Prejudiced against that nation": Baxter harbors a stereotypically British Francophobia, or anti-French prejudice and anxiety; this sort of Francophobia was promoted and circulated by conservative anti-French propagandists and politicians, including the ruling U.S. Federalist Party, during the conservative wave of 1797–1801 during which *Ormond* was written. See the Introduction for more on the novel's response to the conservative and xenophobic wave of the late 1790s.

[5] "An English grenadier at Dettingen and Minden": Baxter (the name suggests Scottish ethnicity) is presented as an elderly former career soldier who served in the British army in the 1740s and 1760s, participating in the Battles of Dettingen (June 27, 1743, at Dettingen in Bavaria, part of the War of the Austrian Succession, 1740–1748) and Minden (August 1, 1759, at Minden in Westphalia, part of the Seven Years' War, 1756–1763). Many soldiers in the Seven Years' War's North American theater (the French and Indian War) stayed behind after the conflict ended, and Baxter is presumably this type of soldier, settling in British North America after years of service in British imperial conflicts worldwide. Both the War of the Austrian Succession and the Seven Years' War involved pan-European coalitions led by England, France, Prussia, and the Austrian Habsburg Empire, and the two battles mentioned were immense, historically significant contests: at Dettingen about sixty thousand troops engaged, with eight thousand killed or wounded; at Minden about ninety-five thousand engaged, with ten thousand killed or wounded, meaning that Baxter would have seen his fair share of battlefield gore and burial, what is shortly described as a "theatre of human calamity."

"Grenadiers" were originally soldiers specialized in siege assault and grenade-throwing, but by the eighteenth century grenades were no longer in use and the name designated specially chosen groups of the largest and most powerful soldiers in each regiment, who then led assaults in open battle. The overall implication, developed in the next sentence, is that Baxter is a big, rugged, battle-scarred man, accustomed to physical danger and death within the conventions of military discipline, yet "timid," subject to limiting prejudices, and lacking in the capacity for benevolent alliances that Constantia demonstrates repeatedly.

Like Baxter, the historical "Count de la Lippe," mentioned in Brown's footnote in Chapter 14, fought at Dettingen and Minden (see note 14.5).

others, and her eyes were always fixed upon the ground. One evening Baxter was passing the pump while she was drawing water. The sadness which her looks betokened, and a suspicion that her father might be sick, had a momentary effect upon his feelings. He stopped and asked how her father was. She paid a polite attention to his question, and said something in French. This and the embarrassment of her air, convinced him that his words were not understood. He said no more (what indeed could he say?) but passed on.

Two or three days after this, on returning in the evening to his family, his wife expressed her surprise in not having seen Miss Monrose in the street that day. She had not been at the pump, nor had gone, as usual, to market. This information gave him some disquiet; yet he could form no resolution. As to entering the house and offering his aid, if aid were needed, he had too much regard for his own safety, and too little for that of a frog-eating Frenchman, to think seriously of that expedient. His attention was speedily diverted by other objects, and Monrose was, for the present, forgotten.

Baxter's profession was that of a porter. He was thrown out of employment by the present state of things. The solicitude of the guardians of the city was exerted on this occasion, not only in opposing the progress of disease, and furnishing provisions to the destitute, but in the preservation of property. For this end the number of nightly watchmen was increased. Baxter entered himself in this service. From nine till twelve o'clock at night it was his province to occupy a certain post.

On this night he attended his post as usual. Twelve o'clock arrived, and he bent his steps homeward. It was necessary to pass by Monrose's door. On approaching this house, the circumstance mentioned by his wife recurred to him. Something like compassion was conjured up in his heart by the figure of the lady, as he recollected to have lately seen it. It was obvious to conclude that sickness was the cause of her seclusion. The same, it might be, had confined her father. If this were true, how deplorable might be their present condition! Without food, without physician or friends, ignorant of the language of the country, and thence unable to communicate their wants or solicit succour; fugitives from their native land, neglected, solitary, and poor.

His heart was softened by these images. He stopped involuntarily when opposite their door. He looked up at the house. The shutters were closed, so that light, if it were within, was invisible. He stepped into the porch, and put his eye to the keyhole. All was darksome and waste. He listened and imagined that he heard the aspirations of grief. The sound was scarcely articulate, but had an electrical effect upon his feelings. He retired to his home full of mournful reflections.[6]

He was willing to do something for the relief of the sufferers, but nothing could be done that night. Yet succour, if delayed till the morning, might be ineffectual. But

---

[6] "His heart was softened by these images ... key-hole ... mournful reflections": an example of the operation of sympathy in a curious audience, as Baxter's prejudice and antagonism are modulated by considerations of presumed suffering. Baxter searches for information by gazing through a key-hole (twice in this chapter), acting like an audience at a theatrical performance. Incidents of spying, secret witnessing, and gazing through keyholes recur throughout the novel.

how, when the morning came, should he proceed to effectuate his kind intentions? The guardians of the public welfare, at this crisis, were distributed into those who counselled and those who executed. A set of men, self-appointed to the generous office, employed themselves in seeking out the destitute or sick, and imparting relief. With this arrangement, Baxter was acquainted. He was resolved to carry tidings of what he had heard and seen to one of those persons early the next day.

Baxter, after taking some refreshment, retired to rest. In no long time, however, he was awakened by his wife, who desired him to notice a certain glimmering on the ceiling. It seemed the feeble and flitting ray of a distant and moving light, coming through the window. It did not proceed from the street, for the chamber was lighted from the side, and not from the front of the house. A lamp borne by a passenger, or the attendants of an hearse, could not be discovered in this situation. Besides, in the latter case, it would be accompanied by the sound of the vehicle, and probably, by weeping and exclamations of despair. His employment, as the guardian of property, naturally suggested to him the idea of robbery. He started from his bed, and went to the window.

His house stood at the distance of about fifty paces from that of Monrose. There was annexed to the latter, a small garden or yard, bounded by an high wooden fence. Baxter's window overlooked this space. Before he reached the window, the relative situation of the two habitations occurred to him. A conjecture was instantly formed that the glimmering proceeded from this quarter. His eye, therefore, was immediately fixed upon Monrose's back door. It caught a glimpse of an human figure, passing into the house, through this door. The person had a candle in his hand. This appeared by the light which streamed after him, and which was perceived, though faintly, through a small window of the dwelling, after the back door was closed.

The person disappeared too quickly to allow him to say whether it was male or female. This scrutiny confirmed, rather than weakened the apprehensions that first occurred. He reflected on the desolate and helpless condition of this family. The father might be sick; and what opposition could be made by the daughter to the stratagems or violence of midnight plunderers. This was an evil which it was his duty, in an extraordinary sense, to obviate. It is true, the hour of watching was passed, and this was not the district assigned to him; but Baxter was, on the whole, of a generous and intrepid spirit: In the present case, therefore, he did not hesitate long in forming his resolution. He seized an hanger that hung at his bed-side, and which had hewn many an Hungarian and French hussar to pieces. With this he descended to the street. He cautiously approached Monrose's house. He listened at the door, but heard nothing. The lower apartment, as he discovered through the key-hole, was deserted and dark. These appearances could not be accounted for. He was, as yet, unwilling to call or to knock. He was solicitous to obtain some information by silent means, and without alarming the persons within, who, if they were robbers, might thus be put upon their guard, and enabled to escape. If none but the family were there, they would not understand his signals, and might impute the disturbance to the cause which he was desirous to obviate. What could he do? Must he patiently wait till some incident should happen to regulate his motions?

In this uncertainly, he bethought himself of going round to the back part of the dwelling, and watching the door which had been closed. An open space, filled with rubbish and weeds, adjoined the house and garden on one side. Hither he repaired, and raising his head above the fence, at a point directly opposite the door, waited with considerable impatience for some token or signal, by which he might be directed in his choice of measures.

Human life abounds with mysterious appearances. A man, perched on a fence, at midnight, mute and motionless, and gazing at a dark and dreary dwelling, was an object calculated to rouse curiosity. When the muscular form, and rugged visage, scarred and furrowed into something like ferocity, were added; when the nature of the calamity, by which the city was dispeopled, was considered, the motives to plunder, and the insecurity of property, arising from the pressure of new wants on the poor, and the flight or disease of the rich, were attended to, an observer would be apt to admit fearful conjectures.

I know not how long Baxter continued at this post. He remained here, because he could not, as he conceived, change it for a better. Before his patience was exhausted, his attention was called by a noise within the house. It proceeded from the lower room. The sound was that of steps, but this was accompanied with other inexplicable tokens. The kitchen door at length opened. The figure of Miss Monrose, pale, emaciated, and haggard, presented itself. Within the door stood a candle. It was placed on a chair within sight, and its rays streamed directly against the face of Baxter, as it was reared above the top of the fence. This illumination, faint as it was, bestowed a certain air of wildness on features which nature, and the sanguinary habits of a soldier, had previously rendered, in an eminent degree, harsh and stern. He was not aware of the danger of discovery, in consequence of this position of the candle. His attention was, for a few seconds, engrossed by the object before him. At length he chanced to notice another object.

At a few yards distance from the fence, and within it, some one appeared to have been digging. An opening was made in the ground, but it was shallow and irregular. The implement which seemed to have been used, was nothing more than a fire shovel, for one of these he observed lying near the spot. The lady had withdrawn from the door, though without closing it. He had leisure, therefore, to attend to this new circumstance, and to reflect upon the purpose for which this opening might have been designed.

Death is familiar to the apprehensions of a soldier. Baxter had assisted at the hasty interment of thousands, the victims of the sword or of pestilence. Whether it was because this theatre of human calamity was new to him, and death, in order to be viewed with his ancient unconcern, must be accompanied in the ancient manner, with halberts[7] and tents, certain it is, that Baxter was irresolute and timid in every thing that respected the yellow fever. The circumstances of the time suggested that this was a grave, to which some victim of this disease was to be consigned. His teeth

---

[7] "Halberts": a halbert is a combined spear and battle-ax.

chattered when he reflected how near he might now be to the source of infection: yet his curiosity retained him at his post.

He fixed his eyes once more upon the door. In a short time the lady again appeared at it. She was in a stooping posture, and appeared to be dragging something along the floor. His blood ran cold at this spectacle. His fear instantly figured to itself a corpse, livid and contagious. Still he had no power to move. The lady's strength, enfeebled as it was by grief, and perhaps by the absence of nourishment, seemed scarcely adequate to the task which she had assigned herself.

Her burthen, whatever it was, was closely wrapt in a sheet. She drew it forward a few paces, then desisted, and seated herself on the ground apparently to recruit her strength, and give vent to the agony of her thoughts in sighs. Her tears were either exhausted or refused to flow, for none were shed by her. Presently she resumed her undertaking. Baxter's horror increased in proportion as she drew nearer to the spot where he stood, and yet it seemed as if some fascination had forbidden him to recede.

At length the burthen was drawn to the side of the opening in the earth. Here it seemed as if the mournful task was finished. She threw herself once more upon the earth. Her senses seemed for a time to have forsaken her. She sat buried in reverie, her eyes scarcely open and fixed upon the ground, and every feature set to the genuine expression of sorrow. Some disorder, occasioned by the circumstance of dragging, now took place in the vestment of what he had rightly predicted to be a dead body. The veil by accident was drawn aside, and exhibited, to the startled eye of Baxter, the pale and ghastly visage of the unhappy Monrose.

This incident determined him. Every joint in his frame trembled, and he hastily withdrew from the fence. His first motion in doing this produced a noise by which the lady was alarmed: she suddenly threw her eyes upward, and gained a full view of Baxter's extraordinary countenance, just before it disappeared. She manifested her terror by a piercing shriek. Baxter did not stay to mark her subsequent conduct, to confirm or to dissipate her fears, but retired, in confusion, to his own house.

Hitherto his caution had availed him. He had carefully avoided all employments and places from which he imagined imminent danger was to be dreaded. Now, through his own inadvertency, he had rushed, as he believed, into the jaws of the pest. His senses had not been assailed by any noisome effluvia.[8] This was no unplausible ground for imagining that this death had some other cause than the yellow fever. This circumstance did not occur to Baxter. He had been told that Frenchmen were not susceptible of this contagion. He had hitherto believed this assertion, but now regarded it as having been fully confuted. He forgot that Frenchmen were undoubtedly mortal, and that there was no impossibility in Monrose's dying, even at this time, of a malady different from that which prevailed.

---

[8] "Effluvia": an "effluvium" is a stream of particles producing a smell, usually unpleasant. The term is commonly used in the period's yellow fever writings to describe fever-associated odors and emanations.

Before morning he began to feel very unpleasant symptoms. He related his late adventure to his wife. She endeavoured, by what arguments her slender ingenuity suggested, to quiet his apprehensions, but in vain. He hourly grew worse, and as soon as it was light, dispatched his wife for a physician. On interrogating this messenger, the physician obtained information of last night's occurrences, and this being communicated to one of the dispensers of the public charity, they proceeded, early in the morning, to Monrose's house. It was closed as usual. They knocked and called, but no one answered. They examined every avenue to the dwelling, but none of them were accessible. They passed into the garden, and observed, on the spot marked out by Baxter a heap of earth. A very slight exertion was sufficient to remove it and discover the body of the unfortunate exile beneath.

After unsuccessfully trying various expedients for entering the house, they deemed themselves authorised to break the door. They entered, ascended the staircase, and searched every apartment in the house, but no human being was discoverable. The furniture was wretched and scanty, but there was no proof that Monrose had fallen a victim to the reigning disease. It was certain that the lady had disappeared. It was inconceivable whither she had gone.

Baxter suffered a long period of sickness.—The prevailing malady appeared upon him in its severest form. His strength of constitution, and the careful attendance of his wife, were insufficient to rescue him from the grave. His case may be quoted as an example of the force of imagination. He had probably already received, through the medium of the air, or by contact of which he was not conscious, the seeds of this disease. They might perhaps have lain dormant, had not this panic[9] occurred to endow them with activity.

---

[9] "This panic": another example of the wider phenomena of self-destructive panic and fear-related behavior first emphasized in Chapter 3; see note 3.14.

Chapter VIII

SUCH were the facts circumstantially communicated by Sarah. They afforded to Constance a theme of ardent meditation. The similitude between her own destiny and that of this unhappy exile, could not fail to be observed. Immersed in poverty, friendless, burthened with the maintenance and nurture of her father, their circumstances were nearly parallel. The catastrophe of her tale, was the subject of endless but unsatisfactory conjecture.

She had disappeared between the flight of Baxter and the dawn of day. What path had she taken? Was she now alive? Was she still an inhabitant of this city? Perhaps there was a coincidence of taste as well as fortunes between them. The only friend that Constantia ever enjoyed, congenial with her in principles, sex and age, was at a distance that forbad communication. She imagined that Ursula Monrose would prove worthy of her love, and felt unspeakable regret at the improbability of their ever meeting.

Meanwhile the dominion of cold began to be felt, and the contagious fever entirely disappeared. The return of health was hailed with rapture, by all ranks of people. The streets were once more busy and frequented. The sensation of present security seemed to shut out from all hearts the memory of recent disasters. Public entertainments were thronged with auditors. A new theatre had lately been constructed, and a company of English Comedians had arrived during the prevalence of the malady. They now began their exhibitions, and their audiences were overflowing.[1]

Such is the motly and ambiguous condition of human society, such is the complexity of all effects from what cause soever they spring, that none can tell whether this destructive pestilence was, on the whole, productive of most pain or most pleasure. Those who had been sick and had recovered, found, in this circumstance, a source of exultation. Others made haste, by new marriages, to supply the place of wives, husbands and children, whom the scarcely extinguished pestilence had swept away.

Constance, however, was permitted to take no share in the general festivity. Such was the colour of her fate, that the yellow fever, by affording her a respite from toil, supplying leisure for the acquisition of a useful branch of knowledge, and leading her to the discovery of a cheaper, more simple, and more wholesome method of subsistence, had been friendly, instead of adverse, to her happiness. Its disappearance, instead of relieving her from suffering, was the signal for the approach of new cares.

---

[1] "A new theatre … overflowing": a reference to the elaborate "New Theatre" built by impresario Thomas Wignell and partners in 1792–1793 on Chestnut Street between Sixth and Seventh. The ship carrying the theater's first company of fifty-six actors from London (the "English Comedians" noted here) arrived in the Delaware River in August 1793, but the company stayed on board the ship while the fever epidemic ran its course. Because of the epidemic, the company eventually disembarked and traveled to Baltimore, only returning to Philadelphia to begin performances the following winter; thus theatrical performances were delayed by the yellow fever epidemic until February 17, 1794. Novelist Susanna Rowson, author of the first U.S. bestseller *Charlotte Temple* (London, 1791; Philadelphia, 1794), was one of the actors in the troupe that arrived in this manner.

Of her ancient customers, some were dead, and others were slow in resuming their ancient habitations, and their ordinary habits. Meanwhile two wants were now created and were urgent. The season demanded a supply of fuel, and her rent had accumulated beyond her power to discharge. M'Crea no sooner returned from the country, than he applied to her for payment. Some proprietors, guided by humanity, had remitted their dues, but M'Crea was not one of these. According to his own representation, no man was poorer than himself, and the punctual payment of all that was owing to him, was no more than sufficient to afford him a scanty subsistence.

He was aware of the indigence of the Dudleys, and was therefore extremely importunate for payment, and could scarcely be prevailed upon to allow them the interval of a day, for the discovery of expedients. This day was passed by Constantia in fruitless anxieties. The ensuing evening had been fixed for a repetition of his visit. The hour arrived, but her invention was exhausted in vain. M'Crea was punctual to the minute. Constance was allowed no option. She merely declared that the money demanded she had not to give, nor could she foresee any period at which her inability would be less than it then was.

These declarations were heard by her visitant, with marks of unspeakable vexation. He did not fail to expatiate on the equity of his demands, the moderation and forbearance he had hitherto shewn, notwithstanding the extreme urgency of his own wants, and the inflexible rigour with which he had been treated by *his* creditors. This rhetorick was merely the prelude to an intimation that he must avail himself of any lawful means, by which he might gain possession of *his own*.

This insinuation was fully comprehended by Constance, but it was heard without any new emotions. Her knowledge of her landlord's character taught her to expect but one consequence. He paused to observe what effect would be produced by this indirect menace. She answered, without any change of tone, that the loss of habitation and furniture, however inconvenient at this season, must be patiently endured. If it were to be prevented only by the payment of money, its prevention was impossible.

M'Crea renewed his regrets that there should be no other alternative. The law sanctioned his claims and justice to his family, which was already large, and likely to increase, required that they should not be relinquished, yet such was the mildness of his temper and his aversion to proceed to this extremity, that he was willing to dispense with immediate payment on two conditions. First, that they should leave his house within a week, and secondly, that they should put into his hands some trinket or moveable, equal in value to the sum demanded, which should be kept by him as a pledge.

This last hint suggested an expedient for obviating the present distress. The lute with which Mr. Dudley was accustomed to solace his solitude, was, if possible, more essential to his happiness than shelter or food. To his daughter it possessed little direct power to please. It was inestimable merely for her father's sake. Its intrinsic value was at least equal to the sum due, but to part with it was to bereave him of a good, which nothing else could supply. Besides, not being a popular and saleable instrument, it would probably be contemptuously rejected by the ignorance and avarice of M'Crea.

There was another article in her possession, of some value in traffic, and of a kind which M'Crea was far more likely to accept. It was the miniature portrait of her friend, executed by a German artist, and set in gold.[2] This image was a precious though imperfect substitute for sympathy and intercourse with the original. Habit had made this picture a source of a species of idolatry. Its power over her sensations was similar to that possessed by a beautiful Madonna over the heart of a juvenile enthusiast. It was the mother of the only devotion which her education had taught her to consider as beneficial or true.

She perceived the necessity of parting with it on this occasion, with the utmost clearness, but this necessity was thought upon with indescribable repugnance. It seemed as if she had not thoroughly conceived the extent of her calamity till now. It seemed as if she could have endured the loss of eyes with less reluctance than the loss of this inestimable relique. Bitter were the tears which she shed over it as she took it from her bosom, and consigned it to those rapacious hands, that were stretched out to receive it. She derived some little consolation from the promises of this man, that he would keep it safely till she was able to redeem it.

The other condition, that of immediate removal from the house, seemed at first sight impracticable. Some reflection, however, shewed her, that the change might not only be possible but useful. Among other expedients for diminishing expence, that of limiting her furniture and dwelling to the cheapest standard, had often occurred. She now remembered, that the house occupied by Monrose, was tenantless; that its antiquity, its remote and unpleasant situation, and its small dimensions, might induce M'Crea, to whom it belonged, to let it at a much lower price than that which he now exacted. M'Crea would have been better pleased if her choice had fallen on a different house, but he had powerful though sordid reasons for desiring the possession of this tenement. He assented therefore to her proposal, provided her removal took place without delay.

In the present state of her funds this removal was impossible. Mere shelter, would not suffice during this inclement season. Without fuel, neither cold could be excluded, nor hunger relieved. There was nothing, convertible into money, but her lute. No sacrifice was more painful, but an irresistible necessity demanded it.

Her interview with M'Crea took place while her father was absent from the room. On his return she related what had happened, and urged the necessity of parting with his favorite instrument. He listened to her tale with a sigh. Yes, said he, do what

---

[2] "Portrait of her friend … set in gold": a precious image and keepsake, in other words, of the narrator S.C., or Sophia Courtland, who uses this paragraph and following scene to assert that Constantia longs for "sympathy and intercourse" with herself. This literal visual portrait will be juxtaposed with the verbal, figurative "portrait" of Ursula Monrose in the remainder of the chapter, anticipating the triangulation of these two characters with Constantia that was hinted at in the first paragraph of this chapter and that will be amplified in the latter part of the novel. The portrait itself will figure in an important plot turn in Chapter 25, where the "German artist" noted here will be identified as the painter John (Johann) Eckstein, then a recent émigré from Prussia (see notes 25.1–2).

thou wilt, my child. It is unlikely that any one will purchase it. It is certain that no one will give for it what I gave: but thou may'st try.

It has been to me a faithful friend. I know not how I should have lived without it. Its notes have cheered me with the sweet remembrances of old times. It was, in some degree, a substitute for the eyes which I have lost, but now let it go, and perform for me perhaps the dearest of its services. It may help us to sustain the severities of this season.

There was no room for delay. She immediately set out in search of a purchaser. Such an one was most likely to be found in the keeper of a musical repository, who had lately arrived from Europe. She entertained but slight hopes that an instrument, scarcely known among her neighbours, would be bought at any price, however inconsiderable.

She found the keeper of the shop engaged in conversation with a lady, whose person and face instantly arrested the attention of Constance. A less sagacious observer would have eyed the stranger with indifference. But Constance was ever busy in interpreting the language of features and looks. Her sphere of observation had been narrow, but her habits of examining, comparing and deducing, had thoroughly exhausted that sphere. These habits were eminently strong, with relation to this class of objects. She delighted to investigate the human countenance, and treasured up numberless conclusions as to the coincidence between mental and external qualities.[3]

She had often been forcibly struck by forms that were accidentally seen, and which abounded with this species of mute expression. They conveyed at a single glance, what could not be imparted by volumes. The features and shape sunk, as it were, into perfect harmony with sentiments and passions. Every atom of the frame was pregnant with significance. In some, nothing was remarkable but this power of the outward figure to exhibit the internal sentiments. In others, the intelligence thus unveiled, was remarkable for its heterogeneous or energetic qualities; for its tendency to fill her heart with veneration or abhorrence, or to involve her in endless perplexities.[4]

---

[3] "Language of features and looks … coincidence between mental and external qualities ": Constantia is interested in contemporary parascientific theories of physiognomy, the interpretation of character from outward facial and physical features. Earlier theories about interpreting personality through bodily features were reinterpreted and popularized by Swiss scientist Johann Kaspar Lavater (1741–1801), whose influential *Essays on Physiognomy* (first published 1775–1778; English translation 1789) was well known throughout the late-eighteenth century. Lavater's daughter was married to the American-born Count Rumford, mentioned in Brown's footnote to Chapter 6 (see note 6.3). Constantia's interest in reading faces relates the portrait of Sophia Courtland in the previous passage to her active interpretation of Monrose's (Martinette's) face in the paragraphs that follow.

[4] "Heterogeneous or energetic qualities … veneration or abhorrence … endless perplexities": the French-speaking woman confounds Constantia's physiognomic assumption that there is a correspondence between superficial public appearance and private identity. The "power of the outward figure to exhibit the internal sentiments" is scrambled by the woman's "heterogeneous" aspects, by her mind or spirit's refusal to act in ways that her female physique would indicate. Neoclassical order is threatened by this energy, which, according to the narrator, creates both admiration and abhorrence in Constantia.

The accuracy and vividness with which pictures of this kind presented themselves to her imagination, resembled the operations of a sixth sense. It cannot be doubted, however, that much was owing to the enthusiastic tenor of her own conceptions, and that her conviction of the truth of the picture, principally flowed from the distinctness and strength of its hues.

The figure which she now examined, was small but of exquisite proportions. Her complexion testified the influence of a torrid sun, but the darkness veiled, without obscuring, the glowing tints of her cheek. The shade was remarkably deep, but a deeper still was required to become incompatible with beauty. [5] Her features were irregular, but defects of symmetry were amply supplied by eyes that anticipated speech and positions which conveyed that to which language was inadequate.

It was not the chief tendency of her appearance to seduce or to melt. Her's were the polished cheek and the mutability of muscle, which belong to woman, but the genius conspicuous in her aspect, was heroic and contemplative. The female was absorbed, so to speak, in the rational creature, [6] and the emotions most apt to be excited in the gazer, partook less of love than of reverence.

Such is the portrait of this stranger, delineated by Constance. I copy it with greater willingness, because if we substitute a nobler stature, and a complexion less uniform

---

[5] "The shade was remarkably deep … incompatible with beauty": using the period's coded references to racial distinction, the narrator's description of the woman's tanned but not extremely dark skin insinuates that she may be mixed race, a "mulatta." This possibility is confirmed by the intertext of Brown's "A Portrait of an Emigrant," in which a similarly depicted French-speaking woman is explicitly labeled as of mixed African and European descent. This raises the possibility, at this point in the narrative, that the woman might be a "free person of color" from Haiti and mistress to the man previously described by Baxter as her father. Earlier in 1793, Philadelphia and other eastern cities received a large influx of white Creoles fleeing the racial conflict in the Haitian Revolution. Many of these refugees brought slaves and mixed-race mistresses as well, with whom they would walk affectionately in Philadelphia's streets. The unashamed display of miscegenation and the cosmopolitan fashion sense of the French men and women was sensational, especially in Philadelphia, due to the cultural legacy of Quakers, who favored a plainer style of dress. This is to say that the woman Constantia sees combines both voluptuous beauty and hints of erotic license with masculine features (see the next note, below), to present a hermaphroditic confusion of gender and racial types, a move that upends physiognomic certainties. Subsequent revelations by this character orient her mixed-race potential to the Eastern Mediterranean, where northern and southern European, Turkish, North African, and near-Eastern cultures continually intermixed. For more on the impact of French émigrés in Philadelphia, see "Portrait of an Emigrant" and "French Mores in 1790s Philadelphia" in Related Texts.

[6] "The genius … was heroic and contemplative. The female was absorbed … in the rational creature": the novel's "first take" on Monrose (Martinette) echoes Mary Wollstonecraft's feminist arguments, suggesting that she has overcome the imposed social conditioning of gender to make herself into a "rational creature" in a manner that will be developed and clarified when she explains her story in Chapters 19–21. Similar Wollstonecraftian language about overcoming the limitations of imposed "feminine" weakness will be used in the conversation between Ormond and Constantia in Chapter 15 (see note 15.4).

and delicate, it is suited, with the utmost accuracy, to herself.[7] She was probably unconscious of this resemblance, but this circumstance may be supposed to influence her in discovering such attractive properties in a form thus vaguely seen. These impressions, permanent and cogent as they were, were gained at a single glance. The purpose which led her thither was too momentous to be long excluded.

Why, said the master of the shop, this is lucky. Here is a lady who has just been enquiring for an instrument of this kind. Perhaps the one you have will suit her. If you will bring it to me, I will examine it, and if it is compleat, will make a bargain with you.—He then turned to the lady who had first entered, and a short dialogue in French ensued between them. The man repeated his assurances to Constance, who, promising to hasten back with the instrument, took her leave. The lute, in its structure and ornaments, has rarely been surpassed. When scrutinized by this artist, it proved to be compleat, and the price demanded for it was readily given.

By this means the Dudleys were enabled to change their habitation, and to supply themselves with fuel. To obviate future exigences, Constantia betook herself, once more, to the needle. They persisted in the use of their simple fare, and endeavoured to contract their wants and methodize their occupations, by a standard as rigid as possible. She had not relinquished her design of adopting a new and more liberal profession, but though, when indistinctly and generally considered, it seemed easily effected, yet the first steps which it would be proper to take, did not clearly or readily suggest themselves. For the present she was contented to pursue the beaten tract, but was prepared to benefit by any occasion that time might furnish, suitable to the execution of her plan.

---

[7] "Utmost accuracy, to herself": the narrator Sophia's claim is that the two women resemble each other despite the fact that one is older, smaller, and has a delicate, more conventionally female physique, while Constantia is younger, with a hardier build and more variegated complexion.

Chapter IX

IT may be asked, if a woman of this character did not attract the notice of the world. Her station, no less than her modes of thinking, excluded her from the concourse of the opulent and the gay. She kept herself in privacy, her engagements confined her to her own fire-side, and her neighbours enjoyed no means of penetrating through that obscurity in which she wrapt herself. There were, no doubt, persons of her own sex, capable of estimating her worth, and who could have hastened to raise so much merit from the indigence to which it was condemned. She might, at least, have found associates and friends, justly entitled to her affection. But whether she were peculiarly unfortunate in this respect, or whether it arose from a jealous and unbending spirit that would remit none of its claims to respect, and was backward in its overtures to kindness and intimacy, it so happened that her hours were, for a long period, enlivened by no companion but her father and her faithful Lucy. The humbleness of her dwelling, her plain garb, and the meanness of her occupation, were no passports to the favor of the rich and vain. These, added to her youth and beauty, frequently exposed her to insults, from which, though productive for a time of mortification and distress, she, for the most part, extricated herself by her spirited carriage, and presence of mind.

One incident of this kind it will be necessary to mention. One evening her engagements carried her abroad. She had proposed to return immediately, finding by experience the danger that was to be dreaded by a woman young and unprotected. Somewhat occurred that unavoidably lengthened her stay, and she set out on her return at a late hour. One of the other sex offered her his guardianship, but this she declined, and proceeded homeward alone.

Her way lay through streets but little inhabited, and whose few inhabitants were of the profligate class. She was conscious of the inconveniences to which she was exposed, and therefore tripped along with all possible haste. She had not gone far before she perceived, through the dusk, two men standing near a porch before her. She had gone too far to recede or change her course without exciting observation, and she flattered herself that the persons would behave with decency. Encouraged by these reflections, and somewhat hastening her pace, she went on. As soon as she came opposite the place where they stood, one of them threw himself round, and caught her arm, exclaiming, in a broad tone, "Whither so fast, my love, at this time of night?"— The other, at the same time, threw his arms round her waist, crying out, "A pretty prize, by G—: just in the nick of time."

They were huge and brawny fellows, in whose grasp her feeble strength was annihilated. Their motions were so sudden, that she had not time to escape by flight. Her struggles merely furnished them with a subject of laughter. He that held her waist, proceeded to pollute her cheeks with his kisses, and drew her into the porch. He tore her from the grasp of him who first seized her, who seemed to think his property invaded, and said, in a surly tone: "What now, Jemmy?[1] Damn your heart, d'ye think

---

[1] "Jemmy": slang for James.

I'll be fobbed. Have done with your slabbering, Jemmy. First come, first served;" and seemed disposed to assert his claims by force.

To this brutality, Constantia had nothing to oppose but fruitless struggles and shrieks for help. Succour was, fortunately, at hand. Her exclamations were heard by a person across the street, who instantly ran, and with some difficulty disengaged her from the grasp of the ruffians. He accompanied her the rest of the way, bestowed on her every polite attention, and, though pressed to enter the house, declined the invitation. She had no opportunity of examining the appearance of her new friend. This, the darkness of the night and her own panick, prevented.

Next day a person called upon her whom she instantly recognized to be her late protector. He came with some message from his sister. His manners were simple and unostentatious, and breathed the genuine spirit of civility. Having performed his commission, and once more received the thanks which she poured forth with peculiar warmth, for his last night's interposition, he took his leave.

The name of this man was Balfour.[2] He was middle-aged, of a figure neither elegant nor ungainly, and an aspect that was mild and placid, but betrayed few marks of intelligence. He was an Adventurer[3] from Scotland, whom a strict adherence to the maxims of trade had rendered opulent. He was governed by the principles of mercantile integrity in all his dealings, and was affable and kind, without being generous, in his treatment of inferiors. He was a stranger to violent emotions of any kind, and his intellectual acquisitions were limited to his own profession.

His demeanour was tranquil and uniform. He was sparing of words, and these were uttered in the softest manner. In all his transactions, he was sedate and considerate. In his dress and mode of living, there were no appearances of parsimony,[4] but there were, likewise, as few traces of profusion.

His sister had shared in his prosperity. As soon as his affairs would permit, he sent for her to Scotland, where she had lived in a state little removed from penury, and had for some years, been vested with the superintendance of his houshold. There was a considerable resemblance between them in person and character. Her profession, or those arts in which her situation had compelled her to acquire skill, had not an equal tendency to enlarge the mind, as those of her brother, but the views of each were

---

[2] "Balfour": a recognizable Scottish clan name. In a later example, Robert Louis Stevenson used his mother's maiden name for David Balfour, the young hero of *Kidnapped* (1886).

[3] "Adventurer": a businessman involved in long-distance commerce, an adventurer in the sense that he risks money in commercial ventures and mercantile speculation. In this sense, the term does not have a negative connotation, but is simply descriptive of his kind of trade. On the other hand, since the slave-trading British Royal African Company was originally known as the Company of Royal Adventurers Trading to Africa, it is possible that Balfour's trade is directly or indirectly dependent on Atlantic slavery.

[4] "Parsimony": thriftiness, frugality, often with the negative connotation of stinginess. This was a long-held stereotype for Scots.

limited to one set of objects. His superiority was owing, not to any inherent difference, but to accident.[5]

Balfour's life had been a model of chastness and regularity: though this was owing more to constitutional coldness, and a frugal spirit, than to virtuous forbearance; but, in his schemes for the future, he did not exclude the circumstance of marriage. Having attained a situation secure, as the nature of human affairs will admit, from the chances of poverty, the way was sufficiently prepared for matrimony. His thoughts had been for some time employed in the selection of a suitable companion, when this rencounter happened with Miss Dudley.

Balfour was not destitute of those feelings which are called into play by the sight of youth and beauty in distress. This incident was not speedily forgotten. The emotions produced by it were new to him. He reviewed them oftener, and with more complacency, than any which he had before experienced. They afforded him so much satisfaction, that, in order to preserve them undiminished, he resolved to repeat his visit. Constantia treated him as one from whom she had received a considerable benefit. Her sweetness and gentleness were uniform, and Balfour found that her humble roof promised him more happiness than his own fire-side, or the society of his professional brethren.

He could not overlook, in the course of such reflections as these, the question relative to marriage, and speedily determined to solicit the honor of her hand. He had not decided without his usual foresight and deliberation; nor had he been wanting in the accuracy of his observations and enquiries. Those qualifications, indeed, which were of chief value in his eyes, lay upon the surface. He was no judge of her intellectual character, or of the loftiness of her morality. Not even the graces of person, or features, or manners, attracted much of his attention. He remarked her admirable economy of time, and money, and labour, the simplicity of her dress, her evenness of temper, and her love of seclusion. These were essential requisites of a wife in his apprehension. The insignificance of his own birth, the lowness of his original fortune, and the efficacy of industry and temperance to confer and maintain wealth, had taught him indifference as to birth or fortune in his spouse. His moderate desires in this respect were gratified, and he was anxious only for a partner that would aid him in preserving, rather than in enlarging his property. He esteemed himself eminently fortunate in meeting with one in whom every matrimonial qualification concentred.

He was not deficient in modesty, but he fancied that, on this occasion, there was no possibility of miscarriage. He held her capacity in deep veneration, but this circumstance rendered him more secure of success. He conceived this union to be even more eligible with regard to her than to himself; and confided in the rectitude of her understanding, for a decision favorable to his wishes.

---

[5] "His superiority was owing ... to accident": that is, the brother's "superior" knowledge and experience are a result of his superior opportunities as a male, not to any inherent superiority over a female with similar talent and potential. Another example of Brown's general emphasis on the way that social position and circumstances shape and limit character.

Before any express declaration was made, Constantia easily predicted the event from the frequency of his visits, and the attentiveness of his manners. It was no difficult task to ascertain this man's character. Her modes of thinking were, in few respects, similar to those of her lover. She was eager to investigate, in the first place, the attributes of his mind. His professional and household maxims were not of inconsiderable importance, but they were subordinate considerations. In the poverty of his discourse and ideas, she quickly found reasons for determining her conduct.

Marriage she had but little considered, as it is in itself. What are the genuine principles of that relation, and what conduct with respect to it, is prescribed to rational beings, by their duty, she had not hitherto investigated: But she was not backward to enquire what are the precepts of duty, in her own particular case. She knew herself to be young; she was sensible of the daily enlargement of her knowledge; every day contributed to rectify some error or confirm some truth. These benefits she owed to her situation, which, whatever were its evils, gave her as much freedom from restraint as is consistent with the state of human affairs. Her poverty fettered her exertions, and circumscribed her pleasures. Poverty, therefore, was an evil, and the reverse of poverty to be desired. But riches were not barren of constraint, and its advantages might be purchased at too dear a rate.[6]

Allowing that the wife is enriched by marriage, how humiliating were the conditions annexed to it in the present case? The company of one with whom we have no sympathy, nor sentiments in common, is, of all species of solitude, the most loathsome and dreary. The nuptial life is attended with peculiar aggravations, since the tie is infrangible, and the choice of a more suitable companion, if such an one should offer, is for ever precluded. The hardships of wealth are not incompensated by some benefits, but these benefits, false and hollow as they are, cannot be obtained by marriage. Her acceptance of Balfour would merely aggravate her indigence.

Now she was at least mistress of the product of her own labour. Her tasks were toilsome, but the profits, though slender, were sure, and she administered her little property in what manner she pleased. Marriage would annihilate this power. Henceforth she would be bereft even of personal freedom. So far from possessing property, she herself would become the property of another.

She was not unaware of the consequences flowing from differences of capacity; and, that power, to whomsoever legally granted, will be exercised by the most addressful;[7] but she derived no encouragement from these considerations. She would not stoop to gain her end by the hateful arts of the sycophant; and was too wise to place an unbounded reliance on the influence of truth. The character, likewise, of this man sufficiently exempted him from either of those influences.

---

[6] "Marriage … as it is in itself … too dear a rate": this passage introduces an important consideration of marriage, conveying the Woldwinite critique of the conventional marriage institution that makes women the property of men, thus a form of compulsion likened to racial slavery. For more, see the discussion of marriage in Brown's *Alcuin* (in Related Texts) and the Introduction.

[7] "Addressful": skillful, clever, adroit.

She did not forget the nature of the altar-vows. To abdicate the use of her own understanding, was scarcely justifiable in any case, but to vow an affection that was not felt, and could not be compelled, and to promise obedience to one, whose judgment was glaringly defective, were acts atrociously criminal. Education, besides, had created in her an insurmountable abhorrence of admitting to conjugal privileges, the man who had no claim upon her love. It could not be denied that a state of abundant accommodation was better than the contrary, but this consideration, though in the most rational estimate, of some weight, she was not so depraved and effeminate as to allow to overweigh the opposite evils. Homely liberty was better than splendid servitude.

Her resolution was easily formed, but there were certain impediments in the way of its execution. These chiefly arose from deference to the opinion, and compassion for the infirmities of her father. He assumed no controul over her actions. His reflections in the present case, were rather understood than expressed. When uttered it was with the mildness of equality, and the modesty of persuasion. It was this circumstance that conferred upon them all their force. His decision, on so delicate a topic, was not wanting in sagacity and moderation; but, as a man, he had his portion of defects, and his frame was enfeebled by disease and care; yet he set no higher value on the ease and independance of his former condition, than any man of like experience. He could not endure to exist on the fruits of his daughter's labour. He ascribed her decision to a spirit of excessive refinement, and was, of course, disposed to give little quarter to maiden scruples. They were phantoms, he believed, which experience would dispel. His morality, besides, was of a much more flexible kind; and the marriage vows were, in his opinion, formal and unmeaning, and neither in themselves, nor in the apprehension of the world, accompanied with any rigorous obligation. He drew more favorable omens from the known capacity of his daughter, and the flexibility of her lover.

She demanded his opinion and advice. She listened to his reasonings, and revolved them with candour and impartiality. She stated her objections with simplicity, but the difference of age and sex was sufficient to preclude agreement. Arguments were of no use but to prolong the debate; but, happily, the magnanimity of Mr. Dudley would admit of no sacrifice. Her opinions, it is true, were erroneous; but he was willing that she should regulate her conduct by her own conceptions of right, and not by those of another. To refuse Balfour's offers was an evil; but an evil inexpressibly exceeded by that of accepting them contrary to her own sense of propriety.

Difficulties, likewise, arose from the consideration of what was due to the man who had already benefited her, and who, in this act, intended to confer upon her further benefit. These, though the source of some embarrassments, were not sufficient to shake her resolution. Balfour could not understand her principal objections. They were of a size altogether disproportioned to his capacity. Her moral speculations were quite beyond the sphere of his reflections. She could not expatiate, without a breach of civility, on the disparity of their minds, and yet this was the only or principal ground on which she had erected her scruples.

Her father loved her too well not to be desirous of relieving her from a painful task, though undertaken without necessity, and contrary to his opinion. Refer him to me, said he; I will make the best of the matter, and render your refusal as palatable as possible, but do you authorize me to make it absolute, and without appeal?—

My dear father! how good you are! but that shall be my province. If I err, let the consequences of my mistake be confined to myself. It would be cruel indeed, to make you the instrument in a transaction which your judgment disapproves. My reluctance was a weak and foolish thing. Strange, indeed, if the purity of my motives will not bear me out on this, as it has done on many more arduous occasions.—

Well, be it so; that is best I believe. Ten to one but I, with my want of eyes, would blunder, while yours will be of no small use, in a contest with a lover. They will serve you to watch the transitions in his placid physiognomy, and overpower his discontents.

She was aware of the inconveniences to which this resolution would subject her, but since they were unavoidable, she armed herself with the requisite patience. Her apprehensions were not without reason. More than one conference was necessary to convince him of her meaning, and in order to effect her purpose, she was obliged to behave with so much explicitness, as to hazard giving him offence. This affair was productive of no small vexation. He had put too much faith in the validity of his pretensions, and the benefits of perseverance, to be easily shaken off.

This decision was not borne by him with as much patience as she wished.[8] He deemed himself unjustly treated, and his resentment exceeded those bounds of moderation which he prescribed to himself on all other occasions. From his anger, however, there was not much to be dreaded, but, unfortunately, his sister partook of his indignation and indulged her petulance, which was enforced by every gossiping and tatling propensity, to the irreparable disadvantage of Constantia.

She owed her support to her needle. She was dependant therefore on the caprice of customers. This caprice was swayable by every breath, and paid a merely subordinate regard, in the choice of workwomen, to the circumstances of skill, cheapness and diligence. In consequence of this, her usual sources of subsistence began to fail.

Indigence, as well as wealth, is comparative. He, indeed, must be wretched, whose food, cloathing and shelter are limited, both in kind and quantity, by the standard of mere necessity; who, in the choice of food, for example, is governed by no consideration but its cheapness, and its capacity to sustain nature. Yet to this degree of wretchedness was Miss Dudley reduced.

As her means of subsistence began to decay, she reflected on the change of employment that might become necessary. She was mistress of no lucrative art, but that which now threatened to be useless. There was but one avenue through which she could hope to escape from the pressure of absolute want. This, she regarded with an aversion, that nothing but extreme necessity, and the failure of every other expedient, would be able to subdue. This was the hiring herself as a servant. Even that could not

---

[8] "This decision was not borne … with as much patience as she wished": the mediocre, unintelligent Balfour is the second suitor Constantia has rejected (see note 2.4 for the first). The resentment of Balfour and his sister will consequently bring Constantia and her father to their lowest point in the paragraphs that follow.

answer all her purposes. If a subsistence were provided by it for herself, whither should her father, and her Lucy betake themselves for support.

Hitherto her labour had been sufficient to shut out famine and the cold. It is true she had been cut off from all the direct means of personal or mental gratification: But her constitution had exempted her from the insalutary effects of sedentary application. She could not tell how long she could enjoy this exemption, but it was absurd to anticipate those evils which might never arrive. Meanwhile, her situation was not destitute of comfort. The indirect means of intellectual improvement, in conversation and reflection, the inexpensive amusement of singing, and, above all, the consciousness of performing her duty, and maintaining her independance inviolate, were still in her possession. Her lodging was humble, and her fare frugal, but these, temperance and a due regard to the use of money, would require from the most opulent.

Now, retrenchments must be made even from this penurious provision. Her exertions might somewhat defer, but could not prevent the ruin of her unhappy family. Their landlord was a severe exacter of his dues. The day of quarterly payment was past, and he had not failed in his usual punctuality. She was unable to satisfy his demands, and Mr. Dudley was officially informed, that unless payment was made before a day fixed, resort would be had to the law, in that case made and provided.

This seemed to be the completion of their misfortunes. It was not enough to soften the implacability of their landlord. A respite might possibly be obtained from this harsh sentence. Intreaties might prevail upon him to allow of their remaining under this roof for some time longer; but shelter at this inclement season was not enough. Without fire they must perish with the cold; and fuel could be procured only for money, of which the last shilling was expended. Food was no less indispensible, and, their credit being gone, not a loaf could be extorted from the avarice of the bakers in the neighbourhood.

The sensations produced by this accumulation of distress may be more easily conceived than described. Mr. Dudley sunk into despair, when Lucy informed him that the billet of wood she was putting on the fire was the last. Well, said he, the game is up. Where is my daughter?— The answer was, that she was up stairs.

Why, there she has been this hour. Tell her to come down and warm herself. She must needs be cold and here is a cheerful blaze. I feel it myself. Like the lightning that precedes death, it beams thus brightly, though, in a few moments, it will be extinguished forever. Let my darling come, and partake of its comforts before they expire.

Constantia had retired in order to review her situation, and devise some expedients that might alleviate it. It was a sore extremity to which she was reduced. Things had come to a desperate pass, and the remedy required must be no less desperate. It was impossible to see her father perish. She herself would have died before she would have condescended to beg. It was not worth prolonging a life which must subsist upon alms. She would have wandered into the fields at dusk, have seated herself upon an unfrequented bank, and serenely waited the approach of that death, which the rigours of the season would have rendered sure. But, as it was, it became her to act in a very different manner.

During her father's prosperity, some mercantile intercourse had taken place between him and a merchant of this city. The latter, on some occasion, had spent a few nights at her father's house. She was greatly charmed with the humanity that shone forth in his conversation and behaviour. From that time to this, all intercourse had ceased. She was acquainted with the place of his abode, and knew him to be affluent. To him she determined to apply as a suppliant in behalf of her father. She did not inform Mr. Dudley of this intention, conceiving it best to wait till the event had been ascertained, for fear of exciting fallacious expectations. She was further deterred by the apprehension of awakening his pride, and bringing on herself an absolute prohibition.

She arrived at the door of Mr. Melbourne's house, and enquiring for the master of it, was informed that he had gone out of town, and was not expected to return within a week.

Her scheme, which was by no means unplausible, was thus compleatly frustrated. There was but one other resource, on which she had already deliberated, and to which she had determined to apply, if that should fail. That was to claim assistance from the superintendants of the poor. She was employed in considering to which of them, and in what manner she should make her application, when she turned the corner of Lombard and Second Streets. That had scarcely been done, when, casting her eyes mournfully round her, she caught a glimpse of a person whom she instantly recognized, passing into the market-place. She followed him with quick steps, and, on a second examination, found that she had not been mistaken. This was no other than Thomas Craig, to whose malignity and cunning, all her misfortunes were imputable.

She was at first uncertain what use to make of this discovery. She followed him almost instinctively, and saw him at length enter the Indian Queen Tavern.[9] Here she stopped. She entertained a confused conception, that some beneficial consequences might be extracted from this event. In the present hurry of her thoughts she could form no satisfactory conclusion: But it instantly occurred to her that it would, at least be proper to ascertain the place of his abode. She stept into the inn, and made the suitable enquiries. She was informed that the gentleman had come from Baltimore, a month before, and had since resided at that house. How soon he meant to leave the city, her informant was unable to tell.

Having gained this intelligence, she returned home, and once more shut herself in her chamber to meditate on this new posture of affairs.

---

[9] "Indian Queen Tavern": on Fourth Street between Chestnut and Market streets, one of the city's best-known inns (earlier, for example, the meeting place of Benjamin Franklin's own social club, the Junto).

Chapter X

CRAIG was indebted to her father. He had defrauded him by the most attrocious and illicit arts. On either account he was liable to prosecution, but her heart rejected the thought of being the author of injury to any man. The dread of punishment, however, might induce him to refund, uncoercively, the whole or some part of the stolen property. Money was at this moment necessary to existence, and she conceived herself justly entitled to that, of which her father had been perfidiously despoiled.

But the law was formal and circuitous. Money itself was necessary to purchase its assistance. Besides, it could not act with unseen virtue and instantaneous celerity. The co-operation of advocates and officers was required. They must be visited, and harangued, and importuned. Was she adequate to the task? Would the energy of her mind supply the place of experience, and, with a sort of miraculous efficacy, afford her the knowledge of official processes and dues? As little, on this occasion, could be expected from her father, as from her. He was infirm and blind. The spirit that animated his former days was flown. His heart's blood was chilled by the rigours of his fortune. He had discarded his indignation and his enmities, and, together with them, hope itself had perished in his bosom. He waited in tranquil despair, for that stroke which would deliver him from life, and all the woes that it inherits.

But these considerations were superfluous. It was enough that justice must be bought, and that she had not the equivalent. Legal proceedings are encumbered with delay, and her necessities were urgent. Succour, if withheld till the morrow, would be useless. Hunger and cold would not be trifled with. What resource was there left in this her uttermost distress? Must she yield, in imitation of her father, to the cowardly suggestions of despair?

Craig might be rich. His coffers might be stuffed with thousands. All that he had, according to the principles of social equity, was her's; yet he, to whom nothing belonged, rioted in superfluity, while she, the rightful claimant, was driven to the point of utmost need. The proper instrument of her restoration was law, but its arm was powerless, for she had not the means of bribing it into activity.[1] But was law the only instrument?

Craig, perhaps, was accessible. Might she not, with propriety, demand an interview, and lay before him the consequences of his baseness? He was not divested of the last remains of humanity. It was impossible that he should not relent at the picture of those distresses of which he was the author. Menaces of legal prosecution she meant not to use, because she was unalterably resolved against that remedy. She confided in the efficacy of her pleadings to awaken his justice. This interview she was determined immediately to seek. She was aware that by some accident her purpose might be frustrated. Access to his person, might, for the present, be impossible, or might be denied. It was proper therefore to write him a letter, which might be substituted in

---

[1] "Law ... bribing it into activity": another denunciation of law as a set of institutions and practices that deny instead of enacting justice. For the novel's first passage on this topic, see note 2.3.

place of an interview. It behoved her to be expeditious, for the light was failing, and her strength was nearly exhausted by the hurry of her spirits. Her fingers, likewise, were benumbed with the cold. She performed her task, under these disadvantages, with much difficulty. This was the purport of her letter:

Thomas Craig,

AN hour ago I was in Second-Street, and saw you. I followed you till you entered the Indian Queen-Tavern. Knowing where you are, I am now preparing to demand an interview. I may be disappointed in this hope, and therefore write you this.

I do not come to upbraid you, to call you to a legal, or any other account for your actions. I presume not to weigh your merits. The God of equity be your judge. May he be as merciful, in the hour of retribution, as I am disposed to be.

It is only to inform you that my father is on the point of perishing with want. You know who it was that reduced him to this condition. I persuade myself I shall not appeal to your justice in vain. Learn of this justice to afford him instant succour.

You know who it was that took you in, an houseless wanderer; protected and fostered your youth, and shared with you his confidence and his fortune. It is he who now, blind and indigent, is threatened, by an inexorable landlord, to be thrust into the street; and who is, at this moment, without fire and without bread.

He once did you some little service: now he looks to be compensated. All the retribution he asks, is to be saved from perishing. Surely you will not spurn at his claims. Thomas Craig has done nothing that shews him deaf to the cries of distress. He would relieve a dog from such suffering.

Forget that you have known my father in any character but that of a supplicant for bread. I promise you that, on this condition, I, also, will forget it. If you are so far just, you have nothing to fear. Your property and reputation shall both be safe. My father knows not of your being in this city. His enmities are extinct, and if you comply with this request, he shall know you only as a benefactor.

C. Dudley.

Having finished and folded this epistle, she once more returned to the tavern. A waiter informed her that Craig had lately been in, and was now gone out to spend the evening. Whither had he gone? she asked.

How was he to know where gentlemen eat their suppers? Did she take him for a witch? What, in God's name, did she want with him at that hour? Could she not wait, at least, till he had done his supper? He warranted her pretty face would bring him home time enough.

Constantia was not disconcerted at this address. She knew that females are subjected, through their own ignorance and cowardice, to a thousand mortifications. She set its true value on base and low-minded treatment. She disdained to notice this ribaldry, but turned away from the servant to meditate on this disappointment.

A few moments after, a young fellow smartly dressed, entered the apartment. He was immediately addressed by the other, who said to him, Well, Tom, where's your master. There's a lady wants him, pointing to Constantia, and laying a grinning emphasis on the word lady. She turned to the new-comer: Friend,[2] are you Mr. Craig's servant?

The fellow seemed somewhat irritated at the bluntness of her interrogatory. The appellation of servant sat uneasily, perhaps, on his pride, especially as coming from a person of her appearance. He put on an air of familiar ridicule, and surveyed her in silence. She resumed, in an authoritative tone, where does Mr. Craig spend this evening? I have business with him of the highest importance, and that will not bear delay. I must see him this night.—He seemed preparing to make some impertinent answer, but she anticipated it. You had better answer me with decency. If you do not, your master shall hear of it.

This menace was not ineffectual. He began to perceive himself in the wrong, and surlily muttered, Why, if you must know, he is gone to Mr. Ormond's. And where lived Mr. Ormond? In Arch-Street; he mentioned the number on her questioning him to that effect.

Being furnished with this information, she left them. Her project was not to be thwarted by slight impediments, and she forthwith proceeded to Ormond's dwelling. Who was this Ormond? she enquired of herself as she went along: whence originated, and of what nature is the connection between him and Craig? Are they united by union of designs and sympathy of character, or is this stranger a new subject on whom Craig is practising his arts? The last supposition is not impossible. Is it not my duty to disconcert his machinations, and save a new victim from his treachery? But I ought to be sure before I act. He may now be honest, or tending to honesty, and my interference may cast him backward, or impede his progress.

The house to which she had been directed was spacious and magnificent. She was answered by a servant, whose uniform was extremely singular and fanciful, and whose features and accents bespoke him to be English, with a politeness to which she knew that the simplicity of her garb gave her no title. Craig, he told her, was in the drawing-room above stairs. He offered to carry him any message, and ushered her, meanwhile, into a parlour. She was surprized at the splendour of the room. The ceiling was painted with a gay design, the walls stuccoed in relief, and the floor covered with a Persian carpet, with suitable accompaniments of mirrors, tables and sofas.[3]

Craig had been seated at the window above. His suspicions were ever on the watch. He suddenly espied a figure and face on the opposite side of the street, which an alteration of garb and the improvements of time, could not conceal from his knowledge. He was startled at this incident, without knowing the extent of its consequences. He saw her cross the way opposite this house, and immediately after

---

[2] "Friend": a greeting associated with the Society of Friends (Quakers), possibly suggesting that the Dudleys have links to the group.

[3] "Stuccoed ... Persian carpet ... tables and sofas": Ormond's furnishings are expensive and produce cosmopolitan, vaguely Eastern (Levantine or Ottoman) associations distinct from those of the city's ordinarily Anglo gentleman class, such as the magistrate Melbourne.

heard the bell ring. Still he was not aware that he himself was the object of this visit, and waited, with some degree of impatience, for the issue of this adventure.

Presently he was summoned to a person below, who wished to see him. The servant shut the door, as soon as he had delivered the message, and retired.

Craig was thrown into considerable perplexity. It was seldom that he was wanting in presence of mind and dexterity, but the unexpectedness of this incident, made him pause. He had not forgotten the awful charms of his summoner. He shrunk at the imagination of her rebukes. What purpose could be answered by admitting her? It was, undoubtedly, safest to keep at a distance, but what excuse should be given for refusing this interview? He was roused from his reverie by a second and more urgent summons. The person could not conveniently wait; her business was of the utmost moment, and would detain him but a few minutes.

The anxiety which was thus expressed to see him, only augmented his solicitude to remain invisible. He had papers before him which he had been employed in examining. This suggested an excuse. Tell her that I am engaged just now, and cannot possibly attend to her. Let her leave her business. If she has any message you may bring it to me.

It was plain to Constance that Craig suspected the purpose of her visit. This might have come to his knowledge by means impossible for her to divine. She now perceived the wisdom of the precaution she had taken. She gave her letter to the servant with this message: Tell him I shall wait here for an answer, and continue to wait till I receive one.

Her mind was powerfully affected by the criticalness of her situation. She had gone thus far, and saw the necessity of persisting to the end. The goal was within view, and she formed a sort of desperate determination not to relinquish the pursuit. She could not overlook the possibility that he might return no answer, or return an unsatisfactory one. In either case, she was resolved to remain in the house till driven from it by violence. What other resolution could she form? To return to her desolate home, penniless, was an idea not to be endured.

The letter was received, and perused. His conscience was touched, but compunction was a guest, whose importunities he had acquired a peculiar facility of eluding. Here was a liberal offer. A price was set upon his impunity. A small sum, perhaps, would secure him from all future molestation.—She spoke, to be sure, in a damned high tone. 'Twas a pity that the old man should be hungry before supper-time. Blind too! Harder still, when he cannot find his way to his mouth. Rent unpaid, and a flinty-hearted landlord. A pretty pickle to be sure. Instant payment she says. Won't part without it. Must come down with the stuff. I know this girl: When her heart is once set upon a thing, all the devils will not turn her out of her way. She promises silence. I can't pretend to bargain with her. I'd as lief be ducked, as meet her face to face. I know she'll do what she promises. That was always her grand failing. How the little witch talks! Just the dreamer she ever was! Justice! Compassion! Stupid fool! One would think she'd learned something of the world by this time.

He took out his pocket book. Among the notes it contained the lowest was fifty dollars. This was too much, yet there was no alternative, something must be given.

She had detected his abode, and he knew it was in the power of the Dudleys to ruin his reputation, and obstruct his present schemes. It was probable, that if they should exert themselves, their cause would find advocates and patrons. Still the gratuitous gift of fifty dollars,[4] sat uneasily upon his avarice. One idea occurred to reconcile him to the gift. There was a method he conceived of procuring the repayment of it with interest. He inclosed the note in a blank piece of paper and sent it to her.

She received the paper, and opened it with trembling fingers. When she saw what were its contents, her feelings amounted to rapture. A sum like this was affluence to her in her present condition. At least it would purchase present comfort and security. Her heart glowed with exultation, and she seemed to tread with the lightness of air, as she hied homeward. The langour of a long fast, the numbness of the cold, were forgotten. It is worthy of remark how much of human accommodation was comprized within this small compass; and how sudden was this transition from the verge of destruction to the summit of security.

Her first business was to call upon her landlord and pay him his demand. On her return she discharged the little debts she had been obliged to contract, and purchased what was immediately necessary. Wood she could borrow from her next neighbour, and this she was willing to do, now that she had the prospect of repaying it.

---

[4] "The gratuitous gift of fifty dollars": a large sum in the 1790s, when laborers earned $200–300 per annum.

Chapter XI

ON leaving Mr. Ormond's house, Constance was met by that gentleman. He saw her as she came out, and was charmed with the simplicity of her appearance. On entering, he interrogated the servant as to the business that brought her thither.

So, said he, as he entered the drawing-room, where Craig was seated, you have had a visitant. She came, it seems, on a pressing occasion, and would be put off with nothing but a letter.

Craig had not expected this address, but it only precipitated the execution of a design that he had formed. Being aware of this or similar accidents, he had constructed and related on a previous occasion to Ormond, a story suitable to his purpose.

Aye, said he, in a tone of affected compassion, it is a sad affair enough. I am sorry 'tis not in my power to help the poor girl. She is wrong in imputing her father's misfortunes to me, but I know the source of her mistake. Would to heaven it was in my power to repair the wrongs they have suffered, not from me, but from one whose relationship is a disgrace to me.

Perhaps, replied the other, you are willing to explain this affair.

Yes, I wish to explain it. I was afraid of some such accident as this. An explanation is due to my character. I have already told you my story. I mentioned to you a brother of mine. There is scarcely thirteen months difference in our ages. There is a strong resemblance between him and me, in our exterior, though I hope there is none at all in our minds. This brother was a partner of a gentleman, the father of this girl, at New-York. He was, a long time, nothing better than an apprentice to Mr. Dudley, but he advanced so much in the good graces of his master, that he finally took him into partnership. I did not know till I arrived on the continent, the whole of his misconduct. It appears that he embezzled the property of the house, and fled away with it, and the consequence was, that his quondam master was ruined. I am often mistaken for my brother, to my no small inconvenience: but all this I told you formerly. See what a letter I just now received from this girl.

Craig was one of the most plausible of men. His character was a standing proof of the vanity of physiognomy.[1] There were few men who could refuse their confidence to his open and ingenuous aspect. To this circumstance, perhaps, he owed his ruin. His temptations to deceive were stronger than what are incident to most other men. Deception was so easy a task, that the difficulty lay, not in infusing false opinions respecting him, but in preventing them from being spontaneously imbibed. He contracted habits of imposture imperceptibly. In proportion as he deviated from the practice of truth, he discerned the necessity of extending and systematizing his efforts, and of augmenting the original benignity and attractiveness of his looks, by studied additions. The further he proceeded, the more difficult it was to return. Experience

---

[1] "Vanity of physiognomy": as the French woman's appearance did in Chapter 8 (see notes 8.3–6), Ormond confutes physiognomic assumptions. Although his face engenders a sympathetic response of trust, he is actually a master of disguise, deception, and imposture.

and habit added daily to his speciousness, till at length, the world perhaps might have been searched in vain for his competitor.

He had been introduced to Ormond under the most favorable auspices. He had provided against a danger which he knew to be imminent, by relating his own story as if it were his brother's. He had, however, made various additions to it, serving to aggravate the heinousness of his guilt. This arose partly from policy, and partly from the habit of lying, which was prompted by a fertile invention, and rendered inveterate by incessant exercise. He interwove in his tale, an intrigue between Miss Dudley and his brother. The former was seduced, and this man had employed his skill in chirographical[2] imitation, in composing letters from Miss Dudley to his brother, which sufficiently attested her dishonor. He and his brother, he related, to have met in Jamaica, where the latter died, by which means his personal property and papers came into his possession.

Ormond read the letter which his companion presented to him on this occasion. The papers which Craig had formerly permitted him to inspect, had made him familiar with her hand-writing. The penmanship was, indeed, similar, yet this was written in a spirit not quite congenial with that which had dictated her letters to her lover. But he reflected that the emergency was extraordinary, and that the new scenes through which she had passed, had, perhaps, enabled her to retreave her virtue and enforce it. The picture which she drew of her father's distresses, affected him and his companion very differently. He pondered on it for some time, in silence; he then looked up, and with his usual abruptness said, I suppose you gave her something?

No. I was extremely sorry that it was not in my power. I have nothing but a little trifling silver about me. I have no more at home than will barely suffice to pay my board here, and my expenses to Baltimore. Till I reach there I cannot expect a supply. I was less uneasy I confess, on this account, because I knew you to be equally willing and much more able to afford the relief she asks.

This, Mr. Ormond had predetermined to do. He paused only to deliberate in what manner it could, with most propriety, be done. He was always willing, when he conferred benefits, to conceal the author. He was not displeased when gratitude was misplaced, and readily allowed his instruments to act as if they were principals. He questioned not the veracity of Craig, and was, therefore, desirous to free him from the molestation that was threatened in the way which had been prescribed. He put a note of one hundred dollars into his hand, and enjoined him to send it to the Dudleys that evening, or early the next morning. I am pleased, he added, with the style of this letter: It can be of no service to you; leave it in my possession.

Craig would much rather have thrown it into the fire; but he knew the character of his companion, and was afraid to make any objection to his request. He promised to send, or carry the note, the next morning, before he set out on his intended journey.

This journey was to Baltimore, and was undertaken so soon merely to oblige his friend, who was desirous of remitting to Baltimore a considerable sum in English guineas, and who had been for some time in search of one who might execute this

---

[2] "Chirographical": concerning handwriting, or chirography.

commission with fidelity. The offer of Craig had been joyfully accepted, and next morning had been the time fixed for his departure, a period the most opportune for Craig's designs, that could be imagined.—To return to Miss Dudley.

The sum that remained to her after the discharge of her debts, would quickly be expended. It was no argument of wisdom to lose sight of the future in the oblivion of present care. The time would inevitably come when new resources would be necessary. Every hour brought nearer the period without facilitating the discovery of new expedients. She related the recent adventure to her father. He acquiesced in the propriety of her measures, but the succour that she had thus obtained consoled him but little. He saw how speedily it would again be required, and was hopeless of a like fortunate occurrence.

Some days had elapsed, and Constantia had been so fortunate as to procure some employment. She was thus engaged in the evening when they were surprised by a visit from their landlord. This was an occurrence that foreboded them no good. He entered with abruptness and scarcely noticed the salutations that he received. His bosom swelled with discontent, which seemed ready to be poured out upon his two companions. To the enquiry as to the condition of his health and that of his family, he surlily answered; Nevermind how I am: None the better for my tenants I think. Never was a man so much plagued as I have been; what with one putting me off from time to time: What with another quarrelling about terms, and denying his agreement, and another running away in my debt, I expect nothing but to come to poverty, God help me, at last: but this was the worst of all. I was never before treated so in all my life. I don't know what or when I shall get to the end of my troubles. To be fobbed out of my rent and twenty five dollars into the bargain! It is very strange treatment, I assure you, Mr. Dudley.

What is it you mean? replied that gentleman. You have received your dues, and—

Received my dues, indeed! High enough too! I have received none of my dues. I have been imposed upon. I have been put to very great trouble and expect some compensation. There is no knowing the character of one's tenants. There is nothing but knavery in the world, one would think. I'm sure no man has suffered more by bad tenants than I have. But this is the strangest treatment I ever met with. Very strange indeed Dudley, and I must be paid without delay. To lose my rent and twenty five dollars into the bargain, is too hard. I never met with the equal of it, not I: Besides, I wou'dn't be put to all this trouble for twice the sum.

What does all this mean, Mr. M'Crea? You seem inclined to scold, but I cannot conceive why you came here for that purpose. This behaviour is improper—

No, its very proper, and I want payment of my money. Fifty dollars you owe me. Miss comes to me to pay me my rent as I thought. She brings me a fifty dollar note; I changes it for her, for I thought to be sure, I was quite safe: but, behold, when I sends it to the bank to get the money, they sends me back word that it's forged, and calls on me, before a magistrate to tell them where I got it from. I'm sure I never was so flustered in my life. I would not have such a thing for ten times the sum.

He proceeded to descant on his loss without any interruption from his auditors, whom this intelligence had struck dumb. Mr. Dudley instantly saw the origin, and full extent of this misfortune. He was, nevertheless, calm, and indulged in no invectives against Craig. It is all of a piece, said he: Our ruin is inevitable. Well, then, let it come.

After M'Crea had railed himself weary, he flung out of the house, warning them that, next morning he should distrain[3] for his rent, and, at the same time, sue them for the money that Constance had received in exchange for her note.

Miss Dudley was unable to pursue her task. She laid down her needle, and fixed her eyes upon her father. They had been engaged in earnest discourse when their landlord entered. Now there was a pause of profound silence, till the affectionate Lucy, who sufficiently comprehended this scene, gave vent to her affliction in sobs. Her mistress turned to her:

Cheer up, my Lucy. We shall do well enough my girl. Our state is bad enough, without doubt, but despair will make it worse.

The anxiety that occupied her mind related less to herself, than to her father. He, indeed, in the present instance, was exposed to prosecution. It was he who was answerable for the debt, and whose person would be thrown into durance by the suit that was menaced. The horrors of a prison had not hitherto been experienced, or anticipated. The worst evil that she had imagined was inexpressibly inferior to this. The idea had in it something of terrific and loathsome. The mere supposition of its being possible was not to be endured. If all other expedients should fail, she thought of nothing less than desperate resistance. No. It was better to die than to go to prison.

For a time, she was deserted of her admirable equanimity. This no doubt, was the result of surprise. She had not yet obtained the calmness necessary to deliberation. During this gloomy interval, she would, perhaps, have adopted any scheme, however dismal and atrocious, which her father's despair might suggest. She would not refuse to terminate her own and her father's unfortunate existence, by poison or the chord.

This confusion of mind could not exist long. It gradually gave place to cheerful prospects. The evil perhaps was not without its timely remedy. The person whom she had set out to visit, when her course was diverted by Craig, she once more resolved to apply to; to lay before him, without reserve, her father's situation, to entreat pecuniary succour, and to offer herself as a servant in his family, or in that of any of his friends who stood in need of one. This resolution, in a slight degree, consoled her; but her mind had been too thoroughly disturbed to allow her any sleep during that night.

She equipped herself betimes, and proceeded with a doubting heart to the house of Mr. Melbourne. She was informed that he had risen, but was never to be seen at so early an hour. At nine o'clock he would be disengaged, and she would be admitted. In the present state of her affairs, this delay was peculiarly unwelcome. At breakfast, her suspense and anxieties would not allow her to eat a morsel, and when the hour approached, she prepared herself for a new attempt.

As she went out, she met at the door a person whom she recognized, and whose office she knew to be that of a constable. Constantia had exercised, in her present

---

[3] "Destrain": or distrain, a legal term meaning to seize property for unpaid rent or debts.

narrow sphere, that beneficence which she had formerly exerted in a larger. There was nothing, consistent with her slender means, that she did not willingly perform for the service of others. She had not been sparing of consolation and personal aid in many cases of personal distress that had occurred in her neighbourhood. Hence, as far as she was known, she was reverenced.

The wife of their present visitant had experienced her succour and sympathy, on occasion of the death of a favorite child. The man, notwithstanding his office, was not of a rugged or ungrateful temper. The task that was now imposed upon him, he undertook with extreme reluctance. He was somewhat reconciled to it by the reflection that another might not perform it with that gentleness and lenity which he found in himself a disposition to exercise on all occasions, but particularly on the present.

She easily guessed at his business, and having greeted him with the utmost friendliness, returned with him into the house. She endeavoured to remove the embarrassment that hung about him, but in vain. Having levied what the law very properly calls a distress, he proceeded, after much hesitation, to inform Dudley that he was charged with a message from a Magistrate, summoning him to come forthwith, and account for having a forged bank-note in his possession.

M'Crea had given no intimation of this. The painful surprise that it produced, soon yielded to a just view of this affair. Temporary inconvenience and vexation was all that could be dreaded from it. Mr. Dudley hated to be seen or known. He usually walked out in the dusk of evening, but limited his perambulations to a short space: At all other times, he was obstinately recluse. He was easily persuaded by his daughter to allow her to perform this unwelcome office in his stead. He had not received, nor even seen the note. He would have willingly spared her the mortification of a judicial examination, but he knew that this was unavoidable. Should he comply with this summons himself, his daughter's presence would be equally necessary.

Influenced by these considerations, he was willing that his daughter should accompany the messenger, who was content that they should consult their mutual convenience in this respect. This interview was to her, not without its terrors, but she cherished the hope that it might ultimately conduce to good. She did not foresee the means by which this would be effected, but her heart was lightened by a secret and inexplicable faith in the propitiousness of some event that was yet to occur. This faith was powerfully enforced when she reached the magistrate's door, and found that he was no other than Melbourne, whose succour she intended to solicit. She was speedily ushered, not into his office, but into a private apartment, where he received her alone.

He had been favorably prepossessed with regard to her character by the report of the officer, who, on being charged with the message, had accounted for the regret which he manifested, by dwelling on the merits of Miss Dudley. He behaved with grave civility, requested her to be seated, and accurately scrutinized her appearance. She found herself not deceived in her preconceptions of this gentleman's character, and drew a favorable omen as to the event of this interview, by what had already taken place. He viewed her in silence for some time, and then, in a conciliating tone, said:

It seems to me, madam, as if I had seen you before. Your face, indeed, is of that kind which, when once seen, is not easily forgotten. I know it is a long time since, but I cannot tell when or where. If you will not deem me impertinent, I will venture to ask you to assist my conjectures. Your name as I am informed, is Acworth—I ought to have mentioned that Mr. Dudley on his removal from New-York, among other expedients to obliterate the memory of his former condition, and conceal his poverty from the world, had made this change in his name.[4]

That, indeed, said the lady, is the name, which my father, at present, bears. His real name is Dudley. His abode was formerly in Queen-Street,[5] New-York. Your conjecture, Sir, is not erroneous. This is not the first time we have seen each other. I well recollect your having been at my father's house in the days of his prosperity.

Is it possible? exclaimed Mr. Melbourne, starting from his seat in the first impulse of his astonishment: Are you the daughter of my friend Dudley, by whom I have so often been hospitably entertained. I have heard of his misfortunes, but knew not that he was alive, or in what part of the world he resided.

You are summoned on a very disagreeable affair, but I doubt not you will easily exculpate your father. I am told that he is blind, and that his situation is by no means as comfortable as might be wished. I am grieved that he did not confide in the friendship of those that knew him. What could prompt him to conceal himself?

My father has a proud spirit. It is not yet broken by adversity. He disdains *to beg*, but I must now assume *that office* for his sake. I came hither this morning to lay before you his situation, and to entreat your assistance to save him from a prison. He cannot pay for the poor tenement he occupies, and our few goods are already under distress. He has, likewise, contracted a debt. He is, I suppose, already sued on this account, and must go to gaol unless saved by the interposition of some friend.

It is true, said Melbourne, I yesterday granted a warrant against him at the suit of Malcolm M'Crea. Little did I think that the defendant was Stephen Dudley; but you may dismiss all apprehensions on that score. That affair shall be settled to your father's satisfaction: Meanwhile, we will, if you please, dispatch this unpleasant business respecting a counterfeit note, received in payment from you by this M'Cea.

Miss Dudley satisfactorily explained that affair. She stated the relation in which Craig had formerly stood to her father, and the acts of which he had been guilty. She slightly touched on the distresses which the family had undergone during their abode in this city, and the means by which she had been able to preserve her father from want. She mentioned the circumstances which compelled her to seek his charity as the last resource, and the casual encounter with Craig, by which she was for the present diverted from that design. She laid before him a copy of the letter she had written, and explained the result in the gift of the note which now appeared to be a

---

[4] "Acworth … change in his name": the narrator Sophia now explains that the Dudleys have been living under an assumed name because of the self-imposed shame that led Dudley to leave New York and isolate himself in Chapter 2, after Craig's initial embezzlement. For the description of Dudley's self-isolation and shame, see note 2.1.

[5] "Queen-Street": after the Revolution, many British street names in Manhattan were changed to remove monarchical associations. Queen Street is now Pearl Street. Unsurprisingly, Dudley lived in a wealthy mercantile neighborhood.

counterfeit. She concluded with stating her present views, and soliciting him to receive her into his family, in quality of servant, or use his interest with some of his friends to procure a provision of this kind. This tale was calculated deeply to affect a man of Mr. Melbourne's humanity.

No, said he, I cannot listen to such a request. My inclination is bounded by my means. These will not allow me to place you in an independent situation; but I will do what I can. With your leave, I will introduce you to my wife, in your true character. Her good sense will teach her to set a just value on your friendship. There is no disgrace in earning your subsistence by your own industry. She and her friends will furnish you with plenty of materials, but if there ever be a deficiency, look to me for a supply.

Constantia's heart overflowed at this declaration. Her silence was more eloquent than any words could have been. She declined an immediate introduction to his wife, and withdrew, but not till her new friend had forced her to accept some money.

Place it to account, said he. It is merely paying you before hand, and discharging a debt at the time when it happens to be most useful to the creditor.

To what entire and incredible reverses is the tenor of human life subject. A short minute shall effect a transition from a state utterly destitute of hope, to a condition where all is serene and abundant. The path, which we employ all our exertions to shun, is often found, upon trial, to be the true road to prosperity.

Constantia retired from this interview with an heart bounding with exultation. She related to her father all that had happened. He was pleased on her account, but the detection of his poverty by Melbourne was the parent of new mortification. His only remaining hope relative to himself, was that he should die in his obscurity, whereas, it was probable that his old acquaintance would trace him to his covert. This prognostic filled him with the deepest inquietude, and all the reasonings of his daughter were insufficient to appease him.

Melbourne made his appearance in the afternoon. He was introduced, by Constantia, to her father. Mr. Dudley's figure was emaciated, and his features corroded by his ceaseless melancholy. His blindness produced in them a woeful and wildering expression. His dress betokened his penury, and was in unison with the meanness of his habitation and furniture. The visitant was struck with the melancholy contrast, which these appearances exhibited, to the joyousness and splendour that he had formerly witnessed.

Mr. Dudley received the salutations of his guest with an air of embarrassment and dejection. He resigned to his daughter the task of sustaining the conversation, and excused himself from complying with the urgent invitations of Melbourne, while at the same time, he studiously forbore all expressions tending to encourage any kind of intercourse between them.

The guest came with a message from his wife, who intreated Miss Dudley's company to tea with her that evening, adding that she should be entirely alone. It was impossible to refuse compliance with this request. She cheerfully assented, and, in the evening, was introduced to Mrs. Melbourne, by her husband.

Constantia found in this lady nothing that called for reverence or admiration, though she could not deny her some portion of esteem. The impression which her own appearance and conversation made upon her entertainer, was much more powerful and favorable. A consciousness of her own worth, and disdain of the malevolence of fortune, perpetually shone forth in her behaviour. It was modelled by a sort of mean between presumption on the one hand, and humility on the other. She claimed no more than what was justly due to her, but she claimed no less. She did not soothe our vanity nor fascinate our pity by diffident reserves and flutterings. Neither did she disgust by arrogant negligence, and uncircumspect loquacity.

At parting, she received commissions in the way of her profession, which supplied her with abundant and profitable employment. She abridged her visit on her father's account, and parted from her new friend just early enough to avoid meeting with Ormond, who entered the house a few minutes after she had left it.

What pity, said Melbourne to him, you did not come a little sooner. You pretend to be a judge of beauty. I should like to have heard your opinion of a face that has just left us.

Describe it, said the other.

That is beyond my capacity. Complexion, and hair, and eyebrows may be painted, but these are of no great value in the present case. It is in the putting them together, that nature has here shewn her skill, and not in the structure of each of the parts, individually considered. Perhaps you may at some time meet each other here. If a lofty fellow like you, now, would mix a little common sense with his science, this girl might hope for an husband, and her father for a natural protector.

Are they in search of one or the other?

I cannot say they are. Nay, I imagine they would bear any imputation with more patience than that, but certain I am, they stand in need of them. How much would it be to the honor of a man like you rioting in wealth, to divide it with one, lovely and accomplished as this girl is, and struggling with indigence.

Melbourne then related the adventure of the morning. It was easy for Ormond to perceive that this was the same person of whom he already had some knowledge—but there were some particulars in the narrative that excited surprise. A note had been received from Craig, at the first visit in the evening, and this note was for no more than fifty dollars. This did not exactly tally with the information received from Craig. But this note was forged. Might not this girl mix a little imposture with her truth? Who knows her temptations to hypocrisy? It might have been a present from another quarter, and accompanied with no very honorable conditions.[6] Exquisite wretch! Those whom honesty will not let live, must be knaves. Such is the alternative offered by the wisdom of society.

He listened to the tale with apparent indifference. He speedily shifted the conversation to new topics, and put an end to his visit sooner than ordinary.

---

[6] "A present … accompanied with no very honourable conditions": in other words, Ormond wonders whether the money was payment for prostitution.

Chapter XII

I KNOW no task more arduous than a just delineation of the character of Ormond.[1] To scrutinize and ascertain our own principles are abundantly difficult. To exhibit these principles to the world with absolute sincerity, can scarcely be expected. We are prompted to conceal and to feign by a thousand motives; but truly to pourtray the motives, and relate the actions of another, appears utterly impossible. The attempt, however, if made with fidelity and diligence, is not without its use.

---

[1] "The character of Ormond": with this introduction, the narrator Sophia begins a portrait of the novel's title character.

Brown reuses the name Ormond throughout his fiction-writing career. In the eighteenth century Ormond (or Ormonde) is associated with the aristocratic Irish Butler family, titled Earls and Dukes of Ormond, with interruptions, from 1328 to 1715. By the 1790s, the best-known Ormond was James Butler, 2nd Duke of Ormond (1665–1745), often praised as a rebellious hero in popular writing. This Ormond took part in the failed (Catholic) Jacobite rebellion or "rising" in 1715 and subsequently fled into exile at Avignon, then a sovereign territory near the Mediterranean in France. His status as a failed conspirator caused the Duke of Ormond title to be attainted and declared forfeit or suspended after 1715. Brown refers to this family in Chapter 26 (note 26.4) and in several other fictions. The female protagonist of Brown's tale "A Lesson on Sensibility" (*Weekly Magazine*, May 19, 1798) is presented as a Butler-Ormond, "a daughter of a family more distinguished for their pride of birth than their wealth. The Butlers claimed an alliance with the House of Ormond." Similarly, a character in the only surviving fragment of Brown's first novel *Sky-Walk* (completed March 1798, but never printed and subsequently lost) is named "Ormond Courtney" and the related name "Orme" is important in Brown's 1803–1806 *Historical Sketches*.

Two other more contemporary and topical references may also have particular relevance for this novel:

Brown was likely familiar with the widely publicized case of American-born imposter James Molesworth Hubbard (or Hobart; c. 1760s–1793), who presented himself in England under several aliases, notably Duke of Ormond, in 1790–1792. Hubbard was tried and executed for his impostures in 1793, and numerous versions of his story were printed in newspaper accounts in England and the U.S., or in book form through the rest of the 1790s. See for example John Colley's *Life and Adventures of James Molesworth Hobart (alias Lord Massey, alias Duke of Ormond)*, etc. (London: I. Hawkins, 1793). Hubbard's case, like the contemporary U.S. notoriety of swindler and scam artist Stephen Burroughs, may resonate in the novel's character Craig.

Second, given the emphasis the novel will increasingly place on female same-sex friendship, cross-dressing, and collectivity, it seems likely that Brown was familiar with Lady Eleanor Butler-Ormond (1739–1829) and Sarah Ponsonby (1755–1832), a couple who fled their aristocratic Irish families in 1778 (after being previously separated by them) to live together romantically in a Welsh cottage. The couple became Romantic-era cultural celebrities as the "Ladies of Llangollen" (their village in Wales) and received notable visitors, from Edmund Burke to Percy Shelley, well into the nineteenth century. British writer Anna Seward (1747–1809) made her poem praising the couple the title-piece of her collection *Llangollen Vale, with Other Poems* (London: G. Sael, 1796). Articles on the couple appeared in British and U.S. newspapers as early as 1790, with titles such as "Extraordinary Female Affection" (New York *Daily Gazette*, October 11, 1790); "Men Haters" (*Connecticut Journal*, November 17, 1790); or "Anecdotes of Miss Butler and Miss Ponsonby" (*Weekly Visitor, or Ladies' Miscellany*, August 25, 1804).

To comprehend the whole truth, with regard to the character and conduct of another, may be denied to any human being, but different observers will have, in their pictures, a greater or less portion of this truth. No representation will be wholly false, and some though not perfectly, may yet be considerably exempt from error.

Ormond was, of all mankind, the being most difficult and most deserving to be studied. A fortunate concurrence of incidents has unveiled his actions to me with more distinctness than to any other. My knowledge is far from being absolute, but I am conscious of a kind of duty, first to my friend, and secondly to mankind, to impart the knowledge I possess.[2]

I shall omit to mention the means by which I became acquainted with his character, nor shall I enter, at this time, into every part of it. His political projects are likely to possess an extensive influence on the future condition of this western world.[3] I do not conceive myself authorized to communicate a knowledge of his schemes, which I gained, in some sort, surreptitiously, or at least, by means of which he was not apprized. I shall merely explain the maxims by which he was accustomed to regulate his private deportment.

No one could entertain loftier conceptions of human capacity than Ormond, but he carefully distinguished between men, in the abstract, and men as they are.[4] The former were beings to be impelled, by the breath of accident, in a right or a wrong

---

[2] "The knowledge I possess": in the chapter's first four paragraphs, narrator Sophia Courtland develops an elaborate justification for the portrait that follows. Sophia first noted in her preface "To I. E. Rosenberg" that the portrait is drawn from secret sources and cannot be "unerring and compleat" (see note 0.4). This repeated insistence on the inscrutable, secretive nature of both the portrait's object (Ormond) and the portrait's sources and motivation (the narrator's sources and motivations) reminds the reader that this narrative framing is a significant factor in evaluating Sophia's perspective on Ormond and the larger tale she is shaping. For more on implications of the novel's narrative structure, see the Introduction.

[3] "Political projects ... this western world": Sophia uses suggestive language that, for contemporary readers, clearly associates Ormond with 1790s anxieties about the Illuminati. These associations will be emphasized repeatedly, for example when she alludes again to Ormond's "projects ... instruments and coadjutors" near the end of this chapter or in Chapter 18; see note 18.1. The Illuminati were originally a small Bavarian and later German group dedicated to progressive ideals but by the late 1790s conservative propagandists had inflated the group into a fearsome international secret society ostensibly plotting to overthrow church and state institutions throughout the Atlantic world. In 1797–1801, at the time of the novel's appearance, the Illuminati scare was a major, ongoing episode of political fearmongering and scapegoating used by opponents of the French Revolution (and, in the U.S., by political and clerical supporters of the ruling Federalist Party) to demonize their opponents as dangerous, godless radicals. For more on the Illuminati scare, see the discussion and selections in Related Texts.

[4] "Men as they are": Sophia associates Ormond with unconventional ideas about the status quo ("things as they are") by echoing a phrase commonly associated in the 1790s with Woldwinite radical-democratic narratives. *Things As They Are* was the original title of Godwin's radical novel of social critique *Caleb Williams* (1794). *Man As He Is* (1792) was the title of radical Robert Bage's first novel, and *Man As He Is Not* the subtitle of his second novel *Hermsprong* (1796). These are all key literary and intellectual sources for Brown and his New York circle. Here, however, Sophia's

road, but whatever direction they should receive, it was the property of their nature to persist in it. Now this impulse had been given. No single being could rectify the error. It was the business of the wise man to form a just estimate of things, but not to attempt, by individual efforts, so chimerical an enterprize as that of promoting the happiness of mankind. Their condition was out of the reach of a member of a corrupt society to controul. A mortal poison pervaded the whole system by means of which every thing received was converted into bane and purulence. Efforts designed to ameliorate the condition of an individual, were sure of answering a contrary purpose. The principles of the social machine must be rectified, before men can be beneficially active. Our motives may be neutral or beneficent, but our actions tend merely to the production of evil.

The idea of total forbearance was not less delusive. Man could not be otherwise than an cause of perpetual operation and efficacy. He was part of a machine, and as such had not power to withhold his agency. Contiguousness to other parts, that is, to other men, was all that was necessary to render him a powerful concurrent. What then was the conduct incumbent on him? Whether he went forward, or stood still, whether his motives were malignant, or kind, or indifferent, the mass of evil was equally and necessarily augmented. It did not follow from these preliminaries that virtue and duty were terms without a meaning, but they require us to promote our own happiness and not the happiness of others. Not because the former end is intrinsically preferable, not because the happiness of others is unworthy of primary consideration, but because it is not to be attained. Our power in the present state of things is subjected to certain limits. A man may reasonably hope to accomplish his end, when he proposes nothing but his own good: Any other point is inaccessible.

He must not part with benevolent desire: This is a constituent of happiness. He sees the value of general and particular felicity; he sometimes paints it to his fancy, but if this be rarely done, it is in consequence of virtuous sensibility, which is afflicted on observing that his pictures are reversed in the real state of mankind. A wise man will relinquish the pursuit of general benefit, but not the desire of that benefit, or the perception of that in which this benefit consists, because these are among the ingredients of virtue and the sources of his happiness.

Principles, in the looser sense of that term, have little influence on practice. Ormond was, for the most part, governed, like others, by the influences of education and present circumstances. It required a vigilant discernment to distinguish whether the stream of his actions flowed from one or the other. His income was large, and he managed it nearly on the same principles as other men. He thought himself entitled to all the splendour and ease which it would purchase, but his taste was elaborate and correct. He gratified his love of the beautiful, because the sensations it afforded were

---

implication is that Ormond's ideas are dangerous and subversive of right order. The following paragraphs detailing his ideas on "the principles of the social machine," "benevolent desire," conventional "etiquette" and titles, and "sincerity," will all echo Woldwinite keywords and passages from Godwin's *Enquiry Concerning Political Justice* (1793) in a similar disapproving manner. For more on Brown's use of Woldwinite ideas, see the Introduction and Related Texts.

pleasing, but made no sacrifices to the love of distinction. He gave no expensive en-tertainments for the sake of exciting the admiration of stupid gazers, or the flattery or envy of those who shared them. Pompous equipage and retinue were modes of ap-propriating the esteem of mankind which he held in profound contempt. The garb of his attendants was fashioned after the model suggested by his imagination, and not in compliance with the dictates of custom.

He treated with systematic negligence, the etiquette that regulates the intercourse of persons of a certain class. He, every where, acted, in this respect, as if he were alone, or among familiar associates. The very appellations of Sir, and Madam, and Mister, were, in his apprehension, servile and ridiculous, and as custom or law had annexed no penalty to the neglect of these, he conformed to his own opinions. It was easier for him to reduce his notions of equality to practice than for most others. To level himself with others was an act of condescension and not of arrogance. It was requi-site to descend rather than to rise; a task the most easy, if we regard the obstacles flowing from the prejudice of mankind, but far most difficult, if the motives of the agent be considered.

That in which he chiefly placed his boast, was his sincerity. To this he refused no sacrifice. In consequence of this, his deportment was disgusting to weak minds, by a certain air of ferocity and haughty negligence. He was without the attractions of can-dour, because he regarded not the happiness of others, but in subservience to his sin-cerity. Hence it was natural to suppose that the character of this man was easily understood. He affected to conceal nothing. No one appeared more exempt from the instigations of vanity. He set light by the good opinions of others, had no compas-sion for their prejudices, and hazarded assertions in their presence which he knew would be, in the highest degree, shocking to their previous notions. They might take it, he would say, as they list. Such were his conceptions, and the last thing he would give up was the use of his tongue. It was his way to give utterance to the suggestions of his understanding. If they were disadvantageous to him in the opinions of others, it was well. He did not wish to be regarded in any light, but the true one. He was contented to be rated by the world, at his just value. If they esteemed him for quali-ties he did not possess, was he wrong in rectifying their mistake: But in reality, if they valued him for that to which he had no claim, and which he himself considered as contemptible, he must naturally desire to shew them their error, and forfeit that praise which, in his own opinion, was a badge of infamy.

In listening to his discourse, no one's claim to sincerity appeared less questionable. A somewhat different conclusion would be suggested by a survey of his actions. In early youth he discovered in himself a remarkable facility in imitating the voice and gestures of others.[5] His memory was eminently retentive, and these qualities would

---

[5] "Imitating the voices and gestures of others": Ormond's skill in ventriloquism and pantomime re-calls the character Carwin in Brown's then-recently published *Wieland* (September 1798). Though there is no direct link, the similarity of their attributes and descriptions suggests that Ormond may be considered as an older Carwin or another version of the potentials associated with Carwin.

have rendered his career, in the theatrical profession, illustrious, had not his condition raised him above it. His talents were occasionally exerted for the entertainment of convivial parties, and private circles, but he gradually withdrew from such scenes, as he advanced in age, and devoted his abilities to higher purposes.

His aversion to duplicity had flowed from experience of its evils. He had frequently been made its victim; In consequence of this his temper had become suspicious, and he was apt to impute deceit on occasions when others, of no inconsiderable sagacity, were abundantly disposed to confidence. One transaction had occurred in his life, in which the consequences of being misled by false appearances were of the utmost moment to his honor and safety. The usual mode of solving his doubts, he deemed insufficient, and the eagerness of his curiosity tempted him, for the first time, to employ, for this end, his talents at imitation. He therefore assumed a borrowed character and guise, and performed his part with so much skill as fully to accomplish his design. He whose mask would have secured him from all other attempts, was thus taken through an avenue which his caution had overlooked, and the hypocrisy of his pretensions unquestionably ascertained.

Perhaps, in a comprehensive view, the success of this expedient was unfortunate. It served to recommend this method of encountering deceit, and informed him of the extent of those powers which are so liable to be abused. A subtlety much inferior to Ormond's would suffice to recommend this mode of action. It was defensible on no other principle than necessity. The treachery of mankind compelled him to resort to it. If they should deal in a manner as upright and explicit as himself, it would be superfluous. But since they were in the perpetual use of stratagems and artifices, it was allowable, he thought, to wield the same arms.

It was easy to perceive, however, that this practice was recommended to him by other considerations. He was delighted with the power it conferred. It enabled him to gain access, as if by supernatural means, to the privacy of others, and baffle their profoundest contrivances to hide themselves from his view. It flattered him with the possession of something like Omniscience. It was besides an art, in which, as in others, every accession of skill, was a source of new gratification. Compared with this the performance of the actor is the sport of children. This profession he was accustomed to treat with merciless ridicule, and no doubt, some of his contempt arose from a secret comparison, between the theatrical species of imitation and his own. He blended in his own person the functions of poet and actor, and his dramas were not fictitious but real. The end that he proposed was not the amusement of a play-house mob. His were scenes in which hope and fear exercised a genuine influence, and in which was maintained that resemblance to truth, so audaciously and grossly violated on the stage.

It is obvious how many singular conjunctures must have grown out of this propensity. A mind of uncommon energy like Ormond's, which had occupied a wide sphere of action, and which could not fail of confederating its efforts with those of minds like itself, must have given birth to innumerable incidents, not unworthy to be exhibited by the most eloquent historian. It is not my business to relate any of these. The fate of Miss Dudley is intimately connected with his. What influence he obtained over her destiny, in consequence of this dexterity, will appear in the sequel.

It arose from these circumstances, that no one was more impenetrable than Ormond, though no one's real character seemed more easily discerned. The projects that occupied his attention were diffused over an ample space; and his instruments and coadjutors were culled from a field, whose bounds were those of the civilized world. To the vulgar eye, therefore, he appeared a man of speculation and seclusion, and was equally inscrutable in his real and assumed characters. In his real, his intents were too lofty and comprehensive, as well as too assiduously shrowded from profane inspection, for them to scan. In the latter, appearances were merely calculated to mislead and not to enlighten.

In his youth he had been guilty of the usual excesses incident to his age and character. These had disappeared and yielded place to a more regular and circumspect system of action. In the choice of his pleasures he still exposed himself to the censure of the world. Yet there was more of grossness and licentiousness in the expression of his tenets, than in the tenets themselves. So far as temperance regards the maintainance of health, no man adhered to its precepts with more fidelity, but he esteemed some species of connection with the other sex as venial, which mankind in general are vehement in condemning.

In his intercourse with women, he deemed himself superior to the allurements of what is called love. His inferences were drawn from a consideration of the physical propensities of an human being. In his scale of enjoyments the gratifications which belonged to these, were placed at the bottom. Yet he did not entirely disdain them, and when they could be purchased without the sacrifice of superior advantages, they were sufficiently acceptable.

His mistake on this head was the result of his ignorance. He had not hitherto met with a female worthy of his confidence. Their views were limited and superficial, or their understandings were betrayed by the tenderness of their hearts. He found in them no intellectual energy,[6] no superiority to what he accounted vulgar prejudice, and no affinity with the sentiments which he cherished with most devotion. Their presence had been capable of exciting no emotion which he did not quickly discover to be vague and sensual; and the uniformity of his experience at length instilled into him a belief, that the intellectual constitution of females was essentially defective. He denied the reality of that passion which claimed a similitude or sympathy of minds as one of its ingredients.[7]

---

[6] "Intellectual energy": one of Wollstonecraft's chief complaints in the *Vindication* about the social constraints placed on women is that it limited the development of their "power of mind." Readers will recall that intellectual energy was the chief notable feature of the mysterious French-speaking woman whose features were observed and interpreted in Chapter 8.

[7] "Denied the reality of that passion ... ingredients": in other words, love. Sophia's description of Ormond's skepticism about love and her comments on its relation to his erotic-romantic relations in the following chapters alludes to Godwin's famous critique of marriage in the *Enquiry Concerning Political Justice*, and to conservative accusations that he hypocritically violated his principles by marrying Mary Wollstonecraft in 1797. For more on Brown's presentation of Woldwinite ideas on women's lives and the institution of marriage in *Alcuin, Ormond*, and other writings, see Introduction and Related Texts.

Chapter XIII

HE resided in New-York some time before he took up his abode in Philadelphia. He had some pecuniary concerns with a merchant of that place. He occasionally frequented his house, finding, in the society which it afforded him, scope for amusing speculation, and opportunities of gaining a species of knowledge of which at that time he stood in need. There was one daughter of the family who of course constituted a member of the domestic circle.

Helena Cleves[1] was endowed with every feminine and fascinating quality. Her features were modified by the most transient sentiments and were the seat of a softness at all times blushful and bewitching. All those graces of symmetry, smoothness and lustre, which assemble in the imagination of the painter when he calls from the bosom of her natal deep, the Paphian divinity,[2] blended their perfections in the shape, complexion and hair of this lady. Her voice was naturally thrilling and melodious, and her utterance clear and distinct. A musical education had added to all these advantages the improvements of art, and no one could swim in the dance with such airy and transporting elegance.

It is obvious to enquire whether her mental, were, in any degree, on a level with her exterior accomplishments. Should you listen to her talk, you would be liable to be deceived in this respect. Her utterance was so just, her phrases so happy, and her language so copious and correct, that the hearer was apt to be impressed with an ardent veneration of her abilities, but the truth is, she was calculated to excite emotions more voluptuous than dignified. Her presence produced a trance of the senses rather than an illumination of the soul. It was a topic of wonder how she should have so carefully separated the husk from the kernel, and be so absolute a mistress of the vehicle of knowledge, with so slender means of supplying it: Yet it is difficult to judge but from comparison. To say that Helena Cleves was silly or ignorant would be hatefully unjust. Her understanding bore no disadvantageous comparison with that of the majority of her sex, but when placed in competition with that of some eminent females or of Ormond, it was exposed to the risque of contempt.

This lady and Ormond were exposed to mutual examination. The latter was not unaffected by the radiance that environed this girl, but her true character was easily discovered, and he was accustomed to regard her merely as an object charming to the

---

[1] "Helena Cleves": the name evokes associations with cloistered lives, aristocratic passions, and the tragic results of duplicity by echoing the historical figure Anne of Cleves (1515–1557), fourth wife of Henry VIII, and Madame de La Fayette's important historical novel, *La Princesse de Clèves* (1678).

[2] "Paphian divinity": Aphrodite or Venus, goddess of love. Venus is the "Paphian divinity" because her cult was centered at a temple at Paphos, on the island Cyprus in the eastern Mediterranean. By extension, a "paphian" is a prostitute or promiscuous woman and the adjective "paphian" used alone means "relating to love and sexual desire; especially … engaging in illicit sexual acts, prostitution, etc." (*OED*).

senses. His attention to her was dictated by this principle. When she sung or talked, it was not unworthy of the strongest mind to be captivated with her music and her elocution: But these were the limits which he set to his gratifications. That sensations of a different kind, never ruffled his tranquility must not be supposed, but he too accurately estimated their consequences to permit himself to indulge them.

Unhappily the lady did not exercise equal fortitude. During a certain interval Ormond's visits were frequent, and she insensibly contracted for him somewhat more than reverence. The tenour of his discourse was little adapted to cherish her hopes. In the declaration of his opinions he was never withheld by scruples of decorum, or a selfish regard to his own interest. His matrimonial tenets were harsh and repulsive. A woman of keener penetration would have predicted from them, the disappointment of her wishes, but Helena's mind was uninured to the discussion of logical points and the tracing of remote consequences. His presence inspired feelings which would not permit her to bestow an impartial attention on his arguments. It is not enough to say that his reasonings failed to convince her: The combined influence of passion and an unenlightened understanding hindered her from fully comprehending them. All she gathered was a vague conception of something magnificent and vast in his character.

Helena was destined to experience the vicissitudes of fortune. Her father died suddenly and left her without provision. She was compelled to accept the invitations of a kinswoman, and live, in some sort, a life of dependance.[3] She was not qualified to sustain this reverse of fortune, in a graceful manner. She could not bear the diminution of her customary indulgences, and to these privations were added the inquietudes of a passion which now began to look with an aspect of hopelessness.

These events happened in the absence of Ormond. On his return he made himself acquainted with them. He saw the extent of this misfortune to a woman of Helena's character, but knew not in what manner it might be effectually obviated. He esteemed it incumbent on him to pay her a visit in her new abode. This token at least of respect or remembrance his duty appeared to prescribe.

This visit was unexpected by the lady. Surprise is the enemy of concealment. She was oppressed with a sense of her desolate situation. She was sitting in her own apartment in a museful posture. Her fancy was occupied with the image of Ormond, and her tears were flowing at the thought of their eternal separation, when he entered softly and unperceived by her. A tap upon the shoulder was the first signal of his presence. So critical an interview could not fail of unveiling the true state of the lady's heart. Ormond's suspicions were excited, and these suspicions speedily led to an explanation.

Ormond retired to ruminate on this discovery. I have already mentioned his sentiments respecting love. His feelings relative to Helena did not contradict his principles, yet the image which had formerly been exquisite in loveliness, had now

---

[3] "Life of dependance": like Constantia, Helen suffers a loss of status due to patriarchal insecurity, but unlike Constantia she cannot bear to forgo the comforts of a genteel lifestyle or to labor directly for wages.

suddenly gained unspeakable attractions. This discovery had set the question in a new light. It was of sufficient importance to make him deliberate. He reasoned somewhat in the following manner.

Marriage is absurd. This flows from the general and incurable imperfection of the female character. No woman can possess that worth which would induce me to enter into this contract, and bind myself, without power of revoking the decree, to her society. This opinion may possibly be erroneous, but it is undoubtedly true with respect to Helena, and the uncertainty of the position in general, will increase the necessity of caution in the present case. That woman may exist whom I should not fear to espouse. This is not her. Some accident may cause our meeting. Shall I then disable myself, by an irrevocable obligation, from profiting by so auspicious an occurrence?

This girl's society was to be enjoyed in one of two ways. Should he consult his inclination there was little room for doubt. He had never met with one more highly qualified for that species of intercourse which he esteemed rational. No man more abhored the votaries of licentiousness.[4] Nothing was more detestable to him than a mercenary alliance. Personal fidelity and the existence of that passion, of which he had, in the present case, the good fortune to be the object, were indispensible in his scheme. The union was indebted for its value on the voluntariness with which it was formed, and the entire acquiescence of the judgment of both parties in its rectitude. Dissimulation and artifice were wholly foreign to the success of his project. If the lady thought proper to assent to his proposal, it was well. She did so because assent was more eligible than refusal.

She would, no doubt, prefer marriage. She would deem it more conducive to happiness. This was an error. This was an opinion, his reasons for which he was at liberty to state to her; at least it was justifiable in refusing to subject himself to loathsome and impracticable obligations. Certain inconveniences attended women who set aside, on these occasions, the sanction of law, but these were imaginary. They owed their force to the errors of the sufferer. To annihilate them, it was only necessary to reason justly, but allowing these inconveniences their full weight and an indestructible existence, it was but a choice of evils. Were they worse in this lady's apprehension, than an eternal and hopeless separation? Perhaps they were. If so, she would make her election accordingly. He did nothing but lay the conditions before her. If his scheme should obtain the concurrence of her unbiassed judgment he should rejoice. If not, her conduct should be uninfluenced by him. Whatever way she should decide, he would assist her in adhering to her decision, but would, meanwhile, furnish her with the materials of a right decision.

This determination was singular. Many will regard it as incredible. No man, it will be thought can put this deception on himself, and imagine that there was genuine

---

[4] "Votaries of licentiousness … mercenary alliance": in other words prostitution, direct payment for sexual favors. Ormond rejects marriage, but also impersonal encounters with prostitutes. He prefers to support a mistress in a more lasting arrangement.

beneficence in a scheme like this. Would the lady more consult her happiness by adopting than by rejecting it? There can be but one answer. It cannot be supposed that Ormond, in stating this proposal, acted with all the impartiality that he pretended; that he did not employ falacious exaggerations and ambiguous expedients; that he did not seize every opportunity of triumphing over her weakness, and building his success rather on the illusions of her heart than the convictions of her understanding. His conclusions were specious but delusive, and were not uninfluenced by improper byasses; but of this he himself was scarcely conscious, and it must be, at least, admitted that he acted with scrupulous sincerity.

An uncommon degree of skill was required to introduce this topic so as to avoid the imputation of an insult. This scheme was little in unison with all her preconceived notions. No doubt, the irksomeness of her present situation, the allurements of luxury and ease, which Ormond had to bestow, and the revival of her ancient independance and security, had some share in dictating her assent.

Her concurrence was by no means cordial and unhesitating. Remorse and the sense of dishonor pursued her to her retreat, though chosen with a view of shunning their intrusions, and it was only when the reasonings and blandishments of her lover were exhibited, that she was lulled into temporary tranquility.

She removed to Philadelphia.[5] Here she enjoyed all the consolations of opulence. She was mistress of a small but elegant mansion. She possessed all the means of solitary amusement, and frequently enjoyed the company of Ormond. These however were insufficient to render her happy. Certain reflections might, for a time, be repressed or divested of their sting, but they insinuated themselves at every interval, and imparted to her mind, a hue of dejection from which she could not entirely relieve herself.

She endeavoured to acquire a relish for the pursuits of literature, by which her lonely hours might be cheered; but of this, even in the blithsomeness and serenity of her former days, she was incapable. Much more so now when she was the prey of perpetual inquietude. Ormond perceived this change, not without uneasiness. All his efforts to reconcile her to her present situation were fruitless. They produced a momentary effect upon her. The softness of her temper and her attachment to him, would, at his bidding, restore her to vivacity and ease, but the illumination seldom endured longer than his presence, and the novelty of some amusement which he had furnished her.

At his next visit, perhaps, he would find that a new task awaited him. She indulged herself in no recriminations or invectives. She could not complain that her lover had deceived her. She had voluntarily and deliberately accepted the conditions prescribed. She regarded her own disposition to repine as a species of injustice. She laid no claim to an increase of tenderness. She hinted not a wish for a change of situation:

---

[5] "She removed to Philadelphia": like Constantia, Helena has suffered a loss of status and family wealth after a father's mercantile failure in New York, and similarly has moved to Philadelphia in a manner calculated to disguise perceived shame or dishonor.

yet she was unhappy. Tears stole into her eyes, and her thoughts wandered into gloomy reverie, at moments when least aware of their reproach, and least willing to indulge them.

Was a change to be desired? Yes; provided that change was equally agreeable to Ormond, and should be seriously proposed by him, of this she had no hope. As long as his accents rung in her ears, she even doubted whether it were to be wished. At any rate, it was impossible to gain his approbation to it. Her destiny was fixed. It was better than the cessation of all intercourse, yet her heart was a stranger to all permanent tranquility.

Her manners were artless and ingenuous. In company with Ormond her heart was perfectly unveiled. He was her divinity to whom every sentiment was visible, and to whom she spontaneously uttered what she thought, because the employment was pleasing; because he listened with apparent satisfaction; and because, in fine, it was the same thing to speak and to think in his presence. There was no inducement to conceal from him the most evanescent and fugitive ideas.

Ormond was not an inattentive or indifferent spectator of those appearances. His friend was unhappy. She shrunk aghast from her own reproaches and the contumelies of the world. This morbid sensibility he had endeavoured to cure, but hitherto in vain. What was the amount of her unhappiness? Her spirits had formerly been gay, but her gaiety was capable of yielding place to soul-ravishing and solemn tenderness. Her sedateness was, at those times, the offspring not of reflection but of passion. There still remained much of her former self. He was seldom permitted to witness more than the traces of sorrow. In answer to his enquiries, she, for the most part, described sensations that were gone, and which she flattered himself and him would never return; but this hope was always doomed to disappointment. Solitude infallibly conjured up the ghost which had been laid, and it was plain that argument was no adequate remedy for this disease.

How far would time alleviate its evils? When the novelty of her condition should disappear, would she not regard it with other eyes? By being familiar with contempt, it will lose its sting; but is that to be wished? Must not the character be thoroughly depraved, before the scorn of our neighbours shall become indifferent? Indifference, flowing from a sense of justice, and a persuasion that our treatment is unmerited, is characteristic of the noblest minds, but indifference to obloquy[6] because we are habituated to it, is a token of peculiar baseness. This therefore was a remedy to be ardently deprecated.

He had egregiously over-rated the influence of truth and his own influence. He had hoped that his victory was permanent. In order to the success of truth, he was apt to imagine, that nothing was needful but opportunities for a compleat exhibition of it. They that enquire and reason with sufficient deliberateness and caution, must inevitably accomplish their end. These maxims were confuted in the present case. He had formed no advantageous conceptions of Helena's capacity. His aversion to

---

[6] "Obloquy": slander, insults, verbal abuse.

matrimony arose from those conceptions, but experience had shewn him that his conclusions, unfavorable as they were, had fallen short of the truth. Convictions, which he had conceived her mind to be sufficiently strong to receive and retain, were proved to have made no other, than a momentary impression. Hence his objections to ally himself to a mind inferior to his own were strengthened rather than diminished. But he could not endure the thought of being instrumental to her misery.

Marriage was an efficacious remedy, but he could not as yet bring himself to regard the aptitude of this cure as a subject of doubt. The idea of separation sometimes occurred to him. He was not unapprehensive of the influence of time and absence, in curing the most vehement passion, but to this expedient the lady could not be reconciled. He knew her too well to believe that she would willingly adopt it. But the only obstacle to this scheme did not flow from the lady's opposition. He would probably have found upon experiment as strong an aversion to adopt it in himself as in her.

It was easy to see the motives by which he would be likely to be swayed into a change of principles. If marriage were the only remedy, the frequent repetition of this truth must bring him insensibly to doubt the rectitude of his determinations against it. He deeply reflected on the consequences which marriage involves. He scrutinized with the utmost accuracy, the character of his friend, and surveyed it in all its parts. Inclination could not fail of having some influence on his opinions. The charms of this favorite object tended to impair the clearness of his view, and extenuate or conceal her defects. He entered on the enumeration of her errors with reluctance. Her happiness had it been wholly disconnected with his own, might have had less weight in the ballance, but now, every time the scales were suspended, this consideration acquired new weight.

Most men are influenced, in the formation of this contract, by regards purely physical. They are incapable of higher views. They regard with indifference every tie that binds them to their contemporaries, or to posterity. Mind has no part in the motives that guide them. They chuse a wife as they chuse any household moveable, and when the irritation of the senses has subsided, the attachment that remains is the offspring of habit.

Such were not Ormond's modes of thinking. His creed was of too extraordinary a kind not to merit explication. The terms of this contract were, in his eyes, iniquitous and absurd. He could not think with patience of a promise which no time could annul, which pretended to ascertain contingencies and regulate the future. To forego the liberty of chusing his companion, and bind himself to associate with one whom he despised, to raise to his own level one whom nature had irretrievably degraded; to avow, and persist in his adherence to a falsehood, palpable and loathsome to his understanding; to affirm that he was blind, when in full possession of his senses; to shut his eyes and grope in the dark, and call upon the compassion of mankind on his infirmity, when his organs were, in no degree, impaired, and the scene around him was luminous and beautiful, was an height of infatuation that he could never attain. And why should he be thus self-degraded? Why should he take a laborious circuit to reach a point which, when attained, was trivial, and to which reason had pointed out a road short and direct?

A wife is generally nothing more than a household superintendant. This function could not be more wisely vested than it was at present. Every thing, in his domestic system, was fashioned on strict and inflexible principles. He wanted instruments and not partakers of his authority. One whose mind was equal and not superior to the cogent apprehension and punctual performance of his will. One whose character was squared, with mathematical exactness, to his situation. Helena, with all her faults, did not merit to be regarded in this light. Her introduction would destroy the harmony of his scheme, and be, with respect to herself, a genuine debasement. A genuine evil would thus be substituted for one that was purely imaginary.

Helena's intellectual deficiencies could not be concealed. She was a proficient in the elements of no science. The doctrine of lines and surfaces was as disproportionate with her intellects as with those of the mock-bird. She had not reasoned on the principles of human action, nor examined the structure of society. She was ignorant of the past or present condition of mankind. History had not informed her of the one, nor the narratives of voyagers, nor the deductions of geography of the other. The heights of eloquence and poetry were shut out from her view. She could not commune in their native dialect, with the sages of Rome and Athens. To her those perennial fountains of wisdom and refinement were sealed. The constitution of nature, the attributes of its author, the arrangement of the parts of the external universe, and the substance, modes of operation, and ultimate destiny of human intelligence, were enigmas unsolved and insoluble by her.

But this was not all. The superstructure could for the present be spared. Nay it was desirable that the province of rearing it, should be reserved for him. All he wanted was a suitable foundation; but this Helena did not possess. He had not hitherto been able to create in her the inclination or the power. She had listened to his precepts with docility. She had diligently conned the lessons which he had prescribed, but the impressions were as fleeting as if they had been made on water. Nature seemed to have set impassable limits to her attainments.

This indeed was an unwelcome belief. He struggled to invalidate it. He reflected on the immaturity of her age. What but crude and hasty views was it reasonable to expect at so early a period. If her mind had not been awakened, it had proceeded, perhaps, from the injudiciousness of his plans, or merely from their not having been persisted in. What was wanting but the ornaments of mind to render this being all that poets have feigned of angelic nature. When he indulged himself in imaging the union of capacious understanding with her personal loveliness, his conceptions swelled to a pitch of enthusiasm, and it seemed as if no labour was too great to be employed in the production of such a creature. And yet, in the midst of his glowings, he would sink into sudden dejection at the recollection of that which passion had, for a time, excluded. To make her wise it would be requisite to change her sex. He had forgotten that his pupil was a female, and her capacity therefore limited by nature. This mortifying thought was outbalanced by another. Her attainments, indeed, were suitable to the imbecility of her sex; but did she not surpass, in those attainments, the ordinary rate of women? They must not be condemned, because they are outshone by qualities that are necessarily male births.[7]

Her accomplishments formed a much more attractive theme. He overlooked no article in the catalogue. He was confounded at one time, and encouraged at another, on remarking the contradictions that seemed to be included in her character. It was difficult to conceive the impossibility of passing that barrier which yet she was able to touch. She was no poet. She listened to the rehearsal, without emotion, or was moved, not by the substance of the passage, by the dazzling image or the magic sympathy, but by something adscititious:[8] yet usher her upon the stage, and no poet would wish for a more powerful organ of his conceptions. In assuming this office, she appeared to have drank in the very soul of the dramatist. What was wanting in judgment, was supplied by memory, in the tenaciousness of which, she has seldom been rivalled.

Her sentiments were trite and undigested, but were decorated with all the fluences and melodies of elocution. Her musical instructor had been a Sicilian,[9] who had formed her style after the Italian model. This man had likewise taught her his own language. He had supplied her chiefly with Sicilian compositions, both in poetry and melody, and was content to be unclassical, for the sake of the feminine and voluptuous graces of his native dialect.

Ormond was an accurate judge of the proficiency of Hellen, and of the felicity with which these accomplishments were suited to her character. When his pupil personated the victims of anger and grief, and poured forth the fiery indignation of Calista, or the maternal despair of Constance, or the self-contentions of Ipsipile,[10] he could not deny the homage which her talents might claim.

---

[7] "Limited by nature ... imbecility of her sex ... qualities that are by nature male births": Sophia attributes to Ormond the ultraconventional, un-Wollstonecraftian assumption that women are inferior to men as the result of biological nature, rather than of social and ideological conditioning.

[8] "Adscititious": assumed, adopted from the outside; "taken in to complete something else, though originally extrinsic; supplemental; additional" (*OED*). Helena is said to enjoy poetry not because of its intrinsic merits, but because of external factors such as its pleasing sympathetic form or its celebration by others.

[9] "Sicilian": in the novel's symbolic language concerning classicism and its others, to be trained in modern Italian styles is to be aligned with the "feminine and voluptuous" rather than with the masculine rationality of (classical) history and science. An example of the kind of music she is taught might be the influential late baroque–early classical style of Naples-born Alessandro Scarlatti (1660–1725). In this period Naples and Sicily are part of one sovereign state, The Kingdom of the Two Sicilies.

[10] "Calista ... Constance ... Ipsipile": tragic heroines of plays and operas familiar to eighteenth century Anglophone audiences. Calista (from Greek *kalistos*, most beautiful) is a conventional name for many heroines throughout the century. The allusion here is likely to the much-suffering protagonist of Nicholas Rowe's "she-tragedy" *The Fair Penitent* (1703). The "maternal despair of Constance" refers to the mother figure in Shakespeare's *King John* (c. 1593) who grieves for her dead son. The "self-contentions of Ipsipile" are the self-doubts of the anguished lover of Jason the Argonaut in

Her Sicilian tutor had found her no less tractable as a votary of painting. She needed only the education of Angelica,[11] to exercise as potent and prolific a pencil. This was incompatible with her condition, which limited her attainments to the elements of this art. It was otherwise with music. Here there was no obstacle to skill, and here the assiduities of many years, in addition to a prompt and ardent genius, set her beyond the hopes of rivalship.

Ormond had often amused his fancy with calling up images of excellence in this art. He saw no bounds to the influence of habit, in augmenting the speed and multiplying the divisions of muscular motion. The fingers, by their form and size, were qualified to outrun and elude the most vigilant eye. The sensibility of keys and wires had limits, but these limits depended on the structure of the instrument, and the perfection of its structure was proportioned to the skill of the artist. On well constructed keys and strings, was it possible to carry diversities of movement and pressure too far. How far they could be carried was mere theme of conjecture, until it was his fate to listen to the magical performances of Hellen, whose volant finger seemed to be self-impelled. Her touches were creative of a thousand forms of *Piano*, and of numberless transitions from grave to quick, perceptible only to ears like her own.

In the selection and arrangement of notes, there are no limits to luxuriance and celerity. Hellen had long relinquished the drudgery of imitation. She never played but when there were motives to fervour, and when she was likely to ascend without impediment, and to maintain for a suitable period her elevation, to the element of new ideas. The lyrics of Milton and of Metastasio,[12] she sung with accompaniments

---

Issipile (1724), an opera seria or tragic opera with lyrics by poet and librettist Metastasio, who will be mentioned three paragraphs further on. Metastasio's libretto was set to music by at least fourteen different composers by the 1790s, and regularly staged in London.

[11] "The education of Angelica": artistic training like that of Angelica Kauffmann (1741–1807), a Swiss-Austrian painter widely known and associated with female genius in the arts. Already popular during her early career in Rome and Florence, she worked in London from the late 1760s to 1781, earning wide renown in Anglophone culture and across late-Enlightenment Europe. She was one of the "Bluestockings" group of female intellectuals that included Lady Mary Wortley Montagu, the mother of the "Wortley Montagu" named in Brown's footnote in Chapter 14 (see note 14.5). Among other artists, she worked with engraver Francesco Bartolozzi, mentioned as one of Stephen Dudley's artistic mentors in Chapter 1 (see note 1.1). After 1781 Angelica married a Venetian artist and relocated to Rome for the last phase of her career, where she continued to be celebrated by luminaries such as the German writer Goethe.

[12] "Lyrics of Milton and Metastasio": Helena improvises on songs that use the lyrics of John Milton (1608–1674) and Metastasio (pseudonym of Pietro Antonio Domenico Trapassi, 1698–1782, author of the *Issipile* mentioned three paragraphs earlier). These names reiterate the contrast between Helena's impressive but strangely "superficial" or "light" artistic skill, and works reputed to be profound or serious, since both of these poets are primarily known for their accomplishments in high genres such as epic and tragic opera.

that never tired, because they were never repeated. Her harp and clavichord[13] supplied her with endless combinations, and these in the opinion of Ormond were not inferior to the happiest exertions of Handel and Arne.[14]

Chess was his favorite amusement. This was the only game which he allowed himself to play. He had studied it with so much zeal and success, that there were few with whom he deigned to contend. He was prone to consider it as a sort of criterion of human capacity. He who had acquired skill in this *science*, could not be infirm in mind; and yet he found in Hellen, a competitor not unworthy of all his energies. Many hours were consumed in this employment, and here the lady was sedate, considerate, extensive in foresight, and fertile in expedients.

Her deportment was graceful, inasmuch as it flowed from a consciousness of her defects. She was devoid of arrogance and vanity, neither imagining himself better than she was, and setting light by those qualifications which she unquestionably possessed. Such was the mixed character of this woman.

Ormond was occupied with schemes of a rugged and arduous nature. His intimate associates and the partakers of his confidence, were embued with the same zeal, and ardent in the same pursuits. Helena could lay no claim to be exalted to this rank. That one destitute of this claim should enjoy the privileges of his wife, was still a supposition truly monstrous: Yet the image of Helena, fondly loving him, and a model as he conceived of tenderness and constancy, devoured by secret remorse, and pursued by the scorn of mankind; a mark for slander to shoot at, and an outcast of society, did not visit his meditations in vain. The rigour of his principles began now to relent.

He considered that various occupations are incident to every man. He cannot be invariably employed in the promotion of one purpose. He must occasionally unbend, if he desires that the springs of his mind should retain their due vigour. Suppose his life were divided between business and amusement. This was a necessary

---

[13] "Clavichord": a light, portable keyboard instrument popular from the sixteenth to the eighteenth centuries, primarily in German-speaking countries. Clavichords do not produce enough volume for concert performance and were ordinarily reserved for practice, teaching, or composition of repertoire intended for harpsichord or organ. Soon after the 1790s clavichords began to fall out of general use as the piano was redesigned in its modern form and gained currency in middle-class parlors. Clavichords thus cannot easily create the dynamic spectrum expected from a piano (short for pianoforte; i.e., *piano e forte*, soft and loud). Helena's playing adjures monumental and stirring "loud" registers and favors lulling, soft sounds.

[14] "Handel and Arne": two of the best-known composers of the eighteenth century, particularly in the Anglophone world. The Saxon-born but naturalized English Georg Friderich Handel (1685–1759) was primarily known for operas, oratorios, and orchestral court entertainments. Englishman Thomas Augustine Arne (1710–1778) was a prolific composer especially of stage works (operas, masques, pantomimes, musical plays) because he was Catholic and thus cut off from lucrative Church of England patronage. Although little known today, Arne was extremely popular in the period, when he was considered the only Englishman to rival pan-European stars such as Handel, Haydn, or Pleyel, and celebrated as a key figure in reviving Anglophone opera after the 1730s.

distribution, and sufficiently congenial with his temper. It became him to select with skill his sources of amusement. It is true that Helena was unable to participate in his graver occupations; What then? In whom were blended so many pleasurable attributes? In her were assembled an exquisite and delicious variety. As it was, he was daily in her company. He should scarcely be more so, if marriage should take place. In that case, no change in their mode of life would be necessary. There was no need of dwelling under the same roof. His revenue was equal to the support of many household establishments. His personal independence would remain equally inviolate. No time, he thought, would diminish his influence over the mind of Helena, and it was not to be forgotten that the transition would to her be happy. It would reinstate her in the esteem of the world, and dispel those phantoms of remorse and shame by which she was at present persecuted.

These were plausible considerations. They tended at least to shake his resolutions. Time would probably have compleated the conquest of his pride, had not a new incident set the question in a new light.

Chapter XIV

THE narrative of Melbourne[1] made a deeper impression on the mind of his guest than was at first apparent. This man's conduct was directed by the present impulse, and however elaborate his abstract notions, he seldom stopped to settle the agreement between his principles and actions. The use of money was a science like every other branch of benevolence, not reducible to any fixed principles. No man, in the disbursement of money, could say whether he was conferring a benefit or injury. The visible and immediate effects might be good, but evil was its ultimate and general tendency. To be governed by a view to the present, rather than the future, was a human infirmity from which he did not pretend to be exempt. This, though an insufficient apology for the conduct of a rational being, was suitable to his indolence, and he was content in all cases to employ it. It was thus that he reconciled himself to beneficent acts, and humorously held himself up as an object of censure, on occasions when most entitled to applause.

He easily procured information as to the character and situation of the Dudleys. Neighbours are always inquisitive, and happily, in this case, were enabled to make no unfavorable report. He resolved, without hesitation, to supply their wants. This he performed in a manner truly characteristic. There was a method of gaining access to families, and marking them in their unguarded attitudes more easy and effectual than any other: It required least preparation and cost least pains: The disguise, also, was of the most impenetrable kind. He had served a sort of occasional apprenticeship to the art, and executed its functions with perfect case. It was the most entire and grotesque metamorphosis imaginable. It was stepping from the highest to the lowest rank in society, and shifting himself into a form, as remote from his own, as those recorded by Ovid.[2] In a word, it was sometimes his practice to exchange his complexion and habiliments for those of a negro and a chimney-sweep,[3] and to call at

---

[1] "The narrative of Melbourne": after pausing to provide sketches of Ormond and Helena, the narrator Sophia picks up her narrative thread by returning to the conversation between Melbourne and Ormond that took place at the end of Chapter 11.

[2] "Ovid": Publius Ovidius Naso (43 B.C.E.–17 C.E.), the Roman poet best known for his *Metamorphoses*, or tales of fantastic mythological transformations. *Ormond*'s transformations and masquerades can be read as modern versions of Ovid.

[3] "A negro and a chimney-sweep": to spy on the Dudleys, Ormond disguises himself as a black chimney sweep. Exchanging his elite status for the appearance of an impoverished and despised African worker, this startling transformation or episode of racial passing is another of the novel's many disguises and secret identities, and recalls Chapter 5's reference to debates about race during the yellow fever epidemic (see note 5.6).

Chimney sweeping was extremely dangerous work (sweepers tended to die quickly from work-related cancers or breathing coal dust) reserved for the most disempowered laborers in this period, often abandoned or vagrant orphans and, in the U.S., African children. Thus chimney sweeping is frequently evoked in the period as a powerful example of barbaric labor conditions and socially sanctioned cruelty, for example in William Blake's chimney-sweeper poems (in his *Songs of*

certain doors for employment. This he generally secured by importunities, and the cheapness of his services.

When the loftiness of his port, and the punctiliousness of his nicety[4] were considered, we should never have believed, what yet could be truly asserted, that he had frequently swept his own chimneys, without the knowledge of his own servants.* It was likewise true, though equally incredible, that he had played at romps with his scullion, and listened with patience to a thousand slanders on his own character.

In this disguise he visited the house of Mr. Dudley. It was nine o'clock in the morning. He remarked, with critical eyes, the minutest circumstance in the appearance

*Similar exploits are related of Count de la Lippe and Wortley Montague.[5]

Innocence and Experience, 1794) or in an article "On the Condition of Chimney-Sweepers" that Brown published (and possibly wrote) in his *Literary Magazine* in April, 1805. Pamphlets drawing attention to the destructive nature of the work were widely circulated, for example James Pettit Andrews' *An Appeal to the Humane, on Behalf of the most Deplorable Class of Society, the Climbing Boys, Employed by the Chimney-Sweepers* (London: John Stockdale, 1788). Lady Mary Wortley Montagu, mother of the "Wortley Montagu" mentioned in Brown's note to the next paragraph, was an early activist in drawing attention to the plight of chimney sweeps.

[4] "The punctiliousness of his nicety": that is, his usual insistence on neatness and formality. "Punctilio" is excessive concern with formalities or other details, and "nicety" in this usage means fastidiousness or formality.

[5] "Count de la Lippe and Wortley Montague": two aristocrats noted for extensive travels and adventurous reputations, including episodes of self-transformation or disguise as lowly chimney sweeps or beggars.

Edward Wortley Montagu (1713–1776), son of notable female intellectual and Bluestocking Lady Mary Wortley Montagu (1689–1762), was known in this period for his wide travels throughout Europe, the Mediterranean, and Middle East, during which he married and abandoned a long series of women while continually changing identities and religions (from Protestant to Catholic to Muslim). In the fictionalized *Memoirs of the Late Edw. W—ly M—tague, Esq; with Remarks on the Manners and Customs of the Oriental World; Collected and Published from Original Posthumous Papers* (London: J. Wallis, 1777), his first adventure, on running away from Westminster school as an adolescent, occurs when he "changes cloathes with a Chimney Sweep, and Commences Brother of the Brush" (vol. 1, ch. 4). For more on the novel's reference to this volume, see the Related Text on Female Transvestism.

William (or Wilhelm), Count of Schaumberg-Lippe and Bückeburg (1724–1777) was a London-born, Anglo-German general and ruler of the small Principality of Schaumberg-Lippe in lower Saxony. He was an important commander in the Seven Years' War and, like the common soldier Baxter in Chapter 7, participated in the battles of Dettingen and Minden. He was also well known for reorganizing and modernizing the army of Portugal in collaboration with the Marquis of Pombal, the Portuguese reformer that Brown discusses in his key essay "Walstein's School of History" (see Related Texts). In Johann Zimmermann's *Solitude Considered with Respect to its Influence upon the Mind and the Heart* (London: C. Dilly, 1791), in a section that was often reprinted as a separate anecdote, Lippe appears as a learned strategist whose opponents often failed to take him seriously because of his unconventional appearance and manner. Zimmermann relates that, as a youth, Lippe "not only traversed the greatest part of that kingdom [England] on foot, but travelled in company with a German prince through several of the countries in the character of a beggar" (193–94).

and demeanour of his customers, and glanced curiously at the house and furniture. Every thing was new and every thing pleased. The walls, though broken into roughness, by carelessness or time, were adorned with glistening white. The floor, though loose and uneven, and with gaping seams, had received all the improvements which cloth and brush could give. The pine tables, rush chairs, and uncurtained bed, had been purchased at half price, at vendue,[6] and exhibited various tokens of decay, but care and neatness and order were displayed in their condition and arrangement.

The lower apartment was the eating and sitting room. It was likewise Mr. Dudley's bed chamber.[7] The upper room was occupied by Constance and her Lucy. Ormond viewed every thing with the accuracy of an artist, and carried away with him a catalogue of every thing visible. The faded form of Mr. Dudley that still retained its dignity, the sedateness, graceful condescension and personal elegance of Constantia, were new to the apprehension of Ormond. The contrast between the house and its inhabitants, rendered the appearance more striking. When he had finished his task, he retired, but returning in a quarter of an hour, he presented a letter to the young lady. He behaved as if by no means desirous of eluding her interrogatories, and when she desired him to stay, readily complied. The letter, unsigned and unsuperscribed, was to this effect.

"The writer of this is acquainted with the transaction between Thomas Craig and Mr. Dudley. The former is debtor to Mr. Dudley in a large sum. I have undertaken to pay as much of this debt, and at such times as suits my convenience. I have had pecuniary engagements with Craig. I hold myself, in the sum inclosed, discharging so much of his debt. The future payments are uncertain, but I hope they will contribute to relieve the necessities of Mr. Dudley."

Ormond had calculated the amount of what would be necessary for the annual subsistence of this family, on the present frugal plan. He had regulated his disbursements accordingly.

It was natural to feel curiosity as to the writer of this epistle. The bearer displayed a prompt and talkative disposition. He had a staring eye and a grin of vivacity forever at command. When questioned by Constantia, he answered that the gentleman had forbidden him to mention his name or the place where he lived. Had he ever met with the same person before? O yes. He had lived with him from a child. His mother lived with him still and his brothers. His master had nothing for him to do at home, so he sent him out sweeping chimneys, taking from him only half the money that he earned, that way. He was a very good master.

Then the gentleman had been a long time in the city?

---

[6] "Vendue": public auction, where used goods might be bought, and where ship captains could sell their goods directly to the public, cutting out American merchants.

[7] "Bed chamber": it was common for nonelite homes to have the front or visiting room double as a bedroom.

O yes. All his life he reckoned. He used to live in Walnut-Street,[8] but now he's moved down town. Here he checked himself, and added, but I forgets. I must not tell where he lives. He told me I mustn't.

He has a family and children, I suppose?

O yes. Why don't you know Miss Hetty and Miss Betsy —— there again. I was going to tell the name, that he said I must not tell.

Constantia saw that the secret might be easily discovered, but she forbore. She disdained to take advantage of this messenger's imagined simplicity. She dismissed him with some small addition to his demand, and with a promise always to employ him in this way.

By this mode, Ormond had effectually concealed himself. The lady's conjectures, founded on this delusive information, necessarily wandered widely from the truth. The observations that he had made during this visit afforded his mind considerable employment. The manner in which this lady had sustained so cruel a reverse of fortune, the cheerfulness' with which she appeared to forego all the gratifications of affluence; the skill with which she selected her path of humble industry, and the steadiness with which she pursued it, were proofs of a moral constitution, from which he supposed the female sex to be debarred. The comparison was obvious between Constantia and Hellen, and the result was by no means advantageous to the latter. Was it possible that such an one descended to the level of her father's apprentice? That she sacrificed her honor to a wretch like that? This reflection tended to repress the inclination he would otherwise have felt for cultivating her society, but it did not indispose him to benefit her in a certain way.

On his next visit to his "bella Siciliana," as he called her, he questioned her as to the need in which she might stand of the services of a seamstress, and being informed that they were sometimes wanted, he recommended Miss Acworth to her patronage. He said that he had heard her spoken of in favorable terms, by the gossips at Melbourne's. They represented her as a good girl, slenderly provided for, and he wished that Hellen would prefer her to all others.

His recommendation was sufficient. The wishes of Ormond, as soon as they became known, became hers. Her temper made her always diligent in search of novelty. It was easy to make work for the needle. In short she resolved to send for her the next day. The interview accordingly took place on the ensuing morning, not without mutual surprise, and, on the part of the fair Sicilian, not without considerable embarrassment.

This circumstance arose from their having changed their respective names, though from motives of a very different kind. They were not strangers to each other, though no intimacy had ever subsisted between them. Each was merely acquainted with the name, person, and general character of the other. No circumstance in Constantia's situation tended to embarrass her. Her mind had attained a state of serene

---

[8] "Walnut-Street": then a financial and relatively genteel section of Philadelphia, the northern border of the Society Hill neighborhood that was home to residents of the gentlemen class.

composure, incapable of being ruffled by an incident of this kind. She merely derived pleasure from the sight of her old acquaintance. The aspect of things around her was splendid and gay. She seemed the mistress of the mansion, and her name was changed. Hence it was unavoidable to conclude that she was married.

Helena was conscious that appearances were calculated to suggest this conclusion. The idea was a painful one. She sorrowed to think that this conclusion was fallacious. The consciousness that her true condition was unknown to her visitant, and the ignominiousness of that truth, gave an air of constraint to her behaviour, which Constance ascribed to a principle of delicacy.

In the midst of reflections relative to herself, she admitted some share of surprise at the discovery of Constance, in a situation so inferior to that in which she had formerly known her. She had heard, in general terms, of the misfortunes of Mr. Dudley, but was unacquainted with particulars; but this surprize, and the difficulty of adapting her behaviour to circumstances, was only in part the source of her embarrassment, though by her companion it was wholly attributed to this cause.

Constance thought it her duty to remove it by open and unaffected manners. She therefore said, in a sedate and cheerful tone, You see me, Madam, in a situation somewhat unlike that in which I formerly was placed. You will probably regard the change as an unhappy one, but I assure you, I have found it far less so than I expected. I am thus reduced not by my own fault. It is this reflection that enables me to conform to it without a murmur. I shall rejoice to know that Mrs. Eden[9] is as happy as I am.

Helena was pleased with this address, and returned an answer full of sweetness. She had not, in her compassion for the fallen, a particle of pride. She thought of nothing but the contrast between the former situation of her visitant and the present. The fame of her great qualities had formerly excited veneration, and that reverence was by no means diminished by a nearer scrutiny. The consciousness of her own frailty, meanwhile, diffused over the behaviour of Hellen, a timidity and dubiousness uncommonly fascinating. She solicited Constantia's friendship in a manner that shewed she was afraid of nothing but denial. An assent was eagerly given, and thenceforth a cordial intercourse was established between them.

The real situation of Helena was easily discovered. The officious person who communicated this information, at the same time cautioned Constance against associating with one of tainted reputation. This information threw some light upon appearances. It accounted for that melancholy which Hellen was unable to conceal. It explained that solitude in which she lived, and which Constantia had ascribed to the death or absence of her husband. It justified the solicitous silence she had hitherto

---

[9] "Mrs. Eden": besides moving from New York to Philadelphia to mask her change in status (see note 13.5), Helena has also disguised herself by changing her name (from Cleves to Eden) and posing as a married woman ("Mrs."). In this tendency to disguise and masquerade she resembles the Dudleys (see note 11.4) and the other main female characters in the novel, the narrator Sophia and Martinette de Beauvais, all of whom adopt multiple names and guises.

maintained respecting her own affairs, and which her friend's good sense forbad her to employ any sinister means of eluding.

No long time was necessary to make her mistress of Helena's character. She loved her with uncommon warmth, though by no means blind to her defects. She formed no expectations, from the knowledge of her character, to which this intelligence operated as a disappointment. It merely excited her pity, and made her thoughtful how she might assist her in repairing this deplorable error.

This design was of no ordinary magnitude. She saw that it was previously necessary to obtain the confidence of Helena. This was a task of easy performance. She knew the purity of her own motives and the extent of her powers, and embarked in this undertaking with full confidence of success. She had only to profit by a private interview, to acquaint her friend with what she knew, to solicit a compleat and satisfactory disclosure, to explain the impressions which her intelligence produced, and to offer her disinterested advice. No one knew better how to couch her ideas in words, suitable to the end proposed by her in imparting them.

Hellen was at first terrified, but the benevolence of her friend quickly entitled her to confidence and gratitude that knew no limits. She had been deterred from unveiling her heart by the fear of exciting contempt or abhorrence: But when she found that all due allowances were made, that her conduct was treated as erroneous in no atrocious or inexpiable degree, and as far from being insusceptible of remedy; that the obloquy with which she had been treated, found no vindicator or participator in her friend, her heart was considerably relieved. She had been long a stranger to the sympathy and intercourse of her own sex. Now, this good, in its most precious form, was conferred upon her, and she experienced an increase, rather than diminution of tenderness, in consequence of her true situation being known.

She made no secret of any part of her history. She did full justice to the integrity of her lover, and explained the unforced conditions on which she had consented to live with him. This relation exhibited the character of Ormond in a very uncommon light. His asperities wounded, and his sternness chilled. What unauthorised conceptions of matrimonial and political equality did he entertain! He had fashioned his treatment of Helena on sullen and ferocious principles. Yet he was able, it seemed, to mould her, by means of them, nearly into the creature that he wished. She knew too little of the man justly to estimate his character. It remained to be ascertained whether his purposes were consistent and upright, or were those of a villain and betrayer.

Meanwhile what was to be done by Hellena? Marriage had been refused on plausible pretences. Her unenlightened understanding made her no match for her lover. She would never maintain her claim to nuptial privileges in his presence, or if she did, she would never convince him of their validity.

Were they indeed valid? Was not the disparity between them incurable? A marriage of minds so dissimilar could only be productive of misery immediately to him, and by a reflex operation, to herself. She could not be happy in a union that was the source of regret to her husband. Marriage therefore was not possible, or if possible, was not, perhaps, to be wished. But what was the choice that remained?

To continue in her present situation was not to be endured. Disgrace was a dæmon that would blast every hope of happiness. She was excluded from all society but that of the depraved. Her situation was eminently critical. It depended, perhaps, on the resolution she should now form whether she should be enrolled among the worst of mankind. Infamy is the worst of evils. It creates innumerable obstructions in the path of virtue. It manacles the hand, and entangles the feet that are active only to good. To the weak it is an evil of much greater magnitude. It determines their destiny, and they hasten to merit that reproach, which, at first it may be, they did not deserve.

This connection is intrinsically flagitious. Hellen is subjected by it to the worst ills that are incident to humanity, the general contempt of mankind, and the reproaches of her own conscience. From these, there is but one method from which she can hope to be relieved. The intercourse must cease.

It was easier to see the propriety of separation, than to project means for accomplishing it. It was true that Helena loved; but what quarter was due to this passion when divorced from integrity? Is it not in every bosom a perishable sentiment? Whatever be her warmth, absence will congeal it. Place her in new scenes, and supply her with new associates. Her accomplishments will not fail to attract votaries. From these she may select a conjugal companion suitable to her mediocrity of talents.

But alas! What power on earth can prevail on her to renounce Ormond? Others may justly entertain this prospect, but it must be invisible to her. Besides, is it absolutely certain that either her peace of mind or her reputation will be restored by this means? In the opinion of the world her offences cannot, by any perseverance in penitence, be expiated. She will never believe that separation will exterminate her passion. Certain it is, that it will avail nothing to the reestablishment of her fame: But if it were conducive to these ends, how chimerical[10] to suppose that she will ever voluntarily adopt it? If Ormond refuse his concurrence, there is absolutely an end to hope. And what power on earth is able to sway his determinations? At least what influence was it possible for her to obtain over them?

Should they separate, whither should she retire? What mode of subsistence should she adopt? She has never been accustomed to think beyond the day. She has eaten and drank, but another has provided the means. She scarcely comprehends the principle that governs the world, and in consequence of which, nothing can be gained but by giving something in exchange for it. She is ignorant and helpless as a child, on every topic that relates to the procuring of subsistence. Her education has disabled her from standing alone.

But this was not all. She must not only be supplied by others, but sustained in the enjoyment of a luxurious existence. Would you bereave her of the gratifications of

---

[10] "Chimerical": highly unrealistic, based on chimeras or delusions. A chimera was originally an imaginary creature that combined parts of different animals and, by the late enlightenment, was synonymous with superstition or delusion. In Brown's work the term is a keyword that identifies a process of thinking that is fundamentally flawed or irrational.

opulence? You had better take away her life. Nay, it would ultimately amount to this. She can live but in one way.

At present she is lovely, and, to a certain degree, innocent, but expose her to the urgencies and temptations of want, let personal pollution be the price set upon the voluptuous affluences of her present condition, and it is to be feared there is nothing in the contexture of her mind to hinder her from making the purchase. In every respect therefore the prospect was an hopeless one. So hopeless that her mind insensibly returned to the question which she had at first dismissed with very slight examination, the question relative to the advantages and probabilities of marriage. A more accurate review convinced her that this was the most eligible alternative. It was, likewise, most easily effected. The lady, of course, would be its fervent advocate. There did not want reasons why Ormond should finally embrace it. In what manner appeals to his reason or his passion might most effectually be made, she knew not.

Hellen was illy qualified to be her own advocate. Her unhappiness could not but be visible to Ormond. He had shewn himself attentive and affectionate. Was it impossible that, in time, he should reason himself into a spontaneous adoption of this scheme? This, indeed, was a slender foundation for hope, but there was no other on which she could build.

Such were the meditations of Constantia on this topic. She was deeply solicitous for the happiness of her friend. They spent much of their time together. The consolations of her society were earnestly sought by Helena, but to enjoy them, she was for the most part obliged to visit the former at her own dwelling. For this arrangement, Constance apologized by saying, You will pardon my requesting you to favor me with your visits, rather than allowing me mine. Every thing is airy and brilliant within these walls. There is, besides, an air of seclusion and security about you that is delightful. In comparison, my dwelling is bleak, comfortless, and unretired, but my father is entitled to all my care. His infirmity prevents him from amusing himself, and his heart is cheered by the mere sound of my voice, though not addressed to him. The mere belief of my presence seems to operate as an antidote to the dreariness of solitude; and now you know my motives, I am sure you will not only forgive but approve of my request.

Chapter XV

WHEN once the subject had been introduced, Helena was prone to descant upon[1] her own situation, and listened with deference to the remarks and admonitions of her companion. Constantia did not conceal from her any of her sentiments. She enabled her to view her own condition in its true light, and set before her the indispensible advantages of marriage, while she, at the same time, afforded her the best directions as to the conduct she ought to pursue in order to effect her purpose.

The mind of Helena was thus kept in a state of perpetual and uneasy fluctuation. While absent from Ormond, or listening to her friend's remonstrances, the deplorableness of her condition, arose in its most disastrous hues, before her imagination. But the spectre seldom failed to vanish at the approach of Ormond. His voice dissipated every inquietude.

She was not insensible of this inconstancy. She perceived and lamented her own weakness. She was destitute of all confidence in her own exertions. She could not be in the perpetual enjoyment of his company. Her intervals of tranquility therefore were short, while those of anxiety and dejection were insupportably tedious. She revered, but, believed herself incapable to emulate the magnanimity of her monitor. The consciousness of inferiority, especially in a case like this, in which her happiness so much depended on her own exertions, excited in her the most humiliating sensations.

While indulging in fruitless melancholy, the thought one day occurred to her, why may not Constantia be prevailed upon to plead my cause? Her capacity and courage are equal to any undertaking. The reasonings that are so powerful in my eyes, would they be trivial and futile in those of Ormond? I cannot have a more pathetic[2] and disinterested advocate.

This idea was cherished with uncommon ardour. She seized the first opportunity that offered itself to impart it to her friend. It was a wild and singular proposal and was rejected at the first glance. This scheme, so romantic and impracticable as it at first seemed, appeared to Hellen in the most plausible colours. She could not bear to relinquish her new born hopes. She saw no valid objection to it. Every thing was easy to her friend, provided her sense of duty and her zeal could be awakened. The subject was frequently suggested to Constantia's reflections. Perceiving the sanguineness[3] of her friend's confidence, and fully impressed with the value of the end to be accomplished, she insensibly veered to the same opinion. At least, the scheme was worthy of a candid discussion before it was rejected.

Ormond was a stranger to her. His manners were repulsive and austere. She was a mere girl. Her personal attachment to Helena was all that she could plead in excuse for taking part in her concerns. The subject was delicate. A blunt and irregular

---

[1] "Descant upon": complain or whine about.

[2] "Pathetic": emotionally expressive, able to arouse emotion (pathos).

[3] "Sanguineness": "hopefulness, confidence of success" (*OED*).

character like Ormond's, might throw an air of ridicule over the scene. She shrunk from the encounter of a boisterous and manlike spirit.

But were not these scruples effeminate and puerile? Had she studied so long in the school of adversity, without conviction of the duty of a virtuous independence? Was she not a rational being, fully imbued with the justice of her cause?[4] Was it not ignoble to refuse the province of a vindicator of the injured, before any tribunal, however tremendous or unjust? And who was Ormond, that his eye should inspire terror?

The father or brother of Helena might assume the office without indecorum. Nay, a mother or sister might not be debarred from it. Why then should she who was actuated by equal zeal, and was engaged, by ties stronger than consanguinity,[5] in the promotion of her friend's happiness? It is true she did not view the subject in the light in which it was commonly viewed by brothers and parents. It was not a gust of rage that should transport her into his presence. She did not go to awaken his slumbering conscience, and abash him in the pride of guilty triumph, but to rectify deliberate errors and change his course by the change of his principles. It was her business to point out to him the road of duty and happiness, from which he had strayed with no sinister intentions. This was to be done without raving and fury, but with amicable soberness, and in the way of calm and rational remonstrance. Yet there were scruples that would not be shut out, and continually whispered her, What an office is this for a girl and a stranger to assume!

In what manner should it be performed? Should an interview be sought, and her ideas be explained without confusion or faultering, undismayed by ludicrous airs or insolent frowns? But this was a point to be examined. Was Ormond capable of such behaviour? If he were, it would be useless to attempt the reformation of his errors. Such a man is incurable and obdurate. Such a man is not to be sought as the husband of Helena; but this surely is a different being.

The medium through which she had viewed his character was an ample one, but might not be very accurate. The treatment which Helena had received from him, exclusive of his fundamental error, betokened a mind to which she did not disdain to be allied. In spite of his defects she saw that their elements were more congenial, and the points of contract, between this person and herself, more numerous, than between her and Helena, whose voluptuous sweetness of temper and mediocrity of understanding, excited in her bosom no genuine sympathy.

Every thing is progressive in the human mind. When there is leisure to reflect, ideas will succeed each other in a long train, before the ultimate point be gained. The attention must shift from one side to the other of a given question many times before it settles. Constantia did not form her resolutions in haste, but when once formed,

---

[4] "Was she not a rational being … her cause?": the language recalls Constantia's earlier, Wollstonecraft-like perception of Ursula Monrose, who likewise seemed to rise above the limitations of imposed "feminine" weakness to make herself into a "rational creature" (see note 8.6). Ormond will use the same phrase as he challenges Constantia in the scene that follows.

[5] "Consanguinity": blood relation and, by extension, family kinship.

they were exempt from fluctuation. She reflected before she acted, and therefore acted with consistency and vigour. She did not apprise her friend of her intention. She was willing that she should benefit by her interposition, before she knew it was employed.

She sent her Lucy with a note to Ormond's house. It was couched in these terms:

"Constance Dudley requests an interview with Mr. Ormond. Her business being of some moment, she wishes him to name an hour when most disengaged."

An answer was immediately returned, that at three o'clock, in the afternoon, he should be glad to see her.

This message produced no small surprise in Ormond. He had not withdrawn his notice from Constance, and had marked, with curiosity and approbation, the progress of the connexion between the two women. The impressions which he had received from the report of Hellen, were not dissimilar to those which Constance had imbibed, from the same quarter, respecting himself; but he gathered from them no suspicion of the purpose of a visit. He recollected his connection with Craig. This lady had had an opportunity of knowing that some connection subsisted between them. He concluded, that some information or enquiry respecting Craig, might occasion this event. As it was, it gave him considerable satisfaction. It would enable him more closely to examine one, with respect to whom he entertained great curiosity.

Ormond's conjecture was partly right. Constantia did not forget her having traced Craig to this habitation. She designed to profit by the occasion, which this circumstance afforded her, of making some enquiry respecting Craig, in order to introduce, by suitable degrees, a more important subject.

The appointed hour having arrived, he received her in his drawing-room. He knew what was due to his guest. He loved to mortify, by his negligence, the pride of his equals and superiors, but a lower class had nothing to fear from his insolence. Constantia took the seat that was offered to her, without speaking. She had made suitable preparations for this interview, and her composure was invincible. The manners of her host were by no means calculated to disconcert her. His air was conciliating and attentive.

She began with naming Craig, as one known to Ormond, and desired to be informed of his place of abode. She was proceeding to apologize for this request, by explaining in general terms, that her father's infirmities prevented him from acting for himself, that Craig was his debtor to a large amount, that he stood in need of all that justly belonged to him, and was in pursuit of some means for tracing Craig to his retreat. Ormond interrupted her, examining, at the same time, with a vigilance, somewhat too unsparing, the effects which his words should produce upon her.

You may spare yourself the trouble of explaining. I am acquainted with the whole affair between Craig and your family. He has concealed from me nothing. I know *all* that has passed between you.

In saying this, Ormond intended that his looks and emphasis should convey his full meaning. In the style of her comments he saw none of those corroborating symptoms that he expected.

Indeed! He has been very liberal of his confidence. Confession is a token of penitence, but, alas! I fear he has deceived you. To be sincere was doubtless his true interest, but he is too much in the habit of judging superficially. If he has told you all, there is, indeed, no need of explanation. This visit is, in that case, sufficiently accounted for. Is it in your power, Sir, to inform us whither he has gone?

For what end should I tell you? I promise you you will not follow him. Take my word for it, he is totally unworthy of you. Let the past be no precedent for the future. If you have not made that discovery yourself, I have made it for you. I expect, at least, to be thanked for my trouble.

This speech was unintelligible to Constance. Her looks betokened a perplexity unmingled with fear or shame.

It is my way, continued he, to say what I think. I care little for consequences. I have said that I know *all*. This will excuse me for being perfectly explicit. That I am mistaken is very possible; but I am inclined to place that matter beyond the reach of a doubt. Listen to me, and confirm me in the opinion I have already formed of your good sense, by viewing, in a just light, the unreservedness with which you are treated. I have something to tell, which, if you are wise, you will not be offended at my telling so roundly. On the contrary you will thank me, and perceive that my conduct is a proof of my respect for you. The person whom you met here is named Craig, but, as he tells me, is not the man you look for. This man's brother, the partner of your father, and, as he assured me, your own accepted and illicitly gratified lover, is dead.

These words were uttered without any extenuating hesitation or depression of tone. On the contrary, the most offensive terms were drawn out in the most deliberate and emphatic manner. Constantia's cheeks glowed and her eyes sparkled with indignation, but she forbore to interrupt. The looks with which she listened to the remainder of the speech, shewed that she fully comprehended the scene, and enabled him to comprehend it. He proceeded.

This man is a brother of that. Their resemblance in figure occasioned your mistake. Your father's debtor died, it seems, on his arrival at Jamaica. There he met with this brother, and bequeathed to him his property and papers. Some of these papers are in my possession. They are letters from Constantia Dudley, and are parts of an intrigue which, considering the character of the man, was not much to her honor. Such was this man's narrative told to me some time before your meeting with him at this house. I have a right to judge in this affair, that is, I have a right to my opinion. If I mistake, and I half suspect myself, you are able, perhaps, to rectify my error, and in a case like this, doubtless you will not want the inclination.

Perhaps if the countenance of this man had not been characterized by the keenest intelligence, and a sort of careless and overflowing good will, this speech might have produced different effects. She was prepared, though imperfectly, for entering into his character. He waited for an answer, which she gave without emotion.

You are deceived. I am sorry for your own sake, that you are. He must have had some end in view, in imposing these falsehoods upon you, which, perhaps, they have enabled him to accomplish. As to myself, this man can do me no injury. I willingly make you my judge. The letters you speak of will alone suffice to my vindication. They never were received from me, and are forgeries. That man always persisted till he made himself the dupe of his own artifices. That incident in his plot, on the introduction of which he probably the most applauded himself, will most powerfully operate to defeat it.

Those letters never were received from me, and are forgeries. His skill in imitation extended no farther in the present case, than my hand-writing. My modes of thinking and expression were beyond the reach of his mimicry.

When she had finished, Ormond spent a moment in ruminating. I perceive you are right, said he. I suppose he has purloined from me two hundred guineas, which I entrusted to his fidelity. And yet I received a letter:—but that may likewise be a forgery. By my soul, continued he, in a tone that had more of satisfaction than disappointment in it, this fellow was an adept at his trade. I do not repine. I have bought the exhibition at a cheap rate. The pains that he took did not merit a less recompense. I am glad that he was contented with so little. Had he persisted he might have raised the price far above its value. 'Twill be lamentable if he receive more than he stipulated for; if, in his last purchase, the gallows should be thrown into the bargain. May he have the wisdom to see that an halter, though not included in his terms, is only a new instance of his good fortune: But his cunning will hardly carry him thus far. His stupidity will, no doubt, prefer a lingering to a sudden exit.

But this man and his destiny are trifles. Let us leave them to themselves. Your name is Constance. 'Twas given you I suppose that you might be known by it. Pr'ythee, Constance, was this the only purpose that brought you hither? If it were, it has received as ample a discussion as it merits. You *came* for this end, but will remain, I hope, for a better one. Having dismissed Craig and his plots, let us now talk of each other.

I confess, said the lady, with an hesitation she could not subdue, this was not my only purpose. One much more important has produced this visit.

Indeed! pray let me know it. I am glad that so trivial an object as Craig, did not occupy the first place in your thoughts. Proceed I beseech you.

It is a subject on which I cannot enter without hesitation. An hesitation unworthy of me.—

Stop, cried Ormond, rising and touching the bell, nothing like time to make a conquest of embarrassment. We will defer this conference six minutes, just while we eat our dinner.

At the same moment a servant entered, with two plates and the usual apparatus for dinner. On seeing this she rose in some hurry, to depart. I thought, Sir, you were disengaged. I will call at some other hour.

He seized her hand, and held her from going, but with an air by no means disrespectful. Nay, said he, what is it that scares you away? Are you terrified at the mention of victuals? You must have fasted long when it comes to that. I told you true. I am disengaged, but not from the obligation of eating and drinking. No doubt *you* have dined. No reason why I should go without my dinner. If you do not chuse to partake with me, so much the better. Your temperance ought to dispense with two meals in an hour. Be a looker-on, or, if that will not do, retire into my library, where, in six minutes, I will be with you; and lend you my aid in the arduous task of telling me what you came with an intention of telling.

This singular address disconcerted and abashed her. She was contented to follow the servant silently into an adjoining apartment. Here she reflected with no small surprize on the behaviour of this man. Though ruffled, she was not heartily displeased with it. She had scarcely time to recollect herself, when he entered. He immediately seated her, and himself opposite to her. He fixed his eyes without scruple on her face. His gaze was steadfast, but not insolent or oppressive. He surveyed her with the looks with which he would have eyed a charming portrait. His attention was occupied with what he saw, as that of an Artist is occupied when viewing a Madonna of Rafaello.[6] At length he broke silence.

At dinner I was busy in thinking what it was you had to disclose. I will not fatigue you with my guesses. They would be impertinent, as long as the truth is going to be disclosed—He paused, and then continued: But I see you cannot dispense with my aid. Perhaps your business relates to Hellen. She has done wrong, and you wish me to rebuke the girl.

Constantia profited by this opening, and said, Yes, she has done wrong. It is true, my business relates to her. I came hither as a suppliant in her behalf. Will you not assist her in recovering the path from which she has deviated? She left it from confiding more in the judgment of her guide than her own. There is one method of repairing the evil. It lies with you to repair that evil.

During this address, the gaiety of Ormond disappeared. He fixed his eyes on Constance with new and even pathetic earnestness. I guessed as much, said he. I have often been deceived in my judgment of characters. Perhaps I do not comprehend your's: Yet it is not little that I have heard respecting you. Something I have seen. I begin to suspect a material error in my theory of human nature. Happy will it be for Hellen if my suspicions be groundless.

You are Hellen's friend. Be mine also, and advise me. Shall I marry this girl or not? You know on what terms we live. Are they suitable to our respective characters? Shall I wed this girl, or shall things remain as they are? I have an irreconcilable aversion to a sad brow and a sick bed. Hellen is grieved, because her neighbours sneer and point at her. So far she is a fool, but that is a folly of which she never will be cured. Marriage, it seems, will set all right. Answer me, Constance, shall I marry?

There was something in the tone, but more in the tenor of this address that startled her. There was nothing in this man but what came upon her unaware. This sudden

---

[6] "A Madonna of Rafaello": a painting of a beautiful woman by Raphael (Raffaello Sanzio, 1483–1520), the painter from Tuscany and Rome who was one of the masters of the Italian Renaissance.

effusion of confidence, was particularly unexpected and embarrassing. She scarcely knew whether to regard it as serious or a jest. On observing her indisposed to speak, he continued:

Away with these impertinent circuities and scruples. I know your meaning. Why should I pretend ignorance, and put you to the trouble of explanation? You came hither with no other view than to exact this question, and furnish an answer. Why should not we come at once to the point? I have for some time been dubious on this head. There is something wanting to determine the balance. If you have that something, throw it into the proper scale.

You err if you think this manner of addressing you is wild or improper. This girl is the subject of discourse. If she was not to be so, why did you favor me with this visit? You have sought me, and introduced yourself. I have, in like manner, overlooked ordinary forms: A negligence that has been systematic with me; but, in the present case, particularly justifiable by your example. Shame upon you, presumptuous girl, to suppose yourself the only rational being among mankind. And yet, if you thought so, why did you thus unceremoniously intrude upon my retirements? This act is of a piece with the rest. It shews you to be one whose existence I did not believe possible.

Take care. You know not what you have done. You came hither as Hellen's friend. Perhaps time may shew that in this visit, you have performed the behest of her bitterest enemy. But that is out of season. This girl is our mutual property. You are her friend; I am her lover. Her happiness is precious in my eyes and in your's. To the rest of mankind she is a noisome weed, that cannot be shunned too cautiously, nor trampled on too much. If we forsake her, infamy that is now kept at bay, will seize upon her, and while it mangles her form, will tear from her her innocence. She has no arms with which to contend against that foe. Marriage will place her at once in security. Shall it be? You have an exact knowledge of her strength and her weakness. Of me, you know little. Perhaps, before that question can be satisfactorily answered, it is requisite to know the qualities of her husband. Be my character henceforth the subject of your study. I will furnish you with all the light in my power. Be not hasty in deciding, but when your decision is formed, let me know it.—He waited for an answer, which she, at length, summoned resolution enough to give.

You have come to the chief point which I had in view in making this visit. To say truth, I came hither to remonstrate with you on withholding that which Helena may justly claim from you. Her happiness will be unquestionably restored, and increased by it. Your's will not be impaired. Matrimony will not produce any essential change in your situation. It will produce no greater or different intercourse than now exists. Helena is on the brink of a gulf which I shudder to look upon. I believe that you will not injure yourself by snatching her from it. I am sure that you will confer an inexpressible benefit upon her. Let me then persuade you to do her and yourself justice.

No persuasion, said Ormond, after recovering from a fit of thoughtfulness, is needful for this end; I only want to be convinced. You have decided, but I fear hastily. By what inscrutable influences are our steps guided. Come, proceed in your exhortations. Argue with the utmost clearness and cogency. Arm yourself with all the irresistibles of eloquence. Yet you are building nothing. You are only demolishing. Your argument is one thing. Its tendency is another; and is the reverse of all you expect and desire. My assent will be refused with an obstinacy proportioned to the force that you exert to obtain it, and to the just application of that force.

I see, replied the lady, smiling and leaving her seat, you can talk in riddles, as well as other people. This visit has been too long. I shall, indeed, be sorry, if my interference, instead of serving my friend, has injured her. I have acted an uncommon, and, as it may seem, an ambiguous part. I shall be contented with construing my motives in my own way. I wish you a good evening.

'Tis false, cried he, sternly, you do not wish it.

How? Exclaimed the astonished Constance.

I will put your sincerity to the test. Allow me to spend this evening in your company: Then it will be well spent, and I shall believe your wishes sincere: Else, continued he, changing his affected austerity into a smile, Constance is a liar.

You are a singular man. I hardly know how to understand you.

Well. Words are made to carry meanings. You shall have them in abundance. Your house is your citadel. I will not enter it without leave. Permit me to visit you when I please. But that is too much. It is more than I would allow you. When will you permit me to visit you?

I cannot answer when I do not understand. You cloathe your thoughts in a garb so uncouth, that I know not in what light they are to be viewed.

Well, now, I thought you understood my language, and were an English-woman, but I will use another. Shall I have the honor (bowing with a courtly air of supplication) of occasionally paying my respects to you at your own dwelling. It would be cruel to condemn those who have the happiness of knowing Miss Dudley, to fashionable restraints. At what hour will she be least incommoded by a visitant?

I am as little pleased with formalities, replied the lady, as you are. My friends I cannot see too often. They need to consult merely their own convenience. Those who are not my friends I cannot see too seldom. You have only to establish your title to that name, and your welcome at all times, is sure. Till then you must not look for it.

Chapter XVI

HERE ended this conference. She had, by no means, suspected the manner in which it would be conducted. All punctilios were trampled under foot, by the impetuosity of Ormond. Things were, at once, and without delay, placed upon a certain footing. The point, which ordinary persons would have employed months in attaining, was reached in a moment. While these incidents were fresh in her memory, they were accompanied with a sort of trepidation, the offspring at once of pleasure and surprise.

Ormond had not deceived her expectations, but hearsay and personal examination, however uniform their testimony may be, produce a very different impression. In her present reflections, Hellen and her lover approached to the front of the stage, and were viewed with equal perspicuity. One consequence of this was, that their characters were more powerfully contrasted with each other, and the eligibility of marriage, appeared not quite so incontestible as before.

Was not equality implied in this compact? Marriage is an instrument of pleasure or pain in proportion as this equality is more or less. What, but the fascination of his senses is it, that ties Ormond to Hellen. Is this a basis on which marriage may properly be built?

If things had not gone thus far, the impropriety of marriage could not be doubted; but, at present, there is a choice of evils, and that may now be desirable, which at a former period, and in different circumstances, would have been clearly otherwise.

The evils of the present connection are known; those of marriage are future and contingent; Hellen cannot be the object of a genuine and lasting passion; another may; this is not merely possible; nothing is more likely to happen: This event, therefore, ought to be included in our calculation. There would be a material deficiency without it. What was the amount of the misery that would, in this case, ensue?

Constantia was qualified, beyond most others, to form an adequate conception of this misery. One of the ingredients in her character was a mild and steadfast enthusiasm.[1] Her sensibilities to social pleasure, and her conceptions of the benefits to flow from the conformity and concurrence of intentions and wishes, heightening and refining the sensual passion, were exquisite.

There, indeed, were evils, the foresight of which tended to prevent them, but was there wisdom in creating obstacles in the way of a suitable alliance. Before we act, we must consider not only the misery produced, but the happiness precluded by our measures.

---

[1] "A mild and steadfast enthusiasm": Sophia is saying that Constantia is characterized by her dedication to higher principles. Enthusiasm, in this sense, is a keyword in early-modern discussions of idealistic dedication to religious, political, or other causes. From Greek for inspiration or possession by a god (having a *theos* within), the word could mean "ill-regulated or misdirected religious emotion" (*OED*) in a negative sense. Its more general sense, however, was "intensity of feeling in favor of a person, principle, cause"; "passionate eagerness in any pursuit, proceeding from an intense conviction of the worthiness of the object" (*OED*). In the following sentence, Constantia is said to be interested in how this intellectualized or "higher" energy can refine and be combined with "the sensual passion," or sexual desire.

In no case, perhaps, is the decision of an human being impartial, or totally uninfluenced by sinister and selfish motives. If Constantia surpassed others, it was not, because, her motives were pure, but, because, they possessed more of purity than those of others. Sinister considerations flow in upon us through imperceptible channels, and modify our thoughts in numberless ways, without our being truly conscious of their presence. Constance was young, and her heart was open at a thousand pores, to the love of excellence. The image of Ormond occupied the chief place in her fancy, and was endowed with attractive and venerable qualities. A bias was hence created that swayed her thoughts, though she knew not that they were swayed. To this might justly be imputed, some part of that reluctance which she now felt to give Ormond to Hellen. But this was not sufficient to turn the scale. That which had previously mounted, was indeed heavier than before, but this addition did not enable it to outweigh its opposite. Marriage was still the best upon the whole, but her heart was tortured to think that, best as it was, it abounded with so many evils.

On the evening of the next day, Ormond entered with careless abruptness, Constantia's sitting apartment. He was introduced to her father. A general and unrestrained conversation immediately took place. Ormond addressed Mr. Dudley with the familiarity of an old acquaintance. In three minutes, all embarrassment was discarded. The lady and her visitant were accurate observers of each other. In the remarks of the latter, and his vein was an abundant one, there was a freedom and originality altogether new to his hearers. In his easiest and sprightliest sallies were tokens of a mind habituated to profound and extensive views. His associations were formed on a comprehensive scale.

He pretended to nothing, and studied the concealments of ambiguity more in reality than in appearance. Constantia, however, discovered a sufficient resemblance between their theories of virtue and duty. The difference between them lay in the inferences arbitrarily deduced, and in which two persons may vary without end, and yet never be repugnant. Constantia delighted her companion by the facility with which she entered into his meaning, the sagacity she displayed in drawing out his hints, circumscribing his conjectures, and thwarting or qualifying his maxims. The scene was generally replete with ardour and contention, and yet the impression left on the mind of Ormond was full of harmony. Her discourse tended to rouse him from his lethargy, to furnish him with powerful excitements, and the time spent in her company, seemed like a doubling of existence.

The comparison could not but suggest itself, between this scene and that exhibited by Hellen. With the latter voluptuous blandishments, musical prattle, and silent but expressive homage, composed a banquet delicious for a while, but whose sweetness now began to pall upon his taste. It supplied him with no new ideas, and hindered him, by the lulling sensations it inspired, from profiting by his former acquisitions. Helena was beautiful. Apply the scale, and not a member was found inelegantly disposed, or negligently moulded. Not a curve that was blemished by an angle or ruffled by asperities. The irradiations of her eyes were able to dissolve the knottiest fibres, and their azure was serene beyond any that nature had elsewhere exhibited. Over the rest of her form the glistening and rosy hues were diffused with prodigal luxuriance, and mingled in endless and wanton variety. Yet this image had fewer attractions even to the senses than that of Constance. So great is the difference between forms animated by different degrees of intelligence.

The interviews of Ormond and Constance grew more frequent. The progress which they made in the knowledge of each other was rapid. Two positions, that were favorite ones with him, were quickly subverted. He was suddenly changed, from being one of the calumniators of the female sex, to one of its warmest eulogists. This was a point on which Constantia had ever been a vigorous disputant, but her arguments, in their direct tendency, would never have made a convert of this man. Their force, intrinsically considered, was nothing. He drew his conclusions from incidental circumstances. Her reasonings might be fallacious or valid, but they were so composed, arranged and delivered, were drawn from such sources, and accompanied with such illustrations, as plainly testified a manlike energy in the reasoner. In this indirect and circuitous way, her point was unanswerably established.

Your reasoning is bad, he would say; Every one of your conclusions is false. Not a single allegation but may be easily confuted, and yet I allow that your position is uncontrovertibly proved by them. How bewildered is that man who never thinks for himself! Who rejects a principle merely because the arguments brought in support of it are insufficient. I must not reject the truth, because another has unjustifiably adopted it. I want to reach a certain hill-top. Another has reached it before me, but the ladder he used is too weak to bear me. What then? Am I to stay below on that account? No: I have only to construct one suitable to the purpose, and of strength sufficient.

A second maxim had never been confuted till now. It inculcated the insignificance and hollowness of love.[2] No pleasure he thought was to be despised for its own sake. Every thing was good in its place, but amorous gratifications were to be degraded to the bottom of the catalogue. The enjoyments of music and landscape, were of a much higher order. Epicurism[3] itself was entitled to more respect. Love, in itself, was in his opinion, of little worth, and only of importance as the source of the most terrible of intellectual maladies. Sexual sensations associating themselves, in a certain way, with our ideas, beget a disease, which has, indeed, found no place in the catalogue, but is a case of more entire subversion and confusion of mind than any other.

---

[2] "Insignificance and hollowness of love": Sophia refers again to the skepticism about emotionalized love she mentioned at the end of Chapter 12 (see note 12.7).

[3] "Epicurism": the doctrines of Greek philosopher Epicurus (341–270 B.C.E.), conventionally understood as valorizing the pursuit of rational pleasure. Epicurus was an atomist and important in the development of scientific method, teaching that nothing should be believed that cannot be empirically tested or logically demonstrated. His thinking was in vogue during the late Enlightenment, widely praised by progressive thinkers of the period, including the British Woldwinites, and referenced in Brown's earlier writings. A slogan associated with Epicurus' teachings is "*lathe biosas*," "live secretly" or "unnoticed," meaning that one should live a good life in ordinary and ethical ways, for example in supportive friendships, rather than risking the corruption caused by the pursuit of public power, celebrity, or glory.

The victim is callous to the sentiments of honor and shame, insensible to the most palpable distinctions of right and wrong, a systematic opponent of testimony, and obstinate perverter of truth.

Ormond was partly right. Madness like death can be averted by no foresight or previous contrivance. This probably is one of its characteristicks. He that witnesses its influence on another, with most horror, and most fervently deprecates its ravages, is not therefore more safe. This circumstance was realized in the history of Ormond.

This infatuation, if it may so be called, was gradual in its progress. The sensations which Hellen was now able to excite, were of a new kind. Her power was not merely weakened, but her endeavours counteracted their own end. Her fondness was rejected with disdain, or borne with reluctance. The lady was not slow in perceiving this change. The stroke of death would have been more acceptable. His own reflections were too tormenting, to make him willing to discuss them in words. He was not aware of the effects produced by this change in his demeanour, till informed of it by herself.

One evening he displayed symptoms of uncommon dissatisfaction. Her tenderness was unable to dispel it. He complained of want of sleep. This afforded an hint, which she drew forth into one of her enchanting ditties. Habit had almost conferred upon her the power of spontaneous poesy, and while she pressed his forehead to her bosom, she warbled forth a strain airy and exuberant in numbers, tender and exstatic in its imagery.

> Sleep, extend thy downy pinion,
> Hasten from thy Cell with speed;
>   Spread around thy soft dominion;
> Much those brows thy balmy presence need.
>
> Wave thy wand of slumberous power,
> Moistened in Lethèan dews,
>   To charm the busy spirits of the hour,
> And brighten memory's malignant hues.
>
> Thy mantle, dark and starless, cast
> Over my selected youth;
>   Bury, in thy womb, the mournful past,
> And soften, with thy dreams, th' asperities of truth.
>
> The changeful hues of his impassioned sleep,
> My office it shall be to watch the while;
>   With thee, my love, when fancy prompts, to weep,
> And when thou smile'st, to smile.
>
> But sleep! I charge thee, visit not these eyes,
> Nor raise thy dark pavillion here,
>   Till morrow from the cave of ocean rise,
> And whisper tuneful joy in nature's ear.

> But mutely let me lie, and sateless gaze
> At all the soul that in his visage sits,
> While spirits of harmonious air,——

Here her voice sunk, and the line terminated in a sigh. Her museful ardours were chilled by the looks of Ormond. Absorbed in his own thoughts, he appeared scarcely to attend to this strain. His sternness was proof against her accustomed fascinations. At length she pathetically complained of his coldness, and insinuated her suspicions, that his affection was transferred to another object. He started from her embrace, and after two or three turns across the room, he stood before her. His large eyes were steadfastly fixed upon her face.

Aye, said he, thou hast guessed right. The love, poor as it was, that I had for thee, is gone. Henceforth thou art desolate indeed. Would to God thou wert wise. Thy woes are but beginning; I fear they will terminate fatally; If so, the catastrophe cannot come too quickly.

I disdain to appeal to thy justice, Hellen, to remind thee of conditions solemnly and explicitly assumed. Shall thy blood be upon thy own head? No. I will bear it myself. Though the load would crush a mountain, I will bear it.

I cannot help it; I make not myself; I am moulded by circumstances: Whether I shall love thee or not, is no longer in my own choice. Marriage is, indeed, still in my power. I may give thee my name, and share with thee my fortune. Will these content thee? Thou canst not partake of my love. Thou canst have no part in my tenderness. These are reserved for another more worthy than thou.

But no. Thy state is, to the last degree, forlorn: Even marriage is denied thee. Thou wast contented to take me without it; to dispense with the name of wife, but the being who has displaced thy image in my heart, is of a different class. She will be to me a wife, or nothing, and I must be her husband, or perish.

Do not deceive thyself, Hellen. I know what it is in which thou hast placed thy felicity. Life is worth retaining by thee, but on one condition. I know the incurableness of thy infirmity; but be not deceived. Thy happiness is ravished from thee. The condition on which thou consentedst to live, is annulled. I love thee no longer.

No truth was ever more delicious; none was ever more detestable. I fight against conviction, and I cling to it. That I love thee no longer, is at once a subject of joy and of mourning. I struggle to believe thee superior to this shock: That thou wilt be happy though deserted by me. Whatever be thy destiny, my reason will not allow me to be miserable on that account: Yet I would give the world; I would forfeit every claim but that which I hope upon the heart of Constance,[4] to be sure that thy tranquillity will survive this stroke.

But let come what will, look no longer to me for offices of love. Henceforth, all intercourse of tenderness ceases. Perhaps all personal intercourse whatever. But though

---

[4] "Constance": as he affirms his love for Constantia, Ormond begins to use the same familiar form, "Constance," that the narrator Sophia introduced suggestively in her "To I. E. Rosenberg" preface (see note 0.3).

this good be refused, thou art sure of independence. I will guard thy ease and thy honor with a father's scrupulousness. Would to heaven a sister could be created by adoption. I am willing, for thy sake, to be an imposter. I will own thee to the world for my sister, and carry thee whither the cheat shall never be detected.[5] I would devote my whole life to prevarication and falsehood, for thy sake, if that would suffice to make thee happy.

To this speech Helena had nothing to answer. Her sobs and tears choked all utterance. She hid her face with her handkerchief, and sat powerless and overwhelmed with despair. Ormond traversed the room uneasily. Sometimes moving to and fro with quick steps, sometimes standing and eyeing her with looks of compassion. At length he spoke:

It is time to leave you. This is the first night that you will spend in dreary solitude. I know it will be sleepless and full of agony; but the sentence cannot be recalled. Henceforth regard me as a brother. I will prove myself one. All other claims are swallowed up in a superior affection.— In saying this, he left the house, and almost without intending it, found himself in a few minutes at Mr. Dudley's door.

---

[5] "Own thee to the world for my sister … never be detected": Ormond's affirmation that he would masquerade as Helena's brother in order to protect her will be echoed at the end of the novel when the narrator Sophia introduces dramatic claims or revelations concerning a sister of Ormond's. See note 29.5.

Chapter XVII

THE politeness of Melbourne had somewhat abated Mr. Dudley's aversion to society. He allowed himself sometimes to comply with urgent invitations. On this evening he happened to be at the house of that gentleman. Ormond entered, and found Constantia alone. An interview of this kind was seldom enjoyed, though earnestly wished for by Constantia, who was eager to renew the subject of her first conversation with Ormond. I have already explained the situation of her mind. All her wishes were concentred in the marriage of Helena. The eligibility of this scheme, in every view which she took of it, appeared in a stronger light. She was not aware that any new obstacle had arisen. She was free from the consciousness of any secret bias. Much less did her modesty suspect, that she herself would prove an insuperable impediment to this plan.

There was more than usual solemnity in Ormond's demeanour. After he was seated, he continued, contrary to his custom, to be silent. These singularities were not unobserved by Constance. They did not, however, divert her from her purpose.

I am glad to see you, said she. We so seldom enjoy the advantage of a private interview. I have much to say to you. You authorize me to deliberate on your actions, and, in some measure, to prescribe to you. This is a province which I hope to discharge with integrity and diligence. I am convinced that Hellen's happiness and your own, can be secured in one way only. I will emulate your candour, and come at once to the point. Why have you delayed so long the justice that is due to this helpless and lovely girl? There are a thousand reasons why you should think of no other alternative. You have been pleased to repose some degree of confidence in my judgment. Hear my full and deliberate opinion. Make Helena your wife. This is the unequivocal prescription of your duty.

This address was heard by Ormond without surprise; but his countenance betrayed the acuteness of his feelings. The bitterness that overflowed his heart, was perceptible in his tone when he spoke.

Most egregiously are you deceived. Such is the line with which human capacity presumes to fathom futurity. With all your discernment, you do not see that marriage would effectually destroy me. You do not see that, whether beneficial, or otherwise, in its effects, marriage is impossible. You are merely prompting me to suicide; but how shall I inflict the wound? Where is the weapon? See you not that I am powerless? Leap, say you, into the flames. See you not that I am fettered? Will a mountain move at your bidding, sooner than I in the path, which you prescribe to me?

This speech was inexplicable. She pressed him to speak less enigmatically. Had he formed his resolution? If so, arguments and remonstrances were superfluous. Without noticing her interrogatories, he continued:

I am too hasty in condemning you. You judge, not against, but without knowledge. When sufficiently informed, your decision will be right: Yet how can you be ignorant? Can you, for a moment, contemplate yourself and me, and not perceive an insuperable bar to this union?

You place me, said Constantia, in a very disagreeable predicament. I have not deserved this treatment from you. This is an unjustifiable deviation from plain dealing. Of what impediment do you speak? I can safely say that I know of none.

Well, resumed he, with augmented eagerness, I must supply you with knowledge. I repeat, that I perfectly rely on the rectitude of your judgment. Summon all your sagacity and disinterestedness, and chuse for me. You know in what light Hellen has been viewed by me. I have ceased to view her in this light. She has become an object of indifference: Nay, I am not certain that I do not hate her. Not indeed for her own sake, but because I love another. Shall I marry her whom I hate, when there exists one whom I love with unconquerable ardour?

Constantia was thunderstruck with this intelligence. She looked at him with some expression of doubt. How is this? said she: Why did you not tell me this before?

When I last talked with you on this subject, I knew it not myself. It has occurred since. I have seized the first occasion that has offered, to inform you of it. Say now, since such is my condition, ought Hellen to be my wife?

Constantia was silent. Her heart bled for what she foresaw, would be the sufferings and forlorn destiny of Hellen. She had not courage to enquire further into this new engagement.

I wait for your answer, Constance. Shall I defraud myself of all the happiness which would accrue, from a match of inclination? Shall I put fetters on my usefulness? This is the style in which you speak. Shall I preclude all the good to others, that would flow from a suitable alliance? Shall I abjure the woman I love, and marry her whom I hate?

Hatred, replied the lady, is an harsh word. Hellen has not deserved that you should hate her. I own this is a perplexing circumstance. It would be wrong to determine hastily. Suppose you give yourself to Hellen, will more than yourself be injured by it? Who is this lady? Will she be rendered unhappy by a determination in favor of another? This is a point of the utmost importance.

At these words, Ormond forsook his seat, and advanced close up to Constantia. You say true. This is a point of inexpressible importance. It would be presumption in me to decide. That is the lady's own province. And now, say truly, are you willing to accept Ormond with all his faults. Who but yourself could be mistress of all the springs of my soul? I know the sternness of your probity. This discovery will only make you more strenuously the friend of Hellen. Yet why should you not shun either extreme? Lay yourself out of view. And yet, perhaps, the happiness of Constance, is not unconcerned in this question. Is there no part of me in which you discover your own likeness? Am I deceived, or is it an incontroulable destiny that unites us?

This declaration was truly unexpected by Constance. She gathered from it nothing but excitements of grief. After some pause, she said. This appeal to me has made no change in my opinion. I still think that justice requires you to become the husband of Hellen. As to me, do you think my happiness rests upon so slight a foundation? I cannot love, but when my understanding points out to me the propriety of love. Ever since I have known you, I have looked upon you as rightfully belonging to another.

Love could not take place in my circumstances. Yet I will not conceal from you my sentiments. I am not sure that in different circumstances, I should not have loved. I am acquainted with your worth. I do not look for a faultless man. I have met with none whose blemishes were fewer.

It matters not, however, what I should have been. I cannot interfere, in this case, with the claims of my friend. I have no passion to struggle with. I hope, in every vicissitude, to enjoy your esteem, and nothing more. There is but one way in which mine can be secured, and that is by espousing this unhappy girl.

No, exclaimed Ormond. Require not impossibilities. Hellen can never be any thing to me. I should, with unspeakably more willingness, assail my own life.

What, said the lady, will Hellen think of this sudden and dreadful change. I cannot bear to think upon the feelings that this information will excite.

She knows it already. I have this moment left her. I explained to her, in few words, my motives, and assured her of my unalterable resolution. I have vowed never to see her more, but as a brother, and this vow she has just heard.

Constantia could not suppress her astonishment and compassion at this intelligence. No surely, you could not be so cruel! And this was done with your usual abruptness, I suppose. Precipitate and implacable man! Cannot you foresee the effects of this madness? You have planted a dagger in her heart. You have disappointed me. I did not think you could act so inhumanly.

Nay, beloved Constance, be not so liberal of your reproaches. Would you have me deceive her? She must shortly have known it. Could the truth be told too soon?

Much too soon, replied the lady, fervently. I have always condemned the maxims by which you act. Your scheme is headlong and barbarous. Could you not regard, with some little compassion, that love which sacrificed for your unworthy sake, honest fame and the peace of virtue? Is she not a poor outcast, goaded by compunction, and hooted at by a malignant and misjudging world, and who was it that reduced her to this deplorable condition? For whose sake, did she willingly consent to brave evils, by which the stoutest heart is appalled? Did this argue no greatness of mind? Who ever surpassed her in fidelity and tenderness? But thus has she been rewarded. I shudder to think what may be the event. Her courage cannot possibly support her, against treatment so harsh; so perversely and wantonly cruel. Heaven grant, that you are not shortly made, bitterly to lament this rashness.

Ormond was penetrated with these reproaches. They persuaded him for a moment that his deed was wrong; that he had not unfolded his intentions to Helena, with a suitable degree of gentleness and caution. Little more was said on this occasion. Constantia exhorted him, in the most earnest and pathetic manner, to return and recant, or extenuate his former declarations. He could not be brought to promise compliance. When he parted from her, however, he was half resolved to act as she advised. Solitary reflection made him change this resolution, and he returned to his own house.

During the night, he did little else, than ruminate on the events of the preceding evening. He entertained little doubt of his ultimate success with Constance. She gratified him in nothing, but left him every thing to hope. She had hitherto, it seems, regarded him with indifference, but this had been sufficiently explained. That conduct would be pursued, and that passion be entertained, which her judgment should previously approve. What then was the obstacle? It originated in the claims of Hellen, but what were these claims? It was fully ascertained that he should never be united to this girl. If so, the end contemplated by Constance, and for the sake of which only, his application was rejected, could never be obtained. Unless her rejection of him, could procure a husband for her friend, it would, on her own principles, be improper and superfluous.

What was to be done with Hellen? It was a terrible alternative to which he was reduced; to marry her or see her perish: But was this alternative quite sure? Could not she, by time or by judicious treatment, be reconciled to her lot? It was to be feared that he had not made a suitable beginning; And yet, perhaps, it was most expedient, that an hasty and abrupt sentence should be succeeded by forbearance and lenity. He regretted his precipitation, and though unused to the melting mood, tears were wrung from him, by the idea of the misery which he had probably occasioned. He was determined to repair his misconduct as speedily as possible, and to pay her a conciliating visit the next morning.

He went early to her house. He was informed by the servant that her mistress had not yet risen. Was it usual, he asked, for her to lie so late? No, he was answered; She never knew it happen before, but she supposed her mistress was not well. She was just going into her chamber to see what was the matter.

Why, said Ormond, do you suppose that she is sick?

She was poorly last night. About nine o'clock she sent out for some physic to make her sleep.

To make her sleep? exclaimed Ormond, in a faultering and affrighted accent.

Yes, she said, she wanted it for that. So I went to the pothecary's. When I come back, she was very poorly indeed. I asked her if I mightn't set up with her. No she says: I do not want any body. You may go to bed as soon as you please, and tell Fabian to do the same. I shall not want you again.

What did you buy?

Some kind of water, laud'num[1] I think they call it. She wrote it down and I carried the paper to Mr. Eckhart's, and he gave it to me in a bottle, and I gave it to my mistress.

'Tis well: Retire: I will see how she is myself.

Ormond had conceived himself fortified against every disaster. He looked for nothing but evil, and, therefore, in ordinary cases, regarded its approach without fear or surprise. Now, however, he found that his tremors would not be stilled. His perturbations increased, with every step that brought him nearer to her chamber. He knocked, but no answer was returned. He opened, advanced to the bed side, and

---

[1] "Laud'num": laudanum, a liquid preparation of opium. Helena's choice to kill herself with an overdose of this drug may be a suggestive recollection of the song she sang to Ormond in Chapter 16, which counseled "sleep" as a way to "bury, in thy womb, the mournful past."

drew back the curtains. He shrunk from the spectacle that presented itself—Was this the Hellen, that a few hours before, was blithsome with health and radiant with beauty! Her visage was serene, but sunken and pale. Death was in every line of it. To his tremulous and hurried scrutiny every limb was rigid and cold.

The habits of Ormond tended to obscure the appearances, if not to deaden the emotions of sorrow. He was so much accustomed to the frustration of well intended efforts, and confided so much in his own integrity, that he was not easily disconcerted. He had merely to advert, on this occasion, to the tumultuous state of his feelings, in order to banish their confusion and restore himself to calm. Well, said he, as he dropped the curtain and turned towards another part of the room, this, without doubt, is a rueful spectacle: Can it be helped? Is there in man the power of recalling her? There is none such in me.

She is gone: Well then, she is gone. If she were fool enough to die, I am not fool enough to follow her. I am determined to live, and be happy notwithstanding. Why not?

Yet, this is a piteous sight. What is impossible to undo, might be easily prevented. A piteous spectacle! But what else, on an ampler scale, is the universe? Nature is a theatre of suffering. What corner is unvisited by calamity and pain? I have chosen, as became me. I would rather precede thee to the grave, than live to be thy husband.

Thou hast done my work for me. Thou hast saved thyself and me from a thousand evils. Thou hast acted as seemed to thee best, and I am satisfied.

Hast thou decided erroneously? They that know thee, need not marvel at that. Endless have been the proofs of thy frailty. In favor of this last act, something may be said: It is the last thou wilt ever commit. Others only will experience its effects: Thou hast, at least, provided for thy own safety.

But what is here? A letter for me? Had thy understanding been as prompt as thy fingers, I could have borne with thee. I can easily divine the contents of this epistle.

He opened it, and found the tenor to be as follows:

"You did not use, my dear friend, to part with me in this manner. You never before treated me so roughly. I am sorry, indeed I am, that I ever offended you. Could you suppose that I intended it? And if you knew that I meant not offence, why did you take offence?

I am very unhappy, for I have lost you, my friend. You will never see me more, you say. That is very hard. I have deserved it to be sure, but I do not know how it has happened. No body more desired to please than I have done. Morning, noon and night, it was my only study; but you will love me no more; you will see me no more. Forgive me, my friend, but I must say it is very hard.

You said rightly; I do not wish to live without my friend. I have spent my life happily, heretofore. 'Tis true, there have been transient uneasinesses, but your love was a reward and a cure for every thing. I desired nothing better in this world. Did you ever hear me murmur? No: I was not so unjust. My lot was happy, infinitely beyond my deserving. I merited not to be loved by you. O that I had suitable words to express my gratitude, for your kindness! but this last meeting—how different from that which went before? Yet even then, there was something on your brow like discontent, which I could not warble nor whisper away, as I used to do. But, sad as this was, it was nothing like the last.

Could Ormond be so stern and so terrible? You knew that I would die, but you need not have talked as if I were in the way, and as if you had rather I should die than live. But one thing I rejoice at: I am a poor silly girl, but Constance is a noble and accomplished one. Most joyfully do I resign you to her, my dear friend. You say you love her: She need not be afraid of accepting you. There will be no danger of your preferring another to her. It was very natural and very right for you to prefer her to me. She and you will be happy in each other: It is this that sweetens the cup I am going to drink. Never did I go to sleep, with more good will, than I now go to death. Fare you well, my dear friend."

This letter was calculated to make a deeper impression on Ormond, than even the sight of Hellen's corpse. It was in vain, for some time, that he endeavoured to reconcile himself to this event. It was seldom that he was able to forget it. He was obliged to exert all his energies, to enable him to support the remembrance. The task was, of course, rendered easier by time.

It was immediately requisite to attend to the disposal of the corpse. He felt himself unfit for this mournful office. He was willing to relieve himself from it, by any expedient. Helena's next neighbour, was an old lady, whose scruples made her shun all direct intercourse with this unhappy girl; yet she had performed many acts of neighbourly kindness. She readily obeyed the summons of Ormond, on this occasion, to take charge of affairs, till another should assume it. Ormond returned home, and sent the following note to Constance.

"You have predicted aright. Hellen is dead. In a mind like yours every grief will be suspended, and every regard absorbed in the attention due to the remains of this unfortunate girl. *I* cannot attend to them."[2]

Constantia was extremely shocked by this intelligence, but she was not unmindful of her duty. She prepared herself with mournful alacrity, for the performance of it. Every thing that the occasion demanded, was done with diligence and care. Till this was accomplished, Ormond could not prevail upon himself to appear upon the stage. He was informed of this by a note from Constance, who requested him to take possession of the unoccupied dwelling and its furniture.

---

[2] "*I* cannot attend to them": although Ormond is presented to the reader as a forceful and fearless individual, he is unable to manage the physical necessities of death in the way that Constantia did repeatedly during the yellow fever with Whiston's corpse in Chapter 5, or Baxter's in Chapter 6. This apparent paradox may echo an analogous situation in Chapter 7, when the experienced soldier Baxter was frightened while watching Ursula Monrose (Martinette) dispose of a corpse. In all these scenes the emotional strength of the novel's women is favorably contrasted with that of its men.

Among the terms of his contract with Helena, Ormond had voluntarily inserted the exclusive property of an house and its furniture in this city, with funds adequate to her plentiful maintainance. These he had purchased and transferred to her. To this he had afterwards added a rural retreat, in the midst of spacious and well cultivated fields, three miles from Perth-Amboy, and seated on the right bank of the sound.[3] It is proper to mention that this farm was formerly the property of Mr. Dudley; had been fitted up by him, and used as his summer abode during his prosperity. In the division of his property it had fallen to one of his creditors, from whom it had been purchased by Ormond. This circumstance, in conjunction with the love, which she bore to Constance, had suggested to Hellen a scheme, which her want of foresight would, in different circumstances, have occasioned her to overlook. It was that of making her testament, by which she bequeathed all that she possessed to her friend. This was not done without the knowledge and cheerful concurrence of Ormond, who, together with Melbourne and another respectable citizen, were named executors. Melbourne and his friend were induced by their respect for Constantia, to consent to this nomination.

This had taken place before Ormond and Constance had been introduced to each other. After this event, Ormond had sometimes been employed in contriving means for securing to his new friend and her father, a subsistence, more certain than the will of Helena could afford. Her death he considered as an event equally remote and undesirable. This event, however unexpectedly, had now happened, and precluded the necessity of further consideration on this head.

Constantia could not but accept this bequest. Had it been her wish to decline, it was not in her power, but she justly regarded the leisure and independence thus conferred upon her, as inestimable benefits. It was a source of unbounded satisfaction on her father's account, who was once more seated in the bosom of affluence. Perhaps in a rational estimate, one of the most fortunate events that could have befallen those persons, was that period of adversity through which they had been doomed to pass. Most of the defects that adhered to the character of Mr. Dudley, had, by this means, been exterminated. He was now cured of those prejudices which his early prosperity had instilled, and which had flowed from luxurious indulgences. He had learned to

---

[3] "Three miles from Perth Amboy ... on the right bank of the sound": Perth Amboy, a township in Middlesex County, east-central New Jersey, situated opposite the southern end of Staten Island, at the confluence of Raritan Bay and the narrow Staten Island Sound (or Arthur Kill), that separates Staten Island from mainland New Jersey. The novel's final scenes will take place at this house in Chapters 26–29.

Brown's close friend, theater manager and playwright William Dunlap, owned a farm in Perth Amboy where Brown and other associates from the New York circle often visited (see the excerpt from Elihu Hubbard's Smith's diary in Related Texts); this is where Brown went to recover after he contracted yellow fever during the New York epidemic of August–September 1798, just before he began writing *Ormond*. Like a number of other motifs in this novel (Stephen Dudley's training as a painter in London and blindness, etc.), this detail makes an "inside" allusion to aspects of Dunlap's life. For more on the function of such allusions, see the Introduction.

estimate himself at his true value, and to sympathize with sufferings which he himself had partaken.

It was easy to perceive in what light Constantia was regarded by her father. He never reflected on his relation to her without rapture. Her qualities were the objects of his adoration. He resigned himself with pleasure to her guidance. The chain of subordination and duties was reversed. By the ascendancy of her genius and wisdom, the province of protection and the tribute of homage, had devolved upon her. This had resulted from incessant experience of the wisdom of her measures, and the spectacle of her fortitude and skill in every emergency.

It seemed as if but one evil adhered to the condition of this man. His blindness was an impediment to knowledge and enjoyment, of which, the utmost to be hoped was, that he should regard it without pungent regret, and that he should sometimes forget it: That his mind should occasionally stray into foreign paths, and lose itself in sprightly conversations, or benign reveries. This evil, however, was, by no means, remediless.

A surgeon of uncommon skill had lately arrived from Europe. He was one of the numerous agents and dependants of Ormond, and had been engaged to abdicate his native country for purposes widely remote from his profession. The first use that was made of him, was to introduce him to Mr. Dudley. The diseased organs were critically examined, and the patient was, with considerable difficulty, prevailed upon to undergo the necessary operation. His success corresponded with Constantia's wishes, and her father was once more restored to the enjoyment of light.[4]

These were auspicious events—Constantia held herself amply repaid by them, for all that she had suffered. These sufferings had indeed been light, when compared with the effects usually experienced by others in a similar condition. Her wisdom had extracted its sting from adversity, and without allowing herself to feel much of the evils of its reign, had employed it as an instrument by which the sum of her present happiness was increased. Few suffered less, in the midst of poverty, than she. No one ever extracted more felicity from the prosperous reverse.

---

[4] "Restored to the enjoyment of light": surgery to repair cataracts, identified as the cause of Dudley's blindness in Chapter 2, was performed regularly in the eighteenth century, although with a very uneven rate of success. See, for example, the discussion of eye surgery, with a chapter on cataract removal, in a standard period work such as Benjamin Bell's *A System of Surgery* (Edinburgh: Charles Elliott, 1783; six editions by 1796).

Chapter XVIII

WHEN time had somewhat mitigated the memory of the late disaster, the inter-course between Ormond and Constance was renewed. The lady did not overlook her obligations to her friend: It was to him that she was indebted for her father's restoration to sight, and to whom both owed, essentially, though indirectly, their present affluence. In her mind, gratitude was no perverse or ignoble principle. She viewed this man as the authour of extensive benefits, of which her situation enabled her to judge with more accuracy than others. It created no bias on her judgment, or, at least, none of which she was sensible. Her equity was perfectly unfettered, and she decided in a way contrary to his inclination, with as little scruple as if the benefits had been received, not by herself, but by him. She, indeed, intended his benefit, though she thwarted his inclinations.

She had few visitants beside himself. Their interviews were daily and unformal. The fate of Hellen never produced any reproaches on her part. She saw the uselessness of recrimination, not only because she desired to produce emotions different from those which invective is adapted to excite, but because it was more just to soothe than to exasperate, the inquietudes which haunted him.

She now enjoyed leisure. She had always been solicitous for mental improvement. Any means subservient to this end were valuable. The conversation of Ormond was an inexhaustible fund. By the variety of topics and the excitements to reflection it supplied, a more plenteous influx of knowledge was produced, than could have flowed from any other source. There was no end to the detailing of facts, and the canvassing of theories.

I have already said, that Ormond was engaged in schemes of an arduous and elevated nature. These were the topics of epistolary discussion between him and a certain number of coadjutors, in different parts of the world. In general discourse, it was proper to maintain a uniform silence respecting these, not only because they involved principles and views, remote from vulgar apprehension, but because their success, in some measure, depended on their secrecy.[1] He could not give a stronger proof of his confidence in the sagacity and steadiness of Constance than he now gave, by imparting to her his schemes, and requesting her advice and assistance in the progress of them.

His disclosures, however, were imperfect. What knowledge was imparted, instead of appeasing, only tended to inflame her curiosity. His answers to her enquiries were prompt, and at first sight, sufficiently explicit, but upon reconsideration, an obscurity

---

[1] "Depended on their secrecy": the narrator Sophia again suggests that Ormond is part of a secret, Illuminati-like organization; for an earlier example see note 12.3. By discussing such plans with Constantia, Ormond may be slowly guiding her toward admission within the secret group and knowledge of its plans. For more on the Illuminati scare, see Related Texts.

seemed to gather round them, to be dispelled by new interrogatories.[2] These, in like manner, effected a momentary purpose, but were sure speedily to lead into new conjectures, and re-immerse her in doubts. The task was always new, was always in the point of being finished, and always to be re-commenced.

Ormond aspired to nothing more ardently than to hold the reins of opinion.[3] To exercise absolute power over the conduct of others, not by constraining their limbs, or by exacting obedience to his authority, but in a way of which his subjects should be scarcely conscious. He desired that his guidance should controul their steps, but that his agency, when most effectual, should be least suspected.

If he were solicitous to govern the thoughts of Constantia, or to regulate her condition, the mode which he pursued had hitherto been admirably conducive to that end. To have found her friendless and indigent, accorded, with the most fortunate exactness, with his views. That she should have descended to this depth, from a prosperous height, and therefore be a stranger to the torpor which attends hereditary poverty,[4] and be qualified rightly to estimate, and use the competence to which, by his means, she was now restored, was all that his providence would have prescribed.

Her thoughts were equally obsequious to his direction. The novelty and grandeur of his schemes could not fail to transport a mind, ardent and capacious, as that of Constance. Here his fortune had been no less propitious. He did not fail to discover, and was not slow to seize the advantages flowing thence. By explaining his plans, opportunity was furnished to lead and to confine her meditations to the desirable tract. By adding fictitious embellishments, he adapted it with more exactness to his purpose. By piece-meal and imperfect disclosures, her curiosity was kept alive.

I have described Ormond as having contracted a passion for Constance. This passion certainly existed in his heart, but it must not be conceived to be immutable, or to operate independently of all those impulses and habits which time had interwoven in his character. The person and affections of this woman, were the objects sought by him, and which it was the dearest purpose of his existence to gain. This was his supreme good, though the motives to which it was indebted for its pre-eminence in his imagination, were numerous and complex.

---

[2] "Interrogatories": questions. Ormond is said to be gaining influence over Constantia by illumination, silently encouraging her desire for "mental improvement," or training her to think actively through a set of questions, rather than passively accept a set of doctrinaire propositions that he otherwise might frankly state.

[3] "Hold the reins of opinion": by looking to influence popular social and cultural beliefs, Ormond and his organization downplay the importance of merely political power or the direct overthrow of governments. For him, the noncoercive influence of ideas (ideology) is potentially more powerful than weapons or physical violence. In a projective form, this was also a key concern of the conservative anti-Illuminati fantasists in power in the U.S.

[4] "Hereditary poverty": Ormond distinguishes between those who are born into poverty and those who fall into it. Because she has already experienced changes in her social status, Constantia might be more willing to consider the possibility of other social changes.

I have enumerated his opinions on the subject of wedlock. The question will obviously occur, whether Constantia was sought by him, with upright or flagitious[5] views. His sentiments and resolutions, on this head, had for a time fluctuated, but were now steadfast. Marriage was, in his eyes, hateful and absurd as ever. Constance was to be obtained by any means. If other terms were rejected, he was willing, for the sake of this good, to accept her as a wife; but this was a choice to be made, only when every expedient was exhausted, for reconciling her to a compact of a different kind.

For this end, he prescribed to himself, a path suited to the character of this lady. He made no secret of his sentiments and views. He avowed his love and described, without scruple, the scope of his wishes. He challenged her to confute his principles, and promised a candid audience and profound consideration to her arguments. Her present opinions he knew to be adverse to his own, but he hoped to change them, by subtilty and perseverance. His further hopes and designs, he concealed from her. She was unaware, that if he were unable to effect a change in her creed, he was determined to adopt a system of imposture. To assume the guise of a convert to her doctrines, and appear as devout as herself in his notions of the sanctity of marriage.

Perhaps it was not difficult, to have foreseen the consequence of these projects. Constantia's peril was imminent. This arose not only from the talents and address of Ormond, but from the community of sentiment, which already existed between them. She was unguarded in a point, where, if not her whole, yet, doubtless, her principal security and strongest bulwark would have existed. She was unacquainted with religion. She was unhabituated to conform herself to any standard, but that connected with the present life. Matrimonial, as well as every other human duty, was disconnected in her mind, with any awful or divine sanction. She formed her estimate of good and evil, on nothing but terestrial and visible consequences.

This defect in her character, she owed to her father's system of education. Mr. Dudley was an adherent to what he conceived to be true religion. No man was more passionate in his eulogy of his own form of devotion and belief, or in his invectives against Atheistical dogmas; but he reflected that religion assumed many forms, one only of which is salutary or true, and that truth in this respect, is incompatible with infantile and premature instruction.[6]

To this subject, it was requisite to apply the force of a mature and unfettered understanding. For this end he laboured to lead away the juvenile reflections of

---

[5] "Flagitious": "extremely wicked or criminal; heinous or villainous" (*OED*).

[6] "True religion … premature instruction": intellectualized belief outside specific doctrines or dogmas. Constantia has been brought up outside of any particular (Christian) doctrines, especially those that insist on submission to codes of behavior. Instead, Dudley has raised her according to the view that every individual grows to recognize the true form of their own chosen spiritual belief system, which might not even take a Christian form. Since Dudley has brought up Constantia within the belief that every individual is responsible for forming their own mature opinion regarding divinity and moral conduct, the narrator fears that she lacks the armor that a premade religious doctrine might provide against Ormond's skepticism toward traditional social codes, especially the one that prescribes marriage as the device for legitimizing the sexual gratification of heterosexual passion.

Constantia, from religious topics, to detain them in the paths of history and eloquence. To accustom her to the accuracy of geometrical deduction, and to the view of those evils, that have flowed in all ages, from mistaken piety.[7]

In consequence of this scheme, her habits rather than her opinions, were undevout. Religion was regarded by her, not with disbelief, but with absolute indifference. Her good sense forbad her to decide before enquiry, but her modes of study and reflection, were foreign to, and unfitted her for this species of discussion. Her mind was seldom called to meditate on this subject, and when it occurred, her perceptions were vague and obscure. No objects, in the sphere which she occupied, were calculated to suggest to her the importance of investigation and certainty.

It becomes me to confess, however reluctantly, thus much concerning my friend. However abundantly endowed in other respects, she was a stranger to the felicity and excellence flowing from religion. In her struggles with misfortune, she was supported and cheered by the sense of no approbation, but her own. A defect of this nature, will perhaps be regarded as of less moment, when her extreme youth is remembered. All opinions in her mind were mutable, inasmuch as the progress of her understanding was incessant.

If was otherwise with Ormond. His disbelief was at once unchangeable and strenuous. The universe was to him, a series of events, connected by an undesigning and inscrutable necessity, and an assemblage of forms, to which no begining or end can be conceived. Instead of transient views and vague ideas, his meditations, on religious points, had been intense. Enthusiasm was added to disbelief, and he not only dissented but abhorred.

He deemed it prudent, however, to disguise sentiments, which, if unfolded in their full force, would wear to her the appearance of insanity:[8] But he saw and was eager to improve the advantage, which his anti-nuptial creed derived from the unsettled state of her opinions. He was not unaware, likewise, of the auspicious and indispensible co-operation of love. If this advocate were wanting in her bosom, all his efforts would be in vain. If this pleader were engaged in his behalf, he entertained no doubts of his ultimate success. He conceived that her present situation, all whose comforts were the fruits of his beneficence, and which afforded her no other subject of contemplation than himself, was as favorable as possible to the growth of this passion.

Constance was acquainted with his wishes. She could not fail to see, that she might speedily be called upon to determine a momentous question. Her own sensations and the character of Ormond, were, therefore, scrutinized with suspicious attention. Marriage could be justified in her eyes, only by community of affections and

---

[7] "Mistaken piety": Dudley's distrust of institutionalized religion does not rely on a sentimental notion that individuals can "naturally" or "spontaneously" learn spiritual truth, as Rousseau might claim. Instead, he insists on the power of abstract reason ("geometrical deduction") to protect against religious superstition and errors. The narrator Sophia, on the other hand, bemoans Constantia's lack of religious indoctrination and presents it as a defect in her education.

[8] "Insanity": the first suggestion that the narrator Sophia may see Ormond as deranged.

opinions. She might love without the sanction of her judgment, but while destitute of that sanction, she would never suffer it to sway her conduct.[9]

Ormond was imperfectly known. What knowledge she had gained, flowed chiefly from his own lips, and was therefore unattended with certainty. What portion of deceit or disguise was mixed with his conversation, could be known, only by witnessing his actions with her own eyes, and comparing his testimony with that of others. He had embraced a multitude of opinions, which appeared to her erroneous. Till these were rectified, and their conclusions were made to correspond, wedlock was improper. Some of these obscurities might be dispelled, and some of these discords be resolved into harmony by time. Meanwhile it was proper to guard the avenues to her heart, and screen herself from self-delusion.

There was no motive to conceal her reflections, on this topic, from her father. Mr. Dudley discovered, without her assistance, the views of Ormond. His daughter's happiness was blended with his own. He lived, but in the consciousness of her tranquility. Her image was seldom absent from his eyes, and never from his thoughts. The emotions which it excited, sprung but in part from the relationship of father. It was gratitude and veneration, which she claimed from him, and which filled him with rapture.

He ruminated deeply on the character of Ormond. The political and anti-theological tenets of this man, were regarded, not merely with disapprobation, but antipathy. He was not ungrateful for the benefits which had been conferred upon him. Ormond's peculiarities of sentiment, excited no impatience, as long as he was regarded merely as a visitant. It was only as one claiming to posses his daughter, that his presence excited in Mr. Dudley, trepidation and loathing.

Ormond was unacquainted with what was passing in the mind of Mr. Dudley. The latter conceived his own benefactor and his daughter's friend, to be entitled to the most scrupulous and affable urbanity. His objections to a nearer alliance, were urged with frequent and pathetic vehemence, only in his private interviews with Constance. Ormond and he seldom met: Mr. Dudley, as soon as his sight was perfectly retrieved, betook himself with eagerness to painting, an amusement, which his late privations had only contributed to endear to him.

Things remained nearly on their present footing for some months. At the end of this period, some engagement obliged Ormond to leave the city. He promised to return with as much speed as circumstances would admit. Meanwhile his letters supplied her with topics of reflection. These were frequently received, and were models of that energy of style, which results from simplicity of structure, from picturesque epithets, and from the compression of much meaning into few words. His arguments seldom imparted conviction, but delight never failed to flow from their lucid order and cogent brevity. His narratives were unequaled for rapidity and comprehensiveness. Every sentence was a treasury to moralists and painters.

---

[9] "Sway her conduct": Constantia insists that reason should take precedence over her emotions. In the next paragraphs she goes on to indicate that individual reason is not sufficient by itself, for intellectual clarity must come about through dialogue or group conversation that juxtaposes multiple points of view, in this case with her father.

Chapter XIX

DOMESTIC and studious occupations did not wholly engross the attention of Constance. Social pleasures were precious to her heart, and she was not backward to form fellowships and friendships, with those around her. Hitherto she had met with no one, entitled to an uncommon portion of regard, or worthy to supply the place of the friend of her infancy.[1] Her visits were rare, and as yet, chiefly confined to the family of Mr. Melbourne. Here she was treated with flattering distinctions, and enjoyed opportunities of extending as far as she pleased, her connections with the gay and opulent. To this she felt herself by no means inclined, and her life was still eminently distinguished by love of privacy, and habits of seclusion.

One morning, feeling an indisposition to abstraction, she determined to drop in, for an hour, on Mrs. Melbourne. Finding Mrs. Melbourne's parlour unoccupied, she proceeded unceremoniously, to an apartment on the second floor, where that lady was accustomed to sit. She entered, but this room was likewise empty. Here she cast her eyes on a collection of prints, copied from the Farnese collection, and employed herself, for some minutes, in comparing the forms of Titiano and the Caracchi.[2]

---

[1] "Friend of her infancy": another instance in which the narrator refers to herself in such a way as to suggest that she is closer to Constantia than anyone else. For previous examples see notes 2.10 and 8.2.

[2] "Farnese collection ... Titiano and the Caracchi": well-known examples of classical and Renaissance art (for prior reference to classical and Italianate art, see note 1.2).

The massive Farnese collection in Rome was built up by aristocratic patron Alessandro Farnese (1520–1589), a diplomat, cardinal, and grandson of Pope Paul III (1468–1549; also known as Alessandro Farnese before assuming the papacy). The Farnese family had long been noted as patrons of the arts, but Alessandro vastly increased the family holdings and transformed its Roman palace, the Palazzo Farnese, into a sort of arts academy. A notable aspect of the collection was the recreation of classical (Greek and Roman) sculptures and the commissioning of paintings from notable artists such as Tiziano Vecellio (c. 1488–1576), better known as Titian or Titiano, and Annibale Carracci (1560–1609), who designed an immense fresco, *The Loves of the Gods* (1597–1608), for the palace's ceiling. Thus the prints Constantia examines are reproductions of images by Titian and Carracci held in the Farnese. Many of these images are drawn from classical mythology and depict idealized nude bodies allegorizing erotic themes of longing, abandon, or rape. The central theme of Carracci's fresco, for example, is drawn from Ovid's *Metamorphoses*, the collection of mythological legends cited in Chapter 14 (see note 14.2), and depicts a riotous Bacchus and Ariadne on their way to bed, an image that sexualizes the traditional theme of triumphal military procession.

Brown was certainly aware of the erotic associations of images drawn from Ovid and classical mythology. In Chapter 11 of his novel *Arthur Mervyn, Second Part* (1800) he places one of these images on the wall of a brothel. Given that Constantia's viewing leads immediately, in the next sentence, to music that reintroduces another sexually free woman, Brown may also be alluding to a 1798 print edition of ribald sonnets by Pietro Aretino (1492–1650), a close friend of Titian's. Arentino wrote the poetry to accompany a famous but now lost 1524 edition of engravings taken from a series of paintings of sexual positions by Marcantonio Raimondi (1480–1534). The 1798 edition — *L'Aretin d'Augustin Carrache; ou, Recueil de postures érotiques* (Paris: P. Didot, 1798) — had illustrations attributed to Agostino Carracci (1557–1602), brother to Annibale, whose work was also in the Farnese collections.

Suddenly, notes of peculiar sweetness, were wafted to her ear from without. She listened with surprise, for the tones of her father's lute were distinctly recognized. She hied to the window, which chanced to look into a back court. The music was perceived to come from the window of the next house. She recollected her interview with the purchaser of her instrument, at the musical shop, and the powerful impression which the stranger's countenance had made upon her.[3]

The first use she had made of her recent change of fortune, was to endeavour the recovery of this instrument. The musical dealer, when reminded of the purchase, and interrogated as to the practicability of regaining the lute, for which she was willing to give treble the price, answered that he had no knowledge of the foreign lady, beyond what was gained at the interview which took place in Constantia's presence. Of her name, residence, and condition, he knew nothing, and had endeavoured in vain to acquire knowledge.

Now this incident seemed to have furnished her with the information she so earnestly sought. This performer was probably the stranger herself. Her residence so near the Melbournes, and in an house which was the property of the Magistrate,[4] might be means of information as to her condition, and perhaps of introduction to a personal acquaintance.

While engaged in these reflections, Mrs. Melbourne entered the apartment. Constantia related this incident to her friend, and stated the motives of her present curiosity. Her friend willingly imparted what knowledge she possessed relative to this subject. This was the sum.

This house had been hired, previously to the appearance of yellow fever, by an English family, who left their native soil, with a view to a permanent abode in the new world. They had scarcely taken possession of the dwelling, when they were terrified by the progress of the epidemic. They had fled from the danger, but this circumstance, in addition to some others, induced them to change their scheme. An evil so unwonted as pestilence, impressed them with a belief of perpetual danger, as long as they remained on this side of the ocean. They prepared for an immediate return to England.

---

[3] "Back court ... stranger's countenance ... upon her": the way Constantia gazes into a neighbor's backyard recalls the Baxter episode in Chapter 7, and the music reminds Constantia of the mysterious, French-speaking Ursula Monrose whose face made a powerful impression when she bought Stephen Dudley's lute in Chapter 8 (see note 8.4).

[4] "Property of the Magistrate": the shortly to be named Martinette de Beauvais rents her apartment from Constantia's new friends the Melbournes and thereby extends a pattern of earlier indirect associations and encounters with Constantia. This coincidence and hidden proximity may hint at the identity of Monrose and Martinette, which will be revealed explicitly later in this chapter (see note 19.11). But both cases, and likewise the scene in which the lute is sold, emphasize the manner in which Constantia's relations to other women often pass through financial transactions that benefit men. This pattern will be broken in the following interaction with Martinette de Beauvais, in which the two women exchange the lute between them free of any charge.

For this end their house was relinquished, and their splendid furniture destined to be sold by auction. Before this event could take place, application was made to Mr. Melbourne, by a lady, whom his wife's description, shewed to be the same with her of whom Constantia was in search. She not only rented the house, but negociated by means of her landlord, the purchase of the furniture.

Her servants were blacks, and all but one, who officiated as steward, unacquainted with the English language.[5] Some accident had proved her name to be Beauvais. She had no visitants, very rarely walked abroad, and then only in the evening with a female servant in attendance.[6] Her hours appeared to be divided between the lute and the pen. As to her previous history or her present sources of subsistence, Mrs. Melbourne's curiosity had not been idle, but no consistent information was obtainable. Some incident had given birth to the conjecture, that she was wife, or daughter, or sister of Beauvais, the partizan of Brissot, whom the faction of Marat had lately consigned to the scaffold, but this conjecture was unsupported by suitable evidence.[7]

---

[5] "Unacquainted with the English language": since Martinette will explain in Chapter 21 that, during the fever, she lived among the city's French-speaking refugees from the slave revolution in Haiti (St. Domingue), the servants here are implicitly French- and African-language-speaking free blacks or slaves from that community. In Chapter 20 she explains that she previously traveled through Haiti on her way to fight in the American Revolution.

[6] "Only in the evening with a female servant in attendance": a Creole woman strolling at night with a black female servant could easily be taken for a prostitute or procuress (a female pimp). For more, see the excerpts from Moreau de Saint-Méry in Related Texts.

[7] "Conjecture … Beauvais … Brissot … Marat … scaffold … evidence": that is, although her identity is mysterious, Martinette seems to be closely linked with a recently executed member of the French revolutionary Girondin faction. For more on the Girondin connection, see Related Texts.

The name Beauvais here refers to Benoît Lesterpt-Beauvais (1750–1793; usually identified simply as "Beauvais" in the 1790s Anglophone histories familiar to Brown), a delegate to the National Convention who was executed along with twenty-one other Girondins on October 31, 1793, during the Terror phase of the French Revolution. In January 1794, U.S. and English newspapers reported the event and listed the executed delegates. The Girondins were a bourgeois party that led the French revolutionary process in its early phase, but then lost control to the more radical Jacobins and sansculottes (laboring-class) factions, who subsequently attacked and executed the Girondin leaders as enemies of the Revolution. Because one of their leaders was Jacques-Pierre Brissot (1754–1793; also executed along with Beauvais), Girondins were also styled "partisans of Brissot" or "Brissotins." Anglophone progressives and radicals, including Brown and like-minded friends, almost unanimously regarded the Girondins as revolutionary heroes and martyrs, and condemned the Jacobin faction for descending into violent partisanship and executing their opponents. Crudely put, the Girondins typically appear in Anglophone progressive writings of the 1790s as "good" revolutionaries, while the Jacobins are stigmatized as the "bad" or fallen side of the revolution.

Jean-Paul Marat (1743–1793) was a former physician, political publicist, and leader in the Jacobin faction, who played a central role in the downfall of the Girondins. In early 1793 the Girondins attempted to prosecute Marat, but he was acquitted and returned to the National Convention with greatly increased power, which he used to weaken the Girondins. Marat was famously assassinated in his bathtub on July 13, 1793, by female Girondin sympathizer Charlotte Corday (1768–1793), a young woman from Normandy. Corday was then tried and guillotined four days later. This

This tale by no means diminished Constantia's desire of personal intercourse. She saw no means of effecting her purpose. Mrs. Melbourne was unqualified to introduce her, having been discouraged in all the advances she had made towards a more friendly intercourse. Constance reflected, that her motives to seclusion, would probably induce this lady to treat others as her friend had been treated.

It was possible, however, to gain access to her, if not as a friend, yet as the original proprietor of the lute. She determined to employ the agency of Roseveldt, the musical-shopman, for the purpose of re-buying this instrument. To enforce her application, she commissioned this person, whose obliging temper entitled him to confidence, to state her inducements for originally offering it for sale, and her motives for desiring the repossession on any terms which the lady thought proper to dictate.

Roseveldt fixed an hour in which it was convenient for him to execute her commission. This hour having passed, Constance, who was anxious respecting his success, hastened to his house. Roseveldt delivered the instrument, which the lady, having listened to his pleas and offers, directed to be gratuitously restored to Constance. At first, she had expressed her resolution to part with it on no account, and at no price. Its music was her only recreation, and this instrument surpassed any she had ever before seen, in the costliness and delicacy of its workmanship. But Roseveldt's representations produced an instant change of resolution, and she not only eagerly consented to restore it, but refused to receive any thing in payment.

Constantia was deeply affected by this unexpected generosity. It was not her custom to be outstripped in this career. She now condemned herself for her eagerness to regain this instrument. During her father's blindness, it was a powerful, because the only solace of his melancholy. Now he had no longer the same anxieties to encounter, and books and the pencil were means of gratification always at hand. The lute, therefore, she imagined could be easily dispensed with by Mr. Dudley, whereas its power of consoling might be as useful to the unknown lady, as it had formerly been to her father. She readily perceived in what manner it became her to act. Roseveldt was

---

assassination, in turn, contributed to the atmosphere that led to the arrest and execution of the Girondins as State enemies in September and October.

In the context of *Ormond*, it is notable in symbolic terms that the Terror and Girondin-Jacobin struggles occur simultaneously with the novel's earlier action and yellow fever epidemic. The execution of Beauvais and Brissot on October 31 occurs near the height of the 1793 epidemic in Philadelphia, providing yet another parallel between biological and political convulsions.

Finally, because Martinette takes refuge during the fever with the (mixed-race) community of refugees from the slave revolution in Haiti, it is significant that Beauvais is also the name of an important general in the Haitian revolution, Louis-Jacques Beauvais (1760–1799), mentioned in U.S. newspaper articles available to Brown throughout the 1790s as a "mulatto general" leading revolutionary blacks. This Beauvais, like the fictional Martinette, fought alongside French troops in the American Revolution, notably in the Siege of Savannah (October 1779) as part of the Fontages Legion, a contingent of "free men of color" from Haiti. It was these officers, returning to the Caribbean from early training and experience in the context of the American Revolution, who formed the core of the black military expertise and leadership that allowed the Haitians to overthrow French and then British colonialists during the 1790s.

commissioned to re-deliver the lute, and to intreat the lady's acceptance of it. The tender was received without hesitation, and Roseveldt dismissed without any enquiry relative to Constance.

These transactions were reflected on by Constance with considerable earnestness. The conduct of the stranger, her affluent and lonely state, her conjectural relationship to the actors in the great theatre of Europe, were mingled together in the fancy of Constance, and embellished with the conceptions of her beauty, derived from their casual meeting at Roseveldt's. She forgot not their similitude in age and sex, and delighted to prolong the dream of future confidence and friendship to take place between them. Her heart sighed for a companion fitted to partake in all her sympathies.

This strain, by being connected with the image of a being like herself, who had grown up with her from childhood, who had been entwined with her earliest affections, but from whom she had been severed from the period at which her father's misfortunes commenced, and of whose present condition she was wholly ignorant, was productive of the deepest melancholy. It filled her with excruciating, and for a time irremediable sadness. It formed a kind of paroxysm, which like some febrile affections, approach and retire without warning, and against the most vehement struggles.

In this mood, her fancy was thronged with recollections of scenes, in which her friend had sustained a part. Their last interview was commonly revived in her remembrance so forcibly, as almost to produce a lunatic conception of its reality. A ditty which they sung together on that occasion, flowed to her lips. If ever human tones were qualified to convey the whole soul, they were those of Constance when she sung;—

> The breeze awakes, the bark prepares,
> To waft me to a distant shore:
> But far beyond this world of cares,
> We meet again to part no more.[8]

These fits, were accustomed to approach and to vanish by degrees. They were transitory but not infrequent, and were pregnant with such agonizing tenderness, such heart breaking sighs, and a flow of such better yet delicious tears, that it were not easily decided whether the pleasure or the pain surmounted. When symptoms of their coming were felt, she hastened into solitude, that the progress of her feelings might endure no restraint.

On the evening of the day, on which the lute had been sent to the foreign lady, Constantia was alone in her chamber, immersed in desponding thoughts. From these

---

[8] "Part no more": like Helena's song in Chapter 16, this quatrain is Brown's. The narrator claims that Constantia's desire for female companionship leads to thoughts of herself, Constantia's "childhood friend" (in the previous paragraph), from whom Constantia was separated sometime around 1789–1790 (the dates of the separation are clarified in Chapter 21). This melancholy leads her to her sing a lover's suicidal song that looks forward to reunification with the beloved in the afterlife.

she was recalled by Fabian, her black servant,[9] who announced a guest. She was loath to break off the thread of her present meditations, and enquired with a tone of some impatience, Who was the guest? The servant was unable to tell; It was a young lady whom he had never before seen; She had opened for herself, and entered the parlour without previous notice.

Constance paused at this relation. Her thoughts had recently been fixed upon Sophia Westwyn.[10] Since their parting four years before, she had heard no tidings of this woman. Her fears imagined no more probable cause of her friend's silence than her death. This, however, was uncertain. The question now occurred, and brought with it, sensations that left her no power to move; Was this the guest?

Her doubts were quickly dispelled, for the stranger, taking a light from the table, and not brooking the servant's delays, followed Fabian to the chamber of his mistress. She entered with careless freedom, and presented, to the astonished eyes of Constantia, the figure she had met at Roseveldt's, and the purchaser of her lute.[11]

The stranger advanced towards her with quick steps, and mingling tones of benignity[12] and sprightliness, said:

I have come to perform a duty. I have received from you to-day a lute, that I valued almost as my best friend. To find another in America, would not, perhaps, be possible; but, certainly, none equally superb and exquisite as this can be found. To shew how highly I esteem the gift, I have come in person to thank you for it.—There she stopped.

Constance could not suddenly recover from the extreme surprize into which the unexpectedness of this meeting, had thrown her. She could scarcely sufficiently suppress this confusion, to enable her to reply to these rapid effusions of her visitant, who resumed, with augmented freedom:

---

[9] "Fabian, her black servant": Helena mentioned a servant named Fabian before she committed suicide in Chapter 17, and the implication is that Constantia has inherited the servant along with the rest of the household and staff after Helena's death. In this period, elite Roman or classicizing names like this one—e.g., Pompey, Fabian, Caesar, Hannibal—were frequently chosen by whites for African servants and slaves, partly because of the paradoxical or antithetical turn that occurs when the name of an eminent general is given to a lowly slave.

[10] "Sophia Westwyn": the first appearance of the maiden name of the narrator Sophia. Her names and marriage will be explained when her backstory is provided in Chapters 23–24. Possibly "Westwyn" suggests a playful echo of "Sophia Western," the gentry heiress character in Henry Fielding's comic novel *Tom Jones* (1749), or of Giustiniana Wynne, Countess Rosenberg, the Anglo-Venetian author of enlightened essays who is likely alluded to in Sophia's note "To I. E. Rosenberg" at the beginning of the narrative (see note 0.1). Brown also used the name Sophia for characters in several lesser fiction fragments from the 1790s that were published posthumously.

As she did in Chapter 8, when she highlights her own portrait before explaining Constantia's verbal portrait of Ursula Monrose, Sophia here competitively asserts her own importance to Constantia immediately before explaining how Constantia meets and is again fascinated by Martinette.

[11] "Purchaser of her lute": the first confirmation that Martinette de Beauvais is the same person Constantia has previously encountered and heard about as Ursula Monrose.

[12] "Benignity": kindness.

I came, as I said, to thank you, but, to say the truth, that was not all. I came likewise to see you. Having done my errand, I suppose I must go. I would fain stay longer and talk to you a little: Will you give me lieve?

Constance, scarcely retrieving her composure, stammered out a polite assent. They seated themselves, and the visitant, pressing the hand which she had taken, proceeded in a strain so smooth, so flowing, sliding from grave to gay, blending vivacity with tenderness, interpreting Constantia's silence with so keen sagacity, and accounting for the singularities of her own deportment, in a way so respectful to her companion, and so worthy of a steadfast and pure mind in herself, that every embarrassment and scruple, were quickly banished from their interview.

In an hour the guest took her lieve. No promise of repeating her visit, and no request that Constantia would repay it, was made. Their parting seemed to be the last; Whatever purpose having been contemplated, appeared to be accomplished by this transient meeting. It was of a nature deeply to interest the mind of Constance. This was the lady who talked with Roseveldt, and bargained with Melbourne, and they had been induced by appearances, to suppose her ignorant of any language but French; but, her discourse, on the present occasion, was in English, and was distinguished by unrivalled fluency. Her phrases and habits of pronouncing, were untinctured with any foreign mixture, and bespoke the perfect knowledge of a native of America.[13]

On the next evening, while Constantia was reviewing this transaction, calling up and weighing the sentiments which the stranger had uttered, and indulging some regret at the unlikelihood of their again meeting, Martinette (for I will henceforth call her by her true name) entered the apartment as abruptly as before. She accounted for the visit, merely by the pleasure it afforded her, and proceeded in a strain even more versatile and brilliant, than before. This interview ended like the first, without any tokens, on the part of the guest, of resolution or desire to renew it, but a third interview took place on the ensuing day.

Henceforth Martinette became a frequent but hasty visitant, and Constantia became daily more enamoured of her new acquaintance. She did not overlook peculiarities in the conversation and deportment of this woman. These exhibited no tendencies to confidence, or traces of sympathy. They merely denoted large experience, vigourous faculties and masculine attainments. Herself was never introduced, except as an observer, but her observations, on government and manners, were profound and critical.

Her education seemed not widely different, from that which Constantia had received. It was classical and mathematical, but to this was added a knowledge of political and military transactions, in Europe, during the present age, which implied the possession of better means of information, than books. She depicted scenes and characters, with the accuracy of one who had partaken and witnessed them herself.

---

[13] "English ... fluency ... native of America": although she pretended otherwise during the exchange of the lute in Chapter 8, Martinette speaks English with the fluency of a native speaker.

Constantia's attention had been chiefly occupied by personal concerns. Her youth had passed in contention with misfortune, or in the quietudes of study. She could not be unapprized of contemporary revolutions and wars, but her ideas respecting them were indefinite and vague. Her views and her inferences on this head, were general and speculative. Her acquaintance with history was exact and circumstantial, in proportion as the retired back ward from her own age. She knew more of the siege of Mutina than of that of Lisle;[14] more of the machinations of Cataline and the tumults of Clodius, than of the prostration of the Bastile, and the proscriptions of Marat.[15]

She listened, therefore, with unspeakable eagerness to this reciter, who detailed to her, as the occasion suggested, the progress of action and opinion, on the theatre of France and Poland.[16] Conceived and rehearsed as this was, with the energy and copiousness of one who sustained a part in the scene, the mind of Constantia was always kept at the pitch of curiosity and wonder.

But while this historian described the features, personal deportment, and domestic character of Antonelle, Mirabeau and Robespierre,[17] an impenetrable veil was drawn

---

[14] "Siege of Mutina … Lisle": Constantia's education is one-sided; she knows more about ancient events than about contemporary history. Both "sieges" occurred during struggles over the fate of republics. The Siege of Mutina (present-day Modena, Italy) in 43 B.C.E. was part of the struggle for power during the Roman civil war following Julius Caesar's assassination in 44. The military assault on Lisle (Lille) in northern France in 1792 was part of the French Revolutionary Wars. Habsburg Austrian forces attacked the city but gave up their bombing after ten days to settle into their winter quarters, and the people of Lille were thereafter celebrated for their valor in defending the Republic.

[15] "Cataline … Clodius … Bastile … Marat": Again, Constantia knows more about Roman history than about the ongoing history of her own time, the revolutionary 1790s. Catiline (Lucius Sergius Catilina; 108–62 B.C.E.) was denounced by Cicero for a conspiracy to overthrow the Roman Republic, and Publius Clodius Pulcher (93–52 B.C.E.) was a bitter enemy of Cicero. Conversely, the storming of the Bastille prison in Paris on July 14, 1789, usually given as the inaugural date of the French Revolution, and Marat's condemnation of the Girondins in 1793, previously mentioned in this chapter (see note 19.7), were already well-known French revolutionary events. Both the "tumults of Clodius" and the death of Marat involved transvestism and female masquerade in favor of political violence and intrigue. For more on the assassination of Marat, see the selection from Helen Maria Williams in Related Texts.

[16] "The theatre of France and Poland": the view of contemporary geopolitics opened up by Martinette, in keeping with novel's wider emphasis, is figured as a "theatre" of events. Cosmopolitan interest in France's revolution was followed by concern for Polish independence. Throughout the eighteenth century, Poland was targeted for imperial acquisition by Prussia, Russia, and Austria. Its first partition in 1772 left Polish-Lithuania smaller, but still existing as a political entity. The Second Partition in 1793 reduced it to a rump state and the Third Partition in 1795 ended its existence. Nothing that we are told about or by Martinette suggests a personal presence in Poland, unlike her personalized knowledge of France.

[17] "Antonelle, Mirabeau and Robespierre": French revolutionary notables associated with the Jacobin and early constitutionalist factions. If Martinette encountered these three figures, she came into contact with a left spectrum of revolutionary politicians, many of whom were hostile to the Girondin faction of her possible husband or lover Beauvais. For more on the Girondin-Jacobin distinction, see "Narratives of French Girondin Heroism" in Related Texts.

over her own condition. There was a warmth and freedom in her details which bespoke her own co-agency in these events, but was unattended by transports of indignation or sorrow, or by pauses of abstraction, such as were likely to occur in one whose hopes and fears had been intimately blended with public events.

Constance could not but derive humiliation from comparing her own slender acquirements with those of her companion. She was sensible that all the differences between them, arose from diversities of situation. She was eager to discover in what particulars this diversity consisted. She was for a time withheld by scruples, not easily explained, from disclosing her wishes. An accident however occurred, to remove these impediments.

One evening, this unceremonious visitant discovered Constance busily surveying a chart of the Mediterranean Sea. This circumstance led the discourse to the present state of Syria and Cyprus.[18] Martinette was copious in her details. Constance listened

---

Pierre-Antoine Antonelle (1747–1817) was born in Arles to a noble family, but came to support the Revolution's radicalism and anticlericalism. As president of the Jacobins, he was presiding officer for the revolutionary trials of Marie Antoinette and then the Girondin delegates including Beauvais. The Jacobins mistrusted Antonelle's hesitation in the latter trial and imprisoned him, but he escaped the guillotine after the Jacobins lost power in 1794. He later joined the Conspiracy of Equals, often considered the first class-aware group, the movement from which modern anarchist, socialist, and communist organizations descend. Antonelle luckily escaped the Equals trial and execution in 1797. After Napoleon's rise he was exiled back to Arles. Although some later editions of *Ormond* change the name in this passage to "Antoinette," the novel's pattern of well-informed allusions to Girondin-Jacobin conflicts suggests that the first edition's typographical error ("Antonette") was likely a compositor's mistake for "Antonelle" in the manuscript.

Honoré-Gabriel Mirabeau (1749–1791) came from a merchant family that purchased a noble title. He rose to prominence after publishing a scandalous exposé of the Berlin court following his time as a diplomat there in the 1780s. In the early years of the Revolution he was a moderately progressive constitutionalist, but died before the turn to internecine conflict. His reputation fell almost immediately after his death when he was revealed to have been more sympathetic to the king than previously known. In the paranoid mythology of the Illuminati panic, Mirabeau plays a key role as the primary conductor of German conspiracy into French politics in the years before the Revolution.

Maximilien Robespierre (1758–1794), a lawyer from Arras, quickly rose through the Revolution to lead the Jacobin faction, which took power in 1793. After he was elected to the Committee of Public Safety, Robespierre wielded dictatorial power and the Committee presided over the revolutionary phase known as the Terror (September 1793 to July 1794), during which thousands of politically suspect individuals on both the right and left were tried for treason and guillotined. Called "The Incorruptible" for his strident moralizing, Robespierre also tried to install a form of deism as the state religion. The Terror ended when he himself was executed in July 1794, in the event known as Thermidor. In the 1790s Robespierre's name is commonly used as a synonym for the Terror, for remorseless commitment to political abstractions, or for the use of revolutionary violence in defense of radical ideals.

In 1797, Brown's closest friends William Dunlap and Elihu Hubbard Smith began to write a play titled *The Fall of Robespierre*. They may have been familiar with a similarly titled 1794 verse drama by Samuel Taylor Coleridge and Robert Southey.

[18] "Syria and Cyprus": as described in works by Volney and Mariti (see following note), Syria and Cyprus are of dual interest here. Both suffered fever epidemics, presumably similar to those of Philadelphia and other North American port cities, and both were Ottoman provinces and thus

for a time, and when a pause ensued, questioned her companion as to the means she possessed of acquiring so much knowledge. This question was proposed with diffidence, and prefaced by apologies.

Instead of being offended by your question, replied the guest, I only wonder that it never before occurred to you. Travellers tell us much. Volney and Mariti would have told you nearly all that I have told.[19] With these I have conversed personally, as well as read their books, but my knowledge is, in truth, a species of patrimony. I inherit it.

Will you be good enough, said Constance, to explain yourself?

My mother was a Greek of Cyprus. My father was a Sclavonian of Ragusa, and I was born in a garden at Aleppo.[20]

---

examples of local populations constrained by Turkish "despotism" or political subordination. Brown published numerous political and anthropological articles concerning Ottoman rule, such as "Interesting Account of the Character and Political State of the Modern Greeks [from a Survey of the Turkish Empire &c., by W. Eton, Esq.]" (*Monthly Magazine* 2.6, May 1800).

[19] "Volney and Mariti … all that I have told": authors of important recent accounts of the Middle East, sources for Brown's knowledge of it, and, in Volney's case, an émigré resident in Philadelphia during the 1790s.

C. F. Volney (1757–1820) was a widely read French *philosophe* and historian who published an account of Middle Eastern travels in the 1780s, *Voyage en Egypte et en Syrie* (1787), immediately translated as *Travels Through Syria and Egypt, in the years 1783, 1784, and 1785* (London: Robinson). This work was influential as a source of inspiration for Napoleon in his 1798 invasion of Egypt. In 1788 he published *Considérations sur la guerre actuelle des Turcs avec les Russes* (*Considerations on the current war between Turkey and Russia*), likely a source for Brown's references to that war in Chapter 20. During the Revolution Volney was a delegate to the National Assembly but was imprisoned by the Jacobins until Robespierre's fall. During the first phase of the Revolution he wrote his best-known work, a radical allegory of future political transformation titled *Les Ruines, ou Méditations sur les révolutions des empires* (1791; *The Ruins, or a Survey of the Revolutions of Empires*). In 1795 he traveled through North America and later published a geographical account of the United States, *Tableau du climat et du sol des Etats-Unis* (1803), which Brown translated in 1804. Brown and his friends knew Volney while he lived in Philadelphia briefly in 1797–1798, before he was forced to leave the United States as a result of the reactionary Alien and Sedition Acts. For more on Volney, see Related Texts.

Giovanni Mariti (1736–1806) was a Livorno-based, enlightened anthropological writer who also published influential accounts of the Mediterranean and Middle East. His *Travels through Cyprus, Syria, and Palestine: with a general history of the Levant* (London, 1791) was based on his residence in Cyprus during the 1760s.

[20] "Greek of Cyprus … Sclavonian of Ragusa … a garden at Aleppo": the implication is that Martinette is from a family based in the cosmopolitan, multiethnic merchant networks of the Eastern Mediterranean and Levant. The following passage will explain that Martinette's father was a Ragusan merchant who traded from the Italian peninsula to Syria.

Slavonia (Sclavonia) is the eastern, inland region of present-day Croatia, bordering on Hungary; in the eighteenth century it was a province of the Habsburg Empire. Ragusa is present-day Dubrovnik, then a city-state on the Adriatic coast of present-day Croatia. After the Crusades, Ragusa was controlled by Venice, but from 1358 to 1808 it was an autonomous free state with a cosmopolitan population, and one of the few mercantile shipping rivals to Venice. Ragusan traders renounced involvement with the slave trade as early as the fifteenth century and often sailed under a white flag to signal their lack of interest in gaining imperial control over trading partners.

That was a singular concurrence.

How singular? That a nautical vagrant like my father, should sometimes anchor in the bay of Naples. That a Cyprian merchant should carry his property and daughter beyond the reach of a Turkish Sangiack, and seek an asylum so commodious as Napoli;[21] That my father should have dealings with this merchant, see, love, and marry his daughter, and afterwards procure, from the French government, a consular commission to Aleppo; that the union should, in due time, be productive of a son and daughter, are events far from being singular. They happen daily.

And may I venture to ask if this be your history?

The history of my parents. I hope you do not consider the place of my birth as the sole or the most important circumstance of my life.

Nothing would please me more than to be enabled to compare it with other incidents. I am apt to think that your life is a tissue of surprising events. That the daughter of a Ragusan and Greek, should have seen and known so much; that she should talk English with equal fluency and more correctness than a native; that I should now be conversing with her in a corner so remote from Cyprus and Sicily,[22] are events more wonderful than any which I have known.

Wonderful! Pish! Thy ignorance, thy miscalculation of probabilities is far more so. My father talked to me in Sclavonic: My mother and her maids talked to me in Greek. My neighbours talked to me in a medley of Arabic, Syriac[23] and Turkish. My father's secretary was a scholar. He was as well versed in Lysias and Xenophon,[24] as

---

Aleppo is a cosmopolitan trading city in northern Syria, one of the oldest in the region, and suffered epidemic outbreaks throughout the eighteenth century. Additionally, the well-known allegorical female warrior and sorceress Armida—a central character in *Jerusalem Delivered* by Torquato Tasso (1544–1595), widely known in countless paintings and operas of the seventeenth and eighteenth centuries that were familiar to Brown and his circle—leads Syrian troops and enchants the Christian champion Rinaldo at her magical garden in Syria. Thus Martinette's claims of birth in a "garden in Aleppo" may connect her with this Amazonian legend. For another contemporary use of this tale, see Peale's double portrait of Benjamin and Elizabeth Ridgely Laming in Related Texts.

[21] "Turkish Sangiack ... Napoli": Sanjaks were secondary divisions of territory (not provinces, but subsections of provinces) in the Ottoman Empire. The implication is that Martinette's Greek maternal grandfather left Cyprus, an island in the eastern Mediterranean, for Naples (Napoli) in order to escape the authority of the Turkish governor on that island.

[22] "Ragusan and Greek ... Cyprus and Sicily": Martinette reemphasizes the consequences and implications of her cosmopolitan background. The daughter of a Ragusan (Balkan) merchant and an ethnically Greek woman from Cyprus, Martinette is born in Syria and formed by a world that, in ethnic, linguistic, and sociopolitical senses, is deeply and thoroughly transnational and transcultural.

[23] "Syriac": classical Syriac was a form of Aramaic spoken from Egypt to Iraq in the fourth to eighth centuries. This classical form was an important literary language and the dominant language in the Middle East before the emergence of modern Arabic after the eighth century. A modern form exists, but is spoken only by small, isolated diasporic groups.

[24] "Lysias and Xenophon": Lysias (c. 445–380 B.C.E.) was an Athenian orator born in Sicily. His simplicity of diction made his speeches models for classical Greek and ideal texts for learning the language. Xenophon (c. 431–352 B.C.E.) was a student of Socrates, known for his history of the

any of their contemporaries. He laboured for ten years to enable me to read a language, essentially the same with that I used daily to my nurse and mother. Is it wonderful then that I should be skilful in Sclavonic, Greek, and the jargon of Aleppo? To have refrained from learning was impossible. Suppose a girl, prompt, diligent, inquisitive, to spend ten years of her life partly in Spain; partly in Tuscany; partly in France, and partly in England. With her versatile curiosity and flexible organs, would it be possible for her to remain ignorant of each of these languages?[25] Latin is the mother of them all, and presents itself, of course, to her studious attention.

I cannot easily conceive motives which should lead you, before the age of twenty, through so many scenes.

Can you not? You grew and flourished, like a frail Mimosa, in the spot where destiny had planted you. Thank my stars, I am somewhat better than a vegetable. Necessity, it is true, and not choice, set me in motion, but I am not sorry for the consequences.

Is it too much, said Constance, with some hesitation, to request a detail of your youthful adventures?

Too much to give, perhaps, at a short notice. To such as you, my tale might abound with novelty, while to others, more acquainted with vicissitudes, it would be tedious and flat. I must be gone in a few minutes. For that and for better reasons, I must not be minute. A summary, at present, will enable you to judge how far a more copious narrative is suited to instruct or to please you.

Greek retreat from Persia. Like Lysias, Xenophon was known for stylistic clarity and widely read by students of classical Greek.

[25] "Versatile curiosity and flexible organs ... languages": Martinette's phrase ties intellectual excitement to bodily metamorphoses, a recurring theme for her. Here she claims fluency in English and all the major languages of the Mediterranean basin east and west.

Chapter XX

MY father, in proportion as he grew old and rich, became weary of Aleppo. His natal soil, had it been the haunt of Calmucks or Bedwins,[1] his fancy would have transformed into Paradise. No wonder that the equitable aristocracy, and the peaceful husbandmen of Ragusa, should be endeared to his heart by comparison with Egyptian plagues and Turkish tyranny.[2] Besides, he lived for his children as well as himself. Their education and future lot required him to seek a permanent home.

He embarked with his wife and offspring, at Scanderoon.[3] No immediate conveyance to Ragusa offering, the appearance of the plague in Syria, induced him to hasten his departure. He entered a French vessel for Marseilles. After being three days at sea, one of the crew was seized by the fatal disease, which had depopulated all the towns upon the coast. The voyage was made with more than usual dispatch, but before we reached our port, my mother and half the crew perished. My father died in the Lazzaretto,[4] more through grief than disease.

My brother and I were children and helpless. My father's fortune was on board this vessel, and was left by his death to the mercy of the captain. This man was honest, and consigned us and our property to the merchant with whom he dealt. Happily for us, our protector was childless and of scrupulous integrity. We henceforth became his adopted children. My brother's education and my own, were conducted on the justest principles.

At the end of four years, our protector found it expedient to make a voyage to Cayenne.[5] His brother was an extensive proprietor in that colony, but his sudden death made way for the succession of our friend. To establish his claims, his presence

---

[1] "Calmucks or Bedwins": two traditionally nomadic peoples. Kalmyks (spelled variously) are a Western Mongolian people who flourished in the region around the Caspian Sea (present-day Georgia and Azerbaijan). They were historically Buddhists, associated with Tibetan lamas. The Bedouin are primarily Muslim peoples of the Arabian Peninsula.

[2] "Egyptian plagues and Turkish tyranny": Martinette's family history, like her present, is formed by efforts to escape urban epidemics and nondemocratic, aristocratic, and oppressive forms of government.

[3] "Scanderoon": present-day Iskenderun, a port on the Turkish-Syrian border, the closest port to Aleppo, and an important stop on Mediterranean trade routes in the eighteenth century. Volney's account (see note 19.18) describes the city as prone to epidemics.

[4] "Lazzaretto": a quarantine station for seagoing arrivals and an institution for containing the spread of infectious diseases that was often discussed in the period's yellow-fever literature. Brown mentions the "lazaretto of Naples" in installment IV of his "Man at Home" essay series (Philadelphia *Weekly Magazine,* February 24, 1798) and was familiar with John Howard's *An Account of the Principal Lazarettos of Europe,* etc. (1789), which was extracted and discussed in the same magazine. The Philadelphia Lazaretto, the first quarantine hospital in the U.S., was planned and built in response to the 1793 epidemic. It opened in 1799, the year *Ormond* appeared.

[5] "Cayenne": colonial capital of French Guiana, on the northeast coast of South America. In 1790s Cayenne, slaves outnumbered whites by a factor of nearly ten to one. Martinette's protector has undoubtedly inherited a slave plantation, possibly for cotton rather than sugarcane.

was necessary on the spot. He was little qualified for arduous enterprizes, and his age demanded repose, but his own acquisitions, having been small, and being desirous of leaving us in possession of competence, he cheerfully embarked.

Meanwhile, my brother was placed at a celebrated seminary in the Pais de Vaud, and I was sent to a sister who resided at Verona.[6] I was at this time fourteen years old, one year younger than my brother, whom, since that period, I have neither heard of nor seen.

I was now a woman, and qualified to judge and act for myself.[7] The character of my new friend was austere and devout, and there were so many incongenial points between us, that but little tranquillity was enjoyed under her controul. The priest who discharged the office of her confessor, thought proper to entertain views with regard to me, grossly inconsistent with the sanctity of his profession. He was a man of profound dissimulation and masterly address. His efforts, however, were repelled with disdain. My security against his attempts lay in the uncouthness and deformity which nature had bestowed upon his person and visage, rather than in the firmness of my own principles.

The courtship of Father Bartoli, the austerities of Madame Roselli, the disgustful or insipid occupations to which I was condemned, made me impatiently wish for a change, but my father, so I will call him, had decreed that I should remain under his sister's guardianship till his return from Guiana. When this would happen was uncertain. Events unforeseen might protract it for years, but it could not arrive in less than a twelve-month.

I was incessantly preyed upon by discontent. My solitude was loathsome. I panted after liberty and friendship,[8] and the want of these were not recompensed by luxury and quiet, and by the instructions in useful science, which I received from Bartoli, who, though detested as an hypocrite and lover, was venerable as a scholer: He would fain have been an Abelard, but it was not his fate to meet with an Heloise.[9]

Two years passed away in this durance. My miseries were exquisite. I am almost at a loss to account for the unhappiness of that time, for, looking back upon it, I perceive

---

[6] "Seminary in the Pais de Vaud ... Verona": Pays de Vaud, the present-day Canton of Vaud in Switzerland around Lausanne on Lake Geneva. The current University of Lausanne was originally a Protestant seminary founded in 1537, renowned as the only French-language center for Protestant theology. Verona is a city in Veneto, northern Italy, still part of the Venetian Republic at the time of the novel's events; after Napoleon ended the Venetian Republic in 1797 it became part of the Austrian Habsburg Empire.

[7] "I was now a woman ... myself": at age fourteen, Martinette has reached the age of consent in the eighteenth century.

[8] "Panted after liberty and friendship": Martinette links freedom with intimacy.

[9] "Abelard ... Heloise": a legendary pair of lovers. Peter Abelard (1079–1144) was a French monastic scholar who, despite his lack of conventional beauty, seduced, impregnated, and secretly married his female student Heloise. The affair ended with Abelard castrated on the orders of Heloise's uncle, and with Heloise becoming a nun. The couple's love letters are a common reference for later writers, from Chaucer to Pope and Rousseau.

that an equal period could not have been spent with more benefit. For the sake of being near me, Bartoli importunately offered his instructions. He had nothing to communicate but metaphysics and geometry.[10] These were little to my taste, but I could not keep him at distance. I had no other alternative than to endure him as a lover or a teacher. His passion for science was at least equal to that which he entertained for me, and both these passions combined to make him a sedulous[11] instructor. He was a disciple of the newest doctrines respecting matter and mind.[12] He denied the impenetrability of the first, and the immateriality of the second. These he endeavoured to inculcate upon me, as well as to subvert my religious tenets, because he delighted, like all men, in transfusing his opinions, and because he regarded my piety as the only obstacle to his designs. He succeeded in dissolving the spell of ignorance, but not in producing that kind of acquiescence he wished. He had, in this respect, to struggle not only with my principles, but my weaknesses. He might have overcome every obstacle, but my abhorrence of deformity and age. To cure me of this aversion, was beyond his power. My servitude grew daily more painful. I grew tired of chasing a comet to its aphelion, and of untying the knot of an infinite series.[13] A change in my condition became indispensable to my very existence. Langour and sadness, and unwillingness to eat or to move, were at last my perpetual attendants.

Madame Roselli was alarmed at my condition. The sources of my inquietude were incomprehensible to her. The truth was, that I scarcely understood them myself, and my endeavours to explain them to my friend, merely instilled into her an opinion, that I was either lunatic or deceitful. She complained and admonished, but my disinclination to my usual employments would not be conquered, and my health rapidly declined. A physician, who was called, confessed that my case was beyond his power to understand, but recommended, as a sort of desperate expedient,

---

[10] "Metaphysics and geometry": like Constantia, Martinette is educated in topics usually reserved to men. For Constantia's "masculine" education, see notes 3.6 and 3.7.

[11] "Sedulous": dedicated.

[12] "Newest doctrines respecting matter and mind": Bartoli is a student of the radical Enlightenment's secularism and materialism.

[13] "Chasing a comet to its aphelion … knot of an infinite series": Martinette tires of doing advanced mathematics, of calculating orbital motion using Newtonian equations (the aphelion is a planetary object's furthest point from the sun) or of working through the series of problems that Brown refers to in his feminist dialogue *Alcuin* as the "mazes of Dr. Waring," the challenging equations of English analytical mathematician Edward Waring (1736–1798). Waring's work presents "knots" or "mazes" because he is commonly associated with the difficulties of "Waring's Problem" (according to which every positive integer is the sum of not more than nine cubes or the sum of not more than nineteen fourth powers) and "Waring's Prime Number Conjecture" (in which every odd integer exceeding three is either a prime number or the sum of three prime numbers). The theoretical issues raised by both these "knots" were not resolved or superceded until the early twentieth century. For the more explicit reference to Waring in the discussion of female education in Brown's *Alcuin*, Part I, see footnote 15 here in Related Texts.

a change of scene. A succession and variety of objects, might possibly contribute to my cure.[14]

At this time there arrived at Verona, Lady D'Arcy,[15] an English-woman of fortune and rank, and a strenuous Catholic. Her husband had lately died, and in order to divert her grief, as well as to gratify her curiosity in viewing the great seat of her religion, she had come to Italy. Intercourse took place between her and Madame Roselli. By this means she gained a knowledge of my person and condition, and kindly offered to take me under her protection. She meant to traverse every part of Italy, and was willing that I should accompany her in all her wanderings.

This offer was gratefully accepted, in spite of the artifices and remonstrances of Bartoli. My companion speedily contracted for me the affection of a mother. She was without kindred of her own religion, having acquired her faith, not by inheritance, but conversion. She desired to abjure her native country, and to bind herself by every social tie, to a people who adhered to the same faith. Me, she promised to adopt as her daughter, provided her first impressions in my favor, were not belied by my future deportment.

My principles were opposite to her's, but habit, an aversion to displease my friend, my passion for knowledge, which my new condition enabled me to gratify, all combined to make me a deceiver, but my imposture was merely of a negative kind; I deceived her rather by forbearance to contradict, and by acting as she acted, than by open assent and zealous concurrence. My new state was, on this account, not devoid of inconvenience. The general deportment and sentiments of Lady D'Arcy, testified a vigorous and pure mind. New avenues to knowledge, by converse with mankind and with books, and by the survey of new scenes, were open for my use. Gratitude and veneration attached me to my friend, and made the task of pleasing her by a seeming conformity of sentiments, less irksome.

---

[14] "My cure": in the eighteenth century, travel was often recommended as a possible cure for prolonged sadness, for example in the writings of Erasmus Darwin (1731–1802), a basic medical and scientific authority for Brown and his circle. Later references to this common prescription occur in Chapters 23 and 29 (see notes 23.7, 29.4).

[15] "Lady D'Arcy": this name may be intended to evoke some reference to either of two historical Lady D'Arcys, a mother and her daughter. Mary D'Arcy (1720–1801; née Mary Doublet, countess of Mertola), an Anglo-Dutch heiress, married Robert D'Arcy, 4th Earl of Holderness (1718–1778), a diplomat who in the 1740s was British ambassador to Venice. Mary was part of minor political scandal in the late 1760s when she was accused of using her husband's position as "Warden of the Cinque Ports" to profit from smuggling. In 1770 this Lady D'Arcy was appointed Lady of the Bedchamber. The second historical Lady D'Arcy is Mary's daughter Amelia, commonly known in the period press as Lady Amelia D'Arcy (1754–1784), who was born in Venice while her father was ambassador there. Her first marriage to Francis Osborne, Marquess of Carmarthen, ended in scandal in 1778 when she ran off with John "Mad Jack" Byron (1756–1791), an adventurer who later fathered the poet Byron with another wife. Because Robert D'Arcy had no surviving male heirs, Amelia inherited a substantial annual income on his death in 1778. Neither of these historical Lady D'Arcys was Catholic, however. The D'Arcy family holdings were in Holderness, present-day East Yorkshire; the novel's character Thomas Craig claims to be from Yorkshire (see note 1.5).

During this interval, no tidings were received by his sister, at Verona, respecting the fate of Sebastian Roselli. The supposition of his death, was too plausible, not to be adopted. What influence this disaster possessed over my brother's destiny, I know not. The generosity of Lady D'Arcy, hindered me from experiencing any disadvantage from this circumstance. Fortune seemed to have decreed, that I should not be reduced to the condition of an orphan.

At an age and in a situation like mine, I could not remain long unacquainted with love. My abode at Rome, introduced me to the knowledge of a youth from England, who had every property which I regarded as worthy of esteem. He was a kinsman of Lady D'Arcy, and as such admitted at her house on the most familiar footing. His patrimony was extremely slender, but was in his own possession. He had no intention of increasing it by any professional pursuit, but was contented with the frugal provision it afforded. He proposed no other end of his existence, than the acquisition of virtue and knowledge.

The property of Lady D'Arcy was subject to her own disposal, but, on the failure of a testament, this youth was, in legal succession, the next heir. He was well acquainted with her temper and views, but in the midst of urbanity and gentleness, studied none of those concealments of opinion, which would have secured him her favor. That he was not of her own faith, was an insuperable, but the only obstacle, to the admission of his claims.

If conformity of age and opinions, and the mutual fascination of love, be a suitable basis for marriage Wentworth[16] and I were destined for each other. Mutual disclosure added sanctity to our affection, but the happiness of Lady D'Arcy, being made to depend upon the dissolution of our compact, the heroism of Wentworth made him hasten to dissolve it. As soon as she discovered our attachment, she displayed symptoms of the deepest anguish. In addition to religious motives, her fondness for me forbad her to exist but in my society, and in the belief of the purity of my faith. The contention, on my part, was vehement, between the regards due to her felicity and to my own. Had Wentworth left me the power to decide, my decision would doubtless have evinced the frailty of my fortitude, and the strength of my passion, but having informed me fully of the reasons of his conduct, he precipitately retired from Rome. He left me no means of tracing his footsteps and of assailing his weakness, by expostulation and intreaty.

---

[16] "Wentworth": The connection may be slight, but the politically liberal D'arcy Wentworth (1762–1827), born in County Armagh, Ireland, claimed descent from an English aristocratic family from Yorkshire, the home region of the D'Arcy family. Wentworth escaped conviction for highway robberies in 1789 by voluntarily emigrating to Botany Bay, the Australian penal colony, as a surgeon. The *Philadelphia Gazette* of April 2, 1794, printed a political reading of the case against pickpocket George Barrington and Wentworth, presenting them as "victims of justice, for asserting the rights of man in opposition to the letter and spirit of law." Brown uses the name Wentworth again for a significant female character in both parts of his novel *Arthur Mervyn*. Readers of Jane Austen will recognize the names Darcy and Wentworth as belonging to the romantic heroes of *Pride and Prejudice* (1813) and the posthumous *Persuasion* (1818).

Lady D'Arcy was no less eager to abandon a spot, where her happiness had been so iminently endangered. Our next residence was Palermo.[17] I will not dwell upon the sensations, produced by this disappointment, in me. I review them with astonishment and self-compassion. If I thought it possible for me to sink again into imbecility so ignominious, I should be disposed to kill myself.

There was no end to vows of fondness and tokens of gratitude in Lady D'Arcy. Her future life should be devoted to compensate me for this sacrifice. Nothing could console her in that single state in which she intended to live, but the consolations of my fellowship. Her conduct coincided for some time with these professions, and my anguish was allayed by the contemplation of the happiness conferred upon one whom I revered.

My friend could not be charged with dissimulation and artifice. Her character had been mistaken by herself as well as by me. Devout affections seemed to have filled her heart, to the exclusion of any object besides myself. She cherished with romantic tenderness, the memory of her husband, and imagined that a single state was indispensibly enjoined upon her, by religious duty. This persuasion, however, was subverted by the arts of a Spanish Cavalier, young, opulent, and romantic as herself in devotion. An event like this might, indeed, have been easily predicted, by those who reflected that the lady was still in the bloom of life, ardent in her temper and bewitching in her manners.

The fondness she had lavished upon me, was now, in some degree, transferred to a new object, but I still received the treatment due to a beloved daughter. She was solicitous as ever to promote my gratification, and a diminution of kindness would not have been suspected, by those who had not witnessed the excesses of her former passion. Her marriage with the Spaniard removed the obstacle to union with Wentworth. This man, however, had set himself beyond the reach of my enquiries. Had there been the shadow of a clue afforded me, I should certainly have sought him to the ends of the world.

I continued to reside with my friend, and accompanied her and her husband to Spain. Antonio de Leyva[18] was a man of probity. His mind was enlightened by knowledge and his actions dictated by humanity. Though but little older than myself, and young enough to be the son of his spouse, his deportment to me was a model of rectitude and delicacy. I spent a year in Spain, partly in the mountains of Castile and partly at Segovia.[19] New manners and a new language occupied my

---

[17] "Palermo": the largest city in Sicily and, at this time, the second city (after Naples) of the Kingdom of the Two Sicilies, a sovereign territory comprising the southern part of the Italian peninsula and Sicily.

[18] "Antonio de Leyva": there does not seem to be any thematic reference to the sixteenth-century Spanish general Antonio de Leyva (1480–1536). De Leyva was an aristocratic family name in Castile throughout the early modern period.

[19] "Segovia": the capital city of the similarly named region in Castile, northwest of Madrid.

attention for a time, but these, losing their novelty, lost their power to please. I betook myself to books, to beguile the tediousness and diversify the tenor of my life.

This would not have long availed, but I was relieved from new repinings, by the appointment of Antonio de Leyva to a diplomatic office at Vienna. Thither we accordingly repaired. A coincidence of circumstances had led me wide from the path of ambition and study, usually allotted to my sex and age. From the computation of eclipses, I now betook myself to the study of man. My proficiency, when I allowed it to be seen, attracted great attention. Instead of adulation and gallantry, I was engaged in watching the conduct of states, and revolving the theories of politicians.

Superficial observers were either incredulous with regard to my character, or connected a stupid wonder with their belief. My attainments and habits, they did not see to be perfectly consonant with the principles of human nature. They unavoidably flowed from the illicit attachment of Bartoli, and the erring magnanimity of Wentworth. Aversion to the priest was the grand inciter of my former studies; the love of Wentworth whom I hoped once more to meet, made me labour to exclude the importunities of others, and to qualify myself for securing his affections.

Since our parting in Italy, Wentworth had traversed Syria and Egypt, and arrived some months after me at Vienna.[20] He was on the point of leaving the city, when accident informed me of his being there. An interview was effected, and our former sentiments respecting each other, having undergone no change, we were united. Madame de Leyva reluctantly concurred with our wishes, and, at parting, forced upon me a considerable sum of money.

Wentworth's was a character not frequently met with in the world. He was a political enthusiast, who esteemed nothing more graceful or glorious than to die for the liberties of mankind. He had traversed Greece with an imagination full of the

---

[20] "Vienna": Martinette's experiences in Vienna, where she encounters her lover after arriving in the company of an older male guardian with a diplomatic assignment in the Austrian Habsburg capital, may echo numerous intrigues concerning Giustiniana Wynne, Countess Rosenberg, an Anglo-Venetian writer and socialite. Alternatively known in print as "Countess Rosenberg," "Justine Wynne," "Jane Wynne," "Giustiniana Wynne," and "Giustiniana degli Orsini," she was celebrated in the period by British Grand Tour travel writers for her personality and as author of several books in the 1780s, including a widely circulated collection of *Moral and Sentimental Essays* (1785) that defends female education in traditionally male subjects such as history and science, and develops enlightened anecdotes on "plebian heroism" and resistance to female subordination. Wynne-Rosenberg, the daughter of a celebrated Venetian courtesan, was involved in many well-known transnational intrigues (some concerning the gothic novelist Beckford and others on the Grand Tour, for example), and acquired the Rosenberg name via her marriage with an elderly Austrian diplomat, Count Philip Orsini-Rosenberg (1692–1765), who was recalled to Vienna after his marriage with Giustiniana caused a scandal. Her semi-autobiographical *Moral and Sentimental Essays* was reviewed in periodicals commonly read by Brown and his circle and was available to Brown in Philadelphia and New York. For the narrator Sophia's initial use of the Rosenberg name, see note 0.1.

exploits of ancient times, and derived from contemplating Thermopylae and Marathon,[21] an enthusiasm that bordered upon phrenzy.

It was now the third year of the revolutionary war in America,[22] and previous to our meeting at Vienna, he had formed the resolution of repairing thither, and tendering his service to the Congress as a volunteer. Our marriage made no change in his plans. My soul was engrossed by two passions, a wild spirit of adventure, and a boundless devotion to him. I vowed to accompany him in every danger, to vie with him in military ardour; to combat and to die by his side.

I delighted to assume the male dress, to acquire skill at the sword, and dexterity in every boisterous exercise. The timidity that commonly attends women, gradually vanished. I felt as if embued by a soul that was a stranger to the sexual distinction. We embarked at Brest, in a frigate destined for St. Domingo. A desperate conflict with an English ship in the bay of Biscay,[23] was my first introduction to a scene of tumult and danger, of whose true nature I had formed no previous conception. At first I was spiritless and full of dismay. Experience however gradually reconciled me to the life that I had chosen.

A fortunate shot by dismasting the enemy, allowed us to prosecute our voyage unmolested. At Cape François[24] we found a ship which transported us, after various perils, to Richmond in Virginia. I will not carry you through the adventures of four years. You, sitting all your life in peaceful corners, can scarcely imagine that variety of hardship and turmoil, which attends the female who lives in a camp.

Few would sustain these hardships with better grace than I did. I could seldom be prevailed on to remain at a distance and inactive, when my husband was in battle, and more than once rescued him from death by the seasonable destruction of his adversary.

---

[21] "Thermopylae and Marathon": two legendary battles in 480 and 493 B.C.E., respectively, in which citizens of Greek city-states defended themselves against Persian, Middle Eastern invaders. Wentworth idealizes ancient battles in his contemporary context because Greece was struggling against Ottoman rule during the revolutionary age. Classical Greek-Persian struggles were commonly invoked by the romantic generation to symbolize modern democratic Greek resistance to the "tyranny" of the Turkish Ottoman Empire.

[22] "Now the third year of the revolutionary war in America": 1778–1779.

[23] "Brest … St. Domingo … Bay of Biscay": Martinette and Wentworth sail from Brest, the primary Atlantic port on the northwest coast of France, to the French Caribbean sugar colony called St. Domingo or Haiti. The Bay of Biscay is off the southwest coast of France; because France is the main ally of the American Revolution, they travel to fight in that conflict on French vessels via French territories and are challenged by the British navy during the voyage.

[24] "Cape François": or Cap Français, the main city and port of Haiti, known as Cap-Haïtien after 1804. As the colony's capital city during the slave revolt, it was the scene of a 1791 massacre of whites led in part by the Haitian General Beauvais, which set off an anxious outflow of Creole refugees, at least ten thousand of whom sailed to U.S. port cities in 1793–1794, the year of the novel's action.

At the repulse of the Americans at German-Town,[25] Wentworth was wounded and taken prisoner. I attained permission to attend his sick bed and supply that care, without which he would assuredly have died. Being imperfectly recovered, he was sent to England, and subjected to a rigorous imprisonment. Milder treatment might have permitted his compleat restoration to health, but, as it was, he died.

His kindred were noble, and rich and powerful, but it was difficult to make them acquainted with Wentworth's situation. Their assistance when demanded was readily afforded, but it came too late to prevent his death. Me they snatched from my voluntary prison, and employed every friendly art to efface from my mind the images of recent calamity.

Wentworth's singularities of conduct and opinion, had estranged him at an early age from his family. They felt little regret at his fate,[26] but every motive concurred to secure their affection and succour to me. My character was known to many officers, returned from America, whose report, joined with the influence of my conversation, rendered me an object to be gazed at by thousands. Strange vicissitude! Now immersed in the infection of a military hospital, the sport of a wayward fortune, struggling with cold and hunger, with negligence and contumely: A month after passing into scenes of gaiety and luxury, exhibited at operas and masquerades, made the theme of enquiry and encomium at every place of resort, and caressed by the most illustrious among the votaries of science, and the advocates of the American cause.

Here I again met Madame de Leyva. This woman was perpetually assuming new forms. She was a sincere convert to the Catholic religion, but she was open to every new impression. She was the dupe of every powerful reasoner, and assumed with equal facility the most opposite shapes. She had again reverted to the Protestant religion, and governed by an headlong zeal in whatever cause she engaged, she had sacrificed her husband and child to a new conviction.

The instrument of this change, was a man who passed, at that time, for a Frenchman. He was young, accomplished and addressful, but was not suspected of having been prompted by illicit views, or of having seduced the lady from allegiance to her husband as well as to her God. De Leyva, however, who was sincere in his religion as well as his love, was hasty to avenge this injury, and in a contest with the Frenchman, was killed. His wife adopted at once, her ancient religion and country, and was once more an English-woman.

At our meeting, her affection for me seemed to be revived, and the most passionate intreaties were used to detain me in England. My previous arrangements would not suffer it. I foresaw restraints and inconveniences from the violence and caprice of her

---

[25] "Repulse ... at German-town": on October 4, 1777, British troops defeated American revolutionaries at Germantown, then a separate village four miles north of Philadelphia.

[26] "Little regret at this fate": that Wentworth's family is indifferent to his death and "estranged" from him is presumably due to his revolutionary "singularities of thought and opinion." As an English subject, his decision to fight in the American Revolution means that he traveled abroad to join a revolution against the rulers of his own country.

passions, and intended henceforth to keep my liberty inviolate by any species of engagement, either of friendship or marriage. My habits were French, and I proposed henceforward to take up my abode at Paris. Since his voyage to Guiana, I had heard no tidings of Sebastian Roselli. This man's image was cherished with filial emotions, and I conceived that the sight of him would amply reward a longer journey than from London to Marseilles.

Beyond my hopes, I found him in his ancient abode. The voyage and a residence of three years at Cayenne, had been beneficial to his appearance and health. He greeted me with paternal tenderness, and admitted me to a full participation of his fortune, which the sale of his American property had greatly inhanced. He was a stranger to the fate of my brother. On his return home, he had gone to Swisserland with a view of ascertaining his destiny. The youth, a few months after his arrival at Lausanne, had eloped with a companion, and had hitherto eluded all Roselli's searches and enquiries. My father[27] was easily prevailed upon to transfer his residence from Provence to Paris.

Here Martinette paused, and marking the clock, It is time, resumed she, to be gone. Are you not weary of my tale? On the day I entered France, I entered the twenty-third year of my age, so that my promise of detailing my youthful adventures is fulfilled. I must away: Till we meet again, farewell.

---

[27] "Paternal tenderness ... my father": Martinette refers to Roselli loosely as her father because he has been her "protector" since the death of her actual father in the Lazaretto of Marseilles, noted at the beginning of this chapter (see note 20.4).

Chapter XXI

SUCH was the wild series of Martinette's adventures. Each incident fastened on the memory of Constance, and gave birth to numberless reflections. Her prospect of mankind seemed to be enlarged, on a sudden, to double its ancient dimensions. Ormond's narratives had carried her beyond the Missisippi, and into the deserts of Siberia. He had recounted the perils of a Russian war, and painted the manners of Mongals and Naudowessies.[1] Her new friend had led her back to the civilized world, and pourtrayed the other half of the species. Men, in their two forms, of savage and refined, had been scrutinized by these observers, and what was wanting in the delineations of the one, was liberally supplied by the other.

Eleven years, in the life of Martinette, was unrelated.[2] Her conversation suggested the opinion that this interval had been spent in France. It was obvious to suppose, that a woman, thus fearless and sagacious, had not been inactive at a period like the present, which called forth talents and courage, without distinction of sex, and had been particularly distinguished by female enterprize and heroism. Her name easily led to the suspicion of concurrence with the subverters of monarchy, and of participation in their fall. Her flight from the merciless tribunals of the faction that now reigned, would explain present appearances.

Martinette brought to their next interview, an air of uncommon exultation. On this being remarked, she communicated the tidings of the fall of the sanguinary tyranny of Robespierre.[3] Her eyes sparkled, and every feature was pregnant with delight,

---

[1] "A Russian War ... Mongals and Naudowessies": the first mention of Ormond's experience in the Russo-Turkish War of 1787–1792, which will be developed later in this chapter and in Chapters 26–27 (see notes 21.15, 26.1, and 27.3).

Naudowessie was a name given to the Native Americans now commonly known as Sioux or Dakotas. The comparison between the Mongols (Tatars) and the Sioux was a common one at this time. Volney (see note 19.19), in *View of the Climate and Soil of the United Sates of America* (1803), described the region west of the Mississippi as an "American Tartary, which has all the characters of that of Asia." In *The Travels of Captns. Lewis and Clark*, etc. (1809), Meriwether Lewis argued that Tatar refugees traveling through China were the ancestors of Native Americans, and compared Chinese words to those of Naudowessie, "whose language, from their little intercourse with Europeans, is the least corrupted." The other basic source at this time for information on the Sioux was Jonathan Carver's tremendously popular *Travels Through the Interior Parts of North-America, in the Years 1766, 1767, and 1768* (London, 1778, frequently reissued through the 1790s) from which Friedrich Schiller drew the material for one of his best known poems, *Nadowessische Totenklage* (Naudowessie Death Song; 1798).

[2] "Eleven years ... unrelated": the period from 1782–1783, the end of the American Revolution, to 1794, the present of the narrative.

[3] "Tidings of the fall of ... Robespierre": Robespierre was executed in the coup of 9 Thermidor, year 2, in the revolutionary calendar, or July 27, 1794. The first news of this event was reported in U.S. newspapers in New York on October 6, 1794, and in Philadelphia on October 7, locating this scene on or near that date. See for example the news item "Robespierre," in the Philadelphia *Gazette of the United States*, October 7, 1794.

while she unfolded, with her accustomed energy, the particulars of this tremendous revolution. The blood, which it occasioned to flow, was mentioned without any symptoms of disgust or horror.

Constance ventured to ask, if this incident was likely to influence her own condition.

Yes. It will open the way for my return.

Then you think of returning to a scene of so much danger?

Danger, my girl? It is my element. I am an adorer of liberty, and liberty without peril can never exist.

But so much bloodshed, and injustice! Does not your heart shrink from the view of a scene of massacre and tumult, such as Paris has lately exhibited and will probably continue to exhibit?

Thou talkest, Constance, in a way scarcely worthy of thy good sense. Have I not been three years in a camp? What are bleeding wounds and mangled corpses, when accustomed to the daily sight of them for years? Am I not a lover of liberty, and must I not exult in the fall of tyrants, and regret only that my hand had no share in their destruction?

But a woman—how can the heart of women be inured to the shedding of blood?

Have women, I beseech thee, no capacity to reason and infer? Are they less open than men to the influence of habit? My hand never faultered when liberty demanded the victim. If thou wert with me at Paris, I could shew thee a fusil of two barrels,[4] which is precious beyond any other relique, merely because it enabled me to kill thirteen officers at Jemappe. Two of these were emigrant nobles,[5] whom I knew and loved before the revolution, but the cause they had since espoused, cancelled their claims to mercy.

What, said the startled Constance, have you fought in the ranks?

Certainly. Hundreds of my sex have done the same. Some were impelled by the enthusiasm of love, and some by a mere passion for war; some by the contagion of example; and some, with whom I myself must be ranked, by a generous devotion to liberty. Brunswick and Saxe Coburg,[6] had to contend with whole regiments of

---

[4] "Fusil of two barrels": a fusil is a light flintlock musket. A similar weapon plays a significant role in Brown's novel *Edgar Huntly*, which appeared seven months after *Ormond* in August 1799.

[5] "Jemappe. Two ... emigrant nobles": On November 6, 1792, the French revolutionary army defeated outnumbered Austrian forces near Jemappe in Belgium. This was an important victory for the French army against Royalist counterrevolutionary forces. For a female cross-dressing tale available to Brown and concerning two emigrant nobles defeated at Jemappe, see the narrative of Louise Françoise de Houssay in Related Texts.

[6] "Brunswick and Saxe Coburg": two generals and princes who led troops against French revolutionary armies. Charles William Ferdinand, Duke of Brunswick (1735–1806) was a Prussian general and brother-in-law to British King George III. He is known for the "Brunswick Manifesto" of July 25, 1792, that threatened military reprisals if the French Republic harmed King Louis XVI, but which had the opposite effect of emboldening popular attacks on the monarchy because it seemed to give proof that Louis was collaborating with reactionary French émigrés and hostile states. On September 20, 1792, Brunswick lost the Battle of Valmy and abruptly retreated from French

women: Regiments they would have formed, if they had been collected into separate bodies.

I will tell thee a secret. Thou wouldst never have seen Martinette de Beauvais, if Brunswick had deferred one day longer, his orders for retreating into Germany.

How so?

She would have died by her own hand.

What could lead to such an outrage?

The love of liberty.

I cannot comprehend how that love should prompt you to suicide.

I will tell thee. The plan was formed and could not miscarry. A woman was to play the part of a banished Royalist, was to repair to the Prussian camp, and to gain admission to the general. This would have easily been granted to a female and an ex-noble. There she was to assassinate the enemy of her country, and to attest her magnanimity by slaughtering herself. I was weak enough to regret the ignominious retreat of the Prussians, because it precluded the necessity of such a sacrifice.[7]

This was related with accents and looks that sufficiently attested its truth. Constantia shuddered and drew back, to contemplate more deliberately the features of her guest. Hitherto she had read in them nothing that bespoke the desperate courage of a martyr, and the deep designing of an assassin. The image which her mind had reflected, from the deportment of this woman, was changed. The likeness which she had feigned to herself, was no longer seen. She felt that antipathy was preparing to displace love. These sentiments, however, she concealed, and suffered the conversation to proceed.

Their discourse now turned upon the exploits of several women, who mingled in the tumults of the capital and in the armies on the frontiers. Instances were mentioned of ferocity in some, and magnanimity in others, which almost surpassed belief. Constance listened greedily, though not with approbation,[8] and acquired, at every sentence, new desire to be acquainted with the personal history of Martinette. On mentioning this wish, her friend said, that she endeavoured to amuse her exile, by composing her own memoirs, and that, on her next visit, she would bring with her the volume, which she would suffer Constance to read.

---

territory; on the following day the French monarchy was abolished and the First French Republic declared. Despite his reputation as a modernizing general, Brunswick was not successful in the revolutionary wars and resigned his command in 1794.

Frederick Josias of Saxe-Coburg-Saalfeld (1737–1815) was an Austrian Habsburg general who fought the French revolutionary army in a series of engagements until his defeat at the Battle of Fleurus (Belgium) in June 1794. The military cross-dressing narrative of Louise Françoise de Houssay excerpted in Related Texts also includes the battle of Fleurus.

[7] "Such a sacrifice": Martinette's plan to assassinate the Duke of Brunswick recalls Charlotte Corday's assassination of Marat a few months earlier (see note 19.7), and inverts it by directing violence against an enemy of the revolution rather than a revolutionary. From Normandy, a site of counter-revolutionary resistance, Corday came to Paris to murder a revolutionary leader of the popular left. For more, see the excerpt from Helen Maria Williams in Related Texts.

[8] "Approbation": approval.

A separation of a week elapsed. She felt some impatience for the renewal of their intercourse, and for the perusal of the volume that had been mentioned. One evening Sarah Baxter, whom Constance had placed in her own occasional service, entered the room with marks of great joy and surprize, and informed her that she at length had discovered Miss Monrose.[9] From her abrupt and prolix account, it appeared, that Sarah had overtaken Miss Monrose in the street, and guided by her own curiosity, as well as by the wish to gratify her mistress, she had followed the stranger. To her utter astonishment the lady had paused at Mr. Dudley's door, with a seeming resolution to enter it, but, presently, resumed her way. Instead of pursuing her steps further, Sarah had stopped to communicate this intelligence to Constance. Having delivered her news, she hastened away, but returning, in a moment, with a countenance of new surprize, she informed her mistress, that on leaving the house she had met Miss Monrose at the door, on the point of entering. She added that the stranger had enquired for Constance, and was now waiting below.

Constantia took no time to reflect upon an incident so unexpected and so strange, but proceeded forthwith to the parlour. Martinette only was there. It did not instantly occur to her that this lady and Mademoiselle Monrose, might possibly be the same. The enquiries she made speedily removed her doubts, and it now appeared that the woman, about whose destiny she had formed so many conjectures, and fostered so much anxiety, was no other than the daughter of Roselli.[10]

Having readily answered her questions, Martinette enquired in her turn, into the motives of her friend's curiosity. These were explained by a succinct account of the transactions, to which the deceased Baxter had been a witness. Constance concluded, with mentioning her own reflections on the tale, and intimating her wish to be informed, how Martinette had extricated herself from a situation so calamitous.

Is there any room for wonder on that head? replied the guest. It was absurd to stay longer in the house. Having finished the interment of Roselli (soldier-fashion) for he was the man who suffered his foolish regrets to destroy him, I forsook the house. Roselli was by no means poor, but he could not consent to live at ease, or to live at all, while his country endured such horrible oppressions, and when so many of his friends had perished.[11] I complied with his humour, because it could not be changed, and I revered him too much to desert him.

---

[9] "Miss Monrose": on the identity of Martinette and Monrose, see Chapter 19 (note 19.11).

[10] "Daughter of Roselli": as in Chapter 20, Roselli is loosely referred to as the father of Martinette because he became her protector and companion after the death of her biological father (see note 20.27).

[11] "By no means poor … perished": Martinette explains that Roselli chose to live in poverty as a refugee while his French countrymen were suffering in the revolution. Once he dies, Martinette has no such scruples and lives in a furnished mansion surrounded by French-Caribbean servants (or possibly slaves, since many Creole immigrants only emancipated their slaves as a technical means of accommodating Pennsylvania laws regarding slavery). If true, the story explains the radical difference in her life conditions between the scene in which Baxter spies on her in Chapter 7 and the present.

But whither, said Constance, could you seek shelter at a time like that? The city was desolate, and a wandering female could scarcely be received under any roof. All inhabited houses were closed at that hour, and the fear of infection would have shut them against you, if they had not been already so.

Hast thou forgotten that there were at that time, at least ten thousand French in this city, fugitives from Marat and from St. Domingo?[12] That they lived in utter fearlessness of the reigning disease: sung and loitered in the public walks, and prattled at their doors, with all their customary unconcern?[13] Supposest thou that there were none among these, who would receive a countrywoman, even if her name had not been Martinette de Beauvais? Thy fancy has depicted strange things, but believe me, that, without a farthing and without a name, I should not have incurred the slightest inconvenience. The death of Roselli I foresaw, because it was gradual in its approach, and was sought by him as a good. My grief, therefore, was exhausted before it came, and I rejoiced at his death, because it was the close of all his sorrows. The rueful pictures of my distress and weakness, which were given by Baxter, existed only in his own fancy.

Martinette pleaded an engagement, and took her leave, professing to have come merely to leave with her the promised manuscript. This interview, though short, was productive of many reflections, on the deceitfulness of appearances, and on the variety of maxims by which the conduct of human beings is regulated.[14] She was accustomed to impart all her thoughts and relate every new incident to her father. With this view she now hied to his apartment. This hour it was her custom, when disengaged, always to spend with him.

She found Mr. Dudley busy in revolving a scheme, which various circumstances had suggested and gradually conducted to maturity. No period of his life had been equally delightful, with that portion of his youth which he had spent in Italy. The climate, the language, the manners of the people, and the sources of intellectual gratification, in painting and music, were congenial to his taste. He had reluctantly

---

[12] "At least ten thousand ... fugitives from Marat and St. Domingo": French-speaking émigrés from the revolution in France and from the slave revolution in Haiti. Historical scholarship suggests a total closer to five thousand, so Martinette's estimate seems high. See Branson and Patrick, "Étrangers dans un Pays Étrange." This was still a very large population segment in a city whose total number was roughly fifty-five thousand at this time, and far less during the fever epidemic.

[13] "Fearlessness of the reigning disease ... unconcern": for commentary on French joie de vivre (joy in living) and lifestyles that appeared in U.S. cities as a consequence of this wave of French-speaking revolutionary emigration, see Related Texts by Moreau de Saint-Méry and Watson, as well as Brown's "Portrait of an Emigrant." The Caribbean refugees had a less panic-driven relation to yellow fever because it was a common feature of life in their region. This was one source of the mistaken belief, common in the Anglophone community among many like the Francophobic former soldier Baxter in Chapter 7, that Africans and the French alike were immune to yellow fever (see notes 7.3–4).

[14] "Deceitfulness of appearances ... variety of maxims by which the conduct of human beings is regulated": in her friendship with Martinette, that is, Constantia is learning many things and gaining new insights about different ways of being a woman in the world as it is.

forsaken these enchanting seats, at the summons of his father, but, on his return to his native country, had encountered nothing but ignominy and pain. Poverty and blindness had beset his path, and it seemed as if it were impossible to fly too far from the scene of his disasters. His misfortunes could not be concealed from others, and every thing around him seemed to renew the memory of all that he had suffered. All the events of his youth served to entice him to Italy, while all the incidents of his subsequent life, concurred to render disgustful his present abode.

His daughter's happiness was not to be forgotten. This he imagined would be eminently promoted by the scheme. It would open to her new avenues to knowledge. It would snatch her from the odious pursuit of Ormond, and by a variety of objects and adventures, efface from her mind any impression which his dangerous artifices might have made upon it.

This project was now communicated to Constantia. Every argument adapted to influence her choice, was employed. He justly conceived that the only obstacle to her adoption of it, related to Ormond. He expatiated on the dubious character of this man, the wildness of his schemes, and the magnitude of his errors. What could be expected from a man, half of whose life had been spent at the head of a band of Cassacks, spreading devastation in the regions of the Danube, and supporting by flagitious intrigues, the tyranny of Catharine, and the other half in traversing inhospitable countries, and extinguishing what remained of clemency and justice, by intercourse with savages?[15]

---

[15] "Band of Cassacks ... Danube ... Catharine ... savages": a second reference to Ormond's time among Cossacks during the Russo-Turkish war of 1787–1792 and related ambitions among the Naudowessie or Sioux of the North American plains (see notes 21.1, 26.1, and 27.3). Different factions of Cossacks were allied with both sides of the conflict after Russian Empress Catherine II (Catherine the Great; 1729–1796) attempted to diminish Cossack power by forcibly disbanding one of the main Cossack groups, the Zaporozhian Host. Previously Cossack troops had fought on the Russian side of Russo-Turkish conflicts, but after this rift they clashed with Catherine in order to defend their relative autonomy within the Russian Empire.

The Cossacks were a nomadic warrior society, centered in the southern plains (steppe) areas of Russian and Eastern Europe, that played a central role in political transformations throughout the region in the early modern period. During the Enlightenment they were renowned for their aggressive independence and stereotyped for their supposed barbarity. Beginning with the 1648 uprising of the Zaporozhian Cossacks, an important event that inaugurated the gradual dissolution of the Polish Commonwealth, and continuing through periodic uprisings against Russian rule around the turn of the eighteenth century, Cossacks were a key factor in the political transformations of Eastern Europe. After 1734, the Cossacks were absorbed into the military apparatus of the Russian Empire, although not without continued intrigues and conflicts, particularly under Catherine. From the sixteenth century onward, the Cossacks were involved in constant raids and counterraids against the nomadic Tatar peoples ruled by the Ottomans, a long-running border conflict that created tensions between the Ottoman Empire and Eastern European states, above all Russia. The first Russo-Turkish War (1768–1774) began when Cossacks in Russian service advanced into Ottoman territory. The war ended well for Russia, which won territory, access to Black Sea ports, and reparations from the Ottomans. Perhaps because of the Cossacks' political unpredictability, however, in 1775 Catherine forcibly disbanded the Zaporozhian Host in order to better control it within the Russian

It was admitted that his energies were great, but misdirected, and that to restore them to the guidance of truth, was not in itself impossible, but it was so with relation to any power that she possessed. Conformity would flow from their marriage, but this conformity was not to be expected from him. It was not his custom to abjure any of his doctrines or recede from any of his claims. She knew likewise the conditions of their union. She must go with him to some corner of the world, where his boasted system was established. What was the road to it, he had carefully concealed, but it was evident that it lay beyond the precincts of civilized existence.

Whatever were her ultimate decision, it was at least proper to delay it. Six years were yet wanting of that period, at which only she formerly considered marriage as proper.[16] To all the general motives for deferring her choice, the conduct of Ormond superadded the weightiest. Their correspondence might continue, but her residence in Europe and converse with mankind, might enlighten her judgment and qualify her for a more rational decision.

Constantia was not uninfluenced by these reasonings. Instead of reluctantly admitting them, she somewhat wondered that they had not been suggested by her own reflections. Her imagination anticipated her entrance on that mighty scene with emotions little less than rapturous. Her studies had conferred a thousand ideal charms on a theatre, where Scipio and Cæsar had performed their parts.[17] Her wishes were no less importunate to gaze upon the Alps and Pyrenees, and to vivify and chasten the images collected from books, by comparing them with their real prototypes.

---

military. The second Russo-Turkish War (1787–1792) was a failed attempt by the Ottoman Empire to regain land lost in the prior conflict. Although the Cossacks and Tatars were long-term enemies, some "intercourse," as the narrator puts it, occurred between the two groups. After Catherine's 1775 attempt to subordinate the Cossacks more effectively, a breakaway group sought protection under the Ottoman Empire until they were pardoned in 1828 by Russian Emperor Nicholas I (1796–1855).

Brown's interest in the recurrent conflict between Christian Russians and Muslim Ottomans—fought via client populations in the barely regulated Cossacks and Tatars—provides another instance of his general fascination with border regions in which sociopolitical and religious conflict becomes encoded as a struggle between "civilization" (associated with dominant forces and classicism) and "barbarity" (associated with insurrectional energies and new styles).

[16] "Six years ... proper": Constantia's ideas about the appropriate age for marriage were first noted in Chapter 2 (see note 2.7).

[17] "A theatre, where Scipio and Caesar had performed their parts": the novel's emphasis on theatrical images is used to describe large-scale perspectives on transnational historical and geopolitical relations. Scipio is the name of several notable Roman figures, but the connection with Julius Caesar (100–44 B.C.E.) and attention to civil conflicts throughout the novel suggests that Brown intends a reference to Metellus Scipio (c.100–46 B.C.E.), a general of the late Republic who was an important antagonist to Caesar. Scipio was the father-in-law and supporter of Pompey and the Senate in the 49 B.C.E. Civil War against Caesar's rise to dictatorship. Although Constantia is still thinking through the lens of classical history (see notes 19.14–15), after her interaction with Martinette she is also newly conscious of "actors now upon the stage," two paragraphs on. All of these theatrical images lead to the literal drawing aside of a curtain in the chapter's final line.

No social ties existed to hold her to America. Her only kinsman and friend would be the companion of her journies. This project was likewise recommended by advantages of which she only was qualified to judge. Sophia Westwyn had embarked, four years previous to this date, for England, in company with an English lady and her husband. The arrangements that were made forbad either of the friends to hope for a future meeting: Yet now, by virtue of this project, this meeting seemed no longer to be hopeless.

This burst of new ideas and new hopes on the mind of Constance took place in the course of a single hour. No change in her external situation had been wrought, and yet her mind had undergone the most signal revolution. The novelty as well as greatness of the prospect kept her in a state of elevation and awe, more ravishing than any she had ever experienced. Anticipations of intercourse with nature in her most august forms, with men in diversified states of society, with the posterity of Greeks and Romans, and with the actors that were now upon the stage, and above all with the being whom absence and the want of other attachments, had, in some sort, contributed to deify, made this night pass away upon the wings of transport.

The hesitation which existed on parting with her father, speedily gave place to an ardour impatient of the least delay. She saw no impediments to the immediate commencement of the voyage. To delay it a month or even a week, seemed to be unprofitable tardiness. In this ferment of her thoughts, she was neither able nor willing to sleep. In arranging the means of departure and anticipating the events that would successively arise, there was abundant food for contemplation.

She marked the first dawnings of the day and rose. She felt reluctance to break upon her father's morning slumbers, but considered that her motives were extremely urgent, and that the pleasure afforded him by her zealous approbation of his scheme, would amply compensate him for this unseasonable intrusion on his rest. She hastened therefore to his chamber. She entered with blithsome steps, and softly drew aside the curtain.

Chapter XXII

UNHAPPY Constance! At the moment when thy dearest hopes had budded afresh, when the clouds of insecurity and disquiet had retired from thy vision, wast thou assailed by the great subverter of human schemes. Thou sawest nothing in futurity but an eternal variation and succession of delights. Thou wast hastening to forget dangers and sorrows which thou fondly imaginedst were never to return. This day was to be the outset of a new career; existence was henceforth to be embellished with enjoyments, hitherto scarcely within the reach of hope.

Alas! Thy predictions of calamity seldom failed to be verified. Not so thy prognostics of pleasure.[1] These, though fortified by every calculation of contingencies, were edifices grounded upon nothing. Thy life was a struggle with malignant destiny; a contest for happiness in which thou wast fated to be overcome.

She stooped to kiss the venerable cheek of her father, and, by whispering, to break his slumber. Her eye was no sooner fixed upon his countenance, than she started back and shrieked. She had no power to forbear. Her outcries were piercing and vehement. They ceased only with the cessation of breath. She sunk upon a chair in a state partaking more of death than of life, mechanically prompted to give vent to her agonies in shrieks, but incapable of uttering a sound.

The alarm called her servants to the spot. They beheld her dumb, wildly gazing, and gesticulating in a way that indicated frenzy. She made no resistence to their efforts, but permitted them to carry her back to her own chamber. Sarah called upon her to speak and to explain the cause of these appearances, but the shock which she had endured, seemed to have irretrievably destroyed her powers of utterance.

The terrors of the affectionate Sarah were increased. She kneeled by the bed-side of her mistress, and with streaming eyes, besought the unhappy lady to compose herself. Perhaps the sight of weeping in another possessed a sympathetic influence, or nature had made provision for this salutary change: However that be, a torrent of tears now came to her succour, and rescued her from a paroxysm of insanity, which its longer continuance might have set beyond the reach of cure.[2]

Meanwhile, a glance at his master's countenance made Fabian fully acquainted with the nature of the scene. The ghastly visage of Mr. Dudley shewed that he was dead, and that he had died in some terrific and mysterious manner. As soon as this faithful servant recovered from surprize, the first expedient which his ingenuity suggested, was to fly with tidings of this event to Mr. Melbourne. That gentleman instantly obeyed the summons. With the power of weeping, Constantia recovered the power of reflection. This, for a time, served her only as a medium of anguish. Melbourne mingled his tears with hers, and endeavoured, by suitable remonstrances, to revive her fortitude.

---

[1] "Prognostics of pleasure": hopes for future happiness.

[2] "The reach of cure": the narrator Sophia asserts that Sarah Baxter's tears and companionship generate a sympathetic bodily response in Constantia that protects her from lapsing into insanity.

The filial passion is perhaps instinctive to man;[3] but its energy is modified by various circumstances. Every event in the life of Constance contributed to heighten this passion beyond customary bounds. In the habit of perpetual attendance on her father, of deriving from him her knowledge, and sharing with him the hourly fruits of observation and reflection, his existence seemed blended with her own. There was no other whose concurrence and council she could claim, with whom a domestic and uninterrupted alliance could be maintained. The only bond of consanguinity was loosened, the only prop of friendship was taken away.

Others, perhaps, would have observed, that her father's existence had been merely a source of obstruction and perplexity; that she had hitherto acted by her own wisdom, and would find, hereafter, less difficulty in her choice of schemes, and fewer impediments to the execution.—These reflections occurred not to her. This disaster had increased, to an insupportable degree, the vacancy and dreariness of her existence. The face she was habituated to behold, had disappeared forever; the voice, whose mild and affecting tones, had so long been familiar to her ears, was hushed into eternal silence. The felicity to which she clung was ravished away: Nothing remained to hinder her from sinking into utter despair.

The first transports of grief having subsided, a source of consolation seemed to be opened in the belief that her father had only changed one form of being for another: That he still lived to be the guardian of her peace and honor; to enter the recesses of her thought: To forewarn her of evil and invite her to good. She grasped at these images with eagerness, and fostered them as the only solaces of her calamity.[4] They were not adapted to inspire her with cheerfulness, but they sublimed her sensations, and added an inexplicable fascination to sorrow.

It was unavoidable sometimes to reflect upon the nature of that death which had occurred. Tokens were sufficiently apparent that outward violence had been the cause. Who could be the performer of so black a deed, by what motives he was guided were topics of fruitless conjecture. She mused upon this subject, not from the thirst of vengeance, but from a mournful curiosity. Had the perpetrator stood before her, and challenged retribution, she would not have lifted a finger to accuse or to punish. The evil already endured, left her no power to concert and execute projects for extending that evil to others. Her mind was unnerved, and recoiled with loathing from considerations of abstract justice, or political utility, when they prompted to the prosecution of the murderer.[5]

---

[3] "The filial passion is perhaps instinctive to man": in other words, Sophia seems to hypothesize that respect and love for parents, elders, and ancestors is a natural, biological or god-given feature of human thought, as opposed to a social institution.

[4] "Recesses of her thought … grasped at these images … solaces of her calamity": Sophia suggests that Constantia takes comfort in supernatural, religious ideas of an afterlife in this traumatic context. According to Sophia, Constantia believes that despite her father's death his spirit will act as a continuing guide. For more on Sophia's ideas concerning religion, see note 23.2.

[5] "Abstract justice, or political utility … prosecution of the murderer": Constantia explicitly refuses the emotion of revenge and a legalistic search for retribution. The narrator's phrasing echoes

Melbourne was actuated by different views, but, on this subject, he was painfully bewildered. Mr. Dudley's deportment to his servants and neighbours, was gentle and humane. He had no dealings with the trafficking or labouring part of mankind.[6] The fund which supplied his cravings of necessity or habit, was his daughter's. His recreations and employments were harmless and lonely. The evil purpose was limited to his death, for his chamber was exactly in the same state in which negligent security had left it. No midnight footstep or voice, no unbarred door or lifted window afforded tokens of the presence, or traces of the entrance or flight, of the assassin.

The meditations of Constantia, however, could not fail, in some of their circuities, to encounter the image of Craig. His agency in the impoverishment of her father, and in the scheme by which she had like to have been loaded with the penalties of forgery, was of an impervious[7] and unprecedented kind. Motives were unveiled by time, in some degree, accounting for his treacherous proceeding, but there was room to suppose an inborn propensity to mischief. Was he not the authour of this new evil? His motives and his means were equally inscrutable, but their inscrutability might flow from her own defects in discernment and knowledge, and time might supply her defects in this as in former instances.

These images were casual. The causes of the evil were seldom contemplated. Her mind was rarely at liberty to wander from reflection on her irremediable loss. Frequently, when confused by distressful recollections, she would detect herself going to her father's chamber. Often his well known accents would ring in her ears, and the momentary impulse would be to answer his calls. Her reluctance to sit down to her meals, without her usual companion, could scarcely be surmounted.

In this state of mind the image of the only friend who survived, or whose destiny, at least, was doubtful, occurred to her. She sunk into fits of deeper abstraction and dissolved away in tears of more agonizing tenderness. A week after her father's interment, she shut herself up in her chamber, to torment herself with fruitless remembrances. The name of Sophia Westwyn was pronounced, and the ditty that solemnized their parting was sung.[8] Now, more than formerly, she became sensible of the loss of that portrait, which had been deposited in the hands of M'Crea, as a pledge. As soon as her change of fortune had supplied her with the means of redeeming it, she hastened to M'Crea for that end. To her unspeakable disappointment he was absent from the city: He had taken a long journey, and the exact period

---

Godwin's *Enquiry Concerning Political Justice* and thereby implies that this repudiation of revenge motivation is a quasi-Godwinian position. Brown thematizes a Woldwinite renunciation of revenge throughout his other novels *Wieland, Arthur Mervyn,* and *Edgar Huntly.*

[6] "Trafficking or labouring part of mankind": that is, Dudley had no relations with merchants, artisans, or servants that might have motivated violent anger against him. The narrator Sophia's language may imply a somewhat pejorative stereotyping of commercial and laboring-class behavior.

[7] "Impervious": impenetrable, inscrutable, impossible to unravel or understand.

[8] "Only friend … agonizing tenderness … the name of Sophia Westwyn … ditty": Sophia recalls Constantia's song in Chapter 19 (see note 19.8) and again, throughout this paragraph, represents herself as Constantia's "only friend" and as the object of her deepest longings.

of his return could not be ascertained. His clerks refused to deliver the picture, or even, by searching, to discover whether it was still in their master's possession. This application had frequently and lately been repeated, but without success; M'Crea had not yet returned and his family were equally in the dark, as to the day on which his return might be expected.

She determined on this occasion, to renew her visit. Her incessant disappointments had almost extinguished hope, and she made enquiries at his door, with a faultering accent and sinking heart. These emotions were changed into surprize and delight, when answer was made that he had just arrived. She was instantly conducted into his presence.

The countenance of M'Crea easily denoted, that his visitant was by no means acceptable. There was a mixture of embarrassment and sullenness in his air, which was far from being diminished when the purpose of this visit was explained. Constance reminded him of the offer and acceptance of this pledge, and of the conditions with which the transaction was accompanied.

He acknowledged, with some hesitation, that a promise had been given to retain the pledge until it were in her power to redeem it, but the long delay, the urgency of his own wants, and particularly the ill treatment which he conceived himself to have suffered, in the transaction respecting the forged note, had, in his own opinion, absolved him from this promise. He had therefore sold the picture to a goldsmith, for as much as the gold about it was worth.

This information produced, in the heart of Constantia, a contest between indignation and sorrow, that, for a time, debarred her from speech. She stifled the anger that was, at length, rising to her lips, and calmly inquired to whom the picture had been sold.

M'Crea answered that for his part he had little dealings in gold and silver, but every thing of that kind, which fell to his share, he transacted with Mr. D——.[9] This person was one of the most eminent of his profession. His character and place of abode were universally known. The only expedient that remained was to apply to him, and to ascertain, forthwith, the destiny of the picture. It was too probable, that when separated from its case, the portrait was thrown away or destroyed, as a mere incumbrance, but the truth was too momentous to be made the sport of mere probability. She left the house of M'Crea, and hastened to that of the goldsmith.

The circumstance was easily recalled to his remembrance. It was true that such a picture had been offered for sale, and that he had purchased it. The workmanship was curious, and he felt unwilling to destroy it. He therefore hung it up in his shop and indulged the hope that a purchaser would, sometime, be attracted by the mere beauty of the toy.

Constantia's hopes were revived by these tidings, and she earnestly inquired if it were still in his possession.

---

[9] "Mr. D——": Philadelphia city directories indicate that there were two gold and silversmiths with names beginning in D in 1793–1794, both probably French speaking: Abraham Dubois at 65 North Second, and John Baptiste Dumoutet at 71 Elm Street.

No. A young gentleman had entered his shop some months before; the picture had caught his fancy, and he had given a price which the artist owned he should not have demanded, had he not been encouraged by the eagerness which the gentleman betrayed to possess it.

Who was this gentleman? Had there been any previous acquaintance between them? What was his name, his profession, and where was he to be found?

Really, the goldsmith answered, he was ignorant respecting all those particulars. Previously to this purchase, the gentleman had sometimes visited his shop, but he did not recollect to have since seen him. He was unacquainted with his name and his residence.

What appeared to be his motives for purchasing this picture?

The customer appeared highly pleased with it. Pleasure, rather than surprize, seemed to be produced by the sight of it. If I were permitted to judge, continued the artist, I should imagine that the young man was acquainted with the original. To say the truth, I hinted as much at the time, and I did not see that he discouraged the supposition. Indeed, I cannot conceive how the picture could otherwise have gained any value in his eyes.

This only heightened the eagerness of Constance to trace the footsteps of the youth. It was obvious to suppose some communication or connection between her friend and this purchaser. She repeated her enquiries, and the goldsmith, after some consideration, said:— Why, on second thoughts, I seem to have some notion of having seen a figure like that of my customer, go into a lodging house, in Front-Street,[10] some time before I met with him at my shop.

The situation of this house being satisfactorily described, and the artist being able to afford her no further information, except as to stature and guise, she took her leave. There were two motives impelling her to prosecute her search after this person; the desire of regaining this portrait and of procuring tidings of her friend. Involved as she was in ignorance, it was impossible to conjecture, how far this incident would be subservient to these inestimable purposes. To procure an interview with this stranger, was the first measure which prudence suggested.

She knew not his name or his person. He was once seen entering a lodging house. Thither she must immediately repair, but how to introduce herself, how to describe the person of whom she was in search, she knew not. She was beset with embarrassments and difficulties. While her attention was entangled by these, she proceeded unconsciously on her way, and stopped not until she reached the mansion that had been described. Here she paused to collect her thoughts.

---

[10] "Front-street": a north-south street running along the Delaware River wharves, the next street east of Second Street where one of the goldsmith's shops was located. City directories list several boarding houses on North and South Front Street in the 1790s. Since this street was next to the wharves and docks, it was a convenient location for travelers and short-term visitors. Throughout this period the intersection of Front and Market Streets was the epicenter of Philadelphia's urban density and commercial maritime networks. The rural protagonist of Brown's novel *Arthur Mervyn* arrives at this spot in his first encounter with the city, amazed by Philadelphia's urban marvels.

She found no relief in deliberation. Every moment added to her perplexity and indecision. Irresistibly impelled by her wishes, she at length, in a mood that partook of desperate, advanced to the door and knocked. The summons was immediately obeyed by a woman of decent appearance. A pause ensued, which Constantia at length terminated, by a request to see the mistress of the house.

The lady courteously answered that she was the person, and immediately ushered her visitant into an apartment. Constance being seated, the lady waited for the disclosure of her message. To prolong the silence was only to multiply embarrassments. She reverted to the state of her feelings, and saw that they flowed from inconsistency and folly. One vigorous effort was sufficient to restore her to composure and self-command.

She began with apologizing for a visit, unpreceeded by an introduction. The object of her enquiries was a person, with whom it was of the utmost moment that she should procure a meeting, but whom, by an unfortunate concurrence of circumstances, she was unable to describe by the usual incidents of name and profession. Her knowledge was confined to his external appearance, and to the probability of his being an inmate of this house, at the begining of the year.

She then proceeded to describe his person and dress.

It is true, said the lady, such an one as you describe has boarded in this house. His name was Martynne.[11] I have good reason to remember him, for he lived with me three months, and then left the country without paying for his board.

He has gone then? said Constance, greatly discouraged by these tidings.

Yes: He was a man of specious manners and loud pretensions. He came from England, bringing with him forged recommendatory letters, and after passing from one end of the country to the other, contracting debts which he never paid, and making bargains which he never fulfilled, he suddenly disappeared. It is likely that he has returned to Europe.

Had he no kindred, no friends, no companions?

He found none here. He made pretences to alliances in England, which better information has, I believe, since shewn to be false.

This was the sum of the information procurable from this source. Constance was unable to conceal her chagrin. These symptoms were observed by the lady, whose curiosity was awakened in turn. Questions were obliquely started, inviting Constance to a disclosure of her thoughts. No advantage would arise from confidence, and the guest, after a few minutes of abstraction and silence, rose to take her leave.

During this conference, some one appeared to be negligently sporting with the keys of an harpsichord, in the next apartment. The notes were too irregular and faint to make a forcible impression on the ear. In the present state of her mind, Constance was merely conscious of the sound, in the intervals of conversation. Having arisen from her seat, her anxiety to obtain some information that might lead to the point

---

[11] "Martynne": the curious name of this Craig-like figure, a relatively rare spelling of "Martin," may be an Anglicization of the French names Martine or Martienne, recalling that of Martinette.

she wished, made her again pause. She endeavoured to invent some new interrogatory better suited to her purpose, than those which had, already, been employed. A silence on both sides ensued.

During this interval, the unseen musician suddenly refrained from rambling, and glided into notes of some refinement and complexity. The cadence was aerial, but a thunderbolt, falling at her feet, would not have communicated a more visible shock to the senses of Constance. A glance that denoted a tumult of soul bordering on distraction, was now fixed upon the door, that led into the room whence the harmony proceeded. Instantly the cadence was revived, and some accompanying voice, was heard to warble

> Ah! far beyond this world of woes,
> We meet to part—to part no more.[12]

Joy and grief in their sudden onset, and their violent extremes, approach so nearly, in their influence on human beings, as scarce to be distinguished. Constantia's frame was still enfeebled by her recent distresses. The torrent of emotion was too abrupt and too vehement. Her faculties were overwhelmed, and she sunk upon the floor motionless and without sense, but not till she had faintly articulated;

My God! My God! This is a joy unmerited and too great.

---

[12] "Part no more": like the songs of Helen in Chapter 16 and Constantia in Chapter 19, these lines are by Brown and echo Constantia's earlier lyrics.

Chapter XXIII

I MUST be forgiven if I now introduce myself on the stage. Sophia Westwyn is the friend of Constance, and the writer of this narrative. So far as my fate was connected with that of my friend, it is worthy to be known. That connection has constituted the joy and misery of my existence, and has prompted me to undertake this task.[1]

I assume no merit from the desire of knowledge, and superiority to temptation. There is little of which I can boast, but that little I derived, instrumentally, from Constance. Poor as my attainments are, it is to her that I am indebted for them all. Life itself was the gift of her father, but my virtue and felicity are her gifts. That I am neither indigent nor profligate, flows from her bounty.

I am not unaware of the divine superintendence, of the claims upon my gratitude and service, which pertain to my God.[2] I know that all physical and moral agents, are merely instrumental to the purpose that he wills, but though the great author of being and felicity must not be forgotten, it is neither possible nor just to overlook the claims upon our love, with which our fellow-beings are invested.

The supreme love does not absorb, but chasten and enforce all subordinate affections. In proportion to the rectitude of my perceptions and the ardour of my piety, must I clearly discern and fervently love, the excellence discovered in my fellow-beings, and industriously promote their improvement and felicity.

From my infancy to my seventeenth year, I lived in the house of Mr. Dudley. On the day of my birth, I was deserted by my mother. Her temper was more akin to that of tygress than woman:[3] Yet that is unjust, for beasts cherish their offspring. No natures but human, are capable of that depravity, which makes insensible to the claims of innocence and helplessness.

---

[1] "Introduce myself on this stage ... this narrative ... this task": as narrator, Sophia has organized the tale and guided the reader's responses from the start, but she now steps forward to act as an active character in her own right. While her shaping and interpreting influence has been relatively implicit to this point, the emotionally saturated self-portrait that follows brings the question of narrative perspective into focus as a basic and explicit concern. In other words, if the reader has not been aware of Sophia's influence to this point, the question now seems to become unavoidable. For a discussion of the novel's emphasis on questions of narrative perspective, see the Introduction.

[2] "My God": unlike Constantia's, Ormond's, or Martinette's absence of belief in an omniscient, omnipotent guiding hand of God, Sophia insists that a divine force organizes human actions and emotions. In contrast to the radical Enlightenment's critique of religious belief as superstition, and in implicit contrast to the thinking of the novel's other main characters on this point, Sophia's declaration of faith is an element in Brown's portrayal of her ideological position in the period's culture wars.

[3] "Mother ... more akin to tygress than woman": Sophia's intense resentment and condemnation of her mother may be compared to Martinette's response to her female guardian, since both older women are similarly mobile in their travels and heterosexual affections. All three of *Ormond*'s main female characters—Constantia, Martinette, and Sophia—have distant or nearly absent relationships with their mothers. Likewise all three are protected and educated by older men to whom they have no family blood relation.

But let me not recall her to memory. Have I not enough of sorrow? Yet to omit my causes of disquiet, the unprecedented forlornness of my condition, and the persecutions of an unnatural parent, would be to leave my character a problem, and the sources of my love of Miss Dudley unexplored. Yet I must not dwell upon that complication of iniquities, that savage ferocity and unextinguishable hatred of me, which characterized my unhappy mother!

I was not safe under the protection of Mr. Dudley, nor happy in the caresses of his daughter. My mother asserted the privilege of that relation; she laboured for years to obtain the controul of my person and actions; to snatch me from a peaceful and chaste assylum, and detain me in her own house, where, indeed, I should not have been in want of raiment and food, but where —

O my mother! Let me not dishonor thy name! Yet it is not in my power to enhance thy infamy. Thy crimes, unequalled as they were, were, perhaps, expiated by thy penitence. Thy offences are too well known, but perhaps they who witnessed thy freaks of intoxication, thy defiance of public shame, the enormity of thy pollutions, the infatuation that made thee glory in the pursuit of a loathesome and detestable trade, may be strangers to the remorse and the abstinence which accompanied the close of thy ignominious life.[4]

For ten years was my peace incessantly molested, by the menaces or machinations of my mother. The longer she meditated my destruction, the more tenacious of her purpose, and indefatigable in her efforts, she became. That my mind was harrassed with perpetual alarms, was not enough. The fame and tranquility of Mr. Dudley and his daughter, were hourly assailed. My mother resigned herself to the impulses of malignity and rage. Headlong passions and a vigorous, though perverted understanding, were her's. Hence her stratagems to undermine the reputation of my protector, and to bereave him of domestic comfort, were subtle and profound. Had she not herself been careless of that good, which she endeavoured to wrest from others, her artifices could scarcely have been frustrated.

In proportion to the hazard which accrued to my protector and friend, the more ardent their zeal in my defence, and their affection for my person became. They watched over me with ineffable solicitude. At all hours and in every occupation, I was the companion of Constance. All my wants were supplied, in the same proportion as her's. The tenderness of Mr. Dudley seemed equally divided between us. I partook of his instructions, and the means of every intellectual and personal gratification, were lavished upon me.

The speed of my mother's career in infamy, was at length slackened. She left New-York, which had long been the theatre of her vices. Actuated by a new caprice, she determined to travel through the Southern States. Early indulgence was the cause of her ruin, but her parents had given her the embellishments of a fashionable education.

---

[4] "Pollutions … loathesome and detestable trade … ignominious life": in other words, Sophia's mother worked as a prostitute.

She delighted to assume all parts, and personate the most opposite characters.[5] She now resolved to carry a new name and the mask of virtue, into scenes hitherto unvisited.

She journeyed as far as Charleston. Here she met an inexperienced youth, lately arrived from England, and in possession of an ample fortune. Her speciousness and artifices seduced him into a precipitate marriage. Her true character, however, could not be long concealed by herself, and her vices had been too conspicuous, for her long to escape recognition. Her husband was infatuated by her blandishments. To abandon her, or to contemplate her depravity with unconcern, were equally beyond his power. Romantic in his sentiments, his fortitude was unequal to his disappointments, and he speedily sunk into the grave. By a similar refinement in generosity, he bequeathed to her his property.

With this accession of wealth, she returned to her ancient abode. The mask, lately worn, seemed preparing to be thrown aside, and her profligate habits to be resumed with more eagerness than ever, but an unexpected and total revolution was effected, by the exhortations of a Methodist divine. Her heart seemed, on a sudden, to be remoulded, her vices and the abettors of them were abjured, she shut out the intrusions of society, and prepared to expiate, by the rigours of abstinence and the bitterness of tears, the offences of her past life.

In this, as in her former career, she was unacquainted with restraint and moderation. Her remorses gained strength, in proportion as she cherished them. She brooded over the images of her guilt, till the possibility of forgiveness and remission disappeared. Her treatment of her daughter and her husband constituted the chief source of her torment. Her awakened conscience refused her a momentary respite from its persecutions. Her thought became, by rapid degrees, tempestuous and gloomy, and it was at length evident, that her condition was maniacal.[6]

In this state, she was to me an object, no longer of terror, but compassion. She was surrounded by hirelings, devoid of personal attachment, and anxious only to convert her misfortunes, to their own advantage. This evil it was my duty to obviate. My presence for a time, only enhanced the vehemence of her malady, but at length it was only by my attendance and soothing, that she was diverted from the fellest purposes. Shocking execrations and outrages, resolutions and efforts to destroy herself and those around her, were sure to take place in my absence. The moment I appeared before her, her fury abated; her gesticulations were becalmed, and her voice exerted only in incoherent and pathetic lamentations.

These scenes, though so different from those which I had formerly been condemned to witness, were scarcely less excruciating. The friendship of Constantia

---

[5] "Opposite characters": like so many of the novel's characters, Sophia's mother uses different names and identities and enjoys a spirit of metamorphosis.

[6] "Maniacal": Sophia writes that her mother became insane. As with the character Theodore in Brown's earlier novel *Wieland* (September 1798), an episode of madness is tied to an excess of religious, doctrinal enthusiasm.

Dudley was my only consolation. She took up her abode with me, and shared with me every disgustful and perilous office, which my mother's insanity prescribed.

Of this consolation, however, it was my fate to be bereaved. My mother's state was deplorable, and no remedy hitherto employed, was efficacious. A voyage to England, was conceived likely to benefit, by change of temperature and scenes, and by the opportunity it would afford of trying the superior skill of English physicians.[7] This scheme, after various struggles, on my part, was adopted. It was detestable to my imagination, because it severed me from that friend, in whose existence mine was involved, and without whose participation, knowledge lost its attractions, and society became a torment.

The prescriptions of my duty could not be disguised or disobeyed, and we parted. A mutual engagement was formed, to record every sentiment and relate every event that happened, in the life of either, and no opportunity of communicating information, was to be omitted. This engagement was punctually performed on my part. I sought out every method of conveyance to my friend, and took infinite pains to procure tidings from her, but all were ineffectual.

My mother's malady declined, but was succeeded by a pulmonary disease, which threatened her speedy destruction. By the restoration of her understanding, the purpose of her voyage was obtained, and my impatience to return, which the inexplicable and ominous silence of my friend daily increased, prompted me to exert all my powers of persuasion, to induce her to re-visit America.

My mother's frenzy was a salutary crisis in her moral history. She looked back upon her past conduct with unspeakable loathing, but this retrospect only invigorated her devotion and her virtue: but the thought of returning to the scene of her unhappiness and infamy, could not be endured. Besides, life in her eyes, possessed considerable attractions, and her physicians flattered her with recovery from her present disease, if she would change the atmosphere of England for that of Languedoc and Naples.[8]

I followed her with murmurs and reluctance. To desert her in her present critical state would have been inhuman. My mother's aversions and attachments, habits and views were dissonant with my own. Conformity of sentiments and impressions of maternal tenderness, did not exist to bind us to each other. My attendance was assiduous, but it was the sense of duty that rendered my attendance a supportable task.

Her decay was eminently gradual. No time seemed to diminish her appetite for novelty and change. During three years we traversed every part of France, Switzerland and Italy. I could not but attend to surrounding scenes, and mark the progress

---

[7] "A voyage … English physicians": travel was commonly recommended in this period as a remedy for madness or depression. This will not be the last time in the novel that a trip to England is proposed as a form of mental or emotional sedation. See notes 20.14 and 29.4.

[8] "Languedoc and Naples": while the move from England to the Mediterranean takes Sophia's mother to warmer climates, it is also involves different spheres of regional conflict in the revolutionary era.

of the mighty revolution, whose effects, like agitation in a fluid, gradually spread from Paris, the centre, over the face of the neighbouring kingdoms; but there passed not a day or an hour in which the image of Constance was not recalled, in which the most pungent regrets were not felt at the inexplicable silence which had been observed by her, and the most vehement longings indulged to return to my native country. My exertions to ascertain her condition by indirect means, by interrogating natives of America, with whom I chanced to meet, were unwearied, but, for a long period, ineffectual.

During this pilgrimage, Rome was thrice visited. My mother's indisposition was hastening to a crisis, and she formed the resolution of closing her life at the bottom of Vesuvius.[9] We stopped, for the sake of a few day's repose, at Rome. On the morning after our arrival, I accompanied some friends to view the public edifices. Casting my eyes over the vast and ruinous interior of the Coliseo, my attention was fixed by the figure of a young man, whom, after a moment's pause, I recollected to have seen in the streets of New-York. At a distance from home, mere community of country is no inconsiderable bond of affection. The social spirit prompts us to cling even to inanimate objects, when they remind us of ancient fellowships and juvenile attachments.

A servant was dispatched to summon this stranger, who recognized a country-woman with a pleasure equal to that which I had received. On nearer view, this person, whose name was Courtland,[10] did not belie my favorable prepossessions. Our intercourse was soon established on a footing of confidence and intimacy.

---

[9] "Vesuvius": the still-active volcanic Mount Vesuvius, south of Naples, famous for its destruction of the Roman city of Pompeii in 79 C.E. Pompeii was rediscovered in 1748 after being buried for almost 1700 years, and elite tourism to notable ruins such as Pompeii or the Roman Coliseum ("Coliseo") in this period often produced reflections on the transitory nature of once great but now fallen empires at a time of widespread European and Atlantic revolution.

[10] "Courtland": the name of Sophia's future husband may be intended to echo that of "Sinisterus Courtland," a minor villain and undesirable or "sinister" suitor in Judith Sargent Murray's "Story of Margaretta," a sentimental fiction included in her essay series "The Gleaner." The series initially appeared in the Boston *Massachusetts Magazine* in 1792–1794 and was published separately in book form in 1798. Since Murray's brand of feminism and cultural politics was firmly religious and allied with the more conservative, Anglophile Federalist party (the 1798 book edition is dedicated to then-President and Federalist John Adams), somewhat akin to the narrator Sophia's position here, Brown's reference may have an ironic or critical edge.

With regard to possible references to "The Gleaner" it is also notable that, although Murray most often wrote under male pseudonyms, she used "Constantia" for this series and included it on the title-page of the 1798 book edition. Both names may thus refer obliquely to Murray's narrative, although Brown's use of "Constantia" recalls two other factors. First, "Constantia" and "Constance" were common allegorical names for female protagonists in this period, for example in titles such as the anonymous *The School of Woman; or, Memoirs of Constantia* (1753); John Langhorne's *The Correspondence of Theodosius and Constantia* (1765, frequently reprinted through the 1790s); Harriet Lee's *Constantia de Valmont. A Novel* (1799); Helena Whitford's *Constantia Neville; or The West Indian* (1800); or Mrs. Charles Matthews' *Constance; A Novel* (1785). Second, Brown used the name Constantia elsewhere; most

The destiny of Constance was always uppermost in my thoughts. This person's acquaintance was originally sought, chiefly in the hope of obtaining from him some information respecting my friend. On inquiry I discovered that he had left his native city, seven months after me. Having tasked his recollection and compared a number of facts, the name of Dudley at length re-occurred to him. He had casually heard the history of Craig's imposture and its consequences. These were now related as circumstantially as a memory, occupied by subsequent incidents, enabled him. The tale had been told to him, in a domestic circle which he was accustomed to frequent, by the person who purchased Mr. Dudley's lute, and restored it to its previous owner, on the conditions formerly mentioned.

This tale filled me with anguish and doubt. My impatience to search out this unfortunate girl, and share with her her sorrows or relieve them, was anew excited by this mournful intelligence. That Constantia Dudley was reduced to beggary, was too abhorrent to my feelings to receive credit, yet the sale of her father's property, comprising even his furniture and cloathing, seemed to prove that she had fallen even to this depth. This enabled me in some degree to account for her silence. Her generous spirit would induce her to conceal misfortunes from her friend, which no communication would alleviate. It was possible that she had selected some new abode, and that in consequence, the letters I had written, and which amounted to volumes, had never reached her hands.

My mother's state would not suffer me to obey the impulse of my heart. Her frame was verging towards dissolution. Courtland's engagements allowed him to accompany us to Naples, and here the long series of my mother's pilgrimages, closed in death. Her obsequies[11] were no sooner performed, than I determined to set out on my long projected voyage. My mother's property, which, in consequence of her decease, devolved upon me, was not inconsiderable. There is scarcely any good so dear, to a rational being, as competence.[12] I was not unacquainted with its benefits, but this acquisition was valuable to me chiefly as it enabled me to re-unite my fate to that of Constance.

Courtland was my countryman and friend. He was destitute of fortune, and had been led to Europe partly by the spirit of adventure, and partly on a mercantile project.[13] He had made sale of his property, on advantageous terms, in the ports of

---

notably for the primary female character (Constantia Davis) in "Somnambulism. A fragment" (May 1805), and in a short piece entitled "Job Strutt" (January 1805), in which a woman considering baby names selects three names for their "excellencies": "These three were Clara, Sophia, and Constantia."

[11] "Obsequies": funeral rites.

[12] "Competence": in this sense, an income sufficient for living comfortably, an estate or inheritance that raises one to a level of comfort with no obligation to labor. Despite her insistent religiosity, Sophia seems to believe that wealth is the chief "good" that any "rational being" could desire to achieve.

[13] "Mercantile project": although he is apparently not a very successful merchant, Courtland is engaged in the new re-export or carrying trade that produced immense profits for the U.S. economy

France, and resolved to consume the produce in examining this scene of heroic exploits and memorable revolutions. His slender stock, though frugally and even parsimoniously administered, was nearly exhausted, and at the time of our meeting at Rome, he was making reluctant preparations to return.

Sufficient opportunity was afforded us, in an unrestrained and domestic intercourse of three months, which succeeded our Roman interview, to gain a knowledge of each other. There was that conformity of tastes and views between us, which could scarcely fail, at an age, and in a situation like ours, to give birth to tenderness. My resolution to hasten to America, was peculiarly unwelcome to my friend. He had offered to be my companion, but this offer, my regard to his interest obliged me to decline; but I was willing to compensate him for this denial, as well as to gratify my own heart, by an immediate marriage.

So long a residence in England and Italy, had given birth to friendships and connections of the dearest kind. I had no view but to spend my life with Courtland, in the midst of my maternal kindred who were English. A voyage to America, and reunion with Constance were previously indispensable, but I hoped that my friend might be prevailed upon, and that her disconnected situation would permit her, to return with me to Europe. If this end could not be accomplished, it was my inflexible purpose to live and to die with her.[14] Suitably to this arrangement, Courtland was to repair to London, and wait patiently till I should be able to rejoin him there, or to summon him to meet me in America.

A week after my mother's death, I became a wife, and embarked, the next day, at Naples, in a Ragusan ship, destined for New-York. The voyage was tempestuous and tedious. The vessel was necessitated to make a short stay at Toulon. The state of that city, however, then in possession of the English, and besieged by the revolutionary forces, was adverse to commercial views. Happily, we resumed our voyage, on the day previous to that on which the place was evacuated by the British. Our seasonable departure rescued us from witnessing a scene of horrors,[15] of which the history of former wars, furnish us with few examples.

---

in the 1790s, during the revolutionary wars. Because Britain and France enforced blockades on each other's shipping, primarily from the Caribbean sugar colonies, U.S. merchants imported British and French Caribbean cargoes to American ports where they were reclassified as "neutral" and thereby became available for re-export across the Atlantic without fear of embargo or seizure. This carrying trade was tremendously lucrative and produced great profits even on a single journey. Brown gives a more extensive and critical account of the trade in the two parts of his novel *Arthur Mervyn*.

[14] "To live and die with her": Sophia's implies that her marriage to Courtland was tactical in that it allows her to travel to America to seek lifelong companionship with Constantia. Her husband must wait in London until the future of her relationship with Constantia is determined, and she leaves immediately after her marriage, not for a honeymoon with Courtland, but to search for Constantia.

[15] "Toulon … scene of horrors": in contrast to Martinette's radical affirmation of the French Revolution in Chapters 20 and 21, Sophia here identifies with antirevolutionary forces during a notable episode at Toulon, a major port on the Mediterranean coast of France.

Following the arrest of Girondin leaders in Paris in May 1793 (see note 19.7), Jacobin authorities in Toulon were ousted by a royalist faction that invited an Anglo-Spanish fleet to attack and occupy

A cold and boisterous navigation awaited us. My palpitations and inquietudes augmented as we approached the American coast. I shall not forget the sensations which I experienced on the sight of the Beacon at Sandy-Hook.[16] It was first seen at midnight, in a stormy and beclouded atmosphere, emerging from the waves, whose fluctuation allowed it, for some time, to be visible only by fits. This token of approaching land, affected me as much as if I had reached the threshhold of my friend's dwelling.

At length we entered the port, and I viewed, with high-raised, but inexplicable feelings, objects with which I had been from infancy familiar. The flag-staff erected on the battery,[17] recalled to my imagination the pleasures of the evening and morning walks, which I had taken on that spot, with the lost Constantia. The dream was fondly cherished, that the figure which I saw, loitering along the terrace, was her's.

On disembarking, I gazed at every female passenger, in hope that it was she whom I sought. An absence of three years, had obliterated from my memory none of the images which attended me on my departure.

---

the city. Toulon was counterattacked and seized after a long siege by Republican forces under Napoleon Bonaparte in a victory for the revolutionary government. After the city was retaken, the Jacobins enacted an exceptionally bloody revenge and suppression of the counterrevolutionaries. The siege, which Sophia represents here from a reactionary perspective, lasted from September 18 to December 18. Sophia's departure on "the day previous" to British evacuation places her in Toulon on December 16 or 17; this departure date, in turn, means that Sophia arrived in New York to search for Constantia in late February or early March 1794.

[16] "Beacon at Sandy-hook": in the 1760s, a lighthouse was built on Sandy Hook beach, at Fort Hancock, New Jersey, to guide ships into the mouth of New York harbor and the Hudson River.

[17] "The battery": the seawall and promenade at the southern tip of Manhattan island, included in the present day Battery Park, so named because it was the site of artillery batteries intended to defend the harbor during the Dutch, British, and early U.S. republic periods. Figuratively, the ports at both ends of Sophia's trans-Atlantic journey have been wrested from the British imperial navy in revolutionary wars. Brown and his circle often took walks at this location and in 1798–1799, while writing *Ormond* and his other best-known novels, Brown lived just a few minutes away.

Chapter XXIV

AFTER a night of repose rather than of sleep, I began the search after my friend. I went to the house which the Dudleys formerly inhabited, and which had been the asylum of my infancy. It was now occupied by strangers, by whom no account could be given of its former tenants. I obtained directions to the owner of the house. He was equally unable to satisfy my curiosity. The purchase had been made at a public sale, and terms had been settled not with Dudley, but with the Sheriff.

It is needless to say, that the history of Craig's imposture and its consequences, were confirmed by every one who resided at that period in New-York. The Dudleys were well remembered, and their disappearance, immediately after their fall, had been generally noticed, but whither they had retired, was a problem which no one was able to solve.

This evasion was strange. By what motives the Dudleys were induced to change their ancient abode, could be vaguely guessed. My friend's grandfather was a native of the West-Indies. Descendants of the same stock still resided in Tobago.[1] They might be affluent, and to them, it was possible, that Mr. Dudley, in this change of fortune, had betaken himself for relief. This was a mournful expedient, since it would raise a barrier between my friend and myself scarcely to be surmounted.

Constantia's mother was stolen by Mr. Dudley from a Convent at *Amiens*. There were no affinities, therefore, to draw them to France.[2] Her grandmother was a native of Baltimore, of a family of some note, by name Ridgeley.[3] This family might still exist, and have either afforded an asylum to the Dudleys, or, at least, be apprised of their destiny. It was obvious to conclude that they no longer existed within the precincts of New-York. A journey to Baltimore was the next expedient.

This journey was made in the depth of winter, and by the speediest conveyance. I made no more than a day's sojourn in Philadelphia. The epidemic by which that city had been lately ravaged, I had not heard of till my arrival in America. Its devastations were then painted to my fancy in the most formidable colours. A few months only

---

[1] "Tobago": control over the Caribbean island Tobago was frequently contested by European imperial nations. The value of the island lay in its slave labor and sugar plantations. Consequently, Dudley's cousins would likely be wealthy planters or merchants in sugar-industry-related trades.

[2] "Amiens ... affinities ... France": Amiens, in northern France, had convents connected with several different orders, all attached to the city's renowned Gothic cathedral (the tallest extant Gothic cathedral, now a UN World Heritage Site). Recalling the passing glimpse of Constantia's mother, who died from grief in Chapter 2, the detail may remind the reader that Constantia is part French, a Franco-American in terms of her parentage, as it hints that her mother rejected priestly rule to run away with an American suitor, Constantia's father, while he was studying art in Europe. Sophia asserts, however, that this French maternal heritage in no way connects Constantia with that nation, that no "affinities" may attract her there.

[3] "Ridgeley": The Ridgelys were one of Baltimore's wealthiest and most prominent families. They were part of the mercantile elite, owned large urban and country properties, and in the 1790s were among Maryland's largest slave owners.

had elapsed since its extinction, and I expected to see numerous marks of misery and dispopulation.

To my no small surprize, however, no vestiges of this calamity were to be discerned. All houses were open, all streets thronged, and all faces thoughtless or busy. The arts and the amusements of life seemed as sedulously cultivated as ever. Little did I then think what had been, and what, at that moment, was the condition of my friend. I stopt for the sake of respite from fatigue, and did not, therefore, pass much time in the streets. Perhaps, had I walked seasonably abroad, we might have encountered each other, and thus have saved ourselves from a thousand anxieties.

At Baltimore I made myself known, without the formality of introduction, to the Ridgeleys. They acknowledged their relationship to Mr. Dudley, but professed absolute ignorance of his fate. Indirect intercourse only had been maintained, formerly, by Dudley with his mother's kindred. They had heard of his misfortune, a twelve-month after it happened, but what measures had been subsequently pursued, their kinsman had not thought proper to inform them.

The failure of this expedient almost bereft me of hope. Neither my own imagination nor the Ridgeleys, could suggest any new mode by which my purpose was likely to be accomplished. To leave America, without obtaining the end of my visit, could not be thought of without agony, and yet the continuance of my stay promised me no relief from my uncertainties.

On this theme, I ruminated without ceasing. I recalled every conversation and incident of former times, and sought in them a clue, by which my present conjectures might be guided. One night, immersed alone in my chamber, my thoughts were thus employed. My train of meditation was, on this occasion, new. From the review of particulars from which no satisfaction had hitherto been gained, I passed to a vague and comprehensive retrospect.

Mr. Dudley's early life, his profession of a painter, his zeal in this pursuit, and his reluctance to quit it, were remembered. Would he not revert to this profession, when other means of subsistence were gone. It is true, similar obstacles with those which had formerly occasioned his resort to a different path, existed at present, and no painter of his name was to be found in Philadelphia, Baltimore, or New-York. But would it not occur to him, that the patronage denied to his skill, by the frugal and un-polished habits of his countrymen, might with more probability of success, be sought from the opulence and luxury of London? Nay, had he not once affirmed in my hearing, that if he ever were reduced to poverty, this was the method he would pursue?

This conjecture was too bewitching to be easily dismissed. Every new reflection augmented its force. I was suddenly raised by it from the deepest melancholy to the region of lofty and gay hopes. Happiness, of which I had began to imagine myself irretrievably bereft, seemed once more to approach within my reach. Constance would not only be found, but be met in the midst of those comforts which her father's skill could not fail to procure, and on that very stage where I most desired to encounter her. Mr. Dudley had many friends and associates of his youth in London. Filial duty had repelled their importunities to fix his abode in Europe, when summoned home by his father. On his father's death these solicitations had been renewed, but were disregarded for reasons, which he, afterwards, himself confessed, were fallacious. That they would, a third time be preferred, and would regulate his conduct, seemed to me incontestable.

I regarded with wonder and deep regret, the infatuation that had hitherto excluded these images from my understanding and my memory. How many dangers and toils had I endured since my embarkation at Naples, to the present moment? How many lingering minutes had I told since my first interview with Courtland? All were owing to my own stupidity. Had my present thoughts been seasonably suggested, I might long since have been restored to the embraces of my friend, without the necessity of an hour's separation from my husband.

These were evils to be repaired as far as it was possible. Nothing now remained but to procure a passage to Europe. For this end diligent inquiries were immediately set in foot. A vessel was found, which, in a few weeks, would set out upon the voyage. Having bespoken a conveyance, it was incumbent on me to sustain with patience the unwelcome delay.

Meanwhile, my mind, delivered from the dejection and perplexities that lately haunted it, was capable of some attention to surrounding objects. I marked the peculiarities of manners and language in my new abode, and studied the effects which a political and religious system, so opposite to that with which I had conversed, in Italy and Switzerland, had produced. I found that the difference between Europe and America, lay chiefly in this; that, in the former, all things tended to extremes, whereas, in the latter, all things tended to the same level. Genius and virtue, and happiness, on these shores, were distinguished by a sort of mediocrity. Conditions were less unequal, and men were strangers to the heights of enjoyment and the depths of misery, to which the inhabitants of Europe are accustomed.[4]

I received friendly notice and hospitable treatment from the Ridgeleys. These people were mercantile and plodding in their habits. I found in their social circle, little exercises for the sympathies of my heart, and willingly accepted their aid to enlarge the sphere of my observation.

About a week before my intended embarkation, and when suitable preparation had been made for that event, a lady arrived in town, who was cousin to my Constantia. She had frequently been mentioned in favorable terms, in my hearing. She had passed her life, in a rural abode with her father, who cultivated his own domain, lying forty miles from Baltimore.

---

[4] "Difference between Europe and American ... same level ... accustomed": Sophia's suggestion that the United States can be distinguished from Europe (or implicitly the American from the French Revolution) by its apparent lack of civil conflict was already a counterrevolutionary cliché by the late 1790s. Sophia echoes an argument proposed by right-wing writers up to the present who maintain that the American Revolution was concerned with individual liberty and mercantile prosperity (in a "classless" society), whereas the French Revolution focused on collective equality and undesirable or "extreme" transformations. In this manner the pronouncement seems to use a patriotic-sounding affirmation to articulate a deeper commitment to conservative principles. For more, see the Introduction and Related Texts for Brown's explicit rejection of this position in a slightly later review of German counterrevolutionary Friedrich von Gentz's version of the argument.

On an offer being made to introduce us to each other, I consented to know one whose chief recommendation, in my eyes, consisted in her affinity to Constance Dudley. I found an artless and attractive female, unpolished and undepraved by much intercourse with mankind. At first sight, I was powerfully struck by the resemblances of her features to those of my friend, which sufficiently denoted their connection with a common stock.

The first interview afforded mutual satisfaction. On our second meeting, discourse insensibly led to the mention of Miss Dudley, and of the design which had brought me to America. She was deeply affected by the earnestness with which I expatiated on her cousin's merits, and by the proofs which my conduct had given of unlimited attachment.

I dwelt immediately on the measures which I had hitherto ineffectually pursued to trace her footsteps, and detailed the grounds of my present belief, that we should meet in London. During this recital, my companion sighed and wept. When I finished my tale, her tears, instead of ceasing, flowed with new vehemence. This appearance excited some surprize, and I ventured to ask the cause of her grief.

Alas! She replied, I am personally a stranger to my Cousin, but her character has been amply displayed to me by one who knew her well. I weep to think how much she has suffered. How much excellence we have lost!

Nay, said I, all her sufferings will, I hope, be compensated, and I by no means consider her as lost. If my search in London be unsuccessful, then shall I indeed despair.

Despair then, already, said my sobbing companion, for your search will be unsuccessful. How I feel for your disappointment! but it cannot be known too soon. My Cousin is dead!

These tidings were communicated with tokens of sincerity and sorrow, that left me no room to doubt that they were believed by the relater. My own emotions were suspended till interrogations had obtained a knowledge of her reasons for crediting this fatal event, and till she had explained the time and manner of her death. A friend of Miss Ridgeley's father had witnessed the devastations of the yellow fever in Philadelphia. He was apprized of the relationship that subsisted between his friend and the Dudleys. He gave a minute and circumstantial account of the arts of Craig. He mentioned the removal of my friends to Philadelphia, their obscure and indigent life, and finally, their falling victims to the pestilence.

He related the means by which he became apprized of their fate, and drew a picture of their death, surpassing all that imagination can conceive of shocking and deplorable. The quarter where they lived was nearly desolate. Their house was shut up, and, for a time, imagined to be uninhabited. Some suspicions being awakened, in those who superintended the burial of the dead, the house was entered, and the father and child discovered to be dead. The former was stretched upon his wretched pallet, while the daughter was found on the floor of the lower room, in a state that denoted the sufferance, not only of disease, but of famine.

This tale was false. Subsequent discoveries proved this to be a detestable artifice of Craig, who stimulated by incurable habits, had invented these disasters, for the purpose of enhancing the opinion of his humanity, and of furthering his views on the fortune and daughter of Mr. Ridgeley.

Its falsehood, however, I had as yet no means of ascertaining. I received it as true, and at once dismissed all my claims upon futurity. All hopes of happiness, in this mutable and sublunary scene, was fled. Nothing remained, but to join my friend in a world, where woes are at an end and virtue finds its recompence. Surely, said I, there will sometime be a close to calamity and discord. To those whose lives have been blameless, but harassed by inquietudes, to which not their own, but the errors of others have given birth, a fortress will hereafter be assigned, unassailable by change, impregnable to sorrow.

O! my ill-fated Constance! I will live to cherish thy remembrance, and to emulate thy virtue. I will endure the privation of thy friendship and the vicissitudes that shall befall me, and draw my consolation and courage, from the foresight of no distant close to this terrestrial scene, and of ultimate and everlasting union with thee.

This consideration, though it kept me from confusion and despair, could not, but with the healing aid of time, render me tranquil or strenuous. My strength was unequal to the struggle of my passions. The ship in which I engaged to embark, could not wait for my restoration to health, and I was left behind.

Mary Ridgeley was artless and affectionate. She saw that her society was dearer to me than that of any other, and was therefore seldom willing to leave my chamber. Her presence, less on her own account, than by reason of her personal resemblance and her affinity by birth to Constance, was a powerful solace.

I had nothing to detain me longer in America. I was anxious to change my present lonely state, for the communion of those friends, in England, and the performance of those duties, which were left to me. I was informed that a British Packet, would shortly sail from New-York. My frame was sunk into greater weakness, than I had felt at any former period; and I conceived, that to return to New-York, by water, was more commodious than to perform the journey by land.

This arrangement was likewise destined to be disappointed. One morning I visited, according to my custom, Mary Ridgeley. I found her in a temper somewhat inclined to gaiety. She rallied[5] me, with great archness, on the care with which I had concealed from her a tender engagement, into which I had lately entered.

I supposed myself to comprehend her allusion, and, therefore, answered that accident rather than design, had made me silent on the subject of marriage. She had hitherto known me by no appellation, but Sophia Courtland. I had thought it needless to inform her, that I was indebted for my name to my husband, Courtland being his name.

All that, said my friend, I know already, and, So you sagely think that my knowledge goes no farther than that? We are not bound to love our husbands longer than their lives. There is no crime, I believe, in preferring the living to the dead, and most heartily do I congratulate you on your present choice.

---

[5] "Rallied": teased.

What mean you? I confess your discourse surpasses my comprehension.

At that moment, the bell at the door, rung a loud peal. Miss Ridgeley hastened down at this signal, saying, with much significance——

I am a poor hand at solving a riddle. Here comes one who, if I mistake not, will find no difficulty in clearing up your doubts.

Presently, she came up, and said, with a smile of still greater archness:—Here is a young gentleman, a friend of mine, to whom I must have the pleasure of introducing you. He has come for the special purpose of solving my riddle—I attended her to the parlour without hesitation.

She presented me, with great formality, to a youth, whose appearance did not greatly prepossess me in favor of his judgment. He approached me with an air, supercilious and ceremonious, but the moment he caught a glance at my face, he shrunk back, visibly confounded and embarrassed. A pause ensued, in which Miss Ridgeley had opportunity to detect the error into which she had been led, by the vanity of this young man.

How now, Mr. Martynne, said my friend, in a tone of ridicule, is it possible you do not know the lady who is the queen of your affections, the tender and indulgent fair one, whose portrait you carry in your bosom; and whose image you daily and nightly bedew with your tears and kisses?

Mr. Martynne's confusion instead of being subdued by his struggle, only grew more conspicuous, and after a few incoherent speeches and apologies, during which he carefully avoided encountering my eyes, he hastily departed.

I applied to my friend, with great earnestness, for an explanation of this scene. It seems that, in the course of conversation with him, on the preceeding day, he had suffered a portrait which hung at his breast, to catch Miss Ridgeley's eye. On her betraying a desire to inspect it more nearly, he readily produced it. My image had been too well copied by the artist, not to be instantly recognized.

She concealed her knowledge of the original, and by questions, well adapted to the purpose, easily drew from him confessions that this was the portrait of his mistress. He let fall sundry innuendoes and surmizes, tending to impress her with a notion of the rank, fortune and intellectual accomplishments of the nymph, and particularly of the doating fondness and measureless confidence, with which she regarded him.

Her imperfect knowledge of my situation, left her in some doubt as to the truth of these pretensions, and she was willing to ascertain the truth, by bringing about an interview. To guard against evasions and artifice in the lover, she carefully concealed from him her knowledge of the original, and merely pretended that a friend of her's, was far more beautiful than her whom this picture represented. She added, that she expected a visit from her friend the next morning, and was willing, by shewing her to Mr. Martynne, to convince him how much he was mistaken, in supposing the perfections of his mistress unrivalled.

Chapter XXV

MARTYNNE, while he expressed his confidence, that the experiment would only confirm his triumph, readily assented to the proposal, and the interview above described, took place accordingly, the next morning. Had he not been taken by surprize, it is likely the address of a man, who possessed no contemptible powers, would have extricated him from some of his embarrassment.

That my portrait should be in the possession of one, whom I had never before seen, and whose character and manners entitled him to no respect, was a source of some surprise. This mode of multiplying faces is extremely prevalent in this age, and was eminently characteristic of those with whom I had associated in different parts of Europe. The nature of my thoughts had modified my features into an expression, which my friends were pleased to consider as a model for those who desired to personify the genius of suffering and resignation.

Hence among those whose religion permitted their devotion to a picture of a female, the symbols of their chosen deity, were added to features and shape that resembled mine. My own caprice, as well as that of others, always dictated a symbolical, and in every new instance, a different accompaniment of this kind. Hence was offered the means of tracing the history of that picture which Martynne possessed.

It had been accurately examined by Miss Ridgeley, and her description of the frame in which it was placed, instantly informed me that it was the same[1] which, at our parting, I left in the possession of Constance. My friend and myself were desirous of employing the skill of a Saxon painter, by name Eckstein.[2] Each of us were drawn by him, she with the cincture of Venus, and I with the crescent of Dian.[3] This symbol

---

[1] "The same": the same miniature portrait, that is, that Sophia first mentioned in Chapter 8 (see note 8.2).

[2] "Saxon painter … Eckstein": Brown was aware of two painters active in the 1790s named Johann or John Eckstein, possibly father and son. The elder Johann Eckstein (1735–1817) was born in Mecklenburg, Lower Saxony, and worked at the Prussian court of Frederick the Great in Berlin before emigrating to Philadelphia in 1793 or 1794, where he began to use the name John. In April 1795, Brown visited his gallery, "John Eckstein & Sons exhibit room," with three female friends, presumably as the male accompanist for the women's interest. In the May 1805 issue of Brown's *Literary Magazine* there is a notice for an instruction book on drawing by this same Eckstein. Brown also mentions the younger Johann Eckstein (1762–1802), who worked primarily in England as a miniaturist, in "On Painting as a Female Accomplishment" (*The Port-Folio*, October 12, 1802). The Philadelphia Eckstein was noted for female allegorical figures like the ones described here. He designed the reverse side of a 1795–1798 silver dollar coin that featured a female Liberty with flowing hair and a ribbon, a figure possibly similar to the ones Sophia describes in this passage. This elder Eckstein does not seem to have been exceptionally skilled, however. Brown's close friend, William Dunlap, in his *History of the Rise and Progress of the Arts of Design in the United States* (1834) cites the painter Thomas Sully (1783–1872) describing Eckstein as a "thorough-going drudge in the arts" and later critics likewise regard him as an inferior technician.

[3] "Cincture of Venus … crescent of Dian": allegorical and iconographic attributes of the goddesses Venus and Diana, signifying erotic and chaste dimensions of female experience. The cincture is a

was still conspicuous on the brow of that image, which Miss Ridgely had examined, and served to identify the original proprietor.

This circumstance tended to confirm my fears that Constance was dead, since that she would part with this picture during her life, was not to be believed. It was of little moment to discover how it came into the hands of the present possessor. Those who carried her remains to the grave, had probably torn it from her neck and afterwards disposed of it for money.

By whatever means, honest or illicit, it had been acquired by Martynne, it was proper that it should be restored to me. It was valuable to me because, it had been the property of one whom I loved, and it might prove highly injurious to my fame and my happiness, as the tool of this man's vanity and the attester of his falsehood. I, therefore, wrote him a letter, acquainting him with my reasons for desiring the repossession of this picture, and offering a price for it, at least double its value, as a mere article of traffic. Martynne accepted the terms. He transmitted the picture, and with it a note, apologizing for the artifice of which he had been guilty, and mentioning, in order to justify his acceptance of the price which I had offered, that he had lately purchased it for an equal sum of a Goldsmith in Philadelphia.

This information suggested a new reflection. Constantia had engaged to preserve, for the use of her friend, copious and accurate memorials of her life. Copies of these were, on suitable occasions, to be transmitted to me, during my residence abroad. These I had never received, but it was highly probable that her punctuality, in the performance of the first part of her engagement, had been equal to my own.

What, I asked, had become of these precious memorials? In the wreck of her property were these irretrievably ingulfed? It was not probable that they had been wantonly destroyed. They had fallen, perhaps, into hands careless or unconscious of their value, or still lay, unknown and neglected, at the bottom of some closet or chest. Their recovery might be effected by vehement exertions, or by some miraculous accident. Suitable enquiries, carried on among those who were active in those scenes of calamity, might afford some clue by which the fate of the Dudleys, and the disposition of their property, might come into fuller light. These inquiries could be made only in Philadelphia, and thither, for that purpose, I now resolved to repair. There was still an interval of some weeks, before the departure of the packet in which I proposed to embark.

Having returned to the capital, I devoted all my zeal to my darling project. My efforts, however, were without success. Those who administered charity and succour during that memorable season, and who survived, could remove none of my doubts,

---

girdle or belt commonly depicted in allegories of Venus, often covering her genitals. The crescent is a crescent-shaped moon usually depicted as Diana's headdress, since she is a lunar deity. If Sophia is depicted as Diana with the lunar crescent on her head in one of the matching portraits, Constantia's cincture may well have been depicted as a ribbon flowing through her hair. Matching allegorized portraits in this style were common in the eighteenth century, and may have been a model for the coinage representations of Liberty. The confusion of love and liberty may also imply Constantia's implicit desire for the latter.

nor answer any of my inquiries. Innumerable tales, equally disastrous with those which Miss Ridgeley had heard, were related; but, for a considerable period, none of their circumstances were sufficiently accordant with the history of the Dudleys.

It is worthy of remark, in how many ways, and by what complexity of motives, human curiosity is awakened and knowledge obtained. By its connection with my darling purpose, every event in the history of this memorable pest, was earnestly sought and deeply pondered. The powerful considerations which governed me, made me slight those punctilious impediments, which, in other circumstances, would have debarred me from intercourse with the immediate actors and observers. I found none who were unwilling to expatiate on this topic, or to communicate the knowledge they possessed. Their details were copious in particulars, and vivid in minuteness. They exhibited the state of manners, the diversified effects of evil or heroic passions, and the endless forms which sickness and poverty assume in the obscure recesses of a commercial and populous city.

Some of these details are too precious to be lost. It is above all things necessary that we should be thoroughly acquainted with the condition of our fellow-beings. Justice and compassion are the fruit of knowledge. The misery that overspreads so large a part of mankind, exists chiefly because those who are able to relieve it do not know that it exists. Forcibly to paint the evil, seldom fails to excite the virtue of the spectator, and seduce him into wishes, at least, if not into exertions of beneficence.[4]

The circumstances in which I was placed, were, perhaps, wholly singular. Hence the knowledge I obtained, was more comprehensive and authentic than was possessed by any one, even of the immediate actors or sufferers. This knowledge will not be useless to myself or to the world. The motives which dictated the present narrative, will hinder me from relinquishing the pen, till my fund of observation and experience be exhausted. Meanwhile, let me resume the thread of my tale.

The period allowed me before my departure was nearly expired, and my purpose seemed to be as far from its accomplishment as ever. One evening I visited a lady, who was the widow of a physician, whose disinterested exertions had cost him his life. She dwelt with pathetic earnestness on the particulars of her own distress, and listened with deep attention to the inquiries and doubts which I laid before her.

After a pause of consideration, she said, that an incident like that related by me, she had previously heard from one of her friends, whose name she mentioned. This person was one of those whose office consisted in searching out the sufferers, and affording them unsought and unsolicited relief. She was offering to introduce me to this person, when he entered the apartment.

After the usual compliments, my friend led the conversation as I wished. Between Mr. Thomson's tale and that related to Miss Ridgeley, there was an obvious resemblance. The sufferers resided in an obscure alley. They had shut themselves up from

---

[4] "Forcibly to paint the evil … virtue of the spectator … beneficence": a rationale for the beneficial effect of narratives that depict the conditions of modern everyday life. For more on Brown's theory of novel writing and its relation to Woldwinite ideas, see the Introduction and writings by Brown and Godwin in Related Texts.

all intercourse with their neighbours, and had died, neglected and unknown. Mr. Thomson was vested with the superintendence of this district, and had passed the house frequently without suspicion of its being tenanted.

He was at length informed by one of those who conducted an hearse, that he had seen the window in the upper story of this house lifted, and a female shew herself. It was night, and the hearse-man chanced to be passing the door. He immediately supposed that the person stood in need of his services, and stopped.

This procedure was comprehended by the person at the window, who, leaning out, addressed him in a broken and feeble voice. She asked him why he had not taken a different route, and upbraided him for inhumanity in leading his noisy vehicle past her door. She wanted repose, but the ceaseless rumbling of his wheels would not allow her the sweet respite of a moment.

This invective was singular, and uttered in a voice which united the utmost degree of earnestness, with a feebleness that rendered it almost inarticulate. The man was at a loss for a suitable answer. His pause only increased the impatience of the person at the window, who called upon him, in a still more anxious tone, to proceed, and intreated him to avoid this alley for the future.

He answered that he must come whenever the occasion called him. That three persons now lay dead in this alley, and that he must be expeditious in their removal, but that he would return as seldom and make as little noise as possible.

He was interrupted by new exclamations and upbraidings. These terminated in a burst of tears, and assertions, that God and man were her enemies. That they were determined to destroy her, but she trusted that the time would come when their own experience would avenge her wrongs, and teach them some compassion for the misery of others.—Saying this, she shut the window with violence, and retired from it sobbing with a vehemence, that could be distinctly overheard by him in the street.

He paused for some time, listening when this passion should cease. The habitation was slight, and he imagined that he heard her traversing the floor. While he staid, she continued to vent her anguish in exclamations and sighs, and passionate weeping. It did not appear that any other person was within.

Mr. Thomson being next day informed of these incidents, endeavoured to enter the house, but his signals, though loud and frequently repeated, being unnoticed, he was obliged to gain admission by violence. An old man, and a female, lovely in the midst of emaciation and decay, were discovered without signs of life. The death of the latter appeared to have been very recent.

In examining the house, no traces of other inhabitants were to be found. Nothing, serviceable as food, was discovered, but the remnants of mouldy bread scattered on a table. No information could be gathered from neighbours respecting the condition and name of these unfortunate people. They had taken possession of this house, during the rage of this malady, and refrained from all communication with their neighbours.

There was too much resemblance between this and the story formerly heard, not to produce the belief that they related to the same persons. All that remained was to obtain directions to the proprietor of this dwelling, and exact from him all that he knew respecting his tenants.

I found in him a man of worth and affability. He readily related, that a man applied to him for the use of this house, and that the application was received. At the beginning of the pestilence, a numerous family inhabited this tenement, but had died in rapid succession. This new applicant was the first to apprize him of this circumstance, and appeared extremely anxious to enter on immediate possession.

It was intimated to him that danger would arise from the pestilential condition of the house. Unless cleansed and purified, disease would be unavoidably contracted. The inconvenience and hazard, this applicant was willing to encounter, and, at length, hinted that no alternative was allowed him, by his present landlord, but to lie in the street or to procure some other abode.

What was the external appearance of this person?

He was infirm, past the middle age, of melancholy aspect, and indigent garb. A year had since elapsed, and more characteristic particulars had not been remarked or were forgotten. The name had been mentioned, but in the midst of more recent and momentous transactions, had vanished from remembrance. Dudley, or Dolby, or Hadley, seemed to approach more nearly than any other sounds.

Permission to inspect the house was readily granted. It had remained, since that period, unoccupied. The furniture and goods were scanty and wretched, and he did not care to endanger his safety, by meddling with them. He believed that they had not been removed or touched.

I was insensible of any hazard which attended my visit, and, with the guidance of a servant, who felt as little apprehension as myself, hastened to the spot. I found nothing but tables and chairs. Cloathing was nowhere to be seen. An earthen pot, without handle and broken, stood upon the kitchen hearth. No other implement or vessel for the preparation of food, appeared.

These forlorn appearances were accounted for by the servant, by supposing the house to have been long since rifled of every thing worth the trouble of removal, by the villains who occupied the neighbouring houses; this alley, it seems, being noted for the profligacy of its inhabitants.

When I reflected that a wretched hovel like this, had been, probably, the last retreat of the Dudleys, when I painted their sufferings, of which the numberless tales of distress, of which I had lately been an auditor, enabled me to form an adequate conception, I felt as if to lie down and expire on the very spot where Constance had fallen, was the only sacrifice to friendship, which time had left to me.

From this house I wandered to the field, where the dead had been, promiscuously and by hundreds, interred. I counted the long series of graves, which were closely ranged, and, being recently levelled, exhibited the appearance of an harrowed field.[5]

---

[5] "Long series of graves ... harrowed field": a likely reference to what since 1825 has been called Washington Square, originally known as Southeast Square, one of the five original squares of Philadelphia. From 1706 on it functioned as a potter's field, or burial ground for the poor. In the 1770s, during the American Revolution, it served as a burial ground for both American and British soldiers (a Tomb of the Unknown Soldier commemorating this function is located there today). Before Pennsylvania abolished slavery in 1780, it was a site of slave auctions and afterward became a

Methought I could have given thousands, to know in what spot the body of my friend lay, that I might moisten the sacred earth with my tears. Boards hastily nailed together, formed the best receptacle, which the exigences of the time could grant to the dead. Many corpses were thrown into a single excavation, and all distinctions founded on merit and rank, were obliterated. The father and child had been placed in the same cart, and thrown into the same hole.

Despairing, by any longer stay in this city, to effect my purpose, and the period of my embarkation being near, I prepared to resume my journey. I should have set out the next day, but a family, with whom I had made acquaintance, expecting to proceed to New-York within a week, I consented to be their companion, and, for that end, to delay my departure.

Meanwhile, I shut myself up in my apartment, and pursued avocations, that were adapted to the melancholy tenor of my thoughts. The day, preceding that appointed for my journey, arrived. It was necessary to compleat my arrangements with the family, with whom I was to travel, and to settle with the lady, whose apartments I occupied.

On how slender threads does our destiny hang! Had not a momentary impulse tempted me to sing my favorite ditty to the harpsichord, to beguile the short interval, during which my hostess was conversing with her visitor in the next apartment, I should have speeded to New-York, have embarked for Europe, and been eternally severed from my friend, whom I believed to have died in phrenzy and beggary, but who was alive and affluent, and who sought me with a diligence, scarcely inferior to my own. We imagined ourselves severed from each other, by death or by impassable seas, but, at the moment when our hopes had sunk to the lowest ebb, a mysterious destiny conducted our footsteps to the same spot.

I heard a murmuring exclamation; I heard my hostess call, in a voice of terror, for help; I rushed into the room; I saw one stretched on the floor, in the attitude of death; I sprung forward and fixed my eyes upon her countenance; I clasped my hands and articulated—Constance!—

She speedily recovered from her swoon. Her eyes opened, she moved, she spoke: Still methought it was an illusion of the senses, that created the phantom. I could not bear to withdraw my eyes from her countenance. If they wandered for a moment, I fell into doubt and perplexity, and again fixed them upon her, to assure myself of her existence.

The succeeding three days, were spent in a state of dizziness and intoxication. The ordinary functions of nature were disturbed. The appetite for sleep and for food were confounded and lost, amidst the impetuosities of a master-passion. To look and to talk to each other, afforded enchanting occupation for every moment. I would not

---

common burial ground for black Americans, where the free and slave black community would gather. In 1782 former slave James "Oronoco" Dexter petitioned for the section of black graves to be protected with an enclosing fence. For a time the square was also known as Congo Square, a site where Philadelphia's black community drummed and danced in Africanist traditions, often before white audiences who assembled to watch while free blacks vended African cooking. In 1793, the square's burial grounds were used as mass graves for victims of the yellow fever epidemic.

part from her side, but eat and slept, walked and mused and read, with my arm locked in her's, and with her breath fanning my cheek.

I have indeed much to learn. Sophia Courtland has never been wise. Her affections disdain the cold dictates of discretion, and spurn at every limit, that contending duties and mixed obligations prescribe.

And yet, O! precious inebriation of the heart! O! pre-eminent love! What pleasure of reason or of sense, can stand in competition with those, attendant upon thee?— Whether thou hiest to the fanes of a benevolent deity, or layest all thy homage at the feet of one, who most visibly resembles the perfections of our Maker, surely thy sanction is divine; thy boon is happiness!—[6]

---

[6] "O! ... happiness!—": Sophia falls into the poetic diction and style of the literature of Sensibility to convey the emotional intensity of her reunion with Constantia.

Chapter XXVI

THE tumults of curiosity and pleasure did not speedily subside. The story of each other's wanderings, was told with endless amplification and minuteness. Henceforth, the stream of our existence was to mix; we were to act and to think in common: Casual witnesses and written testimony should become superfluous: Eyes and ears were to be eternally employed upon the conduct of each other: Death, when it should come, was not to be deplored, because it was an unavoidable and brief privation to her that should survive. Being, under any modification, is dear, but that state to which death is a passage, is all-desirable to virtue and all-compensating to grief.

Meanwhile, precedent events were made the themes of endless conversation. Every incident and passion, in the course of four years, was revived and exhibited. The name of Ormond, was, of course, frequently repeated by my friend: His features and deportment were described: Her meditations and resolutions, with regard to him, fully disclosed. My counsel was asked, in what manner it became her to act.

I could not but harbour aversion to a scheme, which should tend to sever me from Constance, or to give me a competitor in her affections. Besides this, the properties of Ormond were of too mysterious a nature, to make him worthy of acceptance. Little more was known, concerning him, than what he himself had disclosed to the Dudleys, but this knowledge would suffice to invalidate his claims.

He had dwelt, in his conversations with Constantia, sparingly on his own concerns. Yet he did not hide from her, that he had been left in early youth, to his own guidance: That he had embraced, when almost a child, the trade of arms: That he had found service and promotion in the armies of Potemkin and Romanzow:[1] That he had executed secret and diplomatic functions, at Constantinople and Berlin:[2] That, in the latter city, he had met with schemers and reasoners, who aimed at the new-modelling of the world, and the subversion of all that has hitherto been conceived elementary and fundamental, in the constitution of man and of government: that some of those reformers had secretly united, to break down the military and

---

[1] "Potemkin and Romanzow": more information concerning Ormond's participation in the second Russo-Turkish war of 1787–1792 (see notes 21.1, 21.15, 27.3). Grigory Aleksandrovich Potyomkin (or Potemkin; 1739–1791) was a Russian general and consort of Catherine the Great mainly known for campaigning in the Ukrainian steppes against the Ottoman Empire and their Tatar surrogates. He died during the Second Russo-Turkish War, 1787–1792. Pyotr Alexandrovich Rumyantsev (1725–1796) was another Russian general who commanded Cossack troops and played a leading role in the Russo-Turkish wars of 1768–1774 and 1787–1792. He was governor of Ukraine at the time, but resigned his command due to conflicts with Potemkin.

[2] "Constantinople and Berlin": Constantinople (since 1930, Istanbul) was capital of the Ottoman Empire. Berlin served a similar function for Prussia's Frederick the Great. In the countersubversive mythology surrounding the Illuminati (see Related Texts), Berlin was the locale where Mirabeau, in 1786–1787, became familiar with and was inducted into the German organization (see note 19.17). Afterward he supposedly transmitted the group's ideals and plans to Paris, where they helped catalyze the French Revolution.

monarchical fabric of German policy: That others, more wisely, had devoted their se-cret efforts, not to overturn, but to build: That, for this end, they embraced an ex-ploring and colonizing project: That he had allied himself to these, and, for the promotion of their projects, had spent six years of his life, in journeys by sea and land, in tracts unfrequented, till then, by any European.

What were the moral or political maxims, which this adventurous and visionary sect had adopted, and what was the seat of their newborn empire, whether on the shore of an *Austral* continent, or in the heart of desert America,[3] he carefully con-cealed. These were exhibited or hidden, or shifted, according to his purpose. Not to reveal too much, and not to tire curiosity or over-task belief, was his daily labour. He talked of alliance with the family whose name he bore, and who had lost their hon-ors and estates, by the Hanoverian succession[4] to the crown of England.

I had seen too much of innovation and imposture, in France and Italy, not to regard a man like this, with aversion and fear. The mind of my friend was wavering and un-suspicious. She had lived at a distance from scenes, where principles are hourly put to the test of experiment; where all extremes of fortitude and pusillanimity are accus-tomed to meet; where recluse virtue and speculative heroism give place as if by magic, to the last excesses of debauchery and wickedness; where pillage and murder are engrafted, on systems of all-embracing and self-oblivious benevolence; and the good of mankind is professed to be pursued, with bonds of association and covenants of secrecy. Hence my friend had decided without the sanction of experience, had al-lowed herself to wander into untried paths, and had hearkened to positions, preg-nant with destruction and ignominy.[5]

It was not difficult to exhibit, in their true light, the enormous errors of this man, and the danger of prolonging their intercourse. Her assent to accompany me to

---

[3] "*Austral* continent ... desert America": Sophia asserts that Ormond's group plans a colonial exper-iment in either Australia or North America west of the Mississippi, possibly in the region of the Naudowessie or Sioux-Dakota tribes (see note 21.1). Mysterious, possibly utopian colonization projects in Brown's unfinished fictions "Signior Adini" (c.1793–1796) and *Memoirs of Carwin the Biloquist* (1803–1805) are similarly concerned with Australia as a site of potential implantation.

[4] "Family whose name he bore ... Hanoverian succession": the name Ormond (also Ormonde) is as-sociated with a number of titles that were created and reassigned repeatedly in early modern British history, with two distinct Scottish and Irish groups to which the title could refer. Like Brown's uses of the name in other fictions, this novel's Ormond seems to refer to the Irish title created for the Butler family. James Butler, 2nd Duke of Ormond (1665–1745) was a Dublin-born general who often fought in Continental European conflicts. Involved with Catholic interests, he joined the 1715 Jacobite rebellion that resisted the Protestant House of Hanover's rise to power with the as-cension of George I in 1714. After 1715, his status as a failed conspirator caused the Duke of Or-mond title to be attainted and declared forfeit or suspended. His property was appropriated by throne, leaving the family in a fallen state. For more on the Ormond name, see note 12.1.

[5] "Ignominy": this paragraph displays the narrator Sophia's most overtly reactionary language, de-monizing and condemning the French Revolution and progressive thinking of the late Enlighten-ment in quasi-Burkean terms as inherently evil and duplicitous conspiracies to subvert right (monarchical) order.

England, was readily obtained. Too much dispatch could not be used, but the disposal of her property must first take place. This was necessarily productive of some delay.

I had been made, contrary to inclination, expert in the management of all affairs, relative to property. My mother's lunacy, subsequent disease and death, had imposed upon me obligations and cares, little suitable to my sex and age. They could not be eluded or transferred to others, and, by degrees, experience enlarged my knowledge and familiarized my tasks.

It was agreed that I should visit and inspect my friend's estate, in Jersey,[6] while she remained in her present abode, to put an end to the views and expectations of Ormond, and to make preparation for her voyage. We were reconciled to a temporary separation, by the necessity that prescribed it.

During our residence together, the mind of Constance was kept in perpetual ferment. The second day after my departure, the turbulence of her feelings began to subside, and she found herself at leisure to pursue those measures which her present situation prescribed.

The time prefixed by Ormond for the termination of his absence, had nearly arrived. Her resolutions respecting this man, lately formed, now occurred to her. Her heart drooped as she revolved the necessity of disuniting their fates; but that this disunion was proper, could not admit of doubt. How information of her present views might be most satisfactorily imparted to him, was a question not instantly decided. She reflected on the impetuosity of his character; and conceived that her intentions might be most conveniently unfolded in a letter. This letter she immediately sat down to write. Just then the door opened, and Ormond entered the apartment.

She was somewhat, and for a moment, startled by this abrupt and unlooked for entrance. Yet she greeted him with pleasure. Her greeting was received with coldness. A second glance at his countenance informed her that his mind was somewhat discomposed.

Folding his hands on his breast, he stalked to the window, and looked up at the moon. Presently he withdrew his gaze from this object, and fixed them upon Constance. He spoke, but his words were produced by a kind of effort:

Fit emblem, he exclaimed, of human versatility![7] One impediment is gone. I hoped it was the only one, but no: The removal of that merely made room for another. Let this be removed. Well: Fate will interplace a third. All our toils will thus be frustrated, and the ruin will finally redound upon our heads.—There he stopped.

This strain could not be interpreted by Constance. She smiled, and without noticing his incoherences, proceeded to inquire into his adventures during their separation. He listened to her, but his eyes, fixed upon her's, and his solemnity of aspect were immoveable. When she paused, he seated himself close to her, and grasped her hand with a vehemence that almost pained her, said:

---

[6] "My friend's estate, in Jersey": the property in Perth Amboy, New Jersey, that Constantia inherited from Helena in Chapter 17, after Helena's suicide (see note 17.3).

[7] "Versatility!": in this usage, fickleness or inconstancy, unfaithfulness.

Look at me; steadfastly. Can you read my thoughts? Can your discernment reach the bounds of my knowledge and the bottom of my purposes? Catch you not a view of the monsters that are starting into birth here (and he put his left hand to his forehead.) But you cannot. Should I paint them to you verbally, you would call me jester or deceiver. What pity that you have not instruments for piercing into thoughts!—

I presume, said Constance, affecting cheerfulness which she did not feel, such instruments would be useless to me. You never scruple to say what you think. Your designs are no sooner conceived than they are expressed. All you know, all you wish, and all you purpose, are known to others as soon as to yourself. No scruples of decorum; no foresight of consequences, are obstacles in your way.

True, replied he, all obstacles are trampled under foot, but one.

What is the insuperable[8] one?

Incredulity in him that hears. I must not say what will not be credited. I must not relate feats and avow schemes, when my hearer will say, Those feats were never performed: These schemes are not your's. I care not if the truth of my tenets and the practicability of my purposes, be denied. Still I will openly maintain them: But when my assertions will, themselves, be disbelieved; when it is denied, that I adopt the creed and project the plans, which I affirm to be adopted and projected by me, it is needless to affirm.

Tomorrow, I mean to ascertain the height of the lunar mountains, by travelling to the top of them. Then I will station myself in the tract of the last comet, and wait till its circumvolution suffers me to leap upon it; Then, by walking on its surface, I will ascertain whether it be hot enough to burn my soles. Do you believe that this can be done?

No.

Do you believe, in consequence of my assertion, that I design to do this, and that, in my apprehension, it is easy to be done?

Not; Unless I previously believe you to be lunatic.

Then why should I assert my purposes? Why speak, when the hearer will infer nothing from my speech, but that I am either lunatic or liar?

In that predicament, silence is best.

In that predicament, I now stand. I am not going to unfold myself. Just now, I pitied thee for want of eyes: 'Twas a foolish compassion. Thou art happy, because thou seest not an inch before thee or behind.—Here he was for a moment buried in thought; then breaking from his reverie, he said: So; your father is dead?

True, said Constance, endeavouring to suppress her rising emotions, he is no more. It is so recent an event, that I imagined you a stranger to it.

False imagination! Thinkest thou, I would refrain from knowing what so nearly concerns us both? Perhaps your opinion of my ignorance extends beyond this: Perhaps, I know not your fruitless search for a picture: Perhaps, I neither followed you, nor led you to a being called Sophia Courtland. I was not present at the meeting. I

---

[8] "Insuperable": impossible to overcome.

am unapprized of the effects of your romantic passion for each other. I did not witness the rapturous effusions and inexorable counsels of the new comer. I know not the contents of the letter which you are preparing to write.—

As he spoke this, the accents of Ormond gradually augmented in vehemence. His countenance bespoke a deepening inquietude and growing passion. He stopped at the mention of the letter, because his voice was overpowered by emotion. This pause afforded room for the astonishment of Constance. Her interviews and conversations with me, took place at seasons of general repose, when all doors were fast and avenues shut, in the midst of silence, and in the bosom of retirement. The theme of our discourse was, commonly, too sacred for any ears but our own: Disclosures were of too intimate and delicate a nature,[9] for any but a female audience: they were too injurious to the fame and peace of Ormond, for him to be admitted to partake of them: Yet his words implied a full acquaintance with recent events, and with purposes and deliberations, shrowded, as we imagined, in impenetrable secrecy.

As soon as Constantia recovered from the confusion of these thoughts, she eagerly questioned him: What do you know? How do you know what has happened, or what is intended?

Poor Constance! he exclaimed, in a tone bitter and sarcastic. How hopeless is thy ignorance! To enlighten thee is past my power. What do I know? Every thing. Not a tittle has escaped me. Thy letter is superfluous: I know its contents before they are written. I was to be told that a soldier and a traveller, a man who refused his faith to dreams, and his homage to shadows, merited only scorn and forgetfulness. That thy affections and person were due to another; that intercourse between us was henceforth to cease; that preparation was making for a voyage to Britain, and that Ormond was to walk to his grave alone!

In spite of harsh tones and inflexible features, these words were accompanied with somewhat that betrayed a mind full of discord and agony. Constantia's astonishment was mingled with dejection. The discovery of a passion, deeper and less curable than she suspected; the perception of embarrassments and difficulties in the path which she had chosen, that had not previously occurred to her, threw her mind into anxious suspense.

The measures she had previously concerted, were still approved. To part from Ormond was enjoined by every dictate of discretion and duty. An explanation of her motives and views, could not take place more seasonably than at present. Every consideration of justice to herself and humanity to Ormond, made it desirable that this interview should be the last. By inexplicable means, he had gained a knowledge of her intentions. It was expedient, therefore, to state them with clearness and force. In what words this was to be done, was the subject of momentary deliberation.

Her thoughts were discerned, and her speech anticipated by her companion.— Why droopest thou, and why thus silent, Constance? The secret of thy fate will never

---

[9] "Intimate and delicate a nature": the implication is not only that Ormond has secretly *heard* Constantia's private conversations, but also that he has also *witnessed* her in intimate conditions as well.

be detected. Till thy destiny be finished, it will not be the topic of a single fear. But not for thyself, but me, art thou concerned. Thou dreadest, yet determinest to confirm my predictions of thy voyage to Europe, and thy severance from me.

Dismiss thy inquietudes on that score. What misery thy scorn and thy rejection are able to inflict, is inflicted already. Thy decision was known to me as soon as it was formed. Thy motives were known. Not an argument or plea of thy counsellor, not a syllable of her invective, not a sound of her persuasive rhetorick escaped my hearing. I know thy decree to be immutable. As my doubts, so my wishes have taken their flight. Perhaps, in the depth of thy ignorance, it was supposed, that I should struggle to reverse thy purpose, by menaces or supplications. That I should boast of the cruelty with which I should avenge an imaginary wrong upon myself. No. All is very well: Go. Not a whisper of objection or reluctance, shalt thou hear from me.

If I could think, said Constantia, with tremulous hesitation, that you part from me without anger; that you see the rectitude of my proceeding—

Anger! Rectitude. I pr'ythee peace. I know thou art going. I know that all objection to thy purpose would be vain. Thinkest thou that thy stay, undictated by love, the mere fruit of compassion, would afford me pleasure or crown my wishes? No. I am not so dastardly a wretch. There was something in thy power to bestow, but thy will accords not with thy power. I merit not the boon, and thou refusest it. I am content.

Here Ormond fixed more significant eyes upon her. Poor Constance! he continued. Shall I warn thee of the danger that awaits thee? For what end! To elude it, is impossible. It will come, and thou, perhaps, wilt be unhappy. Foresight, that enables not to shun, only pre-creates the evil.

Come, it will. Though future, it knows not the empire of contingency. An inexorable and immutable decree enjoins it. Perhaps, it is thy nature to meet with calmness what cannot be shunned. Perhaps, when it is passed, thy reason will perceive its irrevocable nature, and restore thee to peace. Such is the conduct of the wise, but such, I fear, the education of Constantia Dudley, will debar her from pursuing.

Fain would I regard it as the test of thy wisdom. I look upon thy past life. All the forms of genuine adversity have beset thy youth. Poverty, disease, servile labour, a criminal and hapless parent, have been evils which thou hast not ungracefully sustained. An absent friend and murdered father, were added to thy list of woes, and here thy courage was deficient. Thy soul was proof against substantial misery, but sunk into helpless cowardice, at the sight of phantoms.

One more disaster remains. To call it by its true name would be useless or pernicious. Useless, because thou wouldst pronounce its occurrence impossible: Pernicious, because, if its possibility were granted, the omen would distract thee with fear. How shall I describe it? Is it loss of fame? No. The deed will be unwitnessed by an human creature. Thy reputation will be spotless, for nothing will be done by thee, unsuitable to the tenor of thy past life. Calumny will not be heard to whisper. All that know thee, will be lavish of their eulogies as ever. Their eulogies will be as justly merited. Of this merit thou wilt entertain as just and as adequate conceptions as now.

It is no repetition of the evils thou hast already endured: It is neither drudgery nor sickness, nor privation of friends. Strange perverseness of human reason! It is an evil:

It will be thought upon with agony: It will close up all the sources of pleasurable recollection: It will exterminate hope: It will endear oblivion, and push thee into an untimely grave. Yet to grasp it is impossible. The moment we inspect it nearly, it vanishes. Thy claims to human approbation and divine applause, will be undiminished and unaltered by it. The testimony of approving conscience, will have lost none of its explicitness and energy. Yet thou wilt feed upon sighs: Thy tears will flow without remission: Thou wilt grow enamoured of death, and perhaps wilt anticipate the stroke of disease.

Yet, perhaps, my prediction is groundless as my knowledge. Perhaps, thy discernment will avail, to make thee wise and happy. Perhaps, thou wilt perceive thy privilege of sympathetic and intellectual activity, to be untouched. Heaven grant the non-fulfilment of my prophecy, thy disenthrallment from error, and the perpetuation of thy happiness.

Saying this, Ormond withdrew. His words were always accompanied with gestures and looks, and tones, that fastened the attention of the hearer, but the terms of his present discourse, afforded, independently of gesticulation and utterance, sufficient motives to attention and remembrance. He was gone, but his image was contemplated by Constance: His words still rung in her ears.[10]

The letter she designed to compose, was rendered, by this interview, unnecessary. Meanings, of which she and her friend alone were conscious, were discovered by Ormond, through some other medium than words: Yet that was impossible: A being, unendowed with preternatural attributes, could gain the information which this man possessed, only by the exertion of his senses.

All human precautions had been used, to baffle the attempts of any secret witness.[11] She recalled to mind, the circumstances, in which conversations with her friend had taken place. All had been retirement, secrecy and silence. The hours usually dedicated to sleep, had been devoted to this better purpose. Much had been said, in a voice, low and scarcely louder than a whisper. To have overheard it at the distance of a few feet, was apparently impossible.

Their conversations had not been recorded by her. It could not be believed, that this had been done by Sophia Courtland. Had Ormond and her friend met, during the interval that had elapsed, between her separation from the latter, and her meeting with the former? Human events are conjoined by links, imperceptible to keenest eyes. Of Ormond's means of information, she was wholly unapprized. Perhaps, accident would, sometime, unfold them. One thing was incontestable. That her schemes and her reasons for adopting them, were known to him.

---

[10] "His words still rung in her ears": although in the next chapter Sophia will suggest that Ormond's words in the preceding passage are inscrutable and mysterious, the period's readers would understand that Ormond has elaborately threatened Constantia with rape. Ormond's foreboding harangue developed the conventional supposition that Constantia will understand rape as a life-ending dishonor, like the heroine of Samuel Richardson's *Clarissa* (1748), the period's best-known representation of female virginity in distress.

[11] "Secret witness": the only appearance in the narrative of the novel's subtitle.

What unforeseen effects had that knowledge produced! In what ambiguous terms had he couched his prognostics,[12] of some mighty evil that awaited her! He had given a terrible, but contradictory description, of her destiny. An event was to happen, akin to no calamity which she had already endured, disconnected with all which the imagination of man is accustomed to deprecate, capable of urging her to suicide, and yet of a kind, which left it undecided, whether she would regard it with indifference.

What reliance should she place upon prophetic incoherencies, thus wild? What precautions should she take, against a danger thus inscrutable and imminent?

---

[12] "Prognostics": foreknowledge.

Chapter XXVII

THESE incidents and reflections were speedily transmitted to me. I had always be-lieved the character and machinations of Ormond, to be worthy of caution and fear. His means of information I did not pretend, and thought it useless to investigate. We cannot hide our actions and thoughts, from one of powerful sagacity, whom the de-tection sufficiently interests, to make him use all the methods of detection in his power. The study of concealment, is, in all cases, fruitless or hurtful. All that duty en-joins, is to design and to execute nothing, which may not be approved by a divine and omniscient observer. Human scrutiny is neither to be solicited, nor shunned. Human approbation or censure, can never be exempt from injustice, because our limited perceptions debar us from a thorough knowledge of any actions and motives but our own.

On reviewing what had passed, between Constantia and me, I recollected nothing incompatible with purity and rectitude. That Ormond was apprized of all that had passed, I by no means inferred from the tenour of his conversation with Constantia, nor, if this had been incontestably proved, should I have experienced any trepidation or anxiety on that account.

His obscure and indirect menaces of evil, were of more importance. His discourse on this topic, seemed susceptible only of two constructions. Either he intended some fatal mischief, and was willing to torment her by fears, while he concealed from her the nature of her danger, that he might hinder her from guarding her safety, by suit-able precautions; or, being hopeless of rendering her propitious to his wishes, his malice was satisfied with leaving her a legacy of apprehension and doubt.

Constantia's unacquaintance with the doctrines of that school, in which Ormond was probably instructed, led her to regard the conduct of this man, with more cu-riosity and wonder, than fear. She saw nothing but a disposition to sport with her ig-norance and bewilder her with doubts.

I do not believe myself destitute of courage. Rightly to estimate the danger and en-counter it with firmness, are worthy of a rational being; but to place our security in thoughtlessness and blindness, is only less ignoble than cowardice. I could not forget the proofs of violence, which accompanied the death of Mr. Dudley. I could not overlook, in the recent conversation with Constance, Ormond's allusion to her mur-dered father. It was possible that the nature of this death, had been accidentally im-parted to him; but it was likewise possible, that his was the knowledge of one who performed the act.

The enormity of this deed, appeared by no means incongruous with the sentiments of Ormond. Human life is momentous or trivial in our eyes, according to the course which our habits and opinions have taken. Passion greedily accepts, and habit readily offers, the sacrifice of another's life, and reason obeys the impulse of education and desire.

A youth of eighteen, a volunteer in a Russian army, encamped in Bessarabia,[1] made prey of a Tartar girl, found in the field of a recent battle: Conducting her to his quarters, he met a friend, who, on some pretence, claimed the victim: From angry words they betook themselves to swords. A combat ensued, in which the first claimant ran his antagonist through the body. He then bore his prize unmolested away, and having exercised brutality of one kind, upon the helpless victim, stabbed her to the heart, as an offering to the *manes* of Sarsefield,[2] the friend whom he had slain. Next morning, willing more signally to expiate his guilt, he rushed alone upon a troop of Turkish foragers, and brought away five heads, suspended, by their gory locks, to his horse's mane. These he cast upon the grave of Sarsefield, and conceived himself fully to have expiated yesterday's offence. In reward for his prowess, the General gave him a commission in the Cossack troops. This youth was Ormond; and such is a specimen of his exploits, during a military career of eight years, in a warfare the most savage and implacable, and, at the same time, the most iniquitous and wanton which history records.[3]

With passions and habits like these, the life of another was a trifling sacrifice to vengeance or impatience. How Mr. Dudley had excited the resentment of Ormond, by what means the assassin had accomplished his intention, without awakening alarm or incurring suspicion, it was not for me to discover. The inextricability of human events, the imperviousness of cunning, and the obduracy of malice, I had frequent occasions to remark.

I did not labour to vanquish the security of my friend. As to precautions they were useless. There was no fortress, guarded by barriers of stone and iron, and watched by centinels that never slept, to which she might retire from his stratagems. If there were such a retreat, it would scarcely avail her against a foe, circumspect and subtle as Ormond.

I pondered on the condition of my friend. I reviewed the incidents of her life. I compared her lot with that of others. I could not but discover a sort of incurable malignity in her fate. I felt as if it were denied to her to enjoy a long life or permanent tranquillity. I asked myself, what she had done, entitling her to this incessant persecution? Impatience and murmuring took place of sorrow and fear in my heart. When

---

[1] "Bessarabia": the Eastern European region just north of the Danube River delta on the Black Sea, roughly the area of present-day Moldova and northeastern Romania. Bessarabia and the Danube delta were major sites of conflict between the Russian and Ottoman Empires and their Cossack and Tatar surrogates.

[2] "*Manes* of Sarsefield": manes (in Latin) are the deified spirits of dead ancestors to whom sacrifices would be made. In Brown's *Edgar Huntly*, the name Sarsefield is used again for an important character involved in imperial conflict between the British and French in India. The captured Tatar girl would be subjected to rape.

[3] "Commission in the Cossack troops ... the most savage and wanton that history records": the novel's final bit of information concerning Ormond's experience among Cossack troops in the Russo-Turkish conflicts. In Sophia's construction of events, Ormond is fully assimilated to the legendary "barbarity" of the Cossack hosts. For previous references, see notes 21.1, 21.15, and 26.1.

I reflected, that all human agency was merely subservient to a divine purpose, I fell into fits of accusation and impiety.

This injustice was transient, and soberer views convinced me that every scheme, comprizing the whole, must be productive of partial and temporary evil. The sufferings of Constance were limited to a moment; they were the unavoidable appendages of terrestrial existence; they formed the only avenue to wisdom, and the only claim to uninterrupted fruition, and eternal repose in an after-scene.

The course of my reflections, and the issue to which they led, were unforeseen by myself. Fondly as I doated upon this woman, methought I could resign her to the grave without a murmur or a tear. While my thoughts were calmed by resignation, and my fancy occupied with nothing but the briefness of that space, and evanescence of that time which severs the living from the dead, I contemplated, almost with complacency, a violent or untimely close to her existence.

This loftiness of mind could not always be accomplished or constantly maintained. One effect of my fears, was to hasten my departure to Europe. There existed no impediment but the want of a suitable conveyance. In the first packet that should leave America, it was determined to secure a passage. Mr. Melbourne consented to take charge of Constantia's property, and, after the sale of it, to transmit to her the money that should thence arise.

Meanwhile, I was anxious that Constance should leave her present abode and join me in New-York. She willingly adopted this arrangement, but conceived it necessary to spend a few days at her house in Jersey. She could reach the latter place without much deviation from the streight road, and she was desirous of re-surveying a spot where many of her infantile days had been spent.

This house and domain I have already mentioned to have once belonged to Mr. Dudley. It was selected with the judgment and adorned with the taste of a disciple of the schools of Florence and Vicenza.[4] In his view, cultivation was subservient to the picturesque, and a mansion was erected, eminent for nothing but chastity of ornaments, and simplicity of structure. The massive parts were of stone; the outer surfaces were smooth, snow-white, and diversified by apertures and cornices, in which a cement uncommonly tenacious was wrought into proportions the most correct and

---

[4] "Schools of Florence and Vicenza": Dudley's former estate, now in Constantia's hands, is built and decorated in the neoclassical and Italianate artistic styles he adopted during his training in Italy. The "School of Vicenzo" is the influential architectural style of Andrea Palladio (1508–1580) and his followers, centered around Vicenzo, the capital of Veneto in northern Italy (very near Verona, where Martinette once lived; see note 20.6). Palladian buildings achieve a spare neoclassical elegance that was tremendously popular in the revolutionary age and among the elites of the U.S. Early Republic. Thomas Jefferson, for example, emphasized Palladian principles and precedents in designing his estate Monticello. The "school of Florence" refers to the High Renaissance painting and sculptural styles of Florentine masters such as Leonardo da Vinci (1452–1519), Michelangelo (1475–1564), or Rosso Fiorentino (1494–1540). For earlier references to Dudley's mixing of rigorously classical and more sensuously Italianate styles, see notes 1.2 and 19.2. For the allusive mixture of classical and modernizing elements in the building's cement materials, see the following note.

forms the most graceful.[5] The floors, walls and ceilings, consisted of a still more exquisitely tempered substance, and were painted by Mr. Dudley's own hand. All appendages of this building, as seats, tables and cabinets, were modelled by the owner's particular direction, and in a manner scrupulously classical.

He had scarcely entered on the enjoyment of this splendid possession, when it was ravished away. No privation was endured with more impatience than this; but, happily, it was purchased by one who left Mr. Dudley's arrangements unmolested, and who shortly after conveyed it entire to Ormond. By him it was finally appropriated to the use of Helena Cleves, and now, by a singular contexture of events, it had reverted to those hands, in which the death of the original proprietor, if no other change had been made in his condition, would have left it. The farm still remained in the tenure of a German emigrant, who held it partly on condition of preserving the garden and mansion in safety and in perfect order.

This retreat was now re-visited by Constance, after an interval of four years. Autumn had made some progress, but the aspect of nature was, so to speak, more significant than at any other season. She was agreeably accommodated under the tenant's roof, and found a nameless pleasure in traversing spaces, in which every object prompted an endless train of recollections.

Her sensations were not foreseen. They led to a state of mind, inconsistent, in some degree, with the projects adopted in obedience to the suggestions of her friend. Every thing in this scene had been created and modelled by the genius of her father. It was a kind of fane,[6] sanctified by his imaginary presence.

To consign the fruits of his industry and invention to foreign and unsparing hands, seemed a kind of sacrilege, for which she almost feared that the dead would rise to upbraid her. Those images which bind us to our natal soil, to the abode of our innocent and careless youth, were recalled to her fancy by the scenes which she now beheld. These were enforced by considerations of the dangers which attended her voyage, from storms and from enemies, and from the tendency to revolution and war, which seemed to actuate all the nations of Europe. Her native country was by no means exempt from similar tendencies, but these evils were less imminent, and its

---

[5] "Cement uncommonly tenacious … correct … graceful": the innovative use of cement in the Dudley mansion, and its connection with classical style, alludes to both architectural history and, in the 1790s, the latest discoveries concerning building materials. Brown was fascinated by architecture and its larger history and cultural associations, referring to them frequently in his fictions and essayistic writings, and even producing many Palladian and Florentine style architectural elevations and plans of his own that may be related to historical fiction projects. Although cement is the most widely used building material in the modern world, the chemical secret of its composition was lost after Roman antiquity and remained unknown for thirteen centuries until its rediscovery and wide circulation in the 1790s. Thus, the Dudley estate's unique materials and architecture (there was no use of cement in buildings, much less mansions, in the U.S. in 1799) make it an innovative, simultaneously classicizing and modernizing setting for the novel's final scene. The first uses of modern cement construction in the U.S. did not occur until the 1820s.

[6] "Fane": temple or shrine.

manners and government, in their present modifications, were unspeakably more favorable to the dignity and improvement of the human race, than those which prevailed in any part of the ancient world.

My solicitations and my obligation to repair to England, overweighed her objections, but her new reflections led her to form new determinations with regard to this part of her property. She concluded to retain possession, and hoped that some future event would allow her to return to this favorite spot, without forfeiture of my society. An abode of some years in Europe, would more eminently qualify her for the enjoyment of retirement and safety in her native country. The time that should elapse before her embarkation, she was desirous of passing among the shades of this romantic retreat.

I was, by no means, reconciled to this proceeding. I loved my friend too well to endure any needless separation without repining. In addition to this, the image of Ormond haunted my thoughts, and gave birth to incessant but indefinable fears. I believed that her safety would very little depend upon the nature of her abode, or the number or watchfulness of her companions. My nearness to her person would frustrate no stratagem, nor promote any other end than my own entanglement in the same fold. Still, that I was not apprized, each hour, of her condition, that her state was lonely and sequestered, were sources of disquiet, the obvious remedy to which was her coming to New-York. Preparations for departure were assigned to me, and these required my continuance in the city.

Once a week, Laffert,[7] her tenant, visited, for purposes of traffic, the city. He was the medium of our correspondence. To him I entrusted a letter, in which my dissatisfaction at her absence and the causes which gave it birth, were freely confessed.

The confidence of safety seldom deserted my friend. Since her mysterious conversation with Ormond, he had utterly vanished. Previously to that interview, his visits or his letters were incessant and punctual; but since, no token was given that he existed. Two months had elapsed. He gave her no reason to expect a cessation of intercourse. He had parted from her with his usual abruptness and informality. She did not conceive it incumbent on her to search him out, but she would not have been displeased with an opportunity to discuss with him more fully the motives of her conduct. This opportunity had been hitherto denied.

---

[7] "Laffert": the name seems to involve an inside allusion to an acquaintance of Brown and his circle. Although the historical Laffert's first name does not appear in the letter and diary that mention him, he was well known to Brown and his close friends Elihu Hubbard Smith, William Dunlap, and Joseph Bringhurst. Laffert seems to have traveled regularly between Philadelphia and New York and to have possessed a "cottage," possibly the point of connection here since the novelistic Laffert's modest "habitation" will be mentioned several times in the remaining chapters. In a letter of May 11, 1796, to Bringhurst, Brown notes that he plans to visit their friend Laffert and "look at his Cottage." Smith's diary records that in May 1797, Brown and Smith together visited with Laffert while Smith was in Philadelphia at a convention of Abolition Societies, on a day when they also paid a visit to Constantin Volney (see note 19.19) but did not find him at home.

Her occupations, in her present retreat, were, for the most part dictated by caprice or by chance. The mildness of Autumn permitted her to ramble, during the day, from one rock and one grove to another. There was a luxury in musing, and in the sensations which the scenery and silence produced, which, in consequence of her long estrangement from them, were accompanied with all the attractions of novelty, and from which she could not consent to withdraw.

In the evening, she usually retired to the mansion, and shut herself up in that apartment, which, in the original structure of the house, had been designed for study, and no part of whose furniture had been removed or displaced. It was a kind of closet on the second floor, illuminated by a spacious window, through which a landscape of uncommon amplitude and beauty was presented to the view. Here the pleasures of the day were revived, by recalling and enumerating them in letters to her friend: She always quitted this recess with reluctance, and, seldom, till the night was half-spent.

One evening she retired hither when the sun had just dipped beneath the horizon. Her implements of writing were prepared, but before the pen was assumed, her eyes rested for a moment on the variegated hues, which were poured out upon the western sky, and upon the scene of intermingled waters, copses and fields. The view comprized a part of the road which led to this dwelling. It was partially and distantly seen, and the passage of horses or men, was betokened chiefly by the dust which was raised by their footsteps.

A token of this kind now caught her attention. It fixed her eye, chiefly by the picturesque effect produced by interposing its obscurity between her and the splendours which the sun had left. Presently, she gained a faint view of a man and horse. This circumstance laid no claim to attention, and she was withdrawing her eye, when the traveller's stopping and dismounting at the gate, made her renew her scrutiny. This was reinforced by something in the figure and movements of the horseman, which reminded her of Ormond.

She started from her seat with some degree of palpitation. Whence this arose, whether from fear or from joy, or from intermixed emotions, it would not be easy to ascertain. Having entered the gate, the visitant, remounting his horse, set the animal on full speed. Every moment brought him nearer, and added to her first belief. He stopped not till he reached the mansion. The person of Ormond was distinctly recognized.

An interview, at this dusky and lonely hour, in circumstances so abrupt and unexpected, could not fail to surprize, and, in some degree, to alarm. The substance of his last conversation was recalled. The evils which were darkly and ambiguously predicted, thronged to her memory. It seemed as if the present moment was to be, in some way, decisive of her fate. This visit, she did not hesitate to suppose, designed for her, but somewhat uncommonly momentous, must have prompted him to take so long a journey.

The rooms on the lower floor were dark, the windows and doors being fastened. She had entered the house by the principal door, and this was the only one, at present, unlocked. The room in which she sat, was over the hall, and the massive door beneath could not be opened, without noisy signals. The question that occurred to her, by what means Ormond would gain admittance to her presence, she supposed would be instantly decided. She listened to hear his footsteps on the pavement, or the creaking of hinges. The silence, however, continued profound as before.

After a minute's pause, she approached the window more nearly, and endeavoured to gain a view of the space before the house. She saw nothing but the horse, whose bridle was thrown over his neck, and who was left at liberty to pick up what scanty herbage the lawn afforded to his hunger. The rider had disappeared.

It now occurred to her, that this visit had a purpose different from that which she at first conjectured. It was easily conceived, that Ormond was unacquainted with her residence at this spot. The knowledge could only be imparted to him, by indirect or illicit means. That these means had been employed by him, she was by no means authorized to infer from the silence and distance he had lately maintained. But if an interview with her, were not the purpose of his coming, how should she interpret it?

Chapter XXVIII

WHILE occupied with these reflections, the light hastily disappeared, and darkness, rendered, by a cloudy atmosphere, uncommonly intense, succeeded. She had the means of lighting a lamp, that hung against the wall, but had been too much immersed in thought, to notice the deepening of the gloom. Recovering from her reverie, she looked around her with some degree of trepidation, and prepared to strike a spark, that would enable her to light her lamp.

She had hitherto indulged an habitual indifference to danger. Now the presence of Ormond, the unknown purpose that led him hither, and the defencelessness of her condition, inspired her with apprehensions, to which she had hitherto been a stranger. She had been accustomed to pass many nocturnal hours in this closet. Till now, nothing had occurred, that made her enter it with circumspection, or continue in it with reluctance.

Her sensations were no longer tranquil. Each minute that she spent in this recess, appeared to multiply her hazards. To linger here, appeared to her the height of culpable temerity. She hastily resolved to return to the farmer's dwelling, and, on the morrow, to repair to New-York. For this end, she was desirous to produce a light. The materials were at hand.

She lifted her hand to strike the flint, when her ear caught a sound, which betokened the opening of the door, that led into the next apartment. Her motion was suspended, and she listened as well as a throbbing heart would permit. That Ormond's was the hand that opened, was the first suggestion of her fears. The motives of this unseasonable entrance, could not be reconciled with her safety. He had given no warning of his approach, and the door was opened with tardiness and seeming caution.

Sounds continued, of which no distinct conception could be obtained, or the cause that produced them assigned. The floors of every apartment being composed, like the walls and ceiling, of cement, footsteps were rendered almost undistinguishable. It was plain, however, that some one approached her own door.

The panic and confusion that now invaded her, was owing to surprize, and to the singularity of her situation. The mansion was desolate and lonely. It was night. She was immersed in darkness. She had not the means, and was unaccustomed to the office, of repelling personal injuries. What injuries she had reason to dread, who was the agent, and what were his motives, were subjects of vague and incoherent meditation.

Meanwhile, low and imperfect sounds, that had in them more of inanimate than human, assailed her ear. Presently they ceased. An inexplicable fear deterred her from calling. Light would have exercised a friendly influence. This, it was in her power to produce, but not without motion and noise, and these, by occasioning the discovery of her being in the closet, might possibly enhance her danger.

Conceptions like these, were unworthy of the mind of Constance. An interval of silence succeeded, interrupted only by the whistling of the blast without. It was sufficient for the restoration of her courage. She blushed at the cowardice which had trembled at a sound. She considered that Ormond might, indeed, be near, but that he was probably unconscious of her situation. His coming was not with the circumspection of an enemy. He might be acquainted with the place of her retreat, and had come to obtain an interview, with no clandestine or mysterious purposes. The noises she had heard, had, doubtless, proceeded from the next apartment, but might be produced by some harmless or vagrant creature.

These considerations restored her tranquillity. They enabled her, deliberately, to create a light, but they did not dissuade her from leaving the house. Omens of evil seemed to be connected with this solitary and darksome abode: Besides, Ormond had unquestionably entered upon this scene. It could not be doubted that she was the object of his visit. The farm-house was a place of meeting, more suitable and safe than any other. Thither, therefore, she determined immediately to return.

The closet had but one door, and this led into the chamber where the sounds had arisen. Through this chamber, therefore, she was obliged to pass, in order to reach the stair-case, which terminated in the hall below.

Bearing the light in her left hand, she withdrew the bolt of the door, and opened. In spite of courageous efforts, she opened with unwillingness, and shuddered to throw a glance forward or advance a step into the room. This was not needed, to reveal to her the cause of her late disturbance. Her eye instantly lighted on the body of a man, supine, motionless, stretched on the floor, close to the door through which she was about to pass.

A spectacle like this, was qualified to startle her. She shrunk back and fixed a more steadfast eye, upon the prostrate person. There was no mark of blood or of wounds, but there was something in the attitude, more significant of death than of sleep. His face rested on the floor, and his ragged locks concealed what part of his visage was not hidden by his posture. His garb was characterized by fashionable elegance, but was polluted with dust.

The image that first occurred to her, was that of Ormond. This instantly gave place to another, which was familiar to her apprehension. It was at first too indistinctly seen to suggest a name. She continued to gaze and to be lost in fearful astonishment. Was this the person whose entrance had been overheard, and who had dragged himself hither to die at her door? Yet, in that case, would not groans and expiring efforts have testified his condition, and invoked her succour? Was he not brought hither in the arms of his assassin? She mused upon the possible motives that induced some one thus to act, and upon the connection that might subsist, between her destiny and that of the dead.

Her meditations, however fruitless, in other respects, could not fail to shew her the propriety of hastening from this spot. To scrutinize the form or face of the dead, was a task, to which her courage was unequal. Suitably accompanied and guarded, she would not scruple to return and ascertain, by the most sedulous examination, the causes of this ominous event.

She stept over the breathless corpse, and hurried to the stair-case. It became her to maintain the command of her muscles and joints, and to proceed without faultering or hesitation. Scarcely had she reached the entrance of the hall, when, casting anxious looks forward, she beheld an human figure. No scrutiny was requisite to inform her, that this was Ormond.

She stopped. He approached her with looks and gestures, placid but solemn. There was nothing in his countenance rugged or malignant. On the contrary, there were tokens of compassion.

So, said he, I expected to meet you. A light, gleaming from the window, marked you out. This, and Laffert's directions, have guided me.

What, said Constance, with discomposure in her accent, was your motive for seeking me?

Have you forgotten, said Ormond, what past at our last interview? The evil that I then predicted is at hand. Perhaps, you were incredulous: You accounted me a madman or deceiver: Now I am come to witness the fulfilment of my words, and the completion of your destiny. To rescue you, I have not come: That is not within the compass of human powers.

Poor Constantia! he continued, in tones that manifested genuine sympathy, look upon thyself as lost. The toils that beset thee are inextricable. Summon up thy patience to endure the evil. Now will the last and heaviest trial betide thy fortitude. I could weep for thee, if my manly nature would permit. This is the scene of thy calamity, and this the hour.

These words were adapted to excite curiosity mingled with terror. Ormond's deportment was of an unexampled tenor, as well as that evil which he had so ambiguously predicted. He offered not protection from danger, and yet gave no proof of being himself an agent or auxiliary. After a minute's pause, Constantia recovering a firm tone, said:

Mr. Ormond! Your recent deportment but ill accords with your professions of sincerity and plain dealing. What your purpose is, or whether you have any purpose, I am at a loss to conjecture. Whether you most deserve censure or ridicule, is a point which you afford me not the means of deciding, and to which, unless on your own account, I am indifferent. If you are willing to be more explicit, or if there be any topic on which you wish further to converse, I will not refuse your company to Laffert's dwelling. Longer to remain here, would be indiscrete and absurd.

So saying, she motioned towards the door. Ormond was passive, and seemed indisposed to prevent her departure, till she laid her hand upon the lock. He then, without moving from his place, exclaimed:

Stay. Must this meeting, which fate ordains to be the last, be so short? Must a time and place so suitable, for what remains to be said and done, be neglected or misused? No. You charge me with duplicity, and deem my conduct either ridiculous or criminal. I have stated my reasons for concealment, but these have failed to convince you. Well. Here is now an end to doubt. All ambiguities are preparing to vanish.

When Ormond began to speak, Constance paused to hearken to him. His vehemence was not of that nature, which threatened to obstruct her passage. It was by intreaty that he apparently endeavoured to detain her steps, and not by violence. Hence arose her patience to listen. He continued:

Constance! thy father is dead. Art thou not desirous of detecting the authour of his fate? Will it afford thee no consolation to know that the deed is punished? Wilt thou suffer me to drag the murderer to thy feet? Thy justice will be gratified by this sacrifice. Somewhat will be due to him who avenged thy wrong in the blood of the perpetrator? What sayest thou? Grant me thy permission, and, in a moment, I will drag him hither.

These words called up the image of the person, whose corpse she had lately seen. It was readily conceived that to him Ormond alluded, but this was the assassin of her father, and his crime had been detected and punished by Ormond! These images had no other effect than to urge her departure: She again applied her hand to the lock, and said:

This scene must not be prolonged. My father's death I desire not to hear explained or to see revenged, but whatever information you are willing or able to communicate, must be deferred.

Nay, interrupted Ormond, with augmented vehemence, art thou equally devoid of curiosity and justice? Thinkest thou, that the enmity which bereft thy father of life, will not seek thy own? There are evils which I cannot prevent thee from enduring, but there are, likewise, ills which my counsel will enable thee and thy friend to shun. Save me from witnessing thy death. Thy father's destiny is sealed; all that remained was to punish his assassin: But thou and thy Sophia still live. Why should ye perish by a like stroke?

This intimation was sufficient to arrest the steps of Constance. She withdrew her hand from the door, and fixed eyes of the deepest anxiety on Ormond;—What mean you? How am I to understand—

Ah! said Ormond, I see thou wilt consent to stay. Thy detention shall not be long. Remain where thou art during one moment; merely while I drag hither thy enemy, and shew thee a visage which thou wilt not be slow to recognize. Saying this, he hastily ascended the staircase, and quickly passed beyond her sight.

Deportment thus mysterious, could not fail of bewildering her thoughts. There was somewhat in the looks and accents of Ormond, different from former appearances: tokens of an hidden purpose and a smothered meaning, were perceptible: A mixture of the inoffensive and the lawless which added to the loneliness and silence that encompassed her, produced a faultering emotion. Her curiosity was overpowered by her fear, and the resolution was suddenly conceived, of seizing this opportunity to escape.

A third time she put her hand to the lock and attempted to open. The effort was ineffectual. The door that was accustomed to obey the gentlest touch, was now immoveable. She had lately unlocked and past through it. Her eager inspection convinced her that the principal bolt was still withdrawn, but a smaller one was now perceived, of whose existence she had not been apprized, and over which her key had no power.

Now did she first harbour a fear that was intelligible in its dictates. Now did she first perceive herself sinking in the toils of some lurking enemy. Hope whispered that this foe was not Ormond. His conduct had bespoken no willingness to put constraint upon her steps. He talked not as if he were aware of this obstruction, and yet his seeming acquiescence might have flowed from a knowledge that she had no power to remove beyond his reach.

He warned her of danger to her life, of which he was her self-appointed rescuer. His counsel was to arm her with sufficient caution; the peril that awaited her was imminent; this was the time and place of its occurrence, and here she was compelled to remain, till the power that fastened, would condescend to loose the door. There were other avenues to the hall. These were accustomed to be locked, but Ormond had found access, and if all continued fast, it was incontestable that he was the authour of this new impediment.

The other avenues were hastily examined. All were bolted and locked. The first impulse led her to call for help from without, but the mansion was distant from Laffert's habitation. This spot was wholly unfrequented. No passenger was likely to be stationed where her call could be heard. Besides, this forcible detention might operate for a short time, and be attended with no mischievous consequences. Whatever was to come, it was her duty to collect her courage and encounter it.

The steps of Ormond above now gave tokens of his approach. Vigilant observance of this man was all that her situation permitted. A vehement effort restored her to some degree of composure. Her stifled palpitations allowed her steadfastly to notice him, as he now descended the stair, bearing a lifeless body in his arms. There, said he, as he cast it at her feet, Whose countenance is that? Who would imagine that features like those, belonged to an assassin and imposter?

Closed eyelids and fallen muscles, could not hide from her lineaments so often seen. She shrunk back and exclaimed—Thomas Craig!

A pause succeeded, in which she alternately gazed at the countenance of this unfortunate wretch and at Ormond. At length, the latter exclaimed:

Well, my girl; hast thou examined him? Dost thou recognize a friend or an enemy?

I know him well; but how came this? What purpose brought him hither? Who was the authour of his fate?

Have I not already told thee that Ormond was his own avenger and thine? To thee and to me he has been a robber. To him thy father is indebted for the loss not only of property but life. Did crimes like these merit a less punishment? And what recompense is due to him whose vigilance pursued him hither, and made him pay for his offences with his blood? What benefit have I received at thy hand to authorize me, for thy sake, to take away his life?

No benefit recieved from me, said Constance, would justify such an act. I should have abhored myself for annexing to my benefits, so bloody a condition. It calls for no gratitude or recompense. Its suitable attendant is remorse. That he is a thief, I know but too well: that my father died by his hands is incredible.—No motives or means—

Why so? interrupted Ormond. Does not sleep seal up the senses? Cannot closets be unlocked at midnight? Cannot adjoining houses communicate by doors? Cannot these doors be hidden from suspicion by a sheet of canvass?—

These words were of startling and abundant import. They reminded her of circumstances in her father's chamber, which sufficiently explained the means by which his life was assailed. The closet, and its canvass-covered wall; the adjoining house untenanted and shut up—but this house, though unoccupied, belonged to Ormond!

From the inferences which flowed hence, her attention was withdrawn by her companion, who continued:

Do these means imply the interposal of a miracle? His motives? What scruples can be expected from a man innured, from infancy, to cunning and pillage? Will he abstain from murder when urged by excruciating poverty, by menaces of persecution: by terror of expiring on the gallows?

Tumultuous suspicions were now awakened in the mind of Constance. Her faultering voice scarcely allowed her to ask: How know you that Craig was thus guilty; that these were his incitements and means?—

Ormond's solemnity now gave place to a tone of sarcasm and looks of exultation: Poor Constance! Thou art still pestered with incredulity and doubts! My veracity is still in question! My knowledge, girl, is infallible. That these were his means of access I cannot be ignorant, for I pointed them out. He was urged by these motives, for they were stated and enforced by me. His was the deed, for I stood beside him when it was done.

These, indeed, were terms that stood in no need of further explanation. The veil that shrouded this formidable being, was lifted high enough to make him be regarded with inexplicable horror. What his future acts should be, how his omens of ill were to be solved, were still involved in uncertainty.

In the midst of the fears for her own safety, by which Constantia was now assailed, the image of her father was revived; keen regret and vehement upbraiding were conjured up:

Craig then was the instrument, and your's the instigation that destroyed my father! In what had he offended you? What cause had he given for resentment?

Cause! replied he, with impetuous accents, Resentment! None. My motive was benevolent: My deed conferred a benefit. I gave him sight and took away his life, from motives equally wise. Know you not that Ormond was fool enough to set value on the affections of a woman? These were sought with preposterous anxiety and endless labour. Among other facilitators of his purpose, he summoned gratitude to his aid. To snatch you from poverty, to restore his sight to your father, were expected to operate as incentives to love.

But here I was the dupe of error. A thousand prejudices stood in my way. These, provided our intercourse were not obstructed, I hoped to subdue. The rage of innovation seized your father: this, blended with a mortal antipathy to me, made him labour to seduce you from the bosom of your peaceful country: to make you enter on a boisterous sea; to visit lands where all is havock and hostility. To snatch you from the influence of my arguments.

This new obstacle I was bound to remove. While revolving the means, chance and his evil destiny threw Craig in my way. I soon convinced him that his reputation and his life were in my hands. His retention of these depended upon my will; on the performance of conditions which I prescribed.

My happiness and your's, depended on your concurrence with my wishes. Your father's life was an obstacle to your concurrence. For killing him, therefore, I may claim your gratitude. His death was a due and disinterested offering, at the altar of your felicity and mine.

My deed was not injurious to him. At his age, death, whose coming, at some period, is inevitable, could not be distant. To make it unforeseen and brief, and void of pain; to preclude the torments of a lingering malady; a slow and visible descent to the grave; was the dictates of beneficence. But of what value was a continuance of his life? Either you would have gone with him to Europe, or have staid at home with me. In the first case, his life would have been rapidly consumed by perils and cares. In the second, separation from you, and union with me, a being so detestable, would equally have poisoned his existence.

Craig's cowardice and crimes, made him a pliant and commodious tool. I pointed out the way. The unsuspected door, which led into the closet of your father's chamber, was made by my direction, during the life of Hellen. By this avenue I was wont to post myself, where all your conversations could be overheard. By this avenue, an entrance and retreat were afforded to the agent of my newest purpose.

Fool that I was! I solaced myself with the belief that all impediments were now smoothed, when a new enemy appeared: My folly lasted as long as my hope. I saw that to gain your affections, fortified by antiquated scruples, and obsequious to the guidance of this new monitor, was impossible. It is not my way to toil after that which is beyond my reach. If the greater good be inaccessible, I learn to be contented with the less.

I have served you with successless sedulity.[1] I have set an engine in act to obliterate an obstacle to your felicity, and lay your father at rest. Under my guidance, this engine was productive only of good. Governed by itself or by another, it will only work you harm. I have, therefore, hastened to destroy it. Lo! it is now before you motionless and impotent.

For this complexity of benefit I look for no reward. I am not tired of well-doing. Having ceased to labour for an unattainable good, I have come hither to possess myself of all that I now crave, and by the same deed to afford you an illustrious opportunity to signalize your wisdom and your fortitude.

During this speech, the mind of Constance became more deeply pervaded with dread of some over-hanging but incomprehensible evil. The strongest impulse was, to gain a safe asylum, at a distance from this spot, and from the presence of this extraordinary being. This impulse was followed by the recollection, that her liberty was taken away: That egress from the hall was denied her, and that this restriction might be part of some conspiracy of Ormond, against her life.

Security from danger like this, would be, in the first place, sought, by one of Constantia's sex and opinions, in flight. This had been rendered, by some fatal chance, or by the precautions of her foe, impracticable. Stratagem or force was all that remained, to elude or disarm her adversary. For the contrivance and exertion of frauds, all the habits of her life and all the maxims of her education, had conspired to unfit her. Her force of muscles would avail her nothing, against the superior energy of Ormond.

---

[1] "Sedulity": dedication or diligence.

She remembered that to inflict death, was no iniquitous exertion of self-defence, and that the pen-knife which she held in her hand, was capable of this service. She had used it to remove any lurking obstruction in the wards of her key,[2] supposing, for a time, this to be the cause of her failing to withdraw the bolt of the door. This resource, was, indeed, scarcely less disastrous and deplorable, than any fate from which it could rescue her. Some uncertainty still involved the intentions of Ormond. As soon as he paused, she spoke:

How am I to understand this prelude? Let me know the full extent of my danger; why it is that I am hindered from leaving this house, and why this interview was sought.

Ah! Constance! This, indeed, is merely prelude to a scene that is to terminate my influence over thy fate. When this is past, I have sworn to part with thee forever. Art thou still dubious of my purpose? Art thou not a woman? And have I not intreated for thy love, and been rejected?

Canst thou imagine that I aim at thy life? My avowals of love were sincere; my passion was vehement and undisguised. It gave dignity and value to a gift in thy power, as a woman, to bestow. This has been denied. That gift has lost none of its value in my eyes. What thou refusedst to bestow, it is in my power to extort. I came for that end. When this end is accomplished, I will restore thee to liberty.

These words were accompanied by looks, that rendered all explanation of their meaning useless. The evil reserved for her, hitherto obscured by half-disclosed and contradictory attributes, was now sufficiently apparent. The truth in this respect unveiled itself with the rapidity and brightness of an electrical flash.

She was silent. She cast her eyes at the windows and doors. Escape through them was hopeless. She looked at those lineaments[3] of Ormond which evinced his disdain of supplication and inexorable passions. She felt that intreaty and argument would be vain. That all appeals to his compassion and benevolence would counteract her purpose, since, in the unexampled conformation of this man's mind, these principles were made subservient to his most flagitious designs. Considerations of justice and pity were made, by a fatal perverseness of reasoning, champions and bulwarks of his most atrocious mistakes.

The last extremes of opposition, the most violent expedients for defence, would be justified by being indispensable. To find safety for her honor, even in the blood of an assailant, was the prescription of duty. The equity of this species of defence, was not, in the present confusion of her mind, a subject of momentary doubt.

To forewarn him of her desperate purpose, would be to furnish him with means of counter-action. Her weapon would easily be wrested from her feeble hand. Ineffectual opposition would only precipitate her evil destiny. A rage, contented with nothing less than her life, might be awakened in his bosom. But was not this to be desired? Death, untimely and violent, was better than the loss of honor.

---

[2] "Wards of her key": the hollow grooves of a skeleton-style key.

[3] "Lineaments": "distinctive features or characteristics" (*OED*).

This thought led to a new series of reflections. She involuntarily shrunk from the act of killing, but would her efforts to destroy her adversary, be effectual? Would not his strength and dexterity, easily repel or elude them? Her power, in this respect, was questionable, but her power was undeniably sufficient to a different end. The instrument, which could not rescue her from this injury, by the destruction of another, might save her from it by her own destruction.

These thoughts rapidly occurred, but the resolution to which they led, was scarcely formed, when Ormond advanced towards her. She recoiled a few steps, and, shewing the knife which she held, said:

Ormond! Beware! Know that my unalterable resolution is, to die uninjured. I have the means in my power. Stop where you are; one step more, and I plunge this knife into my heart. I know that to contend with your strength or your reason, would be vain. To turn this weapon against you, I should not fear, if I were sure of success; but to that I will not trust. To save a greater good by the sacrifice of life, is in my power, and that sacrifice shall be made.

Poor Constance! replied Ormond, in a tone of contempt: So! thou preferrest thy imaginary honor to life! To escape this injury without a name or substance: Without connection with the past or future; without contamination of thy purity or thraldom of thy will; thou wilt kill thyself: Put an end to thy activity in virtue's cause: Rob thy friend of her solace: The world of thy beneficence: Thyself of being and pleasure?

I shall be grieved for the fatal issue of my experiment: I shall mourn over thy martyrdom to the most opprobrious and contemptible of all errors, but that thou shouldst undergo the trial is decreed. There is still an interval of hope, that thy cowardice is counterfeited, or that it will give place to wisdom and courage.

Whatever thou intendest, by way of prevention or cure, it behoves thee to employ with steadfastness. Die with the guilt of suicide and the brand of cowardice upon thy memory, or live with thy claims to felicity and approbation undiminished. Chuse which thou wilt. Thy decision is of moment to thyself, but of none to me. Living or dead, the prize that I have in view shall be mine.—

Chapter XXIX

IT will be requisite to withdraw your attention from this scene for a moment, and fix it on myself. My impatience of my friend's delay, for some days preceding this disastrous interview, became continually more painful. As the time of our departure approached, my dread of some misfortune or impediment increased. Ormond's disappearance from the scene, contributed but little to my consolation. To wrap his purposes in mystery, to place himself at seeming distance, was the usual artifice of such as he; was necessary to the maturing of his project, and the hopeless entanglement of his victim. I saw no means of placing the safety of my friend beyond his reach. Between different methods of procedure, there was, however, room for choice. Her present abode was more hazardous than abode in the city. To be alone, argued a state more defenceless and perilous, than to be attended by me.

I wrote her an urgent admonition to return. My remonstrances were couched in such terms, as, in my own opinion, laid her under the necessity of immediate compliance. The letter was dispatched by the usual messenger, and for some hours I solaced myself with the prospect of a speedy meeting.

These thoughts gave place to doubt and apprehension. I began to distrust the efficacy of my arguments, and to invent a thousand reasons, inducing her, in defiance of my rhetorick, at least to protract her absence. These reasons, I had not previously conceived, and had not, therefore, attempted, in my letter, to invalidate their force. This omission was possible to be supplied in a second epistle, but, meanwhile, time would be lost, and my new arguments, might, like the old, fail to convince her. At least, the tongue was a much more versatile and powerful advocate than the pen, and by hastening to her habitation, I might either compel her to return with me, or ward off danger by my presence, or share it with her. I finally resolved to join her, by the speediest conveyance.

This resolution was suggested, by the meditations of a sleepless night. I rose with the dawn and sought out the means of transporting myself, with most celerity, to the abode of my friend. A stage-boat, accustomed, twice a day, to cross New-York bay to Staten-Island, was prevailed upon, by liberal offers, to set out upon the voyage at the dawn of day. The sky was gloomy, and the air boisterous and unsettled. The wind, suddenly becoming tempestuous and adverse, rendered the voyage at once tedious and full of peril. A voyage of nine miles was not effected in less that eight hours, and without imminent and hair-breadth danger of being drowned.

Fifteen miles of the journey remained to be performed by land. A carriage, with the utmost difficulty, was procured, but lank horses and a crazy vehicle were but little in unison with my impatience. We reached not Amboy-ferry till some hours after nightfall. I was rowed across the sound, and proceeded to accomplish the remainder of my journey, about three miles, on foot.

I was actuated to this speed, by indefinite, but powerful motives. The belief that my speedy arrival was essential to the rescue of my friend from some inexpiable injury, haunted me with ceaseless importunity. On no account would I have consented to postpone this precipitate expedition till the morrow.

I, at length, arrived at Dudley's farm-house. The inhabitants were struck with wonder at the sight of me. My cloathes were stained by the water, by which every passenger was copiously sprinkled, during our boisterous navigation, and soiled by dust: My frame was almost overpowered by fatigue and abstinence.

To my anxious enquiries respecting my friend, they told me that her evenings were usually spent at the mansion, where, it was probable, she was now to be found. They were not apprized of any inconvenience or danger, that betided her. It was her custom sometimes to prolong her absence till midnight.

I could not applaud the discretion nor censure the temerity of this proceeding. My mind was harrassed by unintelligible omens and self-confuted fears. To obviate the danger and to banish my inquietudes, was my first duty. For this end I hastened to the mansion. Having passed the intervening hillocks and copses, I gained a view of the front of the building. My heart suddenly sunk, on observing that no apartment, not even that in which I knew it was her custom to sit at these unseasonable hours, was illuminated. A gleam from the window of the study, I should have regarded as an argument, at once, of her presence and her safety.

I approached the house with misgiving and faultering steps. The gate leading into a spacious court was open. A sound on one side attracted my attention. In the present state of my thoughts, any near or unexplained sound, sufficed to startle me. Looking towards the quarter, whence my panic was excited, I espied, through the dusk, an horse grazing, with his bridle thrown over his neck.

This appearance was a new source of perplexity and alarm. The inference was unavoidable, that a visitant was here. Who that visitant was, and how he was now employed, was a subject of eager but fruitless curiosity. Within and around the mansion, all was buried in the deepest repose. I now approached the principal door, and looking through the key-hole, perceived a lamp, standing on the lowest step of the staircase. It shed a pale light over the lofty ceiling and marble balustrades.[1] No face or movement of an human being was perceptible.

These tokens assured me that some one was within; they also accounted for the non-appearance of light, at the window above. I withdrew my eye from this avenue, and was preparing to knock loudly for admission, when my attention was awakened by some one, who advanced to the door from the inside, and seemed busily engaged in unlocking. I started back and waited with impatience, till the door should open and the person issue forth.

Presently I heard a voice within, exclaim, in accents of mingled terror and grief—O what— what will become of me? Shall I never be released from this detested prison?

The voice was that of Constance. It penetrated to my heart like an ice-bolt. I once more darted a glance through the crevice. A figure, with difficulty recognized to be

---

[1] "Balustrades": short columns or posts supporting the handrail on a stairway, terrace, or balcony. Ordinarily a balustrade is more elaborately and artistically shaped than a banister, which is a simple round or square upright serving the same function.

that of my friend, now appeared in sight. Her hands were clasped on her breast, her eyes wildly fixed upon the ceiling and streaming with tears, and her hair unbound and falling confusedly over her bosom and neck.

My sensations scarcely permitted me to call—Constance! For Heaven's sake what has happened to you? Open the door I beseech you.

What voice is that? Sophia Courtland! O my friend! I am imprisoned. Some dæmon has barred the door, beyond my power to unfasten. Ah! Why comest thou so late? Thy succour would have somewhat profited, if sooner given, but now, the lost Constantia—here her voice sunk into convulsive sobs.—

In the midst of my own despair, on perceiving the fulfilment of my apprehensions, and what I regarded as the fatal execution of some project of Ormond, I was not insensible to the suggestions of prudence. I intreated my friend to retain her courage, while I flew to Laffert's, and returned with suitable assistance to burst open the door.

The people of the farm-house readily obeyed my summons. Accompanied by three men of powerful sinews, sons and servants of the farmer, I returned with the utmost expedition to the mansion. The lamp still remained in its former place, but our loudest calls were unanswered. The silence was uninterrupted and profound.

The door yielded to strenuous and repeated efforts, and I rushed into the hall. The first object that met my sight, was my friend, stretched upon the floor, pale and motionless, supine and with all the tokens of death!

From this object my attention was speedily attracted, by two figures, breathless and supine, like that of Constance. One of them was Ormond. A smile of disdain still sat upon his features. The wound, by which he fell, was secret, and was scarcely betrayed by the effusion of a drop of blood. The face of the third victim was familiar to my early days. It was that of the imposter, whose artifice had torn from Mr. Dudley his peace and fortune.

An explication of this scene was hopeless. By what disastrous and inscrutable fate, a place like this became the scene of such complicated havock, to whom Craig was indebted for his death, what evil had been meditated or inflicted by Ormond, and by what means his project had arrived at this bloody consummation, were topics of wild and fearful conjecture.

But my friend—the first impulse of my fears was, to regard her as dead. Hope and a closer observation, outrooted, or at least, suspended this opinion. One of the men lifted her in his arms. No trace of blood or mark of fatal violence was discoverable, and the effusion of cold water restored her, though slowly, to life.

To withdraw her from this spectacle of death was my first care. She suffered herself to be led to the farm-house. She was carried to her chamber. For a time she appeared incapable of recollection. She grasped my hand, as I sat by her bed-side, but scarcely gave any other tokens of life.

From this state of inactivity she gradually recovered. I was actuated by a thousand forebodings, but refrained from molesting her by interrogation or condolence. I watched by her side in silence, but was eager to collect from her own lips, an account of this mysterious transaction.

At length she opened her eyes, and appeared to recollect her present situation, and the events which led to it. I inquired into her condition, and asked if there were any thing in my power to procure or perform for her.

O! my friend! she answered, what have I done; what have I suffered within the last dreadful hour? The remembrance, though insupportable, will never leave me. You can do nothing for my relief. All I claim, is your compassion and your sympathy.

I hope, said I, that nothing has happened to load you with guilt or with shame.[2]

Alas! I know not. My deed was scarcely the fruit of intention. It was suggested by a momentary frenzy. I saw no other means of escaping from vileness and pollution. I was menaced with an evil worse than death. I forbore till my strength was almost subdued: The lapse of another moment would have placed me beyond hope.

My stroke was desperate and at random. It answered my purpose too well. He cast at me a look of terrible upbraiding, but spoke not. His heart was pierced, and he sunk, as if struck by lightning, at my feet. O much-erring and unhappy Ormond! That thou shouldst thus untimely perish! That I should be thy executioner!

These words sufficiently explained the scene that I had witnessed. The violence of Ormond had been repulsed by equal violence. His foul attempts had been prevented by his death. Not to deplore the necessity which had produced this act was impossible; but, since this necessity existed, it was surely not a deed to be thought upon with lasting horror, or to be allowed to generate remorse.

In consequence of this catastrophe, arduous duties had devolved upon me. The people that surrounded me, were powerless with terror, Their ignorance and cowardice left them at a loss how to act in this emergency. They besought my direction, and willingly performed whatever I thought proper to enjoin upon them.

No deliberation was necessary to acquaint me with my duty. Laffert was dispatched to the nearest magistrate with a letter, in which his immediate presence was intreated, and these transactions were briefly explained. Early the next day the formalities of justice, in the inspection of the bodies and the examination of witnesses, were executed. It would be needless to dwell on the particulars of this catastrophe. A sufficient explanation has been given of the causes that led to it. They were such as exempted my friend from legal animadversion.[3] Her act was prompted by motives which every scheme of jurisprudence known in the world not only exculpates but applauds. To state these motives, before a tribunal hastily formed, and exercising its functions on the spot, was a task not to be avoided, though infinitely painful. Remonstrances, the most urgent and pathetic, could scarcely conquer her reluctance.

This task, however, was easy, in comparison with that which remained. To restore health and equanimity to my friend; to repel the erroneous accusations of her conscience; to hinder her from musing, with eternal anguish, upon this catastrophe;

---

[2] "Shame": Sophia fears Constantia has been raped.

[3] "Legal animadversion": animadversion is criticism or censure, and Sophia's skillful management of the crisis has protected Constantia from any legal jeopardy in Ormond's death. Earlier remarks made it clear, however, that law is often strategically disconnected from justice or truth; see notes 2.3 and 10.1.

to lay the spirit of secret upbraiding by which she was incessantly tormented; which bereft her of repose; empoisoned all her enjoyments, and menaced, not only, the subversion of her peace, but the speedy destruction of her life, became my next employment.

My counsels and remonstrances were not wholly inefficacious. They afforded me the prospect of her ultimate restoration to tranquillity. Meanwhile, I called to my aid, the influence of time and of a change of scene.[4] I hastened to embark with her for Europe. Our voyage was tempestuous and dangerous, but storms and perils at length gave way to security and repose.

Before our voyage was commenced, I endeavoured to procure tidings of the true condition and designs of Ormond. My information extended no further, than that he had put his American property into the hands of Mr. Melbourne, and was preparing to embark for France. Courtland, who has since been at Paris, and who, while there, became confidentially acquainted with Martinette de Beauvais, has communicated facts of an unexpected nature.

At the period of Ormond's return to Philadelphia, at which his last interview with Constance, in that city, took place, he visited Martinette. He avowed himself to be her brother, and supported his pretentions, by relating the incidents of his early life. A separation, at the age of fifteen, and which had lasted for the same number of years, may be supposed to have considerably changed the countenance and figure she had formerly known. His relationship was chiefly proved, by the enumeration of incidents, of which her brother only could be apprized.[5]

He possessed a minute acquaintance with her own adventures, but concealed from her the means by which he had procured the knowledge. He had rarely and imperfectly alluded to his own opinions and projects, and had maintained an invariable silence, on the subject of his connection with Constance and Hellen. Being informed of her intention to return to France, he readily complied with her request to accompany her in this voyage. His intentions in this respect, were frustrated by the dreadful catastrophe that has been just related. Respecting this event, Martinette had collected only vague and perplexing information. Courtland, though able to remove her doubts, thought proper to with-hold from her the knowledge he possessed.

Since her arrival in England, the life of my friend has experienced little variation.[6] Of her personal deportment and domestic habits, you have been a witness. These,

---

[4] "Change of scene": Sophia takes control over Constantia and arranges a voyage and relocation to England as a remedy to effect her friend's "restoration to tranquillity." This kind of cure by travel and change of scenery was referenced earlier; see notes 20.14 and 23.7.

[5] "He avowed himself to be her brother ... apprized": if Ormond is indeed Martinette's sibling, then he is the brother of whom she spoke in Chapter 20, and from whom she was separated when Roselli sent the young Martinette to his sister in Verona, while Martinette's brother was sent to a seminary in Lausanne (see note 20.6). At the end of Chapter 20, Roselli and Martinette were unable to locate the brother after he "eloped" from the school in Lausanne.

[6] "Since her arrival in England ... little variation": in this final paragraph, Sophia closes the narrative frame she opened with the initial address "To I. E. Rosenberg" at the outset of the novel (see notes

therefore, it would be needless for me to exhibit. It is sufficient to have related events, which the recentness of your intercourse with her hindered you from knowing, but by means of some formal narrative like the present. She and her friend only were able to impart to you the knowledge which you have so anxiously sought. In consideration of your merits and of your attachment to my friend, I have consented to devote my leisure to this task.[7]

It is now finished, and, I have only to add my wishes, that the perusal of this tale may afford you as much instruction, as the contemplation of the sufferings and vicissitudes of Constantia Dudley has afforded to me. Farewell.

FINIS

takes own agency
to kill man
attacking her

0.1–5). Now that her story is done, Sophia locates the interaction between Rosenberg, Sophia, and Constantia in England, where Sophia and Constantia have relocated after the events described in the narrative. Whereas Ormond and Martinette are relocated to revolutionary France, Sophia has taken Constantia to England, a center of counterrevolutionary organization, and to a seeming absence of the "variation" or dynamic change she experienced in New York and Philadelphia.

[7] "Your merits ... your attachment to my friend ... this task": Sophia ends by hinting again, as she did in the prefatory note, that the purpose or "task" of her narrative is to establish Constantia's virtue in preparation for an elite marriage. Given the narrative's many paradoxes and emphasis on same-sex friendship and new forms of association, however, it may be notable that Rosenberg's gender is never specified. For more on the narrative's conclusions, see the Introduction.

RELATED TEXTS

1. Charles Brockden Brown, "Walstein's School of History. From the German of Krants of Gotha." *The Monthly Magazine and American Review* 1:5 (August–September 1799)

Published in August–September 1799, at the height of Brown's novelistic phase, "Walstein's School of History" is an important fictionalized essay in which Brown articulates his plan for novel writing, identifying both the rationale for his novels and the themes and techniques he will use to construct them.

Along with "The Difference Between History and Romance," which develops further remarks on the close relation of historical and "romance" narratives that is a central point here, this is a key document for understanding Brown's aims and methods in writing fiction. It also arguably establishes Brown as the first modern U.S. literary critic, in the sense of one who explores how texts construct meaning and function in society rather than simply asserting the relative merits of literary productions judged against an imaginary standard of excellence.

The essay's theory of novel writing is similar to ideas about the relation of history and literature raised by the English Woldwinites (see Godwin's remarks on literature in the Related Texts and in his unpublished 1797 essay "Of History and Romance"), but is presented within a fictional framework that alludes primarily to the late-1790s wave, in English-speaking literary circles, of German literary and cultural sources. This frame concerns the literary productions of Walstein, a professor of history at Jena, a center of intellectual culture in Germany, and of his leading student Engel. Brown's choice of the name Walstein likely refers to the work of Friedrich Schiller (1759–1805), a professor of history and philosophy at Jena and a major figure of the late Enlightenment, whose progressive fictions, histories, dramas, and doctrines about art were well known to Brown and his friends. Schiller's 1791–1793 History of the Thirty Years War, *for example, appeared in English translation in 1799; "Walstein" is an alternate English spelling in the period for Wallenstein, a general that Schiller writes about in that history and in several plays; and the setting in Jena and Weimar recalls several 1799* Monthly Magazine *articles by Brown and his circle on Schiller and August von Kotzebue (1761–1819), another contemporary German writer associated with these cities and their cultural institutions.*

Just as Brown draws on living German writers for character names in Wieland, *the novel that he published in September 1798 three months before* Ormond *appeared in January 1799, this essay similarly draws on recognizable names. The name Engel, given to the pupil of Walstein discussed in the second part of the piece, seems to reference Johann Jakob Engel (1741–1802), a poet, dramatist, and philosopher, who taught in Saxony before becoming Professor in Berlin for moral philosophy, logic, and history; advisor to Frederick the Great; and a contributor to Schiller's magazine* Die Horen *(after initially opposing Schiller's tempestuous Sturm and Drang style of writing). Engel was known as an inspiring, if not entirely original or complex, teacher and writer, whose style conveyed current arguments about sympathy and history in ways that made these topics approachable for nonelite audiences. The story of "Olivo Ronsica" that Engel writes, in this fictional frame, is in fact a summary of the plot of Brown's Philadelphia novel* Arthur Mervyn, *first part (April or May 1799), here transposed to Weimar during the chaos and disease created by the Thirty Years War (1618–1648). In an anagrammatical fashion, Engel's title "Olivo Ronsica" may echo that of C. M. Wieland's novel,* (Der Sieg der Natur über die Schwärmerei oder Die Abenteuer des) Don Silvio von Rosalva (1764), *published in English in 1773 as* Reason Triumphant over Fancy; or the Adventures of Don Silvio of Rosalva.

Brown derives the essay's approach to novel-writing from primarily British Woldwinite models, but the Schillerian frame implicitly joins these two related currents of late-Enlightenment thinking about progressive historical and fictional storytelling. Walstein *provides a first model for the progressive novel by combining history and romance in such a way as to promote "moral and political" engagement while rejecting universal truths: the novel provides models for benevolent action and makes its readers active observers of the social world around them. Walstein's fictions concern classical or elite figures such as the Roman statesman and orator Cicero (who struggled to defend the Roman Republic) and Portugal's Marquis of Pombal (a modernizing Enlightenment reformer who struggled against old-regime aristocratic and religious forces in eighteenth-century Portugal). Engel modernizes Walstein's model by focusing on ordinary, nonelite personages (as the novelist Richardson has done with his* Clarissa*), arguing that a romance, to be effective in today's world, must be addressed to a wide popular audience and draw its characters and dilemmas not from the elite, but from the same lower-status groups (women, laborers, servants, etc.) that will read and be moved by the work. Engel insists that history and romance alike should address issues and situations familiar to their modern audiences, notably the common inequalities arising from sex and property. Thus Engel's modern romances will insert ordinary individuals like "Olivo Ronsica," or Brown's novelistic characters, into situations of stress resulting from contemporary tensions and inequalities related to money and other property relations, and erotic desire and other forms of personal relations. Finally, Engel adds that a thrilling style is also necessary if modern fictions are to hold their reader's interest and move them toward progressive values and behaviors.*

*****

Walstein was professor of history at Jena, and, of course, had several pupils. Nine of them were more assiduous in their attention to their tutor than the others. This circumstance came at length to be noticed by each other, as well as by Walstein, and naturally produced good-will and fellowship among them. They gradually separated themselves from the negligent and heedless crowd, cleaved to each other, and frequently met to exchange and compare ideas. Walstein was prepossessed in their favour by their studious habits, and their veneration for him. He frequently admitted them to exclusive interviews, and, laying aside his professional dignity, conversed with them on the footing of a friend and equal.

Walstein's two books were read by them with great attention. These were justly to be considered as exemplifications of his rules, as specimens of the manner in which history was to be studied and written.

No wonder that they found few defects in the model; that they gradually adopted the style and spirit of his composition, and, from admiring and contemplating, should, at length, aspire to imitate. It could not but happen, however, that the criterion of excellence would be somewhat modified in passing through the mind of each; that each should have his peculiar modes of writing and thinking.

All observers, indeed, are, at the first and transient view, more affected by resemblances than differences. The works of Walstein and his disciples were hastily ascribed to the same hand. The same minute explication of motives, the same indissoluble and well-woven tissue of causes and effects, the same unity and coherence of design, the same power of engrossing the attention, and the same felicity, purity, and compactness of style, are conspicuous in all.

There is likewise evidence, that each had embraced the same scheme of accounting for events, and the same notions of moral and political duty. Still, however, there were marks of difference in the different nature of the themes that were adopted, and of the purpose which the productions of each writer seemed most directly to promote.

We may aim to exhibit the influence of some moral or physical cause, to enforce some useful maxim, or illustrate some momentous truth. This purpose may be more or less simple, capable of being diffused over the surface of an empire or a century, or of shrinking into the compass of a day, and the bounds of a single thought.

The elementary truths of morals and politics may merit the preference: our theory may adapt itself to, and derive confirmation from whatever is human. Newton and Xavier, Zengis and William Tell,[1] may bear close and manifest relation to the system we adopt, and their fates be linked, indissolubly, in a common chain.

The physician may be attentive to the constitution and diseases of man in all ages and nations. Some opinions, on the influence of a certain diet, may make him eager to investigate the physical history of every human being. No fact, falling within his observation, is useless or anomalous. All sensibly contribute to the symmetry and firmness of some structure which he is anxious to erect. Distances of place and time, and diversities of moral conduct, may, by no means, obstruct their union into one homogeneous mass.

I am apt to think, that the moral reasoner may discover principles equally universal in their application, and giving birth to similar coincidence and harmony among characters and events. Has not this been effected by Walstein?

---

[1] "Newton … Xavier … Zengis … Tell": Isaac Newton (1642–1727), the mathematician and physicist who first described the laws of gravitation; Francis Xavier (1506–1552), cofounder of the Jesuit order and Catholic missionary who died trying to extend Jesuit institutions to China; Genghis Khan (c. 1162–1227), architect of the Mongol Empire; William Tell, a legendary hero of Swiss independence supposed to have lived in the fourteenth century (new versions of the Tell legend proliferated in the Romantic era).

Walstein composed two works. One exhibited, with great minuteness, the life of Cicero; the other, that of the Marquis of Pombal.[2] What link did his reason discover, or his fancy create between times, places, situations, events, and characters so different? He reasoned thus:—

Human society is powerfully modified by individual members. The authority of individuals sometimes flows from physical incidents; birth, or marriage, for example. Sometimes it springs, independently of physical relation, and, in defiance of them, from intellectual vigour. The authority of kings and nobles exemplifies the first species of influence. Birth and marriage, physical, and not moral incidents, entitle them to rule.

The second kind of influence, that flowing from intellectual vigour, is remarkably exemplified in Cicero and Pombal. In this respect they are alike. The mode in which they reached eminence, and in which they exercised power, was different, in consequence of different circumstances. One lived in a free, the other in a despotic state. One gained it from the prince, the other from the people. The end of both, for their degree of virtue was the same, was the general happiness. They promoted this end by the best means which human wisdom could suggest. One cherished, the other depressed the aristocracy. Both were right in their means as in their end; and each, had he exchanged conditions with the other, would have acted like that other.

Walstein was conscious of the uncertainty of history. Actions and motives cannot be truly described. We can only make approaches to the truth. The more attentively we observe mankind, and study ourselves, the greater will this uncertainty appear, and the farther shall we find ourselves from truth.

This uncertainty, however, has some bounds. Some circumstances of events, and some events, are more capable of evidence than others. The same may be said of motives. Our guesses as to the motives of some actions are more probable than the guesses that relate to other actions. Though no one can state the motives from which any action has flowed, he may enumerate motives from which it is quite certain, that the action did *not* flow.

The lives of Cicero and Pombal are imperfectly related by historians. An impartial view of that which history has preserved makes the belief of their wisdom and virtue more probable than the contrary belief.

Walstein desired the happiness of mankind. He imagined that the exhibition of virtue and talents, forcing its way to sovereign power, and employing that power for the national good, was highly conducive to their happiness. By exhibiting a virtuous being in opposite conditions, and pursuing his end by the means suited to his own condition, he believes himself displaying a model of right conduct, and furnishing

---

[2] "Cicero … Pombal": Marcus Tullius Cicero (106–43 B.C.E.), the statesman, philosopher, and orator well-known for his role in political struggles over the status of the Roman Republic during Julius Caesar's dictatorship. Pombal is Sebastião José de Carvalho e Melo, Marquis of Pombal (1699–1782), who directed the Portuguese government as an enlightened prime minister, 1750–1777. Both figures were displaced and defeated by political forces that opposed them.

incitements to imitate that conduct, supplying men not only with knowledge of just ends and just means, but with the love and the zeal of virtue.

How men might best promote the happiness of mankind in given situations, was the problem that he desired to solve. The more portraits of human excellence he was able to exhibit the better; but his power in this respect was limited. The longer his life and his powers endured the more numerous would his portraits become. Futurity, however, was precarious, and, therefore, it behoved him to select, in the first place, the most useful theme.

His purpose was not to be accomplished by a brief or meagre story. To illuminate the understanding, to charm curiosity, and sway the passions, required that events should be copiously displayed and artfully linked, that motives should be vividly depicted, and scenes made to pass before the eye. This has been performed. Cicero is made to compose the story of his political and private life from his early youth to his flight from Astura, at the coalition of Antony and Octavius. It is addressed to Atticus, and meant to be the attestor of his virtue, and his vindicator with posterity.[3]

The style is energetic, and flows with that glowing impetuosity which was supposed to actuate the writer. Ardent passions, lofty indignation, sportive elegance, pathetic and beautiful simplicity, take their turns to control his pen, according to the nature of the theme. New and striking portraits are introduced of the great actors on the stage. New lights are cast upon the principal occurrences. Everywhere are marks of profound learning, accurate judgment, and inexhaustible invention. Cicero here exhibits himself in all the forms of master, husband, father, friend, advocate, proconsul, consul, and senator.

To assume the person of Cicero, as the narrator of his own transactions, was certainly an hazardous undertaking. Frequent errors and lapses, violations of probability, and incongruities in the style and conduct of this imaginary history with the genuine productions of Cicero, might be reasonably expected, but these are not found. The more conversant we are with the authentic monuments, the more is our admiration at the felicity of this imposture enhanced.

The conspiracy of Cataline is here related with abundance of circumstances not to be found in Sallust.[4] The difference, however, is of that kind which result from a deeper insight into human nature, a more accurate acquaintance with the facts, more correctness of arrangement, and a deeper concern in the progress and issue of the story.

---

[3] "Astura … Atticus": allusions to details concerning Cicero's political execution in 43 B.C.E. by pro-Caesar forces that he had opposed. After Cicero was proscribed, he fled from his villa at Astura (on the coast near Rome) but was soon captured and executed. Atticus was a close friend and frequent correspondent of Cicero's. Brown included all of these elements in his tale "Death of Cicero, A Fragment" (1800).

[4] "Conspiracy of Cataline … Sallust": Sallust (86–34 B.C.E.) is a Roman historian, along with Cicero the best-known source for information on a conspiracy in 64–62, led by Catiline Lucius Sergius Catalina, 108–62 B.C.E.), to overthrow the Roman government. Cicero was Catiline's greatest political opponent, and his Cataline orations (63 B.C.E.) present the conspirator as the embodiment of the vices that were weakening the Roman Republic.

What is false, is so admirable in itself, so conformable to Roman modes and sentiments, so self-consistent, that one is almost prompted to accept it as the gift of inspiration.

The whole system of Roman domestic manners, of civil and military government, is contained in this work. The facts are either collected from the best antiquarians, or artfully deduced from what is known, or invented with a boldness more easy to admire than to imitate. Pure fiction is never employed but when truth was unattainable. The end designed by Walstein, is no less happily accomplished in the second, than in the first performance. The style and spirit of the narrative is similar; the same skill in the exhibition of characters and deduction of events, is apparent; but events and characters are wholly new. Portugal, its timorous populace, its besotted monks, its jealous and effeminate nobles, and its cowardly prince, are vividly depicted. The narrator of this tale is, as in the former instance, the subject of it. After his retreat from court, Pombal consecrates his leisure to the composition of his own memoirs.

Among the most curious portions of this work, are those relating to the constitution of the inquisition, the expulsion of the Jesuits, the earthquake, and the conspiracy of Daveiro.[5]

The Romish religion, and the feudal institutions, are the causes that chiefly influence the modern state of Europe. Each of its kingdoms and provinces exhibits the operations of these causes, accompanied and modified by circumstances peculiar to each. Their genuine influence is thwarted, in different degrees, by learning and commerce. In Portugal, they have been suffered to produce the most extensive and unmingled mischiefs. Portugal, therefore, was properly selected as an example of moral and political degeneracy, and as a theatre in which virtue might be shewn with most advantage, contending with the evils of misgovernment and superstition.

---

[5] Inquisition … Jesuits … earthquake … Daveiro": allusions to the primary struggles of Pombal's administration. Pombal is generally known as an enlightened reformer who was hated by the older nobility as the son of a country squire. Throughout his administration he fought to wrest political power from the Catholic Church and its Inquisition, which had played a dominant role in Portuguese and Iberian affairs for two hundred years and was synonymous with superstition and tyranny. Pombal's struggles against the Jesuits, the Catholic order founded by Xavier (see note 1), led to their expulsion from Portugal and Portuguese colonies in 1767. The Great Lisbon Earthquake of 1755 amplified political tensions in Portugal, posed major problems for Portuguese colonialism, and became an Enlightenment cause célèbre in debunking myths about a benevolent deity, for example in Voltaire's widely read "Poem on the Lisbon Disaster" (1755) and his parable of enlightened education in *Candide* (1759).

The conspiracy of D'Aveiro refers to the Távora Affair, a political scandal that enveloped the Portuguese court following the earthquake. After the earthquake demolished the Royal Palace, King Joseph I and his court, including Pombal, were installed in a tent city outside Lisbon. After a failed assassination attempt there on the King in September 1758, Pombal's investigation revealed that the noble Távora family, who were plotting to make the Duke d'Aveiro king and diminish Pombal's power, had hired the assassins. D'Aveiro and the male Távoras were executed; the Jesuits were also implicated and publicly denounced as conspirators in the assassination plot, one of the key findings that led to their expulsion from Portuguese territories a few years later. Historians commonly understand the affair as an incident that Pombal used to diminish the authority of old aristocratic families and their allies in the church.

In works of this kind, though the writer is actuated by a single purpose, many momentous and indirect inferences will flow from his story. Perhaps the highest and lowest degrees in the scale of political improvement have been respectively exemplified by the Romans and the Portuguese. The pictures that are here drawn, may be considered as portraits of the human species, in two of the most remarkable forms.

There are two ways in which genius and virtue may labour for the public good: first by assailing popular errors and vices, argumentatively and through the medium of books; secondly, by employing legal or ministerial authority to this end.

The last was the province which Cicero and Pombal assumed. Their fate may evince the insufficiency of the instrument chosen by them, and teach us, that a change of national opinion is the necessary prerequisite of revolutions.

Engel, the eldest of Walstein's pupils, thought, like his master, that the narration of public events, with a certain license of invention, was the most efficacious of moral instruments. Abstract systems, and theoretical reasonings, were not without their use, but they claimed more attention than many were willing to bestow. Their influence, therefore, was limited to a narrow sphere. A mode by which truth could be conveyed to a great number, was much to be preferred.

Systems, by being imperfectly attended to, are liable to beget error and depravity. Truth flows from the union and relation of many parts. These parts, fallaciously connected and viewed separately, constitute error. Prejudice, stupidity, and indolence, will seldom afford us a candid audience, are prone to stop short in their researches, to remit, or transfer to other objects their attention, and hence to derive new motives to injustice, and new confirmations in folly from that which, if impartially and accurately examined, would convey nothing but benefit.

Mere reasoning is cold and unattractive. Injury rather than benefit proceeds from convictions that are transient and faint; their tendency is not to reform and enlighten, but merely to produce disquiet and remorse. They are not strong enough to resist temptation and to change the conduct, but merely to pester the offender with dissatisfaction and regret.

The detail of actions is productive of different effects. The affections are engaged, the reason is won by incessant attacks; the benefits which our system has evinced to be possible, are invested with a seeming existence; and the evils which error was proved to generate, exchange the fleeting, misty, and dubious form of inference, for a sensible and present existence.

To exhibit, in an eloquent narration, a model of right conduct, is the highest province of benevolence. Our patterns, however, may be useful in different degrees. Duties are the growth of situations. The general and the statesman have arduous duties to perform; and, to teach them their duty, is of use: but the forms of human society allow few individuals to gain the station of generals and statesmen. The lesson, therefore, is reducible to practice by a small number; and, of these, the temptations to abuse their power are so numerous and powerful, that a very small part, and these, in a very small degree, can be expected to comprehend, admire, and copy the pattern that is set before them.

But though few may be expected to be monarchs and ministers, every man occupies a station in society in which he is necessarily active to evil or to good. There is a sphere of some dimensions, in which the influence of his actions and opinions is felt. The causes that fashion men into instruments of happiness or misery, are numerous, complex, and operate upon a wide surface. Virtuous activity may, in a thousand ways, be thwarted and diverted by foreign and superior influence. It may seem best to purify the fountain, rather than filter the stream; but the latter is, to a certain degree, within our power, whereas, the former is impracticable. Governments and general education, cannot be rectified, but individuals may be somewhat fortified against their influence. Right intentions may be instilled into them, and some good may be done by each within his social and domestic province.

The relations in which men, unendowed with political authority, stand to each other, are numerous. An extensive source of these relations, is property. No topic can engage the attention of man more momentous than this. Opinions, relative to property, are the immediate source of nearly all the happiness and misery that exist among mankind. If men were guided by justice in the acquisition and disbursement, the brood of private and public evils would be extinguished.

To ascertain the precepts of justice, and exhibit these precepts reduced to practice, was, therefore, the favorite task of Engel. This, however, did not constitute his whole scheme. Every man is encompassed by numerous claims, and is the subject of intricate relations. Many of these may be comprised in a copious narrative, without infraction of simplicity or detriment to unity.

Next to property, the most extensive source of our relations is sex. On the circumstances which produce, and the principles which regulate the union between the sexes, happiness greatly depends. The conduct to be pursued by a virtuous man in those situations which arise from sex, it was thought useful to display.

Fictitious history has, hitherto, chiefly related to the topics of love and marriage. A monotony and sentimental softness have hence arisen that have frequently excited contempt and ridicule. The ridicule, in general, is merited; not because these topics are intrinsically worthless or vulgar, but because the historian was deficient in knowledge and skill.

Marriage is incident to all; its influence on our happiness and dignity, is more entire and lasting than any other incident can possess. None, therefore, is more entitled to discussion. To enable men to evade the evils and secure the benefits of this state, is to consult, in an eminent degree, their happiness.

A man, whose activity is neither aided by political authority nor by the *press,* may yet exercise considerable influence on the condition of his neighbours, by the exercise of intellectual powers. His courage may be useful to the timid or the feeble, and his knowledge to the ignorant, as well as his property to those who want. His benevolence and justice may not only protect his kindred and his wife, but rescue the victims of prejudice and passion from the yoke of those domestic tyrants, and shield the powerless from the oppression of power, the poor from the injustice of the rich, and the simple from the stratagems of cunning.

Almost all men are busy in acquiring subsistence or wealth by a fixed application of their time and attention. Manual or mental skill is obtained and exerted for this end. This application, within certain limits, is our duty. We are bound to chuse that species of industry which combines most profit to ourselves with the least injury to others; to select that instrument which, by most speedily supplying our necessities, leaves us at most leisure to act from the impulse of benevolence.

A profession, successfully pursued, confers power not merely by conferring property and leisure. The skill which is gained, and which, partly or for a time, may be exerted to procure subsistence, may, when this end is accomplished, continue to be exerted for the common good. The pursuits of law and medicine, enhance our power over the liberty, property, and health of mankind. They not only qualify us for imparting benefit, by supplying us with property and leisure, but by enabling us to obviate, by intellectual exertions, many of the evils that infest the world.

Engel endeavored to apply these principles to the choice of a profession, and to point out the mode in which professional skill, after it has supplied us with the means of subsistence, may be best exerted in the cause of general happiness.

Human affairs are infinitely complicated. The condition of no two beings is alike. No model can be conceived, to which our situation enables us to conform. No situation can be imagined perfectly similar to that of an actual being. This exact similitude is not required to render an imaginary portrait useful to those who survey it. The usefulness, undoubtedly, consists in suggesting a mode of reasoning and acting somewhat similar to that which is ascribed to a feigned person; and, for this end, some similitude is requisite between the real and imaginary situation; but that similitude is not hard to produce. Among the incidents which invention will set before us, those are to be culled out which afford most scope to wisdom and virtue, which are most analogous to facts, which most forcibly suggest to the reader the parallel between his state and that described, and most strongly excite his desire to act as the feigned personages act. These incidents must be so arranged as to inspire, at once, curiosity and belief, to fasten the attention, and thrill the heart. This scheme was executed in the life of "Olivo Ronsica."

Engel's principles inevitably led him to select, as the scene and period of his narrative, that in which those who should read it, should exist. Every day removed the reader farther from the period, but its immediate readers would perpetually recognize the objects, and persons, and events, with which they were familiar.

Olivo is a rustic youth, whom domestic equality, personal independence, agricultural occupations, and studious habits, had endowed with a strong mind, pure taste, and unaffected integrity. Domestic revolutions oblige him to leave his father's house in search of subsistence. He is destitute of property, of friends, and of knowledge of the world. These are to be acquired by his own exertions, and virtue and sagacity are to guide him in the choice and the use of suitable means.

Ignorance subjects us to temptation, and poverty shackles our beneficence. Olivo's conduct shews us how temptation may be baffled, in spite of ignorance, and benefits be conferred in spite of poverty.

He bends his way to Weimar. He is involved, by the artifices of others, and, in consequence of his ignorance of mankind, in many perils and perplexities. He forms a connection with a man of a great and mixed, but, on the whole, a vicious character. Semlits is introduced to furnish a contrast to the simplicity and rectitude of Olivo, to exemplify the misery of sensuality and fraud, and the influence which, in the present system of society, vice possesses over the reputation and external fortune of the good.

Men hold external goods, the pleasures of the senses, of health, liberty, reputation, competence, friendship, and life, partly by virtue of their own wisdom and activity. This, however, is not the only source of their possession. It is likewise dependent on physical accidents, which human foresight cannot anticipate, or human power prevent. It is also influenced by the conduct and opinions of others.

There is no external good, of which the errors and wickedness of others may not deprive us. So far as happiness depends upon the retention of these goods, it is held at the option of another. The perfection of our character is evinced by the transient or slight influence which privations and evils have upon our happiness, on the skillfulness of those exertions which we make to avoid or repair disasters, on the diligence and success with which we improve those instruments of pleasure to ourselves and to others which fortune has left in our possession.

Richardson has exhibited in Clarissa,[6] a being of uncommon virtue, bereaved of many external benefits by the vices of others. Her parents and lover conspire to destroy her fortune, liberty, reputation, and personal sanctity.

More talents and address cannot be easily conceived, than those which are displayed by her to preserve and to regain these goods. Her efforts are vain. The cunning and malignity with which she had to contend, triumphed in the contest.

Those evils and privations she was unable to endure. The loss of fame took away all activity and happiness, and she died a victim to errors, scarcely less opprobrious and pernicious, than those of her tyrants and oppressors. She misapprehended the value of parental approbation and a fair fame. She depreciated the means of usefulness and pleasure of which fortune was unable to deprive her.

Olivo is a different personage. His talents are exerted to reform the vices of others, to defeat their malice when exerted to his injury, to endure, without diminution of his usefulness or happiness, the injuries which he cannot shun.

Semlits is led, by successive accidents, to unfold his story to Olivo, after which, they separate. Semlits is supposed to destroy himself, and Olivo returns into the country.

---

[6] "Richardson ... Clarissa": novelist Samuel Richardson (1689–1761) and his best-known work, *Clarissa; or, the History of a Young Lady* (1748), one of the most significant English-language novels of the eighteenth century. This multivolume epistolary novel was a landmark presentation of new models of selfhood and virtue, and inaugurated a new subgenre of "seduction" narratives that explored women's lives for decades to come, for example in the popular best-sellers of the early American Republic. Brown's comments here suggest that Richardson placed too much emphasis on psychologized, inner standards of "virtue" that fetishize traditional categories such as piety and sexual chastity, for example, and not enough emphasis on the modernizing social empowerment of women in the public sphere.

A pestilential disease, prevalent throughout the north of Europe, at that time (1630), appears in the city. To ascertain the fate of one connected, by the ties of kindred and love, with the family in which Olivo resides, and whose life is endangered by residence in the city, he repairs thither, encounters the utmost perils, is seized with the reigning malady, meets, in extraordinary circumstances, with Semlits, and is finally received into the house of a physician, by whose skill he is restored to health, and to whom he relates his previous adventures.

He resolves to become a physician, but is prompted by benevolence to return, for a time, to the farm which he had lately left. The series of ensuing events, are long, intricate, and congruous, and exhibit the hero of the tale in circumstances that task his fortitude, his courage, and his disinterestedness.

Engel has certainly succeeded in producing a tale, in which are powerful displays of fortitude and magnanimity; a work whose influence must be endlessly varied by varieties of character and situation of the reader, but, from which, it is not possible for any one to rise without some degree of moral benefit, and much of that pleasure which always attends the emotions of curiosity and sympathy.

2. Charles Brockden Brown, "The Difference Between History and Romance." *The Monthly Magazine and American Review* 2:4 (April 1800)

Together with "Walstein's School of History," and appearing just a few months after it, this essay outlines the basic interrelation of history and fiction writing that Brown assumes in his novels and later historical writings, and helps explain how the novels are intended to educate readers and move them to greater awareness of their social surroundings. Likening the social relations investigated by historians and romancers to the material relations studied by key early modern scientists such as Isaac Newton (mathematician and physicist who first outlined the theory of gravity), Carl Linnaeus (founder of modern biological taxonomy and ecology), or William Herschel (astronomer who discovered infrared radiation and pioneered advanced telescope technologies such as interferometry), Brown argues that novelists and historians alike are, or should be, social scientists who use narrative to explore their social order and its history, and to educate their readers about it.

The essay rejects the common notion that history and fiction are different because one deals with factual and the other with fictional materials. Rather, Brown argues, history and fiction are best understood as two sides of one coin: history describes and documents the results of actions, while fiction investigates the possible conditions and motives that cause these actions. Whereas the historian endeavors to collect and establish facts about events and behaviors, the "romancer" is more concerned with asking why and how the events and behaviors took place. Thus the writing of romance (Brown's kind of novel) deals in conjecture about the causes and consequences of social actions and events. This imaginative conjecture is useful because it helps clarify the ways in which seemingly unique or personal events and acts (such as the financial ruin of the Dudley family,

Constantia's heroism during the fever, or Helena's suicide) are actually conditioned, although not narrowly determined, by larger social forces.

The difference between history as documentation and romance as interpretation also allows Brown to develop an implicit distinction between "romance" and "novel." Brown's definition here situates romance as the kind of narrative that educates readers and helps them grasp the social processes in which they are embedded. Unlike the nineteenth century's contrast between realism and romance, where romance allows the imaginative flight of fancy from the mundane world (this is the way romance is understood in Nathaniel Hawthorne's prefaces of the 1850s, for example), Brown situates the "novel" as a fiction that seeks to amuse a passive reader, and "romance" as a fiction that seeks to train the reader as an active interpreter and interrogator of society. When Brown's narrator writes in this novel's prefatory statement that she will depict "society and manners" in the U.S., and illustrate "modes of life [and] the influence of public events upon the character and happiness of individuals in America," he is therefore indicating that he has designed the work as a romance, not a novel.

Most basically, then, Brown's ideas about "the difference between history and romance" imply that Constantia's tale, with all of its dramatic crises and reversals, should be read as part of an exploration of the causes of contemporary events and behaviors, rather than simply as a "terrific" tale of sensational wonder (see the excerpt from "Terrific Novels" for Brown's definition of that variety of narrative).

*****

History and romance are terms that have never been very clearly distinguished from each other. It should seem that one dealt in fiction, and the other in truth; that one is a picture of the *probable* and certain, and the other a tissue of untruths; that one describes what *might* have happened, and what has *actually* happened, and the other what never had existence.

These distinctions seem to be just; but we shall find ourselves somewhat perplexed, when we attempt to reduce them to practice, and to ascertain, by their assistance, to what class this or that performance belongs.

Narratives, whether fictitious or true, may relate to the processes of nature, or the actions of men. The former, if not impenetrable by human faculties, must be acknowledged to be, hitherto, very imperfectly known. Curiosity is not satisfied with viewing facts in their disconnected state and natural order, but is prone to arrange them anew, and to deviate from present and sensible objects, into speculations on the past or future; it is eager to infer from the present state of things, their former or future condition.

The observer or experimentalist, therefore, who carefully watches, and faithfully enumerates the appearances which occur, may claim the appellation of historian. He who adorns these appearances with cause and effect, and traces resemblances between the past, distant, and future, with the present, performs a different part. He is a dealer, not in certainties, but probabilities, and is therefore a romancer.

An historian will relate the noises, the sights, and the smells that attend an eruption of Vesuvius. A romancer will describe, in the first place, the *contemporary* ebullitions and inflations, the combustion and decomposition that take place in the bowels of the earth. Next he will go to the origin of things, and describe the centrical, primary, and secondary orbs composing the universe, as masses thrown out of an immense volcano called *chaos*. Thirdly, he will paint the universal dissolution that is hereafter to be produced by the influence of volcanic or internal fire.

An historian will form catalogues of stars, and mark their positions at given times. A romancer will arrange them in *clusters* and dispose them in *strata,* and inform you by what influences the orbs have been drawn into sociable knots and circles.

An electrical historian will describe appearances that happen when hollow cylinders of glass and metal are placed near each other, and the former is rubbed with a cloth. The romancer will replenish the space that exists between the sun and its train of planetary orbs, with a fluid called electrical; and describe the modes in which this fluid finds its way to the surface of these orbs through the intervenient atmosphere.

Historians can only differ in degrees of diligence and accuracy, but romancers may have more or less probability in their narrations. The same man is frequently both historian and romancer in the compass of the same work. Buffon,[1] Linneus, and Herschel, are examples of this union. Their observations are as diligent as their theories are adventurous. Among the historians of nature, Haller[2] was, perhaps, the most diligent: among romancers, he that came nearest to the truth was Newton.

It must not be denied that, though history be a term commonly applied to a catalogue of natural appearances, as well as to the recital of human actions, romance is chiefly limited to the latter. Some reluctance may be felt in calling Buffon and Herschel romancers, but that name will be readily conferred on Quintus Curtius and Sir Thomas More.[3] There is a sufficient analogy, however, between objects and modes, in the physical and intellectual world, to justify the use of these distinctions in both cases.

Physical objects and appearances sometimes fall directly beneath our observation, and may be truly described. The duty of the *natural* historian is limited to this description. *Human* actions may likewise be observed, and be truly described. In this respect, the actions of *voluntary* and *involuntary* agents, are alike, but in other momentous respects they differ.

Curiosity is not content with noting and recording the *actions* of men. It likewise seeks to know the *motives* by which the agent is impelled to the performance of these

---

[1] "Buffon": Georges-Louis Leclerc, Compte de Buffon (1707–1788), French biologist and writer whose work on natural history was an important precedent for Darwin's theory of natural selection. Buffon is best know in a U.S. context as one of the scientists addressed in Thomas Jefferson's *Notes on the State of Virginia* (first published in Paris, 1784).

[2] "Haller": Albrecht von Haller (1708–1777), Swiss physiologist and botanist, and a leading contributor to both fields during the Enlightenment. He was notable for the immense number of his scientific publications, hence the "diligent" reputation to which Brown refers.

[3] "Quintus Curtius ... More": two writers of more hypothetical works that may be contrasted with the scientific work of the previously mentioned figures. Quintus Curtius Rufus was a Roman historian of the first century B.C.E.; his only surviving work is two books of a history of Alexander the Great that are notable for speculating about unknowable aspects of Alexander's character. Thomas More (1478–1535) is the English statesman best known for writing the political allegory *Utopia* (1516).

actions; but motives are modifications of thought which cannot be subjected to the senses. They cannot be certainly known. They are merely topics of conjecture. Conjecture is the weighing of probabilities; the classification of probable events, according to the measure of probability possessed by each.

Actions of different men, or performed at different times, may be alike; but the motives leading to these actions must necessarily vary. In guessing at these motives, the knowing and sagacious will, of course, approach nearer to the truth than the ignorant and stupid; but the wise and the ignorant, the sagacious and stupid, when busy in assigning motives to actions, are not *historians* but *romancers*.

The motive is the cause, and therefore the antecedent of the action; but the action is likewise the cause of subsequent actions. Two contemporary and (so to speak) adjacent actions may both be faithfully described, because both may be witnessed; but the connection between them, that quality which constitutes one the effect of the other, is mere matter of conjecture, and comes with the province, not of *history*, but *romance*.

The description of human actions is of moment merely as they are connected with motives and tendencies. The delineation of tendencies and motives implies a description of the action; but the action is describable without the accompanyment of tendencies and motives.

An action may be simply described, but such descriptions, though they alone be historical, are of no use as they stand singly and disjoined from tendencies and motives, in the page of the historian or the mind of the reader. The writer, therefore, who does not blend the two characters, is essentially defective. It is true, that facts simply described, may be connected and explained by the reader; and that the describer may, at least, claim the merit of supplying the builder with materials. The merit of him who drags stones together, must not be depreciated; but must not be compared with him who hews these stones into just proportions, and piles them up into convenient and magnificent fabrics.

That which is done beneath my own inspection, it is possible for me certainly to know and exactly to record; but that which is performed at a distance, either in time or place, is the theme of foreign testimony. If it be related by me, I relate not what I have witnessed, but what I derived from others who were witnesses. The subject of my senses is merely the existence of the record, and not the deed itself which is recorded. The truth of the action can be weighed in no scales but those of probability.

A voluntary action is not only connected with cause and effect, but is itself a series of motives and incidents subordinate and successive to each other. Every action differs from every other in the number and complexity of its parts, but the most simple and brief is capable of being analyzed into a thousand subdivisions. If it be witnessed by others, probabilities are lessened in proportion as the narrative is circumstantial.

These principles may be employed to illustrate the distinction between history and romance. If history relate what is true, its relations must be limited to what is known by the testimony of our senses. Its sphere, therefore, is extremely narrow. The facts to which we are immediate witnesses, are, indeed, numerous; but time and place merely connect them. Useful narratives must comprise facts linked together by some other circumstance. They must, commonly, consist of events, for a knowledge of which the narrator is indebted to the evidence of others. This evidence, though accompanied with different degrees of probability, can never give birth to certainty. How wide, then, if romance be the narrative of mere probabilities, is the empire of romance? This empire is absolute and undivided over the motives and tendencies of human actions. Over actions themselves, its dominion, though not unlimited, is yet very extensive.

X.

3. Two Statements on the Modern Novel:

a) Charles Brockden Brown, excerpt from "Romances." *The Literary Magazine and American Register* 3:16 (January 1805).

In this article on "romances," which in this case means the novel-like narratives that flourished from the Middle Ages to the 1600s, Brown reiterates the need for contemporary forms of art to focus on themes that are relevant for contemporary audiences. Works of the past may have been tremendous achievements, but their usefulness for the modern reader is limited because new historical conditions demand new ideas and modes of behavior. Brown's argument here suggests that there is no unchanging or eternal, transhistorical standard for values, ideas, or behaviors. The lessons of one age may not be useful for another. Like his contemporaries William Godwin and Thomas Paine, Brown remains skeptical about worshipping past forms of art, society, and government.

****

A tale, agreeable to truth and nature or, more properly speaking, agreeable to *our own* conceptions of truth and nature, may be long, but cannot be tedious. Cleopatra and Cassandra by no means referred to an ideal world; they referred to the manners and habits of the age in which they were written; names and general incidents only were taken from the age of Alexander and Caesar. In that age, therefore, they were not tedious, but the more delighted was the reader the longer the banquet was protracted. In after times, when taste and manners were changed, the tale became tedious, because it was deemed unnatural and absurd, and it would have been condemned as tedious, and treated with neglect, whether it filled ten pages or ten volumes.

Cleopatra and Cassandra are no greater violations of historical veracity and probability, and no more drawn from an ideal world, than Johnson's Rasselas, Hawkesworth's Almoran and Hamet, or Fenelon's Telemachus.[1] In all these, names and incidents, and some machinery, are taken from a remote age and nation, but the

---

[1] "Rasselas ... Almoran and Hamet ... Telemachus": popular adventure tales of the eighteenth century: Samuel Johnson, *The History of Rasselas* (1759); John Hawkesworth, *Almoran and Hamet* (1761); and François Fenélon's *The Adventures of Telemachus, Son of Ulysses* (1699). Hawkesworth was Samuel Johnson's successor at the London *Gentlemen's Magazine* and was also well known as editor of James Cook's account of his South Sea voyages (1773).

manners and sentiments are modeled upon those of the age in which the works were written, as those of the Scuderis[2] were fashioned upon the habits of their own age. The present unpopularity of the romances of the fifteenth and sixteenth centuries is not owing to the satires of Cervantes or of Boileau,[3] but to the gradual revolution of human manners and national taste.

The *"Arabian Nights"* delight us in childhood, and so do the chivalrous romances; but, in riper age, if enlightened by education, we despise what we formerly revered. Individuals, whose minds have been uncultivated, continue still their attachment to those marvelous stories. And yet, must it not be ascribed rather to change of manners than to any other cause, that we neglect and disrelish works which gave infinite delight to sir Philip Sidney, sir Walter Raleigh, and sir Thomas More,[4] to Sully and Daubigne:[5] men whose knowledge of Augustan models, and delight in them, was never exceeded, and the general vigor and capacity of whose minds has never been surpassed.

The works that suited former ages are now exploded by us. The works that are now produced, and which accommodate themselves to our habits and taste, would have been utterly neglected by our ancestors: and what is there to hinder the belief, that they, in their turn, will fall into oblivion and contempt at some future time. We naturally conceive our own habits and opinions the standard of rectitude; but their rectitude, admitting our claim to be just, will not hinder them from giving way to others, and being exploded in their turn.

---

[2] "Scuderis": Georges (1601–1667) and Madeleine (1607–1701) de Scudéry, a brother and sister who were popular romancers throughout seventeenth-century Europe. Madeleine was considered the better of the two writers, and the lengthy, baroque narratives that she produced from the 1640s to the 1670s were widely influential, parodied, and taken as models for traditional "romance" writing well into the next century. Her romance *Clelia*, which appeared in ten volumes, 1648–1651, figures as a significant reference in Brown's novel *Stephen Calvert* (1799–1800).

[3] "Cervantes ... Boileau": Miguel de Cervantes (1547–1616), whose modernizing novel *Don Quixote* (1605) includes a humorous polemic against earlier "romance" styles; and Nicolas Boileau-Despréaux (1636–1711), who struggled to reform verse styles in seventeenth-century France.

[4] "Sidney ... Raleigh ... More": three staples of sixteenth-century English letters and court culture (all knighted by British monarchs): Sidney was author of *Astrophel and Stella* and "A Defence of Poesie" in the 1580s; Raleigh, primarily known as a colonial adventurer, also wrote important poetry in the 1570s and 1580s; More's best-known work is *Utopia* (1516), which Brown references in "The Difference Between History and Romance," included in Related Texts.

[5] "Sully and Daubigne": Maximilien de Béthune, duc de Sully (1560–1641), a finance minister to king Henry IV of France, who published widely read memoirs (1662) and religious-utopian tracts (1638); and Théodore-Agrippa d'Aubigné (1552–1630), another political figure at the court of Henry IV who published widely read histories and tragedies in the 1610s and 1620s. Both were Huguenots whose political and literary careers were entwined with the Reformation-era Catholic-Protestant struggles in France. Brown's point in identifying this series of names is primarily that these are all elite-courtly writers. All of these names represent a pre-Enlightenment world of monarchical cultural production that is out of keeping with the needs and purposes of more modern readers in the Revolutionary age.

b) Charles Brockden Brown, excerpt from "Terrific Novels." *The Literary Magazine and American Register* 3:19 (April 1805)

This passage illustrates Brown's criticism of conventional gothic style and helps explain, by contrast, how his own use of the gothic is oriented toward the representation of modern life. Today the term "gothic" generally describes narratives that use the supernatural to excite fear and suspense in their audience. But in this essay, Brown judges such narratives by their motivation rather than by their form, themes, or effect on their audience. Brown calls novels that use sensational devices of mystery simply to create suspense "terrific" ones because they are intended to generate sensations of terror, rather than a sense of excellence. In keeping with his general emphasis on the development of modern forms suited to modern social conditions, Brown criticizes conventional gothic's emphasis on premodern superstitions rather than the anxieties and stresses of contemporary life. As opposed to castles, monks, and superstitions, Brown's version of the gothic, in Wieland *and his other novels, highlights scenarios and themes that his readers might actually experience: mental illness or psychological symptoms in conditions of extreme anxiety and stress such as the threat of rape, somnambulism, bankruptcy, impoverishment, vulnerability to illnesses like the yellow fever, and so on.*

The excerpt also illustrates the manner in which Brown draws material to support his arguments from contemporary British and European periodicals. As he often does (and as was common in the period) Brown has mixed his prose with that of an earlier reviewer from the London Monthly Review *(January 1802), 28–30. In this paragraph, the first two sentences are Brown's, while the last three are reprinted from an anonymous review of a contemporary "terrific novel," Benjamin Frère's* The Man of Fortitude; or, Schedoni in England *(London: Wallis, 1801).*

✶✶✶✶✶

The Castle of Otranto laid the foundation of a style of novel writing, which was carried to perfection by Mrs. Radcliff,[6] and which may be called the *terrific style.* The great talents of Mrs. Radcliff made some atonement for the folly of this mode of composition, and gave some importance to exploded fables and childish fears, by the charms of sentiment and description; but the multitude of her imitators seem to have thought that description and sentiment were impertinent intruders, and by lowering the mind somewhat to its ordinary state, marred and counteracted those awful feelings, which true genius was properly employed in raising. They endeavor to keep the reader in a constant state of tumult and horror, by the powerful engines of trapdoors, back stairs, black robes, and pale faces: but the solution of the enigma is ever

---

[6] "Otranto ... Mrs. Radcliff": Horace Walpole's *The Castle of Otranto* (1764), generally understood as the novel that inaugurates the gothic genre; and Ann Radcliffe (1764–1823), the preeminent author of gothic romances during the 1790s. Her best-known titles are *The Mystery of Udolpho* (1794) and *The Italian* (1796).

too near at hand, to permit the indulgence of supernatural appearances. A well-written scene of a party at snap-dragon would exceed all the fearful images of these books. There is, besides, no *keeping* in the author's design: fright succeeds to fright, and danger to danger, without permitting the unhappy reader to draw his breath, or to repose for a moment on subjects of character or sentiment.

4. Charles Brockden Brown, "Portrait of an Emigrant. Extracted from a Letter." *The Monthly Magazine and American Review* 1:3 (June 1799)

Despite its brevity, "Portrait of an Emigrant" brings together a complex set of positions on progressive politics and social history, especially concerning race. The immediate context for Brown's sketch is the 1793 flood of French refugees who arrived in U.S. port cities, notably Philadelphia, after fleeing the increasingly violent black slave revolution in Haiti. White French Creole (colony-born) refugees in this group, along with native-born French political exiles arriving from France to escape Jacobin rule, had an immediate impact on American culture far out of proportion to their relatively small numbers as an emigrant group. Unlike the mainly agricultural and laboring-class background of earlier and larger northern-European emigrant groups such as the Germans and Scots-Irish, these Francophone exiles of the 1790s belonged largely to the middle class and planter elites, and consequently tended to be more literate, financially comfortable, and less familiar with manual labor than other groups. With little experience in crafts, the refugees scrambled to survive by helping to establish a market for consumer pleasures—often involving the commercialization of physical appearance and behavior—as hairdressers, dressmakers, cooks, dance instructors, book sellers, and music and theater performers. As they brought a new code of manners and personal dress styles to the plainer, predominately Protestant cultures of American cities, the French strangers were arguably important catalysts or accelerators in this period's shift from self-sufficient, agrarian, household economies toward more modern patterns in which individuals fashion their identity, not by adherence to family or village origins, but through consumer choices in clothes, books, and other cultural commodities. Not only did these French emigrants make new kinds of consumer objects and behaviors available to Americans, they also embodied and modeled for locals a radically new mentality involving comfort with lifeways based on a consumer economy, an orientation that is dramatically different than Puritan ideals of asceticism or Quaker moderation. Brown's "Portrait" begins by highlighting the experience of this transformation and then turns to an implicit claim for the abolition of slavery and the affirmation of a postslavery society based on miscegenation and a "mulatto" culture of racial mixture.

The narrator opens the sketch by emphasizing that social experience is contingent on the changing historical environment, highlighting the Woldwinite claim that we are determined more by cultural environment than by the accident of birth into a particular family and location. Explaining that he has been asked to speak with Mrs. K, the narrator claims that, while the undereducated might not know history and political debates, their familiarity with the world around them nevertheless makes them insightful commentators on the shifts in everyday social history, what Brown calls "the romance of real life." While the woman's tales of her urban neighborhood might seem trivial, the narrator suggests that, as an example of the opinions and attitudes of a newly urbanized population, her thinking ought to be viewed as a more important index to historical transformation and model for virtuous activity than the writings and legislation of political elites. By respectfully listening to and learning from the uneducated female observer, the narrator affirms the need for a more socially inclusive, egalitarian history from the bottom up.

Mrs. K. discusses the everyday behavior of a white Haitian refugee, M. de Lisle (de l'isle = "from the island"; Lisle is also a Brown family name on the maternal side), who is openly and unashamedly living with a mixed-race (or mulatto) woman from the French colony. Such a coupling was common in Haiti, where an increasingly wealthy segment of mixed-race property owners would marry their daughters to white men so that their grandchildren would gain the privileges of whiteness in the colonies. The black slave uprising, however, has forced them to flee, losing their wealth in the process. But instead of holding a revenge grudge against unruly blacks after arriving in 1793, they show benevolence by adopting what is, as indicated by her dialect speech, a black child orphaned possibly by yellow fever. Rather than wallowing in self-pity for their lost status, the couple instead enjoy life, taking pleasure in each other's spirited conversation, and live what appears to be a purely consumer-oriented lifestyle, ordering all their meals in and avoiding manual labor by paying for washing and ignoring housecleaning. Contrary to conventional readerly expectations that Mrs. K will condemn the couple's behavior as shiftless and unacceptable, she instead envies their joie de vivre and insists that "the French are the only people that know how to live." Instead of being shocked by their foreignness and different sexual morality (there is a hint that the woman may be a kept mistress who occasionally dabbles in prostitution), Mrs. K is comfortable with these "exiles and strangers." The implied purpose of the conversation, then, is not so much to document the cultural otherness and racial intermixture of the French, as to record and amplify the affirmative response of the common American. It is Mrs. K's newly emergent cosmopolitanism that the narrator wants to highlight, as she provides evidence of a larger historical shift of mentalities, which makes the case for a peaceful and in fact desirable move toward a mixed-race, postslavery society.

As in many of Brown's writings, seemingly random details and references work together to reinforce the surface meaning of the sketch. The de Lisles order their food from Etienne ("Chrétien") Simonet, a French émigré from Montargis, who had a patisserie and catering business on South Second Street near Lombard. Simonet belonged to St. John's Masonic Lodge, which was presided over by Dr. Jean Devèze, a Creole physician who played a leading role at Bush-Hill hospital during the 1793 yellow fever epidemic and is referred to in Brown's novel Arthur Mervyn. The tightly knit, multiracial émigré community evoked here is the same one in which Martinette de Beauvais takes refuge in Ormond, and hints of Martinette's multiethnic background are further links to the milieu evoked here.

The mention of Madame de Lisle's acting in Lailson's circus seemingly dates the conversation to April–July, 1797. In 1797–1798, French immigrant Philip Lailson established the city's largest circus at Fifth and Prune Streets (across from the Debtor's Prison described in Arthur Mervyn), and staged shows that combined equestrian tricks, burlesque, ballet,

241

pantomimes, and plays. In May 1797, Brown's close friends William Dunlap, Elihu Hubbard Smith, and Samuel Latham Mitchill came to Philadelphia to participate in a convention of state abolition societies. With Brown they attended Lailson's circus during the period when it staged plays and may well have seen a piece with actors like Madame de Lisle called The American Heroine. *This was an adaptation of George Coleman's tremendously successful* Inkle and Yarico *(1787), a tale about an English merchant, Inkle, who is shipwrecked on a Caribbean island and saved by the beautiful aborigine Yarico, who shields him from her people's anger. They exchange marriage vows, but Inkle later decides to sell his Indian wife into slavery, raising the price when he learns she is pregnant. Coleman's play was widely received as an abolitionist attack on mercantile greed and is now recognized as a significant part of the cultural push toward the successful British campaign to abolish slavery. Coleman was also familiar to Brown and his friends as author of* The Iron Chest *(1796), a stage version of William Godwin's novel* Caleb Williams *(1793), a primary model for Arthur Mervyn. As she acts in Lailson's productions, then, Madame de Lisle may be employed in more than simply frivolous entertainment; she may be contributing to a popular art form that conveys progressive political messages to a wide audience. This cultural strategy follows Brown's own as outlined in* "Walstein's School of History," *a Related Text here.*

The sketch may also involve one further allusion and intervention. During Lailson's short run, Susanna Rowson, author of the Francophobic Charlotte Temple, a Tale of Truth *(UK publication 1791, U.S. republication 1794), was in the last stages of her acting career and appeared at Lailson's, to somewhat bad reviews, in a play entitled* The Harlequin Mariner. *Critic Steven Epley has recently argued that the great success of* Charlotte Temple *was based on Rowson's repackaging of* Inkle and Yarico's *thematic elements in ways that stripped the source narrative of its abolitionist political purpose. Thus Brown's affirmative characterization of the de Lisles may signal an oblique criticism of Rowson's brand of xenophobic entertainment and declining career as an actor, for at this time Brown and Smith were interested participants in their friend William Dunlap's rival career and (at that time) successful management of the New Park Theatre in New York.*

*****

I called, as you desired, on Mrs. K——. We had considerable conversation. Knowing, as you do, my character and her's, you may be somewhat inquisitive as to the subject of our conversation. You may readily suppose that my inquiries were limited to domestic and every-day incidents. The state of her own family, and her servants and children being discussed, I proceeded to inquire into the condition of her neighbours. It is not in large cities as it is in villages. Those whose education does not enable and accustom them to look abroad, to investigate the character and actions of beings of a distant age and country, are generally attentive to what is passing under their own eye. Mrs. K—— never reads, not even a newspaper. She is unacquainted with what happened before she was born. She is equally a stranger to the events that are passing in distant nations, and to those which ingross the attention and shake the passions of the statesmen and politicians of her own country; but her mind, nevertheless, is far from being torpid or inactive. She speculates curiously and even justly on the objects that occur within her narrow sphere.

Were she the inhabitant of a village, she would be mistress of the history and character of every family within its precincts; but being in a large city,[*] her knowledge is confined chiefly to her immediate neighbours; to those who occupy the house on each side and opposite. I will not stop to inquire into the reason of this difference in the manners of villagers and citizens. The fact has often been remarked, though seldom satisfactorily explained. I shall merely repeat the dialogue which took place on my inquiry into the state of the family inhabiting the house on the right hand and next to her's.

"M'Culey," said she, "who used to live there, is gone."

"Indeed! and who has taken his place?"

"A Frenchman and his wife. His wife, I suppose her to be, though he is a man of fair complexion, well formed, and of genteel appearance; and the woman is half negro. I suppose they would call her a mestee. They came last winter from the West-Indies, and miserably poor I believe; for when they came into this house they had scarcely any furniture besides a bed, and a chair or two, and a pine table. They shut up the lower rooms, and lived altogether in the two rooms in the second story."

"Of whom does the family consist?"

"The man and woman, and a young girl, whom I first took for their daughter, but I afterwards found she was an orphan child, whom, shortly after their coming here, they found wandering in the streets; and, though poor enough themselves, took her under their care."

"How do they support themselves?"

"The man is employed in the compting-house of a French merchant of this city. What is the exact sort of employment, I do not know, but it allows him to spend a great deal of his time at home. The woman is an actress in Lailson's pantomimes. In the winter she scarcely ever went out in the day-time, but now that the weather is mild and good she walks out a great deal."

"Can you describe their mode of life, what they eat and drink, and how they spend their time?"

"I believe I can. Most that they do can be seen from our windows and yard, and all that they say can be heard. In the morning every thing is still till about ten o'clock. Till that hour they lie a-bed. The first sign that they exist, is given by the man, who comes half dressed, to the back window; and lolling out of it, smokes two or three segars, and sometimes talks to a dog that lies on the out-side of the kitchen door. After sometime passed in this manner he goes into the room over the kitchen, takes a loaf of bread from the closet, and pours out a tumbler of wine; with these he returns to the front room, but begins as soon as he has hold of them, to gnaw at one and sip from the other. This constitutes their breakfast. In half an hour they both reappear at the window. They throw out crums of bread to the dog, who stands below with open mouth to receive it; and talk sometimes to him and sometimes to each

[*] Philadelphia

other. Their tongues run incessantly; frequently they talk together in the loudest and shrillest tone imaginable. I thought, at first, they were quarrelsome; but every now and then they burst into laughter, and it was plain that they were in perfect good humour with each other.

"About twelve o'clock the man is dressed, and goes out upon his business. He returns at three. In the mean time the lady employs herself in washing every part of her body, and putting on a muslin dress, perfectly brilliant and clean. Then she either lolls at the window, and sings without intermission, or plays on a guitar. She is certainly a capital performer and singer. No attention is paid to house or furniture. As to rubbing tables, and sweeping and washing floors, these are never thought of. Their house is in a sad condition, but she spares no pains to make her person and dress clean.

"The man has scarcely entered the house, when he is followed by a black fellow, with bare head and shirt tucked up at his elbows, carrying on his head a tray covered with a white napkin. This is their dinner, and is brought from *Simonet's*. After dinner the man takes his flute, on which he is very skilful; and the woman either sings or plays in concert till evening approaches: some visitants then arrive, and they all go out together to walk. We hear no more of them till next morning."

"What becomes of the girl all this time?"

"She eats, sings, dresses, and walks with them. She often comes into our house, generally at meal times; if she spies any thing she likes, she never conceals her approbation. 'O my, how good *dat* must be! Me wish me had some: will you *gif* me some?' She is a pretty harmless little thing, and one cannot refuse what she asks.

"Next day after they came into this house, the girl, in the morning, while our servant was preparing breakfast, entered the kitchen—'O my!' said she to me, 'what you call dem tings?'

'Buckwheat cakes.'

'Ahah! buckawit cake! O my! how good dey must be! Me likes—will you give me one?'

"Next morning she came again, and we happened to be making *muffins*. 'O my!' cried she, 'you be always baking and baking! What you call dem dere?'

'Muffins.'

'Mofeen? O my! me wish for some, me do.'

"Afterwards she was pretty regular in her visits. She was modest, notwithstanding; and, seeming to be half-starved, we gave her entertainment as often as she claimed it."

"Are not these people very happy?"

"Very happy. When together they are for ever chattering and laughing, or playing and singing in concert. How the man is employed when separate we do not certainly know; but the woman, it seems, is continually singing, and her hands, if not employed in adorning her own person, are playing the guitar. I am apt to think the French are the only people that know how to live. These people, though exiles and strangers, and subsisting on scanty and precarious funds, move on smoothly and at ease. Household cares they know not. They breakfast upon bread and wine, without the ceremony of laying table, and arranging platters and cups. From the trouble of watching and directing servants they are equally exempt. Their cookery is performed abroad. Their clothes are washed in the same way. The lady knows no manual employment but the grateful one of purifying and embellishing her own person. The intervals are consumed in the highest as well as purest sensual enjoyments, in music, in which she appears to be an adept, and of which she is passionately enamoured. When the air is serene and bland, she repairs to the public walks, with muslin handkerchief in one hand, and parti-coloured *parasol* in the other. She is always accompanied by men anxious to please her, busy in supplying her with amusing topics, and listening with complacency and applause to her gay effusions and her ceaseless volubility.

"I have since taken some pains to discover the real situation of this family. I find that the lady was the heiress of a large estate in St. Domingo, that she spent her youth in France, where she received a polished education, and where she married her present companion, who was then in possession of rank and fortune, but whom the revolution has reduced to indigence. The insurrection in St. Domingo destroyed their property in that island. They escaped with difficulty to these shores in 1793, and have since subsisted in various modes and places, frequently pinched by extreme poverty, and sometimes obliged to solicit public charity; but retaining, in every fortune, and undiminished, their propensity to talk, laugh and sing—their flute and their guitar."

Nothing is more ambiguous than the motives that stimulate men to action. These people's enjoyments are unquestionably great. They are innocent: they are compatible, at least, with probity and wisdom, if they are not the immediate fruits of it. Constitutional gaiety may account for these appearances; but as they may flow, in one case, from the absence of reflection and foresight, they may likewise, in another instance, be the product of justice and benevolence.

It is our duty to make the best of our condition; to snatch the good that is within our reach, and to nourish no repinings on account of what is unattainable. The gratifications of sense, of conjugal union, and of social intercourse, are among the highest in the scale; and these are as much in the possession of *de Lisle* and his wife, as of the most opulent and luxuriant members of the community.

As to mean habitation and scanty furniture, their temper or their reason enables them to look upon these things as trifles. They are not among those who witnessed their former prosperity, and their friends and associates are unfortunate like themselves. Instead of humiliation and contempt, adversity has probably given birth to sympathy and mutual respect.

His profession is not laborious; and her's, though not respectable according to our notions, is easy and amusing. Her life scarcely produces any intermission of recreation and enjoyment. Few instances of more unmingled and uninterrupted felicity can be found; and yet these people have endured, and continue to endure, most of the evils which the imagination is accustomed to regard with most horror; and which would create ceaseless anguish in beings fashioned on the model of my character, or of yours. Let you and I grow wise by the contemplation of their example.

B.

5. Charles Brockden Brown, excerpts from Review of *The Origin and Principles of the American Revolution compared with the Origin and Principles of the French Revolution. Translated from the German of Gentz, by an American Gentleman* [John Quincy Adams]. Philadelphia: Dickins, 1800. From *The American Review, and Literary Journal* (Jan. 1, 1801), 55–64

The comparison of the American and French Revolutions has always been an ideologically and politically charged exercise. Already in the 1790s, conservatives attempted to condemn the revolution in France and to derevolutionize the one in America by characterizing the former as an anarchic whirlwind sweeping away the foundations of god-given social and political stability, and the latter as a struggle over economic and political liberty that did not challenge the privileges of commerce or already existing native religious and political hierarchies. Progressive thinkers countered by pointing out that the two revolutions developed in different geopolitical and socioeconomic circumstances, but nevertheless shared fundamental goals and were best understood as related struggles in a single arc of social transformation driven by Enlightenment critique and values. Progressives argued that both revolutions affirmed that social-political transformation was not an exceptional disruption of divine order, but a normal and inevitable process requiring rational management; and that both demolished feudal institutions and replaced the old regime with declarations of popular sovereignty and principles of universal human liberty. As it turned out, neither revolution made it possible to reconcile the egalitarian aspirations of the period's radicals and disempowered majorities—for example with regard to women's rights and abolition—with the revolutionary elite's conviction that republican schemes of government resting on propertied male privilege offered the best institutional means of consolidating and expanding bourgeois civil society.[1] Nevertheless, radicals and bourgeois revolutionaries alike affirmed the fundamental kinship of the American and French revolutions, while monarchists and counterrevolutionaries attempted to distinguish the two and launched a print campaign whose basic goal was to delegitimate the principle of social change and provide a rationale for drawing back the progressive gains of the revolutionary age.

Ormond stages this basic dimension of the period's revolution debates by juxtaposing Martinette's participation in the American and French struggles (Chapters 19–21) with Sophia's attempt to praise the American polity while repeatedly condemning the French (notably in Chapter 24). More generally, the debate appears implicitly in the ongoing

---

[1] For more on the historical distinction between radical and bourgeois-revolutionary positions in the period, see Kramnick, *Republicanism and Bourgeois Radicalism: Political Ideology in Late Eighteenth-Century England and America*; Linebaugh and Rediker, *The Many-Headed Hydra: Sailors, Slaves, Commoners, and the Hidden History of the Revolutionary Atlantic*; and Wallerstein, *After Liberalism*.

contrast between the two characters' many reflections on the revolution in France. But if Brown's implicit commentary in Ormond *was indirect, folded within the novel's complex narrative frame and dramatic action, he provided a more explicit and analytical discussion of the debate in his 1801 review of Friedrich von Gentz's attempt to present the reactionary brief for a fundamental distinction between two Atlantic revolutions (ignoring the third, Haitian slave revolution then under way).*

The Prussian-born Friedrich von Gentz (1764–1832) often described as one of the Napoleonic period's most successful "mercenaries of the pen," was the principle German-language antirevolutionary propagandist, a younger disciple and translator of conservative theorists such as Edmund Burke (1729–1797) and Mallet du Pan (1749–1800). He established himself as an effective and highly paid publicist for British and Prussian interests in the early years of the Revolution with translations of major counterrevolutionary tracts (his was the standard translation of Burke's 1790 Reflections on the Revolution in France*), then gained celebrity in his own right after publishing essays and pamphlets like the one Brown reviews here.*[2] *Bonaparte memorably referred to him as that "wretched scribe named Gentz, one of those men without honor who sell themselves for money." On the basis of these accomplishments, Gentz had a long and lucrative career in Prussian diplomacy and was privy to the highest levels of power in postrevolutionary geopolitics in his capacity as chief assistant, confidant, and advisor to Prince Metternich (1773–1859), the Henry Kissinger of romantic Europe.*[3]

In his review, Brown provides a thorough recapitulation and rejection of Gentz's right-wing arguments. It is notable that, after highlighting Gentz's propagandistic goals and techniques of argumentation, Brown specifically affirms the common radical legacy of both revolutions and negates the attempt to draw a line between the arguments made during the American revolt by bourgeois revolutionaries such as Jefferson, John Adams, John Jay, and John Dickinson, and those put forward by radical thinkers such as Thomas Paine. Additionally, Brown points out that Gentz's attempt to conflate the conservative opinions of the Federalist Party elite with American opinion in general is an attempt to submerge and deny the ongoing force of prorevolutionary thinking in the early U.S. republic (see also the Illuminati debates and tract by Elihu Palmer in Related Texts).

Beneath the surface of Brown's explicit rejection of counterrevolutionary theory, however, the review also develops an implicit polemic, which was quite legible to knowledgeable contemporaries, against the conservative efforts of the Adams family in particular. The "American Gentleman" cited as translator on the pamphlet's title page was future president of the U.S. John Quincy Adams (1767–1848), second son of then-President John Adams. At this time Quincy Adams was U.S. Minister to Prussia (1797–1801), appointed by his father, and Brown was clear on the triangulation of power that facilitated the rapid Philadelphia publication of a Prussian antirevolutionary tract brought into

---

[2] Gentz's essay was originally published in the May and June 1800 issues of his Berlin *Historisches Journal* as "Der Ursprung und die Grundsätze der Amerikanischen Revoluzion, vergleichen mit dem Ursprung und Grundsätze der Französischen" (3–140).

[3] For more on Gentz, see Reiff, *Friedrich Gentz, an Opponent of the French Revolution and Napoleon.*

English by the highborn son of the sitting Federalist president. Hence the subtext of Brown's discrete but audible closing slap at the quality of the translation, both intellectual and stylistic. More substantially, however, the entire review and notably the passage on American revolutionary thinking near the end, stand as an emphatic rejection of the Federalist orthodoxy that Quincy Adams articulates in his introduction to the translation. There, Adams argued that Gentz's discussion was of special interest to Americans because "it contains the clearest account of the rise and progress of the revolution that established their independence, that has ever appeared within so small a compass; and secondly, because it rescues that revolution from the disgraceful imputation of having proceeded from the same principles as that of France. This error has no where been more frequently repeated, no where of more pernicious tendency than in America itself ... ." Quincy Adams concludes by affirming that the distinction between the two events boils down to "the difference between right *and* wrong*" (3–4).*

After Brown's review was published anonymously in the New York American Review, *short-lived successor to the Brown-edited* Monthly Magazine, *Quincy Adams' younger brother Thomas Boylston Adams (1772–1832) wrote to him on November 30, 1802, identifying the review as Brown's and dismissing Brown as a plebian antagonist, "a small, sly Deist, a disguised, but determined Jacobin, a sort of Sammy Har[r]ison Smith in 'shape and size the same'."* [4] *Scornfully likening Brown to Samuel Harrison Smith, editor of the newly established* National Intelligencer, *then the newspaper voice of the Jefferson administration (and husband of Margaret Bayard Smith, 1778–1844, one of Brown's friends from the New York circle), Boylston Adams' letter completes the cycle of public and private political commentary that linked revolution debates and press wars from Berlin and Paris to London and Philadelphia.*

*****

[...]

This writer is influenced not by the ordinary motives of the disinterested historian, but by the formal purposes of proving, not only that the two revolutions differ, but that the American was a lawful and equitable procedure, while the French revolution was invariably wicked and detestable. Having heard it affirmed, by some, that both transactions were similar, and that what was *lawful* in American, at one time, must, ten years after, be proper in Europe—it is this inference which he endeavours to elude, by disproving the premises that sustain it, namely, the similitude between the two events.

It is evident, that this is merely an argument *ad homines:* It is addressed only to those who praise the one event, merely on account of its resemblance to another, or who endeavour to fix the charge of inconsistency on their opponents, by showing, that they judge contrarily in like cases. Gentz is one of these opponents; and the

---

[4] Adams, Thomas Boylston. Letter to John Quincy Adams. 30 November 1802. The Adams Papers Microfilms, reel 401. Boston: Massachusetts Historical Society, n.d.

present publication was made to repel and confute the charge: to demonstrate, that the advocate of *our* revolution must not necessarily be the champion of the French, since the origin and principles of both transactions are unlike each other. Though much pains are taken to prove this contrariety, we cannot allow that the author's aim is accomplished.

It is true that there are some obvious differences between them. One related to three, and the other to twenty-five millions of men. One was the insurrection of a distant portion of that empire against the authority of the remainder; and ended in the separation and independence of a few provinces in relation to the whole. The other was the effort of the whole nation against the reigning prince, and the established form of government. One introduced no change in the customary distinctions and relations of the citizens, and had no hierarchy or nobility to overturn. The other extended to an enormous and complicated system of ancient abuses in religion and property, and hence occasioned more vehement struggles and signal changes. One reminds us of Venice shaking off the supremacy of the Greek princes—Florence and Milan withstanding the claims of the German Empire—Switzerland spurning the tyranny of the House of Austria—the Netherlands breaking the yoke of Spain. The other is a vivid copy of the internal or domestic changes which incessantly occurred in the Greek and Italian republics of former times; the rancour of whose factions, the ferocity of whose revenges, the suddenness and and terrifying havock of whose *reactions*, were faithful counterparts of the modern French revolution, from which they differ only as the theatre of France is larger than that of Venice, Milan, Florence, of Ephesus or Rhodes; as the *actors* are more numerous; and, consequently, that though, in each, murder, imprisonment, or banishment, are equally the agents, yet *more* are banished or murdered in one case than in the other.

These are, however, not the differences which this writer exhibits. His aim is, to show that the American revolution was *lawful*: an epithet wholly inapplicable to the French.

The term *lawful* is a very ambiguous one. It seems, however, to mean, in this place, that the resistance of the colonies sprung from adherence to certain fundamental maxims of government, which they believed to have been consecrated by the consent and practice of their ancestors, and of the mother country. Their claims were founded on the construction of the constitution under which their oppressors lived, and the terms of which were urged by these oppressors themselves, to justify their conduct.

This writer seems to be aware that there was actually a *revolution* in America; that, at the conclusion of the war, things were not merely replaced upon their old foundations, and that the successful party were not contented with merely repelling encroachments and aggressions, and restricting the power that had spurned restraint to its ancient metes and boundaries; that those who were formerly subjects have now become sovereigns, and that subordination which had, for a whole age, been expressly acknowledged to be lawful and constitutional, was finally disowned and annihilated.

Till the declaration of independence, the resistance might, in a certain sense, be termed *lawful*. In the American remonstrances, prior to that event, loyalty was solemnly avowed, and the terms of laws, statutes and charters, were modestly pleaded; but *after* that period, surely, there was a total alteration in their style. The *rights of man*; the origin of government in the will of the people; the right of the people to consult and decide, in all possible cases, for their common happiness; the absolute *nihility* of all noble and royal pretensions to the government of mankind, were then the only popular topics; and these were not merely insisted on by a few silly individuals, or in a few obscure pamphlets, but were echoed to and fro among senates and armies; were placed, in the cogent and explicit terms, at the head of proclamations and laws; were urged as the sole foundation of the conduct of the American leaders; and are actually the only basis on which the old confederation, the constitutions of all the States, and the federal constitution, have been built. These were not merely speculative notions, but practical maxims. To deny *their existence*, is to deny that we have, at this moment, any governments, any constitutions, at all. There are persons who question the equity and *truth* of these principles, but none can question that on *these* are actually reared the fabrics of our state and general governments; for by whom were some of them drawn up and ratified, but by the immediate representatives of the people? and by whose consent and acquiescence do others (that, for instance, of Connecticut) exist?

It is only by proclaiming independence that a *revolution* was effected. Had not the *rights of man*, the pure sovereignty of the people, superseded the fantastic and groundless claims of the *mother* country, of king and parliament, America would have furnished no object of comparison to this writer.

This total and essential change in the reasons of the contest was very well understood at the time. Every one knows the opposition made to it by those whose conscience forbad them to resist *lawful*, though they were strenuous in opposing *unlawful* authority. Something was due to their king, and though he demanded more than his due, they did not think themselves warranted in refusing what was due. Hence almost all the internal and intestine divisions which fettered the triumphant party in the American war. Those who continued to regard kings and charters as sacred, exclaimed, but ineffectually, against those who urged the natural and indefeasible right of mankind to choose their own form of government, and to consult, without restraint or controul from musty charters and hereditary claims, for their own good. The supremacy and prerogative of the king, and the commercial powers of the British legislature, were maintained by the dissidents from independence, as they were originally admitted by *all* the opponents of the parliamentary pretensions.

The progress of the American revolution resembled the progress of the French, and of every change in the political condition of nations, in all essential particulars.

[...]

Those whose judgment is founded upon actual observation, are well acquainted with the popularity of Paine's writings. It is a mistake to imagine that his popularity arose from the truth or agency of his reasonings and positions. It sprung entirely from their accidentally *coinciding* with the *prepossessions* and opinions of the whole body of the people. The universal avidity, and even transport, with which they were received in cities, villages, and camps, are well remembered. Men were delighted to find a champion of a cause they had already made their own; to be furnished with popular and plausible arguments in favor of doctrines they had already adopted. The experience of all ages shows that this is the sole foundation of the popularity of political writings; they do no more than countenance and strengthen the prevailing opinion.

The arguments which our author quotes from "Common Sense," to show the absurdity of that performance, are strong proofs of the dexterity of Paine, in taking advantage of the reigning prejudices, to combat, not the prerogatives of parliament, but the monarchy itself. It was not *such a work* that produced the American revolution, but only the principles and reasonings of that work previously existing in the mass of the people, and which that work contributed to diffuse still more by clothing them in a popular and intelligible garb.

Our author imagines a great difference between Paine's eloquence and that of the *great authorities* of the time, Adams, Jay, Dickenson, &c.[5] These great authorities reasoned like *lawyers* only *before* the Declaration of Independence (July, 1776), that is, only *before* the *revolution.* How greatly is this writer mistaken in imagining that, after that event, they continued to reason, not like Doctors Price, Tucker, and Priestly, but like the partisans in the House of Commons![6] *How* they reasoned may be easily seen in all their proclamations and constitutional instruments, drawn up in defence of an absolute revolution.

The inference he draws from the *unquestionable aversion* of *most* of the great statesmen of America to the French revolution, is a very fallacious inference, even if the premises were granted; but the premises are unfortunately untrue. A politician of Berlin may be excused for being ignorant of the prevailing opinions in America, at

---

[5] "Adams, Jay, Dickenson, &c.": on pages 57–58 of the translation (pages 105–08 in Gentz's original), in the passage that Brown refers to here, Gentz opposes Paine to John Adams (1735–1826), John Jay (1745–1829), and John Dickenson (1732–1808)—along with Franklin, whose name Brown omits here—as examples of American prorevolutionary argumentation that he claims are incompatible with the "wild, extravagant, and rhapsodical declamation of a Paine" (58). Although there is no information to let us know whether Brown had access to Gentz's original German version, it is notable that he focuses in detail on a passage in which the political transformations of John Adams, father of the translator John Quincy Adams, are in question.

[6] "Doctors Price, Tucker, and Priestly … partisans in the House of Commons!": in the same passage, Gentz asserts that, at the time of the American Revolution, radical Thomas Paine was to John Adams as Dr. Richard Price (a defender of the French Revolution) was to Edmund Burke (its leading opponent) in British revolution debates of the 1790s. While Gentz does mention Price in this passage, Brown has added Tucker and Priestly, not mentioned there by Gentz. Josiah Tucker (1713–1799) was a British economist and political theorist who became an advocate of the American Revolution and debated Burke in pamphlets. Joseph Priestly (1733–1804) was a British dissenting clergyman, natural scientist, and political theorist who was well known as a defender of the French Revolution. He left England for Philadelphia after an anti-French Revolution mob burnt down his home and church in 1791.

the opening of the French revolution; and for not knowing that, notwithstanding all the evils that have accompanied it, it has always been approved and exulted in by two (among many others) of the most eminent American revolutionists—the author of the Farmer's Letters, and the writer of the Declaration of Independence.[7]

In fine, we are obliged to conclude that the *origin* of the two revolutions was *different*, but not *opposite*, and that the *principles* of both were *similar*. It is plain enough, however, that to effectuate their principles, the Americans, from peculiar circumstances, were necessitated to make *fewer* changes; to contend with a less formidable internal and external opposition; and incurred calamities of less extent and duration than the French. What proportion this difference bears to the respective numbers of the two nations, and the probable issue of the struggle of the latter, are curious subjects of the investigation, but too important and arduous for us to undertake.

[…] We cannot much applaud the perspicuity or elegance of the translation.

6. Charles Brockden Brown, *Alcuin; A Dialogue*. Parts I and II from *Alcuin; A Dialogue* (New York: T. & J. Swords, April 1798). Part III from William Dunlap, *The Life of Charles Brockden Brown together with Selections from the Rarest of his Printed Works, from his Original Letters, and from his Manuscripts before Unpublished* (Philadelphia: James P. Parke, 1815)

As befits one of the period's more daring feminist tracts, Alcuin; A Dialogue *has a complex publication history. In late 1796 or early 1797, Brown wrote the dialogue's first two parts and sent copies to his close associate Elihu Hubbard Smith, who often read and circulated new works in his New York circle of male and female friends. Smith then paid for the anonymous publication of parts I and II, which appeared on April 27, 1798 as* Alcuin; A Dialogue, *printed by T. & J. Swords, the same firm that printed Brown's novel* Wieland *(September 1798) and numerous other works by the New York circle. Unbeknownst to Smith, Brown also sent manuscripts of parts I and II to the Philadelphia* Weekly Magazine, *where they were published in March and early April as "The Rights of Women," a title that echoed Mary Wollstonecraft's* A Vindication of the Rights of Woman *(1792), the landmark feminist manifesto that was republished throughout the 1790s in England and the U.S. (see Related Texts). The* Weekly Magazine *version*

---

[7] "The author of the Farmer's Letters, and the writer of the Declaration of Independence": that is, the previously mentioned John Dickenson, who published *Letters from a Farmer in Pennsylvania: To the Inhabitants of the British Colonies* (1767–1768) and Thomas Jefferson, who drafted the U.S. Declaration of Independence in 1776.

abridges the version published by Smith[1] and additionally edits out a few details that were apparently considered politically indiscrete or inflammatory by that magazine's editor.[2]

*While Smith was proofreading the first two parts for publication, he received the final parts III and IV from Brown, and consequently included an editorial "advertisement" in the printed volume of parts I and II: "The reception which the present publication shall meet will probably determine the author to withhold or print the continuation." Partly because Smith died from yellow fever during the 1798 New York epidemic, and also likely because their content was perceived as too radical for period publishers (the prevailing political atmosphere in 1798 was one of counterrevolutionary reaction), Alcuin's final sections never appeared during Brown's lifetime. The missing material (discussed by Brown and Smith as parts III and IV) was not published until William Dunlap included some or all of it in his 1815 biographical miscellany of Brown's rare and unpublished writings (*The Life of Charles Brockden Brown together with Selections from the Rarest of his Printed Works, etc.*).[3] But since Dunlap did not number the sections or distinguish between them, scholars now refer to the missing material published by Dunlap as "part III," even though it may (or may not) comprise both of the parts that Brown and Smith knew as III and IV. All of the extant parts of the dialogue were not in fact assembled and published together in a single volume until 1970, over 150 years after the different parts first appeared. What became of part IV? Did Dunlap simply collapse the parts that Brown and Smith discussed as III and IV? The missing material added by Dunlap is as long as parts I and II combined. Or, alternatively, does the abrupt ending of the text as we have it today suggest that the manuscript went on to discuss matters that Dunlap omitted because he feared they would damage Brown's reputation in the culturally conservative 1810s?*

Alcuin *was Brown's first extended prose publication and largely draws its arguments from Woldwinite writings on women's rights, especially the arguments that women are infantilized by their dress and their lack of education in history, politics, philosophy, and*

---

[1] "The Rights of Women" appeared in four *Weekly Magazine* installments on March 17, 24, 31 and April 7, 1798. It differs from the Smith-Swords material primarily by omitting a large portion of Part II, from "The maxims of constitution-makers sound well" to "utility to others which they exclude," and replacing that section with a bridge paragraph (see notes 33–34).

[2] The significant edits in the *Weekly Magazine* version will be mentioned in the footnotes in this edition. Parts I and II also exist in two separate manuscript transcriptions in the notebooks of Brown's father Elijah Brown and thus the text comes to us in four different versions in all. The father's transcriptions do not provide a more authoritative text than the printed versions, however, and thus we do not discuss them here apart from one variant in our note 35. For a full account of the dialogue's textual history and variants, see S. W. Reid's "Textual Essay" and appendices in the Kent State Bicentennial edition of *Alcuin*.

[3] The Dunlap biography was begun and partly drafted by Paul Allen; Dunlap took over the project after Allen failed to complete it. Dunlap inherited the *Alcuin* material now published as "Part III" from the earlier, Allen version. For more, see the Introductions to the two scholarly reprints of Allen's first version of the biography by Bennett, and by Hemenway and Katz.

science; that the ideology of passionate romance is incompatible with egalitarian rights; and that marriage is a form of institutionalized slavery.[4] *While Alcuin clearly draws from Brown's contemporaries on women's rights, it is nevertheless significant and noteworthy in its own right, particularly on account of three new gestures that distinguish Brown's positions from those of his predecessors.*

First, Brown chooses a literary form that fits his argumentative purpose. Unlike most other period calls for women's rights, including Wollstonecraft's, Brown does not use the form of a rhetorical polemic in which the author speaks in her or his own persona against other writers and argues against the injustice of denying rights to women. Alcuin presents its argument in the form of a dialogue, which means that neither the first-person narrator Alcuin nor his interlocutor Mrs. Carter can be understood simply as Brown's puppets or surrogates. Because the Woldwinites believed in the primacy of intimate conversation as a model for mutual pedagogy and transformation, Brown records the exchanges between Alcuin and Mrs. Carter in such a way as to encourage the silent reader to enter into the conversation as she or he considers the sallies between the two. Brown wants his readers to experience the way that the speakers' ideas develop through the course of their dialogue, often reversing and shifting their initial claims. This form of presentation—exchanging public polemics for the more dynamic and supple context of overheard conversation in a semi-public, semi-private salon—enacts Brown's belief that social change emerges from an intimate circle's renovation of its members' personal attitudes and behavior, rather than from the public sphere of publication and political legislation.

Second, while Brown moves away from a traditional "one-sex" model of gender relations, he nevertheless does not introduce a later "two-sex" notion of sexual difference. In early modern "one-sex" accounts, the male was considered the norm and the female defined by its absence, that is, as a person lacking male attributes. In this way of thinking, there was simply one normative sex—the male's—rather than the notion that women and men both have significant gendered attributes and traits. Like progressives today, at the beginning of the twenty-first century, Brown understands the difference between "sex" and "gender," the distinction between (presumably natural and unchanging) anatomical differences of sex on the one hand, and variable cultural codes of masculinity and femininity on the other. While gender codes cement behavioral assumptions to bodies in ways that seem natural and commonsensical but are in fact socially conditioned and subject to historical transformation, the biological category of sex is presumably permanent and given in nature. Yet even progressives like Wollstonecraft tended to use "masculinity" as the ideal and "femininity" as a deformed state. Thus, for example, a brave woman was praised for her masculinity while a servile man was condemned for his effeminacy. While traces of this reversion appear in Ormond *(see the descriptions of Martinette and Helena), it is notable*

---

[4] For discussions of the dialogue, see Arner, "Historical Essay"; Burgett, "Between Speculation and Population"; Davidson, "The Manner and Matter of Charles Brockden Brown's *Alcuin*"; Fleischmann, *A Right View of the Subject* and "Charles Brockden Brown: Feminism in Fiction"; Krause, "Brockden Brown's Feminism in Fact and Fiction"; Schloss, "Intellectuals and Women: Social Rivalry in Charles Brockden Brown's *Alcuin*"; and Vickers, "'Pray Madam, are you a Federalist?': Women's Rights and the Republican Utopia in *Alcuin*."

that Alcuin attempts to move beyond these gender stereotypes, suggesting a more androgy-nous ideal in details such as the modes of dress and shared labor in the described utopia of part III. Utility in performing necessary tasks, rather than coded assumptions about sex or gender, seems to prevail in this description.

Finally, the dialogue implicitly abandons the idea that abstract equality concerning rights or legal status is an adequate approach to questions of gender inequality. Instead, it advocates a more thorough and more transformative understanding of the senses in which both men and women are entrapped by sexual codes. In this argument, it is not enough to advocate the "rights" of woman since, in fact, the current state of society needs changing in a wider sense. This change will come about through the innovation of beliefs, rather than through legislation or a violent revolution in the streets. Although the term "ideology" was not historically available to Brown in 1798, his repeated comments concerning opinion (as a means by which dominant groups exercise power) foreshadow the argument that ideas and cultural beliefs are their own field of social conflict.

In parts I and II, Alcuin and Mrs. Carter initially frame their debate about women in terms of separate spheres. Women enclose themselves within the intimate or domestic sphere of the household, while men can roam the public sphere of political economy and professional training. When women attempt to leave their cloistered state, they usually be-come objects of public scandal, not active participants in public debate. Mrs. Carter ar-gues that this division is a product of unequal access to education, but Alcuin claims that women can learn about the world, albeit indirectly, since worldly events and commodity chains inevitably seep into the most isolated realms. For Alcuin, women can understand the linkage between private acts and public interchanges, thereby revealing the inade-quacy of the prevailing notion of separate spheres. This claim about the connectedness (rather than the separation) of the public and private spheres sets up the remainder of part I as a debate between the competing ideals of individual liberty and social equality. Alcuin insists that while it is unusual for women to enter the professions of medicine, law, and divinity, or to have control over property, there is no structural barrier that absolutely prohibits individual women from these practices. Carter responds by noting that excep-tional cases involving a very few successful women do not disprove the larger social impo-sition of inequality for the great majority, especially nonbourgeois women. Alcuin circumvents this claim by arguing that while social divisions of gendered labor do exist, these are only residues of an aristocratic lifeworld, remnants of the old regime of prerevo-lutionary monarchies. Once (bourgeois) civil society overcomes the old order, he argues, both genders will achieve "eminent virtue and true happiness."

Partly because Alcuin's claims lay the ground for a critique of the then-current political system, the two seemingly hesitate to continue until Alcuin restates the opening question, asking whether Mrs. Carter is a federalist, now understood both in the broad sense of loy-alty to the U.S. system of republican government, as well as the narrow sense of allegiance to a particular political party.[5] Mrs. Carter indicates her unhappiness with a political

---

[5] In the political party terminology of the 1790s, Federalists are the more Anglophile, moneyed elite, and conservative party (the party of the Washington and Adams administrations), and

and legal system that treats women as socially dead, taken out of the "class of existences," or categories that identify subjects as enfranchised citizens. In America, women seem to exist only as child-bearers and -rearers, either for the mechanical purposes of reproduction or as "republican mothers," raising male youth (for this outlook, see Rush in Related Texts). If aristocratic societies were tyrannical, then the contemporary social order is another form of despotism, since it relies on a representative system in which citizens elect politicians to represent their collective interests. Given that the early American republic disenfranchises entire categories of humans, such as the young, recent immigrants, the (laboring) poor who do not earn enough to pay taxes, (free and enslaved) African Americans, and women, Mrs. Carter notes a fundamental contradiction in the early U.S. social order. She observes that the Constitution claims in theory that "all power is derived from the people" and "liberty is every one's birthright," but that in practice the power to participate actively in government is restricted to an elite minority of wealthy, white men. A "republican" despotism may take a different form than an "aristocratic" one, but both remain deeply exclusionary and hierarchical. Because the principles of "equality and liberty" are "openly and grossly violated" by the existing social structure (rather than simply by the idiosyncrasy of particular individuals), as Carter notes at the beginning of part II, she refuses to support the federal union or its political parties, whether "Federalist" or "Democratic-Republican."

Alcuin responds that a government cannot be judged simply by the legal "form" of power; we must also consider its "spirit" or the way that power is exercised. Since "no government is independent of popular opinion," even if its people are not all formally empowered to participate as active citizens, then the exclusion of women must be due to their consent to be ruled and represented by men. Assuming the audience's knowledge that women at this time were not enfranchised—did not have the right to vote—Mrs. Carter reiterates that the principle of sovereignty by the people means that the entire population must be consulted in electoral exercises, not simply incorporated within the wishes of elite groups. Alcuin suggests that it might be better to have smaller republics, where the fraction that is excluded might be smaller, but Carter responds that a smaller unit is not any more or less fair. She also claims that while sexual difference is arbitrary, a female political actor is more shocking to the public than a young, poor, or foreign male. Alcuin responds by arguing that women do not desire change since this would neutralize their sexual attractiveness, which constitutes a distinct form of power. Mrs. Carter archly asks how Alcuin knows what women want. He then admits that notions taken to be commonsensical are not necessarily so because their claims are true, but simply because these claims are believed to be true. Alcuin's strategic retreat appears as he ends part II by arguing that, in this light, Mrs. Carter mistakes the source of political power and the nature of social change. Social change is not catalyzed by changing the legal structure of political government, he asserts, but by transforming cultural attitudes and expectations.

Democratic-Republicans are the more socially and regionally heterogeneous Francophile party (which comes to power after 1800 in the Jefferson and Madison administrations). Alcuin's reference in Part I to conservative publicist William Cobbett (alias Peter Porcupine), for example, is a critical allusion to Federalist Party positions (see notes 19–20).

Part III begins with Alcuin's allegorical claim to have visited an island utopia, "the paradise of women," where women dress no differently than men. Because both dress according to the usefulness of their garb, women are freed from the tyranny of looking pretty for the male gaze. Similarly, women and men receive the same education. The division between gendered forms of mental and manual labor is avoided since all participate in the physical labor of farming and the intellectual labor of learning.

When the discussion turns to marriage, Alcuin pauses for fear that it may be improper to discuss sexual intercourse or interaction in public conversation. Here Mrs. Carter seizes the initiative and increasingly places Alcuin on the defensive. From this point on, she speaks more forcefully and with fewer interruptions from Alcuin, until the discussion concludes with an analysis of the interdependence of public law and private behavior, effectively rejecting the separation of spheres with which the dialogue began.

Carter rejects then-current norms of marriage as forms of institutional slavery for women. The prevailing laws of coverture,[6] she notes, in which a woman's property becomes entirely controlled by her husband, make married women dependent on their spouses. Upon marriage, women lose control of both their prenuptial property and their own liberty. Carter counters that no property should be transferred between spouses or even shared, since it is not necessary for a husband and wife even to live together. She argues for easier divorce laws so that women can regain their liberty. When Alcuin makes a conventional objection that divorce would damage children and lead to moral decline, Carter responds that children are hurt more by living in environments shaped by mutual hostility between parents. As for morality and romance, Carter rejects the idea of romantic marriage, saying that "love" is an "empty and capricious passion" based on "sensual attachment" that vanishes after marriage, forcing the adults to dissimulate their physical interest in one another. It is this normalized insincerity that is morally corrosive, not the frank admission of changing states of attraction. Carter seems to champion the idea of romantic or erotic friendship in a relation that includes sexuality, but which is based on a couple's rational (rather than passionate) attraction and esteem.

Mrs. Carter opposes marriage because it is a contractual state that coerces future behavior. Her argument is that marriage should be based on "free and mutual consent," "friendship," and "personal fidelity"; and that partners should be able to dissolve it at will. With Mrs. Carter's final words, Alcuin reaches well beyond a vision of "equality" feminism, in which women should have the same legal rights as men, to probe a structural reformation of the social institutions and practices that contour the construction of gender.

---

[6] Laws of coverture are the body of early modern English common law regulating women's legal status and personhood in this period. Under Anglo-American common law, women had no legal personhood or formal, statutory independence. A woman's legal identity (and consequently her right to own property, sign contracts, and so on) was absorbed into or "covered" by that of her father, husband, or other male guardian. In the Anglo-Norman legal terminology of this system an unmarried woman was a *feme sole* (a woman alone), a married woman a *feme covert* (a covered woman). Although it abolished titles and primogeniture, the American Revolution did not change these laws concerning women's subordination. For a discussion of coverture and its relation to the period's U.S. reading culture, see Kerber, *Women of the Republic*; and Davidson, *Revolution and the Word*.

In this vision, it is not enough for women to be made legally the same as men, to enjoy the same version of legal personhood or citizen status as their male counterparts. Instead, the entire system of practices and assumptions regulating the "intercourse" of real women and men needs to be reformed for the sake of all.

*****

ADVERTISEMENT

THE following Dialogue was put into my hands, the last spring, by a friend who re-sides at a distance, with liberty to make it public. I have since been informed that he has continued the discussion of the subject, in another dialogue. The reception which the present publication shall meet with will probably determine the author to withhold or print the continuation.

E. H. SMITH.

New-York, March, 1798.

*****

ALCUIN

PART I

I CALLED last evening on Mrs. Carter.[7] I had no previous acquaintance with her. Her brother is a man of letters, who, nevertheless, finds little leisure from the en-

---

[7] "Mrs. Carter": seemingly an allusion to Elizabeth Carter (1717–1806), an English poet, translator, and writer. Thanks to her father's interest in her education, the historical Carter was skilled in classical languages, history, and mathematics, like Constantia and Martinette in *Ormond*. Carter was a core member of the Blue Stockings Society to which *Ormond* also alludes indirectly. Founded in the 1750s, the society was an informal discussion group mainly led by educated women who were often creative producers of writing and images in their own right. Men attended by invitation. Led by writer Elizabeth Montagu (1718–1800) and Elizabeth Vesey (1715–1791), other notable members included poet and writer Anna Letitia Barbauld (1743–1825); artist Angelica Kauffmann (1741–1807, referenced in Chapter 13 of *Ormond*); writer Charlotte Lennox (1720–1804); historian Catherine Macaulay (1731–1791); and writer Hannah More (1745–1833).

The group's name originates in an anecdote. Benjamin Stillingfleet (1702–1771), naturalist and writer, remarked to Vesey that he did not have formal attire to attend a social gathering. Vesey is said to have replied that he should come in his blue stockings, that is, in everyday clothing. The gesture highlights the group's dedication to meritocratic conversational exchange that refuses traditional status barriers signified by dress. Like many of the period's discussion groups, the society forbad discussion of political topics that might disrupt the meeting's amity. It aimed for an atmosphere in which women could engage with cultural and intellectual questions free from the limitations imposed by traditional female "beauty" (enacted in the commitment to informal dress) or traditional codes of "eroticism" in which women gathered around men in an atmosphere of drinking and gambling.

gagements of a toilsome profession. He scarcely spends an evening at home, yet takes care to invite, specially and generally, to his house, every one who enjoys the reputation of learning and probity. His sister became, on the death of her husband, his house-keeper. She was always at home. The guests who came in search of the man, finding him abroad, lingered a little as politeness enjoined, but soon found something in the features and accents[8] of the lady, that induced them to prolong their stay, for their own sake: nay, without any well-defined expectation of meeting their inviter, they felt themselves disposed to repeat their visit. We must suppose the conversation of the lady not destitute of attractions; but an additional, and perhaps, the strongest inducement, was the society of other visitants. The house became, at length, a sort of rendezvous of persons of different ages and conditions, but respectable for talents or virtues. A commodious apartment, excellent tea, lemonade, and ice—and wholesome fruits—were added to the pleasures of instructive society:[9] no wonder that Mrs. Carter's *coterie* became the favourite resort of the liberal and ingenious.

These things did not necessarily imply any uncommon merit in the lady. Skill in the superintendence of a tea-table, affability and modesty, promptness to enquire, and docility to listen, were all that were absolutely requisite in the mistress of the ceremonies. Her apartment was nothing, perhaps, but a lyceum open at stated hours, and to particular persons, who enjoyed, gratis, the benefits of rational discourse, and agreeable repasts. Some one was required to serve the guests, direct the menials, and maintain, with suitable vigilance, the empire of cleanliness and order. This office might not be servile, merely because it was voluntary. The influence of an unbribed inclination might constitute the whole difference between her and a waiter at an inn, or the porter of a theatre.

Books are too often insipid.[10] In reading, the senses are inert and sluggish, or they are solicited by foreign objects. To spur up the flagging attention, or check the rapidity of its flights and wildness of its excursions, are often found to be impracticable. It

---

[8] "Features and accents": Brown and other eighteenth-century writers often use this phrase to indicate the physical and aural affinities created by an individual's welcoming sensibility, which was thought to be capable to overcoming traditional social exclusions of rank and status. In this case, male visitors sympathetically respond to Mrs. Carter's thoughtful intelligence and her cultivation of an "instructive society," a salon organized according to intellectual merit rather than quasi-aristocratic rank.

[9] "Excellent tea, lemonade … instructive society": the list of nonalcoholic drinks and vegetarian repast is a conventional sign that the American Carter's salon follows the behavioral precepts of her English counterparts.

[10] "Insipid": the argument that intellectual enlightenment is best achieved through interpersonal dialogue rather than isolated reflection on objects such as books or solipsistic lecturing is a touchstone of the Woldwinite belief system. It celebrates the practice of rational sentiment, rather than the automatic response to the presence of another body. For similar complaints about the inefficacy of books as instruments of learning, see Godwin in Related Texts as well as Chapter 24 of Brown's novel *Arthur Mervyn, Second Part*.

is only on extraordinary occasions that this faculty is at once sober and vigorous, active and obedient. The revolutions of our minds may be watched and noted, but can seldom be explained to the satisfaction of the inquisitive. All that the caprice of nature has left us, is to profit by the casual presence of that which can, by no spell, be summoned or detained.

I hate a lecturer. I find little or no benefit in listening to a man who does not occasionally call upon me for my opinion, and allow me to canvass every step in his argument. I cannot, with any satisfaction, survey a column, how costly soever its materials, and classical its ornaments, when I am convinced that its foundation is sand which the next tide will wash away. I equally dislike formal debate, where each man, however few his ideas, is subjected to the necessity of drawing them out to the length of a speech. A single proof, or question, or hint, may be all that the state of the controversy, or the reflections of the speaker suggest: but this must be amplified and iterated, till the sense, perhaps, is lost or enfeebled, that he may not fall below the dignity of an orator. Conversation, careless, and unfettered, that is sometimes abrupt and sententious, sometimes fugitive and brilliant, and sometimes copious and declamatory, is a scene for which, without being much accustomed to it, I entertain great affection. It blends, more happily than any other method of instruction, utility and pleasure. No wonder I was desirous of knowing, long before the opportunity was afforded me, how far these valuable purposes were accomplished by the frequenters of Mrs. Carter's lyceum.

In the morning I had met the doctor at the bed-side of a sick friend, who had strength enough to introduce us to each other. At parting I received a special invitation for the evening, and a general one to be in force at all other times. At five o'clock I shut up my little school, and changed an alley in the city—dark, dirty, and narrow, as all alleys are—for the fresh air and smooth footing of the fields. I had not forgotten the doctor and his lyceum. Shall I go (said I to myself), or shall I not? No, said the pride of poverty, and the bashfulness of inexperience. I looked at my unpowdered locks, my worsted stockings, and my pewter buckles.[11] I bethought me of my embarrassed air, and my uncouth gait. I pondered on the superciliousness of wealth

---

[11] "Unpowdered locks … worsted stockings … pewter buckles": the narrator, soon to be self-named as Alcuin, indicates his nonelite status by means of dress codes. He wears his hair naturally, without the white powdered wigs of the gentleman political elites (hence his later critical remarks associating barbers with old regime practices); his leggings are made—possibly self-made—from knitted wool, rather than more expensive and "refined" silk; and he wears pewter buckles instead of buttons made from more expensive metals. The use of buckles also suggests that Alcuin may be Quaker, since traditionally the Society of Friends rejected buttons as prideful clothing that violated their "plain style." Because modes of dress and different types of fabric were important social markers and manifestations of political allegiance in the period, Alcuin clearly does not have the "look" of a Federalist Party partisan. The Federalists then in power had Tory, Anglophile attitudes about behavior and dress that often repeated the social prejudices of the English gentry (see note 3), wearing "old regime" wigs, silk stockings, and so on. The mention of ordinary stockings may also allude to the Blue Stockings Society discussed in note 7.

and talents, the awfulness of flowing muslin,[12] the mighty task of hitting on a right movement at entrance, and a right posture in sitting, and on the perplexing mysteries of tea-table decorum: but, though confused and panic-struck, I was not vanquished.

I had some leisure, particularly in the evening. Could it be employed more agreeably or usefully? To read, to write, to meditate; to watch a declining moon, and the varying firmament, with the emotions of poetry or piety—with the optics of Dr. Young, or of De la Lande[13]—were delightful occupations, and all at my command. Eight hours of the twenty-four were consumed in repeating the names and scrawling the forms of the alphabet, or in engraving on infantile memories that twice three make six; the rest was employed in supplying an exhausted, rather than craving, stomach; in sleep, that never knew, nor desired to know, the luxury of down, and the pomp of tissue;[14] in unravelling the mazes of Dr. Waring;[15] or in amplifying the seducing suppositions of 'if I were a king,' or, 'if I were a lover.' Few, indeed, are as happy as Alcuin.[16] What is requisite to perfect my felicity, but the blessings of health,

---

[12] "Awfulness of flowing muslin": awe-inspiring; that is, not the contemporary sense of inferior. Muslin is a cotton weave often used for dresses.

[13] "Optics of Dr. Young, or of De la Lande": two contemporary astronomers. There is more than one contemporary "Dr. Young," but the reference here is most likely to Dr. Joseph Young (1735–1814), a New York physician and author of one of the first U.S. medical textbooks. His *A New System of Astronomy* (New York: Hopkins, 1800) appeared one year later than *Alcuin* and was reviewed in December 1800 in the Brown-edited New York *Monthly Magazine*. Brown would have known of Young's work before the book's publication through common associates in New York medical circles. Jérôme Lalande (1732–1802) was a French scientist who helped popularize the study of astronomy and who is likewise discussed in articles on astronomy in the *Monthly Magazine*.

[14] "Luxury of down, and the pomp of tissue": expensive down feathers used for stuffing cushions and fragile gauze, in this case used for embroidery of fine bedding.

[15] "Mazes of Dr. Waring": Edward Waring (1736–1798), an English analytical mathematician known for algebraic equations and the treatment of curves and conical sections. His challenging work presents "mazes" because he is commonly associated with the difficulties of "Waring's Problem" (according to which every positive integer is the sum of not more than nine cubes or the sum of not more than nineteen fourth powers) and "Waring's Prime Number Conjecture" (in which every odd integer exceeding three is either a prime number or the sum of three prime numbers). The theoretical issues raised by both these "Problems" were not resolved or superceded until the early twentieth century.

[16] "Alcuin": the only appearance of the narrator's pseudonym or persona (given as "Edwin" in the *Weekly Magazine* version). The historical Alcuin (c. 732–804) was an important intellectual and church scholar at the Court of Charlemagne, noted for his pedagogy, or doctrines concerning teaching and learning. Born in Northumbria (present-day northeast England), he attracted many students to York. Returning from a trip to Rome, he met Charlemagne, who convinced him to take charge of the palace school in France, where Alcuin built up the library and theorized a modern curriculum. Many of his students became major figures of the Carolingian Renaissance in learning. Consequently the historical Alcuin figures as a pre-Enlightenment intellectual who foreshadows later ideals of cosmopolitan curiosity and fellowship among scholars. He provides an apt name for the narrator, suggesting a commitment to scholarly conversation and dialogic learning without the

which is incompatible with periodical head-achs, and the visits of rheumatism; —of peace, which cannot maintain its post against the hum of a school, the discord of cartwheels, and the rhetoric of a notable landlady; —of competence—My trade preserves me from starving and nakedness, but not from the discomforts of scarcity, or the disgrace of shabbiness. Money, to give me leisure; and exercise, to give me health; these are all my lot denies: in all other respects I am the happiest of mortals. The pleasures of society, indeed, I seldom taste: that is, I have few opportunities of actual intercourse with that part of mankind whose ideas extend beyond the occurrences of the neighbourhood, or the arrangements of their household. Not but that, when I want company, it is always at hand. My solitude is populous whenever my fancy thinks proper to people it, and with the very beings that best suit my taste. These beings are, perhaps, on account of my slender experience, too uniform, and somewhat grotesque. Like some other dealers in fiction, I find it easier to give new names to my visionary friends, and vary their condition, than to introduce a genuine diversity into their characters. No one can work without materials. My stock is slender. There are times when I feel a moment's regret that I do not enjoy the means of enlarging it.— But this detail, it must be owned, is a little beside the purpose. I merely intended to have repeated my conversation with Mrs. Carter, but have wandered, unawares, into a dissertation on my own character. I shall now return, and mention that I cut short my evening excursion, speeded homeward, and, after japanning[17] anew my shoes, brushing my hat, and equipping my body in its best geer, proceeded to the doctor's house.

I shall not stop to describe the company, or to dwell on those embarrassments and awkwardnesses always incident to an unpolished wight like me. Suffice it to say, that I was in a few minutes respectfully withdrawn into a corner, and fortunately a near neighbour of the lady. To her, after much deliberation and forethought, I addressed myself thus: "Pray, Madam, are you a federalist?"[18]

The theme of discourse was political. The edicts of Carnot, and the commentary of that profound jurist, Peter Porcupine,[19] had furnished ample materials of

---

burden of fame, doctrinal significance, or theological conquest. Interestingly, the historical Alcuin's writings are the source of the well-known adage *vox populi, vox dei* (the voice of the people is the voice of god), although he wrote the phrase not to affirm this idea but to criticize it.

[17] "Japanning": japanning means varnishing with "japan," a glossy black lacquer; and, by extension, "to polish or cover with black" (*OED*). The term recalls the lacquered objects that reached the Atlantic world through early modern trade with Japan.

[18] "Federalist": the Federalist Party was the ruling political party in the U.S. in 1798, the party of Washington and then-President John Adams (see note 5). Alcuin's question is provocative because it violates the convention, in many of the period's discussion groups, that politics remain off limits in order to preserve the meeting's presumed goodwill. Despite such conventions, however, this meeting seems to encourage political conflict by inviting opinions on the French Revolution, then a notoriously divisive topic.

[19] "Edicts of Carnot ... profound jurist, Peter Porcupine": two notable figures on opposite ends of the period's political spectrum, indicating that the conversation concerns political topics that are

discussion.[20] This was my hint. The question, to be sure, was strange; especially addressed to a lady: but I could not, by all my study, light upon a better mode of beginning discourse. She did not immediately answer. I resumed—I see my question produces a smile, and a pause.

True (said she). A smile may well be produced by its novelty, and a pause by its difficulty.

Is it so hard to say what your creed is on this subject? Judging from the slight observation of this evening, I should imagine that to you the theme was far from being new.

She answered, that she had been often called upon to listen to discussions of this sort, but did not recollect when her opinion had been asked.

Will you favour me (said I) with your opinion notwithstanding?

Surely (she replied) you are in jest. What! ask a woman—shallow and inexperienced as all women are known to be, especially with regard to these topics—her opinion on any political question! What in the name of decency have we to do with politics? If you inquire the price of this ribbon, or at what shop I purchased that set of China, I may answer you, though I am not sure that you would be the wiser for my answer. These things, you know, belong to the women's province. We are surrounded by men and politicians. You must observe that they consider themselves in an element congenial to their sex and station. The daringness of female curiosity[21] is well known; yet it is seldom so adventurous as to attempt to penetrate into the mysteries of government.

It must be owned (said I) there is sufficient reason for their forbearance. Most men have trades; but every woman has a trade. They are universally trained to the use of

---

partisan and polarizing. Lazare Carnot (1753–1823) was a French general, engineer, and politician. During the French Revolution, Carnot was a member of the Jacobin Committee of Public Safety, charged with defending France militarily. After Robespierre's execution ended the Terror in 1794, he continued to occupy leading posts in the Directory phase of the Revolution (1794–1798). The "edict" referred to here is likely Carnot's institution of a military draft, since he established compulsory education and military service for all French men between the age of twenty and twenty-five. "Peter Porcupine" was the pen name of journalist and, at this time, ultra-conservative propagandist William Cobbett (1763–1835). The ironic descriptor "profound jurist" indicates that Alcuin is making fun of Cobbett's extremism. Born in England, Cobbett fled France in 1792 for Philadelphia, where he made a name for himself as a frequently offensive journalist who supported the Federalist Party and incessantly attacked the oppositional Democrat-Republicans led by Vice President Thomas Jefferson. Cobbett left the U.S. in 1800 after Dr. Benjamin Rush—the mentor of Brown's friend Elihu Hubbard Smith, the same friend who paid for the publication of *Alcuin* and signed it as "editor"—successfully sued him for libel. Surprisingly, Cobbett became famous as a laboring-class activist after returning to England.

[20] "The edicts … discussion": the politicized references to Carnot and Porcupine were edited out of the *Weekly Magazine* version, where the sentence read instead: "The present condition of our country had furnished ample materials of discussion."

[21] "Curiosity": curiosity is an important key word in eighteenth-century debates about social history and the pursuit of knowledge, particularly among the Woldwinite writers who are Brown's primary models. The term has an ambivalent meaning: it reflects the Enlightenment desire to learn, but can also lead to unchecked (sexual) excess.

the needle, and the government of a family. No wonder that they should be most willing to handle topics that are connected with their daily employment, and the arts in which they are proficient.—Merchants may be expected to dwell with most zeal on the prices of the day, and those numerous incidents, domestic and foreign, by which commerce is affected. Lawyers may quote the clauses of a law, or the articles of a treaty, without forgetting their profession, or travelling, as they phrase it, out of the record. Physicians will be most attached to livid carcases and sick beds. Women are most eloquent on a fan or a tea-cup—on the furniture of a nursery, or the qualifications of a chambermaid. How should it be otherwise? In so doing, the merchant, the lawyer, the physician, and the matron, may all equally be said to stick to their lasts. Doubtless every one's last requires some or much of his attention. The only fault lies in sometimes allowing it wholly to engross his faculties, and often in overlooking considerations that are of the utmost importance to them, even as members of a profession.

Well (said the lady), now you talk reasonably. Your inference is, that women occupy their proper sphere, when they confine themselves to the tea-table and their work-bag: but this sphere, whatever you may think, is narrow. They are obliged to wander, at times, in search of variety. Most commonly they digress into scandal, and this has been their eternal reproach; with how much reason perhaps you can tell me.

Most unjustly, as it seems to me. Women profit by their opportunities. They are trained to a particular art. Their minds are, of course, chiefly occupied by images and associations drawn from this art. If this be blameable, it is not more so in them, than in others. It is a circumstance that universally takes place. It is by no means clear, that a change in this respect is either possible or desirable. The arts of women are far from contemptible, whether we consider the skill that is required by them, or, which is a better criterion, their usefulness in society. They are more honourable than many professions allotted to the men; those of soldier and barber for example; on one of which we may justly bestow all the contempt, and on the other all the abhorrence that we have to spare.[22] But though we may strive, we can never wholly extinguish in women the best principle of human nature, curiosity. We cannot shut them out from all commerce with the world. We may nearly withhold from them all knowledge of the past, because that is chiefly contained in books; and it is possible to interdict them from reading, or, to speak more accurately, withhold from them those incitements to study, which no human beings bring into the world with them, but must owe to external and favourable occurrences. But they must be, in some degree, witnesses of what is passing. Theirs is a limited sphere, in which they are accurate observers. They see and hear, somewhat of the actions and characters of those around them. These are, of course, remembered; become the topics of reflection; and, when opportunity offers, they delight to produce and compare them. All this is perfectly natural and reasonable. I cannot, for my life, discover any causes of censure in it.

---

[22] "Those of soldier and barber … have to spare": the *Weekly Magazine* version edits out the critical remarks on soldiers and barbers.

Very well, indeed (cried the lady), I am glad to meet with so zealous an advocate. I am ready enough to adopt a plausible apology for the peculiarities of women. And yet it is a new doctrine that would justify triflers and slanderers. According to this system, it would be absurd to blame those who are perpetually prying into other people's affairs, and industriously blazoning every disadvantageous or suspicious tale.

My dear Madam, you mistake me. Artists may want skill; historians may be partial. Far be it from me to applaud the malignant or the stupid. Ignorance and envy are no favourites of mine, whether they have or have not a chin to be shaved: but nothing would be more grossly absurd than to suppose these defects to be peculiar to female artists, or the historians of the tea-table. When these defects appear in the most flagrant degree, they are generally capable of an easy apology. If the sexes had in reality separate interests, and it were not absurd to set more value on qualifications on account of their belonging to one of our own sex, it is the women who may justly triumph. Together with power and property, the men have likewise asserted their superior claim to vice and folly.

If I understand you rightly (said the lady), you are of opinion that the sexes are essentially equal.

It appears to me (answered I), that human beings are moulded by the circumstances in which they are placed. In this they are all alike. The differences that flow from the sexual distinction, are as nothing in the balance.

And yet women are often reminded that none of their sex are to be found among the formers of States, and the instructors of mankind—that Pythagoras, Lycurgus, and Socrates, Newton, and Locke, were not women.[23]

True; nor were they mountain savages, nor helots, nor shoemakers.[24] You might as well expect a Laplander to write Greek spontaneously, and without instruction, as that any one should be wise or skillful, without suitable opportunities. I humbly presume one has a better chance of becoming an astronomer by gazing at the stars through a telescope, than in eternally plying the needle or snapping the scissars. To settle a bill of fare, to lard a pig, to compose a pudding, to carve a goose, are tasks that do not, in any remarkable degree, tend to instil the love, or facilitate the acquisition of literature and science. Nay, I do not form prodigious expectations even of one who reads a novel or comedy once a month, or chants once a day to her harpsichord the hunter's stupid invocation to Phoebus or Cynthia.[25] Women are generally superficial and ignorant, because they are generally cooks and sempstresses. Men are the slaves of habit. It is doubtful whether the career of the species will ever terminate in knowledge. Certain it is, they began in ignorance. Habit has given permanence to errors,

---

[23] "Pythagoras, Lycurgus, and Socrates, Newton, and Locke ... not women": iconic examples of male philosophers, scientists, and lawmakers from the classical Greece to the Enlightenment.

[24] "Nor helots, nor shoemakers": "Nor shoemakers" was omitted in the *Weekly Magazine* version. Helots were the slave class of ancient Sparta.

[25] "The hunter's stupid invocation to Phoebus or Cynthia": that is, a song that is ridiculous and clichéd, using stilted allegorical and classical language such "Phoebus" for the Sun, or "Cynthia" for the Moon.

which ignorance had previously rendered universal. They are prompt to confound things, which are really distinct; and to persevere in a path to which they have been accustomed. Hence it is that certain employments have been exclusively assigned to women, and that their sex is supposed to disqualify them for any other. Women are defective. They are seldom or never metaphysicians, chemists, or lawgivers. Why? Because they are sempstresses and cooks. This is unavoidable. Such is the unalterable constitution of human nature. They cannot read who never saw an alphabet. They who know no tool but the needle, cannot be skillful at the pen.

Yes (said the lady); of all forms of injustice, that is the most egregious which makes the circumstance of sex a reason for excluding one half of mankind from all those paths which lead to usefulness and honour.

Without doubt (returned I) there is abundance of injustice in the sentence; yet it is possible to misapprehend and to overrate the injury that flows from the established order of things. If a certain part of every community must be condemned to servile and mechanical professions, it matters not of what sex they may be. If the benefits of leisure and science be, of necessity, the portion of a few, why should we be anxious to which sex the preference is given? The evil lies in so much of human capacity being thus fettered and perverted. This allotment is sad. Perhaps it is unnecessary. Perhaps that precept of justice is practicable which requires that each man should take his share of the labour, and enjoy his portion of the rest: that the tasks now assigned to a few, might be divided among the whole, and what now degenerates into ceaseless and brutalizing toil, might, by an equitable distribution, be changed into agreeable and useful exercise. Perhaps this inequality is incurable. In either case it is to be lamented, and, as far as possible, mitigated. Now, the question of what sex either of those classes may be composed, is of no importance. Though we must admit the claims of the female sex to an equality with the other, we cannot allow them to be superior. The state of the ignorant, servile, and laborious, is entitled to compassion and relief; not because they are women, nor because they are men; but simply because they are rational.—Among savage nations the women are slaves. They till the ground, and cook the victuals. Such is the condition of half of the community—deplorable, without doubt; but it would be neither more nor less so, if the sexes were equally distributed through each class.

But the burthen is unequal (said Mrs. Carter), since the strength of females is less.

What matters it (returned I) whether my strength be much or little, if I am tasked to the amount of it, and no more; and no task can go beyond.

But nature (said the lady) has subjected us to peculiar infirmities and hardships. In consideration of what we suffer as mothers and nurses, I think we ought to be exempted from the same proportion of labour.

It is hard (said I) to determine what is the amount of your pains as mothers and nurses. Have not ease and luxury a tendency to increase that amount? Is not the sustenance of infant offspring in every view a privilege? Of all changes in their condition, that which should transfer to men the task of nurturing the innocence, and helplessness of infancy, would, I should imagine, be to mothers the least acceptable.

I do not complain of this province. It is not, however, exempt from danger and trouble. It makes a large demand upon our time and attention. Ought not this to be considered in the distribution of tasks and duties?

Certainly. I was afraid you would imagine, that too much regard had been paid to it; that the circle of female pursuits had been too much contracted on this account.

I, indeed (rejoined the lady), think it by far too much contracted. But I cannot give the authors of our institutions credit for any such motives. On the contrary, I think we have the highest reason to complain of our exclusion from many professions which might afford us, in common with men, the means of subsistence and independence.

How far, dear Madam, is your complaint well grounded? What is it that excludes you from the various occupations in use among us? Cannot a female be a trader? I know of no law or custom that forbids it. You may, at any time, draw a subsistence from wages, if your station in life, or your education has rendered you sufficiently robust. No one will deride you, or punish you, for attempting to hew wood or bring water. If we rarely see you driving a team, or beating the anvil, is it not a favorable circumstance? In every family there are various duties. Certainly the most toilsome and rugged do not fall to the lot of women. If your employment be for the most part sedentary and recluse, to be exempted from an intemperate exertion of the muscles, or to be estranged from scenes of vulgar concourse, might be deemed a privilege. The last of these advantages, however, is not yours; for do we not buy most of our meat, herbs, and fruit, of women? In the distribution of employments, the chief or only difference perhaps, is, that those which require most strength, or more unremitted exertion of it, belong to the males: and yet there is nothing obligatory or inviolable in this arrangement. In the country, the maid that milks, and the man that ploughs, if discontented with their present office, may make an exchange, without breach of law, or offence to decorum. If you possess stock, by which to purchase the labour of others—and stock may accumulate in your hands as well as in ours—there is no species of manufacture in which you are forbidden to employ it.

But are we not (cried the lady) excluded from the liberal professions?

Why that may admit of question. You have free access, for example, to the accompting-house. It would be somewhat ludicrous, I own, to see you at the Exchange, or superintending the delivery of a cargo. Yet this would attract our notice, merely because it is singular; not because it is disgraceful or criminal: but if the singularity be a sufficient objection, we know that these offices are not necessary. The profession of a merchant may be pursued with success and dignity, without being a constant visitant of the quay or the coffee-house. In the trading cities of Europe, there are bankers and merchants of your sex, to whom that consideration is attached, to which they are entitled by their skill, their integrity, or their opulence.

But what apology can you make for our exclusion from the class of physicians?

To a certain extent, the exclusion is imaginary. My grandmother was a tolerable physician. She had much personal experience; and her skill was, I assure you, in much request among her neighbours. It is true, she wisely forbore to tamper with diseases of an uncommon or complicated nature. Her experience was almost wholly personal. But that was accidental. She might have added, if she had chosen, the experience of others to her own.

But the law—

True, we are not accustomed to see female pleaders at the bar. I never wish to see them there. But the law, as a science, is open to their curiosity or their benevolence. It may be even practised as a source of gain, without obliging us to frequent and public exhibitions.

Well (said the lady), let us dismiss the lawyer and physician, and turn our eye to the pulpit. That, at least, is a sanctuary which women must not profane.

It is only (replied I) in some sects that divinity, the business of explaining to men their religious duty, is a trade.[26] In such, custom or law, or the canons of their faith, have confined the pulpit to men: perhaps the distinction, wherever it is found, is an article of their religious creed, and, consequently, is no topic of complaint, since the propriety of this exclusion must be admitted by every member of the sect, whether male or female. But there are other sects which admit females into the class of preachers. With them, indeed, this distinction, if lucrative at all, is only indirectly so; and its profits are not greater to one sex than to the other. But there is no religious society in which women are debarred from the privileges of superior sanctity. The Christian religion has done much to level the distinctions of property, and rank, and sex. Perhaps, in reviewing the history of mankind, we shall find the authority derived from a real or pretended intercourse with heaven, pretty generally divided between them. And after all, what do these restrictions amount to? If some pursuits are monopolized by men, others are appropriated to you. If it appear that your occupations have least of toil, are most friendly to purity of manners, to delicacy of sensation, to intellectual improvement, and activity, or to public usefulness; if it should appear that your skill is always in such demand as to afford you employment when you stand in need of it; if, though few in number, they may be so generally and constantly useful, as always to furnish you subsistence; or, at least, to expose you, by their vicissitudes, to the pressure of want as rarely as it is incident to men; you cannot reasonably complain: but, in my opinion, all this is true.

Perhaps not (replied the lady): yet I must own your statement is plausible. I shall not take much pains to confute it. It is evident that for some reason or other, the liberal professions, those which require most vigour of mind, greatest extent of knowledge, and most commerce with books and with enlightened society, are occupied only by men. If contrary instances occur, they are rare, and must be considered as exceptions.

Admitting these facts (said I), I do not see reason for drawing mortifying inferences from them. For my part, I entertain but little respect for what are called the liberal professions, and, indeed, but little for any profession whatever. If their motive be

---

[26] "Is a trade": the *Weekly Magazine* version omits the pejorative "is a trade" with its criticism of greed in the clergy, and substitutes "exclusively belongs to our sex."

gain, and that it is which constitutes them a profession, they seem to be, all of them, nearly on a level in point of dignity. The consideration of usefulness is of more value. He that roots out a national vice, or checks the ravages of a pestilence, is, no doubt, a respectable personage: but it is no man's trade to perform these services. How does a mercenary divine,[27] or lawyer, or physician, differ from a dishonest chimney-sweep? The worst that can be dreaded from a chimney-sweep is the spoiling of our dinner, or a little temporary alarm; but what injuries may we not dread from the abuses of law, medicine, or divinity![28] Honesty, you will say, is the best policy. Whatever it be, it is not the road to wealth. To the purposes of a profession, as such, it is not subservient. Degrees, and examinations, and licences, may qualify us for the trade, but benevolence needs not their aid to refine its skill, or augment its activity. Some portion of their time and their efforts must be employed by those who need, in obtaining the means of subsistence. The less tiresome, boisterous and servile that task is, which necessity enjoins; the less tendency it has to harden our hearts, to benumb our intellects, to undermine our health. The more leisure it affords us to gratify our curiosity and cultivate our moral discernment, the better. Here is a criterion for the choice of a profession, and which obliges us to consider the condition of women as preferable.

I cannot perceive it. But it matters nothing what field may be open, if our education does not qualify us to range over it. What think you of female education? Mine has been frivolous. I can make a pie, and cut out a gown. To this only I am indebted to my teachers. If I have added any thing to these valuable attainments, it is through my own efforts, and not by the assistance or encouragement of others.

And ought it not to be so? What can render men wise but their own efforts? Does curiosity derive no encouragement from the possession of the power and materials? You are taught to read and to write: quills, paper, and books are at hand. Instruments and machines are forthcoming to those who can purchase them. If you be insensible to the pleasures and benefits of knowledge, and are therefore ignorant and trifling, truly, it is not for want of assistance and encouragement.

I shall find no difficulty (said the lady) to admit that the system is not such as to condemn all women, without exception, to stupidity. As it is, we have only to lament that a sentence so unjust is executed on, by far, the greater number. But you forget how seldom those who are most fortunately situated, are permitted to cater for themselves. Their conduct, in this case, as in all others, is subject to the controul of others who are guided by established prejudices, and are careful to remember that we are women. They think a being of this sex is to be instructed in a manner different from those of another. Schools, and colleges,[29] and public instructors are provided in all

---

[27] "Mercenary divine": the condemnation of well-to-do ministers was edited out of the *Weekly Magazine* version, so that the phrase reads "How does a mercenary lawyer, or physician...."

[28] "Or divinity!": again, the *Weekly Magazine* deleted the attack on clerical greed, and the phrasing was limited to "from the abuses of law or medicine."

[29] "Colleges": in the period's parlance, a "college" is a secondary, preparatory school.

the abstruse sciences and learned languages; but whatever may be their advantages, are not women totally excluded from them?

It would be prudent (said I), in the first place, to ascertain the amount of those advantages, before we indulge ourselves in lamenting the loss of them. Let us consider whether a public education be not unfavourable to moral and intellectual improvement; or, at least, whether it be preferable to the domestic method;—whether most knowledge be obtained by listening to hired professors,[30] or by reading books;—whether the abstruse sciences be best studied in a closet, or a college;—whether the ancient tongues be worth learning;—whether, since languages are of no use but as avenues to knowledge, our native tongue, especially in its present state of refinement, be not the best. Before we lament the exclusion of women from colleges, all these points must be settled: unless they shall be precluded by reflecting, that places of public education, which are colleges in all respects but the name, are, perhaps, as numerous for females as for males.

They differ (said the lady) from colleges in this, that a very different plan of instruction is followed. I know of no female school where Latin is taught, or geometry, or chemistry.

Yet, Madam, there are female geometricians, and chemists, and scholars, not a few. Were I desirous that my son or daughter should become either of these, I should not deem the assistance of a college indispensible. Suppose an anatomist should open his school to pupils of both sexes, and solicit equally their attendance, would you comply with the invitation?

No; because that pursuit has no attractions for me. But if I had a friend whose curiosity was directed to it, why should I dissuade her from it?

Perhaps (said I) you are but little acquainted with the real circumstances of such a scene. If your disdain of prejudices should prompt you to adventure one visit, I question whether you would find any inclination to repeat it.

Perhaps not (said she); but that mode of instruction in all the experimental sciences is not, perhaps, the best. A numerous company can derive little benefit from a dissection in their presence. A closer and more deliberate inspection than the circumstances of a large company will allow, seems requisite. But the assembly need not be a mixed one. Objections on the score of delicacy, though they are more specious than sound, and owe their force more to our weakness than our wisdom, would be removed by making the whole company, professor and pupils, female. But this would be obviating an imaginary evil, at the price of a real benefit. Nothing has been more injurious than the separation of the sexes. They associate in childhood without restraint; but the period quickly arrives when they are obliged to take different paths. Ideas, maxims, and pursuits, wholly opposite, engross their attention. Different systems of morality, different languages, or, at least, the same words with a different set

---

[30] "Hired professors": the Weekly Magazine version edits out "hired," so that the phrase reads "listening to professors."

of meanings, are adopted. All intercourse between them is fettered and embarrassed. On one side, all is reserve and artifice; on the other, adulation and affected humility. The same end must be compassed by opposite means. The man must affect a disproportionable ardour; while the woman must counterfeit indifference or aversion. Her tongue has no office, but to belie the sentiments of her heart, and the dictates of her understanding.

By marriage she loses all right to separate property. The will of her husband is the criterion of all her duties. All merit is comprised in unlimited obedience. She must not expostulate or rebel. In all contests with him, she must hope to prevail by blandishments and tears; not by appeals to justice and addresses to reason. She will be most applauded when she smiles with most perseverance on her oppressor, and when, with the undistinguishing attachment of a dog, no caprice or cruelty shall be able to estrange her affection.

Surely, Madam, this picture is exaggerated. You derive it from some other source than your own experience, or even your own observation.

No; I believe the picture to be generally exact. No doubt there are exceptions. I believe myself to be one. I think myself exempt from the grosser defects of women, but by no means free from the influence of a mistaken education. But why should you think the picture exaggerated? Man is the strongest. This is the reason why, in the earliest stage of society, the females are slaves. The tendency of rational improvement is to equalize conditions; to abolish all distinctions, but those that are founded on truth and reason; to limit the reign of brute force, and uncontroulable accidents. Women have unquestionably benefited by the progress that has hitherto taken place. If I look abroad, I may see reason to congratulate myself on being born in this age and country. Women that are no where totally exempt from servitude, no where admitted to their true rank in society, may yet be subject to different degrees or kinds of servitude. Perhaps there is no country in the world where the yoke is lighter than here. But this persuasion, though, in one view, it may afford us consolation, ought not to blind us to our true condition, or weaken our efforts to remove the evils that still oppress us. It is manifest, that we are hardly and unjustly treated. The natives of the most distant regions do not less resemble each other, than the male and female of the same tribe, in consequence of the different discipline to which they are subject. Now this is palpably absurd. Men and women are partakers of the same nature. They are rational beings; and, as such, the same principles of truth and equity must be applicable to both.

To this I replied, Certainly, Madam: but it is obvious to enquire to which of the sexes the distinction is most favourable. In some respects, different paths are allotted to them, but I am apt to suspect that of the woman to be strewed with fewest thorns; to be beset with fewest asperities; and to lead, if not absolutely in conformity to truth and equity, yet with fewest deviations from it. There are evils incident to your condition as women. As human beings, we all lie under considerable disadvantages; but it is of an unequal lot that you complain. The institutions of society have injuriously and capriciously distinguished you. True it is, laws, which have commonly been male births, have treated you unjustly; but it has been with that species of injustice that has given birth to nobles and kings.[31] They have distinguished you by irrational and undeserved indulgences. They have exempted you from a thousand toils and cares. Their tenderness has secluded you from tumult and noise: your persons are sacred from profane violences; your eyes from ghastly spectacles; your ears from a thousand discords, by which ours are incessantly invaded. Yours are the peacefullest recesses of the mansion: your hours glide along in sportive chat, in harmless recreation, or voluptuous indolence; or in labour so light, as scarcely to be termed encroachments on the reign of contemplation. Your industry delights in the graceful and minute: it enlarges the empire of the senses, and improves the flexibility of the fibres.[32] The art of the needle, by the lustre of its hues and the delicacy of its touches, is able to mimic all the forms of nature, and pourtray all the images of fancy: and the needle but prepares the hand for doing wonders on the harp; for conjuring up the 'piano' to melt, and the 'forte' to astound us.

This (cried the lady) is a very partial description. It can apply only to the opulent, and but to few of them. Meanwhile, how shall we estimate the hardships of the lower class? You have only pronounced a panegyric on indolence and luxury. Eminent virtue and true happiness are not to be found in this element.

True (returned I). I have only attempted to justify the male sex from the charge of cruelty. Ease and luxury are pernicious. Kings and nobles, the rich and the idle, enjoy no genuine content. Their lot is hard enough; but still it is better than brutal ignorance and unintermitted toil; than nakedness and hunger. There must be one condition of society that approaches nearer than any other to the standard of rectitude and happiness. For this it is our duty to search; and, having found it, endeavour to reduce every other condition to this desirable mean. It is useful, meanwhile, to ascertain the relative importance of different conditions; and since deplorable evils are annexed to every state, to discover in what respects, and in what degree, one is more or less eligible than another. Half of the community are females. Let the whole community be divided into classes; and let us inquire, whether the wives, and daughters, and single women, of each class, be not placed in a more favourable situation than the husbands, sons, and single men, of the same class. Our answer will surely be in the affirmative.

There is (said the lady) but one important question relative to this subject. Are women as high in the scale of social felicity and usefulness as they may and ought to be?

---

[31] "But it has been with that species of injustice that has given birth to nobles and kings": the *Weekly Magazine* version omits this entire phrase condemning feudal institutions and proceeds immediately from "unjustly;" to "they have distinguished you…."

[32] "Flexibility of the fibres": the notion that women's work relaxes the body and makes it more able to respond sympathetically. This language of fibrous nerves and muscles is likened to musical instruments, like the harp, which can produce soft (piano) or loud (forte) sounds in the following sentence. For an example of the equation of musical instruments and bodies, see the description of Helena Cleves in Chapters 13–16 of *Ormond*.

To this (said I) there can be but one answer: No. At present they are only higher on that scale than the men. You will observe, Madam, I speak only of that state of society which we enjoy. If you had excluded sex from the question, I must have made the same answer. Human beings, it is to be hoped, are destined to a better condition on this stage, or some other, than is now allotted them.

PART II

THIS remark was succeeded by a pause on both sides. The lady seemed more inclined to listen than talk. At length I ventured to resume the conversation.

Pray, Madam, permit me to return from this impertinent digression, and repeat my question—"Are you a federalist?"

And let me (she replied) repeat my answer—What have I, as a woman, to do with politics? Even the government of our own country, which is said to be the freest in the world, passes over women as if they were not. We are excluded from all political rights without the least ceremony. Law-makers thought as little of comprehending us in their code of liberty, as if we were pigs, or sheep. That females are exceptions to their general maxims, perhaps never occurred to them. If it did, the idea was quietly discarded, without leaving behind it the slightest consciousness of inconsistency or injustice. If to uphold and defend, as far as woman's little power extends, the constitution against violence, if to prefer a scheme of union and confederacy, to war and dissention, entitle me to that name, I may justly be stiled a federalist. But if that title be incompatible with a belief that, in many particulars, this constitution is unjust and absurd, I certainly cannot pretend to it. But how should it be otherwise? While I am conscious of being an intelligent and moral being; while I see myself denied, in so many cases, the exercise of my own discretion; incapable of separate property; subject, in all periods of my life, to the will of another, on whose bounty I am made to depend for food, raiment, and shelter: when I see myself, in my relation to society, regarded merely as a beast, or an insect; passed over, in the distribution of public duties, as absolutely nothing, by those who disdain to assign the least apology for their injustice—what though politicians say I am nothing, it is impossible I should assent to their opinion, as long as I am conscious of willing and moving. If they generously admit me into the class of existence, but affirm that I exist for no purpose but the convenience of the more dignified sex; that I cannot be entrusted with the government of myself; that to foresee, to deliberate and decide, belongs to others, while all my duties resolve themselves into this precept, "listen and obey;" it is not for me to smile at their tyranny, or receive, as my gospel, a code built upon such atrocious maxims. No, I am no federalist.

You are, at least (said I), a severe and uncommon censor. You assign most extraordinary reasons for your political heresy. You have many companions in your aversion to the government, but, I suspect, are wholly singular in your motives. There are few, even among your own sex, who reason in this manner.

Very probably; thoughtless and servile creatures! but that is not wonderful. All despotism subsists by virtue of the errors and supineness of its slaves. If their discernment was clear, their persons would be free. Brute strength has no part in the government of multitudes: they are bound in the fetters of opinion.[33]

The maxims of constitution-makers sound well. All power is derived from the people. Liberty is every one's birthright. Since all cannot govern or deliberate individually, it is just that they should elect their representatives. That every one should possess, indirectly, and through the medium of his representatives, a voice in the public councils, and should yield to no will but that of an actual or virtual majority. Plausible and specious maxims! but fallacious. What avails it to be told by any one, that he is an advocate for liberty? we must first know what he means by the word. We shall generally find that he intends only freedom to himself, and subjection to all others. Suppose I place myself where I can conveniently mark the proceedings at a general election: "All," says the code, "are free. Liberty is the immediate gift of the Creator to all mankind, and is unalienable. Those that are subject to the laws should possess a share in their enaction. This privilege can be exercised, consistently with the maintenance of social order, in a large society, only in the choice of deputies." A person advances with his ticket. "Pray," says the officer, "are you twenty-one years of age?"—"No."—"Then I cannot receive your vote; you are no citizen." Disconcerted and abashed, he retires. A second assumes his place. "How long," says the officer, "have you been an inhabitant of this State?"—"Nineteen months and a few days."—"None has a right to vote who has not completed two years residence." A third approaches, who is rejected because his name is not found in the catalogue of taxables. At length room is made for a fourth person. "Man," cries the magistrate, "is your skin black or white?"—"Black."—"What, a sooty slave dare to usurp the rights of freemen?" The way being now clear, I venture to approach. "I am not a minor," say I to myself. "I was born in the State, and cannot, therefore, be stigmatized as a foreigner. I pay taxes, for I have no father or husband to pay them for me. Luckily my complexion is white. Surely my vote will be received. But, no, I am a woman. Neither short residence, nor poverty, nor age, nor colour, nor sex, exempt from the jurisdiction of the laws." "True," says the magistrate; "but they deprive you from bearing any part in their formation." "So I perceive, but I cannot perceive the justice of your pretentions to equality and liberty, when those principles are thus openly and grossly violated."

If a stranger question me concerning the nature of our government, I answer that in this happy climate all men are free: the people are the source of all authority; from them it flows, and to them, in due season, it returns. But in what (says my friend) does this unrivalled and precious freedom consist? Not (say I) in every man's governing himself, literally and individually; that is impossible. Not in the controul of an

---

[33] "Fetters of opinion"; the *Weekly Magazine* version omits everything from this point to "utility to others which they exclude" and substitutes the following bridge paragraph:

"The Lady then proceeded to declaim against the prevailing modifications of society, chiefly as they affect the condition of woman. She maintained with great warmth the justice of admitting the female part of the community to elect and to be electable. In answer to her invectives, I observed, that...."

actual majority; they are by much too numerous to deliberate commodiously, or decide expeditiously. No, our liberty consists in the choice of our governors: all, as reason requires, have a part in this choice, yet not without a few exceptions: for, in the first place, all females are excepted. They, indeed, compose one half of the community; but, no matter, women cannot possibly have any rights. Secondly, those whom the feudal law calls minors, because they could not lift a shield, or manage a pike, are excepted. They comprehend one half of the remainder. Thirdly, the poor. These vary in number, but are sure to increase with the increase of luxury and opulence, and to promote these is well known to be the aim of all wise governors. Fourthly, those who have not been two years in the land: and, lastly, slaves. It has been sagely decreed, that none but freemen shall enjoy this privilege, and that all men are free but those that are slaves. When all these are sifted out, a majority of the remainder are entitled to elect our governor; provided, however, the candidate possess certain qualifications, which you will excuse me from enumerating. I am tired of explaining this charming system of equality and independence. Let the black, the young, the poor, and the stranger, support their own claims. I am a woman. As such, I cannot celebrate the equity of that scheme of government which classes me with dogs and swine.

In this representation (said I) it must be allowed there is some truth; but do you sufficiently distinguish between the form and spirit of a government? The true condition of a nation cannot be described in a few words; nor can it be found in the volumes of their laws. We know little or nothing when our knowledge extends no farther than the forms of the constitution. As to any direct part they bear in the government, the women of Turky, Russia, and America, are alike; but, surely, their actual condition, their dignity, and freedom, are very different. The value of any government lies in the mode in which it is exercised. If we consent to be ruled by another, our liberty may still remain inviolate, or be infringed only when superior wisdom directs. Our master may govern us agreeably to our own ideas, or may restrain and enforce us only when our own views are mistaken.

No government is independent of popular opinion. By that it must necessarily be sustained and modified. In the worst despotism there is a sphere of discretion allotted to each man, which political authority must not violate. How much soever is relinquished by the people, somewhat is always reserved. The chief purpose of the wise is to make men their own governors, to persuade them to practise the rules of equity without legal constraint: they will try to lessen the quantity of government, without changing or multiplying the depositories of it; to diminish the number of those cases in which authority is required to interfere. We need not complain of the injustice of laws, if we refrain, or do not find it needful to appeal to them: if we decide amicably our differences, or refer them to an umpire of our own choice: if we trust not to the subtilty of lawyers, and the prejudice of judges, but to our own eloquence, and a tribunal of our neighbours. It matters not what power the laws give me over the property or persons of others, if I do not chuse to avail myself of the privilege.

Then (said the lady) you think that forms of government are no subjects of contest. It matters not by whom power is possessed, or how it is transferred; whether we bestow our allegiance on a child or a lunatic; whether kings be made by the accident of birth or wealth; whether supreme power be acquired by force, or transmitted by inheritance, or conferred freely and periodically by the suffrages of all that acknowledge its validity?

Doubtless (replied I) these considerations are of some moment; but cannot you distinguish between power and the exercise of power, and see that the importance of the first is derived wholly from the consideration of the last?

But how it shall be exercised (rejoined she) depends wholly on the views and habits of him that has it. Avails it nothing whether the prince be mild or austere, malignant or benevolent? If we must delegate authority, are we not concerned to repose it with him who will use it to the best, rather than the worst purposes? True it is, we should retain as much power over our own conduct, maintain the sphere of our own discretion, as large and as inviolate as possible. But we must, as long as we associate with mankind, forego, in some particulars, our self-government, and submit to the direction of another; but nothing interests me more nearly than a wise choice of master. The wisest member of society should, if possible, be selected for the guidance of the rest.

If an hundred persons be in want of a common dwelling, and the work cannot be planned or executed by the whole, from the want of either skill or unanimity, what is to be done? We must search out one who will do that which the circumstances of the case will not allow us to do for ourselves. Is it not obvious to enquire who among us possesses most skill, and most virtue to controul him in the use of it? Or shall we lay aside all regard to skill and integrity, and consider merely who is the tallest, or richest, or fairest among us, or admit his title that can prove that such an one was his father, or that he himself is the eldest among the children of his father? In an affair which is of common concern, shall we consign the province of deciding to a part, or yield to the superior claims of a majority? If it happen that the smaller number be distinguished by more accurate discernment, or extensive knowledge, and, consequently, he that is chosen by the wiser few, will probably be, in himself considered, more worthy than the favourite of the injudicious many; yet what is the criterion which shall enable us to distinguish the sages from the fools? And, when the selection is made, what means shall we use for expunging from the catalogue all those whom age has enfeebled, or flattery or power corrupted? If all this were effected, could we, at the same time, exclude evils from our system by which its benefits would be overweighed? Of all modes of government, is not the sovereignty of the people, however incumbered with inconveniencies, yet attended by the fewest?

It is true (answered I) that one form of government may tend more than another to generate selfishness and tyranny in him that rules, and ignorance and profligacy in the subjects. If different forms be submitted to our choice, we should elect that which deserves the preference. Suppose our countrymen would be happier if they were subdivided into a thousand little independent democratical republics, than they are under their present form, or, than they would be under an hereditary despot: then it behoves us to inquire by what, if by any means, this subdivision may be effected, and, which is matter of equal moment, how it can be maintained: but these, for the most part, are airy speculations. If not absolutely hurtful, they are injurious, by being of inferior utility to others which they exclude.[34] If women be excluded from political functions, it is sufficient that in this exercise of these functions, their happiness is amply consulted.

Say what you will (cried the lady), I shall ever consider it as a gross abuse that we are hindered from sharing with you in the power of chusing our rulers, and of making those laws to which we equally with yourselves are subject.

We claim the power (rejoined I); this cannot be denied; but I must maintain, that as long as it is equitably exercised, no alteration is desirable. Shall the young, the poor, the stranger, and the females[35] be admitted indiscriminately to political privileges? Shall we annex no condition to a voter but that he be a thing in human shape, not lunatic, and capable of loco-motion; and no qualifications to a candidate but the choice of a majority? Would any benefit result from the change? Will it augment the likelihood that the choice will fall upon the wisest? Will it endow the framers and interpreters of law with more sagacity and moderation than they at present possess?

Perhaps not (said she). I plead only for my own sex. Want of property, youth, and servile condition, may, possibly, be well-founded objections; but mere sex is a circumstance so purely physical; has so little essential influence beyond what has flowed from the caprice of civil institutions on the qualities of mind or person, that I cannot think of it without impatience. If the law should exclude from all political functions every one who had a mole on his right cheek, or whose stature did not exceed five feet six inches, who would not condemn without scruple so unjust an institution? yet, in truth, the injustice would be less than in the case of women. The distinction is no less futile, but the injury is far greater, since it annihilates the political existence of at least one half of the community.

But you appeared to grant (said I) that want of property and servile condition are allowable disqualifications. Now, may not marriage be said to take away both the liberty and property of women? at least, does it not bereave them of that independent judgment which it is just to demand from a voter?

Not universally the property (answered she): so far as it has the effect you mention, was there ever any absurdity more palpable, any injustice more flagrant? But you well know there are cases in which women, by marriage, do not relinquish their property. All women, however, are not wives and wards. Granting that such are disqualified, what shall we say of those who are indisputably single, affluent and independent? Against these no objection, in the slightest degree plausible, can be urged. It would be strange folly to suppose women of this class to be necessarily destitute of those qualities which the station of a citizen requires. We have only to examine the pretentions of

---

[34] "Others which they exclude": this phrase ends the lengthy omission in the *Weekly Magazine* version (see note 33).

[35] "The young, the poor, the stranger, and the females": In Brown's father Elijah's complete manuscript transcription of parts I and II, this line adds "the blacks" so that it reads: "...the young, the poor, the blacks, the stranger, and the females."

those who already occupy public stations. Most of them seem not to have attained heights inaccessible to ordinary understandings; and yet the delegation of women, however opulent and enlightened, would, probably, be a more insupportable shock to the prejudices that prevail among us, than the appointment of a youth of fifteen, or a beggar, or a stranger.

If this innovation be just (said I), the period for making it has not arrived. You, Madam, are singular. Women in general do not reason in this manner. They are contented with the post assigned them. If the rights of a citizen were extended to them, they would not employ them—stay till they desire it.

If they were wise (returned the lady), they would desire it: meanwhile, it is an act of odious injustice to withhold it. This privilege is their due. By what means have you discovered that they would not exercise it, if it were granted? You cannot imagine but that some would step forth and occupy this station, when the obstruction was removed.

I know little of women (said I). I have seldom approached them, much less have I enjoyed their intimate society; yet, as a specimen of the prejudice you spoke of, I must own I should be not a little surprized to hear of a woman proferring her services as president or senator. It would be hard to restrain a smile to see her rise in a popular assembly to discuss some mighty topic. I should gaze as at a prodigy, and listen with a doubting heart: yet I might not refuse devotion to the same woman in the character of household deity. As a mother pressing a charming babe to her bosom; as my companion in the paths of love, or poetry, or science; as partaker with me in content, and an elegant sufficiency, her dignity would shine forth in full splendour. Here all would be decency and grace. But as a national ruler; as busied in political intrigues and cares; as intrenched in the paper mounds of a secretary; as burthened with the gravity of a judge; as bearing the standard in battle; or, even as a champion in senatorial warfare, it would be difficult to behold her without regret and disapprobation. These emotions I should not pretend to justify; but such, and so difficult to vanquish, is prejudice.

Prejudices, countenanced by an experience so specious and universal, cannot be suddenly subdued. I shall tell you, however, my genuine and deliberate opinion on the subject. I have said that this equality of the sexes was all that could be admitted; that the superiority we deny to men can, with as little justice, be ascribed to women: but this, in the strictest sense, is not true: on the contrary, it must be allowed that women are superior.

We cannot fail to distinguish between the qualities of mind and those of person. Whatever be the relation between the thinking principle, and the limbs and organs of the body, it is manifest that they are distinct; insomuch, that when we pass judgment on the qualities of the former, the latter is not necessarily taken into view, or included in it. So, when we discourse of our exterior and sensible qualities, we are supposed to exclude from our present consideration, the endowments of the mind. This distinction is loose, but sufficiently accurate for my purpose.

Have we not abundant reason to conclude that the principle of thought is, in both sexes, the same; that it is subject to like influences; that like motives and situations produce like effects? We are not concerned to know which of the sexes has occupied the foremost place on the stage of human life. They would not be beings of the same nature in whom different causes produced like effects. It is sufficient that we can trace diversity in the effects to a corresponding diversity in the circumstances; that women are such as observation exhibits them, in consequence of those laws which belong to a rational being, and which are common to both sexes: but such, beyond all doubt, must be the result of our inquiries. In this respect, then, the sexes are equal.

But what opinion must be formed of their exterior or personal qualities? Are not the members and organs of the female body as aptly suited to their purposes as those of the male? The same, indeed, may be asserted of a mouse or a grashopper; but are not these purposes as wise and dignified, nay, are they not precisely the same? Considering the female frame as the subject of impressions, and the organ of intelligence, it appears to deserve the preference. What shall we say of the acuteness and variety of your sensations; of the smoothness, flexibility, and compass of your voice?

Beauty is a doubtful quality. Few men will scruple to resign the superiority in this respect to women. The truth of this decision may be, perhaps, physically demonstrated; or, perhaps, all our reasonings are vitiated, by this circumstance, that the reasoner and his auditors are male. We all know in what the sexual distinction consists, and what is the final cause of this distinction. It is easier to conceive than describe that species of attraction which sex annexes to the person. It would be fallacious perhaps to infer female superiority, in an absolute and general sense, from the devotion which, in certain cases, we are prone to pay them; which it is impossible to feel for one of our own sex; and which is mutually felt: yet, methinks, the inference is inevitable. When I reflect on the equality of mind, and attend to the feelings which are roused in my bosom by the presence of accomplished and lovely women; by the mere graces of their exterior, even when the magic of their voice sleeps, and the eloquence of their eyes is mute;—and, for the reality of these feelings, if politeness did not forbid, I might quote the experience of the present moment—I am irresistibly induced to believe that of the two sexes, yours is, on the whole, the superior.

It is difficult, I know, to reason dispassionately on this subject: witness the universal persuasion of mankind, that in grace, symmetry, and melody, the preference is due to women. Yet, beside that opinion is no criterion of truth but to him that harbours it, when I call upon all human kind as witnesses, it is only one half of them, the individuals of one sex, that obey my call.

It may at first appear that men have generally ascribed intellectual pre-eminence to themselves. Nothing, however, can be inferred from this. It is doubtful whether they judge rightly on the question of what is, or is not intrinsically excellent. Not seldom they have placed their superiority in that which, rightly understood, should have been pregnant with ignominy and humiliation. Should women themselves be found to concur in the belief that the other sex surpasses them in intelligence, it will avail but little. We must still remember that opinion is evidence of nothing but its own existence. This opinion, indeed, is peculiarly obnoxious. They merely repeat what they have been taught; and their teachers have been men. The prevalence of this opinion, if it does not evince the incurable defects of female capacity, may, at least, be cited to prove in how mournful a degree that capacity has been neglected or perverted. It is a branch of that prejudice which has so long darkened the world, and taught men that nobles and kings were creatures of an order superior to themselves.

Here the conversation was interrupted by one of the company, who, after listening to us for some time, thought proper at last to approach, and contribute his mite to our mutual edification. I soon after seized an opportunity of withdrawing, but not without requesting and obtaining permission to repeat my visit.

*****

[back cover of the 1798 edition of parts I and II]

☞ Since the last page of these two Parts of "ALCUIN" were put to press, the Editor has received, from the Author, the *third* and *fourth Parts*. They are considerably more lengthy than those now published; but it is proposed to deliver them to Subscribers on the same terms. Such persons, therefore, as are desirous of continuing their subscriptions are requested to leave their names with the Editor, or with the printers.

April 24.

*****

PART III
[or III and IV; published posthumously in Dunlap (1815)]

A WEEK elapsed and I repeated my visit to Mrs. Carter. She greeted me in a friendly manner. I have often, said she, since I saw you, reflected on the subject of our former conversation. I have meditated more deeply than common, and I believe to more advantage. The hints that you gave me I have found useful guides.

And I, said I, have travelled farther than common, incited by a laudable desire of knowledge.

Travelled?

Yes, I have visited since I saw you, the paradise of women; and I assure you have longed for an opportunity to communicate the information that I have collected.

Well: you now enjoy the opportunity; you have engaged it every day in the week. Whenever you had thought proper to come, I could have promised you a welcome.

I thank you. I should have claimed your welcome sooner, but only returned this evening.

Returned! Whence, I pry'thee?

From the journey that I spoke of. Have I not told you that I have visited the paradise of women? The region, indeed is far distant, but a twinkling is sufficient for the longest of my journeys.

You are somewhat mysterious, and mystery is one of the many things that abound in the world, for which I have an hearty aversion.

I cannot help it. It is plain enough to me and to my good genius, who when I am anxious to change the scene, and am unable to perform it by the usual means, is kindly present to my prayers, and saves me from three inconveniences, of travelling toil, delay and expense. What sort of vehicle it is that he provides for me, what intervals of space I have overpassed, and what is the situation of the inn where I repose, relatively to this city or this orb, such is the rapidity with which I move that I cannot collect from my own observation. I may sometimes remedy my ignorance in this respect by a comparison of circumstances; for example, the language of the people with whom I passed most of the last week, was English. This was a strong symptom of affinity. In other respects the resemblance was sufficiently obscure. Methought I could trace in their buildings the knowledge of Greek and Roman models: but who can tell that the same images and combinations may not occur to minds distant and unacquainted with each other, but which have been subject to the same enlightened discipline? In manners and sentiments they possessed little in common with us. Here I confess my wonder was most excited, I should have been apt to suspect that they were people of some other planet, especially as I had never met in my reading with any intimations of the existence of such a people on our own. But on looking around me the earth and sky exhibited the same appearances as with us. It once occurred to me, that I had passed the bourne which we are all doomed to pass, and had reached that spot from which, as the poet assures us, no traveller returns. But since I have returned, I must discard that supposition. You will say perhaps when you are acquainted with particulars that it was no more than a sick man's dream, or a poet's reverie. Though I myself cannot adopt this opinion, for who can discredit the testimony of his senses, yet it must be owned that it would most naturally suggest itself to another, and therefore I shall leave you in possession of it.

So, you would persuade me, said the lady, that the journey you meant to relate, is in your own opinion real, though you are conscious that its improbability will hinder others from believing it.

If my statement answer that end be it so. The worst judge of the nature of his own conceptions is the enthusiast: I have my portion of ardour which solitude seldom fails to kindle into blaze. It has drawn vigour and activity from exercise. Whether it transgress the limits which a correct judgment prescribes it would be absurd to inquire of the enthusiast himself. If the perceptions of the poet be as lively as those of sense, it is a superfluous inquiry whether their objects exist really, and externally. This is a question which cannot be decided, even with respect to those perceptions which have most seeming and most congruity. We have no direct proof that the ordinary objects of sight and touch have a being independent of these senses. When there is no ground for believing that those chairs and tables have any existence but in my own sensorium, it would be rash to affirm the reality of the objects which I met, or seemed to meet with in my late journey. I see and hear is the utmost that can be truly said at any time. All that I can say is, that I saw and heard.

Well, returned the lady, that as you say, is a point of small importance. Let me know what you saw and heard without further ceremony.

I was witness to the transactions of a people, who would probably gain more of your approbation than those around you can hope for. Yet this is perhaps to build too largely on my imperfect knowledge of your sentiments: however that be, few things offered themselves to my observation, which I did not see reason to applaud, and to wonder at.

My curiosity embraced an ample field. It did not overlook the condition of women. That negligence had been equally unworthy of my understanding and my heart. It was evening and the moon was present when I lighted, I know not how or whence, on a smooth pavement encompassed by structures that appeared intended for the accommodation of those whose taste led them either to studious retirement or to cheerful conversation. I shall not describe the first transports of my amazement, or dwell on the reflections that were suggested by a transition so new and uncommon, or the means that I employed to penetrate the mysteriousness that hung around every object, and my various conjectures as to the position of the Isle,[36] or the condition of the people among whom I had fallen. I need not tell how in wandering from this spot, I encountered many of both sexes who were employed in awakening by their notes, the neighbouring echoes, or absorbed in musing silence, or engaged in sprightly debate; how one of them remarking as I suppose, the perplexity of my looks, and the uncouthness of my garb, accosted me and condescended to be my guide in a devious tract, which conducted me from one scene of enchantment to another. I need not tell how by the aid of this benevolent conductor, I passed through halls whose pendent lustres exhibited sometimes a groupe of musicians and dancers, sometimes assemblies where state affairs were the theme of sonorous rhetoric, where the claims of ancient patriots and heroes to the veneration of posterity were examined, and the sources of memorable revolutions scrutinized, or which listened to the rehearsals of annalist or poet, or surveyed the labours of the chemist, or inspected the performances of the mechanical inventor. Need I expatiate on the felicity of that plan, which blended the umbrage of poplars with the murmur of fountains, enhanced by the gracefulness of architecture.

Come, come, interrupted the lady, this perhaps, may be poetry, but though pleasing it had better be dispensed with. I give you leave to pass over these incidents in silence: I desire merely to obtain the sum of your information, disembarrassed from details of the mode in which you acquired it, and of the mistakes and conjectures to which your ignorance subjected you.

Well, said I, these restraints it must be owned are a little hard, but since you are pleased to impose them I must conform to your pleasure. After my curiosity was sufficiently gratified by what was to be seen, I retired with my guide to his apartment. It was situated on a terrace which overlooked a mixed scene of groves and edifices,

---

[36] "Isle": Alcuin invokes the longstanding convention, since Socrates and Plato, which presents Utopia as an island.

which the light of the moon that had now ascended the meridian, had rendered distinctly visible. After considerable discourse, in which satisfactory answers had been made to all the inquiries which I had thought proper to make, I ventured to ask, I pray thee my good friend, what is the condition of the female sex among you? In this evening's excursion I have met with those, whose faces and voices seemed to bespeak them women, though as far as I could discover they were distinguished by no peculiarities of manners or dress. In those assemblies to which you conducted me, I did not fail to observe that whatever was the business of the hour, both sexes seemed equally engaged in it. Was the spectacle theatrical? The stage was occupied sometimes by men, sometimes by women, and sometimes by a company of each. The tenor of the drama seemed to be followed as implicitly as if custom had enacted no laws upon this subject. Their voices were mingled in the chorusses: I admired the order in which the spectators were arranged. Women were, to a certain degree, associated with women, and men with men; but it seemed as if magnificence and symmetry had been consulted, rather than a scrupulous decorum. Here no distinction in dress was observable, but I suppose the occasion dictated it. Was science or poetry, or art, the topic of discussion? The two sexes mingled their inquiries and opinions. The debate was managed with ardour and freedom, and all present were admitted to a share in the controversy, without particular exceptions or compliances of any sort. Were shadows and recesses sought by the studious few? As far as their faces were distinguishable, meditation had selected her votaries indiscriminately. I am not unaccustomed to some degree of this equality among my own countrymen, but it appears to be far more absolute and general among you; pray what are your customs and institutions on this head?

Perhaps, replied my friend, I do not see whither your question tends. What are our customs respecting women? You are doubtless apprised of the difference that subsists between the sexes. That physical constitution which entitles some of us to the appellation of male, and others to that of female you must know. You know its consequences. With these our customs and institutions have no concern; they result from the order of nature, which it is our business merely to investigate. I suppose there are physiologists or anatomists in your country. To them it belongs to explain this circumstance of animal existence.

The universe consists of individuals. They are perishable. Provision has been made that the place of those that perish should be supplied by new generations. The means by which this end is accomplished, are the same through every tribe of animals. Between contemporary beings the distinction of sex maintains; but the end of this distinction is that since each individual must perish, there may be a continual succession of individuals. If you seek to know more than this, I must refer you to books which contain the speculations of the anatomist, or to the hall where he publicly communicates his doctrines.

It is evident, answered I, that I have not made myself understood. I did not inquire into the structure of the human body, but into these moral or political maxims which are founded on the difference in this structure between the sexes.

Need I repeat, said my friend, what I have told you of the principles by which we are governed. I am aware that there are nations of men universally infected by error, or who at least entertain opinions different from ours. It is hard to trace all the effects of a particular belief, which chances to be current among a whole people. I have entered into a pretty copious explanation of the rules to which we conform in our intercourse with each other, but still perhaps have been deficient.

No, I cannot complain of your brevity; perhaps my doubts would be solved by reflecting attentively on the information that I have already received. For that, leisure is requisite; meanwhile I cannot but confess my surprise that I find among you none of those exterior differences by which the sexes are distinguished by all other nations.

Give me a specimen if you please, of those differences with which you have been familiar.

One of them, said I, is dress. Each sex has a garb peculiar to itself. The men and women of our country are more different from each other in this respect, than the natives of remotest countries.

That is strange, said my friend, why is it so?

I know not. Each one dresses as custom prescribes. He has no other criterion. If he selects his garb because it is beautiful or convenient, it is beautiful and commodious in his eyes merely because it is customary.

But wherefore does custom prescribe a different dress to each sex?

I confess I cannot tell, but most certainly it is so. I must likewise acknowledge that nothing in your manners more excites my surprise than your uniformity in this particular.

Why should it be inexplicable? For what end do we dress? Is it for the sake of ornament? Is it in compliance with our perceptions of the beautiful? These perceptions cannot be supposed to be the same in all. But since the standard of beauty whatever it be, must be one and the same: since our notions on this head are considerably affected by custom and example, and since all have nearly the same opportunities and materials of judgment, if beauty only were regarded, the differences among us would be trivial. Differences, perhaps, there would be. The garb of one being would, in some degree, however small, vary from that of another. But what causes there are that should make all women agree in their preference of one dress, and all men in that of another, is utterly incomprehensible; no less than that the difference resulting from this choice should be essential and conspicuous.

But ornament obtains no regard from us but in subservience to utility. We find it hard to distinguish between the useful and beautiful. When they appear to differ, we cannot hesitate to prefer the former. To us that instrument possesses an invincible superiority to every other which is best adapted to our purpose. Convince me that this garment is of more use than that, and you have determined my choice. We may afterwards inquire, which has the highest pretensions to beauty. Strange if utility and beauty fail to coincide. Stranger still, if having found them in any instance incompatible, I sacrifice the former to the latter. But the elements of beauty, though perhaps they have a real existence, are fleeting and inconstant. Not so those principles which enable us to discover what is useful. These are uniform and permanent. So must be the results. Among us, what is useful to one, must be equally so to another. The condition of all is so much alike, that a stuff which deserves the preference of one, because it is obtained with least labour, because its texture is most durable, or most easily renewed or cleansed, is for similar reasons, preferable to all.

But, said I, you have various occupations. One kind of stuff or one fashion is not equally suitable to every employment. This must produce a variety among you, as it does among us.

It does so. We find that our tools must vary with our designs. If the task requires a peculiar dress, we assume it. But as we take it up when we enter the workshop, we of course, lay it aside when we change the scene. It is not to be imagined that we wear the same garb at all times. No man enters society laden with the implements of his art. He does not visit the council hall or the theatre with his spade upon his shoulder. As little does he think of bringing thither the garb which he wore in the field. There are no such peculiarities of attitude or gesture among us, that the vesture that has proved most convenient to one in walking or sitting, should be found unsuitable to others. Do the differences of this kind prevalent among you, conform to these rules? Since every one has his stated employment, no doubt each one has a dress peculiar to himself or to those of his own profession.

No. I cannot say that among us this principle has any extensive influence. The chief difference consists in degrees of expensiveness. By inspecting the garb of a passenger, we discover not so much the trade that he pursues, as the amount of his property. Few labour whose wealth allows them to dispense with it. The garb of each is far from varying with the hours of the day. He need only conform to the changes of the seasons, and model his appearance by the laws of ostentation, in public, and by those of ease in the intervals of solitude. These principles are common to both sexes. Small is the portion of morality or taste, that is displayed by either, but in this, as in most other cases, the conduct of the females is the least faulty. But of all infractions of decorum, we should deem the assuming of the dress of one sex by those of the other, as the most flagrant. It so rarely happens, that I do not remember to have witnessed a single metamorphosis, except perhaps on the stage, and even there a female cannot evince a more egregious negligence of reputation than by personating a man.

All this, replied my friend, is so strange as to be almost incredible. Why beings of the same nature, inhabiting the same spot, and accessible to the same influences, should exhibit such preposterous differences is wonderful. It is not possible that these modes should be equally commodious or graceful. Custom may account for the continuance, but not for the origin of manners.

The wonder that you express, said I, is in its turn a subject of surprise to me. What you now say, induces me to expect that among you, women and men are more similarly treated than elsewhere. But this to me, is so singular a spectacle, that I long to hear it more minutely described by you, and to witness it myself.

If you remain long enough among us you will not want the opportunity. I hope you will find that every one receives that portion which is due to him, and since a diversity of sex cannot possibly make any essential difference in the claims and duties of reasonable beings, this difference will never be found. But you call upon me for descriptions. With what hues shall I delineate the scene? I have exhibited as distinctly as possible the equity that governs us. Its maxims are of various application. They regulate our conduct, not only to each other, but to the tribes of insects and birds. Every thing is to be treated as capable of happiness itself, or as instrumental to the happiness of others.

But since the sexual differences is something, said I, and since you are not guilty of the error of treating different things as if they were the same, doubtless in your conduct towards each other, the consideration of sex is of some weight.

Undoubtedly. A species of conduct is incumbent upon men and women towards each other on certain occasions, that cannot take place between man and man; or between women and women. I may properly supply my son with a razor to remove superfluous hairs from his chin, but I may with no less propriety forbear to furnish my daughter with this impliment, because nature has denied her a beard; but all this is so evident that I cannot but indulge a smile at the formality with which you state it.

But, said I, it is the nature and extent of this difference of treatment that I want to know.

Be explicit my good friend. Do you want a physiological dissertation on this subject or not? If you do, excuse me from performing the task, I am unequal to it.

No. But I will try to explain myself. What for example is the difference which takes place in the education of the two sexes?

There is no possible ground for difference. Nourishment is imparted and received in the same way. Their organs of digestion and secretion are the same. There is one diet, one regimen, one mode and degree of exercise, best adapted to unfold the powers of the human body, and maintain them for the longest time in full vigour. One individual may be affected by some casualty or disease, so as to claim to be treated in a manner different from another individual, but this difference is not necessarily connected with sex. Neither sex is exempt from injury, contracted through their own ignorance, or that of others. Doubtless the sound woman and the sick man it would be madness to subject to the same tasks, or the same regimen. But this is no less true if both be of the same sex. Diseases, on whichsoever they fall, are curable by the same means.

Human beings in their infancy, continued my friend, require the same tendance and instruction: but does one sex require more or less, or a different sort of tendance or instruction than the other? Certainly not. If by any fatal delusion, one sex should imagine its interest to consist in the ill treatment of the other, time would soon detect their mistake. For how is the species to be continued? How is a woman, for example, to obtain a sound body, and impart it to her offspring, but, among other sources, from the perfect constitution of both her parents? But it is needless to argue on a supposition so incredible as that mankind can be benefitted by injustice and oppression.

Would we render the limbs supple, vigorous and active? And are there two modes equally efficacious of attaining this end? Must we suppose that one sex will find this end of less value than the other, or the means suitable to its attainment different? It cannot be supposed.

We are born with faculties that enable us to impart and receive happiness. There is one species of discipline, better adapted than any other to open and improve those faculties. This mode is to be practised. All are to be furnished with the means of instruction, whether these consist in the direct commerce of the senses with the material universe, or in intercourse with other intelligent beings. It is requisite to know the reasonings, actions and opinions of others, if we seek the improvement of our own understanding. For this end we must see them, and talk with them if present, or if distant or dead, we must consult these memorials which have been contrived by themselves or others. These are simple and intelligible maxims proper to regulate our treatment of rational beings. The only circumstance to which we are bound to attend is that the subjects of instruction be rational. If any one observe that the consideration of sex is of some moment, how must his remark be understood. Would he insinuate that because my sex is different from yours, one of us only can be treated as rational, or that though reason be a property of both, one of us possesses less of it than the other. I am not born among a people who can countenance so monstrous a doctrine.

No two persons are entitled in the strictest sense, to the same treatment, because no two can be precisely alike. All the possibilities and shades of difference, no human capacity can estimate. Observation will point out some of the more considerable sources of variety. Man is a progressive being, he is wise in proportion to the number of his ideas, and to the accuracy with which he compares and arranges them. These ideas are received through the inlets of his senses. They must be successively received. The objects which suggest them, must be present. There must be time for observation. Hence the difference is, in some degree, uniform between the old and the young. Between those, the sphere of whose observation has been limited, and those whose circle is extensive. Such causes as these of difference are no less incident to one sex than to the other. The career of both commences in childhood and ignorance. How far and how swiftly they may proceed before their steps are arrested by disease, or death, is to be inferred from a knowledge of their circumstances: such as betide them simply as individuals.

It would, perhaps, be unreasonable to affirm that the circumstance of sex affects in no degree the train of ideas in the mind. It is not possible that any circumstance, however trivial, should be totally without mental influence; but we may safely affirm that this circumstance is indeed trivial, and its consequences, therefore, unimportant. It is inferior to most other incidents of human existence, and to those which are necessarily incident to both sexes. He that resides among hills, is a different mortal from him that dwells on a plain. Subterranean darkness, or the seclusion of a valley, suggest ideas of a kind different from those that occur to us on the airy verge of a promontory, and in the neighbourhood of roaring waters. The influence on my character which flows from my age, from the number and quality of my associates, from the nature of my dwelling place, as sultry or cold, fertile or barren, level or diversified, the art that I cultivate, the extent or frequency of my excursions cannot be of small moment. In comparison with this, the qualities which are to be ascribed to my sex are unworthy of being mentioned. No doubt my character is in some degree tinged by it, but the tinge is inexpressibly small.

You give me leave to conclude then, said I, that the same method of education is pursued with regard to both sexes?

Certainly, returned my philosopher. Men possess powers that may be drawn forth and improved by exercise and discipline. Let them be so, says our system. It contents itself with prescribing certain general rules to all that bear the appellation of human. It permits all to refresh and invigorate their frames by frequenting the purest streams and the pleasantest fields, and by practising those gestures and evolutions that tend to make us robust and agile. It admits the young to the assemblies of their elders, and exhorts the elder to instruct the young. It multiplies the avenues, and facilitates the access to knowledge. Conversations, books, instruments, specimens of the productions of art and nature, haunts of meditation, and public halls, liberal propensities and leisure, it is the genius of our system to create, multiply, and place within the reach of all. It is far from creation, and debasing its views, by distinguishing those who dwell on the shore from those that inhabit the hills; the beings whom a cold temperature has bleached, from those that are embrowned by an hot.

But different persons, said I, have different employments. Skill cannot be obtained in them without a regular course of instruction. Each sex has, I doubt not, paths of its own into which the others must not intrude. Hence must arise a difference in their education.

Who has taught you, replied he, that each sex must have peculiar employments? Your doubts and your conjectures are equally amazing. One would imagine that among you, one sex had more arms, or legs, or senses than the other. Among us there is no such inequality. The principles that direct us in the choice of occupations are common to all.

Pray tell me, said I, what these principles are.

They are abundantly obvious. There are some tasks which are equally incumbent upon all. These demand no more skill and strength than is possessed by all. Men must provide themselves by their own efforts with food, clothing and shelter. As long as they live together there is a duty obliging them to join their skill and their exertions for the common benefit. A certain portion of labour will supply the needs of all. This portion then must be divided among all. Each one must acquire and exert the skill which this portion requires. But this skill and this strength are found by experience to be moderate and easily attained. To plant maize, to construct an arch, to weave a garment, are no such arduous employments but that all who have emerged from the infirmity and ignorance of childhood, may contribute their efforts to the performance.

But besides occupations which are thus of immediate and universal utility, there is an infinite variety of others. The most exquisite of all calamities, results from a vacant mind and unoccupied limbs. The highest pleasure demands the ceaseless activity of both. To enjoy this pleasure it is requisite to find some other occupation of our time, beside those which are enjoined by the physical necessities of our nature. Among these there is ample room for choice. The motives that may influence us in this choice, are endless. I shall not undertake to enumerate them. You can be at no loss to conceive them without my assistance: but whether they be solitary or social, whether speech or books, or observation, or experiment be the medium of instruction, there can be nothing in the distinction of sex to influence our determinations, or this influence is so inconsiderable as not to be worth mention.

What, cried I, are all obliged to partake of all the labours of tilling the ground, without distinction of rank and sex?

Certainly. There are none that fail to consume some portion of the product of the ground. To exempt any from a share in the cultivation, would be an inexpiable injustice, both to those who are exempted and those who are not exempted. The exercise is cheerful and wholesome. Its purpose is just and necessary. Who shall dare to deny me a part in it? But we know full well that the task, which, if divided among many, is easy and salubrious, is converted into painful and unwholesome drudgery, by being confined to a sex. What phrenzy must that be which should prompt us to introduce a change in this respect? I cannot even imagine so great a perversion of the understanding. Common madness is unequal to so monstrous a conception. We must first not only cease to be reasonable, but cease to be men. Even that supposition is insufficient, for into what class of animals must we sink, before this injustice could be realized? Among beasts there are none who do not owe their accommodations to their own exertions.

Food is no less requisite to one sex than to the other. As the necessity of food, so the duty of providing it is common. But the reason why I am to share in the labour, is not merely because I am to share in the fruits. I am a being guided by reason and susceptible of happiness. So are other men. It is therefore a privilege that I cannot relinquish, to promote and contemplate the happiness of others. After the cravings of necessity are satisfied, it remains for me, by a new application of my powers, to enlarge the pleasures of existence. The inlets to this pleasure are numberless. What can prompt us to take from any the power of choosing among these, or to incapacitate him from choosing with judgment. The greater the number of those who are employed in administering to pleasure, the greater will be the product. Since both sexes partake of this capacity, what possible reasons can there be for limiting or precluding the efforts of either?

What I conceive to be unjust, may yet be otherwise; but my actions will conform to my opinions. If you would alter the former, you must previously introduce a change into the latter. I know the opinions of my countrymen. The tenor of their actions will conform to their notions of right. Can the time ever come, will the power ever arise, that shall teach them to endure the oppression of injustice themselves, or inflict it upon others? No.

But in my opinion, said I, the frame of women is too delicate, their limbs too minute for rough and toilsome occupations. I would rather confine them to employments more congenial to the female elements of softness and beauty.

You would rather, would you? I will suppose you sincere, and inquire how you would expect to obtain their consent to your scheme.

The sentiments, said I, of a single individual, would avail nothing. But if all the males should agree to prescribe their employments to women—

What then? interrupted my friend. There are but two methods of effecting this end—by force or by persuasion. With respect to force we cannot suppose human beings capable of it, for any moral purpose; but supposing them capable, we would scarcely resort to force, while our opponents are equal in number, strength and skill to ourselves. The efficacy of persuasion is equally chimerical. That frailty of mind which should make a part of mankind willing to take upon themselves a double portion of the labour, and to convert what is pleasurable exercise to all, into a source of pain and misery to a few. But these are vain speculations, let us dismiss them from our notice.

Willingly, said I, we will dismiss these topics for the sake of one more important.

I presume then, said I, there is such a thing as marriage among you.

I do not understand the term.

I use it to express that relation which subsists between two human beings in consequence of difference of sex.

You puzzle me exceedingly, returned he. You question me as to the existence of that concerning which it is impossible for you to be ignorant. You cannot at this age be a stranger to the origin of human existence.

When I had gotten thus far in my narrative, I paused. Mrs. Carter still continued to favour me with her attention. On observing my silence she desired me to proceed.

I presume, said she, your supernatural conductor allowed you to finish the conversation. To snatch you away just now, in the very midst of your subject, would be doing you and me likewise a very unacceptable office. I beseech you go on with the discourse.

It may not be proper, answered I. This is a topic on which, strange to tell, we cannot discourse in the same terms before every audience. The remainder of our conversation decorum would not perhaps forbid you to read, but it prohibits you from hearing. If you wish it, I will give you the substance of the information I collected on this topic in writing.

What is improper to be said in my hearing, said the lady, it should seem was no less improper to be knowingly addressed to me by the pen.

Then, said I, you do not assent to my offer.

Nay, I do not refuse my assent. I merely object to the distinction, that you have raised. There are many things improper to be uttered, or written, or to be read, or listened to, but the impropriety methinks must adhere to the sentiments themselves, and not result from the condition of the author or his audience.

Are these your real sentiments?

Without doubt. But they appear not to be yours. However write what you please. I promise you to read it, and to inform you of my opinion respecting it. Your scheme, I suspect, will not be what is commonly called marriage, but something in your opinion, better. This footing is a dubious one. Take care, it is difficult to touch without overstepping the verge.

Your caution is reasonable. I believe silence will be the safest. You will excuse me therefore from taking up the pen on this occasion. The ground you say, and I believe, is perilous. It will be most prudent to avoid it.

As you please, but remember that though I may not approve of what you write, your silence I shall approve still less. If it be false, it will enable me at least to know you, and I shall thereby obtain an opportunity of correcting your mistakes. Neither of these purposes are trivial. Are you not aware that no future declaration of yours will be more unfavourable than what you have just said, that silence will be most safe. You are afraid no doubt, of shocking too greatly my prejudices; but you err. I am certainly prepossessed in favour of the system of marriage, but the strength of this prepossession will appear only in the ardour of my compassion for contrary opinions, and the eagerness of my endeavours to remove them.

You would condescend then, said I, to reason on the subject, as if it were possible that marriage was an erroneous institution; as if it were possible that any one could seriously maintain it to be, without entitling himself to the imputation of the lowest profligacy. Most women would think that the opponent of marriage, either assumed the character for the most odious and selfish purposes, and could therefore only deserve to be treated as an assassin: to be detested and shunned, or if he were sincere in his monstrous faith, that all efforts to correct his mistakes would avail nothing with respect to the patient, but might endanger the physician by exposing her to the illusions of sophistry or the contagion of passion.

I am not one of these, said the lady. The lowest stupidity only can seek its safety in shutting its ears. We may call that sophistry, which having previously heard, it fails to produce conviction. Yet sophistry perhaps implies not merely fallacious reasoning, but a fallaciousness of which the reasoner himself is apprised. If so, few charges ought to be made with more caution. But nothing can exceed the weakness that prevents us from attending to what is going to be urged against our opinions, merely from the persuasion that what is adverse to our preconceptions must be false. Yet there are examples of this folly among our acquaintance. You are wrong, said I lately to one of these, if you will suffer me, I will convince you of your error. You may save yourself the trouble, she answered. You may torment me with doubts, but why, when I see the truth clearly already, should I risque the involving of it in obscurity? I repeat, I am not of this class. Force is to be resisted by force, or eluded by flight: but he that argues, whatever be his motives, should be encountered with argument. He cannot commit a greater error than to urge topics, the insufficiency of which is known to himself. To demonstrate this error is as worthy of truth as any other province. To sophistry, in any sense of the term, the proper antidote is argument. Give me leave to take so much interest in your welfare, as to desire to see your errors corrected, and to contribute what is in my power to that end. If I know myself so well as sometimes to listen to others in the hope of profiting by their superior knowledge or sagacity, permit me likewise to be just to myself in other respects, and to believe myself capable sometimes of pointing out his mistakes to another.

You seem, said I, to think it certain that we differ in opinion upon this topic.

No. I merely suspect that we do. A class of reasoners has lately arisen, who aim at the deepest foundation of civil society. Their addresses to the understanding have been urged with no despicable skill. But this was insufficient. It was necessary to subdue our incredulity, as to the effects of their new maxims, by exhibiting those effects in detail, and winning our assent to their truth by engrossing the fancy and charming the affections. The journey that you have lately made, I merely regard as an excursion into their visionary world. I can trace the argument of the parts which you have unfolded, with those which are yet to come, and can pretty well conjecture of what hues, and lines, and figures, the remainder of the picture is intended to consist.

Then, said I, the task that I enjoined on myself is superfluous. You are apprised of all that I mean to say on the topic of marriage, and have already laid in an ample stock of disapprobation for my service.

I frankly confess that I expect not to approve the matter of your narrative, however pleased I may be with the manner. Nevertheless I wish you to execute your first design, that I may be able to unveil the fallacy of your opinions, and rescue one whom I have no reason to disrespect, from specious but fatal illusions.

Your purpose is kind. It entitles you at least to my thanks. Yet to say truth, I did not at first despair of your confidence with me in some of my opinions. I imagined that some of the evils of marriage had not escaped you. I recollect that during our last conversation, you arraigned with great earnestness the injustice of condemning women to obey the will, and depend upon the bounty of father or husband.

Come, come, interrupted the lady, with a severer aspect, if you mean to preserve my good opinion, you must tread on this ground with more caution. Remember the atrociousness of the charge you would insinuate. What! Because a just indignation at the iniquities that are hourly committed on one half of the human species rises in my heart, because I vindicate the plainest dictates of justice, and am willing to rescue so large a portion of human-kind, from so destructive a bondage: a bondage not only of the hands, but of the understanding; which divests them of all those energies which distinguish men from the basest animals, destroys all perception of moral rectitude, and reduces its subjects to so calamitous a state, that they adore the tyranny that rears its crest over them, and kiss the hand that loads them with ignominy! When I demand an equality of conditions among beings that equally partake of the same divine reason, would you rashly infer that I was an enemy to the institution of marriage itself? Where shall we look for human beings who surpass all others in depravity and wretchedness? Are they not to be found in the haunts of female licentiousness. If their vice admits of a darker hue, it would receive it from the circumstance of their being dissolute by theory; of their modelling voluptuousness into a speculative system. Yet this is the charge you would make upon me. You would brand me as an enemy to marriage, not in the sense that a vestal, or widow, or chaste, but deserted maid is an enemy; not even in that sense in which the abandoned victims of poverty and temptation are enemies, but in the sense of that detestable philosophy which scoffs at the matrimonial institution itself, which denies all its pretensions to sanctity, which consigns us to the guidance of a sensual impulse, and treats as phantastic or chimerical, the sacred charities of husband, son, and brother. Beware. Imputations of this kind are more fatal in the consequences than you may be able to conceive. They cannot be indifferent to me. In drawing such inferences, you would hardly be justified by the most disinterested intentions.

Such inferences, my dear Madam, it is far from my intention to draw. I cannot but think your alarms unnecessary. If I am an enemy to marriage far be it from me to be the champion of sensuality. I know the sacredness of this word in the opinions of mankind; I know how liable to be misunderstood are the efforts of him who should labour to explode it. But still, is it not possible to define with so much perspicuity, and distinguish with so much accuracy as to preclude all possibility of mistake? I believe this possible. I deem it easy to justify the insinuation that you yourself are desirous of subverting the marriage state.

Proceed, said the lady. Men are at liberty to annex to words what meaning they think proper. What should hinder you, if you so please, from saying that snow is of the deepest black? Words are arbitrary. The idea that others annex to the word black, you are at liberty to transfer to the word white. But in the use of this privilege you must make your account in not being understood, and in reversing all the purposes of language.

Well, said I, that is yet to appear. Meanwhile, I pray you, what are *your* objections to the present system?

My objections are weighty ones. I disapprove of it, in the first place, because it renders the female a slave to the man. It enjoins and enforces submission on her part to the will of her husband. It includes a promise of implicit obedience and unalterable affection. Secondly, it leaves the woman destitute of property. Whatever she previously possesses, belongs absolutely to the man.

This representation seems not to be a faithful one, said I. Marriage leaves the wife without property, you say. How comes it then that she is able to subsist? You will answer, perhaps, that her sole dependence is placed upon the bounty of her husband. But this is surely an error. It is by virtue of express laws that all property subsists. But the same laws sanction the title of a wife to a subsistence proportioned to the estate of her husband. But if law were silent, custom would enforce this claim. The husband is in reality nothing but a steward. He is bound to make provision for his wife, proportionately to the extent of his own revenue. This is a practical truth, of which every woman is sensible. It is this that renders the riches of an husband a consideration of so much moment in the eye of a prudent woman. To select a wealthy partner is universally considered as the certain means of enriching ourselves, not less when the object of our choice is an husband than when it is a wife.

Notwithstanding all this, said the lady, you will not pretend to affirm that marriage renders the property common.

May I not truly assert, rejoined I, that the wife is legally entitled to her maintenance?

Yes, she is entitled to food, raiment, and shelter, if her husband can supply them. Suppose a man in possession of five thousand pounds a year: from this the wife is entitled to maintenance: but how shall the remainder be administered? Is not the power of the husband, over this, absolute? Cannot he reduce himself to poverty tomorrow? She may claim a certain portion of what she has, but he may, at his own pleasure, divest himself of all that he has. He may expend it on what purposes he pleases. It is his own, and, for the use of it, he is responsible to no tribunal; but in reality, this pompous claim of his wife amounts, in most cases, to nothing. It is the discretion of the husband that must decide, as to the kind and quantity of that provision. He may be niggardly or prodigal, according to the suggestions of his own caprice. He may hasten to poverty himself, or he may live, and compel his partner to live, in the midst of wealth as if he were labouring under extreme indigence. In neither case has the wife any remedy.

But recollect, my good friend, the husband is commonly the original proprietor. Has the wife a just claim to that which, before marriage, belonged to her spouse?

Certainly not. Nor is it less true that the husband has no just claim to that which, previously to marriage, belonged to the wife. If property were, in all respects, justly administered, if patrimonies were equally divided among offspring, and if the various avenues that lead to the possession of property were equally accessible to both sexes, it would be found as frequently and extensively vested in one son as in the other. Marriage is productive of no consequences which justify the transfer of what either previously possessed to the other. The idea of common property is absurd and pernicious; but even this is better than poverty and dependence to which the present system subjects the female.

But, said I, it is not to be forgotten that the household is common. One dwelling, one table, one set of servants may justly be sustained by a single fund. This fund may be managed by common consent. No particle of expense may accrue without the concurrence of both parties, but if there be a difference of opinion, some one must ultimately decide. Why should not this be the husband? You will say that this would be unjust. I answer that, since it is necessary that power should be vested in one or the other the injustice is inevitable. An opposite procedure would not diminish it. If this necessary power of deciding in cases of disagreement were lodged in the wife, the injustice would remain.

But a common fund and a common dwelling is superfluous. Why is marriage to condemn two human beings to dwell under the same roof and to eat at the same table, and to be served by the same domestics? This circumstance alone is the source of innumerable ills. Familiarity is the sure destroyer of reverence. All the bickerings and dissentions of a married life flow from no other source than that of too frequent communication. How difficult is it to introduce harmony of sentiment, even on topics of importance, between two persons? But this difficulty is increased in proportion to the number and frequency, and the connection with our private and personal deportment of these topics.

If two persons are condemned to cohabitation, there must doubtless be mutual accommodation. But let us understand this term. No one can sacrifice his opinions. What is incumbent upon him, in certain cases, is only to forbear doing what he esteems to be right. Now that situation is most eligible in which we are at liberty to conform to the dictates of our judgment. Situations of a different kind will frequently occur in human life. Many of them exist without any necessity. Such, in its present state, is matrimony.

Since an exact agreement of opinions is impossible, and since the intimate and constant intercourse of a married life requires either that the parties should agree in their opinions, or that one should forego his own resolutions, what is the consequence? Controversies will incessantly arise, and must be decided. If argument be insufficient, recourse must be had to legal authority, to brute force, or servile artifices, or to that superstition that has bound itself by a promise to obey. These might be endured if they were the necessary attendants of marriage; but they are spurious additions. Marriage is a sacred institution, but it would argue the most pitiful stupidity to imagine that all those circumstances which accident and custom have annexed to it are likewise sacred. Marriage is sacred, but iniquitous laws, by making it a compact of slavery, by imposing impracticable conditions and extorting impious promises have, in most countries, converted it into something flagitious and hateful.

But the marriage promises, said I, amount to this, that the parties shall love each other till death. Would you impose no restraint on wayward inclinations? Shall this contract subsist no longer than suits the wishes of either party? Would you grant, supposing you exalted into a law-giver, an unlimited power of divorces?

Without the least doubt. What shadow of justice is there in restraining mankind in this particular. My liberty is precious, but of all the ways in which my liberty can be infringed, and my actions be subjected to force, heaven deliver me from this species of constraint. It is impossible to do justice to my feelings on this occasion. Offer me any alternative, condemn me to the workshop of an Egyptian taskmaster, imprison me in chains of darkness, tear me into pieces, subject me to the endless repetition of toil and stripes and contumelies, but allow me, I beseech you, the liberty, at least, of conjugal choice. If you prohibit my intercourse with one on whom my heart dotes, I shall not repine, the injury is inexpressibly trivial. There is scarcely an inconvenience that will be worth enduring for the sake of this prohibited good. My resources must be few, indeed, if they do not afford me consolation under this injustice. But if you subject me to the controul and the nauseous caresses of one whom I hate, or despise, you indeed inflict a calamity which nothing can compensate. There is no form which your injustice can assume more detestable and ugly than this.

According to present modes, the servitude of wives is the most entire and unremitting. She lays aside her fetters not for a moment. There is not an action, however minute, in which her tyrant does not assume the power of prescribing. His eyes are eternally upon her. There is no period, however short, in which she is exempt from his cognizance; no recess, however sacred or mysterious, into which he does not intrude. She cannot cherish the friendship of a human being without his consent. She cannot dispense a charitable farthing without his connivance. The beings who owe their existence to her, are fashioned by his sole and despotic will. All their dignity and happiness is lodged in the hands that superintend their education and prescribe their conduct during the important periods of infancy and youth. But how they shall exist, what shall be taught, and what shall be withholden from them, what precepts they shall hear, and what examples they shall contemplate, it is his province to decide.

An husband is proposed to me. I ruminate on these facts. I ponder on this great question. Shall I retain my liberty or not? Perhaps the evils of my present situation, the pressure of poverty, the misjudging rule of a father, or the rare qualities of him who is proposed to me, the advantages of change of place or increase of fortune, may outweigh the evils of this state. Perhaps I rely on the wisdom of my partner. I am assured that he will, in all cases, trust to nothing but the force of reason; that his arguments will always convince, or his candour be accessible to conviction; that he will never make his appeal to personal or legal coersion, but allow me the dominion of my own conduct when he cannot persuade me to compliance with his wishes. These considerations may induce me to embrace the offer.

If I am not deceived; if no inauspicious revolution take place in his character; if circumstances undergo no material alteration; if I continue to love and to confide as at the first, it is well. I cannot object to a perpetual alliance, provided it be voluntary. There is nothing, in a choice of this kind, that shall necessarily cause it to expire. This alliance will be durable in proportion to the wisdom with which it was formed, and the foresight that was exerted.

But if a change take place, if I were deceived, and find insolence and peevishness, rigour and command, where I expected nothing but sweet equality and unalterable complaisance; or if the character be changed, if time introduce new modes of thinking and new systems of action to which my understanding refuses to assimilate, what is the consequence? Shall I not revoke my choice?

The hardships of constraint in this respect are peculiarly severe upon the female. Her's is the task of submission. In every case of disagreement it is she that must yield. The man still retains, in a great degree, his independence. In the choice of his abode, his occupations, his associates, his tasks and his pleasures, he is guided by his own judgment. The conduct of his wife, the treatment of her offspring, and the administration of her property are consigned to him. All the evils of constraint are aggravated by the present system. But if the system were reformed, if the duties of marriage extended to nothing but occasional interviews and personal fidelity, if each retained power over their own actions in all cases not immediately connected with the sensual intercourse, the obligation to maintain this intercourse, after preference had ceased, would be eminently evil. Less so, indeed, than in the present state of marriage, but still it would be fertile in misery. Have you any objections to this conclusion?

I cannot say that I have many. You know what is commonly urged in questions of this kind. Men, in civil society are, in most cases, subjected to a choice of evils. That which is injurious to one, or a few individuals, may yet be beneficial to the whole. In an estimate, sufficiently comprehensive, the good may overweigh the ill. You have drawn a forcible picture of the inconveniences attending the prohibition of divorces. Perhaps if entire liberty in this respect were granted, the effects might constitute a scene unspeakably more disastrous than any thing hitherto conceived.

As how, I pray you?

Men endeavour to adhere with a good grace to a contract which they cannot infringe. That which is commonly termed love is a vagrant and wayward principle. It pretends to spurn at those bounds which decorum and necessity prescribe to it, and yet, at the same time, is tamely and rigidly observant of those bounds. This passion commonly betides us when we have previously reasoned ourselves into the belief of the propriety of entertaining it. It seldom visits us but at the sober invitation of our judgment. It speedily takes its leave when its presence becomes uneasy, and its gratification ineligible or impossible. Youth and beauty, it is said, have a tendency to excite this passion, but suppose those qualities are discovered in a sister, what becomes of this tendency? Suppose the possession to be already a wife. If chance place us near an object of uncommon loveliness and we are impressed with a notion that she is single and disengaged, our hearts may be in some danger. But suppose better information has precluded this mistake, or that it is immediately rectified, the danger in most cases, is at an end. I am married and have no power to dissolve the contract. Will this consideration have no power over my sensations in the presence of a stranger? If care, accomplishments, and inimitable loveliness attract my notice, after my lot is decided, and chained me to one, with whom the comparison is disadvantageous, I may indulge a faint wish that my destiny had otherwise decreed; a momentary sigh at the irrevocableness of my choice, but my regrets will instantly vanish. Recollecting that my fate is indeed decided, and my lot truly irrevocable, I become cheerful and calm.

It is true that harmony cannot be expected to subsist for ever and in every minute instance between two persons, but how far will the consciousness that the ill is without remedy, and the condition of affairs unchangeable, tend to foster affection and generate mutual compliance. Human beings are distinguished by nothing more than by a propensity to imitation. They contract affection and resemblance with those persons or objects that are placed near them. The force of habit, in this respect, is admirable. Even inanimate objects become, through the influence of this principle, necessary to our happiness. They that are constant companions fail not to become, in most respects, alike, and to be linked together by the perception of this likeness. Their modes of acting and thinking might, at first, have jarred, but these modes are not in their own nature, immutable. The benefits of concurrence, the inconveniences of opposition, and the opportunities of comparing and weighing the grounds of their differences cannot be supposed to be without some tendency to produce resemblance and sympathy.

This is plausible, said the lady, but what is your aim in stating these remarks? Do you mean by them to extenuate the evils that arise from restraining divorces?

If they contribute to that end, answered I, it is proper to urge them. They promote a good purpose. Your picture was so terrible that I am willing to employ any expedient for softening its hues.

If it were just, you ought to have admitted its justice. We see the causes of these evils. They admit of an obvious remedy. A change in the opinions of a nation is all that is requisite for this end. But let us examine your pleas, or rather, instead of reasoning on the subject, let us turn our eyes on the world and its scenes, and mark the effect of this spirit by which human beings are prompted to adopt the opinions, and dote upon the presence of those whom accident has placed beside them. It would be absurd to deny all influence to habit and all force to reflections upon the incurableness of the evil, but what is the effect they produce? In numberless cases the married life is a scene of perpetual contention and strife. A transient observer frequently perceives this, but in cases where appearances are more specious, he that has an opportunity to penetrate the veil which hangs over the domestic scene, is often disgusted with a spectacle of varied and exquisite misery. Nothing is to be found but a disgusting train of mean compliances, despicable artifices, pevishness, recriminations and falsehood. It is rare that fortitude and consideration are exercised by either party. Their misery is heightened by impatience and tormenting recollections, but the few whose minds are capable of fortitude, who estimate the evil at its just value, and profit by the portion of good, whatever it be, that remains to them, experience indeed, sensations less acute, and pass fewer moments of bitterness; but it is from the unhappy that patience is demanded. This virtue does not annihilate the evil that oppresses us, but lightens it. It does not destroy in us the consciousness of privileges of which we are destitute, or of joys which have taken their flight. Its office is to prevent these reflections from leading us to rage and despair; to make us look upon lost happiness without relapsing into phrenzy; to establish in our bosoms the empire of cold and solemn indifference. If the exercise of reason and the enjoyment of liberty be valuable; if the effusions of genuine sympathy and the adherence to an unbiassed and enlightened choice, be the true element of man, what shall we think of that harmony which is the result of narrow views and that sympathy which is the offspring of constraint?

I know that love, as it is commonly understood, is an empty and capricious passion. It is a sensual attachment which, when unaccompanied with higher regards, is truly contemptible. To thwart it is often to destroy it, and sometimes, to qualify the victims of its delusions for Bedlam.[37] In the majority of cases it is nothing but a miserable project of affectation. The languishing and sighing lover is an object to which the errors of mankind have annexed a certain degree of reverence. Misery is our title to compassion, and to men of limited capacities the most delicious potion that can be administered is pity. For the sake of this, hundreds are annually metamorphosed into lovers. It is graceful to languish with an hopeless passion; to court the music of sighs and the secrecy of groves. But it is to be hoped that these chimeras[38] will, at length, take their leave of us.

In proportion as men become wise, their pursuits will be judiciously selected, and that which they have wisely chosen will continue for a certain period, to be the objects of their choice. Conjugal fidelity and constancy will characterize the wise. But constancy is meritorious only within certain limits. What reverence is due to groundless and obstinate attachments? It becomes me to make the best choice that circumstances will admit, but human affairs will never be reduced to that state in which the decisions of the wisest man will be immutable. Allowance must be made for inevitable changes of situation, and for the nature of man, which is essentially progressive: That is evil which hinders him from conforming to these changes, and restrains him from the exercise of his judgment.

Let it be admitted that love is easily extinguished by reflection. Does it follow that he ought to be controuled in the choice of his companion? Your observations imply, that he that is now married to one woman, would attach himself to another, if the law did not interpose. Where are the benefits of interposition? Does it increase the happiness of him that is affected by it? Will its succour be invoked by his present

---

[37] "Bedlam": a madhouse, a lunatic asylum; so called because Bedlam was the common name for the St. Mary of Bethlehem hospital in London, used as an insane asylum.

[38] "Chimeras": "an unreal creature of the imagination; a mere wild fancy" (*OED*). Brown and many writers of the Enlightenment use the term with a progressive or radical inflection to mean delusive, irrational, or "unenlightened" conclusions based on false premises or the illogical linkage of cause and effect.

consort? That a man continues to associate with me contrary to his judgment and inclination is no subject of congratulation. If law or force obliged him to endure my society, it does not compel him to feign esteem, or dissemble hatred or indifference. If the heart of my husband be estranged from me, I may possibly regard it as an evil. If in consequence of this estrangement, we separate our persons and interests, this is a desirable consequence. This is the only palliation of which the evil is susceptible.

It cannot be denied that certain inconveniences result from the disunion of a married pair, according to the present system. You have justly observed that men are reduced, in most cases, to a choice of evils. Some evils are unavoidable. Others are gratuitous and wantonly incurred. The chief evils flowing from the dissolution of marriage, are incident to the female. This happens in consequence of the iniquitous and partial treatment to which women in general are subjected. If marriage were freed from all spurious obligations, the inconveniences, attending the dissolution of it, would be reduced to nothing.

What think you, said I, of the duty we owe to our children. Is not their happiness materially affected by this species of liberty?

I cannot perceive how. I would, however, be rightly understood. I confess that, according to the present system, it would, and hence arises a new objection to this system. The children suffer, but do their sufferings, even in the present state of things, outweigh the evils resulting from the impossibility of separation? The evil that the parents endure, and the evils accruing to the offspring themselves?

If children stand in need of the guidance and protection of their elders, and particularly of their parents, it ought to be granted. The parental relation continues notwithstanding a divorce. Though they have ceased to be husband and wife to each other, they have not ceased to be father and mother to me. My claims on them are the same, and as forcible as ever. The ties by which they are bound to me, are not diminished by this event. My claim for subsistence is made upon their property. But this accident does not annihilate their property. If it impoverish one, the other is proportionably enriched. There is the same inclination and power to answer my claim: The judgment that consulted for my happiness and decided for me, before their separation, is no whit altered or lessened. On the contrary, it is most likely to be improved. When relieved from the task of tormenting each other, and no longer exposed to bickerings and disappointment, they become better qualified for any disinterested or arduous office.

But what effects, said I, may be expected from the removal of this restraint, upon the morals of the people? It seems to open a door to licentiousness and profligacy. If marriages can be dissolved and contracted at pleasure, will not every one deliver himself up to the impulse of a lawless appetite? Would not changes be incessant? All chastity of mind perhaps, would perish. A general corruption of manners would ensue, and this vice would pave the way for the admission of a thousand others, till the whole nation were sunk into a state of the lowest degeneracy.

Pray thee, cried the lady, leave this topic of declamation to the school boys—Liberty, in this respect, would eminently conduce to the happiness of mankind. A partial reformation would be insufficient. Set marriage on a right basis, and the pest that has hitherto made itself an inmate of every house, and ravaged every man's peace, will be exterminated. The servitude that has debased one half and the tyranny that has depraved the other half of the human species will be at an end.

And with all those objections to the present regulations on this subject, you will still maintain that you are an advocate of marriage?

Undoubtedly I retain the term, and am justified by common usage in retaining it. No one imagines that the forms which law or custom, in particular age or nation, may happen to annex to marriage are essential to it. If lawgivers should enlarge the privilege of divorce, and new modify the rights of property, as they are affected by marriage. Should they ordain that henceforth the husband should vow obedience to the wife, in place of the former vow which the wife made to the husband, or entirely prohibit promises of any kind; should they expunge from the catalogue of conjugal duties that which confines them to the same dwelling, who would imagine that the institution itself were subverted? In the east, conjugal servitude has ever been more absolute than with us, and polygamy legally established. Yet, who will affirm that marriage is unknown in the east. Every one knows that regulations respecting property, domestic government, and the causes of divorce are incident to this state, and do not constitute its essence.

I shall assent, said I, to the truth of this statement. Perhaps I may be disposed to adventure a few steps further than you. It appears to me that marriage has no other criterion than custom. This term is descriptive of that mode of sexual intercourse, whatever it may be, which custom or law has established in any country. All the modifications of this intercourse that have ever existed, or can be supposed to exist, are so many species included in the general term. The question that we have been discussing is no other than this: what species of marriage is most agreeable to justice—Or, in other words, what are the principles that ought to regulate the sexual intercourse? It is not likely that any portion of mankind have reduced these principles to practice. Hence arises a second question of the highest moment: what conduct is incumbent upon me, when the species of marriage established among my countrymen, does not conform to my notions of duty.

That indeed, returned she, is going further then I am willing to accompany you. There are many conceivable modes of sexual intercourse on which I cannot bestow the appellation of marriage. There is something which inseparably belongs to it. It is not unallowable to call by this name a state which comprehends, together with these ingredients, any number of appendages. But to call a state which wants these ingredients marriage, appears to me a perversion of language.

I pry'thee, said I, what are these ingredients! You have largely expatiated on the non-essentials of matrimony: Be good enough to say what truly belongs to this state?

Willingly, answered she. Marriage is an union founded on free and mutual consent. It cannot exist without friendship. It cannot exist without personal fidelity. As soon as the union ceases to be spontaneous it ceases to be just. This is the sum. If I were to talk for months, I could add nothing to the completeness of this definition.

7. William Godwin, excerpts from *Enquiry Concerning Political Justice* (1793)

William Godwin (1756–1836) was at the center of British progressive culture and politics in the 1790s. His Political Justice *is a key work of the Woldwinite circle, the most complete articulation of its social principles and program. Along with Mary Wollstonecraft and Thomas Paine, Godwin was tremendously popular and influential among the college-educated young men who formed the core of Brown's associates. These writings operate as the common sense and moral compass for Brown's group, which corresponded with Godwin and Godwin's fellow traveler Thomas Holcroft as early as 1796.*

Brown and his circle were familiar with Political Justice *in its successive editions. They could easily compare and contrast passages from expanded later editions with earlier material. With the exception of the first passage provided here, on the social function of literature, these excerpts follow the second (1796) edition in the Philadelphia printing by Bioren and Madan, the version that was most readily available to Brown during his novelistic years. The first edition sets forth Godwin's belief that reasonable conversation—rational discussion, dialogue, and learning—can generally impart truth to those who participate in it, and that this rationalizing spirit will spread outward from small communities that practice it to peacefully undermine the coercive practices of traditional states and governments, and the abusive superstition imposed by institutionalized religion.*

Literature plays a basic role in this gradual process of progressive action initiated through cultural practices, and Godwin assumes that the political purpose of fiction is to help educate readers about social relations so that they can overcome the retarding limits of traditional beliefs and behaviors that are merely reproduced and imposed by the status quo. Although Godwin removed this entire passage from later editions, he continued to reflect on the relation of literature and politics in his unpublished writings and, implicitly, in his fictions. His reticence to publish essays and make explicit public statements on the link between literature and politics may well be the result of increased repression and political prosecutions against free speech in Great Britain during the 1790s. In a preview of the 1798 U.S Alien and Sedition Acts, British state measures against democratic and dissenting writers resulted in several ideological trials that particularly targeted Godwin's circle. During a well-known but possibly apocryphal exchange, British Prime Minister William Pitt is said to have argued that there was no need to suppress Political Justice *as he had suppressed Thomas Paine's* Rights of Man *(1791) because Godwin's large treatise was too expensive for laboring class militants to purchase.*

Consequently, Godwin and his closest associates, including Mary Wollstonecraft, responded to these pressures by shifting their writing away from explicitly political commentary and toward fiction. The removal of the passage about the political nature of literature after the first edition does not represent any fundamental shift in Godwin's thinking on this topic, in other words, but may be a safeguard against the risk of too openly advertising the purpose of his own literary practices. Contemporary readers understood "literature," of course, to mean print culture in general, all printed books, rather than belles lettres, "art," or the restricted realm of aesthetic distinction.

The remaining excerpts insist on several themes that are important in Brown's theory of novel writing and that are implicitly explored in Ormond: *the social degradation and psychic damage caused by inequalities of wealth; the obligation to struggle for social reform through rational improvements; the power of benevolence as it acts through associative sentiment; and the importance of intimate conversation and transparency of personal motivation in setting the stage for larger social and historical transformations.*

*****

First Edition (1793)

From *Book I. Of the Importance of Political Institutions; Chapter IV. Three Principle Causes of Moral Improvement; I. Literature*

Few engines can be more powerful, and at the same time more salutary in their tendency, than literature. Without enquiring for the present into the cause of this phenomenon, it is sufficiently evident in fact, that the human mind is strongly infected with prejudice and mistake. The various opinions prevailing in different countries and among different classes of men upon the same subject, are almost innumerable; and yet of all these opinions only one can be true. Now the effectual way for extirpating these prejudices and mistakes seems to be literature.

Literature has reconciled the whole thinking world respecting the great principles of the system of the universe, and extirpated upon this subject the dreams of romance and the dogmas of superstition. Literature has unfolded the nature of the human mind, and Locke and others have established certain maxims respecting man, as Newton has done respecting matter, that are generally admitted for unquestionable. Discussion has ascertained with tolerable perspicuity the preference of liberty over slavery; and the Mainwarings, the Sibthorpes, and the Filmers, the race of speculative reasoners in favour of despotism, are almost extinct. Local prejudice had introduced innumerable privileges and prohibitions upon the subject of trade; speculation has nearly ascertained that perfect freedom is most favourable to her prosperity. If in many instances the collation of evidence have failed to produce universal conviction, it must however be considered, that it has not failed to produce irrefragable argument, and that falshood would have been much shorter in duration, if it had not been protected and inforced by the authority of political government.

Indeed, if there be such a thing as truth, it must infallibly be struck out by the collision of mind with mind. The restless activity of intellect will for a time be fertile in paradox and error; but these will be only diurnals, while the truths that occasionally spring up, like sturdy plants, will defy the rigour of season and climate. In proportion as one reasoner compares his deductions with those of another, the weak places of his argument will be detected, the principles he too hastily adopted will be overthrown, and the judgments, in which his mind was exposed to no sinister influence, will be confirmed. All that is requisite in these discussions is unlimited speculation, and a sufficient variety of systems and opinions. While we only dispute about the best way of doing a thing in itself wrong, we shall indeed make but a trifling progress; but, when we are once persuaded that nothing is too sacred to be brought to the touch-stone of examination, science will advance with rapid strides. Men, who turn their attention to the boundless field of enquiry, and still more who recollect the innumerable errors and caprices of mind, are apt to imagine that the labour is without benefit and endless. But this cannot be the case, if truth at last have any real existence. Errors will, during the whole period of their reign, combat each other; prejudices that have passed unsuspected for ages, will have their era of detection; but, if in any science we discover one solitary truth, it cannot be overthrown.

Such are the arguments that may be adduced in favour of literature. But, even should we admit them in their full force, and at the same time suppose that truth is the omnipotent artificer by which mind can infallibly be regulated, it would yet by no means sufficiently follow that literature is alone adequate to all the purposes of human improvement. Literature, and particularly that literature by which prejudice is superseded, and the mind is strung to a firmer tone, exists only as the portion of a few. The multitude, at least in the present state of human society, cannot partake of its illuminations. For that purpose it would be necessary, that the general system of policy should become favourable, that every individual should have leisure for reasoning and reflection, and that there should be no species of public institution, which, having falshood for its basis, should counteract their progress. This state of society, if it did not precede the general dissemination of truth, would at least be the immediate result of it.

But in representing this state of society as the ultimate result, we should incur an obvious fallacy. The discovery of truth is a pursuit of such vast extent, that it is scarcely possible to prescribe bounds to it. Those great lines, which seem at present to mark the limits of human understanding, will, like the mists that rise from a lake, retire farther and farther the more closely we approach them. A certain quantity of truth will be sufficient for the subversion of tyranny and usurpation; and this subversion, by a reflected force, will assist our understandings in the discovery of truth. In the mean time, it is not easy to define the exact portion of discovery that must necessarily precede political melioration. The period of partiality and injustice will be shortened, in proportion as political rectitude occupies a principal share in our disquisition. When the most considerable part of a nation, either for numbers or influence, becomes convinced of the flagrant absurdity of its institutions, the whole will soon be prepared tranquilly and by a sort of common consent to supersede them.

*****

Second Edition (1795)

Book I. Of The Powers Of Man Considered In His Social Capacity; Chapter I. "Introduction"

The object proposed in the following work is an investigation concerning that form of public or political society, that system of intercourse and reciprocal action, extending beyond the bounds of a single family, which shall be found most to conduce to the general benefit. How may the peculiar and independent operation of each individual in the social state most effectually be preserved? How may the security each man ought to possess, as to his life, and the employment of his faculties according to the dictates of his own understanding, be most certainly defended from invasion? How may the individuals of the human species be made to contribute most substantially to the general improvement and happiness?...

Many of the best patriots and most popular writers ... have treated morality and personal happiness as one science, and politics as a different one. ... But, while we confess ourselves indebted to the labours of these writers, and perhaps still more to the intrepid language and behaviour of these patriots, we are incited to enquire whether the topic which engaged their attention be not of higher and more extensive importance than they suspected. Perhaps government is not merely in some cases the defender, and in other the treacherous foe of the domestic virtues. Perhaps it insinuates itself into our personal dispositions, and insensibly communicates its own spirit to our private transactions. Were not the inhabitants of ancient Greece and Rome indebted in some degree to their political liberties for their excellence in art, and the illustrious theatre they occupy in the moral history of mankind? Are not the governments of modern Europe accountable for the slowness and inconstancy of its literary efforts, and the unworthy selfishness that characterizes its inhabitants?

Book I. Of The Powers Of Man Considered In His Social Capacity; Chapter III. Spirit Of Political Institutions

Two of the greatest abuses relative to the interior policy of nations, which at this time prevail in the world, consist in the irregular transfer of property, either first by violence, or secondly by fraud....First then it is to be observed that, in the most refined states of Europe, the inequality of property has risen to an alarming height. Vast numbers of their inhabitants are deprived of almost every accommodation that can render life tolerable or secure. Their utmost industry scarcely suffices for their support....A perpetual struggle with the evils of poverty, if frequently ineffectual, must necessarily render many of the sufferers desperate. A painful feeling of their oppressed situation will itself deprive them of the power of surmounting it. The superiority of the rich, being thus unmercifully exercised, must inevitably expose them to reprisals; and the poor man will be induced to regard the state of society as a state of war, an unjust combination, not for protecting every man in his rights and securing to him the means of existence, but for engrossing all its advantages to a few favoured individuals, and reserving for the portion of the rest want, dependence and misery.

Chapter IV. The Characters Of Men Originate In Their External Circumstances

... I shall attempt to prove two things: first, that the actions and dispositions of mankind are the offspring of circumstances and events, and not of any original determination that they bring into the world; and, secondly, that the great stream of our voluntary actions essentially depends, not upon the direct and immediate impulses of sense, but upon the decisions of the understanding.

Chapter V. The Voluntary Actions Of Men Originate In Their Opinions

The corollaries respecting political truth, deducible from the simple proposition, which seems clearly established by the reasonings of the present chapter, that the voluntary actions of men are in all instances conformable to the deductions of their understanding, are of the highest importance. Hence we may infer what are the hopes and prospects of human improvement. The doctrine which may be founded upon these principles may perhaps best be expressed in the five following propositions: Sound reasoning and truth, when adequately communicated, must always be victorious over error: Sound reasoning and truth are capable of being so communicated: Truth is omnipotent: The vices and moral weakness of man are not invincible: Man is perfectible, or in other words susceptible of perpetual improvement.

Chapter VII. Of the Influence of Luxury

This idea has been partly founded upon the romantic notions of pastoral life and the golden age. Innocence is not virtue. Virtue demands the active employment of an ardent mind in the promotion of the general good. No man can be eminently virtuous who is not accustomed to an extensive range of reflection. He must see all the benefits to arise from a disinterested proceeding, and must understand the proper method of producing those benefits. Ignorance, the slothful habits and limited views of uncultivated life, have not in them more of true virtue, though they may be more harmless, than luxury, vanity and extravagance. Individuals of exquisite feeling, whose disgust has been excited by the hardened selfishness or the unblushing corruption which have prevailed in their own times, have recurred in imagination to the forests of Norway or the bleak and uncomfortable Highlands of Scotland in search of a purer race of mankind. This imagination has been the offspring of disappointment, not the dictate of reason and philosophy.

Book II. Principles of Society; Chapter IV. Of Personal Virtue and Duty

In the first sense I would define virtue to be any action or actions of an intelligent being proceeding from kind and benevolent intention, and having a tendency to contribute to general happiness. Thus defined, it distributes itself under two heads; and, in whatever instance either the tendency or the intention is wanting, the virtue is incomplete. An action, however pure may be the intention of the agent, the tendency of which is mischievous, or which shall merely be nugatory and useless in its character, is not a virtuous action. Were it otherwise, we should be obliged to concede the appellation of virtue to the most nefarious deeds of bigots, persecutors and religious assassins, and to the weakest observances of a deluded superstition. Still less does an action, the consequences of which shall be supposed to be in the highest degree beneficial, but which proceeds from a mean, corrupt and degrading motive, deserve the appellation of virtue. A virtuous action is that, of which both the motive and the tendency concur to excite our approbation.

Book IV. Of The Operation Of Opinion In Societies And Individuals; Chapter I. Of Resistance

The strong hold of government has appeared hitherto to have consisted in seduction. However imperfect might be the political constitution under which they lived, mankind have ordinarily been persuaded to regard it with a sort of reverential and implicit respect. The privileges of Englishmen, and the liberties of Germany, the splendour of the most Christian, and the solemn gravity of the Catholic king, have each afforded a subject of exultation to the individuals who shared, or thought they shared, in the advantages these terms were conceived to describe. Each man was accustomed to deem it a mark of the peculiar kindness of providence that he was born in the country, whatever it was, to which he happened to be long. The time may come which shall subvert these prejudices. The time may come when men shall exercise the piercing search of truth upon the mysteries of government, and view without prepossession the defects and abuses of the constitution of their country. Out of this new order of things a new series of duties will arise. When a spirit of impartiality shall prevail, and loyalty shall decay, it will become us to enquire into the conduct which such a state of thinking shall make necessary. We shall then be called upon to maintain a true medium between blindness to injustice and calamity on the one hand, and an acrimonious spirit of violence and resentment on the other. It will be the duty of such as shall see these subjects in the pure light of truth to exert themselves for the effectual demolition of monopolies and usurpation; but effectual demolition is not the offspring of crude projects and precipitate measures. He who dedicates himself to these may be suspected to be under the domination of passion, rather than benevolence. The true friend of equality will do nothing unthinkingly, will cherish no wild schemes of uproar and confusion, and will endeavour to discover the mode in which his faculties may be laid out to the greatest and most permanent advantage.

Book IV. Chapter III. Of Political Association

There is at present in the world a cold reserve that keeps man at a distance from man. There is an art in the practice of which individuals communicate for ever, without anyone telling his neighbour what estimate he forms of his attainments and character, how they ought to be employed, and how to be improved. There is a sort of domestic tactics, the object of which is to elude curiosity, and keep up the tenour of conversation, without the disclosure either of our feelings or opinions. The friend of justice will have no object more deeply at heart than the annihilation of this duplicity. The man whose heart overflows with kindness for his species will habituate himself to consider, in each successive occasion of social intercourse, how that occasion may be most beneficently improved. Among the topics to which he will be anxious to awaken attention, politics will occupy a principal share. ...

It follows that the promoting the best interests of mankind eminently depends upon the freedom of social communication. Let us figure to ourselves a number of individuals who, having stored their minds with reading and reflection, are accustomed, in candid and unreserved conversation, to compare their ideas, suggest their doubts, examine their mutual difficulties and cultivate a perspicuous and animated manner of delivering their sentiments. Let us suppose that their intercourse is not confined to the society of each other, but that they are desirous extensively to communicate the truths with which they are acquainted. Let us suppose their illustrations to be not more distinguished by impartiality and demonstrative clearness than by the mildness of their temper, and a spirit of comprehensive benevolence. We shall then have an idea of knowledge as perpetually gaining ground, unaccompanied with peril in the means of its diffusion. Their hearers will be instigated to impart their acquisitions to still other hearers, and the circle of instruction will perpetually increase. Reason will spread, and not a brute and unintelligent sympathy.

Book IV. Chapter III, Appendix. Of the Connection Between Understanding and Virtue

A proposition which, however evident in itself, seems never to have been considered with the attention it deserves is that which affirms the connection between understanding and virtue. Can an honest ploughman be as virtuous as Cato? Is a man of weak intellects and narrow education as capable of moral excellence as the sublimest genius or the mind most stored with information and science?

To determine these questions it is necessary we should recollect the nature of virtue. Considered as a personal quality, it consists in the disposition of the mind, and may be defined a desire to promote the happiness of intelligent beings in general, the quantity of virtue being as the quantity of desire.

Book IV. Chapter VI. Of Sincerity

The powerful recommendations attendant upon sincerity are obvious. It is intimately connected with the general dissemination of innocence, energy, intellectual improvement, and philanthropy. [....]

There is a further benefit that would result to me from the habit of telling every man the truth, regardless of the dictates of worldly prudence and custom. I should acquire a clear, ingenuous and unembarrassed air....Sincerity would liberate my mind, and make the eulogiums I had occasion to pronounce, clear, copious and appropriate. Conversation would speedily exchange its present character of listlessness and insignificance, for a Roman boldness and fervour; and, accustomed, at first by the fortuitous operation of circumstances, to tell men of things it was useful for them to know, I should speedily learn to study their advantage, and never rest satisfied with my conduct till I had discovered how to spend the hours I was in their company in the way which was most rational and improving. [...]

What is it that, at this day, enables a thousand errors to keep their station in the world; priestcraft, tests, bribery, war, cabal and whatever else excites the disapprobation of the honest and enlightened mind? Cowardice; the timid reserve which makes men shrink from telling what they know; and the insidious policy that annexes persecution and punishment to an unrestrained and spirited discussion of the true interests of society. Men either refrain from the publication of unpalatable opinions because they are unwilling to make a sacrifice of their worldly prospects; or they publish them in a frigid and enigmatical spirit, stripped of their true character, and incapable of their genuine operation. If every man today would tell all the truth he knew, it is impossible to predict how short would be the reign of usurpation and folly.

Book VI. Effects of the Political Superintendence of Opinion; Chapter I. General Effects of the Political Superintendence of Opinion

The legitimate instrument of effecting political reformation is knowledge. Let truth be incessantly studied, illustrated and propagated, and the effect is inevitable. Let us not vainly endeavour, by laws and regulations, to anticipate the future dictates of the general mind, but calmly wait till the harvest of opinion is ripe. Let no new practice in politics be introduced, and no old one he anxiously superseded, till the alteration is called for by the public voice. The task which, for the present, should occupy the first rank in the thoughts of the friend of man is enquiry, communication, discussion.

Book VIII. Of Property. Appendix. Of Co-operation, Cohabitation and Marriage

The evil of marriage, as it is practiced in European countries, extends further than we have yet described. The method is, for a thoughtless and romantic youth of each sex, to come together, to see each other, for a few times, and under circumstances full of delusion, and then to vow to eternal attachment. What is the consequence of this? In almost every instance they find themselves deceived. They are reduced to make the best of an irretrievable mistake. They are led to conceive it is their wisest policy, to shut their eyes upon realities, happy, if, by any perversion of intellect, they can persuade themselves that they were right in their first crude opinion of each other. Thus the institution of marriage is made a system of fraud; and men who carefully mislead their judgments in the daily affair of their life, must be expected to have a crippled judgment in every other concern.

Add to this, that marriage, as now understood, is a monopoly, and the worst of monopolies. So long as two human beings are forbidden, by positive institution, to follow the dictates of their own mind, prejudice will be alive and vigorous. So long as I seek, by despotic and artificial means, to maintain my possession of a woman, I am guilty of the most odious selfishness. Over this imaginary prize, men watch with perpetual jealousy; and one man finds his desire, and his capacity to circumvent, as much excited, as the other is excited, to traverse his projects, and frustrate his hopes. As long as this state of society continues, philanthropy will be crossed and checked in a thousand ways, and the still augmenting stream of abuse will continue to flow.

The abolition of the present system of marriage, appears to involve no evils. We are apt to represent that abolition to ourselves, as the harbinger of brutal lust and depravity. But it really happens, in this, as in other cases, that the positive laws which are made to restrain our vices, irritate and multiply them. Not to say, that the same sentiments of justice and happiness, which, in a state of equality, would destroy our relish for expensive gratifications, might be expected to decrease our inordinate appetites of every kind, and to lead us universally to prefer the pleasures of intellect to the pleasures of sense.

It is a question of some moment, whether the intercourse of the sexes, in a reasonable state of society, would be promiscuous, or whether each man would select for himself a partner, to whom he will adhere, as long as that adherence shall continue to be the choice of both parties. Probability seems to be greatly in favour of the latter. [...] Friendship, if by friendship we understand that affection for an individual which is measured singly by what we know of his worth, is one of the most exquisite gratifications, perhaps one of the most improving exercises, of a rational mind. Friendship therefore may be expected to come in aid of the sexual intercourse, to refine its grossness, and increase its delight. All these arguments are calculated to determine our judgement in favour of marriage as a salutary and respectable institution, but not of that species of marriage in which there is no room for repentance and to which liberty and hope are equally strangers.

Admitting these principles therefore as the basis of the sexual commerce, what opinion ought we to form respecting infidelity to this attachment? Certainly no ties ought to be imposed upon either party, preventing them from quitting the attachment, whenever their judgement directs them to quit it. With respect to such infidelities as are compatible with an intention to adhere to it, the point of principal importance is a determination to have recourse to no species of disguise. In ordinary cases, and where the periods of absence are of no long duration, it would seem that any inconstancy would reflect some portion of discredit on the person that practised it. It would argue that the person's propensities were not under that kind of subordination which virtue and self-government appear to prescribe. But inconstancy like any other temporary dereliction, would not be found incompatible with a character of uncommon excellence. What, at present, renders it, in many instances, peculiarly loathsome is its being practised in a clandestine manner. It leads to a train of falsehood and a concerted hypocrisy, than which there is scarcely anything that more eminently depraves and degrades the human mind.

8. Debates on Women's Education and Rights

Throughout Ormond, *remarks concerning female education, marriage, and behavior stage an implicit commentary on and dramatization of debates on female education that were an important focus of innovation and resistance during the revolutionary period. The following examples from Benjamin Rush and Mary Wollstonecraft, both figures that Brown's circle followed closely, illustrate the polemical backdrop for this central dimension of Brown's novel.*

8a. Benjamin Rush, excerpts from *Thoughts Upon Female Education, Accommodated to the Present State of Society, Manners and Government, in the United States of America. Addressed to the Visitors of the Young Ladies Academy in Philadelphia, 28 July, 1787, At the Close of the Quarterly Examination* (Philadelphia: Prichard & Hall, 1787)

Benjamin Rush (1745–1813) was a key U.S. political leader, scientist-physician, and public writer in the colonial and early national periods. Although he was a signatory to the Declaration of Independence, Rush never served in elected political office, choosing instead to focus his energies on medical science and treatment. The Philadelphia-based Rush was well known to Brown as a member of abolitionist societies; as a key figure in public health policy and treatment controversies for the 1793 yellow fever epidemic that figures prominently in Brown's novels Ormond *and* Arthur Mervyn; *and as an older associate of Brown's medical friends such as Elihu Hubbard Smith. Rush apparently thought highly of Brown and, in 1803, recommended and praised Brown warmly as an ideal author for a proposed progressive history of prison reform.*[1]

Rush's voice was influential in many contemporary debates, including those concerning women's education and role in the social order, although his understanding of democratic or republican ideals was firmly cemented in a parochial form of patriotism and prejudice against foreign cultures. In his 1786 essay, "Of the Mode of Education Proper in a Republic," Rush championed education less as a human right central to the intellectual Enlightenment than as an institutional instrument for advancing a postaristocratic politics. In this essay he urges both native and immigrant youths to attend U.S. educational institutions so that schools can become engines for creating a homogeneous civil society. Education's goal, in his view, is to transform students into "republican machines" by instilling a love for selfless service that will lead young people to value the common interests of the republic over those of "friends, family, and property": "let our pupil be taught that he does not belong to himself, but that he is public property." Rush also maintains that education should emphasize topics useful for "promoting national prosperity and independence" and that the curriculum should include religious training, since a (Protestant) "Christian cannot fail of being a republican." Rush takes up the question of female education at the end of the essay, because "the opinions and conduct of men are often regulated by the women in the most arduous enterprises of life; and their approbation is frequently the principal reward of the hero's dangers, and the patriot's toils. Besides, the first impressions upon the minds of children are generally derived from the women."

In this manner, Rush's essay epitomizes the late-eighteenth-century view of women's role in the social order that scholars now refer to as "republican motherhood" or "republican womanhood." In this model, women's primary role is to function as agents for the social

---

[1] In an October 19, 1803 letter to Thomas Eddy, responding to Eddy's suggestion that he (Rush) write a history of prison reform, Rush writes: "Of course I must be excused from undertaking the work you have suggested to me. I shall mention it to Charles Brown. He possesses talents more than equal to it. The subject would glow under the eloquent strokes of his masterly pen." See *Letters of Benjamin Rush*, II: 874–76.

and cultural regulation of Christian bourgeois society through their influence as wives and mothers. Shortly after his essay on republican education, Rush expanded his arguments on female education in a Trustee Address delivered at the Young Ladies' Academy of Philadelphia. This academy, founded in 1787–1788 and, as of 1792, the first public chartered school for women in the early Republic, was a pioneering institution in female education. It immediately attracted a large number of students from the U.S. and Caribbean, and later drew students internationally, since it was one of the first schools offering female education above the primary level.

In his "Thoughts upon Female Education" address, Rush distinguishes the United States from England, primarily because the former remains organized along aristocratic lines. In a new, middle-class-dominated society, the American population (or at least its leaders) must be trained to tend and safeguard its property. While the address affirms women's education, Rush imagines women less as public actors than as a "field" to be cultivated for its valuable cultural produce. A woman's main identity is to embody a "natural soil" that can bear infants and ensure the multigenerational inheritance of class attitudes and property values, especially when men die before they can guarantee their children's inheritance of their social status and capital. In an important shift from the earlier essay on male education, the key word "republican" is now displaced by a newer term: "business." Consequently, Rush argues that women need to study "literature," by which he means history, travel accounts, poetry, and moral essays, but not print forms such as novels, since these degraded genres lead their readers away from the realities of everyday material life to the fantasies of an imagined or utopian state of affairs.

Additionally, Rush's essay stands as an early instance of U.S. cultural imperialism and resistance to cosmopolitan cultural orientations, especially when he suggests that immigrants to the new nation should learn English and assumes that any worthwhile foreign language text will naturally be translated into English for the ease of domestic readers. The implicit purpose of such cultural-linguistic gatekeeping is to prevent American women (and men) from being able to encounter alternative attitudes toward the organization of society, class relations, sexuality, and market exchange. If women are wrongly educated, Rush argues, then U.S. society will decline and the extent of its degeneration will be evident in the increasing diffusion of foreign cultural influences and languages within the new nation.

Brown's Ormond *can be read as a polemical reply to Rush's limited notion of women's empowerment, as well as to the insularity of his patriotism and nationalism. While Constantia pursues Rush's preferred curriculum in history, geography, and science, Constantia and the novel as a whole reject the notion that a women's priority is marriage and childbirth, as well as the arguments that familiarity with "foreign" languages, peoples, and lands is irrelevant or pernicious, and that the purpose of life is business, rather than the purpose of business life. With its repeated and spectacular examples of parental neglect and vice,* Ormond *rejects the notion that children are inflexibly determined by their parents' opinions and cannot develop into subjects who think through complex social issues for themselves. Female education improves with exposure to a wide spectrum of diverse ("foreign") cultures throughout the narrative, and both Constantia and Martinette are literally empowered as extraordinarily resourceful and admirable women as a result of their*

311

ability to extend their experience beyond confining local horizons. Despite Sophia's complaints about Constantia's lack of Christianity, Brown represents the novel's protagonist as a woman of exceptional moral and ethical strength.

Indeed, it was not only Brown who seems to have rejected Rush's constraining framework for women; the female graduates of the Young Ladies' Academy did so as well. As historian Margaret Nash observes, in the years immediately following Rush's address the school's valedictorian speakers pointedly ignored and rejected Rush's emphasis on motherhood and exclusion of women from full participation in civic speech and action. In 1793, valedictorian Priscilla Mason complained that there was no theater for women's public speech because "the Church, the Bar, and the Senate are shut against us. Who shut them? Man; despotic man, first made us incapable of the duty, and then forbid us the exercise." The following year, her successor Ann Harker complained about the shackles of marriage and argued for female equality in the pursuit of international liberty: "In opposition to your immortal Paine, we will exalt our Wolstencraft [sic], and the female Iberian Cicero." Given that the Academy published these speeches in their promotional material, Rush's opinions on women might not have been as widely accepted in the 1790s as might become the case later on, in the increasingly conservative early nineteenth century.

*****

GENTLEMEN,

I HAVE yielded with diffidence to the solicitations of the Principal of the Academy, in undertaking to express my regard for the prosperity of this Seminary of Learning, by submitting to your candor a few thoughts upon Female Education.

The first remark that I shall make upon this subject, is that female education should be accommodated to the state of society, manners, and government of the country, in which it is conducted.

This remark leads me at once to add, that the education of young ladies, in this country, should be conducted upon principles very different from what it is in Great Britain, and in some respects different from what it was when we were part of a monarchical empire.

There are several circumstances in the situation, employments, and duties of women, in America, which require a peculiar mode of education.

I. The early marriages of our women, by contracting the time allowed for education, renders it necessary to contract its plan, and to confine it chiefly to the more useful branches of literature.

II. The state of property, in America, renders it necessary for the greatest part of our citizens to employ themselves, in different occupations, for the advancement of their fortunes. This cannot be done without the assistance of the female members of the community. They must be the stewards, and guardians of their husbands' property. That education, therefore, will be most proper for our women, which teaches them to discharge the duties of those offices with the most success and reputation.

III. From the numerous avocations to which a professional life exposes gentlemen in America from their families, a principal share of the instruction of children naturally devolves upon the women. It becomes us therefore to prepare them, by a suitable education, for the discharge of this most important duty of mothers.

IV. The equal share that every citizen has in the liberty, and the possible share he may have in the government of our country, make it necessary that our ladies should be qualified to a certain degree by a peculiar and suitable education, to concur in instructing their sons in the principles of liberty and government.

V. In Great Britain the business of servants is a regular occupation, but in America this humble station is the usual retreat of unexpected indigence; hence the servants in this country possess less knowledge and subordination than are required from them; and hence, our ladies are obliged to attend more to the private affairs of their families than ladies generally do of the same rank in Great Britain. "They are good servants (said an American lady of distinguished merit* in a letter to a favorite daughter) who will do well with good looking after." This circumstance should have great influence upon the nature and extent of female education in America.

The branches of literature most essential for a young lady in this country, appear to be,

I. A knowledge of the English language. She should not only read, but speak and spell it correctly. And to enable her to do this, she should be taught the English grammar, and be frequently examined in applying its rules in common conversation.

II. Pleasure and interest conspire to make the writing of a fair and legible hand, a necessary branch of female education. For this purpose she should be taught not only to shape every letter properly, but to pay the strictest regard to points and capitals.†

I once heard of a man who professed to discover the temper and disposition of persons by looking at their hand writing. Without enquiring into the probability of this story, I shall only remark that there is one thing in which all mankind agree upon this subject, and that is, in considering writing that is blotted, crooked, or illegible, as a mark of a vulgar education. I know of few things more rude or illiberal, than to obtrude a letter upon a person of rank or business which cannot be easily read. Peculiar care should be taken to avoid every kind of ambiguity and affectation in writing *names*. I have now a letter in my possession upon business, from a gentleman of a liberal profession in a neighboring state, which I am unable to answer because I cannot discover the name which is subscribed to it. For obvious reasons I would recommend the writing of the first or Christian name at full length, where it does not consist of more than two syllables. Abbreviations of all kinds in letter-writing, which always denote either haste or carelessness, should likewise be avoided. I have only to add under this head, that the Italian and inverted hands, which are read with difficulty, are by

---

* Mrs. Græme.

† The present mode of writing among persons of taste is to use a capital letter only for the first word of a sentence, and for names of persons, places and months, and for the first word of every line in poetry. The words should be so shaped that a straight line may he drawn between two lines, without touching the extremities of the words in either of them.

no means accommodated to the active state of business in America, or to the simplicity of the citizens of a republic.

III. Some knowledge of figures and bookkeeping is absolutely necessary to qualify a young lady for the duties which await her in this country. There are certain occupations in which she may assist her husband with this knowledge; and should she survive him, and agreeably to the custom of our country be the executrix of his will, she cannot fail of deriving immense advantages from it.

IV. An acquaintance with geography and some instruction in chronology will enable a young lady to read history, biography, and travels, with advantage; and thereby qualify her not only for a general intercourse with the world, but to be an agreeable companion for a sensible man. To these branches of knowledge may be added, in some instances, a general acquaintance with the first principles of astronomy, and natural philosophy, particularly with such parts of them as are calculated to prevent superstition, by explaining the causes, or obviating the effects of natural evil.

V. Vocal music should never be neglected, in the education of a young lady, in this country. Besides preparing her to join in that part of public worship which consists in psalmody, it will enable her to soothe the cares of domestic life. The distress and vexation of a husband—the noise of a nursery, and, even, the sorrows that will sometimes intrude into her own bosom, may all be relieved by a song, where sound and sentiment unite to act upon the mind. I hope it will not be thought foreign to this part of our subject to introduce a fact here, which has been suggested to me by my profession, and that is, that the exercise of the organs of the breast, by singing, contributes very much to defend them from those diseases to which our climate, and other causes, have of late exposed them.—Our German fellow-citizens are seldom afflicted with consumptions, nor have I ever known but one instance of a spitting of blood among them. This, I believe, is in part occasioned by the strength which their lungs acquire by exercising them frequently in vocal music, for this constitutes an essential branch of their education. The music-master of our academy* has furnished me with an observation still more in favor of this opinion. He informed me that, he had known several instances of persons who were strongly disposed to the consumption, who were restored to health, by the moderate exercise of their lungs in singing.

VI. DANCING is by no means an improper branch of education for an American lady. It promotes health, and renders the figure and motions of the body easy and agreeable. I anticipate the time when the resources of conversation shall be so far multiplied, that the amusement of dancing shall be wholly confined to children. But in our present state of society and knowledge, I conceive it to be an agreeable substitute for the ignoble pleasures of drinking, and gaming, in our assemblies of grown people.

VII. The attention of our young ladies should be directed, as soon as they are prepared for it, to the reading of history—travels—poetry—and moral essays. These studies are accommodated, in a peculiar manner, to the present state of society in

---

* Mr. ADGATE.

America, and when a relish is excited for them, in early life, they subdue that passion for reading novels, which so generally prevails among the fair sex. I cannot dismiss this species of writing and reading without observing, that the subjects of novels are by no means accommodated to our present manners. They hold up *life*, it is true, but it is not yet *life*, in America. Our passions have not as yet "overstepped the modesty of nature," nor are they "torn to tatters," to use the expressions of the poet, by extravagant love, jealousy, ambition, or revenge. As yet the intrigues of a British novel are as foreign to our manners as the refinements of Asiatic vice. Let it not be said, that the tales of distress, which fill modern novels, have a tendency to soften the female heart into acts of humanity. The fact is the reverse of this. The abortive sympathy which is excited by the recital of imaginary distress, blunts the heart to that which is real; and, hence, we sometimes see instances of young ladies who weep away a whole forenoon over the criminal sorrows of a fictitious Charlotte or Werter, turning with disdain at two o'clock from the sight of a beggar, who solicits in feeble accents or signs, a small portion only, of the crumbs which fall from their fathers' tables.

VIII. It will be necessary to connect all these branches of education with regular instruction in the christian religion. For this purpose the principles of the different sects of christians should be taught and explained, and our pupils should early be furnished with some of the most simple arguments in favor of the truth of christianity.* A portion of the bible (of late improperly banished from our schools) should be read by them every day, and such questions should be asked, after reading it, as are calculated to imprint upon their minds the interesting stories contained in it.

Rousseau has asserted that the great secret of education consists in "wasting the time of children profitably." There is some truth in this observation. I believe that we often impair their health, and weaken their capacities, by imposing studies upon them, which are not proportioned to their years. But this objection does not apply to religious instruction. There are certain simple propositions in the christian religion, that are suited in a peculiar manner, to the infant state of reason and moral sensibility. A clergyman of long experience in the instruction of youth[†] informed me, that he always found children acquired religious knowledge more easily than knowledge upon other subjects; and that young girls acquired this kind of knowledge more readily than boys. The female breast is the natural soil of christianity; and while our women are taught to believe its doctrines, and obey its precepts, the wit of Voltaire and the style of Bolingbroke, will never be able to destroy its influence upon our citizens.

I cannot help remarking in this place, that Christianity exerts the most friendly influence upon science, as well as upon the morals and manners of mankind. Whether this be occasioned by the unity of truth, and the mutual assistance which truths upon different subjects afford each other, or whether the faculties of the mind be sharpened and corrected by embracing the truths of revelation, and thereby prepared

---

* Baron Haller's letters to his daughter on the truths of the christian religion, and Dr. Beatie's "evidences of the christian religion briefly and plainly stated," are excellent little tracts, and well adapted for this purpose.

† The Rev. Mr. NICHOLAS COLLIN, minister of the Swedish church in Wicocoe.

to investigate and perceive truths upon other subjects, I will not determine, but it is certain that the greatest discoveries in science have been made by christian philosophers, and that there is the most knowledge in those countries where there is the most christianity.* By knowledge I mean truth only; and by truth I mean the perception of things as they appear to the divine mind. If this remark be well founded, then those philosophers who reject christianity, and those christians, whether parents of school-masters, who neglect the religious instruction of their children and pupils, *reject* and *neglect* the most effectual means of promoting knowledge in our country.

IX. If the measures that have been recommended for inspiring our pupils with a sense of religious and moral obligation be adopted, the government of them will be easy and agreeable. I shall only remark under this head, that *strictness* of discipline will always render *severity* unnecessary, and that there will be the most instruction in that school, where there is the most order.

I have said nothing in favour of instrumental music as a branch of female education, because I conceive it is by no means accommodated to the present state of society and manners in America. The price of musical instruments, and the extravagant fees demanded by teachers of instrumental music, form but a small part of my objections to it.

To perform well, upon a musical instrument, requires much time and practice. From two to four hours in a day, for three or four years, appropriated to music, are an immense deduction from that short period of time which is allowed by the peculiar circumstances of our country for the acquisition of the useful branches of literature that have been mentioned. How many useful ideas might be picked up in these hours from history, philosophy, poetry, and the numerous moral essays with which our language abounds, and how much more would the knowledge acquired upon these subjects add to the consequence of a lady, with her husband and with society, than the best performed pieces of music upon a harpsichord or a guittar! Of the many ladies whom we have known, who have spent the most important years of their lives, in learning to play upon instruments of music, how few of them do we see amuse themselves or their friends with them after they become mistresses of families! Their harpsichords serve only as sideboards for their parlors, and prove by their silence, that necessity and circumstances, will always prevail over fashion, and false maxims of education.

Let it not be supposed from these observations that I am insensible of the charms of instrumental music, or that I wish to exclude it from the education of a lady where a musical ear irresistibly disposes to it, and affluence at the same time affords a

---

* This is true in a peculiar manner in the science of medicine. A young Scotch physician of enterprising talents, who conceived a high idea of the state of medicine in the eastern countries, spent two years in enquiries after medical knowledge in Constantinople, and Grand Cairo. On his return to Britain he confessed to an American physician whom he met at Naples, that after all his researches and travels, he "had discovered nothing except a single fact relative to the plague, that he thought worth remembering or communicating." The science of medicine in China, according to the accounts of De Halde, is in as imperfect a state as among the Indians of North-America.

prospect of such an exemption from the usual cares and duties of the mistress of a family, as will enable her to practice it. These circumstances form an exception to the general conduct that should arise upon this subject, from the present state of society and manners in America.

I beg leave further to bear a testimony against the practice of making the French language a part of female education in America. In Britain, where company and pleasure are the principal business of ladies; where the nursery and the kitchen form no part of their care, and where a daily intercourse is maintained with Frenchmen and other foreigners who speak the French language, a knowledge of it is absolutely necessary. But the case is widely different in this country. Of the many ladies who have applied to this language, how great a proportion of them have been hurried into the cares and duties of a family before they had acquired it; of those who have acquired it, how few have retained it after they were married; and of the few who have retained it, how seldom have they had occasion to speak it in the course of their lives! It certainly comports more with female delicacy as well as the natural politeness of the French nation, to make it necessary for Frenchmen to learn to speak our language in order to converse with our ladies, than for our ladies to learn their language in order to converse with them.

Let it not be said in defense of a knowledge of the French language, that many elegant books are written in it. Those of them that are truly valuable, are generally translated; but, if this were not the case, the English language certainly contains many more books of real utility and useful information than can be read, without neglecting other duties, by the daughter, or wife of an American citizen.

It is with reluctance that I object to drawing, as a branch of education for an American lady. To be the mistress of a family is one of the great ends of a woman's being, and while the peculiar state of society in America imposes this station so early, and renders the duties of it so numerous and difficult, I conceive that little time can be spared for the acquisition of this elegant accomplishment.

It is agreeable to observe how differently modern writers, and the inspired author of the proverbs, describe a fine woman. The former confine their praises chiefly to personal charms, and ornamental accomplishments, while the latter celebrates only the virtues of a valuable mistress of a family, and a useful member of society. The one is perfectly acquainted with all the fashionable languages of Europe; the other, "opens her mouth with wisdom" and is perfectly acquainted with all the uses of the needle, the distaff, and the loom. The business of the one, is pleasure; the pleasure of the other, is business. The one is admired abroad; the other is honored and beloved at home. "Her children arise up and call her blessed, her husband also, and he praiseth her." There is no fame in the world equal to this; nor is there a note in music half so delightful, as the respectful language with which a grateful son or daughter perpetuates the memory of a sensible and affectionate mother.

It should not surprise us that British customs, with respect to female education, have been transplanted into our American schools and families. We see marks of the same incongruity, of time and place, in many other things. We behold our houses accommodated to the climate of Great Britain, by eastern and western directions. We behold our ladies panting in a heat of ninety degrees, under a hat and cushion, which were calculated for the temperature of a British summer. We behold our citizens condemned and punished by a criminal law, which was copied from a country where maturity in corruption renders public executions a part of the amusements of the nation. It is high time to awake from this servility——to study our own character—to examine the age of our country—and to adopt manners in every thing, that shall be accommodated to our state of society, and to the forms of our government. In particular it is incumbent upon us to make ornamental accomplishments yield to principles and knowledge, in the education of our women.

A philosopher once said "let me make all the ballads of a country and I care not who makes its laws." He might with more propriety have said, let the ladies of a country be educated properly, and they will not only make and administer its laws, but form its manners and character. It would require a lively imagination to describe, or even to comprehend, the happiness of a country, where knowledge and virtue were generally diffused among the female sex. Our young men would then be restrained from vice by the terror of being banished from their company. The loud laugh, and the malignant smile, at the expence of innocence, or of personal infirmities—the feats of successful mimickry—and the low priced wit, which is borrowed from a misapplication of scripture phrases, would no more be considered as recommendations to the society of the ladies. A double entendre, in their presence, would then exclude a gentleman forever from the company of both sexes, and probably oblige him to seek an asylum from contempt, in a foreign country. The influence of female education would be still more extensive and useful in domestic life. The obligations of gentlemen to qualify themselves by knowledge and industry to discharge the duties of benevolence, would be encreased by marriage; and the patriot—the hero—and the legislator, would find the sweetest reward of their toils, in the approbation and applause of their wives. Children would discover the marks of maternal prudence and wisdom in every station of life; for it has been remarked that there have been few great or good men who have not been blessed with wise and prudent mothers. Cyrus was taught to revere the gods by his mother Mandane—Samuel was devoted to his prophetic office before he was born, by his mother Hannah—Constantine was rescued from paganism by his mother Constantia—and Edward the sixth inherited those great and excellent qualities which made him the delight of the age in which he lived, from his mother, Lady Jane Seymour. Many other instances might be mentioned, if necessary, from ancient and modern history, to establish the truth of this proposition.

I am not enthusiastical upon the subject of education. In the ordinary course of human affairs we shall probably too soon follow the footsteps of the nations of Europe in manners and vices. The first marks we shall perceive of our declension, will appear among our women. Their idleness, ignorance, and profligacy will be the harbingers of our ruin. Then will the character and performance of a buffoon on the theatre, be the subject of more conversation and praise, than the patriot or the minister of the gospel;—then will our language and pronunciation be enfeebled and corrupted by a flood of French and Italian words;—then will the history of romantic amours, be preferred to the immortal writings of Addison, Hawkesworth and Johnson;—then will our churches be neglected, and the name of the supreme being never be called upon, but in profane exclamations;—then will our Sundays be appropriated, only to feasts and concerts;—and then will begin all that train of domestic and political calamities—But, I forbear. The prospect is so painful, that I cannot help, silently, imploring the great arbiter of human affairs, to interpose his almighty goodness, and to deliver us from these evils, that, at least one spot of the earth may be reserved as a monument of the effects of good education, in order to show in some degree, what our species was, before the fall, and what it shall be, after its restoration.

Thus, gentlemen, have I briefly finished what I proposed. If I am wrong in those opinions in which I have taken the liberty of departing from the general and fashionable habits of thinking, I am sure you will discover, and pardon my mistakes. But if I am right, I am equally sure you will adopt my opinions; for to enlightened minds truth is alike acceptable, whether it comes from the lips of age, or the hand of antiquity, or whether it be obtruded by a person, who has no other claim to attention, than a desire of adding to the stock of human happiness.

I cannot dismiss the subject of female education without remarking, that the city of Philadelphia first saw a number of gentlemen associated for the purpose of directing the education of young ladies. By means of this plan, the power of teachers regulated and restrained, and the objects of education are extended. By the separation of the sexes in the unformed state of their manners, female delicacy is cherished and preserved. Here the young ladies may enjoy all the literary advantages of boarding-school, and at the same time live under the protection of their parents.* Here emulation may be excited without jealousy,—ambition without envy,—and competition without strife. The attempt to establish this new mode of education for young ladies was an experiment, and the success of it hath answered our expectations.† Too much praise cannot be given to our principal and his assistants, for the abilities and fidelity with which they have carried the plan into execution. The proficiency which the young ladies have discovered in reading—writing—spelling—arithmetic—grammar—geography—music—and their different catechisms, since the last examination, is a less equivocal mark of the merits of our teachers than anything I am able to express in their favour.

But the reputation of the academy must be suspended, till the public are convinced, by the future conduct and character of our pupils, of the advantages of the institution. To you, therefore,

---

* "Unnatural confinement makes a young woman embrace with avidity every pleasure when she is set free. To relish domestic life one must be acquainted with it; for it is in the house of her parents a young woman acquires the relish." Lord Kaims's thought upon education, and the culture of the heart.

† The number of scholars in the academy at present, amounts to upwards of one hundred.

YOUNG LADIES,

an important problem is committed for solution; and that is, whether our present plan of education be a wise one, and whether it be calculated to prepare you for the duties of social and domestic life. I know that the elevation of the female mind, by means of moral, physical and religious truth, is considered by some men as un-friendly to the domestic character of a woman. But this is the prejudice of little minds, and springs from the same spirit which opposes the general diffusion of knowledge among the citizens of our republics. If men believe that ignorance is fa-vorable to the government of the female sex, they are certainly deceived; for a weak and ignorant woman will always be governed with the greatest difficulty. I have sometimes been led to ascribe the invention of ridiculous and expensive fashions in female dress, entirely to the gentlemen*, in order to divert the ladies from improving their minds, and thereby to secure a more arbitrary and unlimited authority over them. It will be in your power, LADIES, to correct the mistakes and practice of our sex upon these subjects, by demonstrating, that the female temper can only be gov-erned by reason, and that the cultivation of reason in women, is alike friendly to the order of nature, and to private as well as public happiness.

8b. Mary Wollstonecraft, excerpts from *A Vindication of the Rights of Woman: with Strictures on Political and Moral Subjects* (1792)

Mary Wollstonecraft (1759–1797) was a major radical voice of the revolutionary age, re-membered today primarily as a path-breaking feminist. Her ideas and writings on gender and revolutionary cultural politics were central, formative references for Brown and his circle, who frequently discussed her books. Brown's Alcuin; A Dialogue *(included in Re-lated Texts), published just before he wrote* Ormond *and his other novels, rehearses many of the arguments about the social disempowerment of women that appeared in Woll-stonecraft's best known work,* A Vindication of the Rights of Woman. *Along with William Godwin, her lover and then husband (see the Godwin material in Related Texts), and Thomas Paine, Wollstonecraft was affirmed by most of Brown's generation of educated Americans as one the main figures of the English progressive writing that in-formed and energized their imaginations. News of her death (as a result of giving birth to daughter Mary, the later author of* Frankenstein *and wife of poet Percy Shelley) was re-ceived by Brown's circle and other Anglophone progressives as a tragic turn of events.*

*Wollstonecraft's life and sexual attitudes were as widely publicized as her writing, espe-cially after Godwin produced a 1798 memoir about her shortly after she died (*Memoirs of the Author of A Vindication of the Rights of Woman*). Godwin's narrative openly discussed her disastrous affair with American adventurer Gilbert Imlay (1754–1828), their out-of-wedlock child, and Wollstonecraft's suicide attempt after Imlay abandoned her. The reception of this unconventional narrative colored public attitudes about*

---

* The very expensive prints of female dresses which are published annually in France, are invented and executed wholly by GENTLEMEN.

Wollstonecraft for decades to come, and she was widely demonized and condemned by contemporary conservative propagandists.[2]

The London-born Wollstonecraft's early life was marked by strong affinities and concern for women's status outside the narrow confines of conventional female behavior. She convinced her sister to leave an abusive husband and had plans to live in a sort of female commune with a close friend. From the start, her early writing was concerned with the limits placed on women. In the early 1790s, she returned to London, after a period in Ireland as a governess, and Johnson helped secure her housing and steady, if not spectacular, employment as a reviewer for his Analytical Review. *Within this circle, she was quickly introduced to a set of male radicals and the period's wider progressive intellectual currents: she first met Godwin at a party Johnson gave for Thomas Paine's departure to revolutionary France. Responding to Edmund Burke's conservative condemnation of the French Revolution (*Reflections on the Revolution in France, *1790),* Wollstonecraft published A Vindication of the Rights of Men *(1790), a defense of progressive social struggle that appeared even before Paine's now better known* Rights of Man *(1791). She followed this with* A Vindication of the Rights of Woman, *the work for which she is best known today, which criticized Burke and Jean-Jacques Rousseau for their prejudicial idealizations of women.*

As author of A Vindication of the Rights of Woman, *Wollstonecraft is recognized as one of the foremothers of modern feminism. The* Vindication*'s basic point is that women are not born unequal to men, but are made so through custom. Wollstonecraft stands as one of the first critics of the social construction of gender, which separates biological sex from the cultural traits of masculinity and femininity. The core argument of the* Vindication *is that women have been historically subordinated and infantilized by their lack of access to education and pressure to dress and act in submissive ways, arguments illustrated in the excerpts below. Along with Godwin, she held that marriage was an unfair contract that held women in a slave-like condition to men. When Godwin and Wollstonecraft themselves married after several years together, their circle was scandalized at the paradox. Yet Wollstonecraft continued to affirm her autonomy as the two maintained their own apartments.*

Wollstonecraft's writing had an immediate impact on Brown's career as a writer. For his Wollstonecraft-influenced dialogue Alcuin, *see Related Texts here. More generally, most of the primary female characters in Brown's fiction are written to explore the arguments that Wollstonecraft articulates.* Ormond*'s overall focus on the struggles of its primary characters, all women coping in contrasting ways with the social forces that shape and limit their prospects and potentials, illustrates basic themes in the* Vindication. *The radical rejection of conventions concerning female education, marriage, and "softness" that is exhibited primarily in the exploits of Constantia and Martinette seems implicitly to affirm the arguments of Wollstonecraft and extend them toward further reflections on the social transformations that will be necessary to create improved conditions for liberty for both sexes.*

---

[2] See, for example, Chandos, "Mary Wollstonecraft; or, the Female Illuminati: The Campaign against Women and 'Modern Philosophy' in the Early Republic."

*****

Author's Introduction[3]

[...]

Yet, because I am a woman, I would not lead my readers to suppose that I mean violently to agitate the contested question respecting the equality or inferiority of the sex; but as the subject lies in my way, and I cannot pass it over without subjecting the main tendency of my reasoning to misconstruction, I shall stop a moment to deliver, in a few words, my opinion.—In the government of the physical world it is observable that the female, in general, is inferior to the male. The male pursues, the female yields—this is the law of nature; and it does not appear to be suspended or abrogated in favour of woman. This physical superiority cannot be denied—and it is a noble prerogative! But not content with this natural pre-eminence, men endeavour to sink us still lower, merely to render us alluring objects for a moment; and women, intoxicated by the adoration which men, under the influence of their senses, pay them, do not seek to obtain a durable interest in their hearts, or to become the friends of the fellow creatures who find amusement in their society.

I am aware of an obvious inference:—from every quarter have I heard exclamations against masculine women; but where are they to be found? If by this appellation men mean to inveigh against their ardour in hunting, shooting, and gaming, I shall most cordially join in the cry; but if it be against the imitation of manly virtues, or, more properly speaking, the attainment of those talents and virtues, the exercise of which ennobles the human character, and which raise females in the scale of animal being, when they are comprehensively termed mankind;—all those who view them with a philosophical eye must, I should think, wish with me, that they may every day grow more and more masculine.

[...]

My own sex, I hope, will excuse me, if I treat them like rational creatures, instead of flattering their *fascinating* graces, and viewing them as if they were in a state of perpetual childhood, unable to stand alone. I earnestly wish to point out in what true dignity and human happiness consists—I wish to persuade women to endeavour to acquire strength, both of mind and body, and to convince them that the soft phrases, susceptibility of heart, delicacy of sentiment, and refinement of taste, are almost synonymous with epithets of weakness, and that those beings who are only the objects of pity and that kind of love, which has been termed its sister, will soon become objects of contempt.

Dismissing then those pretty feminine phrases, which the men condescendingly use to soften our slavish dependence, and despising that weak elegancy of mind, exquisite sensibility, and sweet docility of manners, supposed to be the sexual characteristics of the weaker vessel, I wish to shew that elegance is inferior to virtue, that the

---

[3] The text is given here as it appears in the second edition (London: J. Johnson, 1792).

first object of laudable ambition is to obtain a character as a human being, regardless of the distinction of sex; and that secondary views should be brought to this simple touchstone.

*****

To M. Talleyrand-Périgord Late Bishop of Autun[4]

[…]

Contending for the rights of woman, my main argument is built on this simple principle, that if she be not prepared by education to become the companion of man, she will stop the progress of knowledge, for truth must be common to all, or it will be inefficacious with respect to its influence on general practice. And how can woman be expected to cooperate unless she knows why she ought to be virtuous? unless freedom strengthens her reason till she comprehend her duty, and see in what manner it is connected with her real good? If children are to be educated to understand the true principle of patriotism, their mother must be a patriot; and the love of mankind, from which an orderly train of virtues spring, can only be produced by considering the moral and civil interest of mankind; but the education and situation of woman, at present, shuts her out from such investigations.

---

[4] Charles Maurice de Talleyrand-Périgord (1754–1838), commonly known simply as Talleyrand, was an important French political leader and diplomat during the Revolutionary and Napoleonic periods. Wollstonecraft "dedicates" the *Vindication* to Talleyrand in a critical sense because her argument is intended to rebut "a pamphlet you have lately published," his earlier statements concerning female education. Talleyrand authored a 1791 French National Assembly "Report on Public Instruction" which, like Benjamin Rush, recommended that female education shape women to fulfill subservient roles as republican helpmates and mothers.

Born into an aristocratic family from Périgord in the south of France (present-day Dordogne), Talleyrand became involved in the revolutionary process in 1789 as a clergy representative to the Estates General. Because he was a nonbeliever and had pursued an ecclesiastical career as a form of political advancement (after his family refused him the right of primogeniture), he resigned his bishopric and was excommunicated early in the revolutionary process. Thus Wollstonecraft's "Late Bishop of Autun" is a rather arch form of address. After traveling to England in 1792 as an unofficial envoy from the Revolutionary Assembly charged with attempting to avert war with England, he was forced to remain in England when accused of treason by enemies in Paris. After a time in London during which he supported himself as a banker involved in commodity and real-estate speculation, he was expelled from England in December 1794 by Prime Minister Pitt and traveled to Philadelphia, where he became one of many French-speaking revolutionary émigrés along with figures such as Volney and Moreau de Saint-Méry (see Related Texts for writings by both). After political accusations against him were rescinded (and his excommunication was lifted by the Pope), Talleyrand returned to Paris from Philadelphia in 1796 as a "Thermidorean" conservative and went on to become Napoleon's foreign minister and a crucial figure in the first French Empire. There is no record of encounters between Brown or his circle and Talleyrand, although it is likely they crossed paths, given the ordinariness of interactions between Brown's circle and other elite groups in Philadelphia during this period.

[…]

Consider, Sir, dispassionately, these observations—for a glimpse of this truth seemed to open before you when you observed, 'that to see one half of the human race excluded by the other from all participation of government, was a political phænomenon that, according to abstract principles, it was impossible to explain.' If so, on what does your constitution rest? If the abstract rights of man will bear discussion and explanation, those of woman, by a parity of reasoning, will not shrink from the same test: though a different opinion prevails in this country, built on the very arguments which you use to justify the oppression of woman—prescription.

[…]

Who made man the exclusive judge, if woman partake with him the gift of reason?

In this style, argue tyrants of every denomination, from the weak king to the weak father of a family; they are all eager to crush reason; yet always assert that they usurp its throne only to be useful. Do you not act a similar part, when you force all women, by denying them civil and political rights, to remain immured in their families groping in the dark? for surely, Sir, you will not assert, that a duty can be binding which is not founded on reason? If indeed this be their destination, arguments may be drawn from reason: and thus augustly supported, the more understanding women acquire, the more they will be attached to their duty—comprehending it—for unless they comprehend it, unless their morals be fixed on the same immutable principle as those of man, no authority can make them discharge it in a virtuous manner. They may be convenient slaves, but slavery will have its constant effect, degrading the master and the abject dependent.

*****

Chapter II. The Prevailing Opinion of a Sexual Character Discussed

[…]

Riches and hereditary honours have made cyphers of women to give consequence to the numerical figure; and idleness has produced a mixture of gallantry and despotism into society, which leads the very men who are the slaves of their mistresses to tyrannize over their sisters, wives, and daughters. This is only keeping them in rank and file, it is true. Strengthen the female mind by enlarging it, and there will be an end to blind obedience; but, as blind obedience is ever sought for by power, tyrants and sensualists are in the right when they endeavour to keep women in the dark, because the former only want slaves, and the latter a play-thing. The sensualist, indeed, has been the most dangerous of tyrants, and women have been duped by their lovers, as princes by their ministers, whilst dreaming that they reigned over them.

[…]

Women ought to endeavour to purify their heart; but can they do so when their uncultivated understandings make them entirely dependent on their senses for employment and amusement, when no noble pursuit sets them above the little vanities of the day, or enables them to curb the wild emotions that agitate a reed over which every passing breeze has power? To gain the affections of a virtuous man is affectation necessary? Nature has given woman a weaker frame than man; but, to ensure her husband's affections, must a wife, who by the exercise of her mind and body whilst she was discharging the duties of a daughter, wife, and mother, has allowed her constitution to retain its natural strength, and her nerves a healthy tone, is she, I say, to condescend to use art and feign a sickly delicacy in order to secure her husband's affection? Weakness may excite tenderness, and gratify the arrogant pride of man; but the lordly caresses of a protector will not gratify a noble mind that pants for, and deserves to be respected. Fondness is a poor substitute for friendship!

In a seraglio, I grant, that all these arts are necessary; the epicure must have his palate tickled, or he will sink into apathy; but have women so little ambition as to be satisfied with such a condition? Can they supinely dream life away in the lap of pleasure, or the languor of weariness, rather than assert their claim to pursue reasonable pleasures and render themselves conspicuous by practising the virtues which dignify mankind? Surely she has not an immortal soul who can loiter life away merely employed to adorn her person, that she may amuse the languid hours, and soften the cares of a fellow-creature who is willing to be enlivened by her smiles and tricks, when the serious business of life is over.

Besides, the woman who strengthens her body and exercises her mind will, by managing her family and practising various virtues, become the friend, and not the humble dependent of her husband; and if she, by possessing such substantial qualities, merit his regard, she will not find it necessary to conceal her affection, nor to pretend to an unnatural coldness of constitution to excite her husband's passions. In fact, if we revert to history, we shall find that the women who have distinguished themselves have neither been the most beautiful nor the most gentle of their sex.

[…]

I own it frequently happens that women who have fostered a romantic unnatural delicacy of feeling, waste their* lives in imagining how happy they should have been with a husband who could love them with a fervid increasing affection every day, and all day. But they might as well pine married as single—and would not be a jot more unhappy with a bad husband than longing for a good one. That a proper education; or, to speak with more precision, a well stored mind, would enable a woman to support a single life with dignity, I grant; but that she should avoid cultivating her taste, lest her husband should occasionally shock it, is quitting a substance for a shadow. To say the truth, I do not know of what use is an improved taste, if the individual is not rendered more independent of the casualties of life; if new sources of enjoyment, only dependent on the solitary operations of the mind, are not opened. People of taste, married or single, without distinction, will ever be disgusted by various things that touch not less observing minds. On this conclusion the argument must not be allowed to hinge; but in the whole sum of enjoyment is taste to be denominated a blessing?

---

* For example, the herd of Novelists.

[...]

But to view the subject in another point of view. Do passive indolent women make the best wives? Confining our discussion to the present moment of existence, let us see how such weak creatures perform their part? Do the women, who, by the attainment of a few superficial accomplishments, have strengthened the prevailing prejudice, merely contribute to the happiness of their husbands? Do they display their charms merely to amuse them? And have women, who have early imbibed notions of passive obedience, sufficient character to manage a family or educate children? So far from it, that, after surveying the history of woman, I cannot help, agreeing with the severest satirist, considering the sex as the weakest as well as the most oppressed half of the species. What does history disclose but marks of inferiority, and how few women have emancipated themselves from the galling yoke of sovereign man?—So few, that the exceptions remind me of an ingenious conjecture respecting Newton: that he was probably a being of superior order, accidentally caged in a human body. In the same style, I have been led to imagine that the few extraordinary women who have rushed in eccentrical directions out of the orbit prescribed to their sex, were *male* spirited, confined by mistake in a female frame. But if it be not philosophical to think of sex when the soul is mentioned, the inferiority must depend on the organs; or the heavenly fire, which is to ferment the clay, is not given in equal portions.

*****

Chapter IV. Observations on the State of Degradation to Which Woman Is Reduced by Various Causes

[...]

Novels, music, poetry, and gallantry, all tend to make women the creatures of sensation, and their character is thus formed during the time they are acquiring accomplishments, the only improvement they are excited, by their station in society, to acquire. This overstretched sensibility naturally relaxes the other powers of the mind, and prevents intellect from attaining that sovereignty which it ought to attain to render a rational creature useful to others, and content with its own station: for the exercise of the understanding, as life advances, is the only method pointed out by nature to calm the passions.

Satiety has a very different effect, and I have often been forcibly struck by an emphatical description of damnation:—when the spirit is represented as continually hovering with abortive eagerness round the defiled body, unable to enjoy any thing without the organs of sense. Yet, to their senses, are women made slaves, because it is by their sensibility that they obtain present power.

[...]

Still, highly as I respect marriage, as the foundation of almost every social virtue, I cannot avoid feeling the most lively compassion for those unfortunate females who are broken off from society, and by one error torn from all those affections and relationships that improve the heart and mind. It does not frequently even deserve the name of error; for many innocent girls become the dupes of a sincere, affectionate heart, and still more are, as it may emphatically be termed, ruined before they know the difference between virtue and vice:—and thus prepared by their education for infamy, they become infamous. Asylums and Magdalenes are not the proper remedies for these abuses. It is justice, not charity, that is wanting in the world!

A woman who has lost her honour, imagines that she cannot fall lower, and as for recovering her former station, it is impossible; no exertion can wash this stain away. Losing thus every spur, and having no other means of support, prostitution becomes her only refuge, and the character is quickly depraved by circumstances over which the poor wretch has little power, unless she possesses an uncommon portion of sense and loftiness of spirit. Necessity never makes prostitution the business of men's lives; though numberless are the women who are thus rendered systematically vicious. This, however, arises, in a great degree, from the state of idleness in which women are educated, who are always taught to look up to man for a maintenance, and to consider their persons as the proper return for his exertions to support them. Meretricious airs, and the whole science of wantonness, has then a more powerful stimulus than either appetite or vanity; and this remark gives force to the prevailing opinion, that with chastity all is lost that is respectable in woman. Her character depends on the observance of one virtue, though the only passion fostered in her heart—is love. Nay, the honour of a woman is not made even to depend on her will.

[…]

Love, considered as an animal appetite, cannot long feed on itself without expiring. And this extinction in its own flame, may be termed the violent death of love. But the wife who has thus been rendered licentious, will probably endeavour to fill the void left by the loss of her husband's attentions; for she cannot contentedly become merely an upper servant after having been treated like a goddess. She is still handsome, and, instead of transferring her fondness to her children, she only dreams of enjoying the sunshine of life. Besides there are many husbands so devoid of sense and parental affection, that during the first effervescence of voluptuous fondness they refuse to let their wives suckle their children. They are only to dress and live to please them: and love—even innocent love, soon sinks into lasciviousness, when the exercise of a duty is sacrificed to its indulgence.

[…]

Friendship is a serious affection; the most sublime of all affections, because it is founded on principle, and cemented by time. The very reverse may be said of love. In a great degree, love and friendship cannot subsist in the same bosom; even when inspired by different objects they weaken or destroy each other, and for the same object can only be felt in succession. The vain fears and fond jealousies, the winds which fan the flame of love, when judiciously or artfully tempered, are both incompatible with the tender confidence and sincere respect of friendship.

*****

Chapter VI. The Effect which an Early Association of Ideas Has upon the Character

Educated in the enervating style recommended by the writers on whom I have been animadverting; and not having a chance, from their subordinate state in society, to recover their lost ground, is it surprising that women every where appear a defect in nature? Is it surprising, when we consider what a determinate effect an early association of ideas has on the character, that they neglect their understandings, and turn all their attention to their persons?

[…]

Education thus only supplies the man of genius with knowledge to give variety and contrast to his associations; but there is an habitual association of ideas, that grows 'with our growth,' which has a great effect on the moral character of mankind; and by which a turn is given to the mind that commonly remains throughout life. So ductile is the understanding, and yet so stubborn, that the associations which depend on adventitious circumstances, during the period that the body takes to arrive at maturity, can seldom be disentangled by reason. One idea calls up another, its old associate, and memory, faithful to the first impressions, particularly when the intellectual powers are not employed to cool our sensations, retraces them with mechanical exactness.

This habitual slavery, to first impressions, has a more baneful effect on the female than the male character, because business and other dry employments of the understanding, tend to deaden the feelings and break associations that do violence to reason. But females, who are made women of when they are mere children, and brought back to childhood when they ought to leave the go-cart for ever, have not sufficient strength of mind to efface the superinductions of art that have smothered nature.

Every thing that they see or hear serves to fix impressions, call forth emotions, and associate ideas, that give a sexual character to the mind. False notions of beauty and delicacy stop the growth of their limbs and produce a sickly soreness, rather than delicacy of organs; and thus weakened by being employed in unfolding instead of examining the first associations, forced on them by every surrounding object, how can they attain the vigour necessary to enable them to throw off that factitious character?—where find strength to recur to reason and rise superiour to a system of oppression, that blasts the fair promises of spring? This cruel association of ideas, which every thing conspires to twist into all their habits of thinking, or, to speak with more precision, of feeling, receives new force when they begin to act a little for themselves; for they then perceive that it is only through their address to excite emotions in men, that pleasure and power are to be obtained. Besides, the books professedly written for their instruction, which make the first impression on their minds, all inculcate the same opinions. Educated then in worse than Egyptian bondage, it is unreasonable, as well as cruel, to upbraid them with faults that can scarcely be avoided, unless a degree of native vigour be supposed, that falls to the lot of very few amongst mankind.

For instance, the severest sarcasms have been levelled against the sex, and they have been ridiculed for repeating 'a set of phrases learnt by rote,' when nothing could be more natural, considering the education they receive, and that their 'highest praise is to obey, unargued' —the will of man. If they be not allowed to have reason sufficient to govern their own conduct—why, all they learn—must be learned by rote! And when all their ingenuity is called forth to adjust their dress, 'a passion for a scarlet coat,' is so natural, that it never surprised me; and, allowing Pope's summary of their character to be just, 'that every woman is at heart a rake,' why should they be bitterly censured for seeking a congenial mind, and preferring a rake to a man of sense? [...]

*****

Chapter IX. Of the Pernicious Effects which Arise from the Unnatural Distinctions Established in Society

From the respect paid to property flow, as from a poisoned fountain, most of the evils and vices which render this world such a dreary scene to the contemplative mind. For it is in the most polished society that noisome reptiles and venomous serpents lurk under the rank herbage; and there is voluptuousness pampered by the still sultry air, which relaxes every good disposition before it ripens into virtue.

[...]

But, to have done with these episodical observations, let me return to the more specious slavery which chains the very soul of woman, keeping her for ever under the bondage of ignorance.

The preposterous distinctions of rank, which render civilization a curse, by dividing the world between voluptuous tyrants, and cunning envious dependents, corrupt, almost equally, every class of people, because respectability is not attached to the discharge of the relative duties of life, but to the station, and when the duties are not fulfilled the affections cannot gain sufficient strength to fortify the virtue of which they are the natural reward. Still there are some loop-holes out of which a man may creep, and dare to think and act for himself; but for a woman it is an herculean task, because she has difficulties peculiar to her sex to overcome, which require almost superhuman powers.

[...]

Women are, in common with men, rendered weak and luxurious by the relaxing pleasures which wealth procures; but added to this they are made slaves to their persons, and must render them alluring that man may lend them his reason to guide their tottering steps aright. Or should they be ambitious, they must govern their tyrants by sinister tricks, for without rights there cannot be any incumbent duties. The laws respecting woman, which I mean to discuss in a future part, make an absurd unit of a man and his wife; and then, by the easy transition of only considering him as responsible, she is reduced to a mere cypher.

The being who discharges the duties of its station is independent; and, speaking of women at large, their first duty is to themselves as rational creatures, and the next, in point of importance, as citizens, is that, which includes so many, of a mother. The rank in life which dispenses with their fulfilling this duty, necessarily degrades them by making them mere dolls. Or, should they turn to something more important than merely fitting drapery upon a smooth block, their minds are only occupied by some soft platonic attachment; or, the actual management of an intrigue may keep their thoughts in motion; for when they neglect domestic duties, they have it not in their power to take the field and march and counter-march like soldiers, or wrangle in the senate to keep their faculties from rusting.

[...]

How strangely must the mind be sophisticated when this sort of state impresses it! But, till these monuments of folly are levelled by virtue, similar follies will leaven the whole mass. For the same character, in some degree, will prevail in the aggregate of society: and the refinements of luxury, or the vicious repinings of envious poverty, will equally banish virtue from society, considered as the characteristic of that society, or only allow it to appear as one of the stripes of the harlequin coat, worn by the civilized man.

In the superiour ranks of life, every duty is done by deputies, as if duties could ever be waved, and the vain pleasures which consequent idleness forces the rich to pursue, appear so enticing to the next rank, that the numerous scramblers for wealth sacrifice every thing to tread on their heels. The most sacred trusts are then considered as sinecures, because they were procured by interest, and only sought to enable a man to keep good company. Women, in particular, all want to be ladies. Which is simply to have nothing to do, but listlessly to go they scarcely care where, for they cannot tell what.

But what have women to do in society? I may be asked, but to loiter with easy grace; surely you would not condemn them all to suckle fools and chronicle small beer! No. Women might certainly study the art of healing, and be physicians as well as nurses. And midwifery, decency seems to allot to them, though I am afraid the word midwife, in our dictionaries, will soon give place to *accoucheur*, and one proof of the former delicacy of the sex be effaced from the language.

They might, also, study politics, and settle their benevolence on the broadest basis; for the reading of history will scarcely be more useful than the perusal of romances, if read as mere biography; if the character of the times, the political improvements, arts, etc. be not observed. In short, if it be not considered as the history of man; and not of particular men, who filled a niche in the temple of fame, and dropped into the black rolling stream of time, that silently sweeps all before it, into the shapeless void called—eternity.—For shape, can it be called 'that shape hath none?'

Business of various kinds, they might likewise pursue, if they were educated in a more orderly manner, which might save many from common and legal prostitution. Women would not then marry for a support, as men accept of places under government, and neglect the implied duties; nor would an attempt to earn their own subsistence, a most laudable one! sink them almost to the level of those poor abandoned creatures who live by prostitution. For are not milliners and mantua-makers reckoned the next class? The few employments open to women, so far from being liberal, are menial; and when a superiour education enables them to take charge of the education of children as governesses, they are not treated like the tutors of sons, though even clerical tutors are not always treated in a manner calculated to render them respectable in the eyes of their pupils, to say nothing of the private comfort of the individual. But as women educated like gentlewomen, are never designed for the humiliating situation which necessity sometimes forces them to fill; these situations are considered in the light of a degradation; and they know little of the human heart, who need to be told, that nothing so painfully sharpens sensibility as such a fall in life.

Some of these women might be restrained from marrying by a proper spirit or delicacy, and others may not have had it in their power to escape in this pitiful way from servitude; is not that government then very defective, and very unmindful of the happiness of one half of its members, that does not provide for honest, independent women, by encouraging them to fill respectable stations? But in order to render their private virtue a public benefit, they must have a civil existence in the state, married or single; else we shall continually see some worthy woman, whose sensibility has been rendered painfully acute by undeserved contempt, droop like 'the lily broken down by a plow-share.'

It is a melancholy truth; yet such is the blessed effect of civilization! the most respectable women are the most oppressed; and, unless they have understandings far superiour to the common run of understandings, taking in both sexes, they must, from being treated like contemptible beings, become contemptible. How many women thus waste life away the prey of discontent, who might have practised as physicians, regulated a farm, managed a shop, and stood erect, supported by their own industry, instead of hanging their heads surcharged with the dew of sensibility, that consumes the beauty to which it at first gave lustre; nay, I doubt whether pity and love are so near akin as poets feign, for I have seldom seen much compassion excited by the helplessness of females, unless they were fair; then, perhaps, pity was the soft handmaid of love, or the harbinger of lust.

How much more respectable is the woman who earns her own bread by fulfilling any duty, than the most accomplished beauty!—beauty did I say?—so sensible am I of the beauty of moral loveliness, or the harmonious propriety that attunes the passions of a well-regulated mind, that I blush at making the comparison; yet I sigh to think how few women aim at attaining this respectability by withdrawing from the giddy whirl of pleasure, or the indolent calm that stupifies the good sort of women it sucks in.

9. William Godwin, excerpts from *Memoirs of the Author of A Vindication of the Rights of Woman* (London: J. Johnson, 1798)

Mary Wollstonecraft's death in childbirth in September 1797 came as a tremendous shock and loss to her admirers, including Brown's circle. When Elihu Hubbard Smith heard the news in early November, he wrote that the event was a "deep wound to my hopes. The loss of 50,000 French & as many Austrians, on the Rhine or in Italy, would have affected me less." Four months after the death, Godwin published a biographical memoir of Woll-stonecraft that was unexpectedly intimate, frankly discussing Wollstonecraft's ill-fated ro-mance with American adventurer Gilbert Imlay, the birth of an illegitimate daughter, her suicide attempts, and other aspects of her emotional life. If Godwin wrote the Mem-oirs *with the intention of cementing Wollstonecraft in the imagination of the Anglophone reading public, he certainly succeeded, but in a negative sense that made Wollstonecraft's name synonymous with revolutionary excess and a target for reactionary attacks for decades to come. The details of Wollstonecraft's refusal to follow the dominant constraints on female desire and propriety became fodder for the conservative press, which aggressively demonized Wollstonecraft and presented her death from puerperal fever as just punish-ment for what they condemned as immorality and infidelity.*

Despite the widespread journalistic campaign against Wollstonecraft's memory and Godwin's judgment in publishing the Memoirs, *it is not necessarily the case that Woll-stonecraft's admirers and other factions of the period's reading public felt the same way. No doubt many were capable of reading Godwin's gesture as an attempt to continue his wife's inquiry into the social construction of femininity and the forces aligned against female liberation. In the passage below, Godwin recounts Wollstonecraft's close emotional bonds with her friend Frances ("Fanny") Blood (1757–1785).*

After the death of her mother, Wollstonecraft lived for two years with Blood's family. She and Frances made plans to live together and to work to support each other mutually. With Wollstonecraft's sister, the two later established a school before Blood left for Portugal as a result of the health concerns described below. Wollstonecraft named her first, illegitimate child with Gilbert Imlay, Frances ("Fanny") in memory of Blood.

Godwin's account of Blood and Wollstonecraft's friendship begins by comparing Mary's attraction to Fanny with the romantic attachment described in the German writer Goethe's 1774 novel Die Leiden des jungen Werther (The Sorrows of Young Werther), *in which a young man falls passionately in love with a married woman. The erotic allu-sion suggests that Wollstonecraft's attraction to Blood will likewise transgress social con-ventions. Frances Blood's attraction to Mary becomes a catalyzing model of female intellectual development and illustrates innovative possibilities for women's expression and responsibility. Balanced against Frances' thrilling aspects, however, were her greater commitment to female subordination in the roles of daughter, wife, and mother. Blood's death in childbirth will, of course, be echoed in the* Memoirs *by Wollstonecraft's own eventual death in an analogous situation. Since Godwin was often considered to be emo-tionally inert or excessively stoic, his decision to include this passage may also involve some degree of self-recrimination.*

The Memoirs *provide a vivid point of reference for Brown's consideration of female in-teraction and development in* Ormond. *Readers of* Ormond *may hear echoes of Woll-stonecraft's attraction to Blood in Constantia's interactions with Martinette, Sophia, and Helena Cleves. The latter, particularly, seems to provide a negative example of a stereo-typical "female" lack of courage because, like Frances Blood, she fails to challenge the lim-its of traditionalized female codes and behaviors.*

*****

From Chapter II, 1775–1783

BUT a connection still more memorable originated about this time, between Mary and a person of her own sex, for whom she contracted a friendship so fervent, as for years to have constituted the ruling passion of her mind. The name of this person was Frances Blood; she was two years older than Mary. Her residence was at that time at Newington Butts, a village near the southern extremity of the metropolis; and the original instrument for bringing these two friends acquainted, was Mrs. Clare, wife of the gentleman already mentioned, who was on a footing of considerable intimacy with both parties. The acquaintance of Fanny, like that of Mr. Clare, contributed to ripen the immature talents of Mary.

The situation in which Mary was introduced to her, bore a resemblance to the first interview of Werter with Charlotte. She was conducted to the door of a small house, but furnished with peculiar neatness and propriety. The first object that caught her sight, was a young woman of a slender and elegant form, and eighteen years of age, busily employed in feeding and managing some children, born of the same parents, but considerably inferior to her in age. The impression Mary received from this spectacle was indelible; and, before the interview was concluded, she had taken, in her heart, the vows of an eternal friendship.

Fanny was a young woman of extraordinary accomplishments. She sung and played with taste. She drew with exquisite fidelity and neatness; and, by the employment of this talent, for some time maintained her father, mother, and family, but ultimately ruined her health by extraordinary exertions. She read and wrote with considerable application; and the same ideas of minute and delicate propriety followed her in these, as in her other occupations.

Mary, a wild, but animated and aspiring girl of sixteen, contemplated Fanny, in the first instance, with sentiments of inferiority and reverence. Though they were much together, yet, the distance of their habitation being considerable, they supplied the want of more frequent interviews by an assiduous correspondence. Mary found Fanny's letters better spelt and better indited than her own, and felt herself abashed. She had hitherto paid but a superficial attention to literature. She had read, to gratify the ardour of an inextinguishable thirst of knowledge; but she had not thought of writing as an art. Her ambition to excel was now awakened, and she applied herself with passion and earnestness. Fanny undertook to be her instructor; and, so far as related to accuracy and method, her lessons were given with considerable skill.

****

From Chapter III, 1783–1785

[...]

I have already said that Fanny's health had been materially injured by her incessant labours for the maintenance of her family. She had also suffered a disappointment, which preyed upon her mind. To these different sources of ill health she became gradually a victim; and at length discovered all the symptoms of a pulmonary consumption.

By the medical men that attended her, she was advised to try the effects of a southern climate; and, about the beginning of the year 1785, sailed for Lisbon.

The first feeling with which Mary had contemplated her friend, was a sentiment of inferiority and reverence; but that, from the operation of a ten years' acquaintance, was considerably changed. Fanny had originally been far before her in literary attainments; this disparity no longer existed. In whatever degree Mary might endeavour to free herself from the delusions of self-esteem, this period of observation upon her mind and that of her friend, could not pass, without her perceiving that there were some essential characteristics of genius, which she possessed, and in which her friend was deficient. The principal of these was a firmness of mind, an unconquerable greatness of soul, by which, after a short internal struggle, she was accustomed to rise above difficulties and suffering. Whatever Mary undertook, she perhaps in all instances accomplished; and, to her lofty spirit, scarcely anything she desired, appeared hard to perform. Fanny, on the contrary, was a woman of a timid and irresolute nature, accustomed to yield to difficulties, and probably priding herself in this morbid softness of her temper. One instance that I have heard Mary relate of this sort, was, that, at a certain time, Fanny, dissatisfied with her domestic situation, expressed an earnest desire to have a home of her own. Mary, who felt nothing more pressing than to relieve the inconveniences of her friend, determined to accomplish this object for her. It cost her infinite exertions; but at length she was able to announce to Fanny that a house was prepared, and that she was on the spot to receive her. The answer which Fanny returned to the letter of her friend, consisted almost wholly of an enumeration of objections to the quitting her family, which she had not thought of before, but which now appeared to her of considerable weight.

The judgment which experience had taught Mary to form of the mind of her friend, determined her in the advice she gave, at the period to which I have brought down the story. Fanny was recommended to seek a softer climate, but she had no funds to defray the expence of such an undertaking. At this time Mr. Hugh Skeys of Dublin, but then resident in the kingdom of Portugal, paid his addresses to her. The state of her health Mary considered as such as scarcely to afford the shadow of a hope; it was not therefore a time at which it was most obvious to think of marriage. She conceived however that nothing should be omitted, which might alleviate, if it could not cure; and accordingly urged her speedy acceptance of the proposal. Fanny accordingly made the voyage to Lisbon; and the marriage took place on the twenty-fourth of February 1785.

The change of climate and situation was productive of little benefit; and the life of Fanny was only prolonged by a period of pregnancy, which soon declared itself. Mary, in the mean time, was impressed with the idea that her friend would die in this distant country; and, shocked with the recollection of her separation from the circle of her friends, determined to pass over to Lisbon to attend her. This resolution was treated by her acquaintance as in the utmost degree visionary; but she was not to be diverted from her point.

[…]

Her residence in Lisbon was not long. She arrived but a short time before her friend was prematurely delivered, and the event was fatal to both mother and child. Frances Blood, hitherto the chosen object of Mary's attachment, died on the twenty-ninth of November 1785.

It is thus that she speaks of her in her Letters from Norway, written ten years after her decease. "When a warm heart had received strong impressions, they are not to be effaced. Emotions become sentiments; and the imagination renders even transient sensations permanent, by fondly retracing them. I cannot, without a thrill of delight, recollect views I have seen, which are not to be forgotten, nor looks I have felt in every nerve, which I shall never more meet. The grave has closed over a dear friend, the friend of my youth; still she is present with me, and I hear her soft voice warbling as I stray over the heath."

10. Female Transvestism in the Revolutionary Era

The two relatively well-known narratives of female cross-dressing excerpted here provide examples of a popular period genre to which Ormond *alludes on several levels.*

During the revolutionary age, accounts of women secretly cross-dressing and serving in armies and navies became increasingly common in Northern Europe and its colonies. Like the behaviors they describe, these cross-dressing tales tend to reinforce narrative and gender stereotypes even as they subversively illustrate how easily the tenuous social conventions of sex-gender may be transgressed. In this manner, these tales provide another source of commentary on and response to the period's debates about women's rights. Just as female protagonists in these tales learn codes of maleness in a more conscious way than men themselves, but do so only to escape limitations imposed on women, cross-dressing tales as a genre simultaneously adopt familiar narrative conventions only to break—or, to use a Brownian term, "explode"—them.

Though often presented as picaresque, episodic travel adventures, in genre terms these tales are closest to (and most disruptive of) the genre of captivity narrative, a popular early-modern form in which Christian Europeans typically experience the trauma of war or cross-cultural conflict and, after being captured by cultural "others" (usually Muslims or Indians), endure various forms of coercion and imprisonment. In the period's cross-dressing tales, women who masquerade (mainly as male sailors and soldiers) seek to escape the constraints of traditional gender roles, but do so in a way that forces them to "hide in plain sight" and continually risk being "recaptured" or returned to female status if their prior gender assignment is discovered. Thus these tales of transvestite imposture focus on the process of changing or challenging gender roles, rather than successfully establishing their subjects in a lasting state of improved conditions. That is, these tales stand not as accounts of gender liberation, but rather as a popular genre that constantly measures the limits of policed gender identities and behaviors.

If these cross-dressing tales are about experiencing transformation, or about being caught up in wider patterns of transformation, this is because they respond to rapidly changing social conditions in the eighteenth-century Atlantic world. The revolutionary age pro-duced rapid urbanization magnetized by the rise of industrialism; a global expansion of commerce and the mercantile and military navies required to support commerce-driven imperialism; and rapid changes in the nature of land warfare. All of these factors created novel conditions that allowed women to escape geographic and social constraints through a variety of strategies, including cross-dressing. As the rural poor were increasingly driven off the land and away from traditional agrarian lifeworlds, smashing the familiar cer-tainties of village culture and local, multigenerational family memory, they were drawn into cities where they sought individualized employment, often in the emerging system of mechanized factories. The influx of workers into growing urban centers gave some women openings to escape from countryside hierarchies and remake themselves in the more confusing and unknown world of the modern city. As industrializing northern Eu-ropean economies pulled in the lower classes from the countryside, however, they also pro-pelled them outward into military-imperial service, as a pool of cheap labor supporting the navies and merchant ships that patrolled distant territories and transported their raw materials back to metropolitan manufacturers and traders. Because these navies routinely drew boys and very young men into service (either by ordinary employment or coerced impressments), they also made it easier for smaller, less muscular and beardless women to pass as men.

As the need for colonial human and natural resources increased, so too did tensions among increasingly belligerent European nation–states vying for dominance. Throughout the century, an almost continuous series of wars between imperial rivals, above all Eng-land, France, and the Austrian Habsburg Empire, changed the nature of warfare in ways that also may have made it easier for women to masquerade their sex. As changes in the process of land war led to the decline of localized mercenary cultures and increasing re-liance on mass national armies, recruiting agents offered not only a way for lower-class men to escape provincial life, but also ways for passing women to blend into masses of male foot soldiers who were more mutually anonymous than previous generations of con-scripts because they were drawn from disparate regions.

The disruptions caused by ongoing wars meant that most of the period's accounts of cross-dressing involve episodes located on either side of a front that extended from the Nether-lands to southern Germany, dividing French revolutionary forces from their British and Habsburg antagonists. Rumors of significant numbers of women secretly enrolled in armies proliferated throughout the period. The actual prevalence of female cross-dressing is difficult to quantify, since the records of this activity discovered by social historians are only the episodes of "failure," or evidence concerning women who were caught and re-vealed as men. Given the logistics of warfare and the collective, open-air nature of otherwise intimate acts of dressing and toiletry, it may also be the case that the number of women who cross-dressed in civilian urban centers, where they had more control over bodily privacy, was as great or greater than the number on the battlefield or ships. Additionally, since most of these fighting women came from working or plebian-class backgrounds, they were probably weakly literate at best and had little access to male-con-trolled print institutions, so that many of their accounts would never reach the printed record. All of this indicates that the actual practice of cross-dressing has both links to and differences from the accounts we can read in the period's journalism, popular ballads, plays, and fiction.[1]

How does Brown register these practices and the popular genre of cross-dressing narratives in Ormond*?*[2] *In Chapter 20, as she explains her experiences as a highly motivated revolutionary soldier to Constantia, Martinette de Beauvais lists three reasons why women might masquerade as men during the revolutionary wars: patriotism or political convictions, curiosity, and the desire to follow their male lovers. With this passage Brown knowingly reproduces some of the rationales provided by the period's female soldiers or sailors when they were captured. Yet the chameleon Martinette seems to leave other motivations unspoken but suggestively implied in her exchange with Constantia. Many transvestite women, for example, moved in the period's criminal subcultures and cross-dressed simply to escape prosecution for other illegal activities. In a related possibility, although Houssay's account below involves political crimes, she makes it clear that her transvestism was enabled by a covert network and community of like-minded people, both men and women. This situation parallels Martinette's claim that an underrecognized Francophone exile community protected her at a time when she might otherwise have been treated as an outcast in Philadelphia. In this case, the performance of gender subversion becomes part of wider patterns of collective resistance to social authority, clustered under the category of "deviance."*

This possibility of a convergence between transvestism and collective resistance is related to the concerns of male authorities during their interrogations of women who had been caught cross-dressing. These questioners generally accepted women's explanations for their cross-dressing at face value, not least because the advantages of male privilege are self-evident. Nevertheless, as in the long interrogation scene from Houssay's narrative (not included here), male examiners were also anxious to learn how women discovered the possibility and techniques of cross-dressing in order to find out whether these acts were merely individual or rather the result of wider organization. Was there possibly a secret society educating and aiding women in their revolts, or other associational activities that might be brewing larger, unforeseen strategies of rebellion?[3]

---

[1] For more on this genre and its appeal in the revolutionary age, see Cohen, *The Female Marine and Related Works: Narratives of Cross-Dressing and Urban Vice in America's Early Republic*; Dekker and Van de Pol, *The Tradition of Female Transvestism in Early Modern Europe*; Dugaw, "Female Sailors Bold: Transvestite Heroines and the Markers of Gender and Class"; Friedli, "'Passing Women': a Study of Gender Boundaries in the Eighteenth Century"; Kahn, *Narrative Transvestism: Rhetoric and Gender in the Eighteenth-Century English Novel*; Levy and Applewhite, "Woman and Militant Citizenship in Revolutionary Paris"; and Wheelwright, *Amazons and Military Maids: Women who Dressed as Men in Pursuit of Life, Liberty and Happiness*.

[2] Brown's awareness of these narratives continued into his post-novelistic phase when he republished a brief example, "Account of Frances Scanagatti, a Milanese Young Lady, Who Served with Reputation as an Ensign and Lieutenant of Three Different Austrian Regiments during the Last War" in his Philadelphia *Literary Magazine* VIII.49 (October 1807), 183–88. The text had previously appeared in the London *Monthly Magazine* 150 (Dec. 1, 1806) 465–68.

[3] For more on the role of interrogations as a motif in these cross-dressing narratives, see Dekker and Van de Pol, *The Tradition of Female Transvestism in Early Modern Europe*.

This type of anxiety about the possibility of larger forms of covert and collective organization is echoed in the way that the novel's narrator Sophia presents both Martinette and Ormond as part of violent political organizations, and also in aspects of period accounts that appear in our readings here. Deborah Sampson's tale emphasizes her patriotism, but it also suggests that another reason for cross-dressing is her desire to participate in intellectual Enlightenment by acquiring knowledge, even scientific and philosophical knowledge, in ways that are otherwise prohibited to women. Her desire for American independence becomes a vehicle for legitimizing her push toward female autonomy.

A final important aspect of these cross-dressing narratives is their relation to the history of erotic desire. Like all genres, tales of female cross-dressing included formulaic scenarios, situations, or scenes. One standard situation in these cross-dressing tales presents a male-dressed woman being courted by another woman who is unaware that her object of desire is not a man. Similarly, the tales often feature scenes in which the protagonist is wounded or disempowered, so that the woman's identity is discovered as she is treated by a surgeon while in a weakened or half-conscious state. As plot points, these situations explain why the cross-dressing ends and becomes public, but obviously they also legitimate a pornographic thrill for (male) readers, since they make it permissible to voyeuristically imagine a woman's body being revealed to the male gaze. But male control of publication did not of course prevent these tales from being read by women, alone or in discussion groups. For women, the tales offered a mechanism for political commentary on female gender constraints and a primer on unruly activity and gender insubordination. Many female readers were thus encouraged, despite initial doubts, to consider transgressing conventional boundaries, and it is this emotional pattern that is presented in Ormond *when Martinette's accounts of her own serial transvestism encourage Constantia to embrace a more assertive style of female independence. Therefore, while male readers could use these tales as opportunities to fantasize about women's bodies, so too could female readers use them to fantasize about bodies and about a world in which they were not held captive by imposed constraints on female behavior and potentials.*

As someone who was exceptionally well versed in the period's multiple subgenres and literary underground, Brown was certainly aware of the homoerotic potential of cross-dressing tales. Indeed, Chapter 14's footnote on Ormond's masquerade as a chimney-sweep likely involves an allusion to a then well-known presentation of these scenarios. In his footnote, Brown refers readers to the pseudonymous Memoirs of the Late Edw. W—ly M—tague, Esq; with Remarks on the Manners and Customs of the Oriental World; Collected and Published from Original Posthumous Papers *(London: J. Wallis, 1777). Edward Wortley Montagu (1713–1776) was well known as a kind of cultural cross-dresser after a series of marriages and religious-cultural conversions (from Protestantism to Catholicism to Islam and back) throughout the Mediterranean and Middle East. His mother, Lady Mary Wortley Montagu (1689–1762), enjoyed a related celebrity after her travels in the Ottoman Empire and well-known letters from Turkey; she was also one of the Bluestockings group and was notoriously attacked by poet Alexander Pope (an unsuccessful suitor), who insulted her by associating her with same-sex sexual practices. The book Brown refers to is a fictional version of Montagu's exploits that is framed by an account of his mother's Ottoman journeys and her experience with exotic, "oriental" sexual mores. The narrative emphasizes Lady Montagu's love of "voluptuous pleasures" and recounts that in Turkey she watched women performing a dance that mimicked orgasm and encouraged female viewers to contemplate "something not to be spoke of," which is one of the period's familiar codes for same-sex sexuality (a code that Brown himself uses in his novel* Memoirs of Stephen Calvert*). Lady Montagu then accedes to the interior of the Emperor's seraglio disguised as a Turkish woman, presumably to secretly observe its female inhabitants, but discovers that the Ottoman ruler has right of sexual possession of any woman there. The Sultan exercises his right and impregnates Lady Montagu, leading to the birth of her son Edward as a bastard, mixed-ethnicity child. The titillating frame story is fictional, but serves to connect female homoerotic passion with transcultural contact and ethno-racial mixture. For more on* Ormond's *allusions to tales of cross-dressing and same-sex relations, see the Introduction.*

10a. Louise Françoise de Houssay, *A Narrative of the Sufferings of Louise Francoise de Houssay, de Bannes, Who served in the Army as a Volunteer, from 1792, to July 21, 1795; when she was made a prisoner at Quiberon, with her Examination at Vannes, from Whence she Made her ESCAPE, the Day before that which was appointed for her EXECUTION.* Translated from the Manuscript of the Author (London: printed for the author and sold by her; T. Boosey &c., 1796)

Little is known about aristocrat Louise Françoise de Houssay, although the fact that she printed and sold her story may indicate that it is a reasonably faithful or only lightly fictionalized account of historical experience. Houssay's Narrative *is the more conventional of our two examples of female cross-dressing tales; it recuperates the genre's subversive energy by subordinating it to gender-normative and counterrevolutionary political principles. The* Narrative *was briefly reviewed in the London* Monthly Review *(vol. 19, April 1796, p. 235), an influential periodical that was a standard reference for Brown and his associates. That review comments that there is "no reason to doubt the authenticity of the narrative" despite the "extraordinary occurrences" it relates.*

Since Houssay's narrative presents a number of details that recur in the backstory of Martinette de Beauvais in Ormond's *Chapters 19–21, this publication may have provided context for elements of Brown's novel. Like Brown's character, Houssay first dresses like a man and fights in the revolutionary wars alongside her husband, then overcomes her fear of combat and continues to fight after the husband's death. Although unlike Martinette she fights on the counterrevolutionary side of the conflict, both women warriors take part in the battle of Jemappe and generally engage along the northern front where the Duke of Brunswick (the target of Martinette's planned assassination) commanded counterrevolutionary forces. Since Martinette asserts that of the thirteen officers she killed at Jemappe "two ... were emigrant nobles, whom I knew and loved before the revolution, but the cause they had since espoused, cancelled their claims to mercy," it is tempting to speculate that this detail may involve a reply to the Houssay narrative, in which the protagonist and her husband are, precisely, two emigrant nobles fighting against the revolution at the battle mentioned by Brown's character.*

Interestingly, Houssay claims that her identity was known to other aristocratic officers, who welcomed her involvement in the fight. And significantly, her narrative is not framed by a male voice; she presents it in the first person and acknowledges that her primary purpose in publishing the story is to raise money.

*****

I am a native of Normandy; my name is *Louise Francoise de Houssay*. My father, who served in the Body Guards of the King of France, very little expected, that two and twenty years after the birth of a son, Heaven should send him a second child; yet it happened to be so, and I am the unfortunate daughter, whose misfortunes seem to be intended as a judgment against her, for having thus been an intruder into this world.
[…]
My husband, being a nobleman, was elected, though he never before had been in the army, Colonel of the National Guard; but he declined the Commission, upon which, he was considered as an Aristocrat. We were both arrested […].
[…]
Three weeks after we had been confined, our Judges entered the prison […]: we had been found guilty, and the next day had been fixed upon for our execution.

> *[They bribe a guard and escape over the Belgian border to*
> *join Royalist armies. Houssay addresses her husband.]*

[…]
You are going, my beloved husband, to take arms in defence of our Religion; for the restoration of our lawful Sovereign; for the protection of the inherited property of our children, against rebels, innovators and usurpers! Can you imagine that such noble motives are not capable of warming a female breast equally with that of one of your own sex? I am no longer permitted to discharge my duty as a mother; I am stronger and taller than the generality of my sex: we are told that nature never exceeds her wants; I am no less inclined to believe that my Creator has permitted I should be endowed with this bodily strength, only, that I might be enabled to keep the oath I have taken never to forsake you. I am determined, therefore, to disguise my sex, to follow your fortunes, and to fight the same battles: the same hand which has delivered me from prison, will aid and support me in the field.
[…]
My brother, a Captain in the regiment of Beuvoisis, […] had sometimes, during the carnival, prevailed upon me to dress in his regimentals, but it was long since, so that at first I really felt uncomfortable. However, as this was but a slight consideration, compared with the thoughts of a more serious nature which employed me: "My dear brother," said I to my husband, "let us take the first fraternal embrace, and from this

moment, till we can see happy days again, let it ever be present to our minds, that we are brothers in arms. We must stifle every other recollection."

[…]

By this time my husband thought it would not be improper to disclose to our commanding officers the secret of my sex. They were much surprised at the intelligence, paid me very high compliments on my resolution, and promised never to abuse my confidence.

[Houssay experiences battle at Thionville, 1792]

[…]

At the time of the attack […] I mounted guard, and was employed in warming the ball: the very word of red-hot shot would have been sufficient to make me shudder in former days; but, in truth, at this period I acted mechanically, without as much as bestowing a thought on what I was doing.

[After the defeat and dispersal of counterrevolutionary forces at Thionville, Houssay flees, hides with sympathizers, and eventually joins another Royalist corps forming in July 1793 at Maastricht.]

[…]

My sex was now generally known: the Count *de Damas* introduced me to his family, who bestowed high compliments upon me for my resolution, courage, and affection to my husband—alas! None of them could foresee how soon I was to lose him.

[Houssay fights at the Battles of Fleurus and Jemappe; her husband is killed at Louvain. Prince Waldek offers her a pension, but she demands to fight on.]

[…]

The Prince would have induced me to renounce my military excursions, but I displayed too eager a desire to avenge my late husband; he did not insist. Proud of not having undergone his disapprobation, I think myself entitled to pay very little attention to such as have attempted to ridicule me.

[Captured at Quiberon, Houssay is imprisoned and interrogated in a dialogue scene. She disguises her noble status, pretending she is a German who dressed as a man and fought to escape poverty. In the prisoner of war camp, she is not classified as a woman and is sentenced to death. She escapes and makes her way to England.]

10b. [Herman Mann] A citizen of Massachusetts, *The Female Review: or, Memoirs of an American Long Lady; whose life and character are peculiarly distinguished—being a continental solder, for nearly three years, in the late American war. During which time, she performed the duties of every department, into which she was called, with punctual exactness, fidelity and honor, and preserved her chastity inviolate, by the most artful concealment of her sex* (Dedham, 1797)

Near the end of the American Revolution in 1782, Uxbridge, Massachusetts native Deborah Sampson (1760–1829) took on the name of her deceased brother Robert Shurtliff, enlisted in the Continental Army, and served in male disguise until her honorable discharge in 1783. Sampson was from a poor family and had been an indentured servant previous to her imposture. On being freed from her indenture at age eighteen, she tried her hand at school teaching, but found it insufficiently adventurous and made a first, unsuccessful attempt at enlisting as a man. After her successful enlistment a few months later, she fought and was wounded in a skirmish near Tarrytown, New York. In summer 1783, her secret was discovered, but not revealed publicly, by a physician treating her for fever. Years later, after marrying and bearing three children, she continued to face financial difficulty and, like Houssay, decided to publicize her military adventure as a means of raising money.[4]

Sampson's tale of American revolutionary experience repeats many of the concerns and stock situations of the European cross-dressing tales. Writer Herman Mann (1771–1833), who worked with Sampson and wrote up her experiences in The Female Review, *mixed what seem to be historically attested events with generic features from earlier accounts of woman warriors such as the popular English tale* The Female Soldier; or, the Surprising Life and Adventures of Hannah Snell *(London, 1750). Mann casts his version of Sampson's cross-dressing in progressive terms, however, making the Sampson tale more compatible with Woldwinite ideas and a narrative like Martinette's. Thus Sampson's cross-dressing and military struggle for American independence are not re-absorbed into a commonsensical norm, but allegorize a female protagonist's wider desire for enlightened social transformation and the expansion of human liberty. Additionally, Mann may have drawn on the developing genre of African American slave narrative. A regular feature of slave narratives is the struggle to gain the tools of literacy, which Mann illustrates by explaining how the indentured servant Sampson used the discarded textbooks of her master's children to educate herself.*

Like Brown's Ormond, *Mann's representation of Sampson encodes a strategy for responding to the rise of dogmatic conservatism. Rather than openly confronting the common sense of religious orthodoxy, as Thomas Paine did in his classic deistic polemic,* The Age of Reason *(1794/1807), Mann's Sampson, like Brown's Martinette, negates ortho-*

---

[4] For fuller accounts of Sampson's story, see Gustafson, "The Genders of Nationalism: Patriotic Violence, Patriotic Sentiment in the Performances of Deborah Sampson Gannett"; Hiltner, "'She Bled in Secret': Deborah Sampson, Herman Mann, and *The Female Review*"; and Young, *Masquerade: The Life and Times of Deborah Sampson, Continental Soldier.*

doxy discretely, through her actions. While the male public sphere of politics and debate is represented as a space of oppressive forces, the narrative presents an independent woman creating an oppositional and semi-covert space that is distinct from conventional female roles.

As concerns same-sex romance, the first, 1797 edition goes to great pains to avoid any enactment of sexual or libidinal activity. After the first edition, Mann worked with Sampson to develop a more complete version but the revised manuscript remained unfinished and unpublished. In the later version, female-female sexuality is more pronounced. Yet, as Alfred F. Young notes, this eroticization may be no more than the trace of Mann's own imagination and changing publication plans. When The Female Review *was republished in 1866 with annotations, the new edition added an appendix that luxuriates in the fantasy of female same-sex sexuality enabled by cross-dressing. Clearly, some readers were eager to chart out the confluence of radical politics, gender-crossing, and erotic energies, whether historically attested or merely imagined and profitably published.*

*****

[...]

My first business, then, with the public, is to inform them, that the FEMALE, who is the subject of the following MEMOIRS, does not only exist in theory and imagination, but in reality.

[...]

EUROPE has exhibited its chivalry and wonders. It now remains for America to do the same [...] It is a wonder, but a truth full of satisfaction, that North America has become *free* and *independent*.

[...]

DEBORAH SAMPSON was born in Plympton, a small village in the county of Plymouth in New England, December 17, 1760.

[The family's fortunes fall; her father dies at sea and her mother is forced to send Deborah and her siblings away; Deborah struggles to educate herself.]

[...]

It was a circumstance peculiarly unhappy with Miss SAMPSON, during her minority, that she found less *opportunity*, than *inclinations*, for learning.

[...]

Her method [of learning literacy] was to listen to every one she heard read and speak with propriety. And when she could, without instruction, catch the formation of a letter from a penman, she gladly embraced it. She used to obtain what school books and copies she could from the children of the family, as models for imitation. Her leisure interims were appropriated to these tasks with as little reluctance, as common children went to play. [...] The anxiety and aspirations of her mind after knowledge, at length, became more notorious to many, who made learning their element.

[...]

It is with peculiar pleasure, I find here occasion to speak of Miss SAMPSON'S *taste* for the study of *Nature*, or *Natural Philosophy*. More agreeable still would be my task, had she enjoyed opportunities, that her proficiency in it might have been equal to her relish for it.

[…] The *philosopher* has been considered as—*not a man of this world; as an unsocial and unfit companion*, and *wanting* in the general *duties* of *life*. Such ideas must have been the result of a very erroneous acceptation of the word; or, of a mind not a little tinctured with prejudice.—I have always conceived that *philosophy* is a *scientific sphere*, in which we are enjoined to act by nature, reason and religion; which serve as a directory, or auxiliaries to accelerate us in it. The *philosopher*, then, instead of being rendered a *useless object* in society, and *wanting* in the general *duties* of life, is the person most eminently qualified for a *useful member* of society, the most agreeably calculated for an *intercourse* and *union* with the sexes, best acquainted with the social and enjoined *duties* of life; and is this preparing himself for a more refined BEING in futurity.

[…] But however reprobated and useless the study of philosophy may have been deemed for the man of sense, and much more dangerous for the other sex; it is certain, that it is now emerging from an obsolete state, to that of a fashionable and reputable employment. Ignorance in it being now the things mostly to be dreaded. And many of both sexes are not ashamed of having the appellation conferred on them in any situation of life.

[…]

I know not whether it was from her mental application to books, instructions from public or private preceptors, or from her own observations on *nature*, that she acquired the most knowledge of philosophy and astronomy.

[Deborah reflects on Christianity, politics, and limits of convention.]

[…]

To have called in question the validity and authenticity of the Scriptures would have only been challenging, at least, one half American, and a quarter of the rest of the globe to immediate combat: For which she had neither abilities, nor inclination. She began to reflect, however, that, the being bound to any set religion, by the force of man, would not only be an infraction against the laws of *Nature*, but a striking and effectual blow at the prime root of that *liberty*, for which our nation was then contending.

[…]

From the maturity of her years, observation and experience, she could determine, with more precision, on the nature of the war [for American Independence] and on the consequence of its termination. This may be said to be her logic:—If it should terminate in our subjection again to England, the abolition of our *Independence* must follow; by which, we not only mean to be *free*, but to gain us the possession of *Liberty* in its truest sense and greatest magnitude […] It was now a crisis with her not often to be experienced: and though it was painful to bear, it was, doubtless, conducive to improvement. Invention being upon the rack, every wheel in the machine is put into motion, and some event must follow. It produced many pertinent thoughts on the education of her sex. Very justly did she consider the female sphere of action, in many respects, too contracted; in others, wanting limits. In general, she deemed their *opportunities*, rather than *abilities*, inadequate for those departments in science and the belles-lettres, in which they are so peculiarly calculated to shine.

[...]

But the public must here be surprised in the contemplation of the machinations and achievements of *female* heroism and virtue: which if not the most unparralleled, are the most singular, that have ever sprung out of Columbia's soil. And it is but reasonable, that we exercise all that candor and charity, that the nature of the circumstances will admit. By ideally putting ourselves in similar circumstances, the reasonableness will be fully evinced. Though independent and free, *custom* in many respects, rules us with despotic sway: And the person who greatly deviates from it, exposes himself to numberless dangers. An indelible stigma may doom him to infamy; though perhaps, his original design was to effect some useful and important event. But on the other hand, *liberty* gives us such ascendancy over old *habit*, that unless it binds us to some apparent and permanent good, its iron bands are subject to dissolution.

[Deborah's embodiment of liberty.]

[...]

But neither the rigor of a parent to induce her marriage with one, whom she did not dislike, nor her own abhorrence of the idea of being considered a *female candidate* for conjugal union, is the cause of her turning volunteer in the American War; as may hereafter, partly, be conjectured by an anonymous writer. This must be the greatest obstacle to the magic charm of the novelist. She did not slight love; nor was she a distracted inamorato. [...] She was a *lover*; but different from those, whose love is only a short epilepsy, or for the gratification of a fantastical and criminal pleasure. [...] Her love extended to all. [...] This is that love, whose original source and motive induced Columbia's sons to venture their property, endearments—their lives! to gain themselves the possession of that heaven-born companion, called *liberty*.

[...]

Her stature is perhaps more than the middle size; that is, five feet and seven inches. The features of her face are regular; but not what a physiognomist would term the most beautiful. Her eye is lively and penetrating. She has a skin naturally clear, and flushed with a blooming carnation. But her aspect is rather masculine and serene, than effeminate and sillily jocose. Her waist might displease a coquette: but her limbs are regularly proportioned. Ladies of taste consider them handsome, when in the masculine garb. Her movement is erect, quick and strong: gestures naturally mild, animating and graceful; speech deliberate, with firm articulation. Her voice is not disagreeable for a female.

[...]

Spring having once more wafted its fragrance from the South, our Heroine leaped from the masculine, to the feminine sphere. Throwing off her martial attire, she once more hid her form with the *dishabille* of FLORA, recommenced her former occupation; and I know not; that she found difficulty in its performance. Whether this was done voluntarily, or compulsively, is to me an enigma. But she continues a phenomenon among the revolutions of her sex.

11. "French" Mores in 1790s Philadelphia

In his novels Ormond *and* Arthur Mervyn, *as well as shorter pieces such as "Portrait of an Emigrant" (here in Related Texts), Brown reflects on the cultural shifts and openings that occurred when a wave of French-speaking refugees from the ongoing revolutions in France and Haiti arrived in Philadelphia during the 1790s. Whereas British troops had occupied the city militarily in the late 1770s when Brown was a boy, twenty years later it was Francophone men and women of all ranks and ethnicities, from Royalists and Girondins fleeing the Revolution in Paris and Creoles escaping the one in Haiti, to "French negroes" and free persons of color, who for a time occupied the city in a more culturally transformative sense. In both of the Brown novels, the lives of central characters, such as Martinette de Beauvais in* Ormond, *are notably linked to revolutionary struggles against the old regime in Paris and the French provinces, to Jacobin-Girondin partisan conflict during the Terror (see Related Texts), and to struggles against slavery and colonialism in Haiti, which brought roughly 5,000 Caribbean refugees of all ethno-racial and political affiliations to Philadelphia (then a city of roughly 55,000). Once in Philadelphia, this community developed its own network of businesses and cultural institutions, and maintained a complex set of relations to metropolitan France, the Caribbean, and the rest of the U.S. French notables such as Talleyrand (1754–1838, soon to be a key Napoleonic minister), Louis Philippe (1773–1850; later king of France between 1830 and 1848), C. F. Volney (1757–1820, a prestigious radical intellectual included in these Related Texts), or Brillat-Savarin (1755–1826, a key figure in the development of haute cuisine, or elite cooking practices) interacted in the city's elite communities with leaders of the U.S. government (Philadelphia was then the national capital), with Philadelphia's already-established Francophone civic leaders (including key figures such as banker Stephen Girard, 1750–1831, and Jewish community leader Benjamin Nones, 1757–1826, both of "Girondin" or Bordeaux origin) and other communities before the conservative wave of the late 1790s chilled relations and led to the departure of many of the French political and intellectual elite. Likewise, free persons of color and former slaves circulated within the important Philadelphia free black community and spread awareness of revolutionary developments through Atlantic African networks.*

The excerpts and images presented here provide several accounts of or documents related to everyday life in and around this community, particularly as it pertains to gender and sexuality. As noted in the earlier discussion of Brown's "Portrait of an Emigrant" and the Introduction, the French community of the 1790s had a cultural impact beyond its numbers, particularly as concerns practices of everyday life and the modernizing transformations of consumerism. This community introduced a demographic and cultural sensibility that was fundamentally distinct from that of the city's predominantly Anglo elite or previous waves of primarily laboring class northern European immigrants. The community's short-lived association with a cultural-revolutionary "opening" of the mid-1790s, registered in Ormond's *cosmopolitan cultural geography and interest in a range of sexual and associational potentials, is a central concern in these documents.*

11a. Moreau de Saint-Méry, excerpts from *Voyage to the United States of America, 1793–98* (1913, compiled c. 1806–1812)

Even by the standards of the revolutionary age, Médéric-Louis Elie Moreau de Saint-Méry (1750–1819) had a turbulent life. Son of a wealthy family in the sugar colony Martinique, Moreau was sent to Paris for legal training. Returning to the Caribbean in the 1770s he practiced as an attorney in Haiti and Martinique, and published on French colonial law, science, anthropology, and archaeology. In 1789 he returned to Paris as a member of the Constituent Assembly for Martinique and was elected president of the electors during the tumultuous first days of the Revolution. He claimed to have accepted, on behalf of revolutionary council, the iconic keys to the Bastille on the night it was seized by revolutionaries, July 14, 1789, and joked that he thereby became "King of Paris during three days."

Three years later, in 1793, however, he barely escaped the Terror and fled with his family to the United States. In Philadelphia he survived by operating a French-language bookstore at the corner of Walnut and Front streets (84 South Front, one short block from Brown's family address during this period, 117 South Second). The shop was not a great financial success, but became a convivial meeting place for other French political refugees and travelers (he worried that they made too much noise for his American neighbors). Like fellow Francophone émigrés C. F. Volney and Talleyrand, he was elected a member of the American Philosophical Society. But also like Volney, he was deported from the U.S. as a suspicious enemy of the State in 1798 under the reactionary Alien and Sedition Acts. When he had friends ask why his name appeared on the lists (Moreau was no radical) he was told that President John Adams replied, "Nothing in particular, but he's too French." On his return to France, he held political posts during the Consulate (thanks to fellow Philadelphia émigré Talleyrand) and was appointed by Napoleon as administrator of Parma. When Napoleon recalled him and revoked his state pension, Moreau had Empress Josephine, his cousin and a fellow Creole from Martinique, intervene to restore his income.[1]

Today Moreau is mainly known as the author of the six-volume, ethnographic A Topographical and Political Description of the Spanish Part of Saint-Domingo: Containing General Observations on the Climate, Population, and Productions, *etc. (first volume published in Philadelphia, 1797, translated by William Cobbet). The* Description *is the most complete account of Haitian society before the Revolution. Most scholarly*

---

[1] For more on Moreau, see his *A Civilization that Perished: The Last Year of White Colonial Rule in Haiti*, as well as Garraway, "Race, Reproduction and Family Romance in Moreau de Saint-Méry's *Description de la Partie Françoise de L'Isle Saint-Domingue.*"

interest today focuses on its account of the many gradations of racializing distinction in the colony. Additionally, well into the nineteenth century, the Description *was the most substantive account of "voodoo" practices among Haitian slaves.*

    Moreau's account of émigré life in Philadelphia documents his fascination with the increase of sexual freedom in the city. In the sections below, Moreau claims to have successfully introduced the sale of condoms (the "medical items" mentioned below) in the United States, offers opinions on abortion and "syringes" of abortificants, the means of procuring a prostitute, and contemporary intersections of sexual practices and racial prejudice. These reports of sexual liberty in Philadelphia can be read alongside Ormond's allusions to prostitution, same-sex companionship, and French styles in the 1790s.

Note: this translation modifies the 1947 version by Kenneth and Anna Roberts, published as Moreau de St. Méry's American Journey, 1793–98.

*****

Residence at Philadelphia

    [December 31, 1794] Since I didn't want to deprive my shop of an advantage, the lack of which in hot climates would not, I think, be without risks; and since my old colleague and friend, the lawyer Geanty, a refugee from Cap François[2] now in Baltimore—who is quite knowledgeable and clever with medical items—offered me a stock of certain small devices so ingenious that the idea is said to have been suggested by the stork; I accepted his offer and carried a complete assortment of them for four years. These were items to which French colonials were accustomed, and the Americans were frequent customers as well, despite their pretenses of shame, to such a degree that the use of this aid on the vast American continent dates from this era. People from San Domingo and the other colonies also had frequent recourse to our stock.

    [January 2, 1795] I was inducted as a *resident* member of the Philosophical Society of Philadelphia.

Description of Philadelphia

I. Of Whites:

… Marriages are all the easier to arrange as they're often settled in a hurry, and many of them are secret.

    I am going to say something that is almost unbelievable. These women, without real love and without passions, give themselves up at an early age to the enjoyment of themselves; and they are quite familiar with that taste which seeks the pleasures of a wandering imagination with persons of their own sex.

---

[2] "Cap François": the main port of Haiti.

Bastards are extremely common in Philadelphia, and there are two principal reasons for this. Firstly, the city has so many religious sects that none of the clergy have any real power of persuasion and find it impossible to inspire shame in women who become mothers for no reason but the pleasure. Secondly, as soon as the infant reaches 12 months the mother can indenture it for 21 years, get rid of it, and do the same thing all over again, nursing another child without even worrying that it will never know her, or that she's using it for a shameful commerce.

Needless to say, with such notions and such heartlessness, abortion is extremely rare.

II. *Of Coloured Persons all Ages and Sexes*

Under this heading I include all persons not white, but free and descended from the African race. The people of color live entirely among themselves without distinguishing between mulattoes, griffes, Negroes, and quadroons, who are extremely rare.[3]

… Women, those of color especially, seduce young white girls and sell them to corruption in their houses. The price for such transactions is ordinarily 30 dollars (180 francs), and the procuress keeps the greater part. It is thus that the colored people partly avenge themselves for the terrible contempt with which they are treated in Philadelphia. Usually they're badly dressed. White children strike children of color. When it snows, colored men passing by are sure to be hit with snowballs thrown by white children.

III. *Of Slaves*

… I must add here that French colored women[4] display a most insolent degree of luxury in Philadelphia, and when you consider that this can only be kept up by French men, and former French colonials at that, the contrast between their condition and the poverty of most of their compatriots is revolting. Generally the Americans don't like to rent their houses to colored girls. Most of them in Philadelphia take their lodgings just outside the city, or in the lesser side streets.

When a Quakeress has lecherous impulses, she lets her husband know about it and does her best to make him share her torment.

The daughters of Quakers are very easy, and prone to accidents.

Quaker youths are frequent visitors in the houses of ill fame, of which there are many in Philadelphia, and frequented at all hours. There is even a certain well-known *gentleman* who leaves his horse tied to the post outside one of these houses,

---

[3] "Griffe": the child of a half-white, half-black (a "mulatto") and a "full-blood" black, or, in other words, someone who is three-quarters black. Méry's point here is that America does not have multiple racial hierarchies among its nonwhite population, but rather a binary distinction between "white" and "black."

[4] "French colored women": in this context, the phrase means mixed-race, free women from the Francophone Caribbean. The category of "free people of color" or "gens libres de couleur" was an ethno-racial and political category in the Francophone Caribbean, situated between free whites on the one hand and African slaves on the other.

so that everyone knows when he is there and exactly how long he stays. There are streetwalkers of every color.

In the extremely rare instances when a Quakeress violates the conjugal tie, she claims that it's the evil spirit which is acting; and after she repents, the mistake is forgiven. These American women might not be badly painted after the portrait that Jean Jacques made of Mme. de Varens.*

In Virginia women visit each other in their homes for long periods, even when they live only short distances apart, sometimes in the same town.

Since 1806 there are streetwalkers of a new sort in Philadelphia. These are very young and very pretty girls, elegantly dressed, who promenade two by two, arm in arm, walking rapidly.

The time of the walks makes it clear that they're not out for a stroll. They are usually found on the south side of Market Street from 4th Street on up.[5] One talks them up and they take you to their place. They pretend to be dressmakers. They do anything you wish for 2 dollar pieces, and supposedly one of the dollars pays for the room.

Another sort is becoming quite common as well. Some women, usually ones who are getting older, are known to procure for younger ones. One gets introduced at their houses by a reliable friend, and asks permission to visit again. And then if these duennas are alone, one asks them to allow you to see a friend, if she's free, and point out which one. Sometimes the duennas themselves suggest which friend to select.

The duennas contact the person one has chosen and report whether or not there is any hope. They arrange the meetings, and it's at their houses that one meets the women or girls whom they debauch in this manner; and the process is repeated as often as one likes. The chosen object can be changed, and the duenna stays just as obliging.

Each woman costs 3 dollars (18 francs); the money is left with the woman who received the favors, and she gives the procuress one dollar for her efforts.

But if one desires a beauty of higher rank, or a more difficult conquest, or one supposedly less experienced in love, higher prices must be paid, either in money or gifts. And through everything the young innocent keeps cold-bloodedly pleading for larger gifts, claiming the duenna is demanding ever higher rewards for her silence. This is the only language her tenderness speaks.

---

* Jean Jacques Rousseau was the acknowledged lover of Mme. De Varens. The portrait that Rousseau drew of her is in the Confessions, and pictures a good-natured, sentimental, fairly intelligent woman given to taking her pleasures wherever she found them. Saintsbury calls her "nominally a converted protestant … in reality, as many women of her time were, a kind of deist, with a theory of noble sentiment and a practice of libertinism tempered by good nature."

---

[5] "South side of Market Street from 4th Street on up": many émigrés resided in this area. Market Street was the city's main thoroughfare, a wide boulevard with market buildings in the middle, and thus very public setting for the streetwalkers' trade. The protagonist of Brown's novel *Arthur Mervyn* arrives in this setting at night on his first visit to the city.

But never, even during the most voluptuous transports, allow yourself to sing the praises of the treasures you're being granted, for the reply will be that in giving in to your desires she never dreamed she'd be considered unchaste; and your pocket-book will be needed once again to dry up the flood of tears shed by such truly virginal modesty.

A greater and more pressing danger occurs if you should meet your little friend anywhere except the place of rendez-vous, and give any sign of knowing her. She'll keep an imperturbable stone face if she recognizes you, and if you insist that you know her, especially in the street, everyone will take her side and only a quick exit can save you from a beating.

It is in a country such as this that syringes, when first imported by French colonials, were regarded as something awful. Later they were displayed for sale by American apothecaries. The Quakers were responsible for this change, and were the first to adopt them.

*****

11b. John F. Watson, excerpts from *Watson's Annals of Philadelphia and Pennsylvania* (1857; compiled 1830–1842)

John Fanning Watson (1779–1860) was well known in the nineteenth century as an amateur but widely read historian of Philadelphia and New York. His father was a Philadelphia-based sea captain and his mother a poet and Methodist mystic. After business ventures that took him to Washington, D.C. and New Orleans in his early twenties, Watson returned to Philadelphia where he worked as a bookseller and then as a bank and railroad functionary in his later years. He was a founder of the Historical Society of Pennsylvania and the Society for the Commemoration of the Landing of William Penn.

Watson articulates an Anglo-conservative and xenophobic perspective on the social mores of the revolutionary age, but his sources transmitted to him vivid recollections of the "French" styles, behaviors, and political tendencies that were widespread in 1790s Philadelphia. Watson's account can be juxtaposed with Moreau's, as well as with Brown's "Portrait of an Emigrant." All three writers develop contrasting accounts of the racial mixture, sexual and associational "liberties," and cultural-political currents that brought Atlantic Francophone revolutionary energies into the streets and private spaces of Brown's Philadelphia.

*****

Chapter 17. HABITS AND STATE OF SOCIETY

"Not to know what has been transacted in former times, is always to remain a child!"
—Cicero

One of the remarkable incidents of our republican principles of equality, is, that hirelings, who in times before the war of Independence were accustomed to accept the name of servants, and to be dressed according to their condition, will now no longer suffer the former appellation; and all affect the dress and the air, when abroad, of genteeler people than their business warrants. Those, therefore, who from affluence have many such dependants, find it a constant subject of perplexity to manage their pride and assumption.

[…]

A lady of my acquaintance, Mrs. H., familiar with those things as they were before the Revolution, has thus expressed her sense of them, viz. In the olden time domestic comfort was not every day interrupted by the pride and the profligacy of servants. There were then but few hired,—black slaves, and German and Irish redemptioners made up the mass. Personal liberty is, unquestionably, the inherent right of every human creature; but the slaves of Philadelphia were a happier class of people than the free blacks now, who exhibit every sort of wretchedness and profligacy in their dwellings. The former felt themselves to be an integral part of the family to which they belonged; they were faithful and contented, and affected no equality in dress or manners with those who ruled them; every kindness was extended to them in return.

[…]

We shall give the reader some little notice of a strange state of our society about the years 1793 to 1798, when the phrenzy of the French Revolution possessed and maddened the boys, without any check or restraint from men half as puerile then as themselves in the delusive politics of the day.

About the year 1793 to '94, there was an extravagant and impolitic affection for France, and hostility to every thing British, in our country generally. It required all the prudence of Washington and his cabinet to stem the torrent of passion which flowed in favour of France to the prejudice of our neutrality. Now the event is passed we may thus soberly speak of its character. This remark is made for the sake of introducing the fact, that the patriotic mania was so high that it caught the feelings of the boys of Philadelphia! I remember with what joy we ran to the wharves at the report of cannon to see the arrivals of the Frenchmen's prizes, —we were so pleased to see the British union down! When we met French marines or officers in the streets, we would cry "Vive la Republique." Although most of us understood no French, we had caught many national airs, and the streets, by day and night, resounded with the songs of boys, such as these…:

[…] About this time, almost every vessel arriving here brought fugitives from the infuriated negroes in Port au Prince,[6] or the sharp axe of the guillotine in Paris, dripping night and day with the blood of Frenchmen, shed in the name of liberty, equality, and the (sacred) rights of man. Our city thronged with French people of all shades from the colonies, and those from Old France, giving it the appearance of one great hotel, or place of shelter for strangers hastily collected together from a raging tempest. The characteristic old school simplicity of the citizens, in manners, habits of

---

[6] "In Port du Prince": that is, in Haiti, during the Haitian revolution.

dress, and modes of thinking and speaking on the subjects of civil rights and forms of government, by the square and rule of reason and argument, and the "rules of the schools," began to be broken in upon by the new enthusiasm of C'ira and Carmagnole,[7] French boarding-houses (pension Française), multiplied in every street. The one at the southeast corner of Race and Second Streets, having some 40 windows, was filled with colonial French to the garret windows, whistling and jumping about, fiddling and singing, as fancy seemed to suggest, like so many crickets and grasshoppers. Groups of both sexes were to be seen seated on chairs, in summer weather, forming semi-circles near the doors, so displayed as sometimes to render it necessary to step into the street to get along;—their tongues, shoulders and hands in perpetual motion, jabbering away, "talkers and no hearers." Mestizo ladies, with complexions of the palest marble, jet black hair, and eyes of the gazelle, and of the most exquisite symmetry, were to be seen, escorted along the pavement by white French gentlemen, both dressed in West India fashion, and of the richest materials; coal black negresses, in flowing white dresses, and turbans of "muchoir de Madras," exhibiting their ivory dominos, in social walk with a white or creole;—altogether, forming a contrast to the native Americans, and the emigrants from Old France, most of whom still kept in the stately old Bourbon style of dress and manner, wearing the head full powdered à la Louis, golden headed cane, silver buckles, and cocked hat, seemingly to express thereby their fierce contempt for the pantaloons, silk shoestring, and "Brutus Crop."[8]

---

[7] "C'ira and Carmagnole": popular revolutionary songs. "Ça ira," was the best-known popular song of the French Revolution. The title, repeated several times in each line of the chorus, means literally "it will go" or "it will work"; figuratively, "we will win." "La Carmagnole," named after a short jacket worn by the sansculottes or laborers, was a song (and dance) that originated in 1792, whose lyrics mocked Marie Antoinette and her Royalist supporters. Both songs became clichés in later Anglophone antirevolutionary representations, not only here in Watson, but in later sentimentalized critiques of the revolution such as Charles Dickens' *A Tale of Two Cities* (1859) or Baroness Orczy's *The Scarlet Pimpernel* (1905). Timothy Dwight refers to "Ça ira" in a similar manner in the excerpt from his anti-Illuminati tract here in Related Texts.

[8] "Brutus Crop": Watson refers to the popular 1790s and Empire (1803–1815) hairstyle known in French as the "Brutus" or "Titus" cut, after Roman republican hero Brutus or, alternatively, Roman Emperor Titus. The cut was a short style with bangs, evoking stereotypical male "roman" hairstyles, sometimes teased or permed slightly to lend volume. Culturally, as Watson notes, it represented revolutionary affiliation and opposition to the old regime, because it abandoned the wigs and hair powder that were a primary sign of male status before the revolution and advertised open identification with revolutionary iconography. Brown and his circle, for example, wore their hair natural and short, and Brown has his fictional schoolmaster Alcuin criticize barbers for their association with old-regime styles (see *Alcuin; A Dialogue* here in Related Texts). These styles *à la Brutus* were first popularized in Paris and London after 1791 by the actor Talma, who wore a wig styled in this manner for his role in the influential revival of Voltaire's *Brutus* (originally 1730). Talma's precedent became a sensation and the style became associated with the mood of emancipatory cultural transformation throughout the theater of Atlantic revolutions. By freeing the hair from old-regime constraints, its conscious unruliness was egalitarian; both Europeans and Africans, and women and men could and did equally sport this hairstyle in the 1790s and 1800s, when it retained its association with the period's Roman and revolutionary iconography.

From *Le paysan perverti* by Rétif de la Bretonne (The Hague & Paris: Esprit, 1776). Image courtesy of the Division of Rare and Manuscript Collections, Carl A. Kroch Library, Cornell University.

11c. Louis-Sébastien Binet, image from Rétif de la Bretonne *The Perverted Peasant* (1776). *Le Paysan perverti ou les dangers de la ville* [The Peasant Perverted; or, The Dangers of the City] (The Hague & Paris: Esprit, 1776). From Volume I, Letter LXIV (219): "Madame Parangon kissing Ursule and Tienette, thanking them for their attachment and devotion."

Nicolas Edme Restif (or Rétif) de la Bretonne (1734–1806) holds a special place in the modern development of sexuality and politics, not least for his introduction or early publication of what are today much-considered key words such as "pornography" and "communism." Born into a provincial farming family, Restif came to Paris where he worked as a printer, publishing hundreds of books. Well before the Revolution, he published Le Pornographe *(1769), calling for publicly regulated centers of prostitution. During the Revolution he survived by publishing erotic novels, left-wing political tracts, and accounts of urban mores. Writers of the time were often divided on him, and described him with epithets ranging from "Rousseau of the gutter" to the "French Richardson." He discusses his foot fetishism in* Le Pied de Fanchette *(Fanchette's Foot, 1769), which was then called "restifism" in the same way that sadism or masochism were named after D. A. F. Sade and Leopold von Sacher-Masoch, authors who wrote about these behaviors. Restif's* Parisian Nights, *or the Nocturnal Spectator (1788–early 1790s) is a contribution to the long eighteenth-century tradition of first-hand accounts of nocturnal enactments of urban working-class and sexual subcultures. Influenced by Rousseau, Bretonne's writing often purveys a simultaneous denunciation of and fascination with urban modernity's transformation of peasant culture. His well-known* Le Paysan Perverti *(The Peasant Perverted) depicts a moralizing and voyeuristic account of rural innocence corrupted by city libertines. These accounts and the well-known illustrations by Parisian Louis-Sébastien Binet (1750–1812)—which often depicted scenes not explicitly described in the actual text—had the double value of condemning sexual practices while describing them in a titillating and profitable manner.*

With Ormond's *declaration of a male voyeur's secret witnessing of the intimacies of a woman's chambers, Brown knowingly invokes the libertine and erotic writings of the period. He would have been familiar with this dimension of print culture through his active search for French-language materials, and also because his New York publisher, French émigré Hocquet Caritat (who handled Brown's first novel* Wieland *and arranged the first British publication of* Ormond *with the popular Minerva Press, as well as the first translation of Brown's novels into French, possibly the first U.S. fiction to be translated) openly advertised the sale of erotically charged material, at first only in his French-language catalog, but shortly afterward in his regular catalogs as well.*

This image of a male gazing on a lesbian orgy comes from a well-known printing that is likely the same edition of Restif's novel that Caritat advertised for sale and that Brown may have himself handled. Describing familiar paintings based on Ovid's Metamorphoses *in the interior of a brothel in his novel* Arthur Mervyn, *or developing* Ormond's *references to Italian traditions of erotic nudes, Brown draws his readers' attention to the long tradition of images that encode sexual desire.*

Charles Willson Peale. *Benjamin and Eleanor Ridgely Laming* (1788). Gift of Morris Schapiro. Image courtesy of the Board of Trustees, National Gallery of Art, Washington, D.C.

11d. Charles Willson Peale, portrait of *Benjamin and Eleanor Ridgely Laming* (1788). National Gallery of Art, Washington, D.C.

Charles Willson Peale (1741–1827) was a prolific painter, committed natural scientist, and ardent U.S. nationalist. Portraiture was one of Peale's most successful genres. He produced likenesses of many notable public figures in the early republic and is widely known for almost sixty portraits of Washington. Born in Maryland, Peale studied in London in the 1760s under Benjamin West (1738–1820), an influential Pennsylvania-born, Quaker painter who flourished in England and identified himself with British rather than American interests. Brown's close friend William Dunlap likewise studied in West's London atelier during the 1780s, after it had become a more conventional destination for American male painters seeking training in metropolitan centers abroad. Peale was based in Philadelphia throughout his mature years; his gallery and natural history exhibits were among the earliest U.S. museum institutions and he was well known to Brown and his circles.

Peale's unorthodox double portrait of the newly married Laming-Ridgely couple differs significantly from his relatively conventional renderings of male political and scientific notables. Benjamin Laming (1750–1792) was a wealthy Baltimore merchant in the Caribbean sugar, rum, and wine trade who married into the Ridgely clan, one of Maryland's most influential families. Whereas traditional portraits rarely eroticize physical contact between elite married couples, here the pair's posture, absorbed gazes, and attributes convey a ready sensuality and inclination to erotic pleasure, indicated most clearly in the way Benjamin's telescope extends from his breeches toward the allegorical fruits held by his partner Eleanor. The portrait celebrates female sexuality with its fruits and flowers, by emphasizing Eleanor's loosely flowing tresses and sashes, which hint at a relaxation of bodily constraints, and by having the woman grasp her partner's arm, actively drawing him and his telescope toward her. The marine background (the Chesapeake waterfront at Baltimore) and exotic parrot inscribe the Caribbean and mercantile origin of Laming's wealth.

Miles and Reinhardt point out that the couple's pose alludes to the passionate Rinaldo and Armida, characters from Gerusalemme Liberata *(1575), an influential Renaissance epic by Torquato Tasso (1544–1595) then familiar in a translation by Edward Fairfax (c. 1580–1635) titled* Godfrey of Bulloigne, or the Recoverie of Jerusalem *(1600).[9]*
Tasso's romance epic about Christian Crusader conquest of the Muslim-governed Holy Lands differs significantly from the traditions embedded within the poetic genre of military conquest and nation building as it interweaves a phobic rejection of cultural difference with a sensual communion between Christian knights and Muslim women, as befits the Italian Renaissance's complicated introduction of non-Christian culture into Europe, despite the Roman Catholic Church's attempt to maintain the feudal period's mental and geographic boundaries against cosmopolitan curiosity. The poem's action is set during the First Crusade and features the tale of a Christian warrior entranced by an Eastern

---

[9] For more on the painting's erotic allegory, see Miles and Reinhardt, " 'Art conceal'd': Peale's Double Portrait of Benjamin and Eleanor Ridgely Laming."

sorceress who allegorizes the "oriental" attractions of the Muslim Ottoman Empire. In Book 14, Armida draws the martial hero into erotic attachment and dreamlike reverie at her magical garden in Syria.[10] *Rinaldo and Armida's tale was widely developed in the seventeenth and eighteenth centuries, when it supplied the scenarios for many operas and became a familiar source of subject matter for elite visual art. The first engraved illustrations were by Agostino Carracci (one of the Carracci whose eroticized prints are referenced in* Ormond's *Chapter 19) and the tale inspired many influential paintings, from the 1640s series by Nicolas Poussin (1594–1665) to the sensual "Tasso cycle" (1742–1745) by Venetian master Giovanni Battista Tiepolo (1696–1770). In the revolutionary period, among others, Benjamin West and Angelica Kauffmann (mentioned in* Ormond's *Chapter 13) treated the scenario, and another of Peale's female portraits alludes to it.*

Tasso's epic was known and read by Brown and his associates, and its tales of cross-ethnic and cross-religious desire may be referenced in Brown's Wieland, *when the female protagonist recalls a ballad about a knight dying under Godfrey's Crusade, and in* Arthur Mervyn, *when a young American male becomes enraptured with a Jewish woman and then proposes in a secluded garden scene.*

While neither Brown nor Dunlap ever mention this particular portrait by Peale, Brown seems to evoke its affirmative spirit in Ormond's *Chapter 24 when Sophia travels to Baltimore to meet Constantia's cousin, who is given the name Mary Ridgeley. When Ridgeley meets Sophia she is amused and assumes (without disapproving) that Sophia is involved in an affair with Martynne, a fraudulent adventurer who has been displaying Sophia's portrait and claiming she is his lover. As one of Sophia's first American encounters after a long sojourn in Europe, the incident may illustrate the contrast between Sophia's nostalgia for an older, more restrictive cultural order and the attitudes of women actually living in the 1790s American republic. In contrast to Sophia's prim and humorless use of melodrama, Mary Ridgeley displays "gayety" and a playful attitude toward romantic dalliances with foreign men outside of and unknown to the status order of local great families. Even when Martynne's fraud is revealed, Ridgely seems unperturbed and allows the con man to escape with embarrassment only, without punishment or any clear indication that he will be excluded from Ridgeley's friendship. Thus the scene seems to telegraph Sophia's fear that, even if she finds Constantia, her beloved friend may have become one of these American woman who easily take foreign partners and are unconcerned with continuing to uphold past behavioral codes, especially those involving feminine propriety. Given that Constantia has indeed befriended Ormond and Martinette (whose name strangely echoes Martynne's), the moment seems to articulate tensions between Sophia's cultural conservatism and new attitudes associated with French-inspired progressivism. Amidst his nationalist portraits of men, Peale's canvas of an Anglo-American couple affirming cultural models conveyed through Italianate visual and musical arts likewise registers the general presence of these two orientations in the early American Republic.*

---

[10] Tasso's epic includes a conspirator whose name is given as both "Ormond" and "Ormondo" in the Fairfax translation (Cantos 19–20).

12. Narratives of French Girondin Heroism

In historical terms, the Girondins were not a political party, but a loosely organized bour-
geois faction that held sway in the French revolutionary process from its beginnings
through the stages of the National and Legislative Assemblies (1789–1792), up until the
general crisis that began with the abolition of the now-constitutional monarchy and re-
lated decisions to declare war on Habsburg Austria and execute Louis XVI (September
1792–January 1793). Because some of the group's early leaders were from Bordeaux, on
the Gironde River, they became known as Girondins.[1] *Led by Jacques-Pierre Brissot*
(1754–1793, who had recently completed a fact-finding mission to Philadelphia and the
U.S.), the group initially gathered at the salon of enlightened memoirist Marie-Jeanne
Roland (1754–1793), wife of Jean Marie Roland (1734–1793), a Girondin delegate,
both of whom were killed in the Terror. Madame Roland's salon functioned as the po-
litical and cultural hub for a wide spectrum of cosmopolitan thinkers and national
liberation leaders, from Anglophone figures such as Thomas Paine and Mary Woll-
stonecraft to Corsican Pasquale Paoli (1725–1807), Venezuelan Francisco de Miranda
(1750–1816), or Haitian Jean-Baptiste Belley (1746–1805), a black representative to
the Assembly who was born in West Africa and was formerly a slave.

Crucially, Brissot and the other Girondins were allied with the Jacobin Club, a large
and at first ideologically diverse group so named because it initially met in a hall formerly
owned by Monks called Jacobin for their association with the Rue St. Jacques. Girondin
delegates and the more numerous Jacobins were fellow travelers: both groups were resolute
in abolishing monarchy and feudalism, included democratic as well as republican princi-
ples in their political outlook, and were willing to embrace violence in achieving revolu-
tionary goals and defending the new republic. But in 1793, in the course of the general
crisis and paranoia that led rapidly to partisan polarization amidst foreign invasion and
provincial rebellion, the more partisan Jacobin elements led by Maximilien Robespierre
(1758–1794), along with sansculotte or laboring-class factions, won over uncommitted
delegates in the Assembly and cast the Girondins, once the revolution's most effective ad-
vocates, as a clear and present danger to its continuation. At this point many Girondin-
identified revolutionaries were guillotined or fled Paris and France,[2] *and, in the notorious*
October 1793 mass execution of Brissot and twenty others—including the lesser-known
delegate Lesterpt-Beauvais mysteriously linked to Martinette in Ormond's *Chapter 19—*
the faction's influence came to a bloody end.

---

[1] In English the form "Girondist" also appears and the group are likewise referred to as "Brissotins" or "partisans of Brissot," after the name of their de facto leader.

[2] Numerous Girondin refugees took up residence in the Philadelphia French émigré community in the 1794–1798 period. Among others these refugees included *philosophe* C. F. Volney, who spent much of his time in exile at Philadelphia, where he was well known to Brown and his associates; see the Introduction, as well as Brown's "Portrait of an Emigrant" and selections from Volney and Moreau de Saint-Méry in Related Texts here.

 Girondin influence was short-lived in historical terms, but after the Terror the group's story took on a life of its own in political debates and cultural representations of the Revolution in poems, tales, and dramas. After 1793 "Girondin" and "Jacobin" increasingly became keywords in the period's culture wars, detached from concrete historical usage. Conservative publicists inflated "Jacobin" into an all-purpose insult or epithet used to tar all progressive ideas as dangerously subversive, for example in the title of a leading conservative journal, the London Anti-Jacobin Review.[3] *Anglophone progressives, on the other hand, clearly distinguished the contending factions and praised the Girondins as a means of affirming the underlying principles of the radical Enlightenment while simultaneously criticizing the violent excesses of the Terror and often worrying about the increasing insubordination of the laboring class. In a crude sense, then, the Girondins tend to appear in Anglophone progressive writings of the 1790s as "good" revolutionaries, while the Jacobins are stigmatized as the "bad" or fallen side of the revolution.*

 These reflections on the Girondins and their downfall loom large in the background of Ormond, *whose main action overlaps suggestively with the September 1793–July 1794 dates of the Terror.[4] Although Martinette's family situation remains mysterious in its detail, Chapter 19 relates her to executed Girondin deputy Lesterpt-Beauvais when the narrator Sophia notes a "conjecture, that she was wife, or daughter, or sister of Beauvais, the partizan of Brissot, whom the faction of Marat had lately consigned to the scaffold...." Later, in Chapter 21, Martinette's association with Girondin actors is cemented when her plan to assassinate the Duke of Brunswick (leader of an Austrian Habsburg royalist army seeking to put down the Revolution by force) alludes to Girondin sympathizer Charlotte Corday's assassination of the Jacobin-aligned editor of the* Ami du peuple *("Friend of the People") Jean-Paul Marat (1743–1793), and as she rejoices at the news of Robespierre's fall and plans her return to the revolutionary struggle.*

 As the two selections presented here indicate, Brown's decision to reference Girondin exploits in Ormond *and his later novel* Arthur Mervyn *places his novels squarely within this larger polemical context about the complex nature of revolution as a social act that cannot merely be denounced. Brown's novels are in tacit dialogue with the currents represented by these two excerpts, adopting their manner of affirming the revolution's general principles while condemning its excesses, and extending the fascination with Girondin tales that Brown and his closest associates had developed in the mid-1790s.*

---

[3] Fittingly, *Ormond* received a scathing response in the *Anti-Jacobin Review* (no. 6.26, August 1800, p. 458), which condemned it and Brown's *Wieland* and *Arthur Mervyn* for containing "much disgusting and pernicious nonsense."

[4] Brown develops a similar overlap between the dates of the Terror and the timeline of his novel *Arthur Mervyn*. In that novel the character Achsa Fielding, like Martinette de Beauvais in *Ormond*, is a Philadelphia émigré tied to Girondin-Jacobin struggles.

12a. Helen Maria Williams on Charlotte Corday, excerpts from *Letters Containing a Sketch of the Politics of France, from the Thirty-first of May 1793, Till the Twenty-eighth of July 1794, and the Scenes which Have Passed in the Prisons of Paris. Vol. I (London: Printed for G.G. and J. Johnson, 1795)*

Daughter of a Scottish army officer and a Welsh mother, Helen Maria Williams (1761–1827) was a poet, novelist, and translator who was a literary celebrity in 1780s London even before she took up residence in Paris as an unaccompanied woman at the outset of the Revolution. Her independent habits (living unmarried with a male partner) and affirmation of revolutionary principles meant that she was subject to the same types of criticism and press abuse as Mary Wollstonecraft. In London her salon had included Godwin and other Woldwinite writers, and she was the subject of William Wordsworth's earliest published poem—"On Seeing Miss Helen Maria Williams Weep at a Tale of Distress" (1787)—that presents her as an epitome of enlightened sensibility. In Paris she established a new salon frequented by revolutionaries including Brissot, Carnot (mentioned notably in Brown's Alcuin*), and Anglophone fellow travelers such as Wollstonecraft and Thomas Paine; aligned herself with Girondin circle; and survived imprisonment during the Terror as a Girondin sympathizer.*

Throughout the 1790s, Williams was widely known for eight successive volumes of commentary on the revolution, published 1790 to 1798, that combine observational reportage, political reflection, and emotionalized narratives, and which are collectively known as her Letters from France. *These volumes had wide influence as first-hand accounts of the twists and turns of the revolutionary process as it unfolded through the decade. They were simultaneously powerful sources of credible eyewitness testimony concerning disputed events; an ongoing intervention in the decade's revolution debates; and influential models for the synthesis of sensibility and progressive thinking in the early-romantic cultural field. The second excerpt below, from the diary of Brown's close friend Elihu Hubbard Smith, illustrates some of their immediate effects within Brown's circle, which followed Williams'* Letters *closely, and read her poems and her 1795 translation of Bernardin de Saint-Pierre's novel* Paul and Virginia *as well.*

The passage presented here is drawn from the sixth of the series' eight books, which addresses the period of the Terror, including the proscription and execution of Madame Roland and other Girondins, and the events of Thermidor (the coup against Robespierre and the ruling Committee for Public Safety which ended the Terror). Williams recounts the much-mythologized incident in which Charlotte Corday (1768–1793) assassinated Jacobin publicist Marat. Countering Jacobin representations of Corday as a monstrous mixture of male and female attributes, Williams presents the female assassin as a martyr of liberty whose personal magnetism oriented those around her to similar self-sacrifice in reported incidents of political and eroticized emulation. In early 1793, as their power was declining, the Girondins attempted to prosecute Marat, but he was acquitted and returned to the Assembly with greatly increased power, which he used to further weaken the Girondins. On July 13, 1793, after traveling from Normandy expressly to kill him for his persecution of the Girondins, Corday gained an interview with Marat and stabbed him.

She was immediately tried and guillotined four days later. This violence, in turn, contributed to the cycle of reprisals that led to the arrest and execution of the Girondin leaders in September and October. The event was widely narrated and fictionalized, notably in Jacques-Louis David's Death of Marat *(1793), one of the crucial paintings of the era.*[5]

Contemporary readers of Ormond *understood that Martinette's "love of liberty" and plan to assassinate the Duke of Brunswick (Chapter 19) allude to Corday's Girondin martyrdom. Because the rise and especially the spectacular fall of the Girondins was memorably chronicled by Williams and Madame Roland, two influential writers whose progressive chronicles also involved the modeling of new potentials and aspirations for women, narratives of Girondin heroism were also tied to ongoing reflections on female liberty and agency in the revolutionary era.*

****

[Charlotte Corday's assassination of Marat linked to the execution of the arrested Girondin deputies]

[…] This calumny, which was refuted by every address received from the departments, formed the basis of the accusation which was framed against the Gironde; and the founders and most strenuous supporters of the republic were soon after dragged to the scaffold as the advocates and protectors of royalty.

[…]

An event also happened at this period, which, from the calumnies to which it gave rise, and the consequences it produced, proved fatal to the arrested deputies. This was the assassination of Marat. In the first dawn of the conspiracy Marat became a principal instrument in the hands of the traitors, who found him well fitted for their purposes […] . [W]hat rendered him useful to the conspirators was his readiness to publish every slander which they framed, and to exhort to every horror which they meditated.—His rage for denunciation was so great that he became the dupe of the idle; and his daily paper contains the names of great criminals who existed only in the imagination of those who imposed on his credulous malignity.

After this first preacher of blood had performed the part allotted to him in the plan of evil, he was confined to his chamber by a lingering disease to which he was subject, and of which he would probably soon have died. But he was assassinated in his bath by a young woman who had travelled with this intention from Caen in Nor-

---

[5] For more on Corday and her cultural reception, see Corazzo and Montfort, "Charlotte Corday: femme-homme"; Gutwirth, *The Twilight of the Goddesses; Women and Representation in the French Revolutionary Era*; Huet, *Rehearsing the Revolution: The Staging of Marat's Death, 1793–1797*; Kindleberger, "Charlotte Corday in Text and Image: A Case Study in the French Revolution and Women's History"; and Outram, *The Body and the French Revolution: Sex, Class and Political Culture*. For discussions of Corday's resonance in *Ormond*, see Lewis, "Attaining Masculinity: Charles Brockden Brown and Woman Warriors of the 1790s"; and Shapiro, "In a French Position: Radical Pornography and Homoerotic Society in Charles Brockden Brown's *Ormond or the Secret Witness*."

mandy. Charlotte Anne Marie Corday was a native of St. Saturnin in the department of the Orne. She appears to have lived in a state of literary retirement with her father, and by the study of antient and modern historians to have imbibed a strong attachment to liberty. She had been accustomed to assimilate certain periods of antient history with the events that were passing before her, and was probably excited by the examples of antiquity to the commission of a deed, which she believed with fond enthusiasm would deliver and save her country.

Being at Caen when the citizens of the department were enrolling themselves to march to the relief of the convention, the animation with which she saw them devoting their lives to their country, led her to execute, without delay, the project she had formed.* Under pretence of going home, she came to Paris, and the third day after her arrival obtained admission to Marat. She had invented a story to deceive him; and when he promised her that all the promoters of the insurrection in the departments should be sent to the guillotine, she drew out a knife which she had purchased for the occasion, and plunged it into his breast.

* Louvet[6] speaks of this extraordinary woman in the following terms:—"A young person came to speak to Barbaroux[7] at the Intendance where we all lodged. She was tall and well shaped, of the most graceful manners and modest demeanour: there was in her countenance, which was beautiful and engaging, and in all her movements, a mixture of softness and dignity, which were evident indications of a heavenly mind. She came always attended by a servant, and waited for Barbaroux in an apartment through which we passed frequently. Since this young woman has fixed on herself the attention of the world, we have each of us recollected the circumstances of her visits, of which it is now clear that some favour solicited for a friend was only a pretence. Her true motive undoubtedly was to become acquainted with some of the founders of the republic, for which she was going to devote herself; and perhaps she was desirous that at some future day her features should be brought to their recollection.

"I declare and solemnly attest, that she never communicated to us a word of her design; and if such actions could be directed, and she had consulted us, would it have been against Marat that we should have pointed her stroke? Did we not know that he was then languishing under a fatal disease, and had but a few days to live?"

---

[6] "Louvet": Jean-Baptiste Louvet (1760–1797), a Girondin publicist and Assembly delegate from Loiret, noted for his bold attacks on Robespierre and other Jacobins. He survived the Terror in hiding and in 1795 published an influential memoir chronicling the sufferings of Girondins who fled Paris in 1793. After distinguishing himself as an antagonist of the Jacobins, he remained a staunch revolutionary and did not, like many, become a "Thermidorean" conservative in the aftermath of the Terror.

[7] "Barbaroux: Charles Barbaroux (1767–1794) was allied with the moderate wing of the Jacobins before the Terror, and a close associate of Brissot and the Rolands. He led the battalion of volunteer soldiers from Marseilles that arrived Paris in 1792 singing the battle song that subsequently become the "Marseillaise," later the national anthem of France. Barbaroux fled Paris during the proscriptions, only to be captured and executed a year after Corday, in June 1794.

She was immediately apprehended, and conduced to the Abbaye prison, from which she was transferred to the Conciergerie, and brought before the revolutionary tribunal.

She acknowledged the deed, and justified it by asserting that it was a duty she owed her country and mankind to rid the world of a monster whose sanguinary doctrines were framed to involve the country in anarchy and civil war, and asserted her right to put Marat to death as a convict already condemned by the public opinion. She trusted that her example would inspire the people with that energy which had been at all times the distinguished characteristic of republicans; and which she defined to be that devotedness to our country which renders life of little comparative estimation.

Her deportment during the trial was modest and dignified. There was so engaging a softness in her countenance, that it was difficult to conceive how she could have armed herself with sufficient intrepidity to execute the deed. Her answers to the interrogatories of the court were full of point and energy. She sometimes surprised the audience by her wit, and excited their admiration by her eloquence. Her face sometimes beamed with sublimity, and was sometimes covered with smiles.

[Corday's execution and republican martyrdom]

[…] [I]t is difficult to conceive the kind of heroism which she displayed in the way to execution. The women who were called furies of the guillotine, and who had assembled to insult her on leaving the prison, were awed into silence by her demeanour, while some of the spectators uncovered their heads before her, and others gave loud tokens of applause. There was such an air of chastened exultation thrown over her countenance, that she inspired sentiments of love rather than sensations of pity.* She ascended the scaffold with undaunted firmness, and, knowing that she

---

* She excited in this interesting situation a very strong and singular passion in a young man of the name of Adam Lux, a commissary from Mayence. He accidentally crossed the street she was passing in her way to execution, and became instantly enamoured not of her only, but, what was more extraordinary, of the guillotine. He published a few days after a pamphlet, in which he proposed raising a statue to her honour, and inscribing on the pedestal "Greater than Brutus,"[8] and invoked her shade wandering through Elysium with those glorious personages who had devoted themselves for their country. He was sent to the prison of the Force, where a friend of mine often saw him, and where he talked of nothing to him but of Charlotte Corday and the guillotine; which, since she had perished, appeared to him transformed into an altar, on which he would consider it as a privilege to be sacrificed, and was only solicitous to receive the stroke of death from the identical instrument by which she had suffered. A few weeks after his imprisonment he was executed as a counter-revolutionist.

---

[8] "Greater than Brutus": greater, that is, than Lucius Junius Brutus, a founder of the Roman Republic, who was celebrated during the early years of the Revolution as an example of stoic, patriarchal

had only to die, was resolved to die with dignity. She had learned from her jailor the mode of punishment, but was not instructed in the detail; and when the executioner attempted to tie her feet to the plank, she resisted, from an apprehension that he had been ordered to insult her; but on his explaining himself she submitted with a smile. When he took off her handkerchief, the moment before she bent under the fatal stroke, she blushed deeply; and her head, which was held up to the multitude the moment after, exhibited this last impression of offended modesty.

12b. Elihu Hubbard Smith, Diary Entry for August 5–6, 1796. *The Diary of Elihu Hubbard Smith (1771–1798)*. Edited by James E. Cronin. Reproduced here by permission of the American Philosophical Society

Elihu Hubbard Smith was one of Brown's closest and most influential associates throughout the 1790s. An enterprising physician and writer from Connecticut, born the same year as Brown, Smith met Brown in 1790–1791 while he was in Philadelphia studying medicine with Benjamin Rush and Brown was still a law apprentice (see the selection by Rush here in Related Texts). He provided crucial encouragement and material support for Brown's development as a writer, publishing Brown's early poetry anonymously in American Poems, Selected and Original, *a volume that he edited in 1793, and introducing Brown into the New York circle where his ambitions expanded in the late 1790s. Smith proofread and paid for the printing of the first half of Brown's first major publication, the feminist dialogue* Alcuin, *in early 1798 (included in its entirety here in Related Texts), and was regularly involved in responding to Brown's manuscripts and preparing them for publication.*

More generally, besides his medical practice, Smith was active in New York literary and professional circles, publishing writings of his own, cofounding the nation's first medical journal, the New York Medical Repository, *and serving as an abolition activist. In 1798, as his novelistic phase began in earnest, Brown shared an apartment with Smith on Pine Street in Manhattan. He was present when Smith died after caring for patients during the September 1798 New York yellow fever epidemic, and memorializes him in aspects of several characters in his novels* Edgar Huntly *and* Arthur Mervyn.

The passage presented here was written in August 1796, when both Smith and Brown were visiting at William Dunlap's home in Perth Amboy (the referent for the Dudley mansion that figures in Ormond's *final scenes) and reading Helen Maria Williams's* Letters. *Smith describes a long walk during which he spins a tale of Girondin heroism inspired by Williams, and discusses it with Dunlap and Brown. Smith's scenario is far more paternalistic and conventional than Williams' or Brown's, since it allegorizes the role of an all-powerful, benevolent, and protecting father and ends with normative unions, but it enacts the group's common interest in affirming revolutionary progress, while*

---

severity in the service of republican principles. Corday's female patriotism is contrasted here to the severity of a male-associated ideal of "incorruptible" ideological purity advocated by Robespierre and his allies. Brutus famously had his own sons killed when they presented a threat to the Republic.

condemning its perversion in violent partisanship.[9] *Five months later, in January 1797, Dunlap and Smith began work on a play titled* The Fall of Robespierre, *which was apparently never completed; they may have been familiar with a similarly titled 1794 verse drama by Samuel Taylor Coleridge and Robert Southey. Brown's female heroines Martinette and, more obliquely, Constantia, seem to be the group's most lasting adaptation of contemporary stagings of Girondin struggle. For more on Brown's engagement with revolution and sex-gender debates, see the Introduction.*

Friday, 5th

Amboy has lost none of its charms, since last year: & the society of the same friends gave it an interest in my mind, new & considerable. We conversed, as may be supposed, on our wonted themes. Man, Morals, Politics, &c. I opened to Charles some views of, at least, a temporary settlement in New York [...].

[...] I sat up till late to read the seventh volume of Helen M. Williams's Letters.

Saturday, 6th

[...] I finished the volume of H. M. Williams's Letters, which I began to read last evening. I also looked at some numbers of the Monthly Review, for 1795, which I had not before seen.

After calling at Dunlap's—we—Dunlap, Brown, & myself—took a walk [...]

As we were walking along, I began to muse on a tale in Miss Williams's Letters, of an old gentleman, in neighborhood of Vaucluse,[10] his niece & son—ruined by the horrible blood-hounds of Robespierre. It struck me as affording, in connection with other circumstances, the basis of a good drama—the outline of which my imagination imperfectly sketched, as follows.

Suppose a Man, animated by the purest spirit of benevolent Philosophy, to obtain, by some means, the place of Commissary in one of the Departments—i.e. be placed in the situation of Lebon, Carrier, &c.[11] I suppose this to happen after the Depart-

---

[9] In addition to Williams' and Wollstonecraft's commentaries, Smith and the group were reading and, in Smith's case translating, two other Girondin-oriented accounts of the revolution that circulated in the late 1790s: Honoré Riouffe's *Revolutionary Justice Displayed; or, an Inside View of the Various Prisons of Paris, under the Government of Robespierre and the Jacobins. Taken Principally from the Journals of the Prisoners Themselves* (Philadelphia: Benjamin Davies, 1795); and François-Xavier Pagès (Francis Page, or de Pages, in some English versions), *The Secret History of the French Revolution, from the Convocation of the Nobles in 1787, to the First of November, 1796,* etc. (London: T. Longman, 1797). These histories reinforced the Girondin perspective derived from the group's other sources. See Smith's *Diary,* 132, 180, 198, 442.

[10] A mountainous Department in Provence, southeastern France, near the Mediterranean. A Department, in France, is the basic administrative unit, akin to a state in the U.S.

[11] "Lebon, Carrier, &c.": Jacobin functionaries notorious for cruelty. Joseph Lebon (1765–1795) was a former priest and professor of rhetoric who became a provincial representative in Pas-de-

ment had been subjected to the fury of some minor villain; & before the invention of *Noyades, fusillades*, &c.[12] Our Commissary's plan is to arrest & imprison, that he may save. His prophetic spirit tells him that the Decemvirs[13] must fall, shortly; & that if he can contrive to preserve their victims for a few months, or weeks, the justice of the Nation will then restore them to their homes & fortunes. From the moment of his arrival at the place of his Mission, he organizes the Tribunals, after the manner of Lebon, with persons who he brings with him, & on whose integrity he can therefore rely. He puts a stop to most single executions. As the denunciations & arrests are very numerous, some instances of persons deserving punishment occur, these are publicly tried & expiate their crimes. But a report is caused to be spread, that numerous victims are recd. into the prisons & never more heard of. Men, women, & children, are dragged from their homes, on the slightest pretence. The cruelty of these wretches would lead them to put their prisoners to immediate death. Our Commissary derides such feeble vengeance—speaks to them of the Noyades of Carrier, of his treacherous Feasts, &c. &c. To conceal his real designs the more effectually, he causes an immense vessel, on the plan of Carrier, to be constructed. He also causes hideous excavations to be made in the courtyard of the prisoners. His addresses to the people breathe the spirit of patriotism; & the young men of the Requisition are eager to depart. Among these is the Lover of Vaucluse. During all this period his prisoners are always spoken to, by the Commissary, with tenderness; & perfectly well treated. They, however, detest him the more—knowing how such arts have terminated. The Jacobins, too, are deceived, & admire the zeal, & address of their supposed leader.

The Drama may be supposed to open before the arrival of the Commissary in his Department. His first business is to dispatch the young men of the Requisition. Our Lover is torn from the arms of his mistress, & the house of his father—& there is interrupted that picture of felicity with which the piece commences. The lover goes with a conviction of the Commissary's goodness. In the mean time, various incidents occur. The father & Mistress of the young man are denounced, arrested, & placed in prison. Being of Noble extraction, & the character of the Commissary being now supposed, universally, to be like that of his employers, a report easily gains credit that the new prisoners are massacred in private. The exterior conduct of the Commissary countenances this belief, while, in fact, he causes them to be treated with all possible

---

Calais, on the English Channel. He was accused of excessive cruelty during the Terror and acquitted; then accused again, convicted, and executed in 1795. Jean-Baptiste Carrier (1756–1794) was known for his suppression of the counterrevolution in Nantes. He put groups of prisoners into damaged boats in the Loire River to be drowned, hence the *noyades* or drownings and specially constructed vessels mentioned farther on.

[12] "*Noyades, fusillades*, &c.": drownings and firing squads, methods of execution employed by Carrier and Lebon.

[13] "Decemvirs": Latin for "ten men," a commission for law making or law enforcement in the Roman republic, used here by extension to designate the Committee for Public Safety, the Jacobin ruling committee during the Terror.

kindness. Their fears, notwithstanding, are boundless. The Lover obtains a furlow. He hastens home, & finds all desolate. He hears of the unprovoked arrestation, & supposed death, of his friends. He determines on revenge. His return from the army affords him a pretext for a private conference with the Commissioner; who suspects his purpose & is prepared. The Lover, tho' torn with contending passions, attempts to poinard the Commissary & is seized. He is ordered to be imprisoned; & is told that his punishment shall be inflicted the next day, & in a summary manner. This proves to be, in restoring the delinquent to his friends, & a full exposition of the true character of the Commissioner; who, at this moment receives the news of the Revolution of the Ninth of Thermidor,[14] enlarges his prisoners, arrests the cut-throats, & proclaims the triumph of Humanity.

Such is the imperfect outline which was suggested to me, in the moment, & which I immediately unfolded to my friends, who bestowed on it marks of approbation.

I dined at Lovegrove's. After dinner I read them the passage which I had translated from Riouffe[15] […] .

13. Illuminati Debates

The Illuminati scare that began in 1797 and spread rapidly through the Atlantic world was a concerted, remarkably effective effort by conservative propagandists to demonize the French Revolution and, by extension, the Enlightenment (or Illumination, an early synonym for Enlightenment) ideas that had driven a major wave of progressive change in all fields over the previous generation. In the United States, the scare also became an effort, by mainly conservative ministers, to reassert their authority by supporting the ruling Federalist party's attempt to safeguard its diminishing power in a time of domestic and international challenges. Our discussion in what follows focuses primarily on the panic, Brown's response to it, and the role that it played in the counterrevolutionary turn of the late 1790s, illustrated by the Dwight-Ogden and Cicero-Demosthenes debates excerpted here.

---

[14] "Revolution of the Ninth of Thermidor": the coup against Robespierre that ended the Terror in late July, 1794.

[15] "The passage which I had translated from Riouffe": at the same time they were reading and discussing Williams, Smith and the group were also reading several other histories and commentaries that presented Girondin perspectives on the Revolution. Smith was particularly interested in Honoré-Jean Riouffe (1764–1813), another Girondin memoirist whose testimonies circulated widely after 1795. Riouffe's *Mémoires d'un détenu; pour servir à l'histoire de la tyrannie de Robespierre* (Memoirs of a Prisoner, illustrating the Tyranny of Robespierre) was printed in French in London in 1795 and translated into English in 1796, in a Philadelphia edition, as *Revolutionary Justice Displayed: or, An Inside View of the Various Prisons of Paris, Under the Government of Robespierre and the Jacobins. Taken principally from the Journals of the Prisoners themselves* (Philadelphia: Benjamin Davies, 1796). Smith made plans to publish his own version of Riouffe. On several occasions like the one noted here, he read unspecified passages from his translation to Brown and other friends in the New York circle, but the translation was never completed or published.

The Illuminati Scare

The eruption of elite reactionary panic in the Illuminati scare is still studied today as a classic case and precedent for many episodes of antimodern political, religious, and cultural demonology that follow the age of democratic revolutions and extend to the present. Scapegoating, projection, and blame were not new strategies of panic in the 1790s, of course. Nor were fears of political conspiracy, which were widespread in early modern political thinking. But the way that these basic processes and themes were linked to fears of modernizing change and exploited as mass political tools in the Illuminati scare is often understood as a landmark event that inaugurates new, postrevolutionary, and media-driven or spectacular forms of political demonology, and that sets the tone for new variations of xenophobic and racist activity in subsequent European and U.S. political history.[1]
Ormond *and Brown's other novels were written at the height of the Illuminati scare and respond to it in on several levels, most generally by foregrounding and consistently rejecting the fears of "foreign" subversive influence that are an important dimension of the larger Illuminati myth. As Brown was writing his novels, anti-Illuminati narratives were being used in the U.S. to aggravate an increasingly partisan crisis atmosphere generated by a threat of impending war against France in 1797, and by the repressive Alien and Sedition Acts (1798–1801), which targeted Irish and French immigrants as perceived subversives, and attempted to silence the opposition press (writing against the Anglophile Federalist administration of John Adams) by reviving old-regime definitions of political critique as unlawful sedition. These drew their inspiration from the similar 1795 British "Two Acts" introduced by the government after it had failed the year before to convict English radicals of treason.*
By 1800, however, the Illuminati panic had failed in the U.S. political sphere. The first-ever transfer of political power occurred with the rise of the Democratic-Republican party and, after his election as President, Thomas Jefferson (the primary political target of the U.S. anti-Illuminati tracts) pardoned those who had been convicted under the Alien and Sedition Acts and allowed the Acts to expire. The groups tarred by association with

---

[1] Scholarship on the episode develops concepts of "countersubversive" extremism, "political demonology," and, more locally, the "paranoid tradition" in U.S. politics. For historical perspectives on the relation of the Illuminati scare to modernization and postrevolutionary shifts, see Garrard, *Counter-Enlightenments: From the Eighteenth Century to the Present*; Koselleck, *Critique and Crisis: Enlightenment and the Pathogenesis of Modern Society*; Leinesch, "The Illusion of the Illuminati: The Counterconspiratorial Origins of Post-Revolutionary Conservatism"; McMahon, *Enemies of the Enlightenment: The French Counter-Enlightenment and the Making of Modernity*; Roberts, *The Mythology of the Secret Societies*. For the scare's impact in Brown's New York circle, see Waterman, *Republic of Intellect: The Friendly Club of New York City and the Making of American Literature*. A related body of scholarship builds on the work of Richard Hofstadter and focuses on the event as a precedent for later U.S. reactionary panics: see Hofstadter, *The Paranoid Style in American Politics*; Davis, *The Fear of Conspiracy: Images of Un-American Subversion from the Revolution to the Present*; Rogin, *Ronald Reagan, the Movie: and other Episodes in Political Demonology*; Stauffer, *New England and the Bavarian Illuminati;* Tise, *The American Counterrevolution*; Wood, "Conspiracy and the Paranoid Style: Causality and Deceit in the Eighteenth Century"; and White, "The Value of Conspiracy Theory."

*the Illuminati waged a successful counterattack in the press that mocked and discredited
the clerical promoters of the panic.*

*The anti-Illuminati narrative and the myths that it created circulated in loose diatribes
and rumors during the early years of the French Revolution, but took their canonical form
with the antirevolutionary propaganda tracts of French Jesuit and monarchist Augustin
Barruel (1741–1820). Barruel, from a family of petty* noblesse de robe *(lesser aristocratic status achieved by rising through the judicial or administrative bureaucracies), was
trained in the Jesuit order and first left France when the order was suppressed there in
1767. After Jesuit assignments in Germany and Austria, he returned to France when the
order was entirely suppressed by Pope Clement XIV in 1773, and began a career as a propagandist for crown and altar. Barruel relocated to London after the French Revolution
began and in 1793–1794 published French and English editions of his first antirevolutionary tract,* The History of the Clergy during the French Revolution. A Work Dedicated to the English Nation. *In 1797, still working from London, he published his
best-known work,* Mémoires pour servir à l'histoire du Jacobinisme, *immediately
translated as* Memoirs, illustrating the History of Jacobinism. *This work developed the
anti-Illuminati narrative in its fullest form, in four books: I,* The Antichristian Conspiracy; *II,* The Antimonarchical Conspiracy; *III,* The Antisocial Conspiracy; *and
IV, a historical appendix to* The Antisocial Conspiracy *that claimed to document conspiratorial activities of German Masonic lodge leaders such as Adam Weishaupt
(1748–1830) and Adolf Knigge (1752–1796).*[2] *At the same time, the narrative was re-
iterated and circulated in Anglophone form by Edinburgh physicist and professor of philosophy John Robison (1739–1805). Like Barruel's* Memoirs, *Robison's* Proofs of a
Conspiracy against all the Religions and Governments of Europe, carried on in the
Secret Meetings of Free-Masons, Illuminati and Reading Societies, etc., collected
from good authorities *(1797), was republished in several editions in England and the
U.S. over the next four years. Together, these two books provided the basic scenario and os-
tensible evidence that was quoted, recirculated, and debated in innumerable forms in the
following years, and which provides the basis for the debates given here.*

*The anti-Illuminati narratives of Barruel and Robison tell a simple story, although at
great length and with great bombast. The "antichristian" and "antimonarchical" conspiracies of Barruel's books I and II are the Enlightenment itself, the influence of rationalizing ideas on religion and society developed throughout the eighteenth century. Barruel
frames critique of the old regime as a disastrous development and blames its influence in
France on intellectuals from Voltaire to Diderot and the Encyclopedists, and in Germany
on modernizing reforms initiated by Frederick the Great. These modernizing ideas, for*

---

[2] Internal conflicts between Knigge and Weishaupt were a key factor in the Illuminati's demise.
When Knigge left the Illuminati in 1784, he may have helped convince the Bavarian Elector to ban
the group. His popular *Über den Umgang mit Menschen* (1788) is ostensibly a manual of manners,
but is also an early sociological study in managing human relations. The relation between the reality of secret societies and gothic fiction appears as this title was first translated as *Practical Philosophy
of Social Life; Or The Art Of Conversing With Men* (1794) by Peter Will, who specialized in horror
fiction.

Barruel, primarily encourage popular hatred against aristocrats and the rich, and have led to antireligious measures such as, notably, the suppression of the Jesuit order. The "antisocial" conspiracy of Barruel's books III and IV is the Masonic movement, and particularly the Masonic lodge in Bavaria (southern Germany) known as the Illuminati. Barruel and Robison claim that this lodge, led by Weishaupt in its earlier development and Knigge in later forms, has been responsible for secretive, conspiratorial plots that have spread via the institutions of print culture; led to the French Revolution itself; and threaten to spread farther, undermining church and state institutions (the old regimes) in other Christian and monarchical nations. Wieshaupt and Knigge were, in fact, dedicated to progressive change, and Weishaupt's "Illuminati" largely ceased to exist after it had been banned as seditious by Bavarian elector Karl Theodore in 1784. Nevertheless, Barruel's narrative seizes on a minor incident from the period's enlightened lodge activism (widely publicized and allegorized in many forms throughout the late Enlightenment, for exam-
ple *Mozart's 1791 opera* The Magic Flute *or the Masonic emblems on the Great Seal of the United States) and inflates it into an epic myth of conspiratorial terror.*

Like so many other sensational effects taken up in the Anglophone world in the 1790s, the Illuminati phenomenon began in Germany during the 1770s and 1780s. Although the order, its suppression, and ensuing print wars around it were real events, as opposed to literary movements, the entire episode deserves to be seen as an analogue to the contemporaneous rise of "Storm and Stress" (Sturm und Drang) writing, involving the young Goethe and Schiller among others, and of the Horror Novels (Schauerroman*) and State Romances, especially as the latter trends utilize the Illuminati legends as well. All of these trends follow a similar time sequence; and after their elaboration in Germany, all are eagerly transported into England in the early 1790s and the U.S. shortly thereafter.*

On May 1, 1776, Adam Weishaupt, the first lay professor of canon law at the University of Ingolstadt (1472–1800), formed a secret society of freethinkers dedicated to speeding the agendas of the rational Enlightenment throughout the globe.[3] *Weishaupt initially called the group the Perfectibilists, but later changed it to the Illuminati Order. The Bavarian university lay on one of the fault lines of the seesaw between the Enlightenment and Counter-Reformation, and Weishaupt lived out these tensions. Raised by a progressive professor of law at Ingolstadt, Weishaupt quickly rose through the academic hierarchy in the university, which had been founded to advance Christian ideals. The suppression of the Jesuit order in 1773 made it possible for Weishaupt to be promoted to professor of canon law, the only professor in the university who did not have a Jesuit background. Undermined by the machinations of the remaining Jesuit faculty, Weishaupt formed the Illuminati. The group was organized on strictly hierarchical lines: the leaders of one cell*

---

[3] For discussions of the historical Illuminati episode, its relation to wider Masonic and lodge elements of the late Enlightenment, and to the scare, see the previously mentioned studies by Koselleck, Leinesch, and Roberts, as well as Hofman, "Opinion, Illusion, and the Illusion of Opinion: Barruel's Theory of Conspiracy" and "The Origins of the Theory of the Philosophe Conspiracy"; as well as Luckert, *Jesuits, Freemasons, Illuminati, and Jacobins: Conspiracy Theories, Secret Societies, and Politics in Late Eighteenth-century Germany.*

initiated others, who remained ignorant about the identity of the group's other leaders, and seeded new cells in turn. Although Weishaupt despised the Jesuits, he followed their organizational system, with its network of spies, and he believed that the ends justified the means in spreading the ideals of the radical Enlightenment.

Under Weishaupt's eccentric academic leadership, the group remained very small until it was reorganized by a Bavarian diplomat and a Hessian noble with contacts in Masonic circles. Thence the group spread through Germany, reaching a peak membership of perhaps 2,000, primarily civil servants, officers, minor nobles, publicists, and academics. Some of its more famous members were Goethe, Herder, and the reformist educationalist Pestalozzi, although it is unlikely that these participants were deeply involved. Increasingly concerned about its influence, the Bavarian Elector Karl Theodor banned the order in 1784–1785. At that point the Illuminati ceased to exist as a functioning group, only to return in ensuing print wars and the paranoid imagination of the late 1790s it generated. The discovery and publication of the group's secret correspondence by the Bavarian authorities in the mid-1780s marked the first public scare concerning its activities, and Weishaupt, in exile at Gotha, one of the Saxon principates, spent the later 1780s writing public defenses of the organization.

Although the actual Illuminati were, in sum, a local episode in the period's vogue for lodge, club, salon, and other private association activism, the grand conspiracy theory put forward by Barruel and Robison, on the other hand (both working from England), blames the French Revolution on progressive French intellectuals and members of this small band of German Masons in Berlin who trained French acolytes, and claims that barbaric social violence is the preconcerted goal and outcome of enlightenment ideas and modernizing social reforms. It is not difficult to see how the scenario is built around basic structures of projection and scapegoating. Viewed historically and analytically, it appears as a fantastic reversal or inversion, a mirror image, of the actual historical situation in the 1790s, when the combined forces of monarchical Europe and its church institutions were focusing their economic, military, political, and ideological resources on the goal of violently crushing the French Revolution and the worldview it represented. In this manner the theory, beyond assigning an absurdly simple cause to complex and systemic historical transformations, projects the organizational and coercive energies of European monarchies onto the reform-minded Enlightenment, and demonizes its representatives as agents of a violence which is being planned and enacted by the monarchies themselves. However implausible, this narrative and its logic of projection and blame was eagerly embraced and amplified by conservatives who were grateful for any means of combating progressive ideas and condemning the social changes associated with the French and American revolutions. English figures such as Edmund Burke and elite U.S. Federalists such as President John Adams or Reverend Timothy Dwight (see excerpt) embraced the theory and used it to malign their political opponents as dangerous, godless extremists.

Shortly after the English publication of Barruel and Robison, the scare was brought to American shores primarily by a number of Congregationalist, New England ministers, including Timothy Dwight and Jedidiah Morse (1759–1826). On May 9, 1798, a day appointed by President Adams as a national fast day for repentance at the nation's "hazardous and afflictive position," Morse delivered the first of several sermons to his Boston *congregation that inveighed against the Illuminati and attempted to associate the scare with the Democratic-Republican political party led by Jefferson. As a result of rebuttals like those of John Ogden and Demosthenes, included here, however, the panic ebbed. These challenges also included published letters from the head of the Hamburg library Christopher Daniel Ebeling (1741–1817) and who denounced Robison's claims as riddled with inaccuracies and complained that because both Barruel and Robison did not know German, they were unfamiliar with the primary sources and context of the Illuminati debate in Germany and Austria.*[4]

Debate and Response

With an understanding of the basic argument and tendency of the anti-Illuminati scenario, it becomes possible to ask how Brown responds to it and how he develops commentary on the Illuminati scare in his novels and other writings. In his essayistic writings, Brown offers only a discreet rejection of the theory, making points that refer to his ideas on the relation of history and fiction writing. In the New York Monthly Magazine *of July, 1799, in his review of an anti-Illuminati oration, Brown points out the implausibility of assigning simple causes to complex events, observing how a grand conspiracy theory obscures thinking by explaining events with a simplistic and tendentious "plot" rather than necessary analysis. In the review's critical and dismissive synopsis of Barruel, Brown dryly observes, for example, how "the Romish religion, and hereditary despotism, were, in the eyes of one of his order and profession, virtue and duty."*[5] *In "Origin of Free-Masonry," a short 1805 article in his* Literary Magazine, *Brown concludes with a brief and critical observation that "the charge of infidel and revolutionary principles, brought by Barruel and Robison, against the lodges of free-masonry, are now generally exploded."*[6] *In addition to his rejection of Barruel in these two magazine pieces, it is notable that nowhere in his*

---

[4] Considered one of the first "Americanists" in Germany and author of internationally respected studies on American geography and history, the seven-volume *Erdbeschreibung und Geschichte von Amerika* (1793–1816), Ebeling already knew, and had found wanting, the geographical work on which Morse had mainly made his reputation. An outspoken and unapologetic defender of the cosmopolitan (and Protestant) Enlightenment, Ebeling was in frequent contact with a wide spectrum of American writers and scholars at the time. His work was mentioned frequently in U.S. newspapers and magazines in the 1790s, including the Brown-edited New York *Monthly Magazine*, and was thus familiar to members of Brown's circle, some of whom were collecting and then shipping over books and maps for Ebeling's collection in Hamburg, which became the most comprehensive one for Americana in Europe at that time. He also created an impressive collection of material relating to the United States for his alma mater, the University of Gottingen, which continues to hold the largest collection of American Studies in Germany today.

[5] See Brown's review of *"An Oration, spoken at Hartford ... by William Brown"* in *Monthly Magazine* July 1799, 289–92. For more on this review's rejection of the anti-Illuminati theories, see Wood, "Conspiracy and the Paranoid Style."

[6] "Origin of Free-Masonry," *Literary Magazine* 4.26 (November 1805), 335.

writings, including Ormond, Wieland, *and* Memoirs of Carwin, *the three texts that address the question most evidently, does Brown use the word Illuminati, and nowhere does he discuss the historical episode or the scare that was built on it, as if to avoid becoming embroiled with reactionary claims concerning the Illuminati or any other specific group. Brown's avoidance of the word seems quite deliberate. Although his hundreds of periodical writings focus on a great many contemporary topics and events, he chooses never to adopt the terms or concerns of this reactionary scare.*

In Ormond, *Brown develops an implicit commentary on the scare in two primary ways. Most evidently, the novel's frame and narrative structure, which ever more pointedly highlights and problematizes narrator Sophia Courtland's counterrevolutionary viewpoint, can be read as a complex reflection on the logic of projection, scapegoating, and blame that is a primary feature of the anti-Illuminati narrative. Sophia's inflationary rhetoric demonizes the mysterious Ormond, insinuating that he belongs to an Illuminati-like organization, but her repeated admission that she cannot reveal the sources of her own secret information mirrors and repeats the bad-faith rhetoric of the major Illuminati fantasists, who likewise failed to produce any evidence, other than rumor, of the Illuminati in America. The wider prejudicial force of Sophia's presentation of events suggests that Brown perceives the way that conservatives seek to naturalize or dehistoricize their assumptions by presenting their positions as commonsensical and thus prior to the complexities of historical causation or critical analysis, even as they condemn progressive arguments as unnatural violations of a supposedly preexisting order. It is notable, in this connection, that Ormond's internationalist plans, glimpsed only fragmentarily, seem to involve Jesuit-like, imperialist occupation of non-European lands, rather than the subversion of existing Atlantic institutions.*

Secondly, the novel's emphasis on the damaging effects of panic and prejudice, most literally in the yellow fever scenes and several characters' unexamined Francophobia, also seems to allegorize the heated amplification of social fault lines and internecine violence envisioned by anti-Illuminati rants.

Timothy Dwight versus John Ogden (1798–1799).

The polemical exchange that follows, between Timothy Dwight and John Ogden, illustrates the ways that the Illuminati scare was received and debated in Brown's immediate context. The anti-Illuminati tract by Dwight begins from the Barruel-Robison narrative, accepting their claims of illicit conspiracies by Weishaupt and Knigge, and argue that extensions of their illuminating and cosmopolitanizing activities pose an immediate threat to U.S. society. The rebuttal from John Ogden points out the outlandish, improbable nature of the anti-Illuminati theories and defends progressive positions by identifying the partisan political and institutional motivations of those who use the Illuminati panic to consolidate their own power and positions in the nation's religious, political, and educational elite.

Timothy Dwight (1752–1817) was well known in the 1790s as a Congregationalist minister, theologian, neoclassical poet, and president of Yale University (1795–1807).

Along with his brother, attorney Theodore Dwight (1764–1846), a possible source for the first name of Theodore Wieland, he was a pillar of the period's Federalist conservative orthodoxy and one of the most visible public amplifiers of the Illuminati scare in the early American republic. Although the Dwights' patrician conservatism did not rule out support for abolitionist activities during the 1780s and early 1790s, when their circles began to overlap with Brown's in New York, they became ideologically polarized as counterrevolutionary extremists in the crisis atmosphere of 1797–1801 and emerged as icons of that moment's "paranoid" style of reactionary, xenophobic polemics and religious-political posturing. Timothy was famously dubbed by his opponents the Federalist "Pope" of Connecticut.[7] John Cosens Ogden (1740–1800) was a Vermont Episcopalian minister who opposed conservative positions in the period's culture wars and acted as a supporter of Democratic-Republican interests. His last book was a commentary on the Moravian community that also figures in the family history outlined in Brown's novel Wieland: An Excursion into Bethlehem and Nazareth in Pennsylvania, in the Year 1799, with a Succinct History of the Society of the United Brethren, commonly called Moravians *(Philadelphia, 1800).*

Dwight's oration and pamphlet on the "Duty of Americans, at the Present Crisis" rehearses the basic anti-Illuminati scenario drawn from Barruel and Robison, arguing that enlightened thinking and social change represent dangerous forms of unchristian subversion. In passages not included here, he attempts to associate these supposed threats with Thomas Jefferson and the Francophile Democratic-Republican party that supported him. Rebutting Dwight's Barruel and Robison-inspired accusations, Ogden's pamphlet counters by ironically reversing and demystifying the basic conspiracy fantasy, identifying Dwight as one of a powerful group of interrelated conservative educational and political administrators that make up a counterrevolutionary "New-England Illuminati." Ogden points out that clerical ideologues like Dwight and his well-connected allies constitute a quasi-aristocratic cabal that combines to found their own networks of wealthy private institutions, notably colleges and universities, in order to further the interests of their own family and class alliances, using their influence to monopolize power and educational opportunities that deliver credentials and contacts for career advancement, and to manipulate and dominate the far more numerous laboring and professional classes who stand to benefit from public institutions and progressive reforms.

Finally, it is interesting to note how Dwight elaborates and further gothicizes the original anti-Illuminati scenario by linking it with local images of plague and pestilence drawn from then-common experience of yellow fever epidemics in U.S. coastal cities. For Dwight, enlightened change, in the demonic form of Illuminati conspiracy, is literally a plague that attacks and sickens the body politic. When Brown takes up this larger metaphor and develops parallels between the yellow fever epidemics and widespread damage in the body politic, however, in his novels Ormond *and* Arthur Mervyn, *he makes the fever into an allegory for the systemic corruptions of market culture, Atlantic slavery, and reactionary extremism.*

---

[7] See Kafer, "The Making of Timothy Dwight: A Connecticut Morality Tale" and Imholt, "Timothy Dwight, Federalist Pope of Connecticut."

*****

Timothy Dwight, *The Duty of Americans, at the Present Crisis, Illustrated in a Discourse, Preached on the Fourth of July, 1798; by the Reverend Timothy Dwight, D.D. President of Yale-College at the Request of the Citizens of New-Haven.* New Haven: Thomas and Samuel Green, 1798

While these measures were advancing the great design with a regular and rapid progress, Doctor Adam Weishaupt, professor of the Canon law in the University of Ingolstadt, a city of Bavaria (in Germany) formed, about the year 1777, the order of Illuminati. This order is professedly a higher order of Masons, originated by himself, and grafted on ancient Masonic Institutions. The secresy, solemnity, mysticism, and correspondence of Masonry, were in this new order preserved and enhanced; while the ardour of innovation, the impatience of civil and moral restraints, and the aims against government, morals, and religion, were elevated, expanded, and rendered more systematical, malignant, and daring.

In the societies of Illuminati doctrines were taught, which strike at the root of all human happiness and virtue; and every such doctrine was either expressly or implicitly involved in their system.

The being of God was denied and ridiculed.

Government was asserted to be a curse, and authority a mere usurpation.

Civil society was declared to be the only apostasy of man.

The possession of property was pronounced to be robbery.

Chastity and natural affection were declared to be nothing more than groundless prejudices.

Adultery, assassination, poisoning, and other crimes of the like infernal nature, were taught as lawful, and even as virtuous actions.

To crown such a system of falsehood and horror all means were declared to be lawful, provided the end was good.

In this last doctrine men are not only loosed from every bond, and from every duty; but from every inducement to perform any thing which is good, and, abstain from any thing which is evil; and are set upon each other, like a company of hellhounds to worry, rend, and destroy. Of the goodness of the end every man is to judge for himself; and most men, and all men who resemble the Illuminati, will pronounce every end to be good, which will gratify their inclinations. The great and good ends proposed by the Illuminati, as the ultimate objects of their union, are the overthrow of religion, government, and human society civil and domestic. These they pronounce to be so good, that murder, butchery, and war, however extended and dreadful, are declared by them to be completely justifiable, if necessary for these great purposes. With such an example in view, it will be in vain to hunt for ends, which can be evil.

Correspondent with this summary was the whole system. No villainy, no impiety, no cruelty, can be named, which was not vindicated; and no virtue, which was not covered with contempt.

The names by which this society was enlarged, and its doctrines spread, were of every promising kind. With unremitted ardour and diligence the members insinuated themselves into every place of power and trust, and into every literary, political and friendly society; engrossed as much as possible the education of youth, especially of distinction; became licensers of the press, and directors of every literary journal; waylaid every foolish prince, every unprincipled civil officer, and every abandoned clergyman; entered boldly into the desk, and with unhallowed hands, and satanic lips, polluted the pages of God; inlisted in their service almost all the booksellers, and of course the printers, of Germany; inundated the country with books, replete with infidelity, irreligion, immorality, and obscenity; prohibited the printing, and prevented the sale, of books of the contrary character; decried and ridiculed them when published in spite of their efforts; panegyrized and trumpeted those of themselves and their coadjutors; and in a word made more numerous, more diversified, and more strenuous exertions, than an active imagination would have preconceived.

[...]

For what end shall we be connected with men, of whom this is the character and conduct? Is it that we may assume the same character, and pursue the same conduct? Is it, that our churches may become temples of reason, our Sabbath a decade, and our psalms of praise Marseillois hymns?[8] Is it, that we may change our holy worship into a dance of Jacobin phrenzy, and that we may behold a strumpet personating a Goddess on the altars of JEHOVAH? Is it that we may see the Bible cast into a bonfire, the vessels of the sacramental supper borne by an ass in public procession, and our children, either wheedled or terrified, uniting in the mob, chanting mockeries against God, and hailing in the sounds of Ca ira[9] the ruin of their religion, and the loss of their souls? Is it, that we may see our wives and daughters the victims of legal prostitution; soberly dishonoured; speciously polluted; the outcasts of delicacy and virtue, and the loathing of God and man? Is it, that we may see, in our public papers, a solemn comparison drawn by an American Mother club between the Lord Jesus Christ and a new Marat;[10] and the fiend of malice and fraud exalted above the glorious Redeemer?

Shall we, my brethren, become partakers of these sins? Shall we introduce them into our government, our schools, our families? Shall our sons become the disciples of

---

[8] "Marseillois hymns": the "Marseillaise," the revolutionary anthem written in 1792, and today the national anthem of the French Republic. Conservative French regimes banned it several times in the early nineteenth century before it was permanently adopted as the national anthem in 1879.

[9] "Ca ira": the best-known popular song of the French Revolution. The title, repeated several times in each line of the chorus, means literally "it will go" or "it will work"; figuratively, "we will win."

[10] "Marat": Jean-Paul Marat (1743–1793), a Swiss-born physician, journalist, and political leader with the Jacobin faction during the French Revolution. His reputation as an extremist and his assassination in 1793 by Charlotte Corday are familiar commonplaces in revolutionary lore, in works such as painter Jacques-Louis David's *The Death of Marat* (1793).

Voltaire, and the dragoons of Marat*; or our daughters the concubines of the Illuminati?

[...]

Some of my audience may perhaps say, "We do not believe such crimes to have existed." The people of Jerusalem did not believe, that they were in danger, until the Chaldeans surrounded their walls. The people of Laish were secure, when the children of Dan lay in ambush around their city. There are in every place, and in every age, persons "who are settled upon their lees," who take pride in disbelief, and "who say in their heart, the Lord will not do good, neither will he do evil." Some persons disbelieve through ignorance; some choose not to be informed; and some determine not to be convinced. The two last classes cannot be persuaded. The first may, perhaps, be at least alarmed, when they are told, that the evidence of all this, and much more, is complete, that it has been produced to the public, and may with a little pains-taking be known by themselves.

There are others, who, admitting the fact, deny the danger. "If others," say they, "are ever so abandoned, we need not adopt either their principles, or their practices." Common sense has however declared, two thousand years ago, and God has sanctioned the declaration, that "Evil communications corrupt good manners." Of this truth all human experience is one continued and melancholy proof. I need only add, that these persons are prepared to become the first victims of the corruption by this very self confidence and security.

Should we, however, in a forbidden connection with these enemies of God, escape, against all hope, from moral ruin, we shall still receive our share of their plagues. This is the certain dictate of the prophetical injunction; and our own experience, and that of nations more intimately connected with them, has already proved its truth.

Look for conviction to Belgium; sunk into the dust of insignificance and meanness, plundered, insulted, forgotten, never to rise more. See Batavia wallowing in the same dust; the butt of fraud, rapacity, and derision, struggling in the last stages of life, and searching anxiously to find a quiet grave. See Venice sold in the shambles, and made the small change of a political bargain. Turn your eyes to Switzerland, and behold its happiness, and its hopes, cut off at a single stroke: happiness, erected with the labour and the wisdom of three centuries; hopes, that not long since hailed the blessings of centuries yet to come. What have they spread, but crimes and miseries; Where have they trodden, but to waste, to pollute, and to destroy?

All connection with them has been pestilential. Among ourselves it has generated nothing but infidelity, irreligion, faction, rebellion, the ruin of peace, and the loss of property. In Spain, in the Sardinian monarchy, in Genoa, it has sunk the national character, blasted national independence, rooted out confidence, and forerun destruction.

---

* [Dwight's footnote:] See a four years Residence in France, lately published by Mr. Cornelius Davis of New-York. This is a most valuable and interesting work, and exhibits the French Revolution in a far more perfect light than any book I have seen. *It ought to be read by every American.*

But France itself has been the chief seat of the evils, wrought by these men. The unhappy and ever to be pitied inhabitants of that country, a great part of whom are doubtless of a character similar to that of the peaceable citizens of other countries, and have probably no voluntary concern in accomplishing these evils, have themselves suffered far more from the hands of philosophists, and their followers, than the inhabitants of any other country. General Danican, a French officer,[11] asserts in his memoirs, lately published, that three millions of Frenchmen have perished in the Revolution. Of this amazing destruction the causes by which it was produced, the principles on which it was founded, and the modes in which it was conducted, are an aggravation, that admits no bound. The butchery of the stall, and the slaughter of the stye, are scenes of deeper remorse, and softened with more sensibility. The siege of Lyons, and the judicial massacres at Nantes, stand, since the crucifixion, alone in the volume of human crimes. The misery of man never before reached the extreme of agony, nor the infamy of man its consummation. Collot D'Herbois[12] and his satellites, Carrier[13] and his associates, would claim eminence in a world of fiends, and will be marked with distinction in the future hissings of the universe. No guilt so deeply died in blood, since the phrenzied malice of Calvary, will probably so amaze the assembly of the final day; and Nantes and Lyons may, without a hyperbole, obtain a literal immortality in a remembrance revived beyond the grave.

In which of these plagues, my brethren, are you willing to share? Which of them will you transmit as a legacy to your children?

*****

John Ogden. *A View of the New-England Illuminati; Who Are Indefatigably Engaged in Destroying the Religion and Government of the United States; Under a Feigned Regard for their Safety—And Under an Impious Abuse of True Religion.* Philadelphia: Printed by James Carey, No. 16, Chesnut-Street, 1799

WHILE clamours and prejudices are excited publicly and artfully against a large and respectable body of our fellow-citizens, under the pretext, that some are secretly embarked with a society in Europe, who are engaged in the destruction of religion and government in general, it is proper to present before the public a society which actually exists in the United States. This is more needful at this time, as these last are

---

[11] "General Danican, a French officer": Louis Michel Auguste Thévenet, known as "Danican" (1764–1848), who was decommissioned after suspected collaboration with antirevolutionary forces in1793. He became a royalist and subsequently took part in antirevolutionary efforts from London.

[12] "Collot d'Herbois": Jean-Marie Collot d'Herbois (1749–1796), an actor, writer, and member of the Jacobin faction during the Revolution. He was a member of the Jacobin Committee for Public Safety that controlled the French government in 1793–1794 and one of the more brutal Terrorists.

[13] "Carrier": Jean-Baptiste Carrier (1756–1794), a Jacobin revolutionary notorious for his suppression of the counterrevolution in Nantes, involving putting groups of prisoners in the Loire River in damaged boats to drown.

indefatigably engaged in destroying the religion and government of *this* country, under a feigned regard for their safety—and under an impious abuse of true religion.

These societies have passed without general scrutiny, until they have nearly destroyed our liberties and happiness at home, and contributed to plunge us into a share of the confusions of Europe.

These are the monthly meetings of the Clergy. As their design, tendency, and effect have been to destroy established law, morals, order, and universal toleration; they too bear near an affinity to the Illuminati Societies of Europe, not be viewed as part of the same: at least, if Professor *Robeson* and Abbé *Barruel* are to be believed, they must be *sister societies*. They have been known by the appellation of *Ministers' Meetings*— But I shall take the liberty of calling them the New-England Illuminati; leaving the reader to decide upon the propriety of the name.

These societies originated about thirty years ago; and were designed to increase the power and influence of the clergy. Success attending this confederacy, certain opulent and leading laymen have fostered and encouraged them, thereby forming that union of Church and State—of laymen and ecclesiastics—which have created an order equally formidable with that body of men in any country in Europe.

[…]

In this way Connecticut, especially, has become almost totally an ecclesiastical state, ruled by the *President* of the *College, as a Monarch*. The caution and politeness of the Governor of that state, the great age of many of the council, the respectful condescension of the members of the lower house, the submission of the clergy, the influence of *clubs*, of *uncles, brothers, cousins*, scribblers, and poets—of former and present pupils, have given him almost unlimited control.—Sufficient to undertake great duties, he does not consider the weight of cares, too difficult for his years, health, or inclination, but has assumed, among a passive people, the dignity of ruling with the united powers of an ecclesiastic and a politician.

[…]

To give the people of the United States a more perfect yet concise view of the proceedings of the Illuminati of Connecticut, and their adherents elsewhere, it is not amiss to recapitulate some things which relate to their arts, to secure religion, learning, the colleges, schools, and public property, to their uses. This is more important, as thereby they have called off the public attention from the schools and children of the yeomanry in general, to the promoting of the children of the Illuminati, and the colleges subservient to them.

A few clergymen artfully attempted to begin a college in Branford, in Connecticut, by depositing a few books. This design fell through, from want of consistency and property; and a new plan was adopted at Saybrook, which the government fostered; and it ended in Yale College. Mr. Yale, Governor of the East-India Company, and a churchman, liberally bestowed such benefactions as led the corporation to call it after his name, and write him a most flattering letter of thanks. Dean Berkley, afterwards Bishop of Coyne, in Ireland, gave an handsome farm on Rhode-Island, and a large library, to this college. The colony and state of Connecticut have erected three buildings and the chapel, and paid large annual sums to help it forward: but the illiberal and contracted doings of the clergy and corporation, caused the government and the generously disposed, to withhold their bounty. Five hundred pounds were left at one time, in this way, and given by a gentleman in England, to Cambridge College, in Massachusetts.

[...]

The sons and favourites of the Illuminati now hold seats in the Senate and House of Representatives in Congress.—They gained and hold their stations thereby: their efforts to gain a sedition law, and carry it into execution in their own state, is too evidently in order to check that *examination into their own affairs*, to which the people of Connecticut are prone, and from which they will not be deterred.

[...]

This gives a short view of a leading law character.—The head of the Illuminati, Doctor *Dwight*, a divine, who has made himself so conspicuous and has been so often animadverted upon publicly, that the nation are very generally acquainted with his character and proceedings.

In his sermon preached on the fourth day of July, 1798, in New-Haven, he has given us a perfect picture of the Illuminati of Connecticut, under his control, in the representation he has made of the Illuminati of Europe. To transcribe it might be useful; but the sermon is in the hands of so many, that it would be needless to swell this tract, by excerpts from it.

Birth, education, elevation, and connections have placed Doctor Dwight at the head of the Edwardean sect[14] and Illuminati. Active, persevering, and undaunted, he proceeds to direct all political, civil, and ecclesiastical affairs. Science, he forsakes, and her institutions he prostrates, to promote party, bigotry, and error. He is making great strides after universal control in Connecticut, New-England, and the United States, over religious opinions and politics. He is seeking the establish the Edwardean system of doctrines and discipline, from pride for his grandfather's (President Edwards') talents and fame; while few indeed of that deceased gentleman's descendents believe in his tenets. With a large salary, paid from the public bounty, he is maintained in his place, and excites and perpetuates party designs. For more than twenty years, he has been a writer in the newspapers upon many points, where he wished to forward alterations. He attacked the constitution of the college, while it was still directed by his predecessor, Dr. Stiles, and ecclesiastics only. Layman are now introduced, to little good purpose; and we must believe, without a violation of charity, that if a President had been elected who was not an Edwardean, he would have zealously sought to place that institution upon the same liberal foundation with other colleges.

---

[14] "Edwardean sect": in the passage that follows, Ogden builds on then commonly understood connections among the New England ministerial elite. Timothy Dwight was a grandson of late-Calvinist theologian and writer Jonathan Edwards (1703–1758), who also served briefly as first president of Princeton University.

Under his administration, and Illuminati influence, expecting favours from this nation, he has frequently disannulled the ties of religion, consanguinity, and friendship. Merit is neglected, and youth taught prejudices by him. These are circulated, to please the President of the College, and gain diplomas and flattering recommendations to schools and colleges.

[…]

14. C. F. Volney, excerpt from *View of the Climate and Soil of the United States of America* (London: J. Johnson, 1804)

French writer and philosophe *Constantin François Volney (1757–1820) was an important influence for Brown throughout his literary career. Like most well-informed readers of their generation, Brown and his circle were familiar with Volney as a celebrated voice of the radical Enlightenment, and they interacted with him personally during Volney's extended residence in Philadelphia in 1796–1797, when he could have regaled them with personal stories about Diderot, Franklin, Pasquale Paoli, the rising Napoleon, and other revolutionary-era notables. Brown immediately translated and annotated Volney's geophysical account of the United States (originally* Tableau du climat et du sol des Etats-Unis*) after it appeared in 1803, even as another English version was published in London. Volney's work may been have one inspiration for Brown's own geographical study,* A Complete System of Geography, *which he advertised just before his death in 1810, although it apparently remained unfinished and no manuscript has survived. Brown's interest in Volney, however, goes back to the early and mid-1790s, before his novelistic period. The diary of Brown's close friend Elihu Hubbard Smith notes that they read Volney's* Ruins *in 1795 and called on Volney socially in 1796–1797.*[1]

Born into a provincial noble family named Boisgirais, Volney created a new and explicitly revolutionary name for himself by combining Voltaire *and* Ferney, *the town on the French-Swiss border where Voltaire (1694–1778) lived at the end of his life. Volney was a delegate to both the Estates-General and National Assembly but, like many on the center-left, was imprisoned by the Jacobins. After surviving the Terror, he became the first professor of history at the newly founded École Normale Supérieure. In 1795, he traveled to the United States, established a friendship with Thomas Jefferson, and lived in Philadelphia where he was active in intellectual circles. Later accused by the Adams administration of being a French spy (after he published a review critical of John Adams' writings), Volney returned to France in August 1798. He was thus one of the first, although not the last, of the city's large French émigré community to abandon the U.S. as a result of the late 1790s right-wing political repression against foreigners and progressives that was legislated in 1798 as The Alien and Sedition Acts.*[2]

---

[1] See *The Diary of Elihu Hubbard Smith*, 48, 119, 152, 302, 305, 315.

[2] For more on the expulsion of French émigrés in the late 1790s, see the Related Text by Moreau de Saint-Méry.

14. C. F. Volney, excerpt from *View of the Climate and Soil of the United States of America*

Volney was best known in the 1790s as a materialist atheist, an opponent of institu-tional Christianity, and author of the widely read 1791 progressive parable The Ruins, or, Meditations on the Revolutions of Empires *(Les ruines, ou méditations sur les révolutions des empires), a book that he supposedly decided to write while visiting with Franklin in Paris. From the moment of its publication,* The Ruins *circulated throughout the Anglophone cultural sphere; fully translated in 1795 as* The Ruins, or a Survey of the Revolutions of Empires, *the work's popularity led to numerous editions in the United Kingdom and United States. Thomas Jefferson began his own translation but abandoned it after he became President in 1801. Not wanting to publicize his part in translating an iconic radical work, Jefferson gave the incomplete manuscript to Joel Bar-low, who completed the translation and published it in Paris in 1802.*

The Ruins *reflects on the decline and fall of ancient empires as a result of tyranny by aristocratic political and priestly elites. It ends with an imagined debate between follow-ers of all the world's religions, Western and Eastern, at a congress that leads to the dele-gates' amicable recognition that their fundamental similarities have been obscured by institutional regulators and doctrinal dogma. As an inquiry into the failure of past civi-lizations,* The Ruins *follows and further radicalizes earlier influential histories such as Edward Gibbon's* The History of the Decline and Fall of the Roman Empire *(1776–1789), which argued that Christian superstition was a key factor in the disinte-gration of the Roman Empire, along with the rise of "barbaric" north Europeans. Along-side its critique of institutional religion,* The Ruins *also presented progressive claims in the form of a debate between the "People" and the "Privileged Class" that condemns tra-ditional social divisions of labor, denounces the repressive power of despotism and priest-craft, and ends with the liberation of newly enlightened peoples. This section was widely influential and frequently republished in pamphlet form for plebian readers by English, Irish, and Welsh radicals.*

While The Ruins *excited Brown's circle, they read Volney's other works as well, several of which are likely sources for the Ottoman, Russian, and Middle Eastern references in* Or-mond. *In the mid-1780s, Volney traveled in Syria and Egypt and published an anthro-pological account as* Voyage en Syrie et en Égypt, pendant les années 1783, 1784 & 1785 *(1787) [Travels through Egypt and Syria in the Years 1783, 1784, and 1785 (New York, 1798)]. He also published an early account of the Russo-Turkish War of 1787–1792 as* Considérations sur la guerre actuelle des Turcs *(Considerations on the Current Turkish War; published in French in London, 1788, but never translated). Brown's circle read the book on Syria (the birthplace of* Ormond's *Martinette de Beau-vais) and the* Considérations *may have been one of Brown's primary references for infor-mation on the Russo-Turkish War referenced in* Ormond's *Chapters 21 and 27–28.*

Also of relevance for the remarks on Cossack-Tatar conflict in Ormond *is Volney's trea-tise on the U.S.,* Tableau du climat et du sol des Etats-Unis *(1803;* View of the Clim-ate and Soil of the United States of America*). In this work, Volney compares the Ukrainian steppes (a site of Russo-Turkish conflict) with the central plains of North America, which he described as an "American Tartary, which has all the characters of that of Asia." Volney's account links the Asian Tatars (Mongols) with the North American Naudowessie (Sioux or Dakota Indians). Although* Ormond *was published four years* *before Volney's account, this linkage of Asian and North American plains peoples had also been developed in earlier Enlightenment historical-anthropological writings.*

The following excerpts are from the preface to the book on American geography. This preface is generally relevant to an understanding of the atmosphere in which Brown wrote Ormond *and his other novels because Volney uses it to reflect on the political atmosphere and rhetoric of Federalist-ruled America in the late 1790s. Unlike conservative commentators, then and now, who are anxious to present the American and French revolutions as fundamentally distinct in their principles and effects, Volney argues that the two are far more similar than different (see Brown's January 1801 statement on this debate here in Related Texts). Volney specifically draws parallels between the Jacobin Terror of 1793 and the U.S. Federalist Party's strategies of partisan repression in the counterrevolutionary wave of 1797–1798, noting that the Federalists' "language and system were truly those of* terrorism*" and that "in the year 1798 different circumstances only were wanting to one party, to have displayed usurpation of power, and a violence of character, altogether counterrevolutionary." Volney's point is that the Jacobins' hunger for political retribution and repression reappeared during the presidency of John Adams and the late-1790s reactionary extremism of the Federalist Party. Fortunately, though, Volney adds that the damage caused by one disastrously partisan presidential regime may be repaired by a new president (then Jefferson) from the opposition party (then the Democratic-Republicans).*

Intended as a critical reply to Adams and the reactionary Federalists that forced him to leave the U.S. in 1798, Volney's preface dismantles several familiar mythologies surrounding the United States; for example, the notion that the U.S. is an "exceptional" nation whose politics differ in their essential dynamics and social interests from those of European or other nations, or the idea that the postrevolutionary years were a period of harmony rather than a series of crises and tumults caused by relentless partisan infighting, the nation's integration into a European-Atlantic mercantile economy, emerging U.S. imperialist designs on neighboring lands, and the problem of slavery. Volney emphasizes the problems and contradictions that beset a country which calls itself a republic even while it allows a violently antidemocratic political party to seize all the levers of power. He rejects the notion that the U.S. is any more fiscally responsible, transparent, moral, or respectful than European powers as he highlights a series of contemporary events such as the large 1794 military expenditures that commissioned new frigates to protect American commercial shipping from Algerian piracy; the pro-British 1794 treaty that ignored popular desires for closer alliance with France in favor of mercantile profit; the violent physical attack on the floor of Congress that occurred in 1798 when Federalist Congressman Roger Griswold of Connecticut assaulted Democratic-Republican Congressman Matthew Lyon of Vermont; and a series of riots by university students against the conservative clerical administrations of the period's universities. In short, Volney provides a catalogue of examples which together indicate that U.S. counterrevolutionary political elites and their rhetoric had less impact on the making of the United States than the country's position within an international political economy and the relative advantages (as to wages and property) that American workers then enjoyed over their European counterparts. Volney upends the ruling party's conservative rhetoric: not only do Federalist rants against foreign influences make it impossible to understand the economic and geopolitical realities underlying the

American situation, but the intemperance of the reactionaries actually damages home-land security by generating irrational hatred and internecine social divisions.

The translation reproduced here is from the first London edition, rather than Brown's version. Although Brown's version of the main, geographical text is accurate, his version of this preface omits Volney's polemical footnotes and moderates the tone of his criticisms of Adams ("a person, who was then all-powerful") and the Federalist reactionaries. Besides Brown's policy of avoiding direct partisan polemics in his magazines, his version moderates Volney's preface because Federalists still wielded considerable power in elite cultural circles in 1803. In the same way that Jefferson passed off his Volney translation to avoid unnecessary political opposition after becoming President, the far more vulnerable Brown moderates his translation of this preface to avoid unnecessary attacks in the U.S. public sphere. Nevertheless, Brown clearly considered this preface an important document and reprinted his translation of it as a separate article, "Volney's Travels in America," in his Literary Magazine in August, 1804.

Although the translator of the London version is not known, the book's publication by Joseph Johnson, the progressive printer and associate of figures such as Thomas Paine, Henry Fuseli (mentioned in the first sentence of Ormond) and the Wollstonecraft-Godwin circle, means that the book was immediately assimilated into progressive circles in England as well.

✶✶✶✶✶

PREFACE.

[…]

Perhaps this would be a proper place for me, to complain of the violent public attacks leveled at me during the latter part of my stay, under the influence of a person, who was then all-powerful; but the election of 1801, making amends for that of 1797, gave me sufficient reparation.*

[…]

In the plan I traced I first laid down as a basis the soil and climate: then, following the method which I conceive to afford the most copious information, a systematic arrangement, I considered the quantity of population, it's distribution over the territory, it's division into different kinds of labour and employment, the habits, that is the *manners*, resulting from these occupations, and the combination of these habits with the ideas and prejudices derived from the parent stock. Tracing this stock through history, language, laws, and customs, I showed the romantic errour of writers, who give the name of a *new and virgin people* to a combination of the inhabitants of old Europe, Germans, Dutch, and particularly English from the three kingdoms. The organization of these ancient and various elements into political bodies led me

---

* I shall point out to the Americans however the absurdity of the principal grievance, by which I was rendered a *suspected person*: (for at that period the language and system were truly those of *terrorism*). I was supposed to be the secret agent of a government, whose axe had not ceased to fall on those like me.[…]

to recapitulate succinctly the formation of each colony: to show in the characters of it's first authors that mental leaven, which has served as a prime mover to almost the whole system of conduct of their successors, according to a moral truth too little observed, that, in '*political bodies*, as in individuals, first habits exercise a predominant influence over all the rest of their existence.' In this leaven would have been seen one of the principal causes of the difference of character and inclination, that appears more and more obvious in the different parts of the Union.

The crisis of independence, obliging me to take a brief view of it's causes and incidents, would have furnished me with new remarks on it's less known and less observed consequences. A number of facts, omitted or misrepresented, would have established a much greater resemblance than is commonly imagined between the American and French revolutions, both in the motives, the means of execution, the conduct of parties, and the fluctuations, even retrograde, of the public mind; and finally even to the character of the three principal assemblies, the first of which in both countries was equally reputed to have advanced a whole generation in knowledge before it's contemporaries, and the last not to have kept pace with the knowledge acquired: so that those great political movements called revolutions seem to have in them something automatic, depending less on the calculations of prudence, than on a mechanical series and progress of the passions.

In treating of the period between the peace that established the independence of America and the formation of the federal government, a period but little known to the public, I should have shown the influence of that time of anarchy on the national character; the alteration of the public mind and it's principles by the return of the discontented loyalists, and the immigration of a number of tory merchants from England; and the change that took place in the primitive honesty and simplicity of the people, occasioned at first by the paper money, and the want of laws and justice, and afterward by the temporary wealth and permanent luxury, that the war of Europe introduced into this neutral country. I should have pointed out the advantages, that every European war procures the United States; the sensible increase they derived from the last, notwithstanding the weak and wavering politics of their government; the national and progressive direction of their ambition toward the West India islands and the continent surrounding them; and the probability of their enlargement, in spite of party divisions and the germes of an internal schism. I should have unfolded the difference of opinion, and even of interest, that divide the Union into eastern states (New England) and southern states, and into an Atlantic country and Mississippi country; the preponderance of the agricultural interest in these, and of the commercial interest in those; and the weakness of one part, occasioned by their slaves, with the strength of the other originating from a free and industrious population. I should have pointed out a still more active source of schism in the collision of two opposite opinions, styled republicanism and federalism: this maintaining the preeminence of the monarchical or rather despotic form of government over every other; the necessity of absolute and arbitrary power in every system, founded on the ignorance, passions, and indocility of the multitude, and the example of most governments and people, ancient and modern; in short all the old politico-religious doctrine of the royal prerogative held by the Stuarts and aramontanes: the other on the contrary arguing, that arbitrary power is a radical principle of disorder and destruction, since it does not exempt rulers from the passions, errours, or ignorance common to other men, but even tends to produce and heighten them; that the faculty of being able to do every thing, as it leads to desiring every thing, has a direct and immediate tendency to extravagance and tyranny; that, if the multitude be ignorant and wicked, it is because it receives such an education from such government; that, supposing men to be born vicious, they can be corrected only by the sway of reason and equity; that this reason and equity cannot be obtained without knowledge, requiring study, labour, and the collision of argument, all which presume an independence of mind, a freedom of opinion, the right to which men derive from Nature herself, &c.; in short, all the modern doctrine of the declaration of rights, on which the independence of the United States was erected. I would have discussed, from what I have heard from the most impartial persons, the consequences these dissensions may have. Whether it be true, that a division into two or three powerful bodies, at a period more or less remote, would be as stormy and disastrous, as is commonly supposed. Whether, on the contrary, too much unity and concentration would not be of fatal consequence to liberty, left destitute of asylum and of choice; and whether too great a degree of security and prosperity would not radically corrupt a *young people**, who, while they affect to give themselves this name, do not so much confess their present weakness, as disclose their schemes of future grandeur; a people particularly deserving this name of *young* for the inexperience and eagerness, with which they give themselves up to the enjoyments of fortune and seductions of flattery.

I should then have considered in a moral view the conduct of this people and it's government, from the period of 1783 to 1798: and I would have proved by incontestible facts, that neither more economy in the finances**, more good faith in public transactions†, more decency in public morals‡, more moderation of party-spirit, nor more care in education and instruction‖, prevailed in the United States, in proportion to their population, the mass of affairs, and the multiplicity of interests, than in most of the old states of Europe: that whatever has been done there of good and useful, and whatever of civil liberty, and security of person and property, exists among them, is owing rather to popular and personal habits, the necessity of labour, and the high price of all kinds of work, than any able measures of sage policy of government: that on almost all these heads the principles of the nation has been retrograde since it's establishment: that in the year 1798 different circumstances only were wanting to one party, to have displayed a usurpation of power, and a violence of character, altogether counterrevolutionary: in a word, that the United States have

* Whenever you point out to the Americans any weakness or imperfection in their social state, arts, or government, their answer is: 'We are but a young people;' tacitly implying 'let us grow.'

** The affair of Algiers, and construction of frigates at 1700000 {70833l.} a piece.

† Jay's treaty compared with that of Paris.

‡ The affair of Mr. Lyons in full congress

‖ Scandalous disorders in the college of Princetown, and nullity of others.

been much more indebted to their insulated situation, their distance from every powerful neighbour and the theatre of war, and the general easiness of their circumstances, than to the essential goodness of their laws, or the wisdom of their administration, for their public prosperity, and civil and individual wealth.

15. Elihu Palmer, excerpts from *The Political Happiness of Nations; An Oration. Delivered at the city of New-York, on the Fourth July, Twenty-Fourth Anniversary of American Independence* (New York, 1800)

Elihu Palmer (1764–1806) belongs to Brown's generation and his background is similar to that of several of Brown's New York associates. Born in Connecticut and educated at Dartmouth for the ministry, he rejected that career path and became one of the early Republic's most energetic advocates for Deism, the skeptical movement to which Brown's close friend, Elihu Hubbard Smith, was likewise attracted. Smith, who was an essential catalyst for Brown's literary career and had a closer relation to his work than any other contemporary reader, aligned Brown's writing with Deism and its implications. Like Brown, Palmer spent the 1790s moving between Philadelphia and New York, and at one point fled Philadelphia to escape mob anger. After being blinded by yellow fever during the Philadelphia epidemic of 1793 (memorialized in both Ormond *and Brown's other fever novel,* Arthur Mervyn*), Palmer devoted his life to writing and speaking in favor of political and religious progress. Unlike many of his age cohort in the U.S. and England during the reactionary cultural turn of the late 1790s, he never recanted his early dedication to the extension of social liberty, and never retreated into the safety of conservative positions.*[1]

While there is no record of direct contact between Brown's circle and Palmer, Brown and his group were in close contact with Palmer's intimates, above all the bookseller Colonel John Fellows (1760–1844), a Revolutionary War veteran, radical Democrat, and American confidant and publisher of Thomas Paine. In 1796–1797, while Brown was developing Wieland *and sharing lodgings with Elihu Hubbard Smith in New York, Smith frequented Fellows' Manhattan bookstore and discussed the possibility of becoming the editor of a Fellows-backed revival of the short-lived* The Lady & Gentleman's Pocket Magazine of Literary and Polite Amusement. *Smith seems to have turned down the position because Fellows could not guarantee an editorial salary independent of sales. Despite its conventional-sounding name, the* Pocket Magazine*'s initial run of four issues in 1796 began with an affirmation of Wollstonecraftian ideals, discussing the "rights and duties of Woman (which have lately been ably pointed out by one of the sex)," included a*

---

[1] For more on Palmer, see French, "Elihu Palmer, Radical Deist, Radical Republican: A Reconsideration of American Free Thought"; Schlereth, "A Tale of Two Deists: John Fitch, Elihu Palmer, and the Boundary of Tolerable Religious Expression in Early National Philadelphia"; and Walters, *Rational Infidels: The American Deists.*

proposal for "Female Universities" (in the September 15, 1796 issue), and may have in-
cluded poetry by Smith.

Fellows later provided a generational bridge for American democratic radicalism: he
dined regularly with Walt Whitman in the 1840s, shortly before his death, and regaled
the poet with personal memories of Thomas Paine.

In the address reprinted here, Palmer challenges the rising tide of religious-backed con-
servatism in the new century, which seeks to reestablish quasi-feudal hierarchies and ap-
propriate the language of patriotism for anti-democratic purposes. The choice of a Fourth
of July oration is a direct rebuttal to well-known ministers like Timothy Dwight, who
used Independence Day sermons as conservative polemics (see Dwight's Illuminati address
in Related Texts), and specifically reverses scare-mongering claims about the Illuminati.
Speaking against Edmund Burke and other theorists and propagandists of conservative
restoration like Friedrich von Gentz (see Brown's review of Gentz in Related Texts), and
reaffirming the radical Enlightenment's positive orientation toward historical transforma-
tion and thirst for universal emancipation, Palmer reminds his audience that the Ameri-
can Revolution should be commemorated as an act of social change, and not as alibi to
prevent further renovations of society. He repeats Woldwinite-like claims that virtuous
acts will sympathetically spread through a population that can learn to emulate beneficial
models. The call to "citizens" echoes the French Revolution's egalitarian language, affirm-
ing that the American Revolution's democratizing project still remains incomplete.

Palmer's unapologetic call for ongoing liberation is a powerfully argued case for the kind
of politics represented in Ormond *by Martinette de Beauvais (who bears the name of an*
executed Girondin deputy), and a summation of the novel's overall staging of antagonistic
tensions between narrator Sophia's reactionary vision and the emancipatory aspirations of
the revolutionary age.

*****

CITIZENS,

THE anniversary which is this day celebrated by the American people, is no less
powerful in its effects, than it is important in its nature and principle. The recognition of that grand thought, the recollection of that immortal sentiment, which gave
birth to a change so essential to the dignity and character of man, will become one of
the most effectual means of giving to the cause of liberty a durable triumph, and of
annihilating the despotism of antiquity. The celebration of this day is not intended as
a business of festivity alone; it includes the resuscitation of some of the finest feelings
that ever warmed the human heart—of some of the noblest sentiments, that in any
age have emanated from the mind of man.

[…]

Impressions made upon the human mind, either by interesting facts, or important
principles, are durable in their consequences; they mould the moral temperament of
intelligent life; they inspire the heart with a justifiable enthusiasm; they impel the
mind to discard error and venerate the truth, and to form individual conduct upon
the basis of eternal justice. The subject in this point of view is doubly interesting; for

while it does justice to the imminent virtues of revolutionary characters, it animates, it exalts, and inspires with a love of genuine republicanism, the juvenile mind throughout the American country.

Cold hearted, misanthropic, or tyrannical men have endeavoured to cast a gloom over the subject, to envelope it in clouds of awful mystery, and tarnish its purity, its glory and excellence by prophetic maledictions, the object of which is the destruction to the sentiment of equal right and the total subversion of liberty throughout the globe. If there be in nature a single human being who merits universal execration, it is that wretch, smithed in wickedness, who deliberately contends for bondage interminable, and whose aggregate faculties are devoted to the accomplishment of such fatal and malignant design—He is a monster in human shape whom posterity will reject—whom they will renounce with the most pointed asseverations, that such specimen of moral deformity certainly never disgraced a race of intellectual agents.

The enemies of liberty in every country have employed the same detestable argument for the purpose of perpetuating the despotism of antiquity. Innovations it is said are dangerous and destructive; the institutions of former ages have been sanctioned by time and authority—they have been venerated by our ancestors—they have been respected by wise and great men, and a desire to subvert them is indicative only of a restless and turbulent spirit, whose element is the confused and disordered state of the moral world. *Innovations it is said are dangerous and destructive,* it ought not to be considered harsh or severe, to declare that such objection can be attributed to no other course than ignorance or tyranny. To what do we owe the present state of human improvement? To what cause shall we ascribe national dignity and happiness so far as they have already been realized in any country? what is it that has the elevated enjoyments of civilized life—to purity of thought, sublimity of conception, strength of mind, extension of science, love of justice, augmentation of felicity, and that combination of circumstances, that discernable connection of cause and effect, which has already mitigated his sufferings, and improved his character—to what are all these effects to be attributed?

[...]

Anti-republicanism has raised a hue and cry, and set on foot a crusade against the immortality of reason, and the divinity of thought! The abettors of antique systems of vice, ignorance, and tyranny are continually vociferating against the liberty of the press; against the doctrine of equal rights; against the capacity of the people to govern themselves; against the universal extension of science, and the triumphant reign of human reason. In our country some Liliputian efforts have been made to annihilate the glorious effects of the American revolution, but they are like to terminate in smoke, and fall a sacrifice to the just resentment of an injured people.

[...]

The illuminati in Europe have been represented as a vicious combination of persons, whose object was the destruction of all the governments and religions of the world. If the writers against the illuminati, mean by governments the monarchies of

Europe, and by religion popular superstition, or systems founded upon the supposed existence of a mysterious intercourse between beings of the earth and celestial powers, they have undoubtedly been right in this respect; for these are the kind of governments and religions, against whose existence reason and philosophy ought to direct their energies… If liberty prevail throughout the globe, the necessity of human energy, in this great cause, would be diminished; and if love of moral virtue were universal, the duty of opposing error would be proportionably lessened. But calculation of action, is generally made upon ground totally different—upon principles directly opposite, and this has kept the world in slavery, ignorance, and misery.

BIBLIOGRAPHY AND WORKS CITED

I. Writings by Brown

Comprehensive bibliographies of Brown's writings and scholarship on Brown are available at the Web site of The Charles Brockden Brown Electronic Edition and Scholarly Archive: http://www.brockdenbrown.ucf.edu.

A. Novels

Brown, Charles Brockden. *Wieland; or The Transformation. An American Tale.* New York: Printed by T. & J. Swords for H. Caritat, 1798.

———. *Arthur Mervyn; or, Memoirs of the Year 1793.* Philadelphia: H. Maxwell, 1799.

———. *Edgar Huntly; or, Memoirs of a Sleep-Walker.* Philadelphia: H. Maxwell, 1799.

———. *Ormond; or The Secret Witness.* New York: Printed by G. Forman for H. Caritat, 1799.

———. *Memoirs of Stephen Calvert.* Published serially in *The Monthly Magazine,* vols. I-II (New York: T. & J. Swords, June 1799-June 1800).

———. *Arthur Mervyn; or, Memoirs of the Year 1793. Second Part.* New York: George F. Hopkins, 1800.

———. *Clara Howard; In a Series of Letters.* Philadelphia: Asbury Dickens, 1801.

———. *Jane Talbot; A Novel.* Philadelphia, John Conrad; Baltimore, M. & J. Conrad; Washington City, Rapin & Conrad, 1801.

———. *The Novels and Related Works of Charles Brockden Brown.* Bicentennial Edition. Six Volumes. Sydney J. Krause and S.W. Reid, eds. Kent, OH: Kent State UP, 1977–1987. *The Bicentennial edition is the modern scholarly text of Brown's seven novels, plus the Wollstonecraftian dialogue* Alcuin *and* Memoirs of Carwin.

B. Essays and Uncollected Fiction

Brown, Charles Brockden. *Alcuin; A Dialogue.* New York: T. & J. Swords, 1798.

———. *Historical Sketches. Short sections published in the* Literary Magazine and American Register*, 1805; most of the project appeared posthumously in the Allen & Dunlap biographies (1811–1815).*

———. *Literary Essays and Reviews.* Alfred Weber and Wolfgang Schäfer, eds. Frankfurt: Peter Lang, 1992.

———. *The Rhapsodist and Other Uncollected Writings.* Harry R. Warfel, ed. Scholar's Delmar, NY: Facsimiles and Reprints, 1977.

————. *Somnambulism and Other Stories.* Alfred Weber, ed. Frankfurt: Peter Lang, 1987.

C. Periodicals and Pamphlets

The three periodicals that Brown edited include hundreds of his own articles and miscellaneous pieces in a variety of genres (essays, short fictions, reviews, dialogues, anecdotes, and other forms) and on a wide range of subjects, from literary and artistic culture to social and political questions, history, geopolitics, and different subfields of science. For a listing of these publications, consult the Comprehensive Bibliography at the Web site of The Charles Brockden Brown Electronic Archive and Scholarly Edition.

Brown, Charles Brockden. *The Monthly Magazine and American Review.* Vols. I–III. New York: T. & J. Swords, April, 1799–December, 1800.

————. *An Address to the Government of the United States, on the Cession of Louisiana to the French.* Philadelphia: John Conrad, 1803.

————. *Monroe's Embassy, or, the Conduct of the Government, in Relation to Our Claims to the Navigation of the Mississippi [sic], Considered.* Philadelphia: John Conrad, 1803.

————. *The Literary Magazine and American Register.* Vols. I–VIII. Philadelphia: C. & A. Conrad, 1803–1806.

————. *The American Register, or General Repository of History, Politics, and Science.* Vols. I–VII. Philadelphia: C. & A. Conrad, 1807–1809.

————. *An Address to the Congress of the United States, on the Utility and Justice of Restrictions upon Foreign Commerce.* Philadelphia: C. & A. Conrad, 1809.

II. Biographies of Brown and Diaries of his Friends Smith, Dunlap, and Cope

Besides the published biographies, an important resource is the unfinished biographical study written 1910–1945 by Daniel Edwards Kennedy, now preserved at the Kent State Institute for Bibliography and Editing. The Smith and Dunlap diaries provide detailed reportage about Brown and his New York circle in the crucial period when Brown was writing his novels. Cope's diary documents Brown's never-accomplished plan, in 1803–1806, to write an abolitionist history of slavery.

Allen, Paul. *The Life of Charles Brockden Brown.* Charles E. Bennett, ed. Delmar, NY: Scholar's Facsimiles and Reprints, 1975 (written 1811–1814). *Allen's unfinished biography is the preliminary version of Dunlap's 1815* Life, *and remained unpublished until the late twentieth century. It prints miscellaneous fictional fragments and other texts by Brown not available elsewhere.*

————. *The Late Charles Brockden Brown.* Edited, with an Introduction, by Robert E. Hemenway and Joseph Katz. Columbia, SC: J. Faust, 1976. *This is a second fac-*

simile edition of the unfinished Allen biography, with additional commentary and information on the circumstances surrounding the influential 1815 Dunlap version.

Clark, David Lee. *Charles Brockden Brown: Pioneer Voice of America.* Durham: Duke UP, 1952.

Cope, Thomas P. *Philadelphia Merchant: the Diary of Thomas P. Cope, 1800–1851.* Edited and with an introduction and appendices by Eliza Cope Harrison. South Bend, IN: Gateway Editions, 1978.

Dunlap, William. *Diary of William Dunlap (1766–1839): The Memoirs of a Dramatist, Theatrical Manager, Painter, Critic, Novelist, and Historian.* 3 volumes. Dorothy C. Barck, ed. New York: The New-York Historical Society, 1930.

———. *The Life of Charles Brockden Brown.* 2 volumes. Philadelphia: James P. Parke, 1815. *A revision and extension of Allen, above. Together, Dunlap and Allen provide the only texts for the* Historical Sketches, *the complete version of* Alcuin, *and other pieces not available elsewhere.*

Kafer, Peter. *Charles Brockden Brown's Revolution and the Birth of American Gothic.* Philadelphia: U of Pennsylvania P, 2004.

Smith, Elihu Hubbard. *The Diary of Elihu Hubbard Smith (1771–1798).* James E. Cronin, ed. Philadelphia: American Philosophical Society, 1973.

Warfel, Harry R. *Charles Brockden Brown: American Gothic Novelist.* Gainesville: U of Florida P, 1949.

III. Brown, *Ormond,* and *Alcuin* in the Wider Context of Cultural and Literary History

Amfreville, Marc. *Charles Brockden Brown: La part du doute.* Paris: Belin, 2000.

Anthony, David. "Banking on Emotion: Financial Panic and the Logic of Male Submission in the Jacksonian Gothic." *American Literature* 76.4 (December 2004): 719–47.

Axelrod, Alan. *Charles Brockden Brown, an American Tale.* Austin: U of Texas P, 1983.

Baker, Jennifer J. *Securing the Commonwealth: Debt, Speculation, and Writing in the Making of Early America.* Baltimore: Johns Hopkins UP, 2006.

Barnes, Elizabeth. *States of Sympathy: Seduction and Democracy in the American Novel.* New York: Columbia UP, 1997.

Bell, Michael Davitt. "'The Double-Tongued Deceiver': Sincerity and Duplicity in the Novels of Charles Brockden Brown." *Early American Literature* 9.2 (1974): 143–63.

Bennett, Charles E. "Charles Brockden Brown's 'Portrait of an Emigrant.'" *College Language Association Journal* 14 (1970): 87–90.

Bradfield, Scott. *Dreaming Revolution: Transgression in the Development of American Romance.* Iowa City: U of Iowa P, 1993.

Cahill, Edward. "An Adventurous and Lawless Fancy: Charles Brockden Brown's Aesthetic State." *Early American Literature* 36.1 (2001): 31–70.

Chase, Richard. *The American Novel and Its Tradition*. New York: Doubleday, 1957.

Christophersen, Bill. *The Apparition in the Glass: Charles Brockden Brown's American Gothic*. Athens: U of Georgia P, 1993.

Clark, David Lee. "Brown and the Rights of Women." *University of Texas Bulletin*, March 1922: 1–48.

Cody, Michael. *Charles Brockden Brown and the Literary Magazine: Cultural Journalism in the Early American Republic*. Jefferson, NC: McFarland, 2004.

Crain, Caleb. *American Sympathy: Men, Friendship, and Literature in the New Nation*. New Haven: Yale UP, 2001.

Dauber, Kenneth. *The Idea of Authorship in America: Democratic Poetics from Franklin to Melville*. Madison: U of Wisconsin P, 1990.

Davidson, Cathy. *Revolution and the Word: The Rise of the Novel in America*. Expanded Edition. New York: Oxford UP, 2004.

Dawes, James. "Fictional Feeling: Philosophy, Cognitive Science, and the American Gothic." *American Literature* 76.3 (2004): 437–66.

Dillon, Elizabeth Maddock. *The Gender of Freedom: Fictions of Liberalism and the Literary Public Sphere*. Stanford: Stanford UP, 2004.

Dillon, James. "'The Highest Province of Benevolence': Charles Brockden Brown's Fictional Theory." *Studies in Eighteenth-Century Culture* 27 (1998): 237–58.

Downes, Paul. *Democracy, Revolution, and Monarchism in Early American Literature*. Cambridge: Cambridge UP, 2002.

Elliott, Emory. *Revolutionary Writers: Literature and Authority in the New Republic, 1725–1810*. New York: Oxford UP, 1986.

Emerson, Amanda. "The Early American Novel: Charles Brockden Brown's Fictitious Historiography." *Novel: A Forum on Fiction* 40.1/2 (2006): 125–50.

Faherty, Duncan. *Remodeling the Nation: The Architecture of American Identity, 1776–1858*. Lebanon: U of New Hampshire P, 2009.

Ferguson, Robert A. *Law and Letters in American Culture*. Cambridge: Harvard UP, 1984.

———. "Yellow Fever and Charles Brockden Brown: The Context of the Emerging Novelist." *Early American Literature* 14 (1980): 293–305.

Fiedler, Leslie A. *Love and Death in the American Novel*. New York: Criterion Books, 1960.

Fleischmann, Fritz. *A Right View of the Subject: Feminism in the Works of Charles Brockden Brown and John Neal*. Erlangen: Palm & Enke, 1983.

Fliegelman, Jay. *Prodigals and Pilgrims: The American Revolution Against Patriarchal Authority*. Cambridge: Cambridge UP, 1982.

Glasenapp, Jörn. *'Prodigies, Anomalies, Monsters': Charles Brockden Brown und die Grenzen der Erkenntnis*. Göttingen: Wallstein Verlag, 2000.

Goddu, Teresa. *Gothic America: Narrative, History, and Nation.* New York: Columbia UP, 1997.

Goudie, Sean X. *Creole America: The West Indies and the Formation of Literature and Culture in the New Republic.* Philadelphia: U of Pennsylvania P, 2006.

Gould, Philip. "Race, Commerce, and the Literature of Yellow Fever in Early National Philadelphia." *Early American Literature* 35 (2000): 157–86.

Grabo, Norman S. *The Coincidental Art of Charles Brockden Brown.* Chapel Hill: U of North Carolina P, 1981.

Hedges, William. "Charles Brockden Brown and the Culture of Contradictions." *Early American Literature* 9 (1974): 107–42.

Hinds, Elizabeth Jane Wall. *Private Property: Charles Brockden Brown's Gendered Economics of Virtue.* Newark: U of Delaware P, 1997.

Kamrath, Mark L. *The Historicism of Charles Brockden Brown: Radical History and the Early Republic.* Kent: Kent State UP, 2010.

Levine, Robert S. *Conspiracy and Romance: Studies in Brockden Brown, Cooper, Hawthorne, and Melville.* Cambridge: Cambridge UP, 1989.

Lindberg, Gary. *The Confidence Man in American Literature.* New York: Oxford UP, 1982.

McNutt, Donald J. *Urban Revelations: Images of Ruin in the American City, 1790–1860.* New York: Routledge, 2006.

Morris, Colin Jeffrey. "To 'Shut out the World': Political Alienation and the Privatized Self in the Early Life and Works of Charles Brockden Brown, 1776–1794." *Journal of the Early Republic* 24.4 (2004): 609–39.

Richards, Jeffrey. *Drama, Theatre, and Identity in the American New Republic.* Cambridge: Cambridge UP, 2005.

Ringe, Donald A. *Charles Brockden Brown.* Revised Edition. Boston: Twayne; G.K. Hall, 1991.

Samuels, Shirley. *Romances of the Republic: Women, the Family, and Violence in the Literature of the Early American Nation.* New York: Oxford UP, 1996.

Shapiro, Stephen. *The Culture and Commerce of the Early American Novel: Reading the Atlantic World-System.* University Park: The Pennsylvania State UP, 2008.

Simpson, Lewis P. "The Symbolism of Literary Alienation in the Revolutionary Age." *The Journal of Politics* 38.3 (Aug., 1976): 79–100.

Slawinski, Scott Paul. *Validating Bachelorhood: Audience, Patriarchy and Charles Brockden Brown's Editorship of the Monthly Magazine and American Review.* New York: Routledge, 2005.

Stern, Julia A. *The Plight of Feeling: Sympathy and Dissent in the Early American Novel.* Chicago: U of Chicago P, 1998.

Stout, Janis P. *Sodoms in Eden: The City in American Fiction before 1800.* Westport, CT: Greenwood Press, 1976.

Teute, Fredrika J. "A 'Republic of Intellect': Conversation and Criticism among the Sexes in 1790s New York." In Philip Barnard, Mark L. Kamrath, and Stephen

Shapiro, eds. *Revising Charles Brockden Brown: Culture, Politics, and Sexuality in the Early Republic*, 149–81. Knoxville: U of Tennessee P, 2004.

———. "The Loves of the Plants; or, the Cross-Fertilization of Science and Desire at the End of the Eighteenth Century." In Robert M. Maniquis, ed., *British Radical Culture of the 1790s*, 63–89. San Marino: Huntington Library, 2002.

Tompkins, Jane. *Sensational Designs: The Cultural Work of American Fiction, 1790–1860*. New York: Oxford UP, 1985.

Traister, Bryce. "Libertinism and Authorship in America's Early Republic." *American Literature* 72.1 (2000): 1–30.

Verhoeven, W. M. "Opening the Text: The Locked-Trunk Motif in Late Eighteenth-Century British and American Gothic Fiction." In Valeria Tinkler-Villani, Peter Davidson, and Jane Stevenson, eds., *Exhibited by Candlelight: Sources and Developments in the Gothic Tradition*, 205–19. Amsterdam: Rodopi, 1995.

Warner, Michael. *Letters of the Republic: Publication and the Public Sphere in Eighteenth-Century America*. Cambridge: Harvard UP, 1990.

Waterman, Bryan. *Republic of Intellect: The Friendly Club of New York City and the Making of American Literature*. Baltimore, MD: The Johns Hopkins UP, 2007.

Watts, Steven. *The Romance of Real Life: Charles Brockden Brown and the Origins of American Culture*. Baltimore: Johns Hopkins UP, 1994.

Weyler, Karen A. *Intricate Relations: Sexual and Economic Desire in American Fiction, 1789–1814*. Iowa City: U of Iowa P, 2004.

Wood, Sarah. *Quixotic Fictions of the USA, 1792–1815*. New York: Oxford UP, 2005.

Ziff, Larzer. *Writing in the New Nation: Prose, Print, and Politics in the Early United States*. New Haven: Yale UP, 1991.

IV. Discussions Primarily of *Ormond*

Bennett, Maurice J. "Charles Brockden Brown and the Question of Art: *Ormond; or, The Secret Witness*." In *An American Tradition: Three Studies, Charles Brockden Brown, Nathaniel Hawthorne, Henry James*. Dissertation: Harvard U, 1978.

Chapman, Mary. "Introduction." In Charles Brockden Brown, *Ormond: or, The Secret Witness*, 9–31. Peterborough, ON: Broadview Press, 1999.

Christophersen, Bill. "Charles Brockden Brown's 'Ormond': The Secret Witness as Ironic Motif." *Modern Language Studies* 10.2 (1980): 37–41.

Comment, Kristin M. "Charles Brockden Brown's *Ormond* and Lesbian Possibility in the Early Republic." *Early American Literature* 40 (2005): 57–78.

Cowell, Pattie. "Class, Gender, and Genre: Deconstructing Social Formulas on the Gothic Frontier." In David Mogen et al., eds., *Frontier Gothic: Terror and Wonder at the Frontier in American Literature*, 126–39. Rutherford, NJ: Fairleigh Dickinson UP, 1993.

Davies, Rosemary Reeves. "Charles Brockden Brown's *Ormond*: A Possible Influence upon Shelley's Conduct." *Philological Quarterly* 43 (1964): 133–37.

Drexler, Michael J. and Ed White. "Secret Witness: or, the Fantasy Structure of Republicanism." *Early American Literature* 44 (2009): 333–63.

Ellis, Scott. "Charles Brockden Brown's *Ormond*, Property Exchange, and the Literary Marketplace in the Early American Republic." *Studies in the Novel* 37 (2005): 1–19.

Hamelman, Steve. "Secret to the Last: Charles Brockden Brown's *Ormond*." *Literature Interpretation and Theory* 11.3 (2000): 305–26.

Hare, Robert Rigby. *Charles Brockden Brown's* Ormond*: The Influence of Rousseau, Godwin, and Wollstonecraft*. Dissertation, U of Maryland, 1967.

Hirsch, David H. "Charles Brockden Brown as a Novelist of Ideas." *Books at Brown* 20 (1965): 165–84.

Krause, Sydney J. "Historical Notes." In Charles Brockden Brown, *Ormond; or The Secret Witness. Vol. 2, The Novels and Related Works of Charles Brockden Brown. Bicentennial Edition*, 389–478. Kent: Kent State UP, 1982.

———. "*Ormond*: How Rapidly and How Well 'Composed, Arranged, and Delivered.'" *Early American Literature* 13 (1978–1979): 238–49.

———. "*Ormond*: Seduction in a New Key." *American Literature* 44.4 (1973): 570–84.

Layson, Hana. "Rape and Revolution: Feminism, Antijacobinism, and the Politics of Injured Innocence in Brockden Brown's *Ormond*." *Early American Studies* 2 (2004): 160–91.

Levine, Robert S. "Villainy and the Fear of Conspiracy in Charles Brockden Brown's *Ormond*." *Early American Literature* 15 (1980): 124–40.

Lewis, Paul. "Attaining Masculinity: Charles Brockden Brown and Woman Warriors of the 1790s." *Early American Literature* 40 (2005): 37–55.

———. "Charles Brockden Brown and the Gendered Canon of Early American Fiction." *Early American Literature* 31 (1996): 167–88.

Lukasik, Christopher. "'The Vanity of Physiognomy': Dissimulation and Discernment in Charles Brockden Brown's *Ormond*." *Amerikastudien/American Studies* 50.3 (2005): 485–505.

Marchand, Ernest. "Introduction." In Charles Brockden Brown, *Ormond*, ix–xliv. New York: American Book Co., 1937.

Monahan, Kathleen Nolan. "Brown's *Arthur Mervyn* and *Ormond*." *Explicator* 45 (1987): 18–20.

Nelson, Carl W. Jr. "A Just Reading of Charles Brockden Brown's *Ormond*." *Early American Literature* 8 (1973): 163–78.

———. "Brown's Manichean Mock-Heroic: The Ironic Self in a Hyperbolic World." *West Virginia University Philological Papers* 20 (1973): 26–42.

Nye, Russell B. "Historical Essay." In Charles Brockden Brown, *Ormond; or The Secret Witness. Vol. 2, The Novels and Related Works of Charles Brockden Brown. Bicentennial Edition*, 295–341. Kent: Kent State UP, 1982.

Patrick, Marietta S. "Charles Brockden Brown's *Ormond*: A Psychological Portrait of Constantia Dudley." *Journal of Evolutionary Psychology* 5.1–2 (1984): 112–28.

———. "Mythic Images in Charles Brockden Brown's *Ormond.*" *The University of Mississippi Studies in English* 11–12 (1993): 294–302.

Richards, Jeffrey H. "Tales of the Philadelphia Theatre: *Ormond*, National Performance, and Supranational Identity." In *Drama, Theatre, and Identity in the American New Republic*, 241–58. Cambridge: Cambridge UP, 2005.

Rodgers, Paul C., Jr. "Brown's *Ormond*: The Fruits of Improvisation." *American Quarterly* 26.1 (1974): 4–22.

Roulston, Christine. "Having it Both Ways? The Eighteenth-Century Menage-à-Trois." *British Journal for Eighteenth-Century Studies* 27.2 (2004): 257–77. [Also In Chris Mounsey and Caroline Gonda, eds., *Queer People: Negotiations and Expressions of Homosexuality, 1700–1800*, 261–73. Lewisburg: Bucknell UP, 2007.]

Russo, James. "The Tangled Web of Deception and Imposture in Charles Brockden Brown's *Ormond.*" *Early American Literature* 14 (1979): 205-27.

Scheick, William J. "The Problem of Origination in Brown's *Ormond.*" In Bernard Rosenthal, ed., *Critical Essays on Charles Brockden Brown*, 126–41. Boston: G.K. Hall & Co., 1981.

Seelye, John. "The Jacobin Mode in Early American Fiction: Gilbert Imlay's *The Emigrants.*" *Early American Literature* 22 (1987): 204–12.

Shapiro, Stephen. "In a French Position: Radical Pornography and Homoerotic Society in Charles Brockden Brown's *Ormond or the Secret Witness.*" In Thomas A. Foster, ed., *Long Before Stonewall: Histories of Same-Sex Sexuality in Early America*, 357–83. New York: New York UP, 2007.

Smyth, Heather. "'Imperfect Disclosures': Cross-Dressing and Containment in Charles Brockden Brown's *Ormond.*" In Merril D. Smith, ed., *Sex and Sexuality in Early America*, 24–61. New York: New York UP, 1998.

Stern, Julia. "The State of 'Women' in *Ormond*; or, Patricide in the New Nation." In Philip Barnard, Mark L. Kamrath, and Stephen Shapiro, eds., *Revising Charles Brockden Brown: Culture, Politics, and Sexuality in the Early Republic*, 182–215. Knoxville: U of Tennessee P, 2004.

Stott, G. St. John. "Second Thoughts about *Ormond.*" *Etudes Anglaises* 43 (1990): 157–68.

Tutor, Jonathan C. "Disappointed Expectations: Artistic Strategy in *Ormond.*" *Publications of the Mississippi Philological Association* (1985): 67–80.

Verhoeven, W. M. "Displacing the Discontinuous: Or, The Labyrinths of Reason: Fictional Design and Eighteenth-Century Thought in Charles Brockden Brown's *Ormond.*" In Wil Verhoeven, ed., *Rewriting the Dream: Reflections on the Changing American Literary Canon*, 202–29. Amsterdam: Rodopi, 1992.

Wicke, Anne. "Sophia, Martinette, et Constantia: Des femmes exemplaires?" *Profils Américains* 11 (1999): 103–20.

Witherington, Paul. "Charles Brockden Brown's *Ormond*: The American Artist and His Masquerades." *Studies in American Fiction* 4 (1976): 111–19.

Wood, Sarah F. "Foul Contagion and Perilous Asylums: The Role of the Refugee in *Ormond* and *Arthur Mervyn*." *Overhere: A European Journal of American Culture* 18.3 (1999): 82–92.

Zhang, Dingquan. "The Liberation of Women in America and the Three Female Characters in *Ormond*." *Waiguoyu Journal of Foreign Languages* 6.106 (1996): 75–78.

V. Discussions of *Alcuin; A Dialogue*

Amfreville, Marc. "Un obscur dialogue au siècle des Lumières: *Alcuin*." ["A little-known Enlightenment Dialogue: *Alcuin*"]. *Revue française d'études américaines* 92 (2002), 86–97.

Arner, Robert D. "Historical Essay." In Charles Brockden Brown, *Alcuin: A Dialogue and Memoirs of Stephen Calvert*. Vol. 6, *The Novels and Related Works of Charles Brockden Brown*, 273–312. Kent: Kent State UP, 1987.

Borghi, Liana. *Dialogue in Utopia: Manners, Purpose and Structure in Three Feminist Works of the 1790s*. Pisa, Italy: ETS, 1984.

Burgett, Bruce. "Between Speculation and Population: The Problem of 'Sex' in Thomas Malthus's Essay on Population and Charles Brockden Brown's *Alcuin*." In Philip Barnard, Mark L. Kamrath, and Stephen Shapiro, eds. *Revising Charles Brockden Brown: Culture, Politics, and Sexuality in the Early Republic*, 122–48. Knoxville: U of Tennessee P, 2004.

Davidson, Cathy. "The Manner and Matter of Charles Brockden Brown's *Alcuin*." In Bernard Rosenthal, ed., *Critical Essays on Charles Brockden Brown*, 71–86. Boston: G.K. Hall, 1981.

Edwards, Justin D. "Engendering a New Republic: Charles Brockden Brown's *Alcuin, Carwin* and the Legal Fictions of Gender." *Nordic Journal of English Studies* 2.2 (November 2002): 279–302.

Edwards, Lee R. "Afterword." In Charles Brockden Brown, *Alcuin: A Dialogue*, 92–104. New York: Grossman Publishers, 1971.

Fleischmann, Fritz. "Charles Brockden Brown: Feminism in Fiction." In Fritz Fleischmann, ed., *American Novelists Revisited: Essays in Feminist Criticism*, 6–41. Boston: G.K. Hall, 1982.

Kaplan, Catherine O'Donnell. *Men of Letters in the Early Republic: Cultivating Forms of Citizenship*. Chapel Hill: U of North Carolina P, 2008.

Kierner, Cynthia A. "Introduction." In Charles Brockden Brown, *Alcuin*, 3–38. Albany: NCUP, Inc., 1995.

Kimball, Leroy Elwood. "Introduction." In Charles Brockden Brown, *Alcuin: A Dialogue: A Typescript Facsimile Reprint of the First Edition Printed in 1798*, iii–xxiv. New Haven: Carl and Margaret Rollins, 1935.

Krause, Sydney J. "Brockden Brown's Feminism in Fact and Fiction." In Klaus H. Schmidt and Fritz Fleischmann, *Early America Re-Explored: New Readings in Colonial, Early National, and Antebellum Culture*, 349–84. New York: Peter Lang, 2000.

Reid, S. W. "Textual Essay." In Charles Brockden Brown, *Alcuin: A Dialogue and Memoirs of Stephen Calvert*. Vol. 6, *The Novels and Related Works of Charles Brockden Brown*, 313–66. Kent: Kent State UP, 1987.

Rice, Nancy. "*Alcuin.*" *Massachusetts Review* 14 (Autumn 1973), 802–14.

Schloss, Dietmar. "Intellectuals and Women: Social Rivalry in Charles Brockden Brown's *Alcuin*." In Udo J. Hebel, ed., *The Construction and Contestation of American Identities in the Early National Period*, 355–69. Heidelberg: C. Winter Universitätsverlag, 1999.

Vickers, Anita M. " 'Pray Madam, are you a Federalist?' Women's Rights and the Republican Utopia in *Alcuin*." *American Studies* 39.3 (1998): 89–104.

Violette, Augusta Genevieve. *Economic Feminism in American Literature Prior to 1848*. Orono, ME: University of Maine Studies (2nd series, no. 2), 1925.

Zorzi, Rosella Mamoli. "Introduzione." In Charles Brockden Brown, *Alcuin o il Paradiso delle Donne (1798–1815)*, 5–30. Translation, biographical note, and annotation by Paola Menegazzi. Naples: Guida Editori, 1985.

V. *Ormond*'s Early National and Atlantic Context

A. *Philadelphia's Late Eighteenth-Century Urban Space and Social Structure*

Agnew, Jean-Christophe. *Worlds Apart: The Market and the Theater in Anglo-American Thought, 1550–1750*. New York: Cambridge UP, 1986.

Alexander, John K. *Render Them Submissive: Responses to Poverty in Philadelphia, 1760–1800*. Amherst: U of Massachusetts P, 1980.

Baltzell, E. Digby. *Puritan Boston and Quaker Philadelphia: Two Protestant Ethics and the Spirit of Class Authority and Leadership*. New York: Free Press, 1979.

Blumin, Stuart. *The Emergence of the Middle Class: Social Experience in the American City, 1760–1900*. New York: Cambridge UP, 1989.

Campbell, William Burke. *Old Towns and Districts of Philadelphia*. Philadelphia: City History Society of Philadelphia, 1942.

Carter, Edward C., II. "A 'Wild Irishman' under Every Federalist's Bed: Naturalization in Philadelphia, 1789–1806." *Proceedings of the American Philosophical Society*, 133.2, *Symposium on the Demographic History of the Philadelphia Region, 1600–1860* (June 1989): 178–89.

Ditz, Toby L. "Secret Selves, Credible Personas: The Problematics of Trust and Public Display in the Writing of Eighteenth-Century Philadelphia Merchants." In Robert Blair St. George, ed., *Possible Pasts: Becoming Colonial in Early America*, 219–242. Ithaca: Cornell UP, 2000.

————. "Shipwrecked; or, Masculinity Imperiled: Mercantile Representations of Failure and Gendered Self in Eighteenth-Century Philadelphia." *Journal of American History* 81.3 (1994): 51–80.

Griffin, Patrick. *The People with No Name: Ireland's Ulster Scots, America's Scots Irish, and the Creation of a British Atlantic World, 1689–1764.* Princeton: Princeton UP, 2001.

Klepp, Susan. *Philadelphia in Transition: A Demographic History of the City and Its Occupational Groups, 1720–1830.* New York: Garland, 1989.

Lemon, James T. *The Best Poor Man's Country; a Geographical Study of Early Southeastern Pennsylvania.* Baltimore: The Johns Hopkins UP, 1972.

————. *Liberal Dreams and Nature's Limits: Great Cities of North America since 1600.* New York: Oxford UP, 1996.

Meranze, Michael. *Laboratories of Virtue: Punishment, Revolution, and Authority in Philadelphia, 1760–1835.* Chapel Hill: U of North Carolina P, 1996.

Middleton, Simon and Billy G. Smith, Eds. *Class Matters: Early North America and the Atlantic World.* Philadelphia: U of Pennsylvania P, 2008.

Nash, Gary. *First City: Philadelphia and the Forging of Historical Memory.* Philadelphia: U of Pennsylvania P, 2002.

Newman, Simon P. *Embodied History: The Lives of the Poor in Early Philadelphia.* Philadelphia: U of Pennsylvania P, 2003.

Salinger, Sharon V. "Artists, Journeymen, and the Transformation of Labor in Late Eighteenth-Century Philadelphia." *The William and Mary Quarterly* 40.1 (Jan. 1983): 62–84.

————. *"To Serve Well and Faithfully": Labor and Indentured Servants in Pennsylvania, 1682–1800.* New York: Cambridge UP, 1987.

Schweitzer, Mary M. "The Spatial Organization of Federalist Philadelphia, 1790." *Journal of Interdisciplinary History* 24.1 (Summer 1993): 31–57.

Shammas, Carole. "The Space Problem in Early United States Cities." *The William and Mary Quarterly* 57.3 (July 2000): 505–42.

Smith, Billy G, ed., *Life in Early Philadelphia: Documents from the Revolutionary and Early National Periods.* University Park: The Pennsylvania State UP, 1995.

————. *"The Lower Sort": Philadelphia's Laboring People, 1750-1800.* Ithaca: Cornell UP, 1990.

————. "The Material Lives of Laboring Philadelphians, 1750 to 1800." *The William and Mary Quarterly* 38.2 (April 1981): 163–202.

Teitelman, S. Robert. *Birch's Views of Philadelphia, with Photographs of the Sites in 1960 and 1982.* Philadelphia: The Free Library of Philadelphia, 2000. Also available online at: http://www.ushistory.org/birch/index.htm

Upton, Dell. *Another City: Urban Life and Urban Spaces in the New American Republic.* New Haven: Yale UP, 2008.

Warner, Sam Bass. *The Private City: Philadelphia in Three Periods of its Growth.* Philadelphia: U of Pennsylvania P, 1987.

B. *The 1793 Yellow Fever Epidemic*

Arnebeck, Bob. *Destroying Angel: Benjamin Rush, Yellow Fever and the Birth of Modern Medicine.* Online book: http://www.geocities.com/bobarnebeck/fever1793.html.

Estes, J. Worth, and Billy G. Smith, eds. *A Melancholy Scene of Devastation: The Public Response to the 1793 Philadelphia Yellow Fever Epidemic.* Canton, MA: Published for the College of Physicians of Philadelphia and the Library Company of Philadelphia by Science History Publications, 1997.

Kopperman, Paul E. "'Venerate the Lancet': Benjamin Rush's Yellow Fever Therapy in Context." *Bulletin of the History of Medicine* 78.3 (Fall 2004): 539–74.

Kornfield, Eve. "Crisis in the Capital: The Cultural Significance of Philadelphia's Great Yellow Fever Epidemic." *Pennsylvania History* 51 (1984): 189–205.

Lee, Debbie. "Yellow Fever and the Slave Trade: Coleridge's *The Rime of the Ancient Mariner.*" *English Literary History* 65.3 (1998): 675–700.

Miller, Jacquelyn C. *The Body Politic: Passions, Pestilence, and Political Culture in the Age of the American Revolution.* Dissertation. New Brunswick, NJ: Rutgers U, 1995.

Pernick, Martin S. "Politics, Parties, and Pestilence: Epidemic Yellow Fever in Philadelphia and the Rise of the First Party System." *The William and Mary Quarterly* 29.4 (October 1972): 559–86.

Powell, J. M. *Bring Out Your Dead: The Great Plague of Yellow Fever in Philadelphia in 1793.* Reprinted with a new Introduction by Kenneth R. Foster, et al. Philadelphia: U of Pennsylvania P, 1993 [1949].

Taylor, P. Sean. *"We Live in the Midst of Death": Yellow Fever, Moral Economy, and Public Health in Philadelphia, 1793–1805.* Dissertation. Dekalb, IL: Northern Illinois U, 2001.

C. *Atlantic Slavery, Caribbean Slave Revolution, and the Philadelphia Free Black Community*

Blackburn, Robin. "Haiti, Slavery, and the Age of Democratic Atlantic Revolution." *The William and Mary Quarterly* 63.4 (October 2006): 643–74.

Dain, Bruce. *A Hideous Monster of the Mind: American Race Theory in the Early Republic.* Cambridge: Harvard UP, 2002.

Garraway, Dorris. "Race, Reproduction and Family Romance in Moreau de Saint-Méry's *Description de la Partie Françoise de l'Isle Saint-Domingue.*" *Eighteenth-Century Studies* 38.2 (2005): 227–46.

Gilje, Paul A. and Howard B. Rock. "Sweep O! Sweep O!: African-American Chimney Sweeps and Citizenship in the New Nation." *William and Mary Quarterly* 51.3 (1994): 510–31.

Hudson, Nicholas. "From 'Nation' to 'Race': The Origin of Racial Classification in Eighteenth-Century Thought." *Eighteenth-Century Studies* 29.3 (1996): 247–64.

Linebaugh, Peter and Marcus Rediker. *The Many-Headed Hydra: Sailors, Slaves, Commoners, and the Hidden History of the Revolutionary Atlantic.* London: Verso, 2000.

Matthewson, Tim. *A Proslavery Foreign Policy: Haitian-American Relations during the Early Republic.* Westport, CT: Praeger, 2003.

Meaders, Daniel. "Kidnapping Blacks in Philadelphia: Isaac Hopper's Tales of Oppression." *The Journal of Negro History* 80.2 (1995): 47–65.

Nash, Gary. "Reverberations of Haiti in North America: Black Saint Dominguans in Philadelphia." *Pennsylvania History* 65 (1998): 44–73.

Phillips, George L. *American Chimney-Sweeps: An Historical Account of a Once Important Trade.* Trenton: Past Times Press, 1957.

———. "Mrs. Montagu and the Climbing-Boys." *The Review of English Studies* 25.99 (1949): 237–44.

Stewart, Michael A. Morrison and James Brewar, eds. *Race and the Early Republic: Racial Consciousness and Nation-Building in the Early Republic.* Lantham, MD: Rowman & Littlefield, 2002.

White, Ashli. *"A Flood of Impure Lava": Saint Dominguan Refugees in the United States, 1791–1820.* Dissertation. New York: Columbia University, 2003.

D. The French Émigré Community in 1790s Philadelphia

Boroumand, Ladan. "Emigration and the Rights of Man: French Revolutionary Legislators Equivocate." *Journal of Modern History* 72.1 (2000): 67–108.

Branson, Susan. "St. Domingan Refugees in the Philadelphia Community in the 1790s." *Amerindians, Africans, Americans: Three Papers in Caribbean History,* 69–84. Mona: University of the West Indies, 1993.

Branson, Susan, and Leslie Patrick. "Étrangers dans un pays etrange: Saint-Domingan Refugees of Color in Philadelphia." In David P. Geggus, ed., *The Impact of the Haitian Revolution in the Atlantic World,* 193–208. Columbia: U of South Carolina P, 2001.

Childs, Francis Sergent. *French Refugee Life in the United States, 1790–1800. An American Chapter of the French Revolution.* Baltimore: The Johns Hopkins UP, 1940.

Dun, James Alexander. " 'What avenues of commerce, will you, Americans, not explore!': Commercial Philadelphia's Vantage onto the Early Haitian Revolution. *The William and Mary Quarterly* 62.3 (2005): 473–504.

Fäy, Bernard. *The Revolutionary Spirit in France and America.* New York: Harcourt Brace & Co., 1927.

Hébert, Catherine. "Demise of the American Dream: The French Experience of American Life in the Age of the French Revolution." *Histoire Sociale/Social History* 23 (1990): 219–48.

Jones, Howard Mumford. *America and French Culture, 1750–1848*. Westport, CT: Greenwood Press, 1973.

Kennedy, Robert G. *Orders from France: The Americans and the French in a Revolutionary World, 1780–1820*. Philadelphia: U of Pennsylvania P, 1990.

Meadows, R. Darrell. "Engineering Exile: Social Networks and the French Atlantic Community, 1789–1809." *French Historical Studies* 23.1 (Winter 2000): 67–108.

Moreau de Saint-Méry, Médéric-Louis-Elie. *A Civilization that Perished: The Last Year of White Colonial Rule in Haiti*. Translated, abridged, and edited by Ivor D. Spencer. Lanham, MD: UP of America, 1985.

———. *Voyage aux Etats-Unis d'Amérique, 1793–1798*. Stewart L. Mims., ed. New Haven: Yale UP, 1913. Eng. tr. Kenneth and Anna M. Roberts, *Moreau de St. Méry's American Journey* (New York: Doubleday & Company, 1947).

Nussbaum, F. L. *Talleyrand in America as a Financial Promoter 1784–1796. Unpublished Letters and Memoirs*. 3 vols. Washington, DC: United States Government Printing Office, 1942.

Potofsky, Allan. "The 'Non-Aligned Status' of French Emigrés and Refugees in Philadelphia, 1793–1798." *Transatlantica* 2006.2 (*Révolution)*: http://transatlantica.revues.org/document1147.html.

Wiener, Margerie. *The French Exiles, 1789–1815*. New York: William Morrow and Co., 1966.

E. *Illuminati Scare and Counter-Enlightenment*

Chandos, Michael Brown. "Mary Wollstonecraft; or, the Female Illuminati: The Campaign against Women and 'Modern Philosophy' in the Early Republic. *Journal of the Early Republic* 15 (1995): 389–424.

Christensen, Jerome. "The Detection of the Romantic Conspiracy in England." *South Atlantic Quarterly* 95.3 (1996): 603–27.

Davis, David Brion. *The Fear of Conspiracy: Images of Un-American Subversion from the Revolution to the Present*. Ithaca: Cornell UP, 1971.

Garrard, Graeme. *Counter-Enlightenments: From the Eighteenth Century to the Present*. New York: Routledge, 2006.

Hofman, Amos. "Opinion, Illusion, and the Illusion of Opinion: Barruel's Theory of Conspiracy." *Eighteenth-Century Studies* 27.1 (1993): 27–60.

———. "The Origins of the Theory of the Philosophe Conspiracy." *French History* 2.2 (1988): 152–72.

Hofstader, Richard. *The Paranoid Style in American Politics and Other Essays*. New York: Knopf, 1966.

Koselleck, Reinhard. *Critique and Crisis: Enlightenment and the Pathogenesis of Modern Society*. Cambridge, MA: MIT Press, 1988.

Leinesch, Michael. "The Illusion of the Illuminati: The Counterconspiratorial Origins of Post-Revolutionary Conservatism." In Wil Verhoeven, ed., *Revolutionary*

Histories: Translatlantic Cultural Nationalism, 1775–1815, 152–65. New York: Palgrave, 2002.

Luckert, Steven. *Jesuits, Freemasons, Illuminati, and Jacobins: Conspiracy Theories, Secret Societies, and Politics in Late Eighteenth-century Germany.* Dissertation: University of New York at Binghamton, 1993.

McMahon, Darrin M. *Enemies of the Enlightenment: The French Counter-Enlightenment and the Making of Modernity.* New York: Oxford UP, 2001.

Roberts, J. M. *The Mythology of the Secret Societies.* London: Secker & Warburg, 1972.

Rogin, Michael Paul. *Ronald Reagan, the Movie: and other Episodes in Political Demonology.* Berkeley: U of California P, 1987.

Stauffer, Vernon L. *New England and the Bavarian Illuminati.* New York: Columbia UP, 1918.

Tanner, Jakob. "The Conspiracy of the Invisible Hand: Anonymous Market Mechanisms and Dark Powers." *New German Critique* 103, 35.1 (2008): 51–64.

White, Ed. "The Value of Conspiracy Theory." *American Literary History* 14.1 (2002): 1–31.

Wilson, W. Daniels. "Internalizing the Counter-Revolution: Wieland and the Illuminati Scare." In Ehrhard Bahr and Thomas Saine, eds., *The Internalized Revolution: German Reactions to the French Revolution, 1789–1989*, 33–59. New York: Garland, 1992.

Wood, Gordon S. "Conspiracy and the Paranoid Style: Causality and Deceit in the Eighteenth Century." *William & Mary Quarterly* 39 (1982): 401–41.

F. *Women, Patriarchy, and Sexuality in the Revolutionary Age and Early Republic*

Basch, Norma. "Equity vs. Equality: Emerging Concepts of Women's Political Status in the Age of Jackson." *Journal of the Early Republic* 3.3 (1983): 297–318.

Block, Sharon. *Rape and Sexual Power in Early America.* Chapel Hill: U of North Carolina P, 2006.

Branson, Susan. *Those Fiery Frenchified Dames: Women and Political Culture in Early National Philadelphia.* Philadelphia: U of Pennsylvania P, 2001.

Corazzo, Nina and Catherine R. Montfort. "Charlotte Corday: femme-homme." In Catherine R. Montfort, ed., *Literate Women and the French Revolution of 1789*, 33–54. Birmingham, AL: Summa Publications, Inc., 1994.

Daniels, Christine and Michael V. Kennedy, eds. *Over the Threshold: Intimate Violence in Early America.* New York: Routledge, 1999.

Dolan, Frances E. *Marriage and Violence: the Early Modern Legacy.* Philadelphia: U of Pennsylvania P, 2008.

Fliegelman, Jay. *Prodigals and Pilgrims: The American Revolution Against Patriarchal Authority.* Cambridge, UK: Cambridge UP, 1982.

Gutwirth, Madelyn. *The Twilight of the Goddesses: Women and Representation in the French Revolutionary Era.* New Brunswick: Rutgers UP, 1992.

Hartog, Hendrik. *Man and Wife in America: A History.* Cambridge: Harvard UP, 2000.

Hoffman, Ronald and Peter J. Albert, eds. *Women in the Age of the American Revolution.* Charlottesville: U of Virginia P, 1989.

Huet, Marie-Helen. *Rehearsing the Revolution: The Staging of Marat's Death, 1793–1797.* Berkeley: U of California P, 1982.

Kerber, Linda K. "The Paradox of Women's Citizenship in the Early Republic: The Case of Martin vs. Massachusetts, 1805." *The American Historical Review* 97.2 (1992): 349–78.

———. *Women of the Republic: Intellect and Ideology in the Revolutionary Age.* Chapel Hill: U of North Carolina P, 1997.

Kindleberger, Elizabeth R. "Charlotte Corday in Text and Image: A Case Study in the French Revolution and Women's History." *French Historical Studies* 18.4 (1994): 969–99.

Lockridge, Kenneth A. *On the Sources of Patriarchal Rage: The Commonplace Books of William Byrd and Thomas Jefferson and the Gendering of Power in the Eighteenth Century.* New York: New York UP, 1993.

Miles, Ellen G. and Leslie Reinhardt. "'Art conceal'd': Peale's Double Portrait of Benjamin and Eleanor Ridgely Laming." *The Art Bulletin* 78.1 (1996): 57–74.

Outram, Dorinda. *The Body and the French Revolution: Sex, Class and Political Culture.* New Haven: Yale UP, 1989.

Pateman, Carole. *The Sexual Contract.* Stanford: Stanford UP, 1988.

Rowbotham, Sheila. *Hidden from History: 300 Years of Women's Oppression and the Fight against It.* London: Pluto, 1973.

Samuels, Shirley. *Romances of the Republic: Women, the Family, and Violence in the Literature of the Early American Republic.* New York: Oxford UP, 1996.

Stone, Lawrence. *The Family, Sex, and Marriage in England, 1500–1800.* New York: Harper & Row, 1977.

Welter, Barbara. "The Cult of True Womanhood, 1820–1850." *American Quarterly* 18.2 (1966): 151–74.

Wulf, Karin. *Not All Wives: Colonial Women of Philadelphia.* Ithaca: Cornell UP, 2000.

Zagarri, Rosemarie. *Revolutionary Backlash: Women and Politics in the Early American Republic.* Philadelphia: U of Pennsylvania P, 2009.

G. *Long Eighteenth-Century Matters of Sex-Gender, Transvestism, Same-Sex Sexuality, and Pornography*

Arnebeck, Bob. *Through a Fiery Trial: Building Washington, 1790–1800.* New York: Madison Books, 1991.

Binhammer, Katherine. "The Sex Panic of the 1790s." *Journal of the History of Sexuality* 6.3 (1996): 409–34.

Bray, Alan. *Homosexuality in Renaissance England.* London: Gay Men's Press, 1982.

Bullough, Vern L. and Bonnie Bullough. *Cross Dressing, Sex, and Gender.* Philadelphia: U of Pennsylvania P, 1993.

Cohen, Daniel A. *The Female Marine and Related Works: Narratives of Cross-Dressing and Urban Vice in America's Early Republic.* Amherst: U of Massachusetts P, 1997.

Coward, David. "The Sublimations of a Fetishist: Restif de la Bretonne (1734–1806)." In Robert Purks Maccurbi, ed., *'Tis Nature's Fault: Unauthorized Sexuality During the Enlightenment,* 98–108. Cambridge: Cambridge UP, 1988.

Crain, Caleb. *American Sympathy: Men, Friendship, and Literature in the New Nation.* New Haven: Yale UP, 2001.

Darnton, Robert. *The Forbidden Best-Sellers of Pre-Revolutionary France.* London: HarperCollins, 1996.

Dekker, Rudolf, and Lotte Van de Pol. *The Tradition of Female Transvestism in Early Modern Europe.* Houndmills: Macmillan Press, 1989.

Donoghue, Emma. *Passions Between Women: British Lesbian Culture, 1668–1801.* London: Scarlet Press, 1993.

Dugaw, Dianne. "Female Sailors Bold: Transvestite Heroines and the Markers of Gender and Class." In Margaret S. Creighton and Lise Norling, eds., *Iron Men, Wooden Women: Gender and Seafaring in the Atlantic World, 1700–1920,* 34–54. Baltimore: Johns Hopkins UP, 1996.

Faderman, Lillian. *Surpassing the Love of Men: Romantic Friendship and Love between Women from the Renaissance to the Present.* New York: HarperCollins, 1998.

Foster, Thomas, ed. *Long before Stonewall: Histories of Same-Sex Sexuality in Early America.* New York: New York UP, 2007.

Foxon, David. *Libertine Literature in England 1660-1745.* np: Book Collector, 1963.

Friedli, Lynne. "'Passing Women': A Study of Gender Boundaries in the Eighteenth Century." George S. Rousseau and Roy Porter, eds., *Sexual Underworlds of the Enlightenment,* 234–60. Manchester: Manchester UP, 1987.

Garber, Marjorie. *Vested Interests: Cross-Dressing and Cultural Anxiety.* New York: HarperPerennial, 1993.

Gilfoyle, Timothy J. *City of Eros: New York City, Prostitution, and the Commercialization of Sex, 1790–1920.* New York: Norton, 1992.

Godbeer, Richard. *Sexual Revolution in Early America.* Baltimore: Johns Hopkins UP, 2004.

Goulemot, Jean Marie. *Forbidden Texts: Erotic Literature and its Readers in Eighteenth-Century France.* Oxford: Polity Press, 1994.

Gustafson, Sandra M. "The Genders of Nationalism: Patriotic Violence, Patriot Sentiment in the Performances of Deborah Sampson Gannett." In Robert Blair St.

George, ed., *Possible Pasts: Becoming Colonial in Early America*, 380–400. Ithaca: Cornell UP, 2000.

Haggerty, George. *Queer Gothic*. Urbana: U of Illinois P, 2006.

Hallock, John W. M. *The American Byron: Homosexuality and the Fall of Fitz-Greene Halleck*. Madison: U of Wisconsin P, 2000.

Higgs, David, ed. *Queer Sites: Gay Urban Histories since 1600*. London: Routledge, 1999.

Hiltner, Judith. (1999). "'She Bled in Secret': Deborah Sampson, Herman Mann, and *The Female Review.*" *Early American Literature* 34 (1999): 190–220.

Hunt, Lynn. *The Family Romance of the French Revolution*. Berkeley: U of California P, 1993.

————. "The Many Bodies of Marie Antoinette: Political Pornography and the Problem of the Feminine in the French Revolution." In Lynn Hunt, ed. *Eroticism and the Body Politic*, 108–30. Baltimore: Johns Hopkins UP, 1991.

Kahn, Madeleine. *Narrative Transvestism: Rhetoric and Gender in the Eighteenth-Century English Novel*. Ithaca: Cornell UP, 1991.

Lanser, Susan S. "Befriending the Body: Female Intimacies as Class Acts." *Eighteenth-Century Studies* 32.2 (1998–99): 179–98.

Levy, Darlene Gay and Harriett B. Applewhite (1992). "Woman and Militant Citizenship in Revolutionary Paris." In Sarah E. Meltzer and Leslie W. Rabine, eds., *Rebel Daughters: Women and the French Revolution*, 79–101. Oxford: Oxford UP, 1992.

Lyons, Clare. "Mapping an Atlantic Sexual Culture: Homoeroticism in Eighteenth-Century Philadelphia." *The William and Mary Quarterly* 60.1 (2003): 119–54.

————. *Sex Among the Rabble: An Intimate History of Gender & Power in the Age of Revolution, Philadelphia, 1730–1830*. Chapel Hill: U of North Carolina P, 2006.

Moore, Lisa L. "'Something More Tender Still Than Friendship': Romantic Friendship in Early-Nineteenth-Century England." *Feminist Studies* 18.3 (Fall 1992): 499–520.

Morris, Marilyn. "Transgendered Perspectives on Premodern Sexualities." *Studies in English Literature, 1500–1900* 46.3 (2006): 585–600.

Mounsey, Chris and Caroline Gonda, eds. *Queer People: Negotiations and Expressions of Homosexuality, 1700–1800*. Lewisburg: Bucknell UP, 2007: 261–73.

Mourão, Manuela. "The Representation of Female Desire in Early Modern Pornographic Texts, 1660–1745." *Signs* 24 (1999): 573–602.

Mudge, Bradford K. *The Whore's Story: Women, Pornography, and the British Novel, 1684–1830*. Oxford: Oxford UP, 2000.

Norton, Rictor. *Mother Clap's Molly House: The Gay Subculture in England 1700–1830*. London: Gay Men's Press, 1992.

————. *The Myth of the Modern Homosexual: Queer History and the Search for Cultural Unity*. London: Cassell, 1998.

Shapiro, Stephen. "'Man to Man I Needed Not to Dread His Encounter': *Edgar Huntly's* End of Erotic Pessimism." In Philip Barnard, Mark L. Kamrath, and Stephen Shapiro, eds., *Revising Charles Brockden Brown: Culture, Politics, and Sexuality in the Early Republic*, 216–51. Knoxville: U of Tennessee P, 2004.

Smith-Rosenberg, Carroll. *Disorderly Conduct: Visions of Gender in Victorian America*. New York: Oxford UP, 1985.

Trumbach, Randolph. *Sex and the Gender Revolution, Volume 1: Heterosexuality and the Third Gender in Enlightenment London*. Chicago: U of Chicago P, 1998.

Wagner, Peter. *Eros Revived: Erotica of the Enlightenment in England and America*. London: Secker & Warburg, 1988.

Warner, Michael. "Homo-Narcissism; or, Heterosexuality." In Joseph A. Boone and Michael Cadden, eds., *Engendering Men*, 190–206. London: Routledge, 1990.

Wheelwright, Julie. *Amazons and Military Maids: Women who Dressed as Men in Pursuit of Life, Liberty and Happiness*. London: Pandora Press, 1989.

Wyngaard, Amy. "Libertine Spaces: Anonymous Crowds, Secret Chambers, and Urban Corruption in Retif de la Bretonne." *Eighteenth-Century Life* 22 (1998): 104–122.

Young, Alfred F. *Masquerade: The Life and Times of Deborah Sampson, Continental Soldier*. New York: Vintage, 2005.

H. *Revolution Debates and Counterrevolutionary Backlash in the American 1790s*

Carter, Edward C., II. "A 'Wild Irishman' Under Every Federalist's Bed: Naturalization in Philadelphia, 1789–1806." *Proceedings of the American Philosophical Society* 133.2 (1989): 178–89.

Cotlar, Seth. "The Federalists' Transatlantic Cultural Offensive of 1798 and the Moderation of American Political Discourse." In Jeffrey L. Pasley, Andrew W. Robertson, and David Waldstreicher, eds., *Beyond the Founders: New Approaches to the Political History of the Early American Republic*, 274–99. Chapel Hill: U of North Carolina P, 2004.

Elkins, Stanley, and Eric McKitrick. *The Age of Federalism: The Early American Republic, 1788–1800*. New York: Oxford UP, 1993.

Fischer, David Hackett. *The Revolution of American Conservatism: The Federalist Party in the Era of Jeffersonian Democracy*. New York: Harper & Row, 1965.

Fitzmier, John R. *New England's Moral Legislator: Timothy Dwight, 1752–1817*. Bloomington: Indiana UP, 1998.

French, Roderick S. "Elihu Palmer, Radical Deist, Radical Republican: A Reconsideration of American Free Thought." *Studies in Eighteenth-Century Culture* 8 (1979): 87–108.

Imholt, Robert J. "Timothy Dwight, Federalist Pope of Connecticut." *The New England Quarterly* 73.3 (2000): 386–411.

Kafer, Peter. "The Making of Timothy Dwight: A Connecticut Morality Tale." *The William and Mary Quarterly* 47.2 (1990): 189–209.

Kaplan, Catherine O'Donnell. *Men of Letters in the Early Republic: Cultivating Forms of Citizenship.* Chapel Hill: U of North Carolina P, 2008.

Kramnick, Isaac. *Republicanism and Bourgeois Radicalism: Political Ideology in Late Eighteenth-Century England and America.* Ithaca: Cornell UP, 1994.

Miller, John C. *Crisis in Freedom: The Alien and Sedition Acts.* Boston: Little, Brown, and Company, 1951.

Reiff, Paul F. *Friedrich Gentz, an Opponent of the French Revolution and Napoleon.* Urbana-Champaign: U of Illinois P, 1912.

Rush, Benjamin. *The Letters of Benjamin Rush.* 2 volumes. Edited by L. H. Butterfield. Princeton: Princeton UP, 1951.

Sassi, Jonathan. *Republic of Righteousness: The Public Christianity of the Post-Revolutionary New England Clergy.* New York, Oxford UP, 2001.

Schlereth, Eric. "A Tale of Two Deists: John Fitch, Elihu Palmer, and the Boundary of Tolerable Religious Expression in Early National Philadelphia." *Pennsylvania Magazine of History and Biography* 132.1 (2008): 5–32.

Simpson, Lewis. "Federalism and the Crisis of Literary Order." *American Literature* 32 (1960/61): 253–66.

Tise, Larry E. *The American Counterrevolution: A Retreat from Liberty, 1783–1800.* Mechanicsburg, PA: Stackpole Books, 1998.

Wallerstein, Immanuel. *After Liberalism.* New York: New Press, 1995.

———. "The Bourgeois(ie) as Concept and Reality." *New Left Review* 167 (1988): 91–106.

Walters, Kerry S. *Rational Infidels: The American Deists.* Durango: Longwood Academic, 1992.

White, Ed. *The Backcountry and the City: Colonization and Conflict in Early America.* Minneapolis: U of Minnesota P, 2005.

I. *British Radical-Democratic Novel in the 1790s; Links between Wold-winites and Brown's Circle*

Allen, B. Sprague. "William Godwin and the Stage." *PMLA* (Papers of the Modern Language Association) 35.3 (1920): 358–74.

Bernard, John. *Retrospections of America, 1797–1811.* New York: Harper & Brothers, 1887.

Butler, Marilyn. *Jane Austen and the War of Ideas.* Oxford: Clarendon Press, 1975.

Butler, Marilyn and Janet Todd, eds., *The Works of Mary Wollstonecraft.* London: Pickering, 1989.

Coad, Oral Sumner. *William Dunlap: A Study of His Life and Works of his Place in Contemporary Culture.* New York: Dunlap Society, 1917.

Clemit, Pamela. *The Godwinian Novel: The Rational Fictions of Godwin, Brockden Brown, Mary Shelley.* Oxford: Oxford UP, 1993.

Green, David Bonnell. "Letters of William Godwin and Thomas Holcroft to William Dunlap." *Notes and Queries* 3.10 (1956): 441–43.

Johnson, Nancy E. *The English Jacobin Novel on Rights, Property, and the Law.* New York: Palgrave MacMillan, 2004.

Juengel, Scott. "Godwin, Lavater, and the Pleasures of Surface." *Studies in Romanticism* 35 (1996): 73–97.

Johnson, Nancy E. *The English Jacobin Novel on Rights, Property, and the Law.* New York: Palgrave MacMillan, 2004.

Kelly, Gary. *The English Jacobin Novel 1780–1805.* Oxford: Oxford UP, 1976.

———. *English Fiction of the Romantic Period, 1789–1830.* London: Longman, 1989.

Maniquis, Robert M. ed., *British Radical Culture of the 1790s.* San Marino: Huntington Library Press, 2002.

Peacock, Thomas Love. "Memoir of Percy Bysshe Shelley." In *The Works of Thomas Love Peacock, including his Novels, Poems, Fugitive Pieces, Criticisms, etc.*, III, 385–449. London: R. Bentley, 1875.

Pollin, Burton R. "Godwin's Letter to Ogilvie, Friend of Jefferson, and the Federalist Propaganda." *Journal of the History of Ideas* 28.3 (1967): 432–44.

Smith, Geddeth. *Thomas Abthorpe Cooper: America's Premier Tragedian.* Madison: Fairleigh Dickinson UP, 1996.

Steinman, Lisa M. "Transatlantic Cultures: Godwin, Brown, and Mary Shelley." *Wordsworth Circle* 32.3 (2001): 126–30.

Tompkins, J.M.S. *The Popular Novel in England, 1770–1800.* Lincoln: U of Nebraska P, 1961.

J. Sensibility, Sentiment, Physiognomy, and the Gothic

Barker-Benfield, G. J. *The Culture of Sensibility: Sex and Society in Eighteenth-Century Britain.* Chicago: U of Chicago P, 1992.

Barnes, Elizabeth. *States of Sympathy: Seduction and Democracy in the American Novel.* New York: Columbia UP, 1997.

Botting, Fred. *Gothic.* London: Routledge, 1995.

Burgett, Bruce. *Sentimental Bodies: Sex, Gender, and Citizenship in the Early Republic.* Princeton: Princeton UP, 1998.

Chapman, Mary and Glenn Hendler. *Sentimental Men: Masculinity and the Politics of Affect in American Culture.* Berkeley: U of California P, 1999.

Ellis, Kate Ferguson. *The Contested Castle: Gothic Novels and the Subversion of Domestic Ideology.* Chicago: U of Illinois P, 1989.

Ellis, Markman. *The Politics of Sensibility: Race, Gender, and Commerce in the Sentimental Novel.* Cambridge: Cambridge UP, 1996.

Fincher, Max. *Queering Gothic in the Romantic Age: The Penetrating Eye.* London: Palgrave McMillan, 2007.

Johnson, Claudia L. *Equivocal Beings: Politics, Gender, and Sentimentality in the 1790s—Wollstonecraft, Burney, Radcliffe, Austin.* Chicago: U of Chicago P, 1995.

Jones, Chris. *Radical Sensibility: Literature and Ideas in the 1790s.* London: Routledge, 1993.

Kilgour, Maggie. *The Rise of the Gothic Novel.* London: Routledge, 1995.

Massé, Michelle A. *In the Name of Love: Women, Masochism, and the Gothic.* Ithaca: Cornell UP, 1992.

Monleón, José B. *A Specter is Haunting Europe: A Sociohistorical Approach to the Fantastic.* Princeton: Princeton UP, 1990.

Mullan, John. *Sentiment and Sociability: The Language of Feeling in the Eighteenth Century.* Oxford: Clarendon Press, 1988.

Paulson, Ronald. *Representations of Revolution, 1789–1820.* New Haven: Yale UP, 1983.

Rivers, Christopher. *Face Value: Physiognomical Thought and the Legible Body in Marivaux, Lavater, Balzac, Gautier, and Zola.* Madison: U of Wisconsin P, 1994.

Tennenhouse, Leonard. *The Importance of Feeling English: American Literature and the British Diaspora, 1750-1850.* Princeton: Princeton UP, 2007.

Todd, Janet. *Sensibility: An Introduction.* London: Methuen, 1986.

Watt, James. *Contesting the Gothic: Fiction, Genre, and Cultural Conflict, 1764–1832.* Cambridge: Cambridge UP, 1999.

K. *Questions of Form: Alienation Effect, Classicism, and Genre*

Brecht, Bertolt. *Brecht on Theatre; the Development of an Aesthetic.* Edited and translated by John Willet. New York: Hill and Wang, 1964.

Debord, Guy. *The Society of the Spectacle.* Translated by Donald Nicholson-Smith. New York: Zone Books, 1994.

Gombrich, E. H. "Norm and Form: The Stylistic Categories of Art History and their Origins in Renaissance Ideals." In *Norm and Form: Studies in the Art of the Renaissance,* 81–98. 4th Edition. Oxford: Phaidon Press, 1985.

Jameson, Fredric. *The Political Unconscious: Narrative as a Socially Symbolic Act.* Ithaca: Cornell UP, 1981.

Lacoue-Labarthe, Philippe and Jean-Luc Nancy. *The Literary Absolute: The Theory of Literature in German Romanticism.* Translated by Philip Barnard and Cheryl Lester. Albany: SUNY Press, 1986.

Lukács, Georg. "Schiller's Theory of Modern Literature." In *Goethe and his Age,* 101–35. Translated by Robert Anchor. London: Merlin Press, 1968.

Moretti, Franco. *The Way of the World: The Bildungsroman in European Culture.* Translated by Albert Sbragia. New Edition. London: Verso, 2000.

Constance is alone in house, hears noises,
sees Ormond, he has dead body on floor: Craig,
Craig killed her father (per Ormond's order),
he's known everything thats occurred by being
sneaky/ altering architecture, he threatens to attack her,
long convo, shifts to Sophia, Constance kills Ormond,
she appears dead but revives

who is figure Sophia is writing to/ addressing?